THE LAST CHANCERS

13th Legion • Kill Team • Annihilation Squad

LIEUTENANT KAGE HAS a problem. Well, he has several. One is the fact he's a convicted criminal, looking at execution. Another is the psychotic streak that got him in trouble in the first place. Another, he's the leader of an elite team of convict soldiers known as the 13th Legion or the 'Last Chancers'. And finally, there's his commanding officer, Colonel Schaeffer, who almost certainly wants him dead. For all those missions that are just too dangerous, the objectives it's not worth losing good men over, for the dirtiest jobs in the whole galaxy, it falls to the Last Chancers.

The Last Chancers collects *13th Legion*, *Kill Team* and *Annihilation Squad* into one great value omnibus novel and tells the story of Kage's illustrious career. Can Kage keep his head while everyone is getting theirs shot off? Can he ever redeem himself in the eyes of the cold, inhuman Schaeffer? Things can't get any better, so surely they can't get any worse.

Can they?

A WARHAMMER 40,000 OMNIBUS

THE LAST CHANCERS

Gav Thorpe

A Black Library Publication

13th Legion copyright © 2000, Games Workshop Ltd.
Kill Team copyright © 2001, Games Workshop Ltd.
Annihilation Squad copyright © 2004, Games Workshop Ltd.
Liberty first published in *Inferno!* magazine,
copyright © 2001, Games Workshop Ltd. *Deliverance*
first published in *Inferno!* magazine, copyright © 2002, Games Workshop Ltd.

This omnibus edition published in Great Britain in 2006 by
BL Publishing,
Games Workshop Ltd.,
Willow Road, Nottingham,
NG7 2WS, UK.

10 9 8 7 6 5 4

Cover illustration by Andrea Uderzo.
Annihilation Squad map by Stef Kopinski and Dan Drane.

A CIP record for this book is available from the British Library.

ISBN 13: 978 1 84416 300 7
ISBN 10: 1 84416 300 8

Distributed in the US by Simon & Schuster
1230 Avenue of the Americas, New York, NY 10020, US.

Printed and bound in Great Britain by
CPI Bookmarque, Surrey, UK.

See the Black Library on the Internet at
www.blacklibrary.com

Find out more about Games Workshop
and the world of Warhammer 40,000 at
www.games-workshop.com

IT IS THE 41st millennium. For more than a hundred centuries the Emperor has sat immobile on the Golden Throne of Earth. He is the master of mankind by the will of the gods, and master of a million worlds by the might of his inexhaustible armies. He is a rotting carcass writhing invisibly with power from the Dark Age of Technology. He is the Carrion Lord of the Imperium for whom a thousand souls are sacrificed every day, so that he may never truly die.

YET EVEN IN his deathless state, the Emperor continues his eternal vigilance. Mighty battlefleets cross the daemon-infested miasma of the warp, the only route between distant stars, their way lit by the Astronomican, the psychic manifestation of the Emperor's will. Vast armies give battle in his name on uncounted worlds. Greatest amongst His soldiers are the Adeptus Astartes, the Space Marines, bio-engineered super-warriors. Their comrades in arms are legion: the Imperial Guard and countless planetary defence forces, the ever-vigilant Inquisition and the tech-priests of the Adeptus Mechanicus to name only a few. But for all their multitudes, they are barely enough to hold off the ever-present threat from aliens, heretics, mutants – and worse.

TO BE A man in such times is to be one amongst untold billions. It is to live in the cruellest and most bloody regime imaginable. These are the tales of those times. Forget the power of technology and science, for so much has been forgotten, never to be re-learned. Forget the promise of progress and understanding, for in the grim dark future there is only war. There is no peace amongst the stars, only an eternity of carnage and slaughter, and the laughter of thirsting gods.

CONTENTS

AUTHOR'S INTRODUCTION

'If you steal from one author it's plagiarism; if you steal from many it's research.'

– Wilson Mizner

So, AN AUTHOR's intro for the omnibus edition, eh? Never one to shirk the task of talking about my writing and waxing lyrical on just how much thought needs to go into seemingly mindless violence, here is the Complete and Utter History of the Last Chancers. Bear with me, it goes on for a bit...

I make no great claims of originality concerning the Last Chancers. In fact, their creation and development can be credited to many people. Anyway, let's do this properly and start at the beginning.

Years ago, when I were but a youthful assistant games developer for Games Workshop, we were working on the *Codex: Imperial Guard* supplement for the Warhammer 40,000 game. Another assistant games developer, Ian Pickstock, and I were tasked with creating a 'special character' – a famous (or infamous) named individual.

We came up with the idea of a famous squad, rather than a single person, based on the special forces 'men-on-a-mission' platoon as seen in many action movies. So Major Schaeffer (the real name of Arnie's character in *Predator*) was created, along with a squad of ultra-tough hombres with their specialist skills and weaponry.

9

This was passed on to Rick Priestley, the main author of the codex, who is from a different movie-going generation to Ian and myself, and thus moved the squad into a frame of reference he found more familiar – the Dirty Dozen. Schaeffer was promoted to a colonel, and the squad became members of the 13th Penal Legion.

Now, penal legions were real – both the Germans and Soviets made use of them during World War II, mainly for mine clearance and other such unenviable jobs. In the early iterations of the Warhammer 40,000 universe, through the Rogue Trader game, penal legions had been established as part of the Imperial Guard. However, this being the unforgiving Imperium of Man, these penal legions were human bombs, fitted with explosive collars to ensure discipline or, at a pinch, blow up the enemy! Rick wanted to move the penal legions into a slightly more heroic light for this version of the game, so our men-on-a-mission were hijacked and the Last Chancers were born.

That would have been that, if it were not for Andy Jones, who was in the process of setting up a publishing wing of Games Workshop – which was eventually to grow into the book-spewing behemoth of the Black Library. Back then, Andy was starting up *Inferno!* magazine, with the help of editor Marc Gascoigne. I expressed an interest in doing some fiction as freelance work and a fruitful relationship began – so far it's been a dozen short stories and (not including this collection) eight novels.

Anyway, that part's a bit hazy now, I think I raised the idea of a Last Chancers story, and the Dirty Dozen in space angle was discussed, until we came up with the story of a Last Chancer trying to escape, but in the process unwittingly winning a battle. Andy also introduced me to *Monte Cassino* by Sven Hassel. I loved it, and we agreed on the down-and-dirty, grim and violent style that has characterized the Last Chancers ever since. So, Last Chance was written, edited, rewritten, re-edited until we were happy. The idea was, of course, to do many short stories, and at first the plan was to imbed one story within another, so that as Kage was fighting one battle, he was describing other events from his past. The story eventually was re-edited (again!) into the Typhos Prime chapter of 13th Legion.

The next story continued this theme of desperate action leading to positive results. In *Deliverance* we have Kage and company cornered, almost certainly going to be slaughtered and the only way to survive is to do the bravest and stupidest thing. Another driving concept was to have a brief look at a very strong idea in the Last Chancers series – that of hope, and its eventual pointlessness (well, this is 40K after all). *Deliverance* became a good launching point for the next stage of the Last Chancers' saga.

As it turned out, I did some other short stories before getting back to the Last Chancers; Black Library was going strong and was now looking to create a range of novels, many of them based on characters introduced through *Inferno!* magazine. Always hungry to write (and occasionally actually hungry because I wasn't exactly earning a mint back then) I jumped on the chance to get some experience at authoring a novel. The story-within-a-story format obviously wasn't going to work so well in that format, and was replaced by third-person interludes to provide a bit of an idea of the ongoing back story.

In many ways I still regard *13th Legion* as the definitive Last Chancers book – the short story-style format, the unremitting violence and mayhem, and the evolution of Kage from a desperate survivor looking for a way out, to a battle-shocked soldier that has accepted his fate and is permanently scarred (physically and mentally) is at the heart of the concept. I also feel that the rest of the Last Chancers cast are the most interesting characters. But perhaps that's just me.

Other projects beckoned, more short stories were written, before I returned to Schaeffer and Kage. This time, now working with Marc Gascoigne and Lindsey Priestley as editors, Andy having moved onwards and upwards as Black Library continued its unchecked growth, we decided to tie-in with a special event in the Warhammer 40,000 background – the introduction of a completely new alien race, in the form of the tau. So, we needed a story that would involve a new bunch of misfits and have them experience the tau on their home ground. For me, it was just the opportunity to add some more depth to these new aliens, and in particular to exorcise the horrific scene that plagued my brain from early in the project that became known as 'the infamous kroot barbecue'.

The tau, in typical 40K fashion, are aliens that are more like modern humans than the humans of the Imperium. In some ways, with their enlightened attitude to science and their co-operative ideals of the Greater Good, there was a danger that readers might start to think they're actually... well, nice! Never one to be too comfortable with anything that seems too clean and shiny, I wanted to add a few scuffs and a bit of grime to the underbelly, and so the idea of the tau being not quite so united, and not quite so enlightened with their dealings with aliens, formed the underlying vision. It was also, through the more 'modern' outlook of the tau, a good chance to take an askance view at Kage and his fellow Imperials with all their wonderful medieval superstition and xenophobia.

So, while *13th Legion* is the truest Last Chancers novel, *Kill Team* is a lot more polished; the narrative is stronger, it's filled with plenty of definitive scenes that were a joy to devise, and the violence is more directed.

Now, with *Kill Team* done, we thought it would be a good idea to do a promotional story in *Inferno!* to foreshadow the events that begin *Kill Team*. I had set myself a bit of a task with this though, because at the start of the novel there is a reference to Kage doing something pretty awful during an escape attempt using, of all things, a spoon… In *Liberation* the question is answered.

There was quite a long break between *Liberation* and *Annihilation Squad* as I worked on other projects. I was now feeling that there was one good story left in Kage and then it was time to draw a veil over his exploits (though not necessarily the Last Chancers as a whole). He needed to go out with a bang, and there were ever-decreasing mission objectives he could be trying to achieve. He had blown something up; he had killed someone; so what was left? A rescue mission was the obvious choice, though of course it would never be that simple.

As with the tau in *Kill Team*, I wanted the environment of the war-torn world of Armageddon to be rich and feel like it made sense, even if in a warped kind of way. *Annihilation Squad* required the most research, because a lot has been written about Armageddon over the years and it wasn't all in one place. On top of what was already known, I also wanted to expand on life inside Archeron hive, intrigued by the idea of this massive city under almost voluntary control by the brutal orks. Overlord von Strab, a great villain ever since his introduction during the Battle for Armageddon game, seemed a natural candidate for the mission objective, and the twisted world he has created around himself and wonderful mind-bending environment for the Last Chancers to find themselves in. It also focussed on Schaeffer a bit more, filling in a little of his story.

I think it has worked, and it was gratifying to read fan reviewer 'Squig' describe the story as, 'full of twists and a chapter somewhat reminiscent of *Alice in Wonderland* (tumbling down the rabbit hole), albeit a little twisted'.

So the tale is wrapped up in one place in this omnibus – including the very beginning, never before revealed, in the bonus short story.

One other thing before I go… Erasmus Spooge won me a bet. Nuff said.

GAV

DELIVERANCE

ARAGA STOOD UPON the crest of the hill, leaning on his spearstaff, and looked out across the savannah. The rolling grasslands stretched for kilometres in every direction, a yellow sea swaying gently in the wind, broken only by the occasional tree or rocky outcrop. On the horizon he could make out the darker green of the jungle canopy.

The tribesman took out a red-coloured root from an animal skin pouch around his neck and began to chew it. As he crushed the root between his teeth, he felt its juices spreading their effect across his body, loosening the ties between mortal flesh and spirit. His limbs began to go numb and he felt his mind ready itself for the journey to the world of the gods. He looked vaguely up into the yellow sky, his gaze attracted by movement.

From out of the heavens dropped a star, rapidly falling towards Araga, straight as an arrow towards the ridge. This was an omen, but Araga was not sure if it was good or ill. For almost a hundred heart-beats the tribesman watched the object growing larger and larger, until it impacted into the ground at the base of the hill in a shower of mud and dust. It looked like a gigantic egg, made of thick leathery skin and ribbed bone plates. As Araga watched, the egg cracked open, its upper half peeling apart like a grotesque flower. There was a spray of purplish ichor, and a large, gangling shape flopped from the star-egg onto the ground.

The shape stretched itself up to its full height, the fluids of its cocoon dripping from its body. It was over twice Araga's height, and as it stood on two thick legs it unfolded four upper limbs, two of them wicked-looking claws over a man's height in length. Its purplish flesh was protected by overlapping chitinous plates, and powerful muscle and sinew rippled under its dark skin.

Araga's heart began beating faster and faster and he felt cold sweat prickling all over his body, making him shiver uncontrollably as the creature looked around, seeming to sniff the air. With a sudden snap of its monstrous insect head, the beast fixed its hellish glare on Araga, snaring him in the gaze of its red eyes. With a pace startling for its size, the star-beast bounded up the slope, its forelimbs ripping at the earth to increase its speed.

Araga found himself transfixed, unable to move or shout. He realised this must be one of the creatures from beyond the Void which the newcomers had warned his people about, a predator from beyond the distant stars which had come for his soul.

As the monster sped towards him, Araga felt something nagging at the back of his mind, and realised he could hear a rumbling from off to his right. He wanted to look but could not tear his eyes away from the demon of destruction racing towards him. The creature was only a few great strides away from Araga, its claws arching back to deliver the killing attack.

Without warning, a lightning storm of light lashed into the Void Daemon, blasting it sprawling to the ground, its limbs flailing wildly. Snapped out of the beast's hypnotic spell, Araga span to see metal creatures advancing along the ridge, spitting fire at the monstrous intruder. The Sky Spirits had arrived to save him!

THE NATIVE JUST keeps on staring dumbly at us as we open fire again. I guess it ain't that surprising, considering that to these guys a simple mono-edged knife is a creation of the gods. Dumb locals, if they weren't so stupid they'd be able to fend for themselves and we wouldn't be here risking our necks to protect them. My attention's distracted away from him when the lictor gets to its feet again and the Chimeras have to fire another volley into the creature. I order the rest of the platoon to take up firing positions, keeping up a steady stream of las bolts as we advance. The lictor then leaps at Franx's squad, but even as it races towards them, hissing like some damned Oviran cobra, they tear it apart with their lasguns and heavy bolter. It kind of collapses in on itself, those huge killing claws folding over its body.

I walk up to make sure it's truly dead. You can never tell with these fragging tyranids. Some of them have got powers of regeneration you wouldn't believe. Its dark blood is spattered all over the thin grass, and it certainly looks like a corpse. To make sure, I level my laspistol at its head and fire six shots.

'Okay, Last Chancers!' I call to my platoon. 'Mount up and move out!'

Some of them begin to walk back to the Chimera transports, but Franx, Letts and some others walk over to where I'm standing. It's Letts who speaks first.

'We've been thinking, Kage. We've got the perfect opportunity here. I mean, we've got a great chance to get the hell out of this fragging outfit, once and for all.'

I look at them, not knowing what they mean. 'What've you got in mind?'

'Well,' Franx says, 'it's two leagues to the jungles. The Colonel would never find us in there, and there's plenty of food to forage, shelter, everything we need to survive. We just have to turn the Chimeras south and we're free men again.'

His eyes are intense now beneath his thick curls of hair, and he takes another step forward.

'Think of it!' he continues. 'No more Last Chancers! No more fragging suicide missions for the Colonel. No more spending every minute wondering what of a thousand kinds of hell we're going to end up in next. Free men, lieutenant, free men!'

I can hardly believe it. I've been fighting with Franx for a year, and Letts has been with the XIIIth Penal Legion for twice as long. Like me, like all the Last Chancers, they were thrown out of their regular units for breaking the Imperial Guard's rules in a big way, to serve the rest of their lives in a penal legion. We've walked across a dozen battlefields together, in the worst fighting you can imagine. We've been through them all – suicide assaults, rearguard actions and any other no-hope situation you can think of. It takes more than guts and brawn to survive for that long and I can't believe they're being so stupid now.

'What kind of fraggin' scheme is that?' I snap, and their jaws drop. Franx starts getting angry, and I can see the blood rushing to his face. He's gonna start trouble if I don't do something right now.

'Look, boys,' I say, trying to calm them down, 'you haven't thought this through, really. There's a tyranid hive ship up there, full of specially evolved killing machines, all hungering to eat you up as soon as look at you. The only reason the sky isn't full of mycetic spores yet is 'cause we've managed to pick off the lictors before they found Deliverance, so they ain't sure where to commit their forces.

'But it's just a stalling action, 'cause we can't get them all, no way – and even if we could, as soon as they find out there's more Imperial transports on the way, they'll send every bio-engineered little fragger they've got onto the planet.

'So the way I see it, you've got two choices. There's your plan, which means hanging around in the open, I know it's jungle but they'll still find you when they come down, and then what kind of chance are you gonna have? Or, you can come back with me to Deliverance, where there's a big wall to hide behind, three hundred more Last Chancers, the Battle Sisters and two thousand natives to help us fight. Your choice, but if you ain't going my way I'm gonna have to insist you go on foot. The Colonel would skin me if I let you take the Chimeras. It's only midday, so you've got eight hours walking to sundown, plenty of time for you to hole up and wait for the damn tyranids to come.'

I see realisation dawning on their faces like the sun breaking out from behind a cloud. I thought I'd taught them better than this, but it just goes to show that some people never learn anything unless they get taught the hard way. Unfortunately, when you're in the Last Chancers, most people who learn the hard way are food for the worms.

They don't say anything, they just turn around and start walking back to the Chimeras. I take one last look at the lictor, just to be safe. It's strange, 'cause any other type of cadaver would be crawling with flesh-ants on this damn planet by now, and there'd be a flock of carrion birds circling overhead. But there's nothing; not even the bugs will touch a tyranid. Frag, of all the things in this galaxy, those fraggers make my skin crawl the most.

So WE FINISH the firesweep, and I'm back in Deliverance, debriefing with the Colonel in the central keep. I can see the rest of the missionary station out of the window, the mid-afternoon sun blazing down fiercely. It's not big, little more than a large village really, half a mile across, with a large central compound, some scattered buildings, and of course this keep, which doubles as an Ecclesiarchy shrine. I can see the men walking sentry on the curtain wall and even at this distance I reckon I can feel their tension.

'Kage!' Colonel Schaeffer barks, and I snap back from the outside world. There's him, me and the other two lieutenants – Green and Kronin.

'As I was saying,' the Colonel continues pointedly, 'we've had a contact with the relief force. They are no more than two days away. If we can hold for just forty-eight hours, there will be two whole regiments of Imperial Guard. The wall should be fairly straightforward to defend. It is eighteen feet high, so we just have to worry about their hormagaunts and lictors leaping straight up it; the others we can pick off as they climb up the walls. That leaves only the gate, but that is flanked by two towers with emplaced autocannons, and we can park a Chimera behind the gates themselves to make it harder to force. Any questions?'

Kronin clears his throat nervously and wipes a hand through the thin hair plastered across his scalp. He's a skinny man, kind of jittery in my experience. Emperor alone knows how he had the guts to have his squad incinerate an Imperial temple after stealing the artefacts inside. Even more of surprise is that the Ecclesiarchy didn't demand his head on a pole and his entrails decorating the roadway.

'What about gargoyles, sir?' Kronin asks.

'No problem,' the Colonel assures us. He's ice cold, as usual, as calm as if we weren't going to be fighting for our damned lives in a few days, perhaps even in the next few hours. As always, he's wearing his full dress uniform, clean shaven like he was fresh out of the barracks.

He's a big man, physically I mean, but there's more to him than that. Those cold blue eyes and his own force of will make him seem twice as tall as anyone around. I wouldn't call it 'charisma', 'cause he's a uncommunicative and surly man. He just has this sheer presence that fills the room.

'We have two Hydras and this keep has four point-defence emplacements. If anything tries flying over the walls, we have the firepower to gun them down. In any case, Kage and his platoon are acting as mobile reserve behind the walls. If the tyranids get a breakthrough at the walls or gates, or we get some unexpected visitors dropping down, he'll move in and bolster the defence. Anything else?'

I glance out of the window again and see the sunlight glittering off highly polished armour, which makes me think of something.

'The Sisters. What's the deal there?' I ask, already knowing the answer.

'The Adepta Sororitas are under Ministorum authority, so we have no direct control over their actions. I have spoken to the Sister Superior in charge and outlined our plan. I am sure they will play their part. The same applies to the levies. They will be manning the walls, and we will concentrate our guns around the gatehouse. That is where the fighting will be fiercest.

'If you need to see me, that's where you'll find me.'

No surprise there, then. The Colonel is always in the roughest of the fighting, and he always walks out too. Emperor alone knows what makes him do it. We're here because we did wrong, and got caught. But him? What did he do wrong? I mean, what kind of man would choose to lead an Imperial Guard penal legion? What kind of mind do you need to walk into so many situations where you must be blessed by the Emperor to ever take another breath again, and then march straight out and into the next one? He must be mad, I mean seriously insane.

They say he spends his time on board ship practising ways to kill himself in the event that he's wounded. I take it back about the tyranids. There are some things which are a hell of a lot more scary, because they're in human form. That's what they say he is, a devil in human form, and when he's ready for a fight like now, and you look into his eyes like I'm doing now, you can believe it.

IT'S ABOUT NOON the day after and the tyranids have found us. Maybe a lictor slipped through the net, which wouldn't be surprising considering that for a big brute they can be really sneaky. They can sniff you out ten miles downwind, and they're covered in scales which shift colour so that you can't see them. Or maybe the 'nids just got fed up with waiting and decided to come and get us, wherever we are.

I stood on the wall last night and watched the spores dropping down. Scary sight, believe me. It was like ten meteor storms all at once, these falling stars coming down, wave after wave of them. There's an old saying: If you see a shooting star you can offer a prayer to the Emperor and he'll grant it.

Well, with all of those flaming stars that's one hell of a lot of prayers to be delivered on, but I decided to use them all in one go, for one big, huge prayer to the Emperor. Do you want to know what I prayed for? I prayed that those shooting stars would stop coming down. But they didn't, so I guess a murderer like me hasn't got the right to pray to the Emperor anymore, which is why I'm here fighting now, serving Him in the only way I know.

Frag, being here, in this missionary station with all these Ecclesiarchy types, it must be having an affect on me. I mean, I know the Emperor's our Lord and is watching over us, but I've always figured that those of us who can, have to watch out for ourselves, 'cause he's there to watch out for those who can't watch out for themselves. Just like we're here to defend the tribes people from the tyranids, 'cause all they've got are crappy knives and spears and brave warrior hearts, which is all well and good if you're fighting amongst yourselves, but against the tyranids is going to be about as effective as trying to stop a Sabre shell from blowing you away by holding up your hands.

But I guess, when you've stood there for an hour and watched your doom come down out of the stars in a constant flow, it'd be nice to know that if this is the time when it goes wrong and you end up with your guts torn out on a lictor's flesh hooks, or some hormagaunt stabs those dagger-talons through your chest, it ain't really the end, that there's someone waiting for you and it wasn't all a waste of time.

I know I've got to ditch these morbid thoughts. Got to stay sharp, otherwise this is gonna be my final trip with the Last Chancers. It's hard though, so hard, 'cause I was there on Ichar IV, I saw what they can do to a world, how they fight. There were six thousand Last Chancers back then. Less than five hundred of us made it out. The regular troops, I hear, lost over a million men defending Ichar IV.

There were Titans there, and Space Marines too, if the rumours are true, and even those eldar turned up, I heard someone say once. All those guns, all those men and we only just won the fight. I've seen so much blood and guts spilled in my life I don't have nightmares any more, but if there's one thing that would give me nightmares, it's tyranids. They're just so different to us. Even orks fight for territory and conquest, but the tyranids, they just consume everything, like they're here to wipe out every single living thing in the entire galaxy and they'll never, ever stop until that's done.

Which is why I was stood up on the wall last night, in the freezing wind – you'd never guess that it could be so hot in the day and so cold at night – watching them coming down. Watching my doom come, 'cause I've got a seriously bad feeling about this one. The hairs on my neck prickle constantly and I feel like I'm dead already, it's just my body that's gotta catch up with the plan.

Which is why I'm standing there hoping there really is an Emperor, that he listens to our prayers and comes to our aid. But I can't count on that, which is why I'm here now as the sun starts dipping towards the jungles, ready to fight like I've never had to fight before, ready to do anything I can, because death is stalking across those plains right now.

THE MAIN ASSAULT wave has hit the walls. The sun's low on the horizon and they attack from that direction to blind us. The Colonel was right about the gargoyles, our air defences were more than a match. About a hundred of them came flying in, diving down onto the fort. The guns opened up, blowing them out of the sky. Some managed to get over the walls, and then the Hydras got them, firing high explosive shells into the broods, blasting them apart. That was horrible, pieces of bloodied and charred meat dropping down on you like obscene hailstones. No time to clear up the mess, though, 'cause the rest of the swarm has just arrived. It's hard to tell what's going on from back where we are in reserve, a couple of hundred paces from the wall.

We've cleared ourselves a killing zone, demolishing the buildings inside the perimeter and using them to make a redoubt around the keep, so that if the tyranids get inside we've got a second firing line. Most of the action seems to be going off around the gatehouse, just like the Colonel said it would. The men are three ranks deep on the walls on the south side, while the Battle Sisters are holding the west wall. There's about half as many of the Sororitas as there are Last Chancers but they seem to be holding out better than we are. Then again, give me a bolt gun and power armour and I'd show you just how mean and nasty a Last Chancer can get.

It's about a quarter of an hour since the attack begun when the tyranids get their first breakthrough. I'm watching the eastern end of the south wall when I see a horde of termagants running around and I realise there's nobody else up that end anymore.

'Okay, Last Chancers! Time to die!' I bellow as usual, and then we're running across the killing ground towards the wall, fast as we can. The gunners in the Chimeras take the hint and suddenly there's a fusillade of heavy bolter fire and multilaser shots directed at the termagants. Thirty heart-pounding seconds later and we're leaping up the steps, snapping off shots with our lasguns as we close in. The supporting fire from the Chimeras stops as we reach the top and suddenly I'm surrounded by the creatures.

I see one of them levelling its living gun at me and just manage to take it down before it can fire. All of a sudden, they charge at us, and I rip my chainsword from my belt and get the blades whirling, while the others make ready with their bayonets. The termagants are biting and clawing at everything in their path, and I'd swear they were mindless if it wasn't for the co-ordinated fashion of their attack. As they sweep around me I feel like I'm going to get washed away in the wave, and panic hits me, bile rising out of my stomach as I see those fanged, nightmarish faces all around me. One of the termagants leaps at me, its four upper limbs drawn back ready to attack, but I bring the chainsword round and the blades crash through its carapace, sending thick, alien blood spattering across my face. It tastes foul and I'm almost sick with the stench of it. I put a shot through the bulbous head of another one and then something hits me hard in the back. This thing is latched onto me, and I can't get at it. I feel its claws scrabbling at my flak jacket, hear the material tearing away, and its hot breath is on my neck, a long pointed tongue slithering over my neck. Its jaws latch onto my shoulder and I try to angle my laspistol round for a shot, desperately trying to rip this beast off of me, 'cause I don't want to be killed by some damned termagant. I'm not going to go like this, not like this.

Before it gets the killing blow in, Truko is there, one of Franx's squad, his bayonet skewering the termagant, and I feel it let go and drop to the floor. There's no time to thank him, though, as he gets thrown to the ground, half his face ripped off by a vicious claw. The creature is hunched over him, all six limbs on the ground ready to spring, and its red eyes turn to look up at me. I shoot its legs from beneath it then drive the chainsword into its soft, unprotected guts. Truko's screaming, wailing his head off, but there's no time to give him peace. No rest for the wicked, as they say.

We push them back, inch by bloody inch, to the edge of the wall. I see Franx pick one of them up and hurl it bodily over the parapet, its limbs and tail still flailing around even as it plummets down. I look over the edge of the wall, and I see how they managed to get up. A pile of their bodies stretches two-thirds of the way up the wall, almost three metres high, body upon body upon body, creating a ramp of corpses for the others to run up.

'Grenades! Blow those bodies away from the wall!' I shout, even as I dodge aside to avoid a barbed tail lashing towards my throat. My chainsword bites again, making an ear-piercing screech as it shrieks through chitinous plates. The others heard me, though, and they're tossing frag grenades over the parapet, trying to dislodge the fleshy pile. I see Marshall standing atop the wall, gripping his lasrifle by the barrel and swinging it from side to side like a club, battering away at the brood as it scuttles up towards us. The grenades blossom, sending bits of torn flesh flying, and something gives. The pile of bodies slides outwards along the walls, falling to the ground leaving smears of blood along the rockcrete.

Then the termagants are falling back, away from the wall. But things aren't over yet, there's something else coming towards us, coming at us real fast. With long flea-like leaps and bounds the hormagaunts speed in, almost flying over the litter of corpses leading up to the wall. We're trying to shoot as many of them as possible as they close in, but there's still twenty, maybe thirty of them when they get to the base of the wall. They stop there for half a heartbeat, bunching those powerful leg muscles and then they spring up, clearing the wall by a good two or three feet, those four deadly dagger-talons jabbing out.

One of them punches its claw into Marshall's shoulder and he grabs its arm in one hand, holding it close. He wraps his other arm around the throat of another as it tries to push past, and then throws himself off the wall, taking them both with him. A serrated claw sweeps up towards my groin, but I manage to get there with the chainsword, lopping off the limb, my laspistol scoring a hit through one of its glassy red eyes. The rest of the fight just blurs into a waking nightmare of hacking and slashing and stabbing, kicking and shooting, punching and screaming, bestial faces and hot breath, flailing talons and ripping claws, blood and filth and guts slick across the walkway, a constant fight until your arms are leaden with fatigue and your brain can't process the information anymore, you're just fighting from instinct and nothing else.

WE MANAGE TO stave off the assault and as the tyranids fall back across the plain a cheer starts up by the gatehouse and spreads along the wall. I let my men cheer along as well, though we've got little to celebrate. The shock of the close call with the termagant is beginning to creep up on me and I look around for something to do to keep my mind occupied and not thinking about how close I came to going down this time. I see the Colonel striding along the walkway towards me, his face as grim as ever. I've never seen him break into a smile, not once.

'Kage! Clear away the dead. I'm sending flamer teams to clear the front of the wall.' Then he's gone again, issuing orders, getting the wounded divided into those that can fight and those that need to be given the Emperor's grace. That's it, no thanks, no 'Well done, Kage: you held the wall'. Just more orders, more work, more fighting and dying to be done. I detail some of my men to start throwing the bodies over the parapet, and see that the flamer teams are already at work, jets of fire turning the piles into pyres. I leave them to their dirty work and seek out the Colonel.

I find him outside the keep, talking to Nathaniel, the missionary in charge of the station. They seem to be arguing about something.

'But these men need treating, you cannot make them fight again,' Nathaniel's complaining.

'If these men cannot fight, they are dead, missionary. We need every single man we can have for the walls,' the Colonel replies in that low, grating voice of his. It's the first time I've had a chance to get a proper look at him since the fight began. His uniform is soaked in blood, alien and human, but none of it appears to be his. There's not a scratch on his skin, not a fragging scratch. My spine goes to ice and I try not to think about it.

Nathaniel's still arguing, but the Colonel holds up his hand to stop him.

'These men do not deserve your pity,' he says, his eyes flashing like sun on ice. 'They are thieves, murderers, looters, rapists, insubordinates and heretics. Every sin you can conceive of has been committed by at least one man here. More than that, they are traitors. They once served as free men in the great Imperial army. But they betrayed the trust placed in them by the Emperor and his servants. They have broken the proscriptions of Imperial Law and have profaned the Emperor's benevolence with their selfishness and I will, I must, punish them for it.'

'Only the Emperor can judge our sins,' argues Nathaniel.

'And only in death can we receive the Emperor's judgement,' the Colonel completes the catechism. Nathaniel takes a long look at him, then turns away.

'Remember, Nathaniel,' the Colonel calls after him, 'serve the Emperor today, for tomorrow you may be dead!' And then, just for an instant, a tiny fraction of a second, there's a ghost of a smile on Colonel Schaeffer's lips, a minuscule hint of satisfaction, like he knows something the rest of the galaxy doesn't.

'Kage!' he calls, like he must have sensed I was there, beckoning me over with a finger. 'As I am sure you know, that was just the first assault. I do not know when the next one will come, so stay ready. It is only an hour until the sun goes down, so I think they will wait until nightfall. I want you and your platoon to stay near the gate. This first attack was just to test out our defences, to count our guns. They know we were most hard-pressed around the gate, so they'll throw the bulk of their forces there next time.

'We must hold the gate at all costs, Kage, otherwise it's all over. Stay close to the gate, but wait for my signal. Do not, at any costs, allow yourself to get drawn away from the gate. Is that clear?'

'Perfectly, sir!' I reply, as if I couldn't see the scenario for myself. This time we just faced gargoyles, termagants and hormagaunts.

They're all expendable troops. Next time, it'll be much worse. They'll come in with the warriors, the carnifexes, and maybe even the big bug himself, the hive tyrant.

'You have your orders then, lieutenant. Snap to it, I want clear fire for everyone in half an hour.' Then he's off again, shouting for Green and Kronin.

THE COLONEL WAS right, as I knew he would be. Emperor take him, but he's always so damned right.

Nightfall comes sharply, the tyranids waiting us out for the moment. I help Kronin's platoon rig up some searchlights scavenged from the Chimeras and get them set up on the wall. The constant hum of the portable generators fills the air, but listening won't do us any good, 'cause those tyranids can move as silent as you like when they want to. That's one of the scariest things about them – the silence. No battlecries, no war chants, just waves of them sweeping on towards you. When they're fighting, they hiss a lot, but I doubt if they've got any real language to speak of. They're just animals, bugs, but they're well organised for all that. They're like the wasps I saw on Antreides, who seemed to know what each other were up to. When one of them found you, the rest would soon come buzzing in, just like the lictors finding the prey for the rest of the swarm.

So I'm up on the wall checking everything is okay, when the searchlights blaze on at last. The stupid grunts start angling them far away from the wall, like they want to get the earliest warning possible, which I can understand. Problem is, the light doesn't hit the ground before it's too weak to show anything.

I grab the nearest one and point it further down, about seventy metres out. I catch a glimmer of movement and shout for the others to train on that point. What I see makes my spine tingle with fear. A sensation, I might add, that I'm not all that familiar with, though far too familiar for my own liking. There's a big brood of termagants out there, crawling through the grass on their bellies, sneaking really close. Behind them are crouched the warriors, big beasts twice as tall as a man, their four upper limbs evolved into a variety of deadly ranged and close combat weapons. They're creeping forward, bony joints and chitinous plates shown up in the white glare of the searchlights.

The light glitters off their eyes, countless shining orbs reflected back at me. Those eyes seem dead, there's no emotion, nothing. Not even a touch of hunger, which is what you'd expect considering that this race devours whole planets. No, the only eyes I've ever seen colder than those white-fire stares are Colonel Schaeffer's, and we all know he's not really human.

'Mark your targets! Open fire!' I bellow. I see them opening up, first with the missile launchers and autocannons and then with volleys of lasgun fire as the 'nids realise the game's up and they rise out of the grass and charge towards us, a wave of multi-limbed monstrosities intent on our destruction. I take one last look as they come streaming over the plain, blossoms of fire exploding in their mist, showing up their snarling faces in brief glimpses of hellfire, before jumping down the steps three at a time to get back to my platoon.

'Right, men,' I tell them, 'stay steady. Follow my lead, stay tight. If you get separated, they'll pick you off, no problem. When you shoot, aim for the flesh. Your lasguns will have about as much effect on their carapace as punching a Leman Russ. Watch your ammo counters too, 'cause tonight's gonna be a long haul and I don't want to face those fraggin' bugs with just my bare hands.

'One final thing: don't get yourselves killed, 'cause otherwise I'm gonna have to put up with another fresh draft of no-hopers. If you let me go down, sure as hell I'm gonna make sure I come back and haunt you for the rest of your miserable lives, reminding you just what a bunch of fraggin' slack-jawed sons of orks you are!'

That gets a smile. Personally, I couldn't give a frag about all this pre-battle speech crap, but some of them need it, I can tell. Just like me, they're getting awful nervous. I mean, they're a bunch of hard-nosed, thick-skinned meatheads for the most part, but even when you've got nothing but air between your ears you can't get over the unreasoning horror that the tyranids bring out in you. It's not just like they kill you. They devour you, take everything you are, everything you ever were gonna be, and change it and pervert it into something else. It's a horrible thought, I don't mind telling you.

The fire's still pretty steady from the top of the wall, so I guess we're holding out okay. I give myself the luxury of watching the Battle Sisters for a while, fighting alongside the natives. It's a really bizarre scene, I can tell you. You have a thousand or so of those dark-skinned warriors, hurling spears and firing bows, their skin glistening with sweat, their booming war chants echoing down from the wall. And then there's the Sororitas. They're chanting too, their voices raised in constant prayer to the Emperor, a choir all singing as one. I can't make out the words, but it reaches inside me, lifting my spirits. It's a song of defiance and devotion, and as they sing they fire methodical bursts from their bolters, fusillade after fusillade pouring into the darkness, every round sending a streak of light into the shadows from its internal propellant.

Then I see a swathe of the natives jumping in all directions, screaming like mad, clawing at their faces and chests. That'd be a deathspitter then; fires some kind of explosive bug that sprays acid all over the place. Burn through near enough anything, given time, and against the exposed flesh of the native irregulars it's utterly lethal. Dragging my eyes away from the scene, trying to turn a deaf ear to their agonised screeches, I watch what's happening around the gatehouse.

There's hand-to-hand fighting going on now, and I pick out the Colonel, a glowing power sword in one fist and a bolt pistol in the other. While the others are desperately hacking and slaying, he's just stepping to and fro, felling a foe with every blow or shot, as if the chaos going on around wasn't happening at all. I see the shape of a lictor rise up behind him, but he just turns on the spot, fills its face full of bolts and then chops its legs from underneath it with two swings of the power sword. Calm as you like, as if he were just taking a stroll in the morning airs. Damn, but he's so cold, it makes the Battle Sisters seem positively emotional, and the glance they reserve for scum like us would freeze worse than a night on Valhalla.

Then something appears on the western gatehouse that almost makes me swallow my tongue in terror. Silhouetted against the rising moon is the figure of the hive tyrant. It's almost three times as tall as the men around it. Two arms are moulded into some kind of massive living gun, while the other two end in a whip-like protrusion and a serrated bonesword. A thick tail lashes between its legs, tipped with a sting the size of your arm. Mandibles that can chew a man in two snap hungrily in its jaw and its body is covered in chitinous armour and bony protrusions.

It fires the venom cannon into the packed mass on the gatehouse, blasting apart Guardsmen and tyranids alike. Its head stretches back and lets loose a horrifying bellowing screech, which seems to roll along the wall like a wave, sending men staggering in fear, making them pause in their fight so that they're cut down with ease by the termagants and warriors they're fighting. The tyrant steps down from the parapet, its hoofed feet sending splinters of masonry flying as it stamps down with all of its massive weight.

Gazing around, it fixes its evil eyes on the Colonel as he musters his men for a counter-attack. They charge in, las-bolts bouncing harmlessly off the monster's armoured hide, their bayonets snapping against its chitinous plates. Then the bonesword sweeps down and I see a spray of blood fountain into the air as four men are cut down with that single blow. The whip lashes out, its barbs tearing across the chest of another Guardsmen, his ragged corpse flung from the wall to land in a limp heap in the courtyard.

Surely even the Colonel has met his match this time. He's chopping his way through a brood of warriors to get at the hive tyrant. There's a pause in the fighting and he glances over the parapet to the ground outside. He stops for a moment and looks over to where we're positioned. With a wave of his arms, he signals us to attack.

'Here we go again, Last Chancers!' I shout out, and start heading for the wall. I've taken perhaps five steps when something seems wrong. I realise that I'm alone and I stop and look around. They're all just standing there, looking up at the hive tyrant as it butchers another squad of men.

'What the frag is this?' I howl. I grab Sergeant Feonix by his lapels and push him towards the wall, but he turns round and snarls at me.

'This is madness!' he shouts over the cries from the slaughter on the wall. 'That's a fraggin' hive tyrant, it's gonna kill every one of us! We've gotta get the hell out of here while we can. Deliverance has fallen, Kage, face it.' He calms down a little and fixes me with an intense stare. 'There's nothing more we can do! We've gotta save ourselves. You ain't no fraggin' martyr, Kage, and you know it.'

He's right, but then something catches my eye over their heads. There's lights dropping down from the stars again, curving down from orbit towards Deliverance in a long arc. I glance back at the gatehouse, and see the gates shuddering as some titanic beast tries to break them down. I make a decision.

'Look,' I tell them, pointing up to the pinpricks of light falling to the south. 'There ain't no escaping Deliverance, boys. That's more mycetic spores coming down, we're gonna be surrounded. There's no way we can get clear of the area before those things reach here.'

Kruzo, from Letts's squad, opens his mouth to argue but I cut him off.

'There ain't no getting outta this one, lads. We're all gonna die in Deliverance. Now I see it two ways. You can die running from the fight, like the thieves and cowards everyone thinks we are. Sure, you can do that, just get over the wall and hide out. But it won't take them long to find you, when you're all alone out there in the night, cowering in the grass, trying not to sh…'

A crash from the gatehouse distracts me and a I turn around to have a look. The Chimera behind the gates is rocking heavily on its tracks now, it's gonna go over any second, so I better make this quick.

'For frag's sake! We ain't got anything worth fighting for 'cept our pride. Right now I don't give a frag about the natives, or the Emperor, or the Colonel. But what I do care about is how I'm gonna die, and it ain't gonna be with my back turned or on my knees. I'm gonna go down fighting like a man. If there's any men here with me, then you better come too, otherwise you boys can just go running off to cry, dying on your bellies like the scum you are.'

I spit on the ground in front of them and then start walking towards the gate. I'm taking a hell of a risk, 'cause if they don't follow me I'm gonna be standing in front of the gate on my own when whatever it is that's so big and nasty to batter it's way through three feet of plasteel gets through. Then I hear the thud of boots and they're there with me, so I guess the suckers fell for it.

I look up and see that the hive tyrant's gone from the gate tower, but I can still see the Colonel, slicing away with that big power sword of his. Emperor knows how the frag he managed that one. Well, if I live to see the dawn, I might just find out. With a screech of tearing plasteel the gates are torn apart and the Chimera gets shunted towards us. There's a sound like a tank ramming a building and the personnel carrier is flung upwards, spinning through the air. It crashes down and its fuel goes up, a massive fireball that shoots thirty metres into the air. In the flames and smoke I see a sight that will follow me to my grave, long may it be before I get there.

In the red glare comes this huge tyranid creature, about four metres tall and just as wide. It's some kind of Carnifex, but nothing I've ever seen before. It's got four massive scythe-like arms, but the bony extrusions across its shoulders jut forward, rows of spikes thrust outwards like it's some kind of living battering ram. Nestled between its immense shoulders, its head is kind of fused with its chest, a large fang-ringed mouth open in a permanent roar. Pieces of twisted metal hang from the spines as it stomps through the smoke and flames like some monstrous devil from the pits of hell.

Without pause, it shoulders aside the wreck of the Chimera and I'm horrified to see that some of the burning vehicle tears off along one of the creature's armoured plates. The debris carries on burning, the flames crawling along the Carnifex's carapace but it just keeps advancing steadily as if nothing was happening.

'Blow that bastard away!' I shout, and everyone snaps out of the spell.

Breiden opens up with the lascannon, a bolt of energy powerful enough to cripple battle tanks scoring a wound across the carnifex's armoured skull making thick, dark blood dribble down the exoskeleton of its body. The heavy bolter in Franz's squad kicks in, explosive shells rippling across legs as thick as tree trunks in a shower of detonations.

But it still comes on, the ground shaking as those massive feet thud down into the dirt. It pauses for a second, its beady eyes reflecting the flickering flames and fixes us with a stare. Its arms arch back, spreading wider than the length of a tank and its cavernous mouth opens to bellow forth a roar that can probably be heard offworld. It breaks into a run, gathering momentum. Lasgun fire, heavy bolter shots and lascannon shots bounce off as it lumbers towards us. Once more its mouth opens for another terrifying roar, but Breiden picks his moment precisely, his aim guided by the Emperor I'm sure, and the next lascannon bolt lands in its mouth, smashing its head to a pulp, scattering fragments of skull across the courtyard.

For a moment I think that even that isn't enough to stop it, as it comes rumbling on towards us, but then the rest of the body catches up with what's happening and it collapses to the ground with dark, thick ichor oozing out in a gigantic puddle around the mammoth corpse.

I breathe a sigh of relief, glad that those useless fraggers decided to follow me after all, otherwise I'd be little more than a smear along those claws by now. However, just as my heart rate drops to something just below a million beats a minute, the rest of the tyranids start to pour through the opening. At the front is a brood of warriors, deathspitters and devourers firing as they advance.

Men are going down all around me and a stray spatter of acid splashes onto my arm. The pain is almost unbearable and I stoop to grab a handful of dirt to rub the acid off. My right arm's almost numb, so I drop my laspistol and grab my chainsword in my left hand. The lead warriors go down to fire from the lascannon and heavy bolters, but there's more and more of the things pouring through the gap now. I look around to see how the platoon's holding out, and I see there's only about two dozen of us left now.

Franz catches my gaze and I see his desperation turn into fierce pride in that single glance. As if a subconscious order is given, we all charge forward, throwing ourselves at the tide of beasts sweeping into Deliverance. My chainsword bites flesh and I hear an inhuman shriek of pain. I'm not really looking at what's happening, I'm just chopping left and right, hacking blindly, knowing that I can't miss in the tight press of alien creatures swirling around me.

Then a massive clawed paw, larger than a Cthellan cudbear's, comes out of the darkness, smashing me across the face. My head spins and I only dimly feel a sharp blade cutting across my thigh. I feel something wet and sticky pouring down my legs and I gaze down numbly, seeing my blood spilling to the dirt. I try to take a step forward but all my strength seems to have been sapped from me. I drop to my knees, feeling rough alien skin rasping against me, pushing past, leaving me for dead.

Then a shadow descends and I feel like I'm falling, falling down a deep, dark hole.

My ears pick up singing, my mind ringing to the sound of angelic voices singing the praises of the Emperor. So this is what it's like to die. There is an Emperor after all, and I shall receive my judgement, just like Nathaniel and the Colonel said. My thoughts are getting slow, but for the first time in ten years of fighting I feel proud. I didn't run this time, I stayed. I'm dying, but I went down fighting. Surely that's got to count for something.

I CAN HEAR VOICES, shouting, orders being bellowed. So I guess I'm alive then, and I really was right about those falling lights. I try to open my eyes, but the left one seems closed up. I raise an arm, feeling so weak, and touch my temple. Instant pain tells me that there's a bruise the size of a small moon up there, and it's probably blood crusting up my eye. My right arm is swathed in bandages and won't move at all.

Through my good eye I see there's troops running backwards and forwards, and I watch a line of three Leman Russ tanks warming up, ready to go out of the gate. I guess I'm propped up against the redoubt; I can feel rough stonework poking into my back. I turn my head slowly left and right, wary of dizziness and nausea, and I see that there's others like me, bandaged and bloody, all along the redoubt.

The Colonel walks past and he notices that I'm awake. He strides up and stands in front of me, thankfully blocking out the bright light of the sun. I can't see his face, it's in shadow, but he's looking down at me.

'Still alive then, Kage?' he demands, his voice as gruff as ever.

"Fraid so, sir. Guess I can't kick the habit just yet.' I try to manage a smile, but my face is just a mass of aching and pain.

'I head what happened,' he says, dropping down on one knee so that I can see those icy eyes as they fix me with their stare. 'Tell me one thing, Kage. You could have run out on me, you had the chance and you have done it before. What made you fight?'

I fix him with my good eye, returning his gaze with a steady look of my own.

'Well, sir, it's like this,' I explain. 'I saw the lights coming down, and I knew they were Imperial Guard transports. Mycetic spores just come straight down, but they had a landing trajectory. So I knew that Deliverance was saved. Thing was, though, we had to hold out, 'cause if the tyranids got into the compound we'd all be dead. There's nowhere to run from those creatures.'

The Colonel frowns at me.

'So why did you tell your men that there were more spores coming down, rather than the relief force?' he asks.

'You must know why, sir,' I reply, because it seems so obvious to me. 'If I told them that help was on the way, they'd lose what little stomach they had left. They'd think they could give up, get away from here. But like I said, there wasn't any escape from Deliverance, not a chance. So I did the only thing I could. I stripped them of that false hope, I gave them nothing to live for except life itself.

'You see, sir, when you ain't got frag-all worth fighting for, you'll still fight to be alive. Give a man a chance to back down and he'll take it, but give him nothing and he'll grab what he can with both hands and not let go for as long as he can. He'll fight to his last breath just to take one more breath, to feel his heart beat just once more before he dies. If you stick a man in the middle of a fight and give him a gun, he'll fight like a cornered rat 'cause there's nothing else he can do.

'That's the way the Last Chancers work, sir. It's exactly what you do to us all. We ain't got no choice but to fight, and fight good, 'cause if we don't, we're dead. None of us wants to die so we'll do all we can, everything that's possible including going on your damned suicide mission just to breathe one more time. It's why I fight, why they fight.'

He just grunts and stands up. He turns to walk away but I call after him.

'There's another reason why I'll fight my damnedest, sir!'

He spins around and looks at me, an eyebrow raised in question.

'I–I ain't gonna give you the fragging satisfaction of seeing me dead just yet, sir!'

13th LEGION

THE CHAMBER HUMMED and vibrated with energy that coursed along the thick cables snaking across the low ceiling. Somewhere in the distance could be heard the steady thump-thump-thump of heavy machinery in operation. Glowglobes set at metre intervals around the metal walls of the square room illuminated the scene with a fitful, jaundiced light. With a creak the lock wheel on the door span slowly; thick metal bars to either side of the portal ground through their rusted brackets. The door swung open and a figure stepped inside, swathed in a long black greatcoat, the tall collar obscuring his face. As he paced into the light, his thin face caught the yellow glow giving him a sickly pallor. His dark eyes glanced back over his shoulder before he took another step forward, easing the door closed behind him.

Suddenly the man stopped. His eyes snapped to the artefact stored in the middle of the room. It resembled a coffin, stood on end with a rat's nest of wires springing from it to fasten to hastily rigged connectors that pierced the cabling on the ceiling. The glass front of the coffin lay in shards and splinters across the floor. Of what was contained within, there was no sign. Recovering from his initial shock, the man began to examine the sarcophagus, prodding with an inexpert finger at various dials set into its sides. He stepped back and stroked the fingers of a hand gloved in black velvet through his short goatee beard, brow furrowed in concentration, lips twisted in agitation.

'Emperor-damned stasis chamber,' he muttered to himself, looking around once more. 'I should have got it consecrated by a tech-priest.'

As he walked around to the back of the coffin his gaze was caught by a darker shadow in the top corner of the far wall. He peered closer and saw a ventilation duct. Its corroded grille had been twisted and torn, ripped to one side. Standing on tiptoe he pulled himself up to look into the opening: the faint light from the room illuminated a metre or so of a narrow shaft that swiftly sloped upwards and out of sight. Dropping back to the floor, he banged his fist against his thigh with a short frustrated gesture. He pulled the glove from his right hand and reached into a deep pocket inside his coat, pulling out a device the size of a clenched fist. As he stabbed a button on its surface, the light from the glowglobes caught on a golden ring on his index finger, inscribed with the device of an 'I' inset with a grinning skull.

Raising the device to his lips, the man spoke.

'Third day of Euphistles. I have returned to the stasis generator, which appears to have malfunctioned. The specimen has escaped. I will start immediate investigations to recover or eliminate it. I pray to the Emperor that I can recapture the monster. This mistake could cost us dearly.'

ONE
LEAVING DELIVERANCE

+++ *What is the status of Operation Harvest?* +++

+++ *Operation Harvest is beginning second stage as scheduled.* +++

THE GUARDSMAN'S NOSE explodes with blood as my fist crashes between his eyes. Next, I hit him with a left to the chin, knocking him backwards a step. He ducks out of the next punch, spitting blood from cracked lips. My nose is filled with the smell of old sweat and fresh blood, and perspiration from the blazing sun trickles down my face and throat. All around I can hear chanting and cheering.

'Fraggin' kink his fraggin' neck!' I recognise Jorett's voice.

'Break the son of an ork apart!' Franx yells.

The Guardsmen from Chorek are cheering their man on too, their flushed faces looking dark in contrast to their white and grey camouflage jackets and leggings.

He makes a lunge at me, his face swathed in blood, his dusty uniform covered in red stains. I easily side-step his bullish charge, bringing my knee up hard into his abdomen and feeling some ribs crack under the blow. He's doubled up now, his face a mask of pain, but I'm not going to stop there. I grab the back of his head with both hands and ram my knee up into his face, hearing the snap of his cheek or jaw fracturing. He collapses sideways, and as he falls, the toecap of my standard-issue boot connects with his chin, hurling his head backward into the hard soil. I'm about to lay into him again when I realise everything's gone dead quiet. I look up to see what the hell's happening, panting hard.

Pushing through the Chorek ranks is a massively muscled man, and I spot the insignia of a master sergeant on the blue sleeve of his tunic. He's got the black pelt of some shaggy creature tied as a cloak over his left shoulder and his eyes are fixed on me with murderous intent. In his hand is a sixty-centimetre metal parade baton, red jewels clustered around one end, and as he steps up to me he smashes the point of it into my guts, knocking the wind out of me and forcing me to my knees.

'Penal legion scum!' the Chorek master sergeant barks. 'I'll show you what they should have done to you!'

He pulls his arm back for a good swing at me but then stops in mid-strike. Just try it, I think to myself, I've killed harder men and creatures than you. I'm still fired up from the fight and ready to pounce on this jumped-up bully of an officer. I'll give him the same treatment I've just dealt out to his man. He glances over my head and a shadow falls over me. A prickly sensation starts at the back of my neck and turns into a slight shiver down my spine. I turn to look over my shoulder, still clutching my aching guts, and see that he's there. The Colonel. Colonel Schaeffer, commanding officer of the 13th Penal Legion, known by those unlucky enough to be counted amongst its number as the Last Chancers. The swollen dusk sun's behind him – the sun always seems to be behind him, he's always in shadow or silhouette when you first see him, like it's a talent he's got. All I can see is the icy glitter of his sharp blue eyes, looking at the master sergeant, not me. I'm glad of that because his face is set like stone, a sure sign that he is in a bad mood.

'That will be all, master sergeant,' the Colonel says calmly, just standing there with his left hand resting lightly on the hilt of his power sword.

'This man needs disciplining,' replies the Chorek, arm still raised for the blow. I think this guy is stupid enough to try it as well, and secretly hope he will, just to see what Schaeffer does to him.

'Disperse your troopers from the landing field,' the Colonel tells the master sergeant, 'and mine will then be soon out of your way.'

The Chorek officer looks like he's going to argue some more, but then I see he makes the mistake of meeting the Colonel's gaze and I smirk as I see him flinch under that cold stare. Everyone sees something different in those blue eyes, but it's always something painful and unpleasant that they're reminded of. The Colonel doesn't move or say anything while the master sergeant herds his men away, pushing them with the baton when they turn to look back. He details two of them to drag away the trooper I knocked out and he casts one murderous glance back at me. I know his kind, an unmistakable bully, and the Choreks are going to suffer for his humiliation when they reach their camp.

'On your feet, Kage!' snaps the Colonel, still not moving a muscle. I struggle up, wincing as soreness flashes across my stomach from the master sergeant's blow. I don't meet the Colonel's gaze, but already I'm tensing, expecting the sharp edge of his tongue.

'Explain yourself, lieutenant,' he says quietly, folding his arms like a cross tutor.

'That Chorek scum said we should've all died in Deliverance, sir,' I tell him. 'Said we didn't deserve to live. Well, sir, I've just been on burial detail for nearly a hundred and fifty Last Chancers, and I lost my temper.'

'You think that gutter scum like you deserve to live?' the Colonel asks quietly.

'I know that we fought as hard as any bloody Chorek Guardsman, harder even,' I tell him, looking straight at him for the first time. The Colonel seems to think for a moment, before nodding sharply.

'Good,' he says, and I can't stop my jaw from dropping in surprise. 'Get these men onto the shuttle – without any more fighting, Lieutenant Kage,' the Colonel orders, turning on his heel and marching off back towards the settlement of Deliverance.

I cast an astonished look at the other Last Chancers around me, the glance met with knotted brows and shrugs. I compose myself for a moment, trying not to work out what the hell that was all about. I've learnt it's best not to try to fathom out the Colonel sometimes, it'll just tie your head in knots.

'Well, you useless bunch of fraggin' lowlifes,' I snap at the remnants of my platoon, 'you heard the Colonel. Get your sorry hides onto that shuttle at the double!'

As I JOG towards the blocky shape of our shuttle, Franx falls in on my left. I try to ignore the big sergeant, still annoyed with him from a couple of days ago, when he could have got me into deep trouble with the Colonel.

'Kage,' he begins, glancing down across his broad shoulder at me. 'Haven't had a chance to talk to you since... Well, since before the tyranids attacked.'

'You mean since before you tried to lead the platoon into the jungles on some stupid escape attempt?' I snap back, my voice purposefully harsh. He wasn't going to get off easily, even if I did consider him something of a friend. A friendship he'd pushed to the limits by trying to incite a rebellion around me.

'Can't blame me, Kage,' he says, with a slight whine to his deep voice that irritates me. 'Should've all died back then, you know it.'

'I'm still alive, and I know that if I'd let you take off I wouldn't be,' I reply, not even bothering to look at him. 'The Colonel would've killed me for letting you go, even before the 'nids had a chance.'

'Yeah, I know, I know,' Franx tells me apologetically.

'Look,' I say, finally meeting his eye, 'I can't blame you for wanting out. Emperor knows, it's what we all want. But you've got to be smarter about it. Pick your time better, and not one that's gonna leave me implicated.'

'I understand, Kage,' Franx nods before falling silent. One of the shuttle crewmen, looking hot and bothered in his crisp blue and white Navy uniform, is counting us off as we head up the loading ramp, giving us sullen looks as if he wishes they could just leave us here. It's hot inside the shuttle, which has slowly baked in the harsh sun until the air inside feels like a kiln. I see the others settling into places along the three benches, securing themselves with thick restraint belts that hang from beams that stretch at head height along the shuttle chamber's ten-metre length. As I find a place and strap myself into the restraining harnesses, Franx takes the place next to me.

'How's Kronin?' he asks, fumbling with a metal buckle as he pulls the leather straps tighter across his barrel chest.

'Haven't seen him. He went up on the first shuttle run,' I tell him, checking around to see that everybody else is secured. Seeing that the survivors of my platoon are sitting as tight as a Battle Sister's affections, I give the signal to the naval rating waiting at the end of the seating bay. He disappears through the bulkhead and the red take-off lights flash three times in warning.

'I haven't got the full story about Kronin yet,' I say to Franx, pushing my back against the hard metal of the bench to settle myself. Franx is about to reply when the rumble of thrusters reverberates through the fuselage of the shuttle. The rumbling increases in volume to a roar and I feel myself being pushed further into the bench by the shuttle's take-off. The whole craft starts to shake violently as it gathers momentum, soaring upwards into the sky above Deliverance. My booted feet judder against the mesh decking of the shuttle and my backside slides slightly across the metal bench. My stomach is still painful, and I feel slightly sick as the shuttle banks over sharply to take its new course. The twelve centimetre slash in my thigh begins to throb painfully as more blood is forced into my legs by the acceleration. I grit my teeth and ignore the pain. Through a viewport opposite I can see the ground dropping away, the seemingly haphazard scattering of shuttles and dropships sitting a kilometre beyond the walls of Deliverance. The settlement itself is receding quickly, until I can only dimly make out the line of the curtain wall and the block of the central keep. Then we're into the clouds and everything turns white.

As we break out of the atmosphere the engines turn to a dull whine and a scattering of stars replaces the blue of the sky outside the viewport. Franx leans over.

'They say Kronin is touched,' he says, tapping the side of his head to emphasise his point.

'It's bloody strange, I'll give you that,' I reply. 'Something happened to him when he was in the chapel.'

'Chapel?' Franx asks, scratching his head vigorously through a thick bush of brown curls.

'What did you hear?' I say, curious to find out what rumours had started flying around, only a day after the battle against the tyranids. Gossip is a good way of gauging morale, as well as the reactions to a recent battle. Of course, we're never happy, being stuck in a penal legion until we die, but sometimes some of the men are more depressed than usual. The fight against the alien tyranids at the missionary station was horrific, combating monsters like them always is. I wanted to know what the men were focusing their thoughts on.

'Nothing really,' Franx says, trying unsuccessfully to shrug in the tight confines of the safety harness. 'People are saying that he went over the edge.'

'The way I heard it, he and the rest of 2nd platoon had fallen back to the chapel,' I tell him. 'There were 'nids rushing about everywhere, coming over the east wall. Most of them were the big warriors, smashing at the doors of the shrine with their claws, battering their way in. They crashed through the windows and got inside. There was nowhere to run; those alien bastards just started

hacking and chopping at everything inside. They lost the whole platoon except for Kronin. They must have left him for dead, since the
Colonel found him under a pile of bodies.'

'That's a sure way to crack,' Franx says sagely, a half-smile on his
bulbous lips.

'Anyway,' I continue, 'Kronin is cracked, like you say. Keeps talking
all this gibber, constantly jabbering away about something that no
one could work out.'

'I've seen that sort of thing before,' says Poal, who's been listening
from the other side of Franx. His narrow, chiselled face has a knowing air about it, like he was a sage dispensing the wisdom of the
ancients or something. 'I had a sergeant once whose leg was blown
off by a mine on Gaulis II. He just kept repeating his brother's name,
minute after minute, day after day. He slit his own throat with a
med's scalpel in the end.'

There's a moment of silence as everybody considers this, and I carry
on with the story to distract them from thoughts of self-murder.

'Yeah, that's pretty grim,' I tell them, 'but Kronin's case just gets
weirder. Turns out, he's not mumbling just any old thing, oh no. He's
quoting scripture, right? Nathaniel, the preacher back in Deliverance,
overhears him saying out lines from the Litanies of Faith. Stuff like:
"And the Beast from the Abyss rose up with its multitudes and laid
low the servants of the Emperor with its clawed hands". Things like
that.'

'Fragged if I've ever seen Kronin with a damned prayer book, not in
two fragging years of fighting under the son of an ork,' Jorett
announces from the bench down the middle of the shuttle, looking
around. Everybody's listening in now that we can be heard over the
dimmed noise of the engines. Forty pairs of eyes look towards me in
anticipation of the next twist of the tale.

'Exactly!' I declare with an emphatic nod, beginning to play to the
audience a little bit. I'm enjoying having a new tale to tell for a
change, and it keeps them from falling out with each other, which
usually happens when we wind down from a mission.

'Nathaniel sits down with him for a couple of hours while we bury
the dead,' I continue, passing my gaze over those that can see me. 'I
heard him explaining his view on things to the Colonel. Seems Kronin had a visitation from the Emperor himself while he lay half-dead
in the chapel. Says he has been given divine knowledge. Of course,
he doesn't actually say this, he's just quoting appropriate lines from
the Litanies, like: "And the Emperor appeared with a shimmering

halo and spake unto His people on Gathalamor." And like you say, how in the seven hells does he know any of this stuff?'

'There is nothing mystical about that,' answers Gappo, sitting on his own towards the rear of the shuttle. Nearly everybody seems to give an inward groan, except a couple of the guys who are looking forward to this new development in the entertainment. Myself, I've kind of come to like Gappo – he's not such a meathead as most of the others.

'Oh wise preacher,' Poal says with a sarcastic sneer, 'please enlighten us with your bountiful wisdom.'

'Don't call me "preacher"!' Gappo snarls, a scowl creasing his flat, middle-aged features. 'You know I have left that falsehood behind.'

'Whatever you say, Gappo,' Poal tells him with a disdainful look.

'It's quite simple really,' Gappo begins to explain, patently ignoring Poal now. 'You've all been to Ecclesiarchal services, hundreds even thousands of them. Whether you remember them or not, you've probably heard all of the Litanies of Faith and every line from the Book of Saints twice over. Kronin's trauma has affected his mind, so that he can remember those writings and nothing else. It's the only way he's got left to communicate.'

There are a few nods, and I can see the sense of it. People's heads are half-fragged up anyway, in my experience. It doesn't take much to jog it loose, from what I've seen. Emperor alone knows how many times I've felt myself teetering on the edge of the insanity chasm. Luckily I'm as tough as grox hide and it hasn't affected me yet. Not so as anyone's told me, in any case.

'Well I guess that makes more sense than the Emperor filling him with His divine spirit,' says Mallory, a balding, scrawny malingerer sitting next to Poal. 'After all, I don't think the Emperor's best pleased with our Lieutenant Kronin, 'specially considering the fact that Kronin's in the Last Chancers for looting and burning down a shrine.'

'Of course it makes sense,' Gappo says, his voice dropping to a conspiratorial whisper. 'There might not be an Emperor at all!'

'You shut your fragging mouth, Gappo Elfinzo!' Poal spits, making the sign of the protective eagle over his chest with his right hand. 'I may have murdered women and children and I know I'm a lowlife piece of ork crap, but I still think I shouldn't have to share the same room with a fragging heretic!'

Poal starts to fumble at his straps, having trouble because his left arm ends in a hook instead of a hand. I can see things might be getting out of control.

'That's enough!' I bark. 'You all know the score. Doesn't matter what you did to wind up as one of the Colonel's doomed men, we're all Last Chancers now. Now shut the frag up until we're back on the transport.'

There are a few grumbles, but nobody says anything out loud. More than one of them here has had a cracked skull or a broken nose for answering me back. I'm not a bully, you understand, I just have a short temper and don't like it when my men start getting too disrespectful. Seeing that everybody is calming down, I close my eyes and try to get some sleep; it'll be another two hours before we dock.

THE TRAMP OF booted feet echoes around us as the Navy armsmen march us back to our cells. Left and right, along the seemingly endless corridor are the vaulted archways leading to the cargo bays, modified to carry human cargo in supposedly total security. There are twenty of the massive cells in all. Originally each held two hundred men, but after the past thirty months of near-constant war, nearly all of them stand empty now. It'll be even emptier for the rest of the trip; there's only about two hundred and fifty of us left after the defence of Deliverance. The armsmen swagger around, shotcannons grasped easily in heavily gloved hands or slung over their shoulders. Their faces are covered by the helms of their heavy-duty work suits, and their flash-protective visors conceal their features. Only the name badges stitched onto their left shoulder straps show that the same ten men have been escorting my platoon for the past two and a half years.

I see the Colonel waiting up ahead, with someone standing next to him. As we get closer, I see that it's Kronin, his small, thin body half-hunched as if weighed down by some great invisible burden. The lieutenant's narrow eyes flit and dart from side to side, constantly scanning the shadows, and he flinches as I step up to Schaeffer and salute.

'Lieutenant Kronin is the only survivor of 3rd platoon,' the Colonel tells me as he waves the armsmen to move the others inside, 'so I am putting him in with you. In fact, with so few of you left, you are going to be gathered into a single formation now. You will be in charge; Green was killed in Deliverance.'

'How, sir?' I ask, curious as to what happened to the other lieutenant, one of the hundred and fifty Last Chancers who was alive two days ago and now is food for the flesh-ants of the nameless planet below us.

'He was diced by a strangleweb,' the Colonel says coldly, no sign of any emotion on his face at all. I wince inside – being slowly cut up as you try to struggle out of a constricting mesh of barbed muscle is a nasty way to go. Come to think of it, I've never thought of a nice way to go.

'I am leaving it to you to organise the rest of the men into squads and to detail special duties,' the Colonel says before stepping past me and striding down the corridor. A Departmento flunky swathed in an oversized brown robe hurries down to the Colonel carrying a massive bundle of parchments, and then they are both lost in the distant gloom.

'Inside,' orders an armsman from behind me, his nametag showing him to be Warrant Officer Hopkinsson.

The massive cell doors clang shut behind me, leaving me locked in this room with ten score murderers, thieves, rapists, heretics, looters, shirkers, desecrators, grave-robbers, necrophiles, maniacs, insubordinates, blasphemers and other assorted vermin for company. Still, it makes for interesting conversation sometimes.

'Right!' I call out, my voice rebounding off the high metal ceiling and distant bulkheads. 'All sergeants get your sorry hides over here!'

As the order is passed around the massive holding pen, I gaze over my small force. There's a couple of hundred of us left now, sitting or lying around in scattered groups on the metal decking, stretching away into the gloom of the chamber. Their voices babble quietly, making the metal walls ring slightly and I can smell their combined sweat from several days on the furnace-hot planet below. In a couple of minutes eight men are stood around me. I catch sight of an unwelcome face.

'Who made you a sergeant, Rollis?' I demand, stepping up to stand right in front of his blubbery face, staring straight into his beady black eyes.

'Lieutenant Green did,' he says defiantly, matching my stare.

'Yeah? Well you're just a trooper again now, you piece of dirt!' I snap at him, pushing him away. 'Get out of my sight, you fraggin' traitor.'

'You can't do this!' he shouts, taking a step towards me and half-raising a fist. My elbow snaps out sharply and connects with his throat, sending him gasping to the floor.

'Can't I?' I snarl at him. 'I guess I can't do this either,' I say, kicking him in the ribs. Forget about the murderers, it's the out-and-out traitors like him that make me want to heave. With a venomous glance he gets to his hands and knees and crawls away.

'Right,' I say, turning to the others, putting the fat piece of filth from my mind. 'Where were we?'

ALARM SIRENS are sounding everywhere, a piercing shrill that sets your teeth on edge. I'm standing with a pneu-mattock grasped in both hands, its engine chugging comfortably, wisps of oily smoke leaking from its exhaust vents.

'Hurry up, wreck the place!' someone shouts from behind me. I can hear the sound of machinery being smashed, pipelines being cut and energy coils being shattered. There's a panel of dials in front of me and I place the head of the hammer against it, thumbing up the revs on the engine to full, the air filling with flying splinters of glass and shards of torn metal. Sparks of energy splash across my heavy coveralls, leaving tiny burn marks on the thick gloves covering my hands. I turn the pneu-mattock on a huge gear-and-chain mechanism behind the trashed panel, sending toothed wheels clanging to the ground and the heavy chain whipping past my head.

'They're coming!' the earlier voice calls out over the din of twisting metal and fracturing glass. I look over my shoulder to see a bunch of security men hurrying through an archway to my left, wearing heavy carapace breastplates coloured dark red with the twisted chain and eye mark of the Harpikon Union picked out in bold yellow. They've all got vicious-looking slug guns, black enamelled pieces of metal that catch the light menacingly. People hurrying past jostle me, but it's hard to see their faces, like they're in a mist or something. I get a glimpse of a half-rotten skull resembling a man called Snowton, but I know that Snowton died a year ago fighting pirates in the Zandis Belt. Other faces, faces of men who are dead, flit past. There's a thunderous roar and everybody starts rushing around. I realise that the Harpikon guards are firing. Bullets ricochet all over the place, zinging off pieces of machinery and thudding into the flesh of those around me. I try to run, but my feet feel welded to the floor. I look around desperately for somewhere to hide, but there isn't anywhere. Then I'm alone with the security men, the smoking muzzles of their guns pointing in my direction. There's a blinding flash and the thunder of shooting.

I WAKE UP from the dream gasping for breath, sweat coating my skin despite the chill of the large cell. I fling aside the thin blanket that serves as my bed and sit up, placing my hands on the cold floor to steady myself as dizziness from the sudden movement swamps me.

Gulping down what feels like a dead rat in my mouth, I look around. There's the usual night-cycle activity – mumbles and groans from the sleepless, the odd murmured prayer as some other poor soul is afflicted by the sleep-daemons. It's always the same once you've dropped into the Immaterium.

I've had the same nightmare every night in warpspace for the past three years, ever since I joined the Imperial Guard. I'm always back in the hive on Olympas, carrying out a wreck-raid on a rival factory. Sometimes it's the Harpikon Union, like tonight; other times it's against the Jorean Consuls; and sometimes even the nobles of the Enlightened, though we never dared do that for real. There's always the walking dead as well. Folks from my past come back to haunt me: people I've killed, comrades who have died, my family, all of them appear in the nightmares. Lately I've realised that there's more and more of them after every battle, like the fallen are being added to my dreams. I always end up dying as well, which is perhaps the most disturbing thing. Sometimes I'm blown apart by gunfire, other times I'm sawn in half by a poweraxe or a chainsword, sometimes I'm burnt alive by firethrowers. Several people have told me that the warp is not bound in time like the real universe. Instead, you might see images from your past or your future, all mixed together in strange ways. Interpreting warp dreams is a speciality of Lammax, one of the ex-Departmento men. I think they threw him into the penal legions for blasphemy after he offered to read the dreams of a quartermaster-major. He says it's my fear of death being manifested.

Suddenly there's a demented screaming from the far end of the cargo hold where we're held, down where the lighting has gone fritzy and its arrhythmic pulsing gives you a headache. Nobody's slept down there for months, not since there was enough room for everyone to fit in at this end. With everyone gathered in one cell now, someone must have had to try to get to sleep down there. I push myself to my feet and pull on my boots over my bare feet. As I walk towards the commotion, I rub a hand across my bared chest to wipe off the sweat. My body tingles all over with a bizarre feeling of energy, the map of scars traced out across my torso feels strangely hot under my fingertips. I look down, half-expecting the old wounds to be glowing. They're not.

I tramp into the gloom, watched by most of the others. The screaming's loud enough to wake up the Navy ratings on the next deck up. I understand their suspicion and morbid curiosity, because sometimes when a man starts screaming in warpspace, it's not with his own voice. Luckily it's never happened to anyone I know, but there are guys here who tell tales of men being possessed by creatures from the warp. They either go completely mad and kill a load of people before collapsing and dying, or they get taken over totally becoming a body for some strange creature's mind, in which case they'll stalk along the corridors calmly murdering anyone they come across. And that's even when the Immaterium shielding is still working. You don't want to know what happens on a ship whose warp-wards collapse under the continual assault from formless beings intent on the death of the ship's crew.

'Emperor of Terra, watch over me,' I whisper to myself as I'm halfway towards the source of the screeching. If it is a Touched One, this could be some really serious trouble. They don't allow us anything that can be used as a weapon, so we're virtually defenceless. Still, that's just as well really, because there'd be a hell of a lot less of us left if we were armed. Fights break out a lot, but despite what some people think it takes a while to beat someone to death and somebody usually breaks it up before there's a casualty. That said, if I wanted to kill someone I could, particularly if they're sleeping.

My whole body's shaking, and I'm not quite sure why. I try to tell myself it's the cold, but I'm man enough to admit when I'm scared. Men don't scare me, except perhaps the Colonel. Aliens give me shudders now and then, especially the tyranids, but there's something about the idea of warp creatures that just shivers me the core, even though I've never had to face one. There's nothing that I can think of in the galaxy that's more unholy.

I can see someone thrashing around in a blanket ahead, just where the lights go gloomy. It's hard to see in the intermittent haze of the broken glow-globe, but I think I see Kronin's face twisting and turning. I hear footsteps behind me and turn suddenly, almost lashing out at Franx who's got up and followed me.

'Just warp-dreams,' he tries to reassure me with a crooked smile, his big hands held up in reflex.

'Like that makes me feel better,' I reply shortly, turning back to the writhing figure of Kronin. I can just about make out words in the shrieks bursting from his contorted mouth.

'And from the deeps... there arose a mighty beast, of many eyes... and many limbs. And the beast from the... darkness did set upon the light of mankind... with hateful thirst and unnatural hunger!'

'Don't wake him!' Franx hisses as I reach out a hand towards the struggling figure.

'Why not?' I demand, kneeling down beside Kronin and glaring back at the sergeant.

'Preacher Durant once said that waking a man with warp-dreams empties his mind, allows Chaos to seep in,' he says with an earnest look in his face.

'Well, I'll just have to risk a bit of corruption, won't I?' I tell him, annoyed at what seems like a childish superstition to me. 'If he carries on like that for the rest of the cycle, I'm not going to get any sleep at all.'

I rest a hand on Kronin's shoulder, gently at first but squeezing more firmly when he continues to toss and turn. It still doesn't do any good and I lean over him and slap him hard on the cheek with the back of my hand. His eyes snap open and there's a dangerous light in them for a second, but that's quickly replaced by a vague recognition. He sits up and looks straight at me, eyes squinting in the faltering light.

'Saint Lucius spake unto the masses of Belushidar, and great was their uproar of delight,' he says with a warm smile on his thin lips, but his eyes quickly fill with a haunted look.

'Guess that means thanks,' I say to Franx, standing up as Kronin lowers himself back down onto the blanket, glancing around once more before closing his eyes. I stay there for a couple more minutes until Kronin's breathing is shallow and regular again, meaning he's either really asleep or faking it well enough for me not to care any more.

Why the hell did Green have to get himself killed, I ask myself miserably as I trudge back to my sleeping area? I could do without the responsibility of wet-nursing this bunch of frag-for-brains criminals. It's hard enough just to survive in the Last Chancers without having to worry about everyone else. I guess I'll just have to not worry, let them take care of themselves. Hell, if they can't do that, they deserve to die.

It's a few days after the incident with Kronin, and we're sitting down for mess in the middle of the cell, sprawled on the floor with dishes of protein globs in front of us. We have to spoon it out by hand; they won't let us have any kind of cutlery in case it can be sharpened into a blade of some sort. It's this kind of attitude that can really break a man – them not trusting you to even be able to sit down for a meal without being at each other's throats. The food is also picked to grind you down. I know for a fact that they brought hundreds of horn-heads on board from the plains around Deliverance, but do we see any sign of freshly slaughtered meat? Do we ever. No, it's just the same brown, half-liquid slush that you have to shovel into your mouth with your fingers, feeling it slide horribly down your throat with the consistency of cold vomit. You get used to it after a while, you have to. You just shove it in, swallow and hope you don't gag too much. It doesn't even taste of anything except the brackish water it's mixed with. It's cold and slimy, and more than once I've felt like hurling the stuff back into the armsmen's faces, but that'd just get me a kicking and the chance to go hungry. For all of its lack of delights, it certainly fills your stomach and keeps you going, which is all it's supposed to do.

As usual I'm sitting with Franx and Gappo, who are the closest thing to friends that I've got in this miserable outfit. We spend a few minutes cramming our faces with the sludge, before washing it down with reconstituted fruit juice. For some people, fruit juice might seem like an extravagance, but on board ship, where the air's constantly refiltered over and over, and there's only artificial light and close confines, it's the best way of stopping any diseases. There are tales of whole ships' crews being wiped out by Thalois fever or muritan cholettia, and that's too much of a risk to take when you only need to give a man half a pint of juice a day to stave off the worst.

'Ever thought of trying to get out while on board?' Franx asks, using one of his little fingers to wipe the last bits of protein from the rim of his dish.

'I've heard it isn't impossible,' Gappo says, pushing his dish away before digging into his mouth with a fingernail to extract a fragment of protein chunk lodged somewhere.

'Some of the crew reckon there's places a man can hide forever,' I add before pouring the rest of the fruit juice in my mouth and swilling it around to remove the horrid texture left in there from the goop. 'This ship isn't that big, but there's still hundreds of places where no one goes any more, places between the decks, in the ducting and down by the engines. You can creep out and steal what you need to eat, it wouldn't be difficult.'

'Yeah,' Franx says with a curled lip, 'but it ain't exactly bloody freedom, is it?'

'And what would you call freedom?' Gappo asks, lying back onto his elbows, stretching his long legs out in front of him.

'Not sure,' the sergeant says with a shrug. 'Guess I like to choose what I eat, where I go, who I know.'

'I've never been able to do that,' I tell them. 'In the hive factories it's just as much a matter of survival as it is here. Kill or be killed, win the trade wars or starve, it's that simple.'

'None of us knows what freedom is,' Gappo says, rocking his head from side to side to work out a stiff muscle. 'When I was a preacher, all I knew were the holy scriptures and the dogma of the Ecclesiarchy. They told me exactly how I was supposed to act and feel in any kind of situation. They told me who was right and who was wrong. I realise now that I didn't really have any freedom.'

'You know, I'm from an agri-world,' Franx says. 'Just a farmer, wasn't much hardship. Had lots of machines, single man could tend fifteen hundred hectares. Was always plenty to eat, women were young and healthy, nothing more a man could want.'

'So why the bloody hell did you join the Guard?' Gappo blurts out, sitting bolt upright.

'Didn't get any fragging choice, did I?' Franx says bitterly, a sour look on his face. 'Got listed for the Departmento Munitorum tithe when orks invaded Alris Colvin. I was mustered. That was it, no choice.'

'Yeah,' I butt in, 'but you must've settled in all right, you made major after all.'

'Being in the Guard turned out fine,' the sergeant says, leaning forward to stack his dish on top of Gappo's. 'Tell the truth, I liked the discipline. As a trooper, I didn't have to worry about anything except orders. Got foddered and watered, had the comfort that whatever I was told to do would be the right thing.'

'But as you got promoted, that must have changed,' Gappo interjects, leaning back again.

'Did, that was the problem,' Franx continues, ruffling his curly hair with a hand. 'Higher up the chain of command I got, less I liked it. Soon making decisions that get men killed and maimed. All of a sudden it seemed like it was all my responsibility. Colonel was a born officer, one of the gentry, didn't give a second thought to troopers, was just making sure he could sneak his way up the greasy pole of the upper ranks, hoping to make commander-general or warmaster.'

'That's why you went over the edge?' I ask, knowing that Franx was in the Last Chancers for inciting subordination and disobeying orders.

'Right,' he says, face grim with the memory, voice deep and embittered. 'Stuck in the middle of an ice plain on Fortuna II, been on half rations for a month because the rebels kept shooting down our supply shuttles. Got the order to attack a keep called Lanskar's Citadel, two dozen leagues across bare ice. Officers were dining on stewed horndeer and braised black ox, drinking Chanalain brandy; my men were eating dried food substitutes and making water from snow. Led my two companies into the officers' camp and demanded supplies for the march. Departmento bastards turned us down flat and the men went on the rampage, looting everything. Didn't try to stop them, they were cold and starving. What was I supposed to do? Order them back into the ice wastes to attack an enemy-held fort with empty stomachs?'

'That's kinda what happened to you, Gappo,' I say to the ex-preacher, making a pillow out of my thin blanket and lying down with my hands behind my head.

'The haves and have-nots?' he asks, not expecting an answer. 'I can see why Franx here did what he did, but to this day I have not the faintest clue what made me denounce a cardinal in front of half a dozen Imperial Guard officers.'

'Think you were right,' Franx says. 'Cardinal shouldn't have executed men who were laying down their lives for the defence of his palaces.'

'But you had to go and accuse the whole Ecclesiarchy of being corrupt,' I add with a grin. 'Questioning whether there really was an Emperor. How stupid are you?'

'I cannot believe that such suffering could happen if there were such a divine influence looking over humanity,' Gappo replies emphatically. 'If there is an Emperor, which I doubt, the cardinal and others like him representing such a figure is patently ridiculous.'

'Can't imagine being able to carry on if there wasn't an Emperor,' Franx says, shaking his head, trying to comprehend the idea. 'Would've killed myself as soon as I was hauled in by the Colonel if that was the case.'

'You really believe that you have a soul to save?' Gappo asks with obvious contempt. 'You believe this magnificent Emperor cares one bit whether you die serving the Imperium or as a disobedient looter?'

'Hey!' I snap at both of them. 'Let's drop this topic, shall we?'

It's at that point that Poal walks over, face scrunched up into a vicious snarl.

'He's done it again,' he says through gritted teeth.

'Rollis?' I ask, already knowing the answer, pushing myself to my feet. Poal nods and I follow him towards the far end of the prison chamber, where he and what's left of Kronin's old platoon usually eat now. Kronin is sitting there looking dejected.

'I shall steal from the plate of decadence to feed the mouths of the powerless,' the mad lieutenant says.

'That's the sermons of Sebastian Thor. I know that one,' puts in Poal, standing just behind my right shoulder.

'Where's Rollis?' I demand.

One of the men lounging on the ground nods his head to the right and I see the traitor sat with his back to the cell wall about ten metres away. Trust them to leave it up to me. Most of them hate Rollis, just like I do. They're just scared the treacherous bastard is going to do something to them if they stand up to him, and the Colonel's wrath is another factor. Well, I won't stand for it, having to breathe the same air as him makes me want to rip his lungs out. I march up to stand in front of the scumbag. He's got a half-full bowl in his lap.

I stand there with my hands on my hips. I'm shaking with anger, I detest this man so much.

'Slow eater, aren't you?' I hiss at Rollis. He looks slowly up at me with his tiny black eyes.

'Just because I'm more civilised than you animals, I don't have to put up with these insults,' he says languidly, putting the dish to one side.

'You took Kronin's food again.' A statement, not a question.

'I asked him if he would share his ration with me,' he says with a sly smile. 'He didn't say no.'

'He said: "And the bounties of the Emperor shall go to those who have worked hard in his service",' Poal interjects from behind me. 'Sounds like a big "frag off" if you ask me.'

'I warned you last time, Rollis,' I say heavily, sickened at the sight of his blubbery face. 'One warning is all you get.'

His eyes fill with fear and he opens his mouth to speak, but my boot fills it before he can say anything, knocking bloodied teeth across his lap. He clamps his hands to his jaw, whimpering with pain. As I turn away I hear him move behind me and I look back over my shoulder.

'Bashtard!' he spits at me, halfway to his feet, blood and spittle dribbling down his chin. 'I'll fragging get you back for thish, you shanctimonioush shon-of-an-ork!'

'Keep going and you'll need to ask for soup in future,' I laugh back at him. I'd pity the piece of grox crap if he wasn't such a scumbag piece of sumpfloat. He slumps back down again, probing at a tooth with a finger, eyes filled with pure venom. If looks really could kill, they'd be tagging my toes already.

'If he tries it again,' I tell Poal, 'break the fingers of his left hand. He'll find it even harder to eat then, but he'll still be able to pull a trigger. I'll back you up.'

Poal glances back at the traitor, obviously relishing the thought.

'I just hope he tries it again,' he says darkly, glaring at Rollis. 'I just hope he does…'

IN THE DIM ruddy glow of an old star, the tyranid hive fleet drifted remorselessly onwards. The smaller drone ships huddled under the massive, crater-pocked carapaces of the hive ships, the larger vessels slowly coiling in upon themselves to enter a dormant state that allowed them to traverse the vast distances between stars. The clouds of spores were dispersing, scattering slowly on the stellar winds. One hive ship was still awake, feeder tentacles wrapped around the shattered hull of an Imperial warship, digesting the mineral content, the flesh of the dead crew, leeching off the air contained within to sustain itself.

Across the heavens the flotilla of bio-ships stretched out, impelled by instinct to hibernate again until they found new prey and new resources to plunder. In their wake, a bare rock orbited the star, scoured of every organic particle, stripped of all but the most basic elements. Nothing was left of the farming world of Langosta III. There were no testaments to the humans who had once lived there. Now all that was left was an airless asteroid, the unmarked dying place of three million people. All that remained of them was raw genetic material, stored within the great hive ships, ready to be turned into more hunters, more killing machines.

TWO
FALSE HOPE

*+++ Operation New Sun in place, ready for your
arrival. +++*

*+++ Operation Harvest preparing to progress to
next stage. +++*

+++ Only the Insane can truly Prosper. +++

You COULD SAY that dropping out of warpspace feels like having your body turned inside out by some giant invisible hand. You could say it's like you've been scattered into fragments and then reassembled in the real universe. You could say that your mind buzzes with images of birth and death, each flashing into your brain and then disappearing in an instant. I've heard it described like this, and many other fanciful ways, by other soldiers and travellers. You could say it was like these things, but you'd be lying, because it isn't like any of them. In fact, you hardly notice that you've dropped out of warpspace at all. There's a slight pressure at the back of your mind, and then a kind of release of tension, like you've just had a stimm-shot or something. You relax a little, breathe just a little more easily. Well, that's how it's always been for me, and nobody else seems to have come up with a more accurate description that I know of. Then again, maybe you don't even actually get that; perhaps it's all in your mind. I know that I'm damned well relieved every time we drop back into realspace, because it's a whole lot less dangerous than on the Otherside. Considering the outfit I'm in these days, that's saying a hell of a lot, because each drop is just a prelude to the next blood-soaked battle.

I'm standing in the upper starboard gallery, along with another two dozen Last Chancers. The row of windows to our right continues for several hundred metres. The wood-panelled wall of the inner bulkhead stretches unbroken on the other side, leaving a massive corridor thirty metres wide where we can run back and forth along its length, but without any nooks or crannies in the featureless room to hide behind. There's only one door at each end of the gallery, each protected by a squad of armsmen with loaded shotcannons. Sealed, sterile, contained. Just like the Colonel wanted it. We're fortunate that we're on exercise when the drop happens. The shutters on the massive viewing ports grind out of sight, revealing a distant blue star. We're too far away to see any worlds yet, we've still got to go in-system under ordinary plasma drives.

Poal strides up to me, sweat dripping off him from his physical exertions.

'Where are we?' he asks, wiping his forehead with the back of his good hand.

'Haven't got a fraggin' clue,' I tell him with a deep shrug. I catch the eye of the naval officer watching over us from the near end of the gallery. He walks over with a half-confident, half-nervous look. Don't ask me how he manages it but he seems to convey a sense of superiority, but the look in his eyes doesn't match it. He glances quickly to check that the armsmen are still close at hand as he stops in front of me.

'What do you want?' he demands, his lip curled as if he was talking to a pool of sick.

'Just wondering where we are,' I say to him with a pleasant smile. I'm in a good mood for some reason, most likely because we're out of warpspace, as I said before, and so I'm not up for any Navy-baiting today.

'System XV/108, that's where we are,' he replies with a smirk.

'Oh right,' says Poal, lounging an arm across my shoulder and leaning towards the naval officer. 'XV/108? That's right next to XV/109. I heard of it.'

'Have you?' the lieutenant asks, jerking himself up straight, clearly startled.

'Oh yeah,' says Poal, his voice totally deadpan, his face radiating sincerity. 'I hear that this place is grox-country. Nothing but grox farms as far as the eye can see. They say that folks around here are so keen on grox they live with 'em, sleep with 'em, even have kids by 'em.'

'Really?' the lieutenant asks, his pudgy little face screwed up with genuine repulsion now.

'That's right,' Poal continues, casting a mischievous glance at me that the Navy man doesn't notice. 'In fact, looking at you, are you sure your mother wasn't a grox and your father a lonely farmer?'

'Certainly not, my father was a–' he starts back before he actually realises what Poal's been saying. 'Damn you, penal scum! Schaeffer will hear about this insult!'

'That's *Colonel* Schaeffer to you, grox-baby,' Poal says, suddenly serious, staring intently at the lieutenant. 'You Navy men would do well to remember it.'

'Is that right, trooper?' the lieutenant spits back, taking a step towards us. 'When the lash is taking strips off your back, you would do well to remember that it's a naval rating doing it to you!'

With that, he spins on the spot and marches off, the thick heels of his naval boots thudding loudly on the wood-panelled floor. Poal and I just burst out laughing, and I can see his shoulders tense even more. It's a couple of minutes before we can control ourselves – each time I look at Poal I can see his innocent face and the lieutenant's enraged look.

'Hasn't even got a damned name,' Poal says when he's calmed down a little, standing looking out of the nearest viewport, looking pale against the blackness of the high-arched window that stretches up at least another ten metres above his head.

'That's worrying,' I agree, stepping up beside him. 'Even the newest explored system usually gets a name, even if it's just the same as the ship or the man who found it.'

'No name, no name…' Poal mutters to himself for a moment, before turning to look at me, his hand and hook clasped behind his back like an officer or something. 'I've just had a thought. No name probably means it's a dead system, no life-bearing worlds, right?'

'Could be,' I say, though I wouldn't really know. Unlike Poal who was brought up by the Schola Progenium, my education consisted more of how to work a las-lathe and parry an axe-blow with a crowbar.

'And a dead system is just the place you'd put a penal colony…' he suggests, looking back out of the window, more interested this time.

'You think they're going to offload us?' I ask him with an incredulous look.

'Course not,' he says, still staring out of the viewport. 'But we could be getting some more men in, that'd make sense.'

'I see your point,' I say, turning and leaning back against the thick armoured glass of the port. 'It's been two and half years, and we've not had a single new member.'

'And maybe he's organising us into one big platoon to make room for the fresh faces,' Poal says, his face showing a thoughtful impression.

'Hang on, though,' I say, a sudden thought crossing my mind. 'Wouldn't it be better to have the old-timers in charge of the squads and platoons?'

'What? Have us teaching them all the tricks we've learned?' he says with a laugh. 'The Colonel knows better than that.'

We lounge around and jaw a bit more, strolling back and forth along the gallery after one of the armsmen prompts us to carry on exercising instead of loafing. We're talking about what we'd do if we ever get out of the Last Chancers when there's an interruption.

'Lieutenant Kage!' a voice barks out from behind me and I automatically stand to attention, the parade drills banged into me so hard I still can't stop myself responding to a voice with that much authority.

'Emperor damn me it's the Colonel,' hisses Poal, standing-to on my left. 'That bloody naval bastard has fragged us.'

The Colonel walks up behind us. I can hear his slow, certain steps thudding on the floor.

'Face front, Guardsmen,' he says and we both spin on the spot in perfect unison, moving with instinct rather than thought.

'If it's about that naval lieutenant, sir–' I begin to excuse myself, but he cuts me off with a short, chopping motion with his hand, his gold epaulettes swaying with the motion.

'Between you and me,' he says quietly, leaning forward to look at us face-to-face, 'I do not care what the Imperial Navy thinks of you. It could not be any worse than what I think of you.'

We stand there in silence for a moment as he glances sharply at both of us. Clearing his throat with a short cough he stands up straight again.

'Kage,' he tells me, looking past at the other Last Chancers in the gallery, 'you will be escorted to my chambers after exercise to receive briefing about our next mission.'

'Yes, sir!' I snap back, keeping my face neutral, even though inside I feel like dropping to the deck and beating my head against the wooden planks. The relaxation I've felt in the past hour after dropping from the warp disappears totally and tension seeps into my muscles and bones again. So we're here to fight again. No new recruits, no fresh blood. Just here to fight in some other bloody war. To die, perhaps. Well, that's the life of a Last Chancer. It's all there is left for us.

THE ARMSMAN TAPS politely at the panelled and lacquered door, before opening it inwards and waving me inside with the muzzle of his shotcannon. I step inside, as I've done a dozen times before, and stand to attention, my polished boots sinking into the thick carpet. Behind me I hear the door close and the ring of the armsman's boots standing to attention on the corridor decking.

The Colonel glances up from behind his massive desk and then looks back at the data-slate before him, immediately seeming to forget my presence. He presses his thumb to an identification slate on the side of the data-slate and it makes a whirring noise, which I recognise as the 'erase' function operating. He places the device carefully on the desk in front of him, lying it parallel to the edge closest to me, before looking in my direction again.

'At ease,' he tells me as he stands up and begins to pace up and down behind his high-backed chair for a few moments, hands clasped behind his back. It's then that I realise this was the pose Poal was imitating earlier and I fight hard to hold back a smirk. He stops walking and looks at me sharply and I gulp, thinking for a second that he can read my mind.

'Tyranids, Kage,' he says obtusely, pacing back and forth again, turning his gaze downwards once more.

'What… what about them, sir?' I ask after a moment, realising he was waiting for me to say something.

'Some of them may be in this system,' he tells me, still not looking at me, but from his posture I can tell that somehow every sense he has is still directed towards me.

'So there's probably nothing left for us to do,' I say boldly, hoping that perhaps we'd arrived too late, that for once we'd missed the battle.

'That may be the case, Kage,' he says slowly, stopping now to look directly at me. 'We are here to ascertain why communication with our outpost on the third world has been lost. We suspect that a small scouting fleet from Kraken was heading this way.'

As he turns to his desk to pick up a transparent copy of a terminal readout, I wonder who 'we' was meant to include. As far as I know, we're a bit of a rogue element really, bouncing about across this part of the galaxy and dropping in on any wars we happen to come across. I've not heard anything about who the Colonel's superiors might be, if he has any at all.

'Do you remember the first battle of these Last Chancers?' he asks suddenly, sitting down again, more relaxed than he was a moment before.

'Of course, sir,' I reply immediately, wondering what he meant by 'these Last Chancers'. 'I could never forget Ichar IV. I wish I could, and I've tried, but I'll never forget it.'

He replies with a non-committal grunt and proffers me the transparency. It's covered in lines and circles, and I recognise it as some kind of star chart. There are tiny runes inscribed against crosses drawn in a line that arcs from one end to the other, but it might as well be written in Harangarian for all that I can understand it. I give the Colonel a blank look and he realises I haven't got a clue what I'm holding.

'It seems that defending Ichar IV was not necessarily the best plan in the world,' he says heavily, tugging the readout from my fingers and placing it in a vellum-covered envelope in the centre of his desk.

'Saving a hundred and ninety billion people was a bad plan, sir?' I ask, amazed at what the Colonel is implying.

'If by doing so we cause five hundred billion people to die, then yes,' he says giving me a stern look, a warning not to continue my train of thought.

'Five hundred billion, sir?' I ask, totally confused and unsure what the Colonel is talking about.

'When we broke the tyranid fleet attacking Ichar IV, much of it was not destroyed,' he tells me, leaning forward to rest his elbows on the polished marble of the desk, his black-gloved hands clasped in front of him. 'That part of Hive Fleet Kraken was simply shattered. Much of it we managed to locate and destroy while the tyranids were still reeling from their defeat. However, we believe a sizeable proportion of the survivors that attacked Ichar IV coalesced into a new fleet, heading in a different direction. It is impossible to say exactly where they are heading, but reports from monitoring stations and patrol vessels indicate that its course might lead straight into the heart of the sector we are now in – the Typhon sector. If we had let them have Ichar IV, we might have mustered more of a defence and destroyed the tyranids utterly rather than scattering them to hell and back where we cannot find them and it is impossible to track them down until too late.'

'So instead of losing a planet, we could lose the whole of Typhon sector?' I ask, finally catching on to what the Colonel is implying. 'That's where five hundred billion people might die?'

'Now do you see why it is important that we know exactly where this hive fleet is heading?' he asks, an earnest look on his bony face.

'I certainly do, sir,' I reply, my head reeling with the thought of what could happen. It's so many people you can't picture it. It's far more than a hive, more than an entire hive world. Five hundred billion people, all of them devoured by hideous, unfeeling aliens if the tyranids couldn't be stopped.

THE DREAM'S SLIGHTLY different this time: we're defending one of our own factories, against shapeless green men I've never seen before. They hiss and cackle at me as they charge, their vaguely humanoid bodies shifting and changing, covered with what look like scales.

A sound close by pulls me from my sleep and I glimpse a shadow over me. Before I can do anything something heavy falls on my face and pushes down over my mouth and nose, stifling me. I lash out, but my fist connects with thin air and something hard rams into my gut, expelling what little air is in my lungs. I flail around helplessly for another second; I can hear the other man panting hard, feel the warmth of his body on top of me. The cloth on my face smells rank with old sweat, making me want to gag even more.

Suddenly the weight lifts off me and I hear a shrill titter and gasp. I throw off the thing on my face, noting it's a shirt, and I glance up to see Rollis. Behind him is Kronin, a sock wrapped around the traitor's throat, a knot in it to press hard against his windpipe. The ex-lieutenant giggles again.

'And vengeance shall be the Emperor's, said Saint Taphistis,' Kronin laughs, wrenching harder on the improvised garrotte and pulling Rollis backwards onto the decking. Kronin leans over Rollis's shoulder, twisting the sock tighter, and bites his ear, blood dribbling onto his chin and down Rollis's neck as he looks up and grins at me. Rollis's face is going blue now, his eyes bulging under his heavy-set brow. I clamber to my feet, unsteady, my head still light from being choked.

'Let him go, Kronin,' I say, taking a shaky step towards them. Killing Rollis like this will just get Kronin executed, and me as well probably. The Colonel's ordered it before; he won't hesitate to do it again.

'And the Emperor's thanks for those who had been bountiful in their gifts would be eternal,' he replies, a plaintive look on his narrow face, licking the blood from his lips.

'Do it,' I say quietly. With another pleading look, Kronin lets go and Rollis slumps to the deck, panting and clutching his throat. I put a foot against his chest and roll him over, pinning his unresisting body to the floor. I lean forward, crossing my arms and resting them on my knee, putting more weight onto his laboured chest.

'You haven't suffered for your crimes enough yet, it's too soon for you to die,' I hiss at him. 'And when you do, I'm going to be the one that does it.'

'THIS IS NOT a good idea,' Linskrug says, before he gives a deep sigh and takes a swig from his canteen. We're taking a quick rest break from the march, sitting in the jungle mud. All around birds are chattering, whistling and screeching in the trees. Flies the size of your thumb buzz past, and I bat one away that settles on my arm. Who can tell what I might catch if it bit me. Other insects flit around on brightly patterned wings, and a beetle bigger than my foot scuttles into the light on the far side of the track, three metres away. The air is sultry, soaking us in humidity and our own sweat, which pours from every part of my body even though I'm resting.

'What's not a good idea?' I ask with a sour look. 'Marching through this green hellhole, getting slowly eaten by flies, drowning in our own sweat and choking on sulphur fumes? I can't see why that's not a good idea.'

'No, none of that,' he says, waving a dismissive hand. 'I'm talking about following this trail.'

'Finding this trail is the only good thing that's happened since we made planetfall on this Emperor-forsaken jungle world,' I tell him bitterly, pulling my right boot off and massaging my blistered foot. 'It certainly beats hacking our way through the undergrowth. I mean, we've lost eight men already, in just fifteen hours! Drowned in swamps, fallen down hidden crevasses, poisoned by spinethorns, infected by bleed-eye and the black vomit, bitten by snakes and birds. Droken's lost his leg to some damned swamprat-thing, and we're all going to die horribly unless we can find the outpost in the next day or two.'

'Do you know why there's a trail here?' asks Linskrug, glancing sideways at me as he sits down gingerly on a fallen log, his lean, muscled frame showing through the clinging tightness of his sweat-sodden shirt.

'I don't know. Because the Emperor loves us?' I say, teasing the sodden sock from my foot and wringing out the sweat and marsh water.

'Because creatures move along here regularly,' he says, wrinkling his nose at my ministrations on my feet. 'They travel along here frequently, thus forming the trail.'

'Very interesting,' I tell him dryly, slipping on my damp footwear.

'I learnt that hunting back home, on the estate,' he says sagely, screwing the cap back on the water bottle.

I bet you did, I think to myself. Linskrug was once a baron on Korall, and says that his political opponents fragged him good and proper, stitching him up for unlicensed slaving. He's never even been in the Guard before the Last Chancers, so whoever his enemies were, they must have scratched quite a few backs in their time.

'Why's that so useful for hunting?' I ask, switching feet while I wriggle the toes on my right foot inside my clammy boot.

'Because that's where to look for the prey,' he says with exaggerated patience, turning his hawkish features to look at me across his shoulder, his eyes giving me a patronising look.

'But if you know that,' I say slowly, little gears in my head beginning to whirr into slow life, 'then don't the animals know it?'

'The other predators do…' he says quietly.

'What?' I half scream at him. The other Last Chancers around hurriedly glance in my direction, hands reaching instinctively for lasguns. 'You mean that… things will be hunting along here?'

'That's right,' Linskrug says with a slow, nonchalant nod.

'Did you think of letting the Colonel know that?' I ask, desperately trying to keep my temper in check.

'Oh, I'm very sure he knows,' Linskrug says, taking his helmet off and rubbing the sweat out of his long hair. 'He has the look of the hunter about him, does our Colonel.'

'So we must be safer here than in the jungle,' I say, calming down a little. 'I mean, I remember you saying before that the largest predators need a wide territory so there can't be that many around.'

'I can't say that I've noticed the Colonel being overly conscious of our safety,' laughs the baron, slapping his helmet back on his head.

'I guess not,' I agree with a grimace.

'Rest break over!' I hear the Colonel's shout from further up the trail. We're at the back of the column, keeping an eye out for anyone trying to drop away and lose themselves. That said, the Colonel knows anyone dumb enough to think that they can go it alone on a deathworld like this is better off lost.

'Most animals only kill when they're hungry, isn't that right?' I ask Linskrug, seeking a bit more reassurance, as we trudge along the trail, ankle-deep in mud.

'No,' he says, shaking his head vehemently, 'most predators only eat when they're hungry. Some will kill out of sheer maliciousness, while most of them are highly aggressive and will attack anything they see as a threat to their territory.'

'By threat,' I say slowly, pushing my pistol holster further round on my belt to stop it slapping my sore thigh, 'you wouldn't mean two hundred armed men marching along your favourite hunting ground, would you?'

'Well, I couldn't answer for the local beasts,' he says with a smile, 'but back on Korall there is this massive cat called a hookfang, and it'll attack anything man-sized or larger it sees. I can't see any hunting beast trying to survive on a deathworld being any less touchy.'

We march on in silence, and the clouds open up with a fine drizzle of rain. It's been near-constant since we landed yesterday, except for the past few hours. I let my mind wander, forgetting the fatigue in my legs by thinking about our mission. We've come to False Hope, the rather depressing name of this world, because all contact has been lost with the outpost here, nothing at all from two hundred inhabitants. The place is called False Hope because the men who originally landed here suffered a warp engine malfunction and were unceremoniously dumped back into realspace. The ship was badly damaged by the catastrophe and they thought they were doomed until they happened across a habitable world. They managed to land safely, and set up camp. A Navy patrol vessel came across their auto-distress call seventy-five years later, and the landing party found nothing left except the ship, almost swallowed up by the jungle. Apparently the captain had kept a diary, which told of how five hundred crew had died in about a year. He was the last to go. The final line in the diary went something like *It appears that what we thought was our salvation has turned out to be nothing but false hope.* The name just kind of stuck, I guess.

I learnt this from one of the shuttle crew, a rating called Jamieson. Quite a nice guy really, despite him being Navy. We get on a whole lot better with the regular ratings than we do the armsmen, and a lot better than we do with the officers. I guess it's because most of them never wanted to be there either, just got caught up in the press-gangs. Still, they soon get it bludgeoned into their heads by their superiors that the Navy is better than the Guard. I don't know how long the enmity between the Navy and Guard has lasted, probably since they were split up right after the Great Heresy. That was one of the first things I learned when I joined the Imperial Guard – Navy and Guard don't mix. I mean, how can you respect the Navy when they think that they can deal with anything, just by stopping the threat before it reaches a planet. Half the fraggin' time they don't even know there's a threat until it's too late. And then their answer is just to frag everything to the warp and back from orbit with their big guns. I'm no strategist, but without the Guard to fight the ground wars, I reckon the Navy'd be next to useless. All they're good for is getting us from one warzone to the next relatively intact.

The rain patters irritatingly across my face. There don't seem to be any storms here, but there's an almost constant shower, so it's next to impossible to keep anything dry. Some of the men have complained about finding pungent-smelling mould growing in their packs, it's that bad.

Anyway, we've lost contact with False Hope Station, and the Colonel, and whoever the mysterious 'we' is, think the tyranids might have been here, just a little ship. It's blatantly obvious that nothing as big as a hive ship has got here, otherwise the whole planet would be stripped bare by now. They'd be having a total banquet with all those different animals to eat up and mutate. But the Colonel reckons that where you get a few 'nids, more follow soon after. I know that from Ichar IV and Deliverance. They send out scouts: on planetside they use these slippery fraggers we call lictors to find out where the greatest concentration of prey is. These lictors, they're superb predators, they say. It's been reckoned they can track a single man across a desert, and if that wasn't bad enough, they're deadly, with huge scything claws that can rip a man in two, fast as lightning too. When they find somewhere worth visiting, then the rest of the swarm comes along to join in the party. Don't ask me how they keep in contact with all these scouting fleets and beasties, they just manage it somehow. If there are tyranids here, in the Typhon sector, it's our job to hunt them down and kill them before they do their transmitting thing, or whatever it is they do. If we don't, the Colonel informs me, then there's going to be upwards of a hundred hive ships floating this way over the next couple of years, gearing up to devour everything for a hundred light years in every direction.

'Kage!' Linskrug hisses in my ear, breaking my reverie.

'What?' I snarl, irritated at him derailing my thoughts.

'Shut up and listen!' he snaps back as he stops, putting a finger to his lips, his eyes narrowed.

I do as he says, slowly letting out my breath, trying to tune in to the sounds of the jungle around us. I can just hear the pattering of the rain on leaves and splashing onto the muddy trail, the slack wind sighing through the treetops around us.

'I don't hear anything,' I tell him after a minute or so of standing around.

'Exactly,' he says with an insistent nod. 'The whole place has been veritably screaming with insects and birds since we landed, now we can't hear a thing!'

'Sergeant Becksbauer!' I call to the nearest man in front of us, who's stopped and is looking at us, probably wondering if we've decided to make a break for it, despite the odds against surviving for long in this place. 'Go and get the Colonel from the head of the column. There might be trouble coming.'

He gives a wave and then sets off double-stepping up the trail, tapping guys on the shoulder as he goes past, directing them back towards us with a thumb. I see Franx is among them and he breaks into a trot and starts heading towards us. He's jogging through the rain and puddles when suddenly his eyes go wide and he opens his mouth to scream but doesn't utter a sound. He tries to stop suddenly and his feet slide out from underneath him, pitching the sergeant onto his back in the mud. I hear a strangled gulp from Linskrug and look over my shoulder. My heart stops beating for an eternity at what I see.

About fifty metres behind us, poking from between the jungle trees, is a massive reptilian head, almost as long as I am tall. Its plate-sized yellow eye is glaring straight at us, black pupil nothing but a vertical slit.

'Stay still,' Linskrug tells me out of the corner of his mouth. 'Some lizards can't see you if you don't move.'

A trickle of sweat runs down my back, chilling my spine and making me want to shiver.

'What the frag do we do?' I asked in a strained voice, slowly edging my right hand towards the laspistol hanging in the holster at my belt.

'Do you think that's going to hurt it?' Linskrug whispers.

The beast stamps forward two paces, massively muscled shoulders bending aside the trunks of two trees to force its way through. It's covered in scales the size of my face, green and glistening, perfectly matching the round, rain-drenched leaves of the surrounding trees. The camouflage is near-perfect, we could have walked straight past it for all I know. It takes another step and I can see its nostrils flaring as it sniffs the air.

'Any chance that it eats bushes and stuff?' I whisper to Linskrug, not particularly hopeful. As if in reply, the creature's huge jaw opens revealing row after row of serrated teeth, obviously used for stripping flesh and crushing bones.

'I don't think so,' says Linskrug, taking a slow step backwards, shuffling his foot through the mud rather than picking it up. I follow suit, sliding my boots through the puddles as we slowly back away.

'What's the delay?' I hear someone calling, but I daren't look around to see who it is.

The enormous reptile's head swings left and right, trying to look with both eyes down the trail at us. It gives a snort and then breaks into a waddling run on its four tremendous legs, its thick hide scraping bark off the trees along both sides of the trail, its tail swinging in a wide arc from side to side and smashing through branches as thick as my arm.

'Can we run now?' I ask Linskrug, my jaw tight with fear, a trembling starting in my legs and working upwards.

'Not yet,' he says, and I can hear him breathing heavily but steadily, as if calming himself. 'Not yet.'

This thing's pounding down the trail at us, gathering momentum and I can feel the ground shuddering under the impact of its huge weight. It's bigger than a battle tank, easily eleven metres long, not including its tail. I can hear its deep breathing, a constant growling, growing louder by the second. It's speeding up, now moving about as fast as a man can comfortably run and still getting faster. It's only about ten metres away when I feel Linskrug moving.

'Now!' he bellows in my ear, shoving me sideways into the treeline, landing on top of me and knocking my breath out. The predator's head swings in our direction and it snaps its jaw at us as it charges past, but it's going too fast to stop. As it thunders along the trail, we pick ourselves up and jump back onto the track – I've already learnt that it's suicide to lie around in the undergrowth on False Hope.

Ahead of us the other Last Chancers are scattering like flies from a snapping greel, leaping in every direction, some of them turning to try to outpace the beast. I see Franx dodging to one side, but the creature's tail lashes out, crashing across his chest and flinging him bodily through the air for a dozen metres before he thumps awkwardly against a tree trunk.

The sound of lasguns crackles up ahead, and I pull my pistol from its holster and begin snapping off shots at the beast's hindquarters, the flashes of laser impacting on its thick hide with little visible effect. Linskrug is snapping off shots from the hip with his lasgun too, as we hurry side-by-side after the giant reptile. The lasgun fire increases in intensity, accompanied by screams of pain and shouts of terror. It's hard to see past the vast bulk of the monster, all I can see are half-glimpses of Guardsmen dodging to and fro. Now and then one of them is caught up in the beast's immense jaws, crushed and tossed aside or cleaved in half by its huge fangs. It's still thundering along, and I see a clawed foot descend onto the chest of a trooper trying to crawl into the bushes, flattening him in a explosion of pulverised organs and splashing blood.

'Any smart ideas?' I shout to Linskrug, stopping and trying to level a shot at the beast's head as it snakes from side to side.

'Run away?' he suggests, stopping next to me and pulling the power pack from the bottom of his lasrifle. He glances around as he slams another one home, perhaps looking for inspiration.

'Lasfire isn't having much effect, we need to hit and run,' he says, unhooking his bayonet from his belt and twisting it onto the mounting on the end of his lasgun.

'Hand-to-hand? I thought it was Kronin who'd gone mad!' I shout at him, my heart faltering at the thought of voluntarily going any nearer to that murderous mass of muscles and teeth.

'Work a blade in under the scales, in the direction of the head, and push deep,' Linskrug says with a grin, obviously relishing the whole situation, before setting off again along the track. At least half a dozen mashed corpses litter the trail now, and a few more men lie battered, groaning in pain. The monster has stopped its rampage now and is standing four square in the trail, head lunging forward at the Guardsmen in front. Linskrug ducks neatly under its swishing tail and rams his bayonet into the yellowish scales of its underbelly. I see him spread his legs wider and brace himself, and with his teeth gritted with strain he levers the bayonet further into the creature's flesh. It gives a roar of pain and tries to turn round and attack us, but it's too bulky to turn quickly, its massive flanks jamming against trees, its neck not long enough to bend back to attack us. It takes a step back, pushing Linskrug to the ground as it shifts its feet to get into a better position.

'What the frag,' I hear myself saying before I leap forward, grabbing Linskrug's collar in one hand and dragging him free. I can hear the shouts of the other men from across its broad, flat back, bellowed commands from the Colonel cutting through their hysterical yelling. The reptile shuffles forward a little, now almost at right angles to the track, its back hunching up to give it more room. I roll forwards between its legs and make a grab for the rifle still hanging from its midriff. I miss at the first attempt and as the creature shifts its weight the rifle butt cracks painfully against my knuckles. Spitting incoherent curses I duck forward again, narrowly stepping aside as it backs up once again, and manage to get one hand on the lasgun. I put my shoulder to the stock and heave upwards, straining every muscle in my back and legs, my fleet slipping and sliding in the mud. My efforts are rewarded by a plaintive howl of pain and it thrashes around even more violently. Its rear legs become entangled in the thorns of a bush next to the trail and it slips for a moment. The vast bulk of its underside crashes down onto the top of my helmet, knocking me flat to my chest, my face in a puddle. The lasgun slips from my grip once more.

Dark red blood spills freely from the wound now, splashing onto my head and shoulders. The lizard's heaving itself backwards and forwards, left and right, trying to angle its head under, either to attack me or perhaps to pull the bayonet free, I'm not sure which. I roll sideways just as a back foot thuds into the mud where I was lying, spinning out from underneath the monstrous reptile.

I'm covered head to toe in mud and blood, spluttering and spitting dirty water from my mouth. Through grime-filled eyes I see the Colonel leaping through the rain, power sword clenched in his fist, the rain hissing off its searing blue blade. Without a sound he lunges forward, the power sword sheering through the creature's muzzle, a great hunk of burnt flesh flopping to the floor. It rears up, slashing its front claws through the space the Colonel occupied a moment before, but he's already side-stepped to the left. As the lizard lowers its head again, looking for its prey, the Colonel's arm stabs outward with a precise move, plunging the power sword through its right eye. I see the point of the blade protruding a few centimetres from the top of the giant beast's skull and it thrashes wildly for a moment, tearing the sword from the Colonel's grasp and forcing him to take a step backwards. Everyone jumps back hurriedly as its death throes continue, and I have to push myself to my feet and leap aside again as it stumbles towards where I lay. With a thud that reverberates along the ground the monstrosity finally collapses, the air of its last breath whistling out of its ruined face.

The Colonel marches up to the gigantic corpse and pulls his power sword free, as easily as if he were sliding it out of the scabbard, and with no more ceremony either. He looks around at us, slipping the sword back into its sheath. He glances down and, with a casualness I would have thought forced if I didn't know the Colonel, wipes flecks of blood from its basket hilt with a handkerchief pulled from one of his deep greatcoat pockets.

'All right, men,' he says, adjusting how the scabbard hangs against his leg. 'Find out who is dead and who can carry on.' And with that, the whole incident is over, just a few more deaths in the bloody history of the Last Chancers.

WE STUMBLE INTO False Hope Station later the same day, just as the sun is setting. One minute we're in thick jungle, the next there's a rough pathway and buildings to either side. The whole outpost is covered with vines and trailing leaves, woven around the walls and roofs of the rockcrete shelters in a near-continuous mass. What passes for the roads are little more than mud tracks, the odd slab of stone showing through the dense moss underfoot. There's no sign of life at all, just the normal sounds of the jungle. It looks like a ghost town, deserted for a while, succumbing to the eternal predations of the surrounding plants. It's eerie, and I shiver, despite the boiling heat. It's like the people here have disappeared, snatched up by the hand of an unknown god. Something unholy is at work here, I can feel it in my bones.

Deciding to see if there's anyone around, I force open the nearest door, leading into a square building just to my left. Inside it's dark, but from the fitful light coming from the doorway I can see that the building is deserted. There are a few scattered pieces of furniture, hewn from wood, probably from the surrounding trees. I see a firepit in the middle of the one-roomed quarters, but the ashes inside are sodden with rain dripping from the imperfectly covered chimney vent above. As I skulk around in the darkness my foot sends something skittering along the floor. I flounder around for a moment to recover whatever it was that I disturbed, and my hand comes to rest on something vaguely oval and leathery.

I bring it outside to have a look, where Kronin and Gappo are waiting, supporting the half-dead form of Franx. The sergeant didn't seem too badly hurt from his encounter with the lizard, just a bruised back and a few broken ribs, but a couple of hours ago he began to get feverish. The lacerations on his chest have begun to mortify; you can smell the disease from several paces away. He's only half-conscious, his moments of lucidity separated by fever-induced delusions and mumbling. He keeps asking for food, but I don't think it's because he's hungry, more likely memories of his time on Fortuna II coming back to life in his head. He sounds stuck in the past at the moment, replaying what was probably the most important event in his life over and over again.

The object in my hands is about thirty centimetres long, and looks very much like a bunch of dead leaves connected together at one end in a small bundle of fibres.

'What is that, a plant or something?' Gappo says, peering over my shoulder.

'Whatever it is, it can wait,' I tell the ex-preacher. 'We need to get the wounded to the infirmary as soon as possible.'

Dropping the strange object into the mud, I grab Franx's legs and heave them onto my shoulder, the other two have an arm each around their necks and we carry him towards what looks like the centre of False Hope Station. The Colonel is there, directing squads to fan out and search the ghost settlement, which is what it looks like at the moment. The other two wounded, Oklar and Jereminus from Franx's squad, have been propped up against the wall of the largest building, Oklar nursing the stump of his right leg, Jereminus holding a ragged bandage to what's left of the side of his face. We left the corpses of seven other men back where we fought the giant lizard.

'Where's Droken, sir?' I ask the Colonel as we step out of a side street into the central square.

'He died of blood loss just before we arrived,' he says calmly. He nods to the building where Oklar and Jereminus are. 'That should be the station's main facility, where you will find the infirmary, communications room and supplies store. Get the wounded sorted out and then see what you can find that might tell us what has happened here.'

It's with a start that I realise that I'd completely forgotten we were hunting 'nids down here. And there was me just barging into a place without even checking what was inside. I almost deserved to have my head clawed off for being so stupid. I see now that the Colonel's

ordered a firesweep of the settlement to make sure there isn't anything nasty still lurking around, and he expects me to sort out the
control centre. I shout for the five survivors of Franx's squad to follow me, before touching the open rune on the door control panel.
With a hiss the portal slides out of sight, letting the twilight spill into
the corridor beyond. I pull my laspistol from its holster and peek
around the corner, seeing nothing out of the ordinary, just a plain
rockcrete-floored corridor stretching away into darkness, a couple of
doors in the wall about five metres down on either side.

'Well, power's still working,' I hear Crunch say loudly from behind
me. I curse inwardly when I realise he's one of the men still alive. We
call him Crunch for his total inability to sneak around anywhere.
He'll always find a twig to tread on, a piece of razorwire to get
snagged in or a glass crucible to knock over, even in the middle of a
desert. Just the man I need to slip undetected into a potentially hostile building!

'Crunch, you stay here and watch the entrance,' I tell him, motioning the others inside with a wave of my laspistol. He nods and stands
to attention by the side of the door, lasgun in the shouldered-arms
position.

'At ease, trooper,' I say to him as I step past, and hear him let out a
sigh and relax. Shaking my head in irritation, I sneak down the corridor in a half-crouch. I can see artificial light under the door to the
right, while a quick check of the left-hand door shows that the lock
has been activated. I haven't got time to worry about that right now
and signal the four men with me to go through the right-hand doorway. Inside is a small administration room, illuminated by a yellow
lightstrip halfway up the far wall. A portable terminal is next to the
door on a rickety-looking wooden table, its screen blank, the inter-
face pad carefully stowed in the recharging pouch on the side of the
storage banks. I make a mental note to come back and try to start the
machine up once we've ensured the rest of the building is clear.
There's a rack of record scrolls on the other side of the doorway, and
I take out the one nearest the bottom, which should be the most
recent. It's written in what looks to be Techna-lingua, the code used
by the tech-priests, but I recognise the date in the top left corner. It's
about forty days old, give or take a few days, so it's safe to assume
that whatever happened occurred roughly six weeks ago, unless
there's another reason why they stopped making records before then.

Remembering the crew of the ship that discovered False Hope, I
wonder if the people in the research station weren't just killed by the

denizens of the horrible world they lived on, rather than there being any tyranids involved. But that didn't make a careful sweep of the building any less necessary.

The next five rooms we check turn out to be dormitories, each with four bunks, though there's no actual bedding to be found. There's also no sign of any personal belongings at all, reinforcing the spookiness of the abandoned settlement, making the hairs on the back of my neck stand up as we look around, like in a graveyard or something. All we keep finding are the same fibrous pods that I picked up in the first building on the outskirts. By the time we've exhausted our search along the corridor, there's a pile of twenty or so by the main entrance. I don't know why they've been left behind when everything else has gone, but that's a puzzle to sort out another time, there's more urgent matters, like making sure I'm safe.

All the other routes explored, I turn my attention back to the locked door. I study the locking mechanism, which is a numberpad next to the door, and it looks like there's no chance of trying to work out what the cipher is.

'Ah, frag it!' I declare to the galaxy in general and loose off a bolt from my laspistol at the panel, which explodes in a shower of green sparks. I hear the noise of something heavy dropping on the other side of the wall and make a push at the door, which swings inwards easily. I peer inside, laspistol held ready, crouched to duck back out of sight in an instant. Inside are more terminals, although these appear to be wired in, standing on rockcrete plinths along the walls of a room roughly twenty metres long and ten wide. There's another door at the far end, already open, and through it I can see more lights, and two rows of beds. Everything is totally still, no noises except those filtering in from outside, no signs of movement or any kind of life. Dead, a worried part of my mind tells me.

There's a closed door to the right, and I decide to check in there first, not wanting to leave a potential hiding place behind me. The large room we're standing in is obviously the main control chamber, probably where the communications array is. We slip through the door to the right, lasweapons at the ready, but there's nobody inside. The side door leads us into a wide space, filled with metal cages on wheels, each full of boxes marked with an Imperial eagle and notations of shipping dates and so on. This is the store room, obviously, and it appears that there's the usual combat rations, water purification tonics, spare uniforms and some technical equipment. The cages are all still closed with simple padlocks and so it doesn't look like anything was taken by force. That probably rules out pirates, which is one of the thoughts that had occurred to me when looking into the sleeping chambers, which seemed as if they might have been looted.

'Okay, let's check out the ward,' I tell the men, pushing my way past them and back into the control room. Two of them hang back, covering us with their lasguns, while the other pair and me stand either side of the door. I take a quick peek inside and see that the beds are all empty, ten of them each side of the narrow room. I duck through the doorway and scuttle behind the nearest to the right, waving the other two with me, Donalson and Fredricks, to the left-hand side. Glancing behind me to check that the troopers behind have followed us to the door, I begin to creep along the space between the two rows of beds, keeping bent, laspistol pointed in front of me. We're about halfway along, seven or eight metres from the door, when a movement to my right catches my attention. At the far end of the room, there's an archway leading into some kind of ante-chamber and I think I can see something moving about inside.

I shuffle to my left to get a better view and can see a high desk inside the small room, in front of a tall bookshelf filled with tomes and rolled parchments. I can hear something scraping on the floor, perhaps something trying to keep out of sight behind the desk. I gesture with my thumb towards the archway and Fredricks gives a nod and begins to slink very slowly towards it, lasgun cradled across his chest. My breath is coming in shallow gasps at the moment, my whole body tensed and ready for action. I can hear my heart beating, the blood coursing through my ears like the rush of a waterfall. It seems like an eternity is passing as Fredricks makes his way crabwise towards the other room.

There's movement in there again and we all react at the same time, a sudden torrent of las-fire flashing through the archway into the room. The air is filled with the crackling of energy. My heart is hammering in my chest, glad for the sudden release, and I can hear myself growling between gritted teeth. There's a shrill screech from the room and we fire another volley, Donalson spitting incomprehensible curses between gritted teeth as he fires, an incoherent yell bursting from my own lips as I pull repeatedly on the trigger of my laspistol.

'Stop shooting, Emperor damn you!' I hear a high-pitched, strained voice cry out from the ante-chamber. The three of us exchange startled glances.

'Who are you?' I shout back, aiming my pistol into the far room in case a target should present itself.

'I'm Lieutenant Hopkins,' the voice calls back and he shuffles into view, hands held high above his head. He's a little older than me, scrawny-looking with lank hair and a straggly beard on his cheeks and chin. He's wearing a crumpled uniform of some sort: dress jacket a deep red with white breeches and knee-high black boots. He has a slightly tarnished epaulette on one shoulder, the frogging hanging from it frayed and lacklustre. I relax only a little and stand up, still pointing the laspistol at him. He grins when he sees our uniforms, lowers his hands and takes a step forward.

'Stay where you fraggin' are!' I shout, taking a step towards him, laspistol now levelled at his head.

'Are you Imperial Guard? Which regiment are you from?' he asks, voice trembling. I can see his whole body shaking with nerves, obviously distressed that the people he thought were his saviours might still turn out to be his killers.

'It's okay,' I tell him, lowering my laspistol, although I leave the safety catch off and don't holster it. 'We're from the 13th Penal Legion. Colonel Schaeffer's Last Chancers.'

'Penal legion?' he says vaguely, lifting his peaked cap and scratching at his head. 'What the hell are you doing here?'

'I think that's a question you should be answering,' I tell him.

DONALSON BRINGS LIEUTENANT Hopkins from where he's been guarding him in the administration room. I'm sat with the Colonel and Sergeants Broker and Roiseland in the command centre. He looks around curiously, seeing the terminals we've managed to reactivate. It's pitch dark outside; all I can see through the small slit windows are reflections of the interior of the command room. Even through the thick walls I can hear the constant chirruping of insects and the occasional screech of some nocturnal bird or whatever.

'You are Lieutenant Hopkins, of the False Hope garrison company,' the Colonel says. 'I am Colonel Schaeffer, commanding the 13th Penal Legion. I would like an explanation of what has happened to False Hope Station.'

Hopkins gives a quick salute, fingers of his right hand hovering by the peak of his cap for a moment, before his arm drops limply back by his side.

'I wish I could offer one, colonel,' he says apologetically, darting a longing look at an empty chair next to Broker. He seems all but dead on his feet, there's darkness around his eyes and his skin hangs loosely from his cheeks. The Colonel nods towards the seat and

Hopkins sits down gratefully, slouching against the high back of the chair with visible relief. I wave Donalson away, and turn my attention to the Colonel. His ice-blue eyes are still fixed on Hopkins, looking right inside him, trying to work out who the man is.

'Records show that at the last count there were seventy-five Guardsmen and one hundred and forty-eight civilians in False Hope Station,' the Colonel says, glancing at a datasheet in his hands. 'Now there is only you. I think you would agree that this situation demands investigation.'

Hopkins looks helplessly back at the Colonel and gives a weak shrug.

'I don't know what happened to the others,' he says miserably. 'I've been stuck here on my own for thirty-five days now, trying to work out how to get the communications assembly working.'

'Tell me what you remember before then,' the Colonel says sternly, handing the datasheet to Roiseland.

'I was ill in the infirmary,' Hopkins tells us, looking through the doorway towards the ward, where Franx and the others are now safely tucked in. We broke into the medicine chest to get more bandages and stimm-needles. None of us is a medico, so it's down to the Emperor whether they live or die. 'I'd come down with blood poisoning, a local plague we call jungle flu. I'd been leading an expedition through to the sulphur marshes about twenty kays west of here and I caught a dose. The men brought me back, I remember Physician Murrays giving me one of his elixirs and then I must have fallen unconscious. When I woke up, the place was as you find it now.'

'Before the expedition,' the Colonel asks him, gaze never wandering for a second, 'was there anything untoward happening? Was there any sign of danger to the settlement?'

'Our commander, Captain Nepetine, had been acting a bit strangely,' Hopkins admits with a frown. 'He'd been doing some exploration towards the Heart of the Jungle with twenty of the men, and came back alone. He said he'd found a better location for a settlement, one that wasn't as hostile as the area we're in.'

'The Heart of the Jungle?' I ask before I can stop myself, earning myself a scowl from the Colonel.

'Yes,' Hopkins says, not noticing the Colonel's annoyance. 'It's the thickest part of the jungle on the whole planet, about three days march further up the equatorial ridge. It was stupid, because there's nowhere near there at all that could be any more hospitable than where we are. I mean, the whole planet is virtually one big jungle, right up to the poles. Every acre is solid with trees and plants, horrible insects, giant predators and countless hideous diseases. I said so, and the other officers, Lieutenants Korl and Paximan, agreed with me.'

'Do you think that Captain Nepetine may have persuaded the others to leave while you were comatose?' the Colonel asks, absent-mindedly tapping a finger on his knee.

'It's unlikely, sir,' Hopkins says with a doubtful look. 'They were both in vehement agreement with me the last time we spoke about it.'

The Colonel gestures to Sergeant Broker, who pulls one of the empty pod things from a sack under his chair and passes it to Hopkins.

'What is this?' the Colonel asks, pointing towards the object in Hopkins's hands.

'I haven't seen anything like it before,' the lieutenant says. 'I'm no bio-magus, but it looks similar to the seed pods that some of the trees around here use for reproducing. I'm afraid that Lieutenant Paximan was liaison to our Adeptus Mechanicus comrades, I had little to do with the study itself. It's a lot bigger than anything I've seen though, I'm sure I would remember a specimen of this size. If it really is a seed pod, the tree or bush it came from must be enormous. Even the pods from trees over thirty metres tall are only the size of my hand, a quarter of the size of this one.'

'Could it be offworld in origin?' the Colonel asks, his face as neutral as ever. I look at him sharply, realising that he thinks it might be some kind of tyranid organism. I feel the urge to glance over my shoulder, wondering what else is lurking in the jungles out there, as well as all the native killers of False Hope.

'I suppose it could be, but I can't say for sure one way or the other,' Hopkins tells us with a sorrowful look. 'I'm not a specialist in plants or anything, I just run, I mean ran, the camp.'

'Can you take us to the Heart of the Jungle?' Schaeffer asks, finally standing up and beginning to pace back and forth. I wondered how long it would take him before being confined to a chair made him too fidgety. He's obviously concocting some kind of plan, otherwise he'd be content just to sit and ask questions.

'I could lead the way,' Hopkins admits with a shallow nod of the head.

'But?' the Colonel adds.

'All the heavy-duty exploration equipment has gone,' he says with a grimace. 'I checked before, thinking the same thing you do, that I could go after them. But without that sort of gear, one man on his own won't last the first night out in the trees.'

'Well,' the Colonel says, looking at each of us in turn. My heart sinks, knowing what he's going to say next. 'We are more than one man, so I am sure we will survive.'

'Sir?' I interject. 'What about the wounded? They won't be able to make another trip into the jungle.'

'If they can march by tomorrow morning, they come with us,' he says meeting my anxious gaze without a hint of compassion in his eyes. 'If not, we leave them here.'

I'VE BEEN ASLEEP only a short while when sounds of footsteps padding across the rockcrete floor wake me up. Someone's coughing violently from the furthest beds, near the chamber where we found Hopkins. I'm bedded down in the control room with Kronin and a couple of the sergeants, ready to act if any communication comes down from our transport in orbit. In the pale glimmer of the moonlight streaming through the narrow windows of the infirmary I can see a shadow gingerly stepping towards me. Thinking it may be Rollis out for some revenge, I put my hand under the pillow, my fingers closing around the grip of my knife. As the figure gets closer, I can see it's too tall to be Rollis and I relax.

'Kage!' I hear Gappo's terse whisper. 'Franx has woken up.'

I sling my blanket to one side and get up. I see Gappo, barefoot and wearing only his fatigues, leaning on the doorframe and peering into the gloom of the control centre. It's sultry inside the command centre, the rockcrete trapping the humidity and heat of the False Hope day, and I'm covered in a light sheen of sweat. I follow Gappo along the row of beds, towards the intense coughing.

'Kill 'im now,' I hear someone murmur from the darkness. 'That coughin's kept me awake for ages.'

'Drop dead yourself!' I snap back, wishing I could identify the culprit, but it's too dark.

Franx looks a state, his face doused in perspiration, his curls plastered across the tight skin of his forehead, his cheeks hollow. Even the gleam of the moonlight cannot hide the yellowish tinge to his features. His breathing comes in wheezes through his cracked lips. Every few seconds he erupts into a spasm of coughing, blood flecks appearing on his lips. But his eyes are brighter than before, with an intelligent look in them that I haven't seen during the past day.

'You look rougher than a flatulent ork's arse,' I tell him, sitting on the end of the bed. He grins at me, and I can see the reddish stains on his teeth from the blood he's been coughing up.

'Nobody's going to paint portraits of you either, scarface!' he manages to retort before his body convulses with more racking coughs.

'Do you think you'll be able to walk, come the morning?' Gappo asks, concern on his face.

'Fresh air will do me good. Hate infirmaries; always full of sick people,' the sergeant jokes.

Gappo looks at me, his expression one of worry. He's a caring soul at heart, I'm amazed he's managed to survive this long, but in battle he's just as steady as the next man.

'Course you can march in the morning,' I say to Franx. 'And if you need a little help, there are those who'll give you a hand.'

He nods without saying anything and settles back into the bed, closing his eyes, his breathing still ragged.

'What about the other two?' I ask Gappo, who appointed himself chief medico as soon as he heard about the Colonel's decree to leave behind anyone who couldn't make the march.

'Oklar's got one leg left. How do you think he's doing?' the former preacher snaps bitterly. 'Jereminus will be fine, he's just badly concussed.'

'Can we pump Oklar full of stimms before we leave, set him up on some kind of crutch?' I ask, trying to figure a way to deny the Colonel another corpse.

'It might work, providing we can take a bagful of stimm-needles with us to keep him and Jereminus going,' Gappo agrees, looking slightly dubious.

'Well, sort it out,' I tell him. 'I'm going back to bed.'

OKLAR SAVED GAPPO the trouble: stabbed himself through the eye with a stimm-needle left by his bed. The point drove into his brain and killed him instantly. We set out just after dawn yesterday, following Hopkins and the Colonel. Turning westward as soon as we left False Hope station, we climbed up onto a high ridge that Hopkins tells us runs the whole length of the planet's equator. We're marching at the front – me, Kronin, Gappo, Linskrug and Franx's squad, taking it in turns to give Franx a shoulder to lean on. He's stopped coughing blood, but is continuously short of breath. Broker's squad is looking after Jereminus, the sergeant taking custody of a dozen stimms smuggled out of the infirmary by Gappo.

The jungle hasn't been too thick, finding it harder to grow on the dense rock of the volcanic ridge. The air gets even hotter, more choked with sulphur and ashes, as we progress. We can't see them through the jungle canopy, but Hopkins tells us that there's two massive volcanoes a few kilometres away to the south, called Khorne's Twins by the False Hope settlers, named by the original ship's crew after some unholy and violent god. Heresy and blasphemy, but I guess they were getting pretty low on faith at the time. The lieutenant assures us they've been dormant recently, but knowing our luck they'll both blow any moment, just so things don't get too easy for us. My head filled with these gloomy thoughts, I sense somebody falling in beside me and glance right to see Hopkins walking alongside.

'He's Sergeant Franx, is that right?' he asks, glancing towards where the sergeant's stumbling along hanging on to Poal. I nod.

'He must have the constitution of a grox,' Hopkins adds, still looking at the half-crippled Franx.

'He used to,' I say, not being able to stop myself. 'But this sodding sump of a planet of yours might kill him yet.'

'It may yet,' agrees Hopkins with a disconsolate look. 'He's got lungrot, and there's not many survive that.'

'Any more encouraging news?' I ask sourly, wishing he'd frag off and leave me alone.

'He's still alive, and that's half a miracle,' he tells me with a smile. 'Most men don't last the first night. He's lasted two, both of them after days of marching. He won't get any better, but I don't think he'll get any worse.'

'If he was any worse, he'd be dead,' I say, looking over at the wasted figure almost draped over Poal's sunburnt shoulders. 'And looking at him, I'm not sure that would be worse.'

'Don't say that!' Hopkins exclaims.

'What?' I snap back at him. 'You think he's going to survive for long in the Last Chancers while he's in that state? Even if he gets out of this cess tank, the next battle'll kill him, that I'm sure.'

'How long does he have left in the penal legion?' Hopkins asks, pulling a canteen from his belt and proffering it towards me. I irritably wave it away.

'We're all here until we either die or get pardoned by the Colonel,' I tell him, my voice harsh.

'And how many people has he pardoned?' asks Hopkins innocently.

'None,' I snarl, quickening my step to leave the annoying lieutenant behind.

DAWN ON THE third day of the march sees us on the ridge above the area Hopkins calls the Heart of the Jungle. From up here it doesn't look any different from the rest of the Emperor-forsaken jungle, but he assures me that inside the undergrowth is a lot thicker, the trees are a lot bigger and closer together.

'That's where our captain was exploring,' he tells me as we stand in the orange glow of the rising sun, pointing southwards at an area that might be a slightly darker green than the surrounding trees.

'This captain of yours, was he a bit mad or something?' I ask, taking a swig of dentclene from a foil pouch and swilling it around my mouth before spitting the foamy liquid into a puddle by the lieutenant's feet.

'Not really,' he says, stepping back from the splash and giving me an annoyed glance. 'As far as I know, he was perfectly stable.'

He hesitates for a second as if he's going to say more, but closes his mouth and turns away to look at the sunrise.

'What is it?' I ask. He turns back, takes his cap off and scratches his head, a gesture I've noticed him using whenever he seems to be worried about something.

'Do you really think that those seed pods could be some kind of tyranid weapon?' he asks, crumpling the top of his cap in his hand.

'I've seen stranger things,' I tell him, leaning closer, as if confiding something secret to him. 'On Ichar IV, the tech-priests are still trying to eradicate swarms of tyranid bugs, which eat anything organic they come across. I've seen bio-titans twenty-five metres tall, great four-legged things that can trample buildings and crush battle tanks in their huge claws. You ever seen a tyranid?'

'I've seen sketches,' he says hesitantly, placing his creased cap back on his head.

'Sketches?' I laugh. 'Sketches are nothing! When you've got a four-metre tall tyranid warrior standing in front of you, then you know what tyranids are like. Its carapace oozes this lubricant slime to keep the plates from chafing, it's got fangs as long as your fingers and four arms. They stink of death, when they're really close it's almost suffocating. They use all kinds of symbiote weapons to blast, tear, cut and grind you apart.'

I remember the first time I saw them, on Ichar IV. Three warriors jumped us as we were doing a firesweep of some old ruins. I can see clearly now their dark blue skin and reddish-black bony plates as they stormed forward. The shock and fear that swept over us when we first saw them, unnatural and unholy in every way. They had guns we call devourers, spitting out a hail of flesh-eating grubs that can chew straight through you, worse than any bullet. Our lasgun shots just bounced off them, and those who didn't fall to the devourers had their heads ripped off and limbs torn free by their powerful claws. It was only Craggon and his plasma gun that saved us, incinerating the alien monstrosities as they carved through us. As it was, those three tyranid warriors killed fifteen men before they were brought down. I remember Craggon died later on Ichar IV, his blood soaking into the ash wastes when a tyranid gargoyle dropped from the skies and tore out his throat.

Hopkins is visibly shaken, his face pale under his deep tan. I point towards my face, or rather the maze of scars criss-crossing it. I still don't think he understands the horror of the tyranids and decide to press the point. People have to know about the abominations we face out here in the stars.

'I got these from a tyranid spore mine,' I say fiercely, wishing he'd never brought up tyranids, wishing that of all the horrors I've faced, I could forget about the carnage of Ichar IV and the terrifying, bowel-loosening horror that the tyranids represent. No one who wasn't there, hasn't fought them, can really understand what they're like, it's like trying to describe the ocean to a blind man. 'Damn thing exploded as close to me as you're standing now, threw me to the ground with the burst of gasses. Bits of razor-sharp carapace shrapnel damn near tore my face off! Franx bound my head up with his shirt to stop the bleeding. I was in agony for weeks, even on regular stimm doses. I'm lucky I've still got both my eyes, Franx tells me. There were men in my platoon who had limbs ripped off in that explosion, had holes punched straight through them. Others lost their skin and muscles to acid from the spore mine, burning through clean to the bone. Do you know what it looks like, a man with bio-acid searing through his body, eating away at him? Do you know what his screams sound like?'

'I... I...' he stutters, looking at me in a new, horrified way.

'Next time you look at one of those sketches,' I tell him scornfully, 'just you remember that, and just you try to imagine it.'

He stands there, mouth hanging open, eyes blank. I snarl wordlessly and stalk off up the ridge, wishing he hadn't reminded me about Ichar IV.

POAL CURSES CONSTANTLY as he hacks with his bayonet at the branches and vines around us. Hopkins wasn't exaggerating when he said this was the worst part of jungle on the whole of False Hope. It's nearly dusk, and we've travelled perhaps two kilometres down the ridge. We're nearly at the bottom, that much I can tell, but if we have to keep going like this for more than another day or two, we're all going to starve or die of thirst. We found one pool, but it was tainted with sulphur from the volcanoes. Franx thought of catching the rain in canteens, but Hopkins told us there are certain plants, parasites way up near the treetops, which dissolve their spores in the rainwater, so that the stuff cascading down through the trees carries a deadly curse.

One man didn't believe him and tried it anyway. His throat swelled up within an hour and he choked to death. We lost another trooper to poisoned thorn bushes, the lacerations on the Guardsman's legs filling with pus almost in minutes. I shot him, after he begged me to. Hopkins agreed, saying that the infection would pass through his bloodstream into his brain, driving him insane before he died. I began to feel a little more respect for Hopkins after that, when I realised he must have seen his fair share of horrors in this place.

'We need to find a campsite for the night,' Hopkins tells the Colonel as we wait for the men to cut a path through the wall of vegetation in front of us.

'We will look for somewhere when we reach the ridge bottom,' he says, dabbing at the sweat on his cheeks with the handkerchief still stained with the giant lizard's blood. At a shout from Poal we turn our attention back to the troopers, who seem to have found some kind of trail. I spy Linskrug among the throng and we exchange a knowing glance. Trails mean bad news in the jungle. Still, the Colonel steps through the opening and I follow, Hopkins close behind. It's almost like a living tunnel, the foliage curves above us to form a solid canopy, and the closeness of the trunks, intertwined with vines as thick as your arm, make a near-impenetrable wall to

either side. With a glance back to check we're following, the Colonel
sets off and we file after him.

IT'S ALMOST IMPOSSIBLE to tell how long we've been in the labyrinth of
plants. The only real light is a kind of glow from the dying sun seeping through and reflecting off the leaves around us. A few patches of
luminous fungi, which grow more frequent the further we press on,
cast a sickly yellow aura across the path and fill the air with a decaying smell. Side tunnels, or that's what I'd call them, branch off now
and then, and it soon becomes obvious we're in an extensive network
of paths. The roots of the trees higher up the ridge jut out of the
ground around us, twisting about each other in the centuries-long
fight with each other for sustenance. There is no sound at all except
our own laboured breathing, because if it was hot before, we're being
boiled in our uniforms now. Sweat constantly runs from every pore
in my body, soaking my fatigues and shirt, making them stick in wet
folds to my body.

The air is still, no chance of a breeze through the layers of greenery
surrounding us. My mouth is full of salt from my own sweat, drying
on my lips, making me want to keep licking them clean. My eyes are
gummed up with sweat as well, forcing me to squint in the half-light
as I shuffle along, trying not to trip on the roots snaking across the
path. Franx is just behind me, recovered enough to be walking on his
own now, but just barely. The moisture in the air is playing hell with
his lungs, making him cough constantly. Still we stumble on, following the stiff-backed outline of the Colonel forging ahead.

All of a sudden we find ourselves in an open space. It's like a massive amount of pressure is lifted, the air seeming to clear slightly.
There's movement in the branches around us, like the wind, and as
the rest of the troopers trudge in behind us, we drop to the floor. I
close my eyes and take a deep lungful of air. The humidity isn't so
bad, but there's another tinge to the atmosphere in here. I take a deep
sniff, trying to identify where I know the scent from. It's like rotting
flesh or something. Perhaps there's a dead animal nearby.

'Kage...' croaks Franx, and I sit up and look over to where he's lying
flat out a few metres to my right.

'What?' I ask, seeing a disturbed look on his face.

'I think I'm having delusions,' he tells me, pointing straight up. 'I
can see people up in the trees.'

I follow his gaze upwards, squinting to look into the canopy
that arches about thirty metres above our heads. I see a tremor of

movement and stare even harder, blinking the sweat from my eyes. A shiver of fear courses through me as I pick out the shape of a woman directly above me, half-cocooned in a nest of leaves and vines.

'C-colonel...' I stammer, seeing more and more bodies hanging in the branches overhead, mind balking at how they could have got there.

'I know,' he says grimly, pulling his power sword from its scabbard, the blue glow of its blade casting shadows in the leafy cavern. The others have noticed too, and they're stumbling about, looking upwards and pointing in disbelief.

'Kage!' shouts Linskrug. I look back. I see what he's seen – the entrance to the chamber has disappeared, there's just a solid wall of branches and leaves all around us.

'Get those flamers burning!' I call out to the men, noticing as I do that about a quarter of them are missing, presumably cut off on the far side of the vegetation.

'Some of them are alive,' hisses someone to my left, and I look up. I see an arm stretched out, withered as if drained of blood or something, but the fingers are slowly clenching. As I look around, I see that the movement in the leaves isn't caused by the breeze, it's more people, almost out of sight, writhing in their torment. I snatch my knife from my belt and run towards the nearest, hacking away at the leaves in between.

My eyes meet those of a young girl, pale grey and staring, her blonde hair covered in mud, twirled around the branches entombing her. She's trapped a metre from the ground. I rip at the leaves around her face with my spare hand and saw at a thick branch curled around her waist. She croaks something, but I can't understand what she's saying. Her face is pinched, the skin dry as parchment. To my left and right, others are tearing at the tree-prison, trying to pull people free. I manage to work my arm around the little girl's waist, trying to avoid her staring, pitiful gaze. I heave and she gives a gasp of pain. Pulling harder, I manage to get her head and chest out of the cocoon, but as she pitches forward I see thorns as long as my forearm but as thin as a finger are imbedded into her back. Her blood is leaking down her backbone. I grab the nearest spine and try to pull it free, but as I do so I feel something slithering around my left leg.

I look down and see a tendril pushing out of the ground, wrapping around my ankle. It tugs and I fall backwards, slamming hard into the mulchy ground, the knife jarred out of my hand. I curl forwards and grab the vine with both hands, trying to wrench my foot free, but the thing is incredibly strong. Suddenly Franx is there, sawing away at the tendril with his bayonet. Between the two of us, we manage to yank my foot free and we both stumble away from the plant. Others are doing the same, congregating around the Colonel where he stands in the middle of the green chamber. Some are too late, I can see them being enveloped by leaves, pushed upwards along the branches until they're a good few metres off the floor.

There's an explosion off to my right where a flamer cylinder is crushed, spewing flames over the branches and suddenly the area around the detonation is thrashing madly, tossing the burning canister away.

'We have to get out,' shouts Poal, glancing around for some avenue of escape. As far as I can see, there isn't one: we're trapped. We're in an unbroken dome of branches, vines and leaves, about sixty metres in diameter. All around us is a solid mass of vegetation, slowly creeping closer and closer, forcing us back to back in a circle. Men start firing their lasguns at the approaching vines, shearing through the tendrils with bolts of compressed light. But for every one that's blasted, another seems to snake forward, the whole of the cavern constricting around us. Something darts past my face and I hear Warnick scream, a fanged leaf slashing at his neck. His blood sprays over me and more of the horrid tentacles fasten on to him. I step away from him, only to feel someone bumping into my back, obviously avoiding something else. Glancing over my shoulder I see that it's the Colonel, teeth gritted, chopping through attacking tendrils with sweeps of his power sword. I'm gripped by a sudden desperation to get out, overwhelmed with the feeling of being trapped like a fly in a web.

Someone else jogs my elbow and I see that it's Hopkins, eyes wide, staring around at our leafy tomb.

'Treacherous bastard!' I spit, my fear suddenly turning to anger. I pull free my laspistol and push it against his temple, forcing him down to his knees. 'You knew what was here! You led us into a trap! You were the bait, weren't you? I'm gonna see you dead before I'm taken!'

He gives a shriek and throws himself down, curling up on the floor. I can hear him sobbing.

'Don't kill me,' he pleads. 'Don't kill me, I didn't know any of this. Please don't shoot me, I don't want to die. I don't want to die!'

It's obvious from his horror that he's telling the truth, that he wasn't left in the station to lure us here. He's just as dead as the rest of us, as well, so there's no point shooting him.

As the living chamber grows smaller, ten or perhaps twelve metres across now, I can see more and more of the poor souls captured inside. Some of them are corpses, that much is obvious from their sunken features and empty eyes. Others are still alive, their mouths opening and shutting with wordless pleas, their eyes full of terror, staring at me, imploring me to do something, but I'm just as helpless as they are.

'That's the captain!' I hear Hopkins shout, and I look to where he's pointing. There's a man in an officer's coat the same colour as Hopkins's jacket, his brown eyes staring intelligently at us, just a few metres away. His skin is almost glowing with health, in stark contrast to the wasted faces of the others trapped by the plant. I take a step towards him, but suddenly there's a dense fog in the air, a cloud of something that fills my mouth and nostrils. It's like the heavy incense the Ecclesiarchy use, almost making me gag. I see brown shapes in the leaves around me, ovals bigger than my head, and recognise them briefly as the same as the seed pods we found back at the station. My head feels stuffed with bandage gauze, I can't think straight with all of the stuff clogging up my throat. It's then that I hear a voice, almost like it's inside my head.

'Don't fight it,' it tells me, strangely melodic. 'The god-plant will make you immortal. Embrace the god-plant and it will reward you. Embrace it as I did. See its divine beauty, become part of the god-plant's great benevolence.'

Around me I dimly see many of the men stop struggling, staring in rapturous awe at the leaves curling down towards them. The air has a purple tint to it, like a haze across my vision, glittering slightly. My limbs feel leaden and I have to fight hard not to lose my grip on the laspistol.

'There is no point struggling,' the voice continues calmly. 'There will be no pain, the god-plant shall see to your needs. It will sustain you, even as you sustain it. Provide for the god-plant and it shall provide for you in return.'

The cloud of spores is thicker than ever, a purplish mist swirling around my head, fogging my vision and mind. I sense a leafy tendril sliding up my arm, curling towards my face. I feel weak at the knees, it would be so easy just to give in. To become one with the god-plant. I can feel its magnificence, spreading out all around me, its alien life coursing through roots and branches for many kilometres in every direction.

I feel tiny pinpricks of sensation on my neck and dumbly look down, seeing a red liquid seeping into the collar of my shirt. Somewhere in the back of my mind a distant voice tells me it's my own blood, but I don't really take any notice. My throat and neck are warming up, building in heat, like relaxing tonic spreading through my body.

The voice – *my* voice, I realise – is nagging at me to wake up, to shake off the plant. I feel very tired, but from deep within me I start to feel a surge of energy, welling up from my stomach. I feel my fingers twitching into life and my head clears a little. I gaze around, trying to look through the haze that has dropped over my eyes. I can see vague outlines of other people, as if through a fog, some of them standing still, others struggling violently. Noises, real noises from outside, filter through the dull humming filling my ears, strangled shouts and violent cursing.

Like waking from a deep sleep I rise to consciousness again, startled awake by the sharp pain in my neck. Shaking off the last vestiges of the dream-like state, I snatch the tendril biting into my neck and tear it free, my blood scattering in crimson droplets over its greeny-yellow leaf. With a snap I'm fully aware of what's going on again. The Colonel is standing to one side of me, slashing back and forth as vines snap towards him. Franx is on the other side, fallen to one knee, both hands fending off another leafy tentacle lunging for his face.

Without actually thinking about it, I begin snapping shots off from my laspistol, bolts of light flaring into the plant around us, severing tendrils and slashing through leaves.

'Kage!' the Colonel barks over his shoulder at me. 'Hold these off. I will deal with Nepetine.'

He takes a step towards the captain and I jump to fill his place, my laspistol spitting bolts of energy into the green, writhing mass still slowly constricting on us. There's a lull in the attack, the god-plant concentrating its alien limbs on picking up the men who are standing around in dumb acquiescence, pulling them away and into the branches above our heads, their limbs dangling lifelessly like dolls. I see the Colonel fighting with Nepetine, the captain's arms flailing weakly at Schaeffer as the Colonel pushes his hands deep into the leafy folds surrounding Nepetine.

'Step back,' orders the Colonel, pushing me and some of the others away from the captain. A second later and there's a roaring noise, a flame blossoms around Nepetine, shredding the god-plant, throwing pulpy vegetation and human flesh all over us, covering us in blood and sticky sap. The god-plant suddenly recoils, the branches thrashing madly as they rapidly draw away into the distance. The dome retreats slightly, giving us room to spread out a little.

'Anybody still got a flamer?' I shout out, casting my gaze over the few dozen of us left, keen to grab the offensive while we still have the chance. 'Repentance' Clain, murderer of seventeen women, steps forward, the ignition flame on his weapon burning with a piercing blue light in the gloom of the god-plant's bowels.

'Burn a way out!' I snarl viciously, pointing vaguely in the direction where we came in. Repentance gives a grim smile and jogs up to the receding walls. With a torrent of flame that hurts my eyes to look at he opens up, the flammable liquid splashing across the leaves and branches, turning them into an instant inferno. He blasts gout after gout of fire into the retreating vegetation, the whoosh of the flamer accompanied by the crack of burning branches and the staccato popping of exploding seed pods. The leafy wall draws back even more rapidly, trying to get away from the deadly flames. The rest of us join him, firing our own weapons around the flames, forcing the god-plant to open up even further. After we've blasted our way a good hundred metres clear of the chamber, there's still no sign of the men who were cut off, presumably they're already dead.

A few tendrils half-heartedly snake towards us from the ceiling, but the Colonel easily hacks them apart with his power sword. Slowly but steadily we push forwards, the god-plant relenting before our ferocious attack, closing behind us but too far away to be dangerous. I don't know how I can tell, but the god-plant seems to be getting more and more desperate, something in the uncoordinated way it flings biting leaves at us, something about the gradually yellowing, sickly colour of its foliage. We press on, letting the flamers do the work.

The air is filled with the stench and smoke of burning plant, choking me and stinging my eyes as I stumble after the flamer teams. Franx is coughing up so hard now that Poal and one of his men have to carry him again. The green light, tinged with sudden bursts of red and yellow from the flamers, is making me feel sick as well. For what seems like half a lifetime, we push our way forwards through the depths of the god-plant, fending off its ever weakening attacks. I feel the ground rising and I realise we are starting up the ridge. I'm surprised by how far this thing extends, how long we were wandering around inside it, oblivious to the peril as it let us get closer and closer to its centre, where I suppose it thought we would never escape.

It's with a shock that we burst through onto the open rock of the ridge. Glancing behind me, I see the others come stumbling out, some turning around to open up with a fusillade of lasfire to drive back the god-plant's alien limbs as they creep towards us. Gasping and cursing, we haul ourselves up the rocky slope. There's no other vegetation around, obviously devoured by the god-plant to make room for itself.

After a few minutes we're far enough away, half way up the ridge, the going a lot easier without the twisting confines of the god-plant's outer reaches to ensnare and misdirect us. I turn and look back and I can see the god-plant contracting. Its outer edges are a sickly yellow colour by now, looking like grass in a drought. It leaves bare, grey dirt in the wake of its retreat, drained of all nutrition.

'Sergeant Poal,' I hear the Colonel saying behind me as I continue to stare at the plant monstrosity, 'get your comms-operator to call down the shuttles, and order a bombardment of that... thing.'

It's the first time I've ever heard the Colonel almost lost for words. Dragging my gaze away from the strange beast, I push myself a few more steps up the ridge to stand next to the Colonel. Hopkins is there, blood pouring down from a cut above his right eye.

'Well, that was something,' the lieutenant pants, gazing in amazement at the god-plant.

'What the hell was it?' Franx asks, flopping down exhaustedly on a patch of mud in front of me. Others are collapsing around us, staring vacantly at the sky. Some fall to their knees, hands clasped in front of them as they offer up thanks to the Emperor. The Colonel steps forward, gazing intently towards the god-plant.

'Whatever it was,' he says with a hint of satisfaction, 'it is going to be dead soon. I am tempted to request this whole world be virus bombed, just to make sure.'

'What did you do, sir?' Hopkins asks, dabbing a cuff gingerly to the cut on his forehead.

'Frag grenades,' the Colonel replies, breaking his gaze from the view to look at the lieutenant. 'I have heard tales of such symbiotic creatures, though I have never heard of them taking plant form. They lie dormant for centuries, perhaps even millennia, until they can ensnare an alien mind. They form a link with their victim, somehow using their intelligence. Captain Nepetine seemed the conduit for that connection, so I blew him apart with fragmentation grenades. I think we were right at its centre, the damage we did was consider-able.'

He looks over all of us, before fastening his gaze on me.

'Those we left behind were weak,' he says sternly. 'To give in to alien domination is one of the greatest acts of treachery against the Emperor. Remember that well.'

I remember how close I came to succumbing and say nothing.

IT'S WITH A good feeling in the pit of my stomach that I look out of the shuttle window as we roar up into the sky of False Hope. Out of the window I can see a raging fire, setting light across hundreds of square kilometres of jungle. Another bright flash descends from orbit into the ground with an explosion as our transport ship, the *Pride of Lothus*, fires another shot from its plasma driver into the god-plant.

'Burn, you alien piece of crap,' I whisper, rubbing the fresh scabs on my neck. 'Burn!'

THREE
BAD LANDINGS

THE FEELING IN the cell is even tenser than normal. Everybody's shaken up by what happened on False Hope, the memory of our fellow Last Chancers being eaten by the god-plant fresh in our memories. To make matters even worse, there's been no sign of the Colonel for the past three weeks. Talking to the ratings, it seems he disappeared on a rapid transport two days after we left False Hope orbit, taking Hopkins with him.

Not wanting to think about the future, determined to leave the past behind, I try to lose myself in the day-to-day drudgery. I've had to reorganise the men again: there are only forty-seven of us left. I've made an ad-hoc command squad out of Franx, Kronin, Gappo, Linskrug, Becksbauer and Fredricks. The other men are organised into four squads, with Poal, Donalson, Jorett and Slavini as the sergeants. Everyone's getting really shaky now; I need the calmest heads in charge if I'm ever going to survive this whole mess. With less than fifty of us left, we're a below-strength platoon, not even a full company of men. There's an unspoken feeling floating around the unit, a feeling that the end is getting very close. Roughly three thousand nine hundred and fifty Last Chancers have died in the past two and a half years, I can't see forty-seven of us surviving the next battle. Not if the Colonel comes back.

The thought of the Colonel's not returning doesn't leave me too optimistic either, I can't help feeling he's dumped us. There are too few of us to do anything useful that I can think of. I mean, given time the Departmento Munitorum can muster regiments numbering thousands of men, so what can four dozen Last Chancers do? In my gossiping with the ratings I've also learnt that we're heading to a system called Hypernol for re-supply. On the face of it, there seems nothing particularly odd about that. On the other hand, I can remember some of the men, dead now, who had been drafted in from a penal colony in the Hypernol system. The Colonel leaving and us being shipped to a penal colony – coincidence? I don't think so. He's left us to rot, I'm sure of it.

I'm not the only one to add two and two. As usual, Franx and Gappo are sitting with me during the sludge-eating gala they call meal time, a few cycles after dropping back into warpspace, some three weeks after leaving False Hope.

'Can't believe that's it,' Franx says vehemently, his voice a ragged whisper since his infection on the deathworld. 'Four thousand men dead, all over? Just like that, all finished? Doesn't make sense. What have we done? Fought in a bunch of wars, lots of men have died, but we haven't achieved anything. Can't believe this is the end.'

'You think there's some grander scheme?' laughs Gappo. 'Don't be naive! We're just meat in the Imperial grinder, nothing more.'

'What do you mean?' I ask the ex-preacher, slightly disturbed at his words.

'Sitting on a prison hulk or in some penal colony, we were just dead meat, carcasses hanging from the body of humanity,' he replies after a moment's thought. 'We're all criminals, according to the Colonel, who have wasted our chance to serve the Imperium. It doesn't matter if we live or die, as long as we're doing something useful. So they give us guns, put us into a war and let us hurl ourselves at the enemy.'

'That's stupid, too,' argues Franx, shaking his head. 'If we're such a waste, why bother sending us anywhere? Why not just kill us? Men are hung and beheaded and shot, all punishments listed in the Codex Imperialis. Having a naval transport at our beck and call is unheard of. Those resources don't come cheap, somebody owes the Navy.'

'That isn't normal, I'll grant you,' Gappo concedes with a thoughtful look. 'Then again, we've all heard the Colonel. He genuinely believes in our Last Chance, in giving us an opportunity to save our souls from Chaos by allowing us to serve the Emperor again.'

'Can't see how the Colonel has enough clout to have a Navy transport seconded to us,' counters Franx, wagging a finger at Gappo. 'For all the Colonel believes in his mission to save our souls, I don't think it's enough of an argument to convince the Lord Admirals to give him a ship that can carry stores for fifty thousand fighting men, to ferry around a few hundred. Logistics don't make sense.'

'It's not just logistics, though,' I tell them, looking at Gappo then Franx. 'If you knew this was going to happen to you, would you have still defied the cardinal or let your men revolt against your superiors?'

'Not sure,' answers Franx, gnawing at his bottom lip in thought. 'Never really thought about it.'

'I know what you mean,' Gappo exclaims excitedly, as if he's just stumbled on some secret truth about the galaxy. 'It's the deterrent, you're saying?'

'We've been in twelve war zones now,' I remind them. 'How many other regiments have we come in contact with? There were at least thirty on our battlefront on Ichar IV; there's the Perditian Outriders from Octo Genesis, the Choreks at Deliverance, and about another ten from other places. They all saw or heard about the dirty jobs we have to do, the massive casualties we suffer. I know for a fact that if I'd seen this coming, my knife would have stayed firmly in my belt that time.'

'Still doesn't explain why there's a few dozen of us left,' Franx argues, his voice rasping and quiet. Gappo's about to answer back but Franx holds up his hand to stop him. He takes a sip of his juice before continuing. 'Throat feels on fire... Anyway, it would make sense to round up convicts as we travel. Four thousand men are as much a deterrent as fifty, much more useful military force.'

'So perhaps that's where the Colonel's gone,' I suggest with a smug smile. 'He's gone ahead to the penal colony to organise some new recruits. They'll be waiting for us when we arrive.'

'I don't know which would be worse,' Gappo laments, looking thoroughly miserable again. 'Getting locked up in a prison some-where for the rest of my life, or dying on a battlefield.'

'I want to go down fighting,' I tell them firmly. 'Whether the Colonel's right or not about my immortal soul, I want to die doing something that's worth a damn. I joined the Guard to fight for the Emperor, I ain't gonna rot in a cell, be sure about that.'

'With you on this one, scarface,' Franx laughs. 'Give me a gun, a googly-eyed alien to shoot it at, and I'll die a happy man.'

IT'S ANOTHER TWENTY cycles before we drop from warp space into the Hypernol system. The tension and uncertainty is almost tearing us apart. A trooper called Dress was shot by the armsmen when he attacked a Navy warrant officer during unarmed combat drill. Another, Krilbourne, got a broken arm from a fight with Donalson, and everyone, including me, has a few bruises and cuts from flaring tempers. I've tried everything to ease the men: drilling them hard so they're too exhausted to scrap, organised a meal time rotation system so that everyone eats with everyone else and the squads don't get too isolated, stuff like that. None of it seems to be working too well, but then again maybe things would be a whole lot worse if I hadn't.

I'm not sure why I'm bothering, to be honest. Actually that's not true, when I think about it. On the face of it, I could quite happily let them strangle each other in their sleep, even Franx and Gappo, and I wouldn't shed a tear. Nearly four thousand in the regiment have died, and I hardly ever give them a second thought, except perhaps in my warp-dreams. No, it's not a concern for them individually that I'm worried about. It's my survival that bothers me. If the Last Chancers are going to keep going, which means I get to keep breathing, they need to stay sharp, need to keep it together as a fighting force. They always fight and bicker, more than even your normal Guardsmen, but in a fight they watch out for each other.

There's something about battle that unites men like us, whether it's for a common cause or, like us, just for survival. You're all in the same crap, and that makes a bond stronger than friendship or family. But as soon as the battle's finished, the cause is gone and they fragment again. I've come to realise a lot about these men, and myself along with them, over the past thirty months. They're born fighters, men who are at their best in combat. Any other situation and they're not worth a damn, but with a knife or a gun in their hands they seem a whole lot happier somehow. I know I am. I like to know that the man in front of me is the enemy and the one behind me is an ally. I can handle that without any problem. It's the rest of it that I can't stand: the politics and personalities, the responsibilities and the frustration and helplessness of it all. If you haven't been there, you might have some clue what I'm talking about, but to really understand you can't just watch, you have to take part.

IT'S WITH CONFUSION and trepidation that we're herded back into the cell after exercise; rumours are flying everywhere that the transport the Colonel left in has come back. My feelings are mixed, and I'm just waiting to see who's come with him, if anyone, before I start worrying about the future.

Sure enough, an hour later the cargo hold door opens and the Colonel steps in. I bark orders to the Last Chancers, forming them up for the unexpected inspection. The Colonel walks along the five ranks, looking intently at each of the men, before standing next to me.

'The men appear to be combat ready, Lieutenant Kage,' he quietly says to me.

'They are, sir,' I reply, keeping my eyes firmly directed forwards as my drill sergeant instructed me back in basic training.

'You have done well, Kage,' he tells me and my heart skips a beat. I barely stop my eyes flicking to the right to see his face. That's the first word of praise I've ever heard slip from the Colonel's lips. It's stupid, I know, but to hear him sound pleased makes me feel good. The praise of this murderous bastard, this unfeeling tyrant, makes me happy. I feel like a traitor to the other Last Chancers, but I can't stop myself.

'You will have to reorganise the squads again,' he tells me. 'You have some new troopers.' He takes a couple of steps back towards the door and gestures to the armsmen waiting in the corridor. Two figures walk into the cell chamber and I stare in amazement at them.

The two of them are almost identical. Both are tall and slender and dressed in urban camouflage fatigues. Even in the yellow light of the cell their skin is incredibly pale, almost white, and so is their hair. Not silvery grey with age, but pure white, cropped about two centimetres long. As they march into the hold and stand to attention in front of the Colonel I can see their eyes, strikingly blue, a lot darker than the icy colour of the Colonel's, but still very disturbing. Looking more closely at them, I see that the one on the left is a woman. I can see the roundness of small, firm breasts under her shirt, and a curve to her hips which is altogether quite pleasing to the eye. There were about forty women in the Last Chancers when we first started out, but the last of them, Aliss, was killed on Promor about a year ago. The only women I've seen since then were the Battle Sisters at Deliverance, and they were always wearing power armour.

'See that they settle in, lieutenant,' the Colonel orders, snapping me from my contemplation of the finer points of the female form. He strides out and everybody relaxes.

'Names?' I ask, walking up to the new pair, my eyes still drawn to the woman.

'I am Loron,' the man says, his voice quiet, almost feminine. He indicates his companion. 'This is Lorii, my sister.'

'I'm Kage. You two will join my squad,' I tell them, pointing towards where Franx and the others are lounging. Without a word they walk off, sitting next to each other near the wall, in the vicinity of the squad, but not really with them. Franx waves me over.

'Who are they?' he asks, staring at the two troopers.

'Loron and Lorii,' I tell him, pointing each one out. 'Twins, I reckon.'

'Not exactly your normal Guardsmen, are they?' Linskrug mutters, stepping up beside Franx, his eyes following our gaze.

'What do you call a normal Guardsman, baron?' Franx asks with venom in his voice. There's always been a bit of a thing between the two of them. I blame Franx's experience with the officers of his regiment for his distrust of anyone from the Imperial aristocracy. Linskrug didn't help himself; he was a bit off-hand when he first arrived a couple of years ago. But since then I think he's realised he's up to his neck in crap, just like the rest of us. Franx doesn't seem to have noticed the change, though.

'One with a bit of colour, I guess,' Linskrug chuckles, slapping Franx jovially on the shoulder. 'They do seem a bit distant though,' he adds.

'Quit staring, the pair of you!' I snap, tearing my own eyes away. 'They'll soon warm up, once they've shared a few meals and exercise periods. They certainly won't settle in with everybody giving them the wide-eyed treatment all the time.'

'Gives me a strange feeling,' Franx says with a mock shudder before strolling off. Linskrug wanders away after another few seconds, leaving me standing there with my own thoughts. I glance at the two again. It's odd, you'd think that combat fatigues would make a woman look more masculine, but to my eye the manly clothing only emphasises her female attributes even more. Giving myself a mental slap to clear my thoughts, I march away, hollering for Poal and Jorett's squads to report for exercise.

'WITCHERY, IT MUST be!' says Slavini, dropping to a crouch and bending his head forward to stretch the muscles in his back.

'I don't think they'd taint us with a thaumist,' I reply casually, continuing my own warm-up exercises.

'But nobody's heard them utter a word to each other,' protests the sergeant, standing up again. 'Twins are more prone to magical infection than others, everyone knows that.'

'Well, they keep themselves to themselves,' I admit, 'but I'd prefer that to more gossiping old women and bad-mouths like you.'

'Ah,' he says with a triumphant look, 'that's something else as well. In the week they've been here have they given you any trouble at all? Any fights started? Tried to steal anything?'

'No,' I tell him, rolling my head back and forth to loosen my neck. 'I wish you were all like them, in that respect.'

'So it stands to reason, doesn't it?' Slavini says emphatically, looking at me for some sign of agreement.

'What stands to reason?' I ask him irritably, wishing he'd talk sense for a change.

'Twins, perfectly behaved,' he says in a frustrated fashion, as if his point is obvious. 'Is there any other reason that they'd end up in the Last Chancers you can think of? Witchery, it has to be.'

'It doesn't have to be anything of the sort!' I argue. 'Perhaps they're cowards, that's why they're so quiet. Maybe they refused the order to attack or something.'

'They certainly don't come across to me as cowards,' Slavini counters, leaning against the wall and pulling a leg up behind him with his free hand. 'There's something hard-edge in there, not fear, when they meet your gaze.'

'Okay,' I admit, 'they don't seem to be cowards, but that doesn't make them psykers.'

'Does to me,' Slavini exclaims, getting the last word in before jogging off along the gantry. Shaking my head in disbelief at his stubbornness, I run after him.

LIKE EVERYONE ELSE, I gaze open mouthed as the albino twins walk back into the cell after their exercise break. Lorii is stripped from the waist up, displaying her perfectly formed chest to all and sundry, a sheen of sweat glistening on her alabaster skin. She's talking quietly to Loron, their heads leaning together as they walk, totally oblivious to all around them.

'Okay, put your eyes back in!' I snap at the men close by, and most of them avert their gaze. I notice Rollis still staring from where he's sat with his back against the wall, and I begin to walk over to remind him who's in charge when I see something even more pressing. Donovan, a real snake from Korolis, is sidling towards the twins, rubbing sweat from his hands on his combats. I head off to intercept him, but I'm too slow and he stands in front of Lorii, stopping her. My stomach gives a lurch of anxiety, because I know that whatever happens next, this is going to turn out bad.

'That's a fine showing, Lorii,' Donovan says with a leer. He reaches forward and places his right hand on her chest, gazing into her eyes.

She snarls, slapping his hand away angrily and trying to step past, but he wraps an arm around her waist and pulls her back with a laugh. I don't see exactly what happens next – they've both got their backs to me – but half a second later Donovan starts screaming his head off and drops to his knees, clutching his face. Lorii spins apart from him and starts to walk away with Loron. I call out Lorii's name and she stops and walks over to me. She smiles sweetly, holding her right hand out, closed around something.

'I don't like being touched by perverts,' she says lightly, her blue eyes staring straight into mine. I feel her place something wet in my hand before she turns and walks off. Looking down, I see one of Donovan's eyes staring back at me from my palm. My interest in her body immediately drops to below zero.

GAZING OUT THROUGH the small round port in the Colonel's office, I can see the world we're orbiting. It's grey and cloudy, not particularly remarkable. The Colonel is watching me intently, as always, and I self-consciously avoid meeting his eyes.

'Hypernol penal colony is on the moon of the planet below us,' he says, confirming my earlier suspicions. 'We will be travelling to the surface at the start of the last pre-midcycle watch. The *Pride of Lothus* will be re-supplying at the orbital marshalling station. When we reach the penal colony, I will be dispensing with the services of certain members of your platoon who have failed to perform satisfactorily.'

'May I ask who, sir?' I inquire, curious about this change of attitude. The Colonel's never mentioned expelling anyone from the Last Chancers before. Up until now the only options for getting out have been death or a pardon. It seems to me we can die just as well as anyone.

'You may not,' the Colonel replies sternly, reminding me that I'm still gutterfilth in his eyes, for all of the recent increases in my responsibilities. He turns to look out of the port, and as I look away from his back I notice something out of the corner of my eye, on Schaeffer's desk. It's a picture of Loron on a file, and with the Colonel's attention elsewhere I lean forward a little to try to sneak a look.

'You could just ask, Kage,' the Colonel says without turning around.

'Sir?' I blurt out, startled.

'You could just ask what crimes Loron and Lorii have committed,' he replies, looking over his shoulder at me.

'What did they do?' I ask uncertainly, wondering if this is some kind of trap or test being set by the Colonel.

'Disobedience,' the Colonel says simply, turning around fully. 'They refused an order.'

'I understand, sir', I assure the Colonel, crowing inside because I was right and Slavini was wrong. Witches indeed!

'I am sure you will, lieutenant,' the Colonel says with an odd look in his eyes. 'Prepare for embarkation on the shuttle in one hour's time,' he adds before dismissing me with a waved hand.

'OKAY,' ADMITS SLAVINI when I tell him as soon as I get back to the holding pen. 'But that doesn't mean that's what really happened, just because that's what the record shows.'

'Emperor, you're a suspicious man, Slavini,' I say sourly, annoyed that he still won't admit that he's wrong. 'Come with me, we'll settle this once and for all.'

I grab the sergeant's arm and drag him over to where Loron is sitting against the wall, staring at the floor. I put him and his sister on different exercise details in the hope that it would force them to communicate more with the others, but it just seems to have annoyed and upset them. Well, I've had it with their introverted ways, they're going to become a part of the unit whether they like it or not.

'What are you in for?' I demand, standing with my hands on my hips in front of Loron. He looks slowly up at me with those deep blue eyes of his, but doesn't say a word.

'As your lieutenant, I'm ordering you to tell me,' I snap at him, furious at his silence. 'Or is that another order you're gonna refuse?' I add viciously. He stands up and looks me straight in the eye.

'It isn't what you think,' he says finally, his glance moving back and forth between me and Slavini.

'So tell us what it really is,' I insist. He looks at us both again and then sighs.

'It's true that Lorii disobeyed an order,' he tells us slowly. I look smugly at Slavini, who scowls back. 'It was an order to retreat, not an order to attack,' he adds, and we both stare at him in astonishment.

'Ordered to withdraw, you refused?' Slavini says incredulously. 'You'll fit in nicely with the Last Chancers. Are you suicide freaks or something?'

'I was wounded in the leg,' Loron explains, face sombre. 'Lorii refused the order for general withdrawal and came back to get me.

She carried me over her shoulders for the kilometre back to the siege lines. They said she had disobeyed orders and dishonourably discharged her at the court martial.'

'They didn't get you on some crappy conspiracy or complicity charge, did they?' I ask, wondering how Loron had ended up joining his sister.

'No,' he replies. 'I insisted I be discharged with her. They refused, so I punched the captain of my company. They were only too happy to throw me out after that.'

'To stay with your sister, you punched your captain?' laughs Slavini. 'No mistake about it you're fragging weird, man.' I look at the albino's sincere face, seeing an odd look in his eyes that makes me wonder even more about them. About where they're from.

'Very well,' I tell him. 'I'll keep you and Lorii together from now on, if that makes you feel happier.'

'It does,' Loron replies with a slight smile. He takes a step to walk past Slavini and then stops. He looks back at the sergeant and the smile on his face is gone.

'I would suggest you don't use words like freak and weird around Lorii,' he says, his voice dropping to a menacing tone. 'She is more sensitive and less reasonable than me.'

I bet she is, I think to myself as Loron walks off, leaving Slavini visibly shaken. In an unconscious gesture, the sergeant rubs his eye with a knuckle and then wanders off, thoughts obviously somewhere else.

'So, Lorii,' Linskrug says, leaning as far forward as the shuttle safety straps will allow to talk across Kronin's chest, 'I bet you didn't think you'd be going back to the penal colony this soon!'

'We've not been in a penal colony,' she corrects him. The twins have begun to lighten up finally, as everybody gets used to them and gives them some space. For their part, they've started talking a bit more, as if the both of them have resolved that they're not going anywhere, so they better at least try to get along with some of the others. In fact, I'd say Lorii has got a soft spot for Linskrug, though I can't think what she sees in the handsome and once wealthy and well-connected baron. Kronin's asleep between the pair of them, snoring gently, as the shuttle takes us down to the moon.

'Sorry?' I say, catching on to what she said. I look over to my right where she's sitting next to the aft bulkhead. 'You mean the Colonel hasn't just picked you up from the penal moon we're going to?'

'No,' she says with a fierce shake of her head. 'We've been fighting with a punishment battalion on Proxima Finalis for the past eighteen months.'

'Why has the Colonel singled you out?' I ask.

'We weren't singled out,' Loron says, and we turn our heads to the left to look at him. 'We were the only ones left.'

'Only ones?' Franx croaks beside me. 'How'd that happen?'

'Cluster bombs from ork fighter-bombers dropped straight into the middle of the battalion as we made an assault,' says Lorii and everyone's gaze shifts back to her. 'Blew apart two hundred troopers – everybody except my brother and me.'

'Woah,' Broker says from the other side of the shuttle, shock showing on his face. 'That's pretty awesome.'

'What happened then?' I ask Lorii, curious as to how they ended up with us.

'The commissars weren't sure what to do with us,' Loron continues the story, dragging our eyes to the other end of the shuttle. 'That's when Colonel Schaeffer turned up again, had a word with the commissars and then brought us here.'

'Turned up again?' Gappo asks, before I get the chance. 'You'd seen him before?'

'Yes,' Loron replies with a nod. 'It was over a year ago, when the punishment battalion was first formed. He came and met the captain. We don't know what they talked about.'

I'm trying to work out what we were doing roughly a year ago. It's not that easy, for a number of reasons. For a start, in the past year or so we've been to five different worlds, and they all blur into one long war after a while. Added to that, what was a year ago for Loron and Lorii might not be the same for us, what with warp time and the rest. It's like this: a ship in the warp can travel so fast because time there doesn't flow the same as it does in the real universe. Well, that's how a tech-priest tried to explain it to me on my first trip off Olympas. In our universe, time passes normally, so the people on the ship might experience only a week to a month, while three months have really passed them by. I've not had any reference to, for want of a proper term, normal time since Ichar IV two of my years ago. For all I know, ten years might have really passed me by in that time.

The shuttle suddenly lurches, slamming my head back against the hull and wrenching me from my reverie. Everybody's glancing about at each other, wondering what's going on.

'What the frag?' I manage to bark out before the shuttle dips to the right sharply, hurling me forward into my harness.

'Turbulence?' suggests Linskrug, the calmest among us. I twist my head over my shoulder to look out the viewport behind me. I can see the circle of the moon below us, too far away for us to be in its atmosphere yet.

'Nope,' I growl, pulling the release on my straps and hauling myself to my feet. 'Stay here!'

I try to work my way to the front bulkhead, leaning on people's knees as I pull myself along. The shuttle shudders and banks the other way, tossing me sideways and pitching me to my hands and knees. Clawing my way forward, I pull myself up the bulkhead and lean against the wall next to the comms-unit connecting us to the forward chamber where the crew and Colonel are. Pushing the switch to activate it, I steady myself some more as the shuttle seems to waggle from side to side for a few seconds.

'What's happening Colonel?' I shout into the pick-up. The link crackles for about a second before I hear the Colonel, his voice distant and tinny.

'Get back to your seat, Kage,' he orders. 'The pilot has suffered a synaptic haemorrhage. Prepare for crash landing.'

Everybody's looking at me, and they've heard what the Colonel said. Almost all of them seem to start talking at once, I can't make out a word they're saying.

'Shut up!' I bellow, flicking the comms-unit off again and leaning with my back to the bulkhead. 'Check your harnesses are tight. Really tight. When we hit, get your arms over your face and keep your ankles and knees together. If we have to ditch after we land, Broker's squad goes first, followed by Donalson, Jorett and Slavini. I'll follow up. Until then, don't say anything.'

The next few minutes pass agonisingly slowly as I stumble back to my place and strap myself in again. We're utterly helpless, just hoping that the pilot's back-up can regain some kind of control. The moon's got enough of an atmosphere to burn us up if we enter wrong, and even if we survive that we'll slam into the surface at something like a thousand kilometres per hour if the landing thrusters don't fire. Even if the thrusters do slow our descent, we could be spun around like crazy, smashing side or top first into the ground. Assuming the plasma chambers don't explode on impact and incinerate all of us, some of us might just get out of this alive.

It's about ten minutes after the first sign of trouble when I feel the hull vibrating with the constant burning of attitude adjusters, altering our roll and pitch as we plunge towards the moon. That at least is a good sign, because it shows that someone's regained some manoeuvrability. Looking out the port again, the moon is looming large, filling it up. It's a sandy yellow colour, orange wisps of cloud drifting through its atmosphere. The anti-glare shutters snap up, blocking my sight, protecting us from the blinding light caused by entry into the atmosphere. Half a minute later and the shuttle starts shaking violently, bouncing me a few centimetres or so up and down on the bench, despite the fact that my harness is biting painfully tight into my gut and shoulders. I hear the whine of the engines turn into the customary roar as the turbo-jets kick in, and I realise we're not going to burn up. That still doesn't help the fact that we were going twice as fast as we should have been. If the pilot hits the retros too hard he could snap the shuttle in half; if he goes too late we'll be flattened on impact.

The warning lights snap on, glowing a constant red, indicating imminent landing.

'Get ready everyone!' I shout. I wait a moment to check they're all braced properly before wrapping my arms across my face, cupping my hands over my ears to stop my ear drums being blown out by any explosive change in pressure. My heart is hammering, my knees trembling as I try to press them together. This has to be the most terrifying experience of my life, because I'm totally helpless to do anything. There's not a single fragging thing I can do to alter whether I live or die, except protect myself and try not to tense up too much. That's easier said than done when you know you're plummeting groundwards at high speed.

The air fills with a high-pitched whistling as we scream down through the air. I grit my teeth until I remember that you're supposed to keep your mouth open. I can hear some of the troopers praying to the Emperor, and I offer a silent one of my own. Please don't kill me this way, I ask him. Keep me safe and I'll never doubt you again, I promise.

With a near-deafening crash we hit, and the impact hurls me backwards. I feel like we're skidding, the shuttle is jumping and lurching, yawing wildly left and right.

'Fragfragfragfragfrag!' I hear Franz wheezing next to me, but I'm relaxing already, realising that we're down and still alive. Then suddenly I feel light again and can sense us plummeting downwards, like we slipped over the edge of a cliff or something. I pitch towards the front of the shuttle as we go into a nose-dive, and a wild screech forms in my throat, but I manage to bite it back in time. Everything is spinning wildly, making me dizzy and sick. There's a sudden jolt and the spinning changes direction. Across from me, Mallory gives a high pitched yelp and then throws up across my boots. Then there's a sudden moment of calm and I can still hear Franx's cursing.

'Fragfragfragfragfragfrag!' he's spitting. I glance at him and see his knuckles are pure white, he's clenching his fists so tightly. It's then that I notice a pain in my palms and realise I've been digging my fingernails into my hand, even through the cloth of my gloves. Forcing myself to unclench my hands, I stare fixedly at my knees, trying to ignore the nausea sweeping through me.

The next impact smashes my knees together and is accompanied by the wrenching sound of torn metal. And then we've stopped. Suddenly it's all over; there's no sense of motion at all.

'Frag me!' Slavini shouts, breaking the silence, punching a fist into the air, his voice shrill, a wild grin across his face. I'm grinning like a madman too. Someone starts whooping, I burst out laughing, other people are crying out with joy. Feeling hysteria threatening to overwhelm us all I bang my head sharply back against the fuselage, the pain jarring some sense back into me.

'Stow the celebrations,' I bark. 'Is everybody okay?'

There's a series of affirmatives, and then I hear Lorii's melodic voice.

'There's something wrong with Crunch,' she says, indicating the burly Guardsman on her left. I release my harness and make my way over to him, telling everybody to stay sitting in case the shuttle shifts or something. Crunch is flopped in his seat, his head against his chest. I crouch down in front of him and look up into his open eyes. There's no sign of consciousness in them. As I stand up again, I notice a massive bruise on the back of his neck. Fearing the worst, I put a finger to his chin and lift his head up. As I suspected, there's no resistance at all.

'Damn,' I curse to no one in particular. 'His neck's snapped.' Letting Crunch's face flop back to his chest, I go along to the comms-panel.

'Everything all right up there, sir?' I ask.

'The pilot is incapacitated, that is all,' the Colonel tells me, his voice crackling from the comms-panel. 'What is your status?'

I glance around for another check before replying.

'One dead, probably a few dislocations, sprains and bruises, but that's all,' I report.

'We seem to have broken through the surface into a cave,' the Colonel's metallic voice tells me. 'Organise ten men for a survey party, I will be with you shortly.'

Switching off the comms-unit I turn back to the cabin. Everyone seems to have got over their initial delight, realising that we're stuck somewhere on this moon. We don't even know if the air outside is breathable, or anything else about this place. There could be a fire in the engines for all we know, still threatening to blow us to the warp.

'Jorett, how's your squad?' I ask, stepping between the benches towards the sergeant. He glances back at them before replying.

'All present and able, Kage,' he tells me with a relieved smile. 'Fraggin' lucky us, eh?'

'Okay, when the Colonel gets here, we'll see where the frag we've ended up,' I say, dropping into the empty place next to Jorett and sighing heavily. Something always happens; the curse of the Last Chancers always manages to strike when you least expect it. Not even a simple shuttle run can go right for us.

'WHAT'S THAT BLOODY noise?' Jorett asks as I hand out the rebreather masks and photolamps. I listen for a moment, brow furrowed, and hear it as well. It's like a scratching on the hull, an intermittent scraping noise.

'Haven't a clue,' I tell him with a shrug, pulling on the headband of my own mask. Apparently the moon's atmosphere isn't breathable, but other than that, and the darkness of being in an underground cave, everything else is tolerable. The Colonel's watching over the men as we attempt some rudimentary repairs to the engines; the power relays were punctured during the crash. The tech-priest pilot is phasing in and out of consciousness, and from his scattered mumbling it's clear we're not going to go anywhere until the engines are back on-line, and a few other things are fixed up. The warrant officer who took over piloting says his last navigational contact placed us about thirty kilometres from the penal colony, well out of marching range. We've only got enough rebreathers for a dozen people, and even if we had one for everybody the tanks last for only half an hour or so before they need refilling from the shuttle's filtering system, and that's at full stretch at the moment, running on auxiliary power. We're going outside to check for any damage to the exterior, but there's been no hull breach as far as we can tell. If the shuttle's contaminant detection systems are working, that is.

We're running on secondary power with the engines offline and so have to hand-crank the ramp down. It's a laborious process, because two sealing bulkheads have to be lowered first to form an air-lock. It's sweaty work and the air circulators in the small boarding cabin are almost at overload with the eleven of us puffing and panting, making the air stale and thin. After about an hour's work we're ready to get the ramp into position.

'Okay, get your masks in place,' I order, pulling down the mouthpiece of my own. I take a few experimental breaths to check it's working properly and then push the two nose plugs up my nostrils. I pull the visor down from my forehead, settling it across the bridge of my nose, and then check everybody else is ready. I get three of the men on each crank wheel, and they start turning, lowering the ramp centimetre by centimetre. I feel the wisp of a breeze blowing in as the air outside flows fitfully inside. Five minutes later the ramp's down and I march down into the cave, switching on my photolamp. In its harsh red glare I can see the strata of different rocks in the jagged wall of the cave. Looking up, the beam disappears into the darkness, so the roof must be more than ten metres above us. I wave the rest down and set off towards the engines, the most vital part of the shuttle at the moment. Grit crunches underfoot, the floor littered with shards of rock brought down by our crash. I can hear the strange scratching noise again as I near the engine pods. The heat emanating from the thrusters makes me break out in a sweat as I approach closer.

I run the beam of the photolamp over the nozzles of the thrusters, looking for any cracks or dents, but don't see anything. I see Jorett walk past me, playing his photolamp over the engine housing on the other side. He takes a step forward for a closer look and then straightens up, a frown on his face.

'Kage,' he says, voice muffled by the mask, waving me over, 'have a look at this.'

Stepping up beside him I look carefully where his photolamp is pointing. In the ruddy glare I can make out a shadow about halfway up the engine housing, just above my head. It looks like a hole and I curse inwardly. If the housing is punctured, it'll need patching up before the men inside can go through to reconnect the relays. Then the hole seems to move, changing shape slightly.

'What the frag?' I hear Jorett murmur. Pulling myself up the grab rail a little, I peer closer. The hole isn't a hole at all. It's some kind of many-legged creature about the size of my hand. I can see its eyes glittering in my photolamp beam. Its ten legs splay outwards, hooking on to the hull of the shuttle. Its three centimetre mandibles work in and out and I see a kind of froth by its mouth. It seems totally oblivious to my presence. I prod it with the photolamp but it doesn't even move. Something else catches my eye and I look further up the fuselage. I can see another two dozen or so of the things clamped to the hull. Bubbling rivulets run down the hull, leaving metallic trails through the heat-blackened paintwork.

'Send two men to the weapons locker in the boarding bay, and bring every flamer we've got,' I order Jorett. He hesitates for a second. 'Now, Jorett!'

'They're eating the shuttle,' I tell the sergeant after he's sent a couple of his guys heading back to the ramp. 'Have a check up front, see how many more of them there are. If they penetrate the fuselage, the air will bleed out and everyone inside will choke to death...'

As he walks off, I turn my attention back to the alien bugs spread across the shuttle. Walking around to the far side of the shuttle, I count twenty more. I guess they must be like the ferro-beasts on Epsion Octarius, digesting metal ore from the rocks. The shuttle must be one hell of a banquet for them, that's for sure.

'There's about forty of the fraggin' things down here!' I hear Jorett's muted shout from the front of the shuttle. The two men sent inside return, each carrying a couple of flamers. I take one from each of them and tell them to get forward with the sergeant.

'Help me burn the little fraggers off,' I say, passing the flamer to Lammax, the dream interpreter. I take a step back and push the firing stud on the ignition chamber, the blue flame springing into life. Tossing my photolamp to one of the others, I take a firm grip of the flamer in both hands, bracing my legs apart, pointing the nozzle up at the top of the shuttle. I pull the trigger and let flames spray out six metres across the shuttle for a couple of seconds. In the pause between bursts I see flickering orange from ahead and know that Jorett's doing the same up front. Lammax opens up and I can see patches of steaming grease where the alien beasties used to be. Lammox redirects the flow of fire and burning flamer fuel slides down the hull, splashing a metre or so to my right.

'Watch where you're fraggin' pointin' that thing!' I cry out and the flames disappear. Opening up the flamer again, I send an orange jet of fire washing over the thrusters, making sure none of the creatures are hiding inside the nozzles. For another minute I make my way sideways along the shuttle sending bursts across the roof every few metres. Patches of flamer oil carry on burning, stuck to the fuselage, illuminating the cave with a flickering orange light.

'Okay, cease fire!' I call out. Swapping the flamer for my photolamp again, I clamber up the grab rails to stand on top of the shuttle. Playing the beam of the photolamp across the roof, I can see blistered, melted paint and nothing else. I turn to call back to the others that it's all clear, when a strange noise starts echoing around the cave, a low continuous scraping. Scanning around with the photolamp, I see that there's a tunnel leading off about twenty metres from the rear of the shuttle. As I look, I see a shadow moving down the tunnel towards us, accompanied by the same scratching sound we heard inside the shuttle, only getting much louder.

'Oh frag,' I whisper as the tide of aliens sweeps into the chamber, spreading across the cave floor like a living carpet.

'Flamers!' I bellow to the oblivious Guardsmen below, pointing to the approaching mass of aliens. Jorett comes running back from the front of the shuttle as once more blazing fires illuminate the cave. He sets himself up next to Lammax and fiddles for a moment with the nozzle of the flamer before sending a wide sheet of fire arcing towards the tunnel. I hastily clamber back to the ground, constantly looking over my shoulder to see what's going on.

'We're bloody holding them,' declares Jorett as he unleashes another burst.

'Yes, but not forever, they're spreading out,' adds Lammax, pausing to point to his left. I see that it's true, the creatures are spilling around the flamer fire, threatening to surround us.

'Darvon! Thensson!' I call out to the troopers with flamers. 'Get yourself over there and push them back to the tunnel.' As they do as I ordered, I step up between Jorett and Lammax. 'We've got to keep the little fraggers contained within the tunnel, where they can't get around us.'

As we force them back, step by step, something else occurs to me.

'Did you see any other tunnels down the front?' I ask Jorett, casting a panicked glance behind me.

'Rest up,' he replies. 'That was the first fraggin' thing I checked.'

Breathing a sigh of relief I step back and let them carry on with their work. A couple of minutes later and we're stood at the mouth of the cave. It's about two and a half metres across and the same high, almost circular.

'I'm out,' calls Thensson, pulling the flamer up to his shoulder.

'Get to the weapons locker, there should be spare canisters inside,' I tell him.

'They've stopped!' exclaims Darvon. Pushing past, I see he's right. There's no sign of them for the twenty metres we can see up the tunnel, before it curves away out of sight.

'They'll be back,' I say heavily. 'They must have a nest or something close by, for that many to get here so quick. We'll go and hunt them down.'

'Are you fraggin' sure?' asks Jorett. 'We've already been out here ten minutes. We've only got twenty minutes of fraggin' air left.'

'Emperor alone knows how many of those things are up there,' I tell them. 'The flamers are almost out of fuel already. Who can tell how many more attacks we can stave off. No, we hit the lair, get them all in one place at the same time.'

'I'm not sure...' Jorett continues, squaring up to me.

'I'm in charge,' I growl at him and he backs down, shaking his head.

I WAS RIGHT: the tunnel led direct to their nest, about two hundred metres from the shuttle. There's a massive cavern, the far wall too distant to see in the light of the photolamps. There's one more refill for each of the flamers, which might not be enough, because there's thousands of the creatures. They seem to be in some disarray, swarming haphazardly all over the place, covering the floor and scuttling along the walls and roof. Like before, they're not paying us any attention and I lead the squad further into the chamber. I can see another four tunnels leading off this cave, some heading up, others heading down, it's quite a network they've chewed themselves out down here. I wonder if the authorities at the penal colony know what's right under their feet.

'Sir,' Jorett attracts my attention with a terse whisper, jerking his head to one side. Looking over in that direction I see a mass of yellow alien eggs, little fleshy sacs about the size of your thumb. They stretch across the floor in a rough circle, spreading beyond the beam of the photolamp, tens of thousands of them. In the ruddy glare of the photolamps I can make out a larger, darker shape. It's about a metre tall, bloated atop dozens of spindly legs, sitting on a pile of eggs at the centre of the nest.

'I reckon that's the breeder,' Darvon says with a meaningful look.

'Let's torch it!' I snarl, grabbing Darvon's flamer and heading towards the mother bug. It turns its head towards us as we reach the edge of the egg-pile, a cluster of eyes staring back at me, a look of intelligence in them. I raise the flamer and point it directly at the breeder, smiling grimly inside my mask. Just then I notice movement to my left and right. The other Guardsmen have noticed it too and start backing away from the eggs. From the side tunnels, another sort of creature is scuttling into view. They stand waist-high on ten many-jointed legs, with vicious-looking horns jutting forward from their insect-like heads. More and more of them are pouring in, hastening behind us to cut off our retreat.

'Run for it!' I bellow, pulling the trigger of the flamer, engulfing the mother alien in flames, seeing it writhe for a moment in the fires before collapsing in on itself. The air is filled with a hissing sound and the soldier bugs, I guess that's what they are, rush towards us, moving rapidly on their many legs. The others are already heading for the tunnel and I pound after them, jetting the flamer to my left and right a couple of times as the aliens get too close.

One of the soldiers scuttles up the wall around the tunnel entrance and hurls itself at Jorett, landing on his shoulders and clamping its legs around his face. He screams as it drives its horns into his throat, spraying blood as the sergeant falls to the floor. In his death-spasm the sergeant's finger tightens on the trigger of his flamer sending a gout of fire searing across the back of one of the other Guardsmen, Mallory. Mallory flounders for a moment as the flames lick up his fatigues and his hair catches fire. He comes flailing towards me, his skin melting and bubbling around his rebreather mask, eyes staring wide through the visor, and I have to leap to my right to stop him grabbing hold of me. He falls flat on his face, a gurgling shriek issuing from his lips. He claws at his face for a moment as his mask melts into the flesh, before collapsing and lying still. I haven't got time to give him a second thought, two of the soldiers are between me and the tunnel, legs constricting, ready to jump. A flame whooshes out from the tunnel, incinerating the aliens in an instant, ashes wafting around in the heat of the fire. I see Thensson standing there, waving me on. Leaping over the charred, smouldering corpses of the soldiers, I head into the tunnel.

WE MAKE A fighting withdrawal down the passage towards the shuttle. Thensson, Lammax and I take it in turns to hold back the pursuing aliens before falling back past the next flamer man. It takes us another ten minutes to get back to the cave, where we make our stand again at the tunnel entrance. Lammax is on point when I see that he's aiming too low; some of the soldiers are scuttling along the roof of the passage. I shout out, but it's too late, one of them drops on to him, spikes piercing his shoulder. Darvon grabs the thing and flings it away and I drag Lammax out of the way as Thensson steps up to take his place, the first burst from his flamer scouring the ceiling.

Lammax is trying to scratch at the wound, but I hold his hand away, kneeling on his chest to stop him thrashing around too much. The puncture is deep, but doesn't look too bad until I see a thick, tar-like substance smeared with the blood – poison probably. Lammax recognises the look on my face and glances at his shoulder, eyes wide with horror. Tears of pain roll down his cheek, pooling at the bottom of his visor. With a lunge, he pushes me off his chest, wrenching the knife from my belt. I make a grab to get it back, but I'm not quick enough; he rams it into his chest up to the hilt.

'Right!' I shout, standing up and pushing the others away from where they've clustered around Lammax's body. 'Everyone share a rebreather and get back on the shuttle. Leave the rest for me.'

'What the frag are you talking about, sir?' demands Thensson over his shoulder.

'We don't know how long it's going to take to fix the shuttle engines,' I explain hurriedly, jabbing a finger down the tunnel to remind Thensson to keep watch. 'One man can hold this tunnel just as well as all of us, and if you give me your masks I'll be able to stay longer than if everyone stands out here together.'

'You get back on board,' insists Darvon, picking up Lammax's flamer, 'and I'll hold 'em off.'

'Don't even think about arguing with me on this one,' I snap back. 'This ain't self-sacrifice crap, I just don't trust you not to get yourselves killed. Now give me that flamer and get your sorry hide onto that shuttle.'

They exchange glances with each other, but when they see the determined look in my eye, I see them give up the fight. Thensson backs away, firing a final burst of fire down the tunnel, before hooking the strap of the flamer off his shoulder and leaning the weapon up against the wall.

'Soon as you run out of fuel or air, get inside,' he says fiercely, staring at me, daring me to contradict him.

'Get out of my sight,' I say, shooing him away with a wave of the flamer.

I'm left on my own, with three flamers and about an hour's worth of air. I just hope it's enough because one way or the other, if either isn't enough I'm a dead man.

I've fended off another half a dozen attacks over quarter of an hour when Thensson comes running up beside me. I've already had to swap masks once, and the tank on the one I'm wearing is getting low.

'What the frag are you doin' here?' I demand, pushing him back towards the shuttle.

'The Colonel sent me to tell you that main power's been restored,' he says, batting my arm away. 'It'll be another half an hour before we can ignite the take-off thrusters. Do you reckon you can hang on that long?'

'This flamer's almost out, the others are both half full,' I reassure him. He nods and heads back to the shuttle, glancing once more over his shoulder. My attention is back on the tunnel as I see another wave of aliens scuttling towards me. I fire the last shot from the flamer and then toss it to one side, grabbing another from beside me and opening up again straight away. It's going to be a long half hour.

I RECKON THERE's four, maybe five, shots left in the last flamer. I'm onto the last rebreather as well, and I glance back towards the shuttle to see any sign that they've succeeded in fixing the thrusters. There isn't. Looking back down the tunnel, I can see a mound of twisted, burnt alien bodies, half-filling it. The creatures are amazing, throwing themselves time and time again into certain death. I can't understand why they do it. They don't look intelligent enough to be out for vengeance for killing their breeder, and the shuttle isn't worth the hundreds of dead they've suffered. Then again, people have asked me why I don't just kill myself rather than stay in the Last Chancers, fighting battle after battle. They've got a point, because if I did it myself I could make sure it's quick, clean and painless, rather than risking agony and mutilation on the battlefield. But for me, that isn't the point. I am not going to die for the Colonel.

Once, I was willing to die for the Emperor and the Imperium, but the more I've seen of what they represent, the more I've decided they aren't worth it. I've been around a fair bit in the last three years, since I signed up for the Imperial Guard, and I've not seen anything that makes me think all the sacrifices are any use. Millions of Guardsmen and Navy guys are dying all the time, and for what? So that ingrate planetary commanders, cardinals and officers can notch up another pointless victory? So that some Departmento Munitorum or Administratum clerk can make a notation on a star chart to say that a worthless lump of rock is still under Imperial control? So that I can be stood here on this stupid moon, facing a swarm of alien beasts on my own so that I can go off and risk my neck in some other damned war?

I'm starting to feel dizzy now; the air from the mask has almost run out. I wipe a hand across the visor of the mask a few times before I realise the spots are in my eyes not on the plastisteel lenses. There's movement on the heap of dead and I see the aliens pouring towards me once again. I lift the flamer up once more, the gun feeling heavier than it did a moment ago. I pull the trigger and a sheet of fire roars down the tunnel, scorching the live aliens into ashes.

I gasp when I try to take my next breath and I realise with panic that the tank's empty, there's just what's left in the mask itself. More of the aliens are streaming down the tunnel and I manage to fire again, my throat tightening as I try to breathe non-existent air. The dizziness floods up into my head and my legs just collapse underneath me. I can hardly move, but I can see the darker shadow of the alien wave getting closer. I'm choking, my chest tightening, but I manage to angle the flamer in front of me and fire again, forcing the soldiers back a final time. All life goes from my fingers and I see rather than feel the weapon slipping from my grasp. I try to push myself up, to find some last reserve of strength, but there's none there this time. There's a roaring in my ears and blackness swirls around me.

I JAR AWAKE, feeling something touching me. Flailing around weakly with my arms, I try to fend off the soldier aliens. One of them rips the mask off and I feel something clamping down on my face. Suddenly my lungs fill with fresh air, and I can feel myself being dragged across the ground. As my vision returns, I see Thensson firing a flamer up the tunnel before grabbing it by the stock and hurling it down the passage, shouting something I can't hear. As I'm bundled up the ramp, I see a wave of blackness pour over and around the Guardsman, flooring him. Spikes rise and fall, stabbing repeatedly into his body, blood spurting from deep wounds. With a whine the ramp begins to close, obscuring the scene.

'We're in!' I hear someone behind me call out. I'm laid flat on my back and I stare at the glowglobe in the ceiling, entranced by its yellow light. It seems blindingly bright after the cave, but I keep staring at it. The floor beneath me begins to shake violently and I feel the increase in weight that indicates we've taken off. Out-of-focus faces cluster into my vision; people talk, but their voices are just a mixed-up burbling. I close my eyes and concentrate on filling my lungs as much as possible.

THE JURY-RIGGED shuttle managed to make it the score of kilometres to the penal colony, where the Colonel commandeered one of theirs to take us back to the *Pride of Lothus*. The tech-priest died from his feedback injury before we reached the colony, and we left the body there. As we're disembarking into the transport's shuttle bay, I approach the Colonel.

'You didn't leave anyone behind, sir,' I point out.

'You are right, I did not,' he replies, watching the Guardsmen plodding exhaustedly down the ramp.

'And we're not getting any new recruits, either?' I suggest, watching his face for some betrayal of what he might be thinking, but there's nothing there at all.

'You are not,' he confirms, finally turning to look at me.

'Why, sir?' I ask after a moment, wondering if I just need to ask, like he said with Loron and Lorii's history.

'None of them were good enough,' is all he says, looking straight at me and then turning to walk away.

'Good enough for what?' I ask, trotting after him.

'You are full of questions today, Kage,' he says, striding across the mesh decking. He looks over his shoulder at me, sizing me up, and then seems to reach a decision. 'Come with me back to my chamber, the armsmen know how to get your men back to the holding pen.'

We walk in silence, my head spinning with thoughts. What was he going to show me? Or was he going to give me a dressing down in private, not wanting to spoil discipline by taking a few lumps off me in front of the troopers? Then again, it's never stopped him before.

The Colonel keeps glancing at me as we ascend through the decks on the ironwork escalator. This sudden turn of events both worries and excites me. As we walk down the corridor towards his study, one of the robe-shrouded flunkies approaches from the other direction. He gives me a startled look but doesn't say anything. We both follow the Colonel inside and he closes the door behind us.

'Show Lieutenant Kage the documents,' Schaeffer tells the clerk, sitting down behind his desk. The robed man pulls a bundle of parchments from a voluminous sleeve and hands them to me.

I unroll the top one and place the others on the corner of the Colonel's desk. It's written in a large, flowing script. It's in High Gothic, so I can't understand much of what's written. However I do recognise the title. It says *Absolvus Imperius Felonium Omna*, which I take it means 'The Emperor absolves all your sins'. At the bottom is a heavy wax seal with the mark of the Commissariat and above it I see Jorett's name. Startled, I look at the others, and they are for Lammax and the rest of them.

'Pardons for dead men?' I ask, confused.

'Absolution can be awarded posthumously,' the clerk tells me with utter sincerity. 'As easily as commendations and medals.'

'Does everyone get one of these?' I ask, turning to the Colonel. He just nods once, staring intently at me.

You really are mad, I think to myself as I look at him, sitting in his leather-bound chair, fingers steepled in front of him.

'Only the Emperor can grant eternal and unbounded absolution,' the scribe murmurs behind me.

'You all know my promise,' the Colonel says, the first words he's uttered to me since we left the shuttle hangar. 'I give you a last chance. If you die in my service, you have earned the right for absolution. It means a number of things; it is not just sophistry. Your name can be entered into the Imperial annals as serving the Emperor and doing your duty. If we know who they are, your children will be cared for by the Schola Progenium; your families will be contacted and told the manner of your death.'

'And if you don't die?' I ask, suddenly worried.

'Everybody dies, lieutenant,' the clerk says quietly from behind me. I whirl around and glare at him. 'Sooner or later,' he adds, completely unfazed. I turn back to the Colonel, about to demand why he wants us all dead, but he speaks first.

'That will be all, Lieutenant Kage,' he says, no hint of emotion at all. I snap my mouth shut and salute, fuming inside. 'Clericus Amadiel here will summon an armsman to return you to your men,' the Colonel finishes, indicating the door with an open hand and a slight tilt of the head.

THE SOUND OF the constant bombardment was dull and muffled inside the command centre, reduced to a distant thudding. Inside the operations room everything was organised chaos as scribes and logisticians scurried to and fro carrying information detailing the latest enemy offensive. In the centre of the room, amid banks of dials and tactical displays, a hololithic projector showed a schematic diagram of the fortress, red blinking icons indicating the positions of enemy formations. Blue symbols represented the defenders, mustering to their places to fend off the assault. Two officers stood beside the hololith, resplendent in their deep blue frock coats and gold braiding. One, with the five studs of a commander-general on his epaulettes, pointed to an area to the south west.

'This looks like a diversionary attack,' he commented to his fellow officer, whose rank markings showed him to be a captain. 'Bring Epsilon Brigade back to the west wall, and push forward with the 23rd along their flank.'

The captain called over a scribe with a wave of his hand and passed on the order in clipped tones. He turned back to his grey-haired superior, his face a picture of worry.

'How can we continue to fight, sir?' he asked, fingers tapping nervously on the golden hilt of the sword hanging against his left thigh. 'They seem to have limitless numbers, and are willing to throw in thousands just to test our reactions.'

'Don't worry, Jonathan,' the commander-general assured him. 'Help is on the way, and when it arrives we shall be safe.'

'And what of the other problem?' the captain inquired in an agitated fashion, voice dropping to a terse whisper. 'What of the enemy within?'

'There is only one of them,' the commander-general replied in the same hushed tones. 'They will be caught and removed, and the small threat will pass. Nothing is going to stop us now.'

FOUR
TREACHERY

+++ Operation Harvest entering Final Stage. What is status of Operation New Sun. +++

+++ New Sun entering pivotal phase. Operation Harvest must be completed as soon as possible, time is short. +++

+++ Will make all speed for New Sun location. +++

I'VE NEVER SEEN the Colonel so angry before. I thought I'd seen him get mad, but that was just mild annoyance compared with his current performance. His eyes are so hard they could chip rockcrete and his skin is almost white, his jaw is clenched so tight I can see the muscles twitching in his cheeks. Captain Ferrin isn't all that happy either. The ship's commander is flushed and sweating, scowling at the Colonel. And there's me, caught in the middle of it. I'd just been reporting the latest weapons stock check to the Colonel when the captain came in and told him we were altering course to respond to a general alarm call. The Colonel told him flat that they weren't going anywhere and to bring us back on to our original heading, and then things started getting ugly.

'You know my standing orders, Colonel Schaeffer,' hisses the captain, leaning on the front of the Colonel's desk with balled fists, his thick shoulders level with his chin.

'May I remind you that this vessel has been seconded to me for transportation, captain,' Schaeffer spits back, standing up from his big chair and pacing to look out of the viewport.

'It is a high treason offence not to respond to a general alarm signal,' the captain barks at his back. 'There is no over-riding situation or a countermanding order from a superior officer.'

'This vessel is at my disposal,' the Colonel says quietly, and that's when I know things are getting really dangerous. The Colonel's one of those men whose voice gets quieter the nearer to going over the edge he is. 'I am giving you a countermanding order, captain.'

'I am still the most senior officer on this vessel, colonel,' the captain tells him, pulling himself up stiffly, clenching and unclenching his fists behind his back. 'This is naval jurisdiction. *I* am in command of this ship.'

'I have the highest authority! You know what I am talking about, captain!' yells the Colonel, spinning on his heel to confront Ferrin. 'I am giving you a direct order, with all of that authority behind it. You will return us to our original course for Typhos Prime!'

'Your authority does not extend to over-ruling the Naval Articles of War, colonel,' the captain says with a shake of his head. 'After we have reported for duty at Kragmeer, I will reconsider. That is my final word on the matter. If you don't like it, you can get out of the nearest airlock and make your own way!'

With that the captain storms out of the study, the heavy door slamming shut behind him. I can't shake the image of the Colonel lining us up and marching us out of an airlock, like Ferrin suggested. He's probably mad enough to do it. The Colonel looks as if he's going to go after Captain Ferrin for a moment before he pulls himself up short. He takes a deep breath, straightens his greatcoat and then turns to me.

'What do we have in the way of cold weather equipment, Kage?' he asks suddenly. I hesitate, taken aback, and he points to the dataslab with the inventory on it in my hand.

'I– er, what for?' I stammer back, regretting it instantly when he glowers at me.

'Get out, Kage!' he snaps at me, snatching the dataslab from my hand and waving me away with it. I give a hurried salute and bolt for the door, glad to be out of the Colonel's sight while he's in this murderous mood.

* * *

ANOTHER TWO WEEKS of warp-dreams end when we drop into the Kragmeer system. We're here to fight orks, the Colonel tells me. On an ice world, unfortunately. Locked in a permanent ice age, Kragmeer is one huge tundra, scoured by snow storms and covered in glaciers and jagged mountains. Fighting orks is bad enough, but fighting them in those harsh conditions is going to be damn near impossible. I've fought orks before, when a group of slavers tried raiding the world I was garrisoned on before I became a Last Chancer. They're huge green monsters, not much taller than a man because they stoop constantly, but really broad and muscular, with long, ape-like arms. They could bite your head off with their massive jaws and they have sharp claws too. They've also got pretty good guns, though their armour usually isn't worth a damn.

Then again, they don't need much armour; they can survive injuries that would cripple or kill a human. I don't know how they do it, but they hardly bleed at all, they don't seem to register pain very much and they can be patched, bolted and stapled back together in the crudest fashion and still fight with almost full effectiveness. I've seen warriors with rough and ready bionics, huge hissing pistons in their arms or legs, actually making them stronger, with guns or slashing blades built into the limb. No mistakes, even a few orks are bad news, and apparently a few thousand dropped onto Kragmeer several weeks ago.

We've still got a week of in-system travel before we reach orbit, so I go through cold weather survival with the few dozen Last Chancers left on board. Once again, the conversation has turned to just how useful we can be, with less than a platoon of men. Apparently there's another penal legion on the surface already, three whole companies. That's about five hundred to a thousand men, depending on the size of the companies. Who knows: maybe the Colonel will just wedge us into their organisation and leave us there?

Somehow, I don't think that's going to happen, though. The more things happen, and Franx agrees with me on this, the more it seems that the Colonel's got something in mind for us. I mean, if he's just trying to get us all killed, Kragmeer is as good a place as any so why the big fight with the ship's captain? And what's this authority he says he has? As far as I know, the only non-naval rank who can command a ship to do something is a warmaster, and that's because it takes the nominations of at least two admirals to make you warmaster to start with. Well, so they told us when they explained the local ranking system when I joined up. And there's also the Colonel's comment about the convicts from the last penal colony not being good enough. It all makes me wonder what's going on.

WE'RE DOWN IN the main launch bay driving Chimera infantry fighting vehicles onto the shuttles ready for transport down to the surface. The steady chugging of well-tuned engines echoes off the high vaulted ceiling, the tang of diesel fumes filling the air. Rating work parties clamber around on the cranes and gantries, preparing them for when they have to launch the shuttles. The Colonel had a Navy tech-priest look over our Chimeras, bearing in mind the freezing conditions they'll be operating in. We've got vegetative processors loaded on board the Chimeras in case we need to chop down trees to fuel them. Blizzard filters have been installed over the intakes and exhausts and double-graded ignition systems fitted to the chargers to make sure they won't ice over. I, for one, wouldn't like to have to foot it across Kragmeer to get wherever we're going. Apparently we're going to have to land near one of the Imperial bases and then get to the frontline from there. The storm season is just starting, making any air travel impossible except right out on the plains where we're landing, some forty-five kilometres from the fighting.

A piercing shrill echoes out across the rumbling of engines, bringing everybody to an instant standstill.

'Attack alert!' shouts one of the ratings helping us with the loading, my half-friend Jamieson. 'Kage! Get your men over to the gantry if they want to see something interesting.'

Everybody crowds up the metal steps to get a view through the massive armoured windows. I can't see anything yet except for the plasma trails of the two frigates that jumped out of the warp just after us. Apparently on the other side of us is the cruiser *Justice of Terra* but I've never had the chance to see her.

'There!' hisses Jamieson, pointing at a movement to his left. I cup my hands around my face as I push my nose against the armaglass, trying to block out the light so I can see better. Then I can see it, nothing more than a shooting star at this range, sweeping past the furthest frigate.

'I hope there aren't too many of the eldar,' Jamieson mutters, shaking his head. 'We're not built for combat; transports usually act as part of a convoy.'

'How the hell do you know it's eldar?' asks Gappo incredulously from my right.

'Watch how they turn,' Jamieson tells us, nodding towards the window. I strain my eyes for a few minutes before I can see the orange-red spark again. Then I see what Jamieson means. The pin-prick of light slows for a second or two and then speeds off in another direction entirely. Even burning retros and working the manoeuvring thrusters to maximum, one of our ships could never turn that tightly. Nowhere near that tightly, in fact.

As I watch, I see a tiny flicker of blue erupt around the blob of light that I identified as one of the frigates. The frigate seems to glow a little bit brighter as its shields absorb the attack. I can feel the engines of the *Pride of Lothus* forcing us away from the battle, a rumbling that seems to react with the pulsing of the ship to create a stomach-churning vibration.

'Frag me...' whispers Franx, looking up. I glance through the uppermost part of the window and see lights moving across my field of vision. I realise it's the *Justice of Terra* powering across us, over the top of the transport just a few kilometres away. She's immense: gallery after gallery, rows and rows of gunports moving into view. Even through the blast-filter tint of the armaglass I can see the directional engines burning briefly into life along her port side, pushing her a bit further from us. Her plasma drives start to come into view, huge cylinders criss-crossed by countless kilometres of massive pipes and cables, feeding vital power from the plasma reactors deep within her armoured hull. The brightness of the plasma trails is almost blinding even through the darkened glass, white hot energy spilling from her engine tubes, hurling her through space at an incredible speed, although her size and weight make her look ponderous. No, not ponderous, it's more stately, a serenity that belies the awesome amounts of energy she's using. She's an inspiring sight, there's no doubt about that, and I can see why many a young man fantasises about growing up to be a ship's captain, commanding one of those deadly behemoths.

Watching the cruiser forging her way towards the eldar, I feel a sense of security. Surely nothing could stand up to the attentions of that gigantic engine of destruction. The Navy may have some strange ideas about strategy and defence, but you have to hand it to them, they know a hell of a lot about firepower. Their anti-ordnance defence turrets have weapons larger than those carried on Titans, their barrels over ten metres long, dozens of the point-defences studding the hull of a ship the size of a cruiser. Their broadsides vary, sometimes they have huge plasma cannons capable of incinerating cities, other times it's mass drivers that can pound metal and rock into oblivion. Short-ranged missile batteries can obliterate a smaller foe in a matter of minutes, while high-energy lasers, which Jamieson tells me are called lances, can shear through three metres of the toughest armour with one devastating shot. Most cruisers carry huge torpedoes as well, loaded with multiple warheads charged with volatile plasma bombs, carrying the power to unleash the energy of a small star on the enemy. It makes my humble laspistol look like spit in an ocean. More like a hundred oceans, actually.

When the *Justice of Terra* becomes nothing more than another spark in the distant battle, we begin to lose interest. There's the flickering of gunfire, but from several thousand kilometres away, it's hard to see anything really happening. I'm sure up on the gun decks and on the bridge they've got ocular sensors and stuff that allows them to have a better view, but down here it's just an incredibly distant and faint light show.

'Okay,' I tell the men as they begin to wander away from the window gallery, 'let's finish loading the Chimeras.'

WE HAVE THREE of the Chimeras on board one of the dropships and are getting ready to take another two onto the other when the ratings start hurrying around us, a sudden panic stirring them into activity. I grab a warrant officer by the arm as he tries to dash past.

'What's going on?' I demand, looking at the naval men as they converge on the lockers at the rear of the shuttle bay.

'We've got the order to prepare for boarders,' he tells me, pulling my hand off his arm with a snarl. 'One of the eldar pirates has doubled back and is coming straight for us. They lured the cruiser away and now we're on our own. Look!' He points out of the windows and I see a swirling shape approaching us speedily. I can't see the ship clearly, it's defended by what we call holo-fields, which twist and bend light so you can't see the exact location and sends augurs and surveyors haywire. Another example of the infernal witchcraft the eldar use in their weapons and machines.

I'm about to ask somebody to get in contact with the Colonel when I see him walking through the blast doors at the far end of the shuttle bay. He glances out of the windows as I hurry over to him.

'We need to get armed, sir,' I tell him. 'They're expecting a boarding action.'

'I know,' he replies turning his attention to me. I see he has his power sword hanging in its scabbard from his belt, and a holster on his other hip for his bolt pistol. 'I have informed the armsmen. They will issue you with weapons when they have finished assembling the naval parties.'

'Where should we be, sir?' I ask as we walk back towards the platoon. 'The Navy boys seem to know what they're doing. Where can we help out?'

'You are right. They can manage without us interfering,' he agrees, pulling his bolt pistol out and cocking the safety off. 'We shall act as a reserve, behind the Navy teams. If they look like they are faltering, we will advance and support them.'

That seems sensible. I'm all for staying behind the ratings and armsmen. After all, they're the ones trained for this sort of thing, in short-range firefights and close melee, and they've got the heavy duty armour to keep them safe in that sort of scrap. While we're waiting for the armsmen to dish out the weapons, I order the dropships secured, more to keep the men busy than because of any fears that having them open will help the eldar.

We're just finishing that when the armsmen bring over a trolley of weapons. They start handing out shotguns and shell bandoleers to everyone. I grab one and sling it over my shoulder and then snatch a bundle of electro-gaffs, calling over the squad sergeants to take one each and keeping one for myself. Looking back out of the windows I can see fire from our measly batteries flaring towards the miasma of colour that is the eldar ship. It doesn't seem to be damaged at all; it changes course to come alongside us, slowing its speed to match ours.

The whole ship shudders violently as the captain orders evasive manoeuvres and retro-jets spring into life, cutting our speed suddenly and hurling us sideways. This gives us a respite for only half a minute or so before a livid purple stream of energy pours out of the cloud of shifting colours, striking us somewhere near the aft section and causing the ship to tremble under detonations.

'They have disabled the engines,' the Colonel says from beside me, his face grim as ever. 'Now they will board.'

I see smaller shapes detach themselves from the multicoloured fog, heading towards us. They must be using assault boats, I deduce. I can see half a dozen of them, and they seem to be heading straight for us. I think it must be an illusion but then I perceive that they are actually heading straight for us. They grow larger and larger in the windows and I hear the clattering of boots on the metal decking as more men pour into the shuttle bay from the surrounding areas of the ship. I push half a dozen cartridges into the chamber of the shot-gun and pump them ready to fire. Holding the electro-gaff under my left arm, I herd the platoon back towards the wall, away from the windows and launch doors.

'Wait for the Colonel's order and follow my lead!' I shout out to them. I see a few of them glancing around, looking to see if there's an opportunity to get away, but as I follow their gazes I see that the doors have all been shut again. Glancing overhead I notice a trio of Navy officers in the control tower, looking out through the massive plate windows at their men below.

'They're here!' I hear someone bellowing from the front of the bay. I can see the sleek, menacing shapes of the assault boats dropping down past the windows, each patterned in strange, flowing stripes of black, purple and red. A few seconds later, patches of the walls to either side of the launch doors glow blue as the assault boats use some kind of energy field to burn their way through. With an explo-sion of light the first breach is made to my right, throwing sparks and debris onto the decking. Almost at once other detonations flare to my left and right and the Navy parties begin to open fire, the thun-der of their shotguns resounding around the large chamber. The flare of gunfire flickers across my vision, joined by the odd burst of light from a lascannon or something similar.

From where I am I can't see anything of our attackers, but I can see men being hurled to the floor by blasts of dark energy, or torn to shreds by hails of fire. Right in front of me I see a pulsing star of blackness burst through the Navy ranks, smashing through a hand-ful of men, tossing their charred bodies into the air and flinging severed limbs and heads in all directions. Everybody seems to be shouting at once, adding to the cacophony of the gunfire. Hoarse screams of agony or panic echo off the walls and the clatter of spent shell cases rings from the decking. The air stinks with the cordite from two hundred shotguns, the stench of burnt flesh and abattoir smell of dismembered and decapitated bodies. As I glance around trying to work out what the hell is going on, everything is in anarchy, flashes of lasfire mixing in with the bark of shotguns and the shrill, whickering noise from the eldar's splinter rifles and cannons.

It's impossible to see how many we're facing, or whether we're holding them back or not. I can see mounds of dead everywhere, men crawling away holding onto mutilated limbs or clasping wounds on their bodies and heads. Another explosion rocks the grates of the decking, a fireball blossoms far to my left where a generator or something goes up. Shots are whistling overhead now, impacting on the ironwork of the control tower support, hissing and bubbling as they melt through the girders holding the control room a dozen metres above the deck. A shuttle to my right bursts into a huge fireball, a hail of shrapnel scything through the men around it, cutting them down with a cloud of sharp-edged debris.

'It is time,' the Colonel says, stepping forward, the pulsing blue of his power sword illuminating his face from beneath. He nods his head towards the right where I can just see the first alien warriors through the thinned ranks of the Navy ratings and armsmen. They're wearing armour striped in the same colours as their attack ships. Their armour is plated and covered in blades and spikes, which glisten in the erratic light of the firefight. They stand about a head taller than the men around them, but are slim to the point of being emaciated. They move with a graceful, flowing motion that seems entirely effortless. With a speed that the most hardened human fighter would find difficult to match, I see them cutting left and right with close combat weapons made of exotic blades and barbed whips. A man's head spins to the ground as one of them tears through his throat with a backhand slash from its sword, before turning on its heel to plunge the blade through the stomach of another Navy man. There's an aura of malice about them, a ruthlessness betrayed by the odd shrill laugh or extravagant gesture.

There's a moment when the aliens in front of us stand on their own, about two dozen of them, with dead and dying Navy men littering the deck around their feet. Without any order being needed everybody opens fire at once, the heat from the volley washing over me and causing sweat to jump out of my skin. I pump the shotgun and fire again, the haft of my gaff wedged between the top of the breach and under my arm, and I see one of the eldar thrown back by the impact, bright blood spattering into the air. To our left, more come leaping towards us, easily cutting through the few men in their path.

There's a thudding of booted feet to our right and a squad of armsmen rush up and join us.

'They're breaking through towards the main corridor!' their petty officer screams, gesturing towards the far end of the bay with his assault shotgun. His visor is pushed back and I see his hate-filled snarl as he opens up with the shotgun, a dozen shots crashing through the approaching eldar in the space of a few seconds. Pulling the drum magazine from the shotgun and flinging it aside, he leads his men past us. I see Donalson leading his squad after them, and I let them go. The Colonel stands to my left, power sword in one hand, bolt pistol levelled at the enemy in the other.

'Fighting withdrawal to the command tower,' he snaps over his shoulder at me before firing a burst of rounds into the eldar as they head towards us.

'Fall back by squads!' I bellow over the din of the fighting. 'Jorett and Command squad up front!' I see the other men falling back towards the rear of the bay as I kneel to slam another six shells into the shotgun. Getting to my feet again I see the other Last Chancers are in position and I begin to walk backwards, firing round after round from the shotgun, the other squad's covering fire blasting past me into the aliens. The dead are heaped everywhere now, ours and theirs, bloodied body parts scattered across the metal decking, the deep crimson of human blood mixing with the brighter red of alien life fluid. I can't tell how many of them are left, but as I pull back past the other squad I can see that fighting is still raging fiercely to my left as the eldar attempt to break through the main doors and into the ship's interior.

'If they get out, they have an almost direct route to the bridge,' the Colonel informs me as he ejects the magazine on his bolt pistol and slides another into place. 'We must stop them getting out of the shuttle bay.'

Glancing over my shoulder I see that we're at the steps to the command tower now. You can follow the trail of our retreat, five dead Last Chancers lie among more than two dozen alien bodies and a swathe of shotgun cases and bolt pistol cartridges litters the floor. A few eldar manage to dart through our fusillade, almost naked except for a few pieces of bladed red armour strapped across vital body parts. Almost skipping with light steps, they duck left and right with unnatural speed. In their hands they hold vicious-looking whips and two-bladed daggers that drip with some kind of venom that smokes as it drops to the metal decking. Their fierce grins show exquisitely white teeth as they close for the kill, their bright oval eyes burning with unholy passion.

The Colonel counter-attacks, followed by Loron and Lorii. Schaeffer ducks beneath a venomed blade and opens fire with his bolt pistol, blasting the face of his attacker. Loron spins on his heel to send the butt of his shotgun crashing into the midriff of another, grabbing the gun double-handed and bringing the muzzle up into the alien's face, snapping its neck with the blow. Lorii side-steps between two of them, weaving to her right as one makes a lunge at her, grabbing the female eldar's arm and whipping it around, sending the slender creature tumbling into the blade of its comrade. One-handed, she fires the shotgun into the stomach of another, spraying shredded entrails across her white skin, dying her hair with bright red blood.

'Get the men to the control tower,' the Colonel orders me, bounding past me up the metal steps. The aliens continue to fire as we hurry up the open stairwell, cutting down two men from Slavini's squad and pitching them over the railing. I see the sergeant turn around and push his squad back down a few steps, returning fire to hold back the aliens as they race across the open deck towards us. My breath explodes out of my mouth in ragged gasps as I pound up the spiral stairs, forcing my aching legs to keep going, pushing at the back of Franx in front of me to keep him moving. Below us I can see that the eldar have almost reached the main gateway. Only a couple of dozen armsmen stand between them and the locked doorway.

It's with a sense of enormous relief that I tumble through the door of the control room, other men piling after me and pitching me onto the floor. The Colonel grabs me by the shoulder of my flak jacket and hauls me to my feet.

'Seal that,' he tells someone behind me, using his spare hand to point over my shoulder at the control room door. The door closes with a hiss of air and a dull thud. Three dazed naval officers stand looking at us with a mixture of surprise and horror.

'How do you blow the launch doors?' the Colonel demands, letting go of me and stepping up to the nearest one.

'Blow the doors? There's men still fighting down there!' the officer responds, his face a mask of horror.

'They will be dead soon anyway,' the Colonel snarls grimly, pushing the man to one side and stepping up to the next. 'The doors, lieutenant?'

'You can't just flick a switch,' he tells us. 'The crank wheel on the back wall is the gateway pressure release valve.' He points to a wheel about three metres across, with twenty spokes. It's connected by a huge chain to a massive series of gears that disappear into the ceiling. 'It's locked into the barring mechanism that keeps the doors shut. Open up the valves and the internal pressure within the bay will blow the doors out completely. This tower is on a separate system, it should be able to maintain pressure balance.'

'Do it!' the Colonel hisses at us over his shoulder, before looking back out at the shuttle bay.

'Slavini and Donalson's squads are still out there!' I argue, a lump in my throat. 'You can't order me to kill my own men.'

'I am giving you a direct order, Lieutenant Kage,' he says as he turns to me, his voice very low, his eyes glittering dangerously. 'We are all dead if they reach the bridge.'

'I... I can't do it sir,' I plead, thinking of Slavini and his men going back to hold off the eldar to make sure we got up here.

'Do it now, Lieutenant Kage,' Schaeffer whispers, leaning very close, right in front of my face, those eyes lasering their way through mine into my brain. I flinch under that terrible gaze.

'Okay, everyone grab a spoke at the wheel!' I call out to the others, turning away from the Colonel's murderous stare. They start to argue but I soon shut them up, using the butt of my shotgun to smash Kordinara across the jaw when he starts shouting obscenities at me.

'Maintain discipline, Kage,' barks Schaeffer from behind me.

'You have five seconds to turn that wheel before I shoot you myself,' I growl at them, wondering if my eyes are filled with the same psychopathic glare I'd just seen in the Colonel's.

Without a further word they hurl themselves at the valve wheel. It creaks and grinds as they turn it; on a panel above their heads the needles on the dials begin to drop. With a sudden release of tension the wheel spins rapidly, throwing them to the floor in all directions. As they get to their feet an ominous creaking noise resounds around us. I look back out of the window and see the launch doors beginning to buckle under the strain. The huge doors, three metres thick, give way with a loud screeching, each one weighing several tons, ripped off their massive hinges and flung into the darkness. All hell breaks loose on the shuttle bay deck as shuttles, dropships, Chimeras, men and eldar are sucked into the air by the escaping atmosphere.

Men are whirled everywhere. Someone who looks like Slavini bounces off the hull of a spinning shuttle, his blood spraying wildly and violently from his face in the low pressure, sucking the life out of him in an instant. I can't hear their screams over the wild rushing of wind, a howling gale tearing around the shuttle bay throwing men and machines into oblivion. It's one of the most horrific sights I've ever seen, seeing everything rushing out of the jagged gap in the far wall, pitching them into the vacuum to a horrible death. Ice begins to form on the outside of the control tower, frosting over the glass, condensation from our breath beading quickly on the inside. I give a worried glance at the Navy officers, but they're staring in a horrified fashion at the carnage in the shuttle bay. I hear several of the Last Chancers behind me swearing and cursing. I look at the Colonel and he's stood there, totally immobile, watching the destruction outside with no sign of any emotion.

Rage boils up inside me. He knew this was going to happen. As soon as the eldar attacked, he knew it'd come to this. Don't ask me how he knew, or how I know that he knew, but he did. I drop the shotgun and electro-gaff and ball my hands into fists. Like a warm flood the anger flows through me, into my legs and arms, filling them with strength, and I'm about to hurl myself at the Colonel when he turns to look at me. I see the twitch of muscles in his jaw and a resigned look in his eyes, and I realise that he's not totally without compassion. He might have seen this coming, but he doesn't look happy about it. The anger suddenly bleeds away into the air around me, leaving me feeling sick and exhausted. I drop to my knees and bury my face in my hands, rubbing at my eyes with my knuckles. Shock sweeps over me as I realise that I killed them. The Colonel made me kill all of them: the aliens, the ratings, the armsmen and the Last Chancers. He made me do it, and I made the others do it. I hate him for that, more than I hate him for anything else he's done to me. I truly wish he was dead.

WE WERE SHUT up in that control tower, twenty-four of us in that horrid room, for the next six hours while pressure-suited repair teams brought in heavy machinery to clamp and weld a solid plate over the breaches. No one said anything for the whole time, just the odd muttered whisper to themselves. When we get back down to the shuttle bay deck, there is nothing to mark the death that had taken place only a watch and a half earlier. Everything has been swept out into space. Every loose machine, every corpse, every living man, every spent shell and piece of debris, all of it blown to the stars. Only the scorch marks from the explosions show there was any fighting at all.

As we walk back to the holding cell I catch snippets of conversation between the armsmen, who I note have different names from those who have escorted us for nearly the past three years. Our regulars must have been in the launching bay. The eldar attack was unerringly accurate. They seemed to know that the shuttle bay would be weakly defended and that they would be able to get access to the main corridors by going through it. The eldar are very smart, of that I'm sure, but this feat of planning seems unlikely even for them.

I ruminate more on this course of events as we settle back into our prison. Nobody says anything at all, the massive open space seems even emptier than the loss of twenty men would suggest. I've never seen them like this before. For that matter, I've never felt this way myself about any of the other Last Chancers. We all expect to die; we learn that after the first battle. It's only twenty men out of four thousand, so what's the big deal this time? It's because they didn't stand a chance. That's what we're here for – our Last Chance. If we fight well, we survive. If we fight poorly, we die. It's that brutally simple. It's like the law of the downhive – the strongest survive, the weak are killed and eaten. That reminds me again of the Colonel's comments about other convicts not being good enough. There is something going on, and I'm almost there, but I can't quite fit the pieces.

My thoughts veer back to the dead men that started the train of thought. But this time, there was no Last Chance. They were just in the wrong place at the wrong time. And we killed them. The other Last Chancers and I turned that wheel and blew the doors. We killed our own comrades and that's treachery of the highest order. The eldar pirates left us no option, left the Colonel no option, but to blow our fellow soldiers into the heavens. None of us wants to think about that. None of us likes to think that we're that lowest of soldiers, the basest of creatures: a killer of comrades, a cold-blooded traitor.

Except one of us, perhaps. One of us has done it before. One of us could do this sort of thing, betray us to monstrous aliens, betray his fellow men. A man who has had his punishment forestalled for a long time. A man who doesn't share an ounce of common humanity that even the most crazed psychopath in the Last Chancers may feel. A man who tried to kill me in my sleep for standing up to him. A man who has slinked, skulked and slithered his way through life, a slimy sump-toad of the worst order. I feel myself filling with righteous anger. I've held off from this moment for so long, but as I dwell on what happened in the launch bay my fury at the Colonel suddenly returns, but this time directed elsewhere, more focused and backed up by three years of loathing and hatred. I almost hear something in my brain snap.

'Never again,' I whisper to myself, and a few others nearby look up at me, their faces worried when they catch the look in my eye.

Fuelled by a sudden ire I dash across the floor of the cell, looking for Rollis. I see him on his own, in his usual place sitting down with his back against the wall. Trust him to survive when better men die. His eyes are closed, his head drooping against his chest. He gives a startled cry as I grab the front of his shirt and haul him to his feet, slamming him back against the bulkhead with the ring of his head against metal.

'Kage!' he splutters, eyes wide. 'Get the frag off of me!'

'You treacherous bastard!' I hiss back at him, grabbing his throat in one hand and forcing his head back. 'You sold us out! You betrayed us to the eldar!'

'What's this?' asks Loron from behind me, and I glance round to see that everybody has gathered around us.

'He's a traitor,' Linskrug speaks up, pushing through the throng to stand next to me. 'That was with eldar as well.'

'I haven't done anything,' gasps Rollis, twisting out of my grip and pushing me backwards a step.

'He was a comms-operator,' continues Gappo, eyes fixed on the traitor scum. 'He deliberately transmitted unciphered orders, letting the aliens know where our troops were moving. He got his whole company killed in an ambush. Everyone except him. Seems a bit strange, doesn't it?'

Lorii then steps forward, a puzzled look on her pretty face.

'How the hell did he tell them anything this time?' she asks. Everyone is quiet for a moment, trying to work it out.

'I know,' wheezes Franx ominously. 'He was driving one of the Chimeras onto the dropship while the assault boats closed. Was still inside while we were battening it down. Could have used the onboard transceiver. Good for fifteen kilometres, plenty of time to send a quick message to his alien accomplices.'

'This is just so fragging crazy!' Rollis spits at us, sneering in contempt. 'You're all deluded.'

There's an angry growl from some of the men as we absorb this theory. I realise I'm among them. I see Slavini's face exploding in blood against the side of the shuttle again and something inside me snaps. Without a thought, I grab Rollis by both shoulders and ram my knee up into his groin. He gives a choked cry and tries to pitch sideways, but my grip is too tight. I butt him between the eyes, my forehead crashing into the bridge of his nose with the crunch of shattering cartilage. I step back, panting with anger, and let go of him. He stands there swaying, stunned from the blows, blood trickling across his lips and down his chin.

'You stupid bastard!' snarls Rollis, lashing out suddenly with his right fist, catching me on the cheek and knocking my head back. He staggers forward a step and raises the other hand, but I react quicker than he can strike, jabbing the fingertips of my right hand into his reddened throat, driving them into his windpipe. As he doubles over gasping for breath, I grab his greasy hair and smash my knee into his face. In a flash of blood-red I can see Slavini's face again, exploding, slowed down in my mind's eye. I see bodies and men tossed into the air like discarded ration packets. I ram my knee into his stomach. Again and again, over and over, crushing his ribs to a pulp with the repeated hammering until he vomits a gout of blood over my fatigues. But I can't stop; I keep getting flashes of those men sucked into the darkness, blood turning to thousands of sparkling crystals in the freezing void. I claw my left hand and rake it down his face, punching the fingers into his eye sockets.

It's then that I realise that I'm not the only one beating him. Fists and feet are pitching in from all around, pummelling him this way and that, driving him to the floor. I stagger back as others force their way into the fray, and all I can see is Rollis writhing under a storm of kicks and stamping boots. A thin trickle of blood oozes out between Kronin's legs as he stands over Rollis, hands on hips, watching the man bleeding to death.

'And they smote the enemies of the Emperor with a righteous fury, for they knew they were doing His work,' the insane lieutenant says, a vicious grin on his face, his eyes lit with madness. He plunges his teeth into the man's fat cheek, sending droplets of blood splashing through the air. Another flurry of blows descends on the traitor, accompanied by the crack of breaking bones.

There's not a sound from Rollis, not even a hoarse breath. It's then that everyone realises that it's all over. Without another word spoken everybody disperses, each making their way back to their regular spots. I look at the broken, battered corpse of Rollis, and I feel nothing. No hate any more, no contempt. I don't feel sorry either. He was a total bastard, and whether or not he betrayed us to the eldar, he had this coming a long time.

Feeling more exhausted than any time in the past three years, I drag myself over to my bedroll and throw myself down. A few minutes later the lights go dim for sleep cycle and as I lie there my stomach grumbles, empty. I realise that in all the excitement that's been going on, they've forgotten to feed us this evening. Ignoring the hunger pains I try to get some sleep.

* * *

I WAKE FROM a nightmare of blood and screaming, with the Colonel laughing at us as we die in front of him. As I roll my neck back and forth to ease out a kink, it dawns on me that I've been woken by the day cycle lights coming back on. It's then that I see the crumpled shape further along the wall, and realise that the part of the nightmare about Rollis wasn't a dream at all. I push myself to my feet and stroll over to have a look at him. Scrawled across the wall in blood over his head is the word 'Traitor'. As I stand there, I feel someone lean on my shoulder and glance round to see Lorii standing there, looking down at him. She turns and looks at me.

'Do you really think he did it?' I say, half-horrified and half-gladdened by what we had done last night.

'Does it matter?' she asks back, her fabulous blue eyes looking deep into mine.

'No,' I decide. 'He never deserved a last chance; he should have been executed a long time ago. Some things are beyond forgiveness. I'm surprised it took a bunch of criminals like us to realise that.'

'Last Chance justice,' she says with a sweet smile.

'ADMIRAL BECKS, YOUR plan is totally unacceptable,' the wizened warmaster said, smoothing the folds in his long black trench coat. 'It is impossible to reduce Coritanorum from orbit.'

'Nothing is impossible to destroy, Warmaster Menitus,' the fleet admiral replied with a smug grin creasing the leathery skin of his hawk-like face. 'It may take a decade of bombardment, but we can annihilate that rebellious fortress and everyone in it.'

'That is not an option, and you know it,' Warmaster Menitus snapped back irritably. 'By ancient decree, as long as Coritanorum still stands, Typhos Prime remains the capital world of the Typhon Sector and the Typhos Supreme Guard are excused off-world duties. My superiors will do nothing to endanger that privileged position.'

'Then you will send in another ten thousand men to be slaughtered in yet another hopeless assault?' Admiral Becks answered sharply. 'If you cannot keep your own house in order, perhaps your privileged position should be reviewed. After all, who could trust a high command that allows their capital to fall to rebels?'

'You should concern yourself with keeping track of Hive Fleet Dagon, admiral,' the warmaster retaliated. 'Or have you lost track of it again? Leave the ground war to us and just make sure you get us more troops here safely.'

'Don't worry about Dagon, general,' Becks assured him with a sneer. 'The Navy will make sure you are well protected. We are the best line of defence, after all...'

'Best line of...' Menitus spluttered, face going red with anger. 'If you spent half the resources getting Imperial Guard regiments into place as you spend shuttling worthless diplomats across the galaxy, there would be no Hive Fleet Dagon left.'

'You dare suggest that the magnificent Imperial Navy should be nothing more than a glorified ferry service?' snarled fleet admiral Becks. 'You Guard have no idea, no idea at all, about just how big the galaxy is. Without the Navy, even mighty Terra itself would have fallen thousands of years ago.

'Well, so be it. You can waste as many Imperial Guard lives as you care, that's your stupidity and not my responsibility.'

FIVE
COLD STEEL

+++ *Operation Harvest nearing completion.* +++

+++ *Good. I expect you soon.* +++

I CAN SEE for about five metres in front of me, then my vision is blocked by the swirling snow. I pull the hood of my winter coat tighter around my face with heavily gloved hands, trudging slowly but steadily through the knee-deep snow. It seems our Chimeras are useless down here after all; the locals use a transport built from a Chimera chassis on top of a set of skis and driven by a giant turbo-fan engine. It's only a kilometre or two's march from the heated landing pad to the entrance to Epsilon Station, where we're joining up with the other penal legion, but I'm exhausted by the effort. From Epsilon Station we're marching to hold a mountain pass against the orks, more than fifty kilometres from where we are at the moment. We're not expected to survive. We're just here to buy time for the defenders to organise. Two stations have already been overwhelmed by the greenskins' attacks, and we're being thrown in the way to stall their advance.

The going isn't too difficult, it's downhill along the valley to the main entrance to the station. Just ahead of me, the black of his long coat almost obscured by the swirling flurries, the Colonel pushes his way through the snow drifts. Beside him rides Captain Olos of the Kragmeer Imperial Guard, riding on top of a bulky, long-haired grey quadruped which he keeps referring to as a ploughfoot. I can see why: the massive paws on the end of its four legs have horny protrusions that carve through the piled snow. The captain is swathed head to foot in thick dark furs, strapped and belted with gleaming black leather bands around his waist, thighs and biceps. He leans over in the saddle from the ploughfoot's high back to talk to the Colonel and I push myself forwards a little quicker to hear what he's saying.

'I've just sent one of my men on ahead to tell Epsilon we're almost there,' Olos yells against the fierce wind. His face is hard-worn by constant patrols in the harsh conditions, the skin tanned, heavy and thick from constant exposure to the freezing environment.

'How far is it?' the Colonel shouts back, cupping a hand to his mouth to be heard over the howling gale. He's wearing his thick black dresscoat, a heavy scarf wrapped around his chin and cap.

'About five hundred metres,' the captain replies loudly. 'Half an hour's march at this pace.'

'Why send a rider? Why not let them know by comms message?' I ask from behind them, jabbing a thumb over my shoulder at the rider on my left who is wearing a bulky comms set on his back.

'It's the storm season,' Olos bellows back. 'The southern polar regions kick up some weird element that fritzes comms transmissions over any distance greater than about two hundred metres. Every station has an astrotelepath to communicate with relay satellites in orbit. In the summer it isn't so bad, but the timing of the ork invasion couldn't have been worse for us.'

Someone else shuffles up beside me and I glance over to see Loron, his pale face almost blue with the cold, peering out of his fur-lined hood. Like the rest of us, he's wearing the long, dun-coloured coat we were given when the shuttle touched down. He cradles his lasgun in bulky mitts fashioned from the same material.

'Why the hell would anyone want to live in this place?' he demands, teeth chattering.

Olos jabs a finger down at the ground a couple of times.

'Ansidium ninety!' he tells us with a grin. 'There's millions of tons of ansidium ore beneath the rock.'

'What's so damn useful about ansidium ninety?' I ask, wondering what could be so important that three million people would live in such an inhospitable environment.

'It produces a catalyst agent used in plasma reactors,' he says, pulling a plasma pistol from its holster among his snow-covered saddlebags. 'It's one of the most stable ignition elements for plasma weapons, for a start. They say a plasma gun made with Kragmeer ansidium has only a forty-five per cent malfunction rate.'

'You seem very comfortable talking to convicted criminals,' the Colonel remarks. I can't see his face but I expect he's giving the captain one of his sternest looks.

'They are serving their punishment?' the captain asks, pushing the plasma pistol back where it came from.

'Yes,' the Colonel answers after a moment's thought, 'they are atoning for their sins.'

'Then they're all right by me,' Olos says with a laugh. 'It's the criminals wandering around unconvicted and unpunished that worry me! At the moment, we're so shafted by the orks I'm happy for any help we can get!'

'You think that twenty-two men can make a difference?' Loron asks, pulling himself free from a particularly deep drift.

'The last time Kragmeer was attacked, about seven years ago,' he tells us, 'ten men held the main gate of Gamma Station for six days against corsairs. In the right situation, ten men are better than a hundred.'

'I'll take your word for it,' I hear Loron mutter as he drops back behind us.

A FEW DOZEN men are working in the entrance chamber when we pass through the large double gates of the station. Half of them stop what they're doing to look at us. If there's one thing that annoys me more than anything else, it's the stares. I don't know why, call it irrational if you like, but why is everyone so Emperor-damned curious when we're around? Okay, so having the Last Chancers on your doorstep isn't an everyday occurrence, but do I gawp like some sloping-browed idiot whenever I see anything I haven't seen before? Of course I don't. I mean, I've got some self-respect. Our reputation seems to precede us more and more these days. I'm not sure if that makes the Colonel happy or annoyed. On the one hand, the more people hear about us, the greater our deterrent value. On the other hand, some people are seeing us just a bit like heroes, and he certainly doesn't want your average Guardsman to think that this is some kind of glamorous career move. They'd be damned stupid if they do. Personally, I don't give a frag either way, as long as they don't stare at me like some kind of freak show.

Even inside the walls of Epsilon Station, hewn from the bare rock of the mountains, it's cold. Damn cold. Outside, they say, you'll freeze in five minutes without a proper suit. I can damn well believe it too, my toes are still numb from the short trek from the landing pad at the top of the valley. We're resting up here tonight and heading off in the morning. As I lead the men to the part of the barracks the Colonel's requisitioned for us, Franx falls in beside me.

'Planet's going to kill me, Kage,' he says sombrely, gloved hands clumsily unfastening the toggles down the front of his heavy winter coat.

'If False Hope didn't get you, this place is a walk in the plaza,' I reassure him.

'False Hope might get me yet,' he says with a grimace. 'Cold is playing havoc with my chest, can hardly breathe.'

'You'll survive,' I say with feeling. 'It's what we're good at.'

'Maybe,' he admits, still looking unconvinced. 'Just a matter of time before we're all dead. If the weather doesn't kill me, orks might. How long can we keep surviving?'

'As long as we want to,' I tell him emphatically, gripping his shoulder. 'Look, my philosophy is that if you give up, you've had it. You need something to hang on to. Me, it's the Colonel. Every time I see him I convince myself again that he's not going to get me killed. I don't want to give him that pleasure. It's worked so far.'

'You believe him about our chance at redemption?' asks Franx, hopefully.

'It ain't what I believe that matters,' I tell him with a shrug. 'It's what you believe that's important. We deal with it in our own way. Linskrug thinks that if he can just survive he'll be able to return and reclaim his barony and get revenge on his enemies. Kronin's gone mental, but he thinks he's the voice of the Emperor now and that's what gets him through. Everyone's got their own thing. The ones who died just didn't believe it enough. If you want to fight for your soul, that's fine by me.'

'EMPEROR, YOU'RE BLOODY scalding me!' Gappo shrieks at the young boy by the water temperature controls. Steam rises from the massive pool, condensing in droplets on the light blue tiles of the walls. He pulls himself up the side so that just his legs are dangling in the bath.

'Keep it nice and hot, boy,' argues Poal, the former storm trooper. 'This weather's bitten clean through to my heart, I need to let the heat seep in.'

'Don't rust your hook,' Gappo sneers back, gingerly lowering himself back into the water.

'Best damn wash I've had in a long while,' I tell them, reaching for one of the bottles of cleansing tonic. 'This ansidium stuff must bring in a good price, they live pretty well here on Kragmeer.'

'By the sounds of it, the Cult Mechanicus give an arm and a leg for the stuff,' agrees Poal, sliding further into the water until it's up to his chin. 'Think what kind of energy it takes to heat water to this when it's freezing cold topside.'

'Push over, give a weak man room!' calls Franx, padding gingerly across the floor, his bare feet reluctant to touch the cold tiles. He's right, he is looking really haggard, his once ample frame clings to his bones now. There's still plenty of muscle there, but the weight's fallen off him completely. He dips a toe in and whips it back with a hiss, much to everyone's amusement.

'Too hot for your delicate skin?' laughs Poal, splashing water at the sergeant. Franx puts a foot on Poal's head, forcing it under the water. When he surfaces again, spluttering and cursing, Franx jumps in beside him.

'Aieee,' he winces, biting his lip. 'Bastard hot!'

'You get used to it!' I reassure him, pouring some lotion into the stubbly growth on my head that passes for hair.

'Don't forget to wash behind your ears,' Gappo chuckles, grabbing the bottle from me, his lunge forward causing waves to lap against the side and splash up onto the floor. I hear someone else coming in and look up to see Kronin, treading cautiously across the water-slicked tiles.

'And there shall be space in the Emperor's heart for all true believers,' he tells us, waiting at the edge, peering suspiciously into the pool.

'That means shift up, Last Chancers,' I tell them, pushing Poal to one side to clear a space on my right. Kronin takes a deep breath and steps off the edge; the small man splashes in and goes completely under. A few seconds later he bursts into view again, face split by one of the widest grins I've seen.

'Could easily stay here for days,' Franx rasps, closing his eyes and leaning his head back against the pool edge. 'Can see why Kragmeerans don't mind cold patrols up top if they come back to this.'

'I think it's Kragmeerites,' Gappo corrects him, tossing the lotion to Poal.

'Kragmeerans, Kragmeerites, whatever,' Franx croaks back sleepily.

'And I'm sure the novelty wears off after a dozen sweeps in the early morning frost,' the ex-preacher continues. 'I met a sergeant from one of their long-range scouting groups. Even the most experienced men die quite regularly. Frostbite, hidden crevasses, ice bears, all kinds of nasty things waiting for the unwary out there.'

'Can't be any worse than False Hope,' I remind them. 'Now there was a hellhole, with no redeeming features.'

'Amen to that,' Franx agrees. He's got more reason than any of us to want to forget that deathworld.

'There was a great light, and all around was the beauty of the Emperor,' chips in Kronin, chasing after a piece of soap as it slithers through his thin fingers.

'Eh? What's that mean?' asks Poal. Our synchronised shrugs cause more ripples to spread across the water, and Kronin looks around, brow furrowed in thought.

'There was rejoicing upon the Square of the Evernight, for the darkness had passed and the light had returned,' he tries again. He sighs in frustration when we shake our heads.

'Try something from the Articles of Thor,' suggests Gappo. 'I studied them. Wrote a treatise published in the Magnamina Liber, actually.'

'I always thought the Articles of Thor were dull,' argues Poal, dropping the lotion bottle over his shoulder onto the tiled floor. 'Give me some stirring hymns from the Crusade Verses.'

'You even think about singing, I'll drown you,' Franx laughs. We all have to put up with Poal's atonal bellowing in the ablution block aboard ship.

'Ah!' exclaims Kronin suddenly, raising a finger excitedly in the air like some ageing scholar who's just discovered the secret of eternal health, youth and attraction to the opposite sex. 'The people gathered about Thor, and fell to their knees in adoration, for they realised that all that had come to pass was gone, and that all that remained was the future, and it was filled with the love of the Emperor!'

'Thor five-six-eight,' Gappo tells us, biting the corner of his lip in thought. 'It's all about how the people of San Sebacle survived the horrors of the Reign of Blood.'

'Going to be all right!' exclaims Franx suddenly, opening his eyes and turning to Kronin. 'Got a good feeling?'

Kronin grins widely again and nods, his thin face bobbing up and down in the water.

'That's comforting,' Poal says. 'Last time Kronin had a good feeling about a mission was on Harrifax. I ended up jumping bunks with Morag Claptin after that one!'

'You mean Lieutenant Claptin? That's how you made sergeant so fast, you wily dog!' Gappo says, his face a picture of shattered innocence. I duck under the water and rinse my head as Poal expands on the details of his conquest. I've heard them before. We've all heard all the stories before, but it doesn't stop us telling them, or listening to them again. Two and a half years together, there isn't that much we don't know about each other. Or anything new to say.

'Damn it!' I hear Poliwicz cursing as I rise up again. He's been busily scrubbing away on the far side of the pool. 'I knew it wouldn't work.'

'What's that?' Poal asks, swimming a few strokes to cross the three or so metres to the other side.

'Wondered if these fancy cleansers might work on the tattoo,' Poliwicz admits, lifting his shoulder out of the water to show where he's rubbed his upper arm raw. He's talking about the penal legion marking we all got tattooed with when we were 'recruited'.

'Ain't nothing gets rid of that,' Poal assures us. "Cept perhaps the worms. Just ask Kage here, look what happened to his,' he adds, swimming back and prodding his hook into my right upper arm. You can't see that much of my tattoo now, there's a scar from a too-near miss of an eldar splinter rifle slashed across it.

'You remember Themper?' I ask them and they nod. 'Remember how he used his bayonet to slice off about three fingers of flesh to get rid of his?'

'That's right!' exclaims Poal. 'Bled like some fragged bastard for weeks, then they just tattooed another one onto his other arm and the Colonel told him if he cut that one out the next one would be across his face!'

'Should've said it'd be on his crotch,' Poliwicz laughs loudly. 'There'd be no way he'd take a blade anywhere near there!'

'He still died of blood poisoning though,' Gappo finishes the sorry saga of Themper. 'That's what happens when you don't change dressings.'

'And that is the importance of cleanliness and hygiene,' I say to them like a stern tutor. And then I grab a wet flannel floating in the pool and fling it at Franx, landing it square across his chin. Franx hurls it back, then Kronin ducks under the water and grabs my leg, pulling me under, and everything devolves into soaking wet anarchy as the others pile in on top.

* * *

As WE GET further into the mountains, the weather gets worse, if you can believe it. The wind gusts so strongly at times the only thing keeping me upright is that I'm standing thigh-deep in snow. The going is really slow sometimes, as we have to force our way up a ridge or slope. They're expecting the orks to reach the pass we'll be defending in about five days, and we've got to cover more than forty-five kilometres in that time. Not only that, we've got to bring all our camp equipment with us. A few dozen ploughfoots haul sledges for the heaviest gear, but the rest of it we're humping on our backs. I've never been so bone-tired before in my life. The past two nights I've just collapsed in my bedroll and fallen asleep almost straight away. At least we're getting some fresh food, roasted snow-ox, Kragmeerian podwheat and other such basics. It's good wholesome stuff. The Colonel realises that we wouldn't be able to carry on in these conditions on a bowl of protein slop a day.

The worst problem is the broken monotony. You can march for an hour or two, happily getting into your stride and letting your mind wander away from all this crap so that you don't notice the biting cold or the continuous aches in your spine and the backs of your legs. But then you have to scale a hill or something, or the snow gets soft and shifts under your feet, or you almost stumble into an ice crevasse, and it breaks your rhythm entirely and you have to work really hard to get back into your comfortable, numbing rut again.

The whole comms-blockage is playing on my mind too. I've been thinking about it while I've been plodding along. No communications with the base or even an army in the next valley. We're totally isolated. We're marching out here just to fight and die. Nobody's expecting us to return, they're just hoping our deaths will make the orks falter for a day or two while they build more barricades and bring in more troops from other stations. Fodder, that's all we are. Fodder for the orks to chew on for a while, maybe to choke on a little, and then it's over. Emperor knows what Kronin was so happy about. The hot bath seems a thousand kilometres and a year ago, though it was only three days.

Kragmeer is two different worlds, if you ask me. There's the one inside the stations. Nice, civilised, heated. Then there's the surface where snow twisters tear across the ice plains, blizzards can rip the skin off a man, and predators the size of battle tanks fight with each other for morsels of precious food. One planet, two worlds. And we have to get stuck in the nasty one.

I've been watching the Colonel closely these past few days and he seems to have changed. He seems more agitated than usual, urging us on with more than even his normal uncaring relentlessness. This whole business about us getting redirected to Kragmeer has unsettled him for some reason, and that worries me. If there's something that unsettles the Colonel, it probably should make me very, very worried. Still, there doesn't seem to be anything that can be done about it, whatever it is, so I try not to get overly concerned. Problem is, just trudging along I've got too much time to think, and that's when I get depressed. I don't like to think about the future, because I never know when I won't have one any more. Not that I've got much of one at the moment either.

BRAXTON DIED TODAY. The stupid fragger slipped out of his tent and tried to make a run for it. He headed the wrong way for a start, legging even further into the wilderness. We found his body a couple of hours along the march. He'd slipped down a narrow ravine, jagged icicles tearing his coat to ribbons. His body was frozen solid just a couple of metres down the crevasse, his face looked very serene considering his blood had frozen in his veins. He must have passed out before he died, that's what Gappo reckons.

It's the end of another long day. Not just in terms of hard work, it really is a long day here. It lasts about half as long again as a Terran day, which is what they use for the shipboard wake and sleep cycle. In the middle of winter, that's still twelve hours of straight slog; you can't really even stop for proper meals or anything, because once you stop, it's so hard to get going again. I'm getting blisters on my feet the size of eyeballs, and Poliwicz reckons he's going to lose a toe or two to frostbite. I told him to check with the Kragmeer guides, to see if he can get some better boots or something. They told him to put ploughfoot crap in his boots, for added insulation. Poal thought they were messing Poliwicz around, but I'll give it a try tomorrow, see if it works. If it gives me another edge, something else that helps keep me alive in this place, I'll do it.

There's self-respect, and there's pride, and some people can't see where the line is drawn. For me the difference is between doing something you don't want to but is necessary, and just plain refusing to do anything unpleasant at all. I won't let anyone tell me I'm worthless, even if I am a criminal. But I'll still put crap in my boots if it means it'll keep my feet warm. That's self-respect, not pride.

Kragmeer's star looks very distant and almost bluish as it sets over the mountains. Everything about this place is cold, even the light. I turn and watch the others rigging up our three storm tents – long, dome-like shapes of reinforced animal hide, designed to let the wind flow over them rather than push them over. Everything has to be done inside, the cooking, cleaning. Even emptying your bowels, which is quite unpleasant for everyone involved because snow ox is quite rich, if you understand me. Better that than freezing your butt off in a blizzard though.

With the camp set up, I tell Gappo to break out the stove. Huddled under the low roof of the tent, a few of us try to get as close as possible to the portable cooker, desperate for any warmth. The others huddle down in their bedrolls instead. Like everything else on Kragmeer, the stoves have been chosen for their suitability for the conditions, using a hot plate rather than an open flame that could set light to the tent. Its red glow is the only illumination, reflecting off the flapping walls to cast ruddy shadows, one moment making the tent seem warm and cosy, the next turning it into a blood-hued vision of hell. I try to concentrate on the warm and cosy look.

'I can't remember the last time I was this cold,' mutters Poal, his good hand held over the hotplate while Gappo digs around in the ration bags.

'Sure you can,' says Poliwicz, pulling back his hood to reveal his flat cheeks and broad nose, a classic example of Myrmidian ancestry. 'It was when you were in bed with Gappo's sister!'

'I don't have a sister,' Gappo says distractedly, pulling a hunk of flesh the size of my forearm from a saddlebag and dusting it off with his sleeve.

'Do they remove your sense of humour in the Ecclesiarchy?' asks Poliwicz, pushing past me to help Gappo with the food preparation.

'Hmm? No, they just bludgeon it out of you,' Gappo replies sincerely. 'Keeping the souls of humanity pure is a serious endeavour, you know.'

'I guess you're right,' Poliwicz concedes, pulling another piece of meat free and slapping it sizzling onto the stove.

'Not as serious as filling the coffers with donations and penances, of course,' Gappo adds darkly.

'Stop it right there!' I snap, before anyone else can say anything. 'Can we talk about something else? I'm too tired to stop you killing each other over religion.'

Everyone sits quiet, only the wind and the sputtering of the food on the stove break the silence. The tent flaps and flutters, the gale singing across the guy ropes in a tuneless fashion. I hear laughter from one of the other tents, where I put Franx in charge. The Colonel's on his own, keeping his solitary counsel as usual. It's been said before that he practises ways of killing himself in case he gets captured. I guess we all occupy our minds during these quiet moments in our own ways. Well, if the orks get him, all he'll have to do is strip naked and he'll be a lifeless icicle in minutes. The smell of the grilling snow ox fills the tent with its thick scent, reminding my stomach how empty it is. Someone else's guts gurgle in appreciation, so I'm not alone.

'I've got a sister,' Poal says finally.

'Oh, yeah?' I ask, expecting this to be the lead up to some crass joke.

'No, seriously,' he tells us. 'She was, is still I hope, in one of the Orders Hospitaller, from the Sisterhood.'

'Patching up wounded soldiers?' Gappo asks.

'That's right,' Poal confirms. 'Last I heard from her, before my unfortunate encounter with that two-timing serving wench, she was in a field surgery over near Macragge.'

'Say what you like about the Ministorum and their tithes, you get it back really,' says Poliwicz.

'In what way?' asks Gappo, the question half an accusation.

'Well,' explains the Myrmidian, settling down among the bags of grain, 'they fund the Schola Progenium abbeys. That's where we get the Sisterhood, the commissars, the storm troopers, the scribes and so on. That's got to be worth something.'

'There are bounties and treasures aplenty for those of the true faith,' Kronin points out, the first thing I've heard him say today. He says less and less these days, I think he's getting more and more isolated, unable to talk properly with the rest of us. This vast, bleak world probably isn't helping him, it's easy to feel unimportant and lonely when faced with such harsh and eternal elements as the ones that rage outside. I can feel a melancholy mood coming on, fuelled by frustration and exhaustion.

'And of all those bounties,' Gappo says, 'we end up with bloody Poal!'

'So there is a sense of humour in there!' exclaims Poliwicz with a laugh as the rest of us chuckle stupidly.

'Shut the frag up, and turn those steaks over, I don't like mine burnt!' Poal snaps, causing another fit of giggles to erupt.

'I wonder if Franx has killed Linskrug yet?' I speculate idly, as Gappo busies himself with handing out mess tins.

'Why did you put them together then?' asks Kyle, sitting up from where he was lying in a bedsack at the far end of the tent.

'Don't you know?' I say, suddenly feeling bitter about being stuck out here in the middle of nowhere, an ugly and painful death lurking not far away. 'It's the same reason we're all here – torment is good for the soul.'

TWO DAYS WE'VE waited for the orks on this Emperor-forsaken mountainside. Two days sitting on our hands, so to speak, in the freezing snow and bone-chilling wind. We're set up just beneath the cloud line, sometimes it drifts down on us and you can't see your hand in front of your face. The air is so thin up here too, causing sickness and dizziness, the lower pressure making your body expel its gases pretty continuously. That caused some laughs the first few times until it became plain uncomfortable. Some of the men have already died from exposure to the elements, killed by sheer altitude.

The only way to cross onto the plains is over a ridge at the top end of the valley, or that's what the guides reckon. A few brave souls have tried to navigate the routes to the north and west, but none ever returned. We've got some explosives rigged up to bring down a good sized chunk of snow and rock on the greenskins, but I expect that'll just get their attention more than anything. I hope these Kragmeer guys know what they're doing because I don't want to get caught up in that mess when it comes tumbling down.

Now that we're here you might be fooled into thinking that the hard slog was over, but you'd be wrong. We've been kept really busy digging trenches in the ice. If you ever thought snow was soft, you're sorely mistaken. The stuff round here has been packed solid for centuries and I swear is harder than the rock. We've only been able to get the trenches maybe a metre and a half deep. Also, the bulky mitts you have to wear make it hard to grip the haft of a pickaxe or a shovel handle, and Poliwicz almost took his foot off earlier this morning. The watery light of the sun is just about above the clouds now, and for once the snow seems to have slackened off. Well, relatively speaking – it's just coming down continuously in big chunks now, instead of almost horizontally in a blizzard.

'The wind's shifted to the south,' one of the guides, Ekul, explains when I ask him about the calming weather. 'But that's actually bad news.'

'Why so?' I ask, wanting to know the worst before I get caught out by it. He looks to the south for a moment, showing the pointed, sharp profile of his nose and chin from out of the grey and white furs he's wearing. Like the rest of the Kragmeerites, his face is battered and weathered, and his dark eyes seem to gaze into the distance as if remembering something. He looks back at me, those eyes regarding me slowly, set above high cheekbones that seem to have been chiselled rather than grown.

'There's a kind of funnel effect in the valleys and that stirs up the storm a lot,' he replies eventually, bending down to draw a spiral with his finger in the snow. 'It builds up and builds up and then whoosh, it breaks up and over the mountaintops and comes rushing up here. We call it the Emperor's Wrath. A bit poetic, but you understand the idea.'

'Bad news to be caught out in it,' I finish for him.

'Seen men blown easily thirty metres clear off the ground, and that's no lying,' he tells me with a sorry shake of his head.

We stand there looking down the pass at the zigzag of trenches being built. We've taken up position on the western side of the valley, the shallower face. The other penal regiment has been split into two contingents, forming a first line and a second line. The plan is for the orks to crash against the first line and when they're thrown back the surviving defenders will pull back and reinforce the second line. I thought it would have been better on the eastern slopes, where the going is steeper and would slow down the ork assault. But of course the Colonel has looked at everything and pointed out a good kilometre of defilade further along the valley, where units on the eastern slope wouldn't be able to target the valley floor. All the orks would have to do would be to rush the gauntlet of fire for the first kilometre and then they'd be in the defilade and in cover. Once they were clear of that they'd be out of range. That said, I've fought orks before, and I can't see them refusing the challenge of six thousand Guardsmen shooting at them without trying an assault. It's the way their minds work – they're brutal beasts, without much thought, just an unquenchable hunger for war and bloodshed. Emperor knows, nature has certainly built them for battle. As I said before, you can shoot them, stab them, chop them, and they don't go down.

I see someone striding up through the snow and it's not difficult to recognise the Colonel. I watch him as he pushes up through the drifts, hauling himself along the rocks towards us at some points where the going is really treacherous. He pulls himself over the lip of the ledge we're standing on and stands there for a moment, catching his breath, glancing back down towards the entrenchments.

'How much warning can you give me?' he asks Ekul, looking around, towards the guide.

'Depends on how fast the orks are moving, sir,' he replies with a shrug. 'A ploughfoot can cover the ground from the pickets in a couple of hours, and assuming the cloud stays up, you should be able to spot a force that size a good ten kilometres away.'

'About five or six hours, then?' the Colonel confirms and the guide nods. 'Why are you here, Kage?' he adds suddenly.

'I was surveying the layout of the trenches, sir,' I reply quickly. It's the truth. I made the back-breaking climb up here with Ekul to get a feel for the lay of the land.

'You would not try to get away, would you lieutenant?' he says darkly.

'And go where?' I can't stop myself answering back. 'Go live with the orks?'

'And what are your conclusions, lieutenant?' the Colonel asks, thankfully ignoring my insubordination this time.

'We need to extend the front trenches on the left flank,' I tell him, indicating the area with a sweep of my arm. 'They should overlap the secondary position by a few hundred metres.'

'And how did you become such a student of military theory?' he asks quietly, looking straight at me.

'Because that's what we ran into when you led us on the forlorn hope assault into Castle Shornigar on Harrifax, sir,' I point out, keeping the bitterness from my voice.

'I remember,' he says back to me. 'There was quite a deadly crossfire, if I recall.'

'There was, sir,' I concur, keeping my tone level. Three hundred and eighteen men and women died in that crossfire, you murderous bastard, I add mentally.

'I will talk to Colonel Greaves about extending his works,' he says with a nod. 'Thank you, lieutenant.'

I think about Greaves, the man in charge of the other penal regiment, as I clamber awkwardly back down the slope. He's a bull of a man, a few centimetres shorter than I am, but with chest and shoulders that would put an ogryn to shame. He constantly lambastes his men, shouting and swearing at them, cursing their heathen souls. He even has some wardens with him – Adeptus Arbites bullies who like to use their shock mauls. Unlike the Last Chancers, the other poor souls on this barren mountain are all civilians, sentenced to serve a term in a penal legion by the judges and magisters.

Their commander couldn't be any more different from ours either. I've never seen Schaeffer hit anyone who hasn't tried to attack him first. There's been a few over the years, and they ended up spitting teeth, let me assure you. He despises us all as criminals on principle, but doesn't seem to hate us as individuals. Unlike Greaves, who seems to delight in broadcasting his charges' shortcomings and inadequacies to everyone. If I were to sum it up, it's a completely different philosophy. Greaves's poor bastards only have to survive a certain length of time and they're out, so he tries to make their lives as miserable as possible while he can. Schaeffer, on the other hand, thinks he has a higher purpose. He does not act as our judge, he leaves that to the Emperor. And that means getting us killed, of course. It's like comparing False Hope to Kragmeer. One is very obviously a death-trap, full of instant death. The other is subtler, slowly leeching your life from you with a thousand tests of strength and endurance. Both are just as deadly of course.

'MOTHER OF DOLAN,' Poal curses from where he's sitting on the lip of the trench. 'There's thousands of them.'

I pull myself up the trench wall and stand next to him. The air has cleared a lot, part of the build-up for the Emperor's Wrath storm brewing to the south, and I can see what he means. At the mouth of the valley, about two kilometres to the south, the ork horde is spilling towards us. There seems to be little organisation or formation, just a solid mass of green-skinned devils marching solidly through the snow. Among the horde are a few tanks, battlewagons we call them. It's hard to make out any details at this range; it's just a dark mass against the snow.

More than a kilometre away, I make out the shapes of Dreadnoughts among the mobs of ork warriors. These giant walking war engines are twice to three times the height of a man, armed with a wild variety of heavy guns and close combat blades, saws and fists. The walls of the valley begin to echo with the noise of their approach. It's like a dull rumbling of thunder, a bass tone of war cries and bellows all merged into one cacophonous roar. As the horde gets closer, I can see that they're mainly wearing dark furs, with black and white checked banners fluttering in their midst, their vehicles picked out in places with the same patterning, oily smoke gouting from noisy engines that add to the gloom and racket.

The orks aren't stupid: they see the trenchlines and slowly the army begins to wheel up the slope, advancing along a diagonal towards us, making less of the slope's incline. The detachment in the primary trenches open fire with their heaviest weapons at about eight hundred metres, the crack of autocannons reverberating off the valley sides. I can see the sporadic flash of fire from the gun pits dug into the trenchlines, about three hundred metres further down the slope from where I am. The orks respond by starting a low chant, which slowly rises in volume as they advance, until it drowns out the fire of heavy bolters and lascannon.

'Waa-ork! Waa-ork! Waa-ork! Waa-ork! Waa-ork! Waa-ork!' they bellow at us, the mountainsides echoing with the battlecry as it gathers in pace and the greenskins work themselves up for the final charge.

Their shouts are joined by a series of muffled detonations. Huge fountains of snow erupt to our right, just above the ork army. As a single mass, an enormous crescent of snow billows out. The slope begins to slide down towards the aliens, boulders rolling along amongst the wave of whiteness, the sparse trees on the mountainside ripped up as the avalanche quickens, its momentum accelerating rapidly. The orks' cries of dismay are swallowed up by the roaring of tons of snow and rock bearing down on them, the slope turned into a death-trap by the cascading ice.

The ork march falters immediately and the army tries to scatter as the snowslide bears down on them. The ground trembles violently, as it does under a bombardment, and I cast a nervous glance up the slope above, to make sure the effect isn't wider than planned. I must admit I breathe a sigh of relief when I see no movement at all, the glistening ice stretches up the mountain completely undisturbed. Ekul and his scouts did well. The gunners in the front trenches continue firing into the panicked horde even as the avalanche hits the orks. One moment there's a dispersing ork horde, the next there's just a solid whiteness, flecked with darker patches as orks and vehicles are hurled skywards, before being engulfed and disappearing from view.

Secondary slides pile up on top of the hill of snow now filling the valley floor, layering more death onto the orks buried under the packed snow. Greaves's men start cheering, their cries of joy replacing the thunder of the avalanche. I notice that none of the Last Chancers join in, they're all watching the valley floor with determined expressions. I know what they're thinking. It's not going to be that easy, one quick avalanche and the orks are dead. It's never that easy for a Last Chancer. Sure enough, as the swirl of scattered snow begins to clear in the air, I can see a sizeable proportion of the ork army left. Stunned and dazed for the moment, but still more than enough to over-run our defences once they gather their wits again. And now they'll be even madder for the fight, eager to even the head count.

In the front trench, Greaves gets his poor charges to continue the fusillade into the orks, giving them no respite. A smart tactic, but I can't help but think that it's just Greaves wanting to shout at his penal troopers some more. A bright orange explosion lights the centre of the ork mob as a Dreadnought's fuel is detonated by a lascannon. A couple of other Dreadnoughts and a single battlewagon survived the avalanche, but Greaves is directing his men well and the lascannons and autocannons soon reduce them to burning wrecks.

An odd thing occurs to me as the orks forge their way back up the slope. Vehicles need fuel, and there's little to be found out in this icy wilderness. The Kragmeerites have one-in-three of their ski-based Chimeras converted into fuel carriers for long range work, and it stands to reason that orks would need some kind of support vehicles. Not only for fuel, but for transporting ammunition and food. It's hard to see how this army, small as it is, relatively speaking, could take a single Kragmeer station, never mind the three that have already fallen. And it's eight hundred kilometres across unbroken ice plains from the nearest to these mountains. Even if they looted everything they could from the fallen stations, they'd have to move it around somehow. Orks are good looters, they can scavenge pretty much anything, and I was half expecting them to turn up in captured, specially modified Chimeras. It doesn't make sense that several thousand orks, hardy as they are, could survive this long without that kind of backup. I don't know what the explanation is, but I start to feel uneasy about this. I'd speak to the Colonel, but I don't have any answers, and I'm sure he's made the same observations.

Lasgun salvoes join the heavy weapons fire as the orks close. The greenskins begin to return fire, flickers of muzzle flare sparkling across the darkness of the horde as it breaks into a charge. Once more, they break into their war chant, faster and louder than ever. The las-fire is almost constant now; Greaves has ordered the troopers to shoot at will rather than volley fire. Orks tumble into the snow in droves, but the rest keep coming on, surging up the mountainside in a living tide of bestial ferocity.

'They won't hold,' Poal says from beside me, his lasgun whining as he powers up its energy cell.

'They might,' I reply, keeping my gaze firmly fixed on the front trench. The orks burst onto Greaves's soldiers like a storm, the poorly trained penal Guardsmen no match for the orks' innate lust for close quarters combat.

'Pull them back now,' I hear Poal whispering insistently. 'Pull them back before it's too bloody late!'

I see what Poal means as more and more orks pour into the trench-line. If Greaves makes a break for it now, we can give enough covering fire to keep the orks off his back. If he goes too late, they'll be all mingled up and we won't be able to pick out friend from foe.

'Now, you fragging idiot!' Poal bellows, clambering to his feet.

For a moment I think that hard-headed Greaves is going to fight to the last man, taking his criminals into hell with him. But then movement from our end of the front trench, the left flank, shows men and women clambering up the back walls before the orks can fight their way along the trench to them. I reckon Greaves's own instincts for self-preservation must have kicked in. I can see him urging his troopers on, waving his arm towards us as he hauls himself through the snow.

'Covering fire!' the order is shouted from further up the trench. Poal starts snapping off shots to our right, spotting a few dozen orks that have broken from the trench and are charging after Greaves's men, trying to cut them off. The staccato roaring of a heavy bolter joins the snap of lasguns, and a hole is torn in the crowd of orks.

Colonel Greaves leads his men to our left. We're on the right flank of the second trench, about five hundred of them, half of the first-line force. The orks don't pause to consolidate their position in the front trench; they pour over the fortifications and spill up towards us. I pull my laspistol free and start snapping off shots – the orks are densely packed, I can't miss, even at this range with a pistol. The greenskins begin to disperse, trying to attack along a wider frontage, some of them breaking to our left in a bid to get around the left flank and encircle us.

Return fire starts sending up sprays of snow and Poal and I jump back down into the trench for shelter. The orks are spread into a thinning line now, concentrated more in front of us, but stretching out to the left and right.

'Prepare for hand-to-hand combat!' The wardens' bellows carry up the trenchline.

'We cannot hold the trench,' I hear Schaeffer say next to me.

'Sir?' I ask, turning to look at him.

'One on one, these men cannot fight orks,' he explains quickly. 'Once the orks are in the trench, we cannot concentrate our numbers on them. And they will be very hard to get out again.'

'Counter-attack, sir?' I suggest, reading the Colonel's mind, horrified by the thought of hastening any confrontation with the brutal aliens, but seeing there's little hope otherwise. 'Hit them in the open?'

'Pass the word for general attack,' the Colonel shouts up the trench to our left. A moment later and he's grabbing the rungs of the trench ladder and hauling himself out. I follow him, and feel the ladder vibrating as others follow.

There's shouting and screams all around as the orks and Guardsmen exchange fire. We're about fifty metres from the orks, charging full speed towards them, men slipping and floundering in the snow, the greenskins encountering similar difficulties. I start firing with my laspistol again, dismayed to see the flashes of energy striking targets but not having too much effect against the tough aliens. They continue roaring their guttural cries as they close, a wave of sound accompanied by the crack of shells and zip of lasguns. A change in the wind wafts their stench over me, and I gasp for breath, hauling myself through the folds of snow. It's a mixture of death and unwashed bodies, utterly foul.

As we close the gap, I can see the greenskins are armed with a variety of crude-looking guns and hefty close combat weapons. Blazes of muzzle flare punctuate the ork mass, and the silvery light glitters off blades lovingly honed to cleave through flesh and bone with a single stroke. I pick out one to engage, pulling my knife from my belt when I'm twenty metres from the greenskin. It's dressed in black mainly, bits of ragged fur stitched onto a kind of jerkin, white checks painted onto metal pads on its broad shoulder and a roughly beaten breastplate which is gouged and dented from previous fighting. I notice with dismay the two human heads dangling from its belt, meat hooks plunged through their lifeless eyes to hold them on. The alien seems to read my thoughts, its red eyes glaring back at me as we close. Everyone and everything else is forgotten as I focus all my attention on the ork, noting the bulge of muscles under its furs, the ragged scar stretching from its wide chin across its fanged mouth and over its left cheek, passing its pug nose. Its skin is dark green and leathery looking, pocked with scars and warts, obviously impervious to the biting cold that would kill a man. It opens its mouth and bellows something, revealing a jawful of yellowing tusks – tusks that can rip through muscles and crush bones with one bite.

At five metres it levels a bulky pistol and fires, but the shots are way off, screaming past my head at least half a metre to my left. In its right hand is a blade like a butcher's cleaver, its head easily a metre long. It pulls back the cleaver and swings at my chest but I dodge to my left, feet slipping in the snow as the blade arcs past. I take a lunge with my knife but the ork easily bats it away with a strong arm, chopping down with the cleaver at the same time. Once more I wriggle sideways, though not quite quick enough, the crude chopper slicing a strip from the left sleeve of my coat. Cold air swirls onto my arm, causing my flesh to prickle all over with the chill, but that goes unnoticed as I bring my pistol up to its face. It ducks to avoid the shot, straight onto my waiting knife, which I jab upwards, plunging the tip into its throat, twisting with all my strength as dark blood, almost black and very thick, gushes into the white snow and over my legs.

I step back and another ork leaps at me, two serrated knives glittering in the cold light. The las-bolt from my pistol takes it squarely in the left eye, smashing out the back of its head, flinging the creature down into the snow.

Poal's fending off another ork with his hook, slashing at its guts with the point, jumping back as it punches back with knuckle-dusters fitted with a couple of short blades. I reverse my knife and plunge it backhanded into the ork's neck, feeling it deflected off the thick bones of its spine, tearing a gash up into the base of its skull. The ork backhands me, knocking me to my knees, and turns around snarling, blood spraying from the open wound. It kicks out, scattering snow, a metal toe-capped boot connecting with my thigh, almost snapping the bone. Poal's hook flashes up, slashing into the ork's mouth and ripping out its cheek. Spitting blood and teeth, the greenskin rounds on Poal, but his next swipe smashes into the ork's nose, the point ramming up its nostril, lacerating its face and plunging into the brain. The ork twitches spasmodically as it crumples to the ground, but neither of us spares it a second glance as we check on how the fight is going. Most of the orks are falling back towards the other trench, taken off guard by the counter-attack. The few that fight on are hopelessly outnumbered and quickly overwhelmed. Hundreds of greenskin corpses, and more humans, lie twisted and ragged, the snow churned up and red with blood. Severed limbs and decapitated bodies are piled waist high in places where the fighting was most fierce.

'CAUGHT OUT BY a pretty simple trick,' Poal says as I describe the fight with the first ork, the two of us collapsed in the trench with the others. 'I thought the orks were smarter than to be caught out with a straightforward feint.'

'Oldest trick in the bloody book,' chips in Poliwicz, cleaning his bayonet in the snow.

'Yeah, the simplest of tricks...' I murmur to myself, an unsettling thought beginning to form in my mind. I look around for the Colonel and see him not much further along the trench, talking to Greaves and Ekul. I push my way through the tired Guardsmen, turning a deaf ear to the groans and moans of the wounded as I barge them aside.

'Sir!' I call to the Colonel as he's about to walk away.

'Yes, Kage?' he asks sharply, turning on his heel.

'I think we've been tricked, sir,' I tell him quickly, glancing back over my shoulder to see what the orks are doing.

'Tricked?' Greaves says from behind the Colonel, disbelief written all over his face. 'What do you mean?'

'This attack is a feint, a diversion,' I explain hurriedly, waving my hands around trying to convey the sudden sense of urgency that fills me. 'It makes sense, now I think about it. They crossed the plains with the support of the main army and then split off.'

'What nonsense is this?' Greaves demands. 'Get back to your place.'

'Wait a moment, colonel,' Ekul says, stepping up beside the Colonel, looking intently at me. 'A diversion for what, Kage?'

'This isn't the main ork army, it's a diversionary attack sent to fool us and keep us occupied while the main force goes around us,' the words spill out quickly, my mind racing with the implications of the situation.

'You could be right,' the Colonel says with a nod. 'This army bears little resemblance to the one in the reports. I thought it might just be a vanguard.'

'Where else can they go?' asks Greaves disdainfully. 'Ekul says no man's ever survived the other passes in this region.'

'No man, sir,' Ekul agrees, 'but the lieutenant may have a point. We are not fighting men. It is possible the orks could forge another route towards Epsilon Station, circumnavigating this valley altogether.'

'What can we do about it? Our orders are to hold this pass,' Greaves says stubbornly. 'And Kage is probably wrong.'

'It is still a distinct possibility,' the Colonel replies, eyes narrowed as he thinks. 'You and your regiment will continue to hold this pass. The loss of my force does not greatly affect that. We must get to Epsilon Station and warn them.'

My hopes rise at the thought of going back to Epsilon. Much easier to survive a siege than an open battle. And we'll be inside, out of this forsaken cold and snow.

'My few mounted men can travel much quicker,' Ekul points out, dashing my hopes to the ground. 'And we know the terrain better.'

'Wouldn't it be better if you and your scouts went looking for the main force?' I suggest, thinking quickly, trying to keep the desperation from my voice.

'They're coming again!' a warden shouts from back down the line.

'We go now!' the Colonel says emphatically. 'Pack what provisions you can, Kage, and muster the men here.'

FIVE MINUTES LATER and the surviving Last Chancers are gathered with me, stowing what we can onto a couple of the ploughfoot sleds. The wind's picked up again, tossing the snow around us, and over its keening can be heard the rattle of autocannons and snap of lasguns as Greaves's soldiers try to hold off the orks as they pour from the forward trench. The Colonel appears through the snow.

'Are you ready?' he asks, glancing back over his shoulder towards the trenches a few dozen metres away. The odd stray ork shot zips past, but not that close. Greaves soon appears too, stamping through the snow to stand in front of the Colonel with his hands on hips.

'You're disobeying orders, Schaeffer,' Greaves says hotly, jabbing at the Colonel with an accusing finger. 'You're abandoning your position.'

'If you get the opportunity, follow us,' the Colonel replies calmly, ignoring the accusation.

'You're a coward, Schaeffer,' the bulky man counters, prodding a finger into the Colonel's chest. 'You're no better than these scum we have to lead.'

'Goodbye, Colonel Greaves,' the Colonel says shortly, and I can tell he's holding his temper in check. 'We probably will not meet again.'

Greaves continues cursing us as we trudge off through the snow, Franx and Loron leading the ploughfoots at the front, the Colonel at the rear.

* * *

As WE NEAR the top of the ridge again the wind starts to really bite, managing to push its way onto my face despite the thick fur lining of my coat's hood. Already my legs are beginning to feel tired, after just a couple of kilometres. The Colonel pushes us hard, not saying a word, just giving us a scathing look when one of us falters or slows down. I trudge on, concentrating all my thoughts on lifting my feet and taking the next step, my eyes focused on Lorii's back in front of me, letting me detach my mind from the real world.

The light begins to fail soon after, the sun dipping beneath the mountains and casting a red glow across the summits. It would be quite beautiful if I hadn't seen the snow back in the valley stained red and black with blood. Now all the sunset reminds me of is hacked limbs and dismembered bodies. It seems there's nothing left that isn't tainted by bloodshed now. I see children and they just remind me of the pile of small corpses we found in Ravensbrost on Carlille Two. Every time I think of something like flowers, I just remember False Hope and the alien beast of the Heart of the Jungle. A sunny day just takes me back to the crushing heat of the Gathalon ash wastes, where two hundred men sank into the shifting ash dunes, the corrosive dust eating away at them even as they were sucked down. As for any kind of bugs, well I guess you know what they remind me of. There are no pleasures left anywhere except the company of my fellow Last Chancers, and those moments are few and far between. Why does everything have to remind me of a war or battlefield somewhere? Does the Colonel realise this? Is this part of the punishment, to have everything stripped away from you? All my comfortable illusions have been torn apart over the past three years. When I joined up, I thought I'd be able to make a difference. Hah, what a joke. I've seen battle with ten thousand men killed in an afternoon, the rockets and shells raining down like explosive hail for hour after hour. I've shot, strangled and stabbed more enemies than I can remember. There's not a sensation I can feel now that hasn't been stained somehow. Even jumping in the tub back in Epsilon Station, my first thoughts were memories of a river crossing on Juno. Mangled bodies floating past as we tried to swim across, men being dragged down by the swift undercurrents, tracer fire screaming through the night towards us.

IT's AROUND MIDNIGHT before the Colonel calls a stop. We don't even bother setting camp or cooking, everybody takes a few bites of salted meat and then collapses with their blankets wrapped around them. I drift into an exhausted sleep, woken occasionally by the Colonel, who's doing the rounds, making sure the cold hasn't got to anyone too much. It must only have been a couple of hours when he kicks us all awake again. It's still pitch dark as we flounder around getting ready, the Colonel snarling at us to get a move on. Once more the march starts, forcing my aching legs to work, at points literally hauling myself through the snow on my hands and knees, sinking into the cold white layer up to my elbows.

A sudden scream of panic has everybody reaching for their guns, but Gappo comes hurrying back to tell the Colonel someone's wandered into a crevasse in the dark. I push myself after the Colonel as he forges ahead, Gappo guiding us to where the hole is. I can see frag all in the dark, and the Colonel asks who it is. There's just a groan in reply, and we do a quick name check of everybody else and find that bloody Poal is missing.

'We cannot afford the time for a rescue,' the Colonel announces, stepping away from the crevasse's edge. 'There is no way of telling how far down he is and we do not have the proper equipment.'

There's a few discontented murmurs, but everyone's too cold to really argue. Gappo stays by the edge after everyone else has gone. When he turns and looks at me, there's a blank look in his eyes.

'It only takes a few minutes,' he says, to himself I think. 'He'll just fall asleep. He won't know what's happening.'

'If it's deep, he's probably out of it already,' I say, laying a hand on his shoulder and pulling him away. He takes a couple of steps, then stops again.

'We have to keep going!' I snap at him, dragging him forward again. 'We reach Epsilon or we *all* die.'

THE COLONEL PUSHES us without a break for the whole of the next day as well. I walked past someone lying in the snow in the afternoon. They were face down, I couldn't tell who it was and didn't have the energy to try to find out. I try to see who's missing when we stop, but my eyes are crusted up and sore, and everyone looks the same in their heavy coats with the hoods pulled tight across their faces. I force myself to gulp down some more preserved meat. Nobody says a word to each other, and even the Colonel is quieter than usual. I sit there shivering, hands clasped across my chest, feeling an ache in every single bone and muscle. My head's just nodding as my body gives up the fight against the cold and sleep begins to take over, when someone's shaking me awake again.

'What the…?' I snarl, slapping the hand away.

'It's Franx,' says Gappo.

That's all he needs to say. He helps me to my feet and we make our way over to where he's lying. I crouch down beside him and peer inside his hood. His face is crusted with ice, and looks extremely pale. A moment later and Lorii joins us, bending close, her cheek next to his mouth.

'Still breathing,' she tells us, straightening out. 'Barely.'

'I can't leave him,' Gappo declares, and I nod in agreement. I kind of promised myself that Franx was going to survive this one. 'What can we do? I'm too tired to carry anything other than this coat.'

'Put him on the sled,' Lorii suggests.

'The ploughfoots are already pulling as much as they're supposed to,' Gappo cautions, stamping his feet to keep himself warm.

'Well, they'll have to work harder. We'll get them to do it in shifts,' I decide. Nobody argues.

THERE'S A STRANGE whinnying of pain from the ploughfoot at the head of the diminishing column. Two men didn't wake up, another two collapsed this morning. The midday sun glares off the snow, making it as difficult to see during the day as it is at night.

'Kage!' I hear the Colonel bellowing, and I shuffle forward. The ploughfoot is lying in the snow, its left hind leg at an odd angle and clearly broken. The sled is over-turned on a rock nearby.

'Sir?' I ask as the Colonel stands up from where he was kneeling next to the stricken animal.

'Organise the men into teams of six, and rig up the harness into drag ropes,' he says. He pulls his bolt pistol from its holster, places the muzzle against the side of the ploughfoot's head and blows its brains out. My first thought is the fresh meat it could provide, but a glance at the Colonel reminds me that we won't be wasting a second. Then I'm filled with a sudden surge of hatred.

'You wouldn't do the same for us,' I snarl at Schaeffer, pointing to the still-smoking bolt pistol.

'If you had also served the Emperor well, you might have deserved some mercy,' he counters, holstering the pistol. 'You have not, and you do not deserve anything.'

THERE'S TWELVE OF us left now, not including the Colonel, and we take it in turns to drag the sled on two-hour stints. The Colonel tried to get me to leave Franx behind, saying the additional weight was

unnecessary, but Gappo, Loron, Lorii and Kronin volunteered to
team up with me and we've been swapping him between our shift
and the remaining ploughfoot's sled.

I soon lose track of the time, even the midnight stops have gone
beyond counting, so we might have been going for only three days or
for a whole week, it's impossible to say. The wind's really picked up
now, and the snow is getting heavier again. I remember Ekul's warnings about the Emperor's Wrath storm, and fear the worst. I let the
others know what's coming and everybody redoubles their efforts,
but it's getting to the point where it takes everything out of you just
to stay awake, never mind keeping walking and pulling the sled.
Soon we've emptied one sled of provisions and we decide to dump
the tents, nobody's had the strength to put them up since we started.
The going gets a little quicker then, with the two teams and the
ploughfoot taking turns with the remaining sled.

'If the orks are up against anything like this, they may never make
it across,' Kyle suggests one evening as we gnaw on half-frozen strips
of meat.

'Don't you believe it,' I say. 'They're tough bastards, you know that.
Besides, they'll have looted and built Emperor knows what before
trying the crossing. If their warlord's smart enough to come up with
the feint, it's definitely got the brains to come prepared. They've
probably got vehicles and everything as well.'

'What if we're too late?' exclaims Kyle, suddenly veering from opti-
mism to total depression in a moment. I've never noticed him having
mood swings like this before, but then I guess we're all swinging
wildly from hope to despair and back again at the moment.

'Then we're bent over backwards, good and proper,' Poliwicz says,
tearing at his salted meat with his teeth.

'Whole Emperor-damned planet looks the same,' curses Kyle. 'I
can't tell where we are, how far we've got to go.'

Nobody bothers replying; it's hard enough to concentrate on the
next few minutes, let alone worry about the next day. I toss the remnants of my rations aside, too tired to chew, and lie back, willing
sleep to claim me quickly and take me away from the pain in every
part of my body.

HOARSE SCREAMING UP ahead snaps me out of my fatigue-induced
sleepwalking.

'What now?' I ask sleepily when I reach the half-dozen Last
Chancers clustered up ahead.

'One of the station's pickets,' the Colonel says. 'I have sent him back with the warning about the orks.' I realise they were shouts of joy, not screams, but in my befuddled state I'd just interpreted them as more pain and misery for some poor soul.

'We're still going on to Epsilon, aren't we?' I ask hurriedly, fearing the Colonel might be about to order us to turn around and go back the way we came.

'Yes we are. This has gone on long enough,' he reassures me, and for the first time I notice how thin and drawn he's looking. There are massive dark rings around his eyes from the sleepless nights, and his whole body looks slumped, like the rest of us.

It takes another two hours' trekking before we reach the gatehouses. A small delegation of officers from the Kragmeer regiments waits for us. Their mood is grim, but they don't look too unkindly on us when, at a word from the Colonel, we fall to the snow a few metres away from them, completely exhausted.

I don't hear what they're saying; my ears have been numb for the past few days, even with the fur-lined coat pulled protectively over my head. They seem to be having some sort of argument, and I'm wondering if they've taken the same line as Greaves, accusing the Colonel of abandoning his command. I see Schaeffer shaking his head violently and point up into the sky. I hear a scattering of words, like 'siege', 'time', 'important', and 'orbit'. None of it makes any sense. One of the Kragmeer officers, bloody high-ranking by all the finery on his uniform, steps forward and makes negative cutting gestures with his hand before pointing over his shoulder back into the station. There are more heated exchanges and the Colonel turns on his heel and stamps over to us.

'On your feet, Last Chancers,' he snaps, before marching off, up the valley and away from the gates.

'Where the frag are we going now?' asks Poliwicz.

'Perhaps we're defending the shuttle pad?' Gappo guesses with a shrug.

After the brief flood of energy once we knew we were close to Epsilon, my tiredness returns with a vengeance. My brain shuts down everything except the bits needed for walking and breathing for the trek up to the shuttle pad, and everything from the past couple of weeks condenses into a blurry white mess.

We reach the shuttle pad to find the gate closed. Peering through the mesh of the high fence, I can see our shuttle still out on the apron, kept clear of snow by the attendants.

'That's a direct order from a superior officer,' I hear the Colonel say and I focus my attention back on him. He's standing at the door of the little guardhouse next to the gate, and there's a Kragmeer sergeant shaking his head.

'I'm sorry, Colonel,' the sergeant says, hands held up in a helpless gesture, 'but without the proper authority I can't let you take the shuttle.'

My brain suddenly clunks into gear. *Take the shuttle?* We're leaving?

'Lieutenant Kage!' barks the Colonel and I quick march over to him, standing to attention as best I can. 'If this man does not open this gate immediately and clear the pad for launch, shoot him.'

The Kragmeerite starts babbling something as I pull my pistol out and point it at his head. I really don't give a frag whether I blow this guy's brains out or not. For one thing, I'm just too tired to care. For another, if this frag-head is stopping me from getting off this ice-frozen hell, I'll happily put a slug in his skull.

He relents under my not-so-subtle coercion, stepping back into the hut to pull a lever which sets the gate grinding open. Klaxons begin to echo off the hills around us, and people start scurrying from the hangars and work barracks.

'We're leaving,' the Colonel announces, stepping through the gateway.

'Leaving?' Linskrug asks. 'Going where?'

'You'll find that out when we get there, trooper,' the Colonel says mysteriously.

SIX

TYPHOS PRIME

+++ Operation Harvest complete. Preparing to commence Operation New Sun. +++

+++ There can be no more delays. New Sun must go ahead on schedule or all will be lost. +++

COMPARED WITH SOME of the places I've been with the Last Chancers, and considering that it's been torn apart by bloody civil war for the past two years, Typhos Prime seems very civilised. After touching down at one of its many spaceports, a Commissariat squad escorts us through busy city streets, with people coming and going as if there weren't battles being fought less than two hundred kilometres away. There are a few telltale signs that everything isn't as cosy as it seems, though. There are air raid warning sirens at every junction – huge hailers atop six-metre poles – and signs marking the route to the nearest shelters. Arbitrators patrol the streets, menacing with their silvered armour over jet-black jump-suits, wielding shock mauls and suppression shields.

As we pass along a wide thoroughfare, there are shuttered windows amongst the stores along both sides of the wide road. There are a few people around, swathed against the autumnal chill and damp in shapeless brown coats and thick felt hats, trailing brightly coloured scarves from their necks. A smog hangs above the city, visible over the squat buildings to either side, mixing with the cloud that stretches across the sky to cast a dismal gloom over the settlement. A column of Chimeras led by two growling Conqueror tanks, resplendent in blue and gold livery, grumbles past along the road, horse carriages and zimmer cars pulling aside to let them pass. In a reinforced underground staging area, we embark on a massive eight-wheeled roadster designed for long-haul troop movements, and the twelve of us spread out, trying to decide in which of the three hundred seats we want to sit. The Colonel parks himself up front with the driver, intently ignoring us.

'Reminds me of tutelage outings,' jokes Franx. 'Head up the back where bad boys hang out!'

I'll take his word for it, I never had that kind of education. I was brought up as part of an extended family, with a dozen brothers, sisters and cousins, and my first memories are of chipping at slag deposits with a rusted chisel and mallet, trying to find nuggets of iron and steel. The roadster jolts into life, the whine of the electric engines soon being relegated to the back of my mind, out of conscious thought. Linskrug and Gappo join us and we sprawl happily, each across a three-wide seating tier.

'This is a bit of a royal treatment, is it not?' suggests Linskrug, peering out of the tinted windows at the low buildings blurring past outside. A faint rain has started, speckling the windows with tiny droplets of moisture. 'It's much more what I'm accustomed to.'

'He wants to keep us contained,' I point out to him. 'Of all the places we've been, this is the best one to get lost in. Billions of people live on Typhos Prime; a man could quite happily disappear here, never to be seen again.'

'Hey!' whispers Gappo urgently from the other side of the aisle. 'There's an emergency exit down these stairs!'

We cluster round and have a look. It's true, there's a small door at the bottom of a flight of four steps.

'Reckon it's locked?' asks Franx in his now-familiar wheeze. I test the handle and it turns slightly. I look at the others and grin widely. Gappo glances over the top of the surrounding seats and then crouches down again.

'No one's paying the blindest bit of notice,' he says with a smile and a mischievous look in his eye. 'I don't think anyone will miss us.'

'We're moving at a pretty rate,' Linskrug says, pointing to the blurred grey shapes of the outside whizzing past the windows.

'Hell,' coughs Franx, rubbing his hands together with glee. 'I can live with a few bruises!'

I look at each of them in turn, and they meet my gaze, trying to gauge my thoughts. They know my track record on escape attempts, and how I keep nagging them not to get stupid. I guess I've been half-hearted in my own attempts to escape, because I think a part of me agrees with the Colonel. Perhaps I have wasted the opportunity the Emperor gave me, reneged on my oaths. I never intended to, of that much I'm certain, I joined up with the purest of intentions, even though I wanted to get the hell off Olympas. But as they say, the road to Chaos is paved with good intentions. But then again, how much blood does the Emperor want from me? It's kind of a tradition that an Imperial Guard regiment serves for a maximum of ten years at which point it can retire, maybe returning home or going off to join the Explorator fleets and help claim a new world for the Emperor. A lot of them won't spend half that time fighting. I've been up to my neck in blood and guts, seeing men and women and children dead and dying, for nearly three years now. Haven't I had my fair share of war? I think I have. I think I've made the most of my Last Chance. The Colonel's never going to let us live; he wants us all dead, that much I'm sure. I'll let the Emperor be my judge, when I die, hopefully in the not so near future.

'Frag, let's do it!' I whisper hoarsely before twisting the door handle fully. The emergency exit swings open and I see the black of the road tearing past the opening. Somewhere at the head of the roadster there's a shrill whining. The door must have been alarmed. I take a deep breath and then drop out of the doorway feet first. Thudding down onto the road, my momentum sends me rolling madly, pitching me into a shin-high kerbstone. Glancing up the road I see the others bailing out after me, slamming uncomfortably to the ground. I jump to my feet and set off towards them at a run.

'We did it!' screams Linskrug, eyes alight with joy. There's a few people walking past on the pavement, swathed in high-collared raincoats. A couple turn to look at us. 'Schaeffer will never get that thing turned around in time to catch us.'

Just then there's a screech of airbrakes and a black-painted armoured car slews to a halt in front of us, twin cannons on its roof pointing in our direction. A man jumps out of the back hatch, bolt pistol in hand, dressed in a commissar's uniform. His face is pinched, thin-lipped mouth curled in a sneer.

'Please try to run,' he growls as he walks towards us, bolt pistol held unwaveringly in front of him. 'It would save me lots of problems.'

None of us make a move. Ten black-clad troopers pour from the armoured car, thick carapace breastplates over their uniforms, faces hidden behind dark visors. The Commissariat provosts have us surrounded in a couple of seconds and our brief moment of freedom is over. I take a deep breath, loving the smoke-tinged air, the feel of the gentle rain splashing down onto my upturned face. I don't want to relinquish this feeling that easily. I can't believe the Colonel will have us in his grip again. I look at the provosts, at the bulky laser carbines pointed at us, and I wonder if we might not still get out of this. The four of us are hardened fighters. These guys are bully-boys, used to Guardsmen being scared of them. But I can see their faces set grimly underneath the black visors of their helmets and I can tell they're not going to hesitate for a second. The commissar had the truth of it – they'd rather we tried something, giving them the excuse to open fire.

'I can't believe that Schaeffer had an escort following us,' Gappo moans as we're shoved into the back of the armoured car. We have to squat in the middle of the floor between the provosts, there's not enough room for everyone to sit or stand. The commissar leans down towards me and grabs my chin between a finger and thumb, turning my face towards him.

'I am sure Colonel Schaeffer will be very pleased to see you again,' the commissar says with a cruel smile. 'Very pleased indeed.'

TRUDGING THROUGH THE mud, rain cascading off my helmet, I realise that perhaps Typhos Prime isn't so nice after all. The roadster dropped us off about sixteen kilometres from the front line, or where they think the front line is, leaving us to foot it the rest of the way. The war's dragged on for a couple of years now, ever since a first abortive assault against the rebel fortress failed, and both sides have drawn up trenchlines a few kilometres from Coritanorum's walls and have since tried to shell each other into submission.

Alongside us is a Mordian marching column, trying to look smart and trim in their nice blue uniforms. The effect is somewhat spoilt by the mud splashes, and the peaks of their caps are starting to lose their stiffness under the downpour of rain, drooping towards their noses in a pathetic fashion. They've steadfastly ignored us for the past eight kilometres as we sauntered forward alongside them. The Colonel didn't even bother shouting at us when Kyle tried to provoke them by calling them toy soldiers and officers' pets.

He seems very distracted at the moment, the Colonel I mean. Franx and I have agreed that this is what we've been building up to, for a year at least, anyway. He's brought us here to do something particularly horrid, of that we're sure, but we can't suss what it might be yet. A dozen Last Chancers isn't a whole heap of a lot in a war where each side has supposedly already lost half a million men.

'Incoming!' shrieks Linskrug and a second later my ears pick up what the baron's sharp ears heard a moment earlier – the whine of an aircraft's engines in a screaming dive. We scatter, hurling ourselves into water-filled craters and behind rocks, peering up into the clouds for a sign of our attacker. I look astonished as the Mordians continue their formed march and then I realise that they won't break formation until one of their officers tells them to. I see a swathe of them knocked to the ground and an instant later the chatter of heavy guns can be heard. Glancing up I see the rebel stratocraft sweeping low, four flashing bursts along its wings showing where light autocannons are spitting out a hail of death. The Mordians march relentlessly on and the aircraft wings over and banks round for another pass. Once more the guns chatter and two dozen or more Mordians, all the men in two ranks of troopers, are torn apart by the fusillade.

'Get down, you fragging idiots!' screams Gappo, the first time I've ever heard him swear. The Mordians don't pay him any notice though and the aircraft makes another attack run, the trail of bullets sending up splashes of mud and water as the hail zigzags towards the marching Guardsmen. It passes over the column and as it does so I realise with horror that it's heading towards us. Before I can react I feel something slamming across my forehead, pitching me backwards into the puddles and stunning me.

'Emperor-damn, we've got men down! Kage is down! The lieutenant's down!' I dimly hear someone screaming, Poliwicz by the broad Myrmidian accent. People splash around me, soaking me further, but I just lie there, still. Dead still. Two opportunities in one day must mean the Emperor approves.

I feel someone wiping the blood from my forehead and hear them curse bitterly – it's Linskrug. He grabs my arms and I try to go as limp as possible. As he folds my arms across my chest someone else pushes my helmet down across my face.

'The Colonel's says we've got to keep going,' I hear Gappo shouting hoarsely, choking back a sob by the sound of it. Sentimental idiot, I think to myself. Linskrug disappears and another shadow falls across my eyelids.

'Unto death, I shall serve him,' says Kronin. 'Unto life again, shall he serve the Emperor.'

I WAIT UNTIL I haven't heard voices for a long time before opening my eyes. Darkness is falling and I can't see anyone around. The rain's still drizzling down from the overcast sky, but I pull off my flak jacket and fatigues, grabbing the uniform from a dead Mordian only a few metres away. It isn't an exact fit, but it'll do. Cramming the cap onto my head, I try to work out which way to go.

It's then that I see Franx, half buried in slick mud at the rim of the crater he was sheltering in. He hangs loosely over the edge of the shell hole, one arm outstretched. I can see three holes in his chest where the bullets from the aircraft hit him, and a dribble of blood from his mouth shows that they punctured his already overworked lungs. I pause for a moment, shocked that Franx is actually dead. He seemed unkillable, all the way through. And this is how it ends, a random victim of a rebel strafing run. No heroics, no glory, just a few bullets from the skies and it's all over. It saddens me, the way it happened, more than the fact that he's dead. He didn't have a chance. Not much of a Last Chance at all, taking on stratocraft. Still, I hope dying like this counts, and that his soul is safe with the Emperor. Poliwicz and Kyle are lying spread-eagled in another pool, not far from where I fell, their rain- and blood-soaked sleeves clinging tightly to their arms. Poliwicz has half his face blown away, shattered teeth leering at me from his exposed skull. At first I can't tell where Kyle's been hit and I roll him over, finding four holes through the back of his flak jacket, right at the base of his spine. They both look like they died quickly, which is a blessing of sorts, I guess.

Pushing thoughts of Franx and the others from my mind to concentrate on my own survival, I try to figure out which way we were heading in. The rain's obscured all the tracks, and I can see lights in almost every direction, so it's impossible to tell which way is the rear area and which way is the front line. Deciding that it's better to be moving than not, I pick a direction at random and start walking.

I'VE WALKED FOR about an hour in the gathering darkness of the night, when I hear voices nearby. Dropping to my belly, I lie very still, ears straining to work out which direction the conversation is coming from. It's just to my left and a little ahead of me. Moving my head slightly, I look in that direction. Sure enough, I can see a faint light, of a cooking stove or something. I worm my way a little bit closer, and after about ten metres can just make out the outline of a couple of men sitting around a dimly glowing camp cooker.

'Emperor-damned rain,' one curses. 'I wish this Emperor-damned patrol were over.'

'You always moan 'bout the weather. Only another two days on this tour,' replies the other in a conciliatory tone. 'Then we can head on back to old Corry and rest up awhile.'

'Still, trust us to draw a sentry roster that gets us four damned shifts outta three,' the other one whines. Their conversation drifts out of my thoughts as my subconscious tries to attract my attention with an important thought. 'Back to old Corry,' one of them had said. They must mean Coritanorum, the citadel under siege. And that means they're rebels! And here's me a few metres away in a Mordian, in other words loyalist, uniform! Oh frag, I've managed to sneak all the way through our own front line without noticing and now I'm at the traitor picket. How the frag did I manage that?

I'm about to shuffle away again when I hear something that adds to my disturbance.

'I hope Renov's commandos get here on time,' one of the rebels says. 'Once we've scouted out the eastern flank, we can tell 'em the route through the traitors' lines and get back home.'

'Yeah, if this weak spot leads right back to their artillery lines, Renov's boys'll have a field day,' the other says with a laugh.

They must be a scouting party or something, and they've found a chink in our siege line. If they can break through, who knows what hell these commandos they're talking about can play? I push myself further into the darkness to have a think, finding a bit of shelter under the blasted stump of a tree. I'm no hero, anyone will tell you that, but if these rebels can carry on with their mission, who knows what damage it could do to the Imperial lines? It's strange, but if the Colonel had ordered me to do something about it, I would have tried everything I could to get out of it. Now I'm on my own, I wonder whether I should try to break up this little party. After all, I joined the Imperial Guard to fight in defence of the Emperor's domains, and though I have strayed a long way over the years, that's still an oath I took. Knowing I would be guilty of a gross treachery if I heard that an incursion by the rebels had been a powerful setback to the siege, costing thousands more lives, I draw the Mordian knife hanging from my belt and rise up into a crouch.

I circle to my right for a bit, until I find the faint glow of the sentries' position again. Slowly, meticulously, I place one foot in front of the other, easing myself towards them, trying not to make a sound. I make my breathing as shallow as possible, though I'm sure they can hear my heart as it hammers in my chest. Step by step, I get closer. In the near-blackness, I can barely make them both out. The one nearest me is heavy set. The other I can't make out at all. Realising they might be able to see my face if I get any closer, I grab a handful of mud and smear it over my skin, covering my face and hands in the stuff. Fat-boy seems to be napping, I can hear his regular, deep breathing, and I circle round some more so that the other one is closest. I gulp down a sudden feeling of fear and then spring forward, wrapping my left hand across the mouth of the rebel and plunging the knife point-first into his throat. He gives a brief spasm, and I feel warm blood splashing across my fingers as I ease his still shuddering body to the ground.

A glance at the other one shows that he hasn't stirred at all. I step over and drop to a crouch in front of him. Leaning closer, I put the blade of the knife against the artery in his throat and blow softly up his nose. His eyelids flutter open and his eyes flicker for a moment before fixing on me and going wide with terror.

'Say anything,' I whisper harshly, 'and I'll slice you to pieces.'

He gives a jerky nod, eyes trying to peer around his blubbery cheek to see the knife at his throat.

'I'm going to ask you some questions,' I tell him, nicking the skin of his throat a little with the dagger to keep his attention as his eyes wander from mine. 'Answer them quickly, quietly and truthfully.'

He nods again, a kind of panicked squeak sounding from the back of his throat.

'How many of you are near here?' I ask, leaning very close so I can hear the merest whisper.

'One squad... twelve men,' he breathes, body trembling all over.

'Where are the other ten?' I say.

'Fifty metres that way,' he tells me, slowly raising a hand and pointing to his right. I notice his whole arm is shaking with fear.

'Thank you,' I tell him with a grin and he begins to relax. With a swift flick of my wrist the knife slashes through his neck, arterial blood spraying from his throat. He slumps backwards, raised arm flopping to the floor.

As I expected, everyone else in the squad is sleeping, murmuring to themselves in their dreams, perhaps imagining themselves to be at home with loved ones and friends. Some people might say cutting their throats in their sleep would be a cruel thing to do, but I don't care. If these bastards hadn't renounced the reign of the Emperor, I wouldn't be here now, soaked with rain and blood, Emperor-knows how far from where I was born. To think of them betraying the oaths they must have sworn makes me sick to my stomach. They deserve everything they get, and I'll enjoy giving it to them. They're the enemy. It's a matter of moments to tread carefully along the lines of men in their waterproof sleeping sacks, jabbing the knife under ribcages and slicing throats. As I plunge the point of the knife into the eyeball of the ninth one, a movement to my left grabs my attention.

'Wass 'appenin'?' someone says sleepily, sitting up slowly in his nightsack. With an inward curse I pounce towards him, but not quickly enough. He rolls to his left and grabs the lasgun lying next to him in the mud. I dodge sideways as the blast of light sears past me and then kick the barrel of the gun away as he lines up for another shot. He tries to trip me with the gun but I'm too sure-footed, dancing past his clumsy attempt, kicking him in the face as I do so. I fall on top of him and he drops the lasgun and grabs my right wrist with both hands, forcing the knife up and away from his face.

I punch him straight in the throat, the knuckle of my middle finger extended slightly to crush his windpipe. He gives a choked cry and his grip weakens slightly. I wrench my knife hand free and plunge it towards his throat but a flailing arm knocks the blow slightly and the blade gouges down one side of his face, ripping across his cheek and hacking a chunk off his ear. He's still too short of breath to scream and I bring the knife back, smashing it through the thin skull at his left temple, plunging it into his brain. He convulses madly for a second with system shock and then goes limp.

Glancing around to make sure nobody else is about, I wipe the knife on the dead rebel's nightsack and snatch the lasgun from the mud, wiping the slushy dirt off with the Typhon's tunic. I don't know why I didn't grab one of the Mordians' lasguns. I guess I was keen to get away.

'Right,' I say to myself, getting my bearings, 'which way now?'

Looking around, I see a break in the gathering storm clouds back from where I came from. In the hazy scattering of stars I can see moving lights, going up and down, instantly recognisable as shuttle runs. Well, where there's shuttles, there's a way out of this warzone. Putting the knife back into its sheath, I set off at a run.

EVER BEEN TEN strides from death? Not a nice feeling. The trench is seventy strides away and in sixty the snipers will trace me and I'm gonna get a bullet trepanning. I was always fast, but you can't outrun fate, as my sarge used to say.

Fifty strides from safety and the first shot whistles past my ear. At forty I drop my lasgun in the mud. Light as they are, they don't let you pump your arms properly for the type of speed I need if I'm going to get myself out of this. If I'm too slow now, having a gun ain't gonna help me a whole lot.

At thirty strides someone calls in the mortars and suddenly there's explosions all around throwing up water and muck, spattering me with dirt. Luckily I'm dodging left and right too, so only luck will help them out, you can't correct a mortar that quick. There's a tremendous roar of thunder, making the ground under my feet shake, and lightning crackles across the sky. Great, all I needs is more light for the snipers to see me.

Something else, larger than a bullet, goes crashing past me and sends up a plume of debris as it explodes. Oh great! Still twenty strides to go and some smart frag-head has grabbed a grenade launcher. Fifteen strides from life, five from death, bet nobody would give me odds on surviving now!

A ball of plasma roars past me, almost blinding me as it explodes against the shattered hull of an abandoned Leman Russ. I'm eight strides off when I feel something punch into my shoulder from the left. Instinct takes over and I dive forward. Oh frag! I'm at the trench! Double frag! I land head first in the mud and I swear I hear my shoulder snap as I hit the ground two metres further down than I thought I would.

A CROWD HAS gathered, rain-blurred faces peering curiously at me as I sit there in the mud at the bottom of the trench. I hear someone bark an order and the throng dissipates instantly revealing a tall man in his early twenties, wearing the uniform of a Mordian lieutenant. The flash on his breast says Martinez. There must be regiments from half a dozen worlds fighting on Typhos Prime, and I fragging have to land in one full of Mordians! Considering I'm wearing a stolen Mordian uniform, this is not a good situation to be in.

Martinez looks at me with distaste, and I can't blame him. My face is caked in mud and blood, and his precious Mordian uniform is worse off than an engineer's rag.

'On your feet, Guardsman!' the lieutenant snaps.

I give him a surly look and push myself to my feet to lean against a trench support batten, seeking shelter from the incessant downpour. Martinez gives me an odd second glance when he sees my face.

Hey, I feel like shouting, I know I'm not that pretty, but have some manners! His eye lingers on the bullet graze across my forehead, which reminds me that I must wash it out or risk getting infection.

'Name, Guardsman!' barks Martinez, false bravado in his voice.

Nausea sweeps through me as I try to straighten out a little, jerked into action by their parade-ground drilling. I haven't slept for a day and a half, let alone eaten.

'Kage,' I manage to mumble, fighting back a wave of dizziness.

'What is the meaning of this?' demands the Mordian. 'You look a total state! I don't know how discipline is maintained in your platoon, Guardsman, but here I expect every soldier to maintain standards appropriate to the regiment. Get yourself cleaned up! And you will address me as "sir", or I'll have you flogged for insubordination. Is that clear?'

'Yes... sir,' I snarl. You don't even want to know about discipline in my regiment, lieutenant, I think, knowing his strait-laced attitude would have got him killed ten times over if he'd spent the past three years with me.

THIS FRAGGING JUMPED-up nobody lieutenant is beginning to grate on my nerves. Still, I only have myself to blame. I know these damned Mordians are really tagged up on being smart and shiny. I should've looked for a corpse more my size rather than grabbing the first uniform I came across. On the other hand, I've made it to the trench in one piece. That's phase one of my plan complete.

Suddenly, I catch the distinctive scent of gun oil close by, hear the snick of a safety being released and feel a cold metal muzzle poking into the back of my neck. I slowly turn round and face a jutting chin big enough to bulldoze buildings with. Glancing up I pass over the face and focus my attention on the commissar's cap, resplendent with its braiding and solid gold eagle. Frag me, this guy looks almost as mean as the Colonel!

'Kage? Your flash says "Hernandez", Guardsman. Just who are you and what are you doing?' The commissar's voice is gravelly, just like all commissars' voices. Do they train them to speak like that, making them chew on razor blades or something? I can't believe I hadn't checked out the dead guy's name before putting on his uniform! Frag, this is getting too hot!

'Lieutenant Kage, sir! I'm special ops, covert operations kinda thing,' I say, thinking on my feet.

'I was not aware of any special units in this sector,' he replies, clearly unconvinced.

'With respect, sir, that's the idea,' I tell him, trying to remember what normal Guardsmen act like. 'Hardly covert if everyone knows you're around.'

Well, I hadn't lied. You don't get much more special than my unit.

'Who is your commanding officer?' he demands.

'I'm sorry, but I cannot disclose that to anyone outside of the unit, sir,' I tell him. Okay, that was a lie, but he's bound to have heard of the Colonel.

'I'm placing you under armed guard, pending confirmation of your story by command headquarters,' the commissar announces. 'Lieutenant Martinez, detail five men to watch this prisoner. If he so much as looks out of this trench, shoot him!'

As the lieutenant nominates a handful of men to watch me, the commissar strides off towards the comms bunker I'd seen when I'd been waiting for the storm to cover my dash. The lieutenant disappears too, ordering everybody back to their duties, leaving me with the five hopeless cases standing around me.

I SLUMP BACK to the bottom of the trench, ignoring the mud and filth that splashes around me. For the first time I check out my shoulder. It's just a flesh wound: the bullet has left a small furrow about a thumb's length across my left shoulder. Flexing it hurts like hell, but I can tell it isn't actually dislocated, just jarred. I pluck a needle and some wire thread from the survival pack inside my left boot and begin stitching, gritting my teeth against the pain.

My guards look on aghast and it's then that I first realise what's been nagging at my brain since I'd first splashed down in the trench. These soldiers are young. I mean really young; some of them look about sixteen years old, the oldest must be twenty at the most. A bunch of wet-backs, freshly drafted in to fight. I then notice a satchel just off to my left, gold-tinged foil packages stuffed in its pockets. With a flick of my head in its direction, I quiz the youngest soldier.

'That a ration pack?' I ask, already knowing the answer. 'Sure looks like one. Do you get fed regular here? Frag, you don't know how grateful I'd be for just a bite to eat. Any chance?'

With a worried look to his comrades the raw recruit shuffles over to the satchel and pulls out a can. With a twist he opens it up and passes me the hard biscuit inside

'Eat it quick,' he says. 'The rain gets them soggy in no time and they're awful if that happens.' His voice is high-pitched and quivering and he shoots a nervous glance over his shoulder at the others and then up the trench. I laugh.

'You mean "Eat it quick before Lieutenant Frag-Brain or that dumb commissar come back", don't you?' My imitation of his nasal whine makes the others grin before they can stop themselves.

The young Guardsman is silent as he steps back and squats down on the opposite side of the trench, his lasgun cradled between his legs. The oldest one speaks up, his voice a little firmer, a little harder.

'Between us, why are you here? Are you really special ops? What's it like?' he asks, eyes curious.

I stare into his narrow brown eyes, sparkling with moisture. Rain runs down his cheeks and makes me realise how thirsty I am. But I wouldn't trust the stuff pouring out of the sky right now. 'You dig out a canteen of water and I'll clear this smoke out of my throat and tell you,' I offer. The flask is in my hand almost instantly and I grin stupidly for a moment as the cool liquid spills down my parched throat. Without handing it back, I flip the cap shut again and wedge it into the mud next to me.

'Oh. I'm definitely very special, boys,' I say with a grin. 'I don't know if you wet-backs have ever heard about us, but you're about to. You see, I'm with the Last Chancers.'

As I EXPECT, this statement is met with blank incomprehension. These rookies don't know anything outside their platoon, but I'm gonna change that, for sure. 'Your lieutenant, he's very keen on discipline, isn't he?' Nods of agreement. 'I expect he's made it very clear what the different punishments for various infractions are. Flogging, staking, firing squad and all the rest. Has he told you about Vincularum? No? well it's a gulag, basically. You're sent to some prison planet to rot away for the rest of your life. Now, there's one of those prison planets, it doesn't have a name, down near the southern rim. That's where I was sent.'

One of the guards, a slim youngster with ridiculously wide eyes, speaks up. 'What had you done?'

'Well, it's kind of a long story,' I say, settling down against the trench wall, making myself more comfortable. 'My platoon were doing sentry on some backwater hole called Stygies, down near Ophelia. It was a real easy number, watching a bunch of degenerate peasants grubbing around in the dirt, making sure nothing nasty happened to them. In those situations you have to provide your own excitement, know what I mean?'

Again the blank stares. Never mind.

'Well,' I continue regardless, 'back on Stygies they have this contest, called the Path of Fate. It's like one of those obstacle courses you must have gone over a thousand times during your training. Only a lot worse. This was one mean fraggin' test, make no mistake. Every month the bravest locals all line up for a race over the Path. There's a pit of boiling water to swing across, deadfall traps, pitfalls with spikes, not to mention the fact that in the final stretch you're allowed to attack the other contenders, right? Anyway, after watching this go on for a few months, my sergeant, he starts running a book on each race. After all, the contenders have to announce their intentions well in advance, and going on past experience he could work out the odds according to their previous form and their local reputation. I mean, these fraggers were hard as nails, but some of them were just rock, you know?'

A few nods this time. Lucky old me...

'We used to gamble rations, that sort of thing,' I say, settling in to the story I'd told two dozen times back on the transport. 'But that kinda gets boring after a while. Then we moved onto more valuable stuff, picked up from the local artisans. Things like gold necklaces, gems and stuff. I mean, all we did was give 'em a few ration packs and they would sell their daughters, it was amazing. Well, speaking of young ladies, I had my eye on one particular sweet little thing.' I grin at the memory. 'The sarge was soft on her too and rather than contest with each other, neither of us liked the idea of sharing you know, we gambled first rights on the next Path of Fate. I won, but the sarge got sour. Fat people often get like that, and he was immense what with all the easy living and free rations. Anyway, he bawls me out one day, threatening to report me to the lieutenant for something he'd made up unless I gave him the wench. That was it, I just pulled my blade and gutted the fat fragger there and then. Course, they hauled me off of there quicker than you can say it and I end up out on this gulag.'

Their open-mouthed astonishment is hilarious. One of them stutters something incomprehensible and continues staring at me like I've grown an extra head or something.

Then the older one pipes up. 'You murdered your sergeant over a woman?'

'Yeah, and I didn't get to have her in the end anyway, did I?' I take another swig of water to moisten my tongue and then cock my head to one side to listen to what's going on outside the trench. 'You boys better move over to this side of the trench.'

They look at me, Wide Eyes frowning, the older one with his mouth half-open, the others not really paying attention.

'Move it! Now!' I snap, seeing if I can pull the parade ground trick as well as any real officer.

The commanding tone in my voice makes them act instantly, leaping across to my side and thudding down in the muck as well. The sound of explosions gets rapidly closer and suddenly the whole trench line is engulfed in a raging torrent of shells. Red fire explodes everywhere, plasma shells spewing a torrent of molten death onto the far side of the trench where the recruits had been lounging.

Stupid fraggers, did nobody tell them to use the lee of the trench to protect themselves during an artillery attack? And it goes without saying that they hadn't heard the pause in the gunfire that suggested a change of aiming point, or the whistle of the first shells heading our way. Emperor's blood, I would have made a brilliant training officer if I didn't have such a lousy temper!

STRANGE AS IT seems, even the thunderous tumult of a barrage soon gets relegated to being background noise, and you learn to ignore the shaking ground.

It's Wide Eyes who speaks first, pulling his collar up as a gust of wind sends the rain spraying beneath the overhang of the trench.

'Why are you here if you're supposed to be on this prison planet?' he asks. First sensible thing anyone else has said so far. 'Did you escape or something?'

'If I'd escaped, do you really think I would end up in this grave-bait war?' I reply with a sour look. 'I don't think so! But I did try to get out once. You have to understand that this world wasn't a prison like the brig aboard ship. There were only a few guards, and they had this massive fortified tower out on the central plains. Apart from that, you were just kicked out into the wastelands and forgotten. I mean, really! It's just like any other world, there're empires and lords and stuff. The meanest fraggers get to the top and the weak are just left by the wayside or killed and preyed upon. If you're strong, you survive, if you ain't…' I let it hang.

'Anyway, I gets into the retinue of this guy called Tagel,' I tell them. One of the many people I've met and wish I hadn't. 'Big fragger from Catachan, and they breed 'em really big deep in that hellhole. He'd directed an artillery barrage on friendly troops 'cause his captain had called him names or some equally petty stupidity. He was fighting against a rag-tag bunch from across the other side of the valley, who had a nice little still going brewing up some really potent juice. Anyway, I kinda led some of Tagel's guys into an ambush on purpose, but before I can get to the other side they're hunting me. It may be a big planet, but when you've got that red-faced fragger chasing you everywhere you start getting the idea that this planet isn't the best place to be, know what I mean?

'Anyway, there's this supply shuttle every few months. I holed up long enough until one was due and then forged my way across the plains. I hid for a few days, waiting nice and patient. Then the shuttle comes in, as I'd hoped. I sneak real close to the station while they're all excited about getting their visitors. Then the gates open so they can let out the latest bunch of sorry malcontents. In the confusion I scrag one of the guards and swipe his uniform. I slip into the complex just as the gates are closing and then it's time to head for the shuttle. I'd just bluffed my way to the landing pad when the body's spotted and the alarm's raised.'

Their eyes are fixed to me like a sniper's sight, hanging on each word. Can I tell a story or what?

'So, I knife a couple more frag-heads to clear a way through and I'm up the ramp and inside. Just as the door's about to close there's someone up ahead of me. Without thinking I thrust with my stained blade into this guy's shoulder. He just takes it, can you believe that? A span of mono-edge in his arm and the guy just takes a pace back. I look up into his face, 'cause this guy is one big meatgrinder, if you take my meaning, and there's these cold blue eyes just staring at me, icy to the core. He backhands me, breaking my jaw as I later find out, and I go down. I get a boot in the crotch and then a pistol butt to the back of my head. Last thing I hear is this guy laughing. Laughing! I hear him say something which I'll never forget.'

Their eyes ask the question before their mouths can move.

'"Just my type of scum!" is what he says!' That's me, the Colonel's scum through and through.

THE BARRAGE FROM Coritanorum has moved on, dropping its payload of death and misery on some other poor souls, not that I give them a second thought. Rations Boy asks the obvious question. 'Who was he? How did he get you here?'

'That was the Colonel,' I say with due reverence. 'Colonel Schaeffer, no less. Commander of the Last Chancers.'

Wide Eyes jumps in with the next obvious question. 'Who are the Last Chancers?'

'The 13th Penal Legion,' I inform them grandly. 'Of course, there's been hundreds more than thirteen raisings, but we've always been called the 13th on account of our bad luck.'

Wide Eyes is full of questions at the moment. He takes his cap off and flicks water from the brim into the trench, revealing his close-cropped blond hair. It's smudged with brown and black from the dirt and muck that this whole Emperor-damned world is covered in.

'What bad luck?' he asks.

'Our bad luck to have the Colonel in command,' I say with a grin. 'We get the dirtiest missions he can find. Suicide strikes, rear-guards, forlorn hope for assaults. You name the nastiest situation you could ever imagine and I'd bet a week's rations the Colonel has been in it. And survived, more importantly. We get a hundred guys gunned down in the first volley and he'll walk through the entire battle without a scratch. Not a fragging scratch!'

One of the others, silent until now, opens his thin-lipped mouth to ask one of the most sensible questions I'd heard in a long time. 'So why are you here? I know I've not had much experience of battle, but I know this isn't a suicide run. I mean, we're new here; why bother raising a whole new regiment just to throw them away?'

'You so sure it ain't a suicide run?' I say back to him, eyebrows raised. 'You seen the lights, flares heading up, to the west?' Nods of agreement. 'They ain't flares. They're landing barges evacuating this battle-zone. There are twenty or thirty transports up there in orbit, waiting to pull out. Guess they've decided to wipe out everything from space – virus bombs, mass drivers and all the rest. Coritanorum is a lost cause now. The rebels are too well dug in. In the past eighteen months, there've been thirty-eight assaults and we haven't advanced one pace. They're pulling back and guess who's left to hold the front line…'

'But we're behind the front, so what're you doing back here?' Thin Lips points out.

There's a distant whine behind us, getting louder and louder. The recruits duck into shelter, but I know what's coming and take a peek over the trench to see the show. Suddenly, there's a howling roar directly overhead and a squadron of Marauders streak across the sky, Thunderbolt fighters spiralling around them in an escort pattern. While the others cower in stupidity, I see a line of fiery blossoms blooming over the enemy positions. Our own artillery has set up a counter-barrage and the incoming fire suddenly stops. Then the attack run of the Marauders hits, sending up a plume of smoke as their bombs detonate and the blinding pulses of lascannon smash through the enemy fortifications and explode their ammo dumps. The ground attack is over in an instant as the planes light their afterburners and scream off into the storm.

'Hey boys!' I call down to them. 'Take a look at this, you won't see another one for a while!'

The recruits timidly poke their heads out, and give me a quizzical look.

'Bombardment, air attack – next comes the orbital barrage.' I tell them. I've seen it half a dozen times, standard Imperial battle dogma. 'Those damned rebels are in for some hot stuff tonight!'

Just as I finish speaking, the clouds are brilliantly lit up in one area and a moment later an immense ball of energy flashes towards Coritanorum. The fusion torpedo smashes into the citadel's armoured walls, smearing along the scarred and pock-marked metal like fiery oil. Several more salvoes rain down through the storm, some shells kicking up huge plumes of steam as they bury themselves in the mud before detonating, others causing rivulets of molten metal to pour down Coritanorum's walls like lava flows.

Then the rebels' anti-strike batteries open up, huge turrets swivel skywards and blasts of laser energy punch through the atmosphere. For almost a minute the return fusillade continues, dissipating the clouds above the fortress with the heat of their attack. The ship in orbit must have pulled out, as no more death comes spilling from the cloud cover.

Half a minute later a siren sounds along the whole trench. Rations Boy looks up, face suddenly pale and lip trembling. 'That's the standby order. Next one sounds the attack,' he tells me.

This is my big chance. In the confusion of the attack, it'll be easy to slip out the other side of the trench and get myself out of here. As stimulating as their company is, I don't want to be anywhere near these recruits for more than another half-minute.

'I'd wish you luck, but I'm afraid I'm hogging that all to myself just for now.' I smile, but they don't look reassured. Never mind.

Just then the grim-faced commissar comes striding round the corner of the trench, his beady eyes fixed on me. 'Bring the prisoner with you when we advance. Let him go and I'll have all of you up on a charge of negligence!'

Frag! Still, an order's one thing, but execution's another.

Then the attack siren sounds. I'm being pushed out first, so I guess my new friends have learnt one thing, at least. I start sprinting cross the open killing ground to the next trench line. The enemy snipers, who I'd avoided so nimbly before, get a second chance at skinning my hide. There's a yell and Wide Eyes goes down as a bullet smashes through his neck, spraying spine and blood over my stolen uniform. I snatch up his lasgun and send a volley of shots from the hip into the sniper's probable hiding place. No more shots ring out for the moment.

Then something grabs my leg. Looking down I see the hard-headed commissar down on his knees coughing blood, broken. He looks at me with those hard eyes and whispers, 'Do something decent with your life for a change, treacherous scum!'

Without a thought I turn the lasgun round and grant him his wish. The beams of murderous light silencing him forever. I must be getting soft. I've never bothered with a mercy killing before now, especially this knee-deep in trouble.

WITH THE COMMISSAR down, this is my chance to break for it. I just have to turn round and run straight back the way we came. I don't think the rebels are going to bother shooting at someone running in the opposite direction. Just then I notice something, probably the enemy, casting a shadow in the lightning, just ahead of us to the right. Damned snipers must be laughing it up tonight. I look about as a shot plucks at my tunic – maybe I was wrong about an easy getaway. There's a ruined farmstead on the left and I head for it. With the resumption of sniper fire, some of the rookie platoon is face down in the mud, hiding or dead, I don't know. The rest are standing around, milling about in confusion. Someone I don't know gets in my way, his eyes strangely vacant with desperation as more and more of the rookies are gunned down by hidden foes. I slam my fist into his weasel face and as he stumbles out of my way he goes down, his chest blown out by a bullet that would have hit me. Another couple of heartbeats and I'm over the wall of the farm and kneeling in some kind of animal pen.

Right, now that I've separated myself from those no-hopers, time to formulate my escape plan. Then there's the thud of boots all around me and I realise that the platoon has followed me into cover instead of carrying on their planned advance to the next trench! A journey, I might add, that they would have never finished.

One of the little soldier boys grabs my collar and shouts in my ear. 'Good thinking, sir! We'd have been butchered if you hadn't brought us here!'

Frag! 'Brought you here?' I almost scream. 'I didn't fraggin' bring you here, you dumb rookies! Frag, you stupid wetbacks are gonna get me killed, hangin' around here with "target" written all over you as badly as if it was in bright lights five metres high! Get outta my face before I skin you, you stupid little fragger!'

Chips of masonry are flying everywhere now as the snipers bring their high-powered rifles to bear on us. Well, as long as these space-heads are around, I might as well use them to my advantage. As Tagel used to say, an iron ball around your leg can still be used to smash someone's head in. Actually, that was probably one of the longest sentences the dumb brute had ever used, so I figure he'd heard it from someone else. Pulling my thoughts back to the problem in hand, I point through the downpour towards the escarpment where the snipers are lying in cover.

'Suppression fire on that ridge!' I bellow.

Drilled for months while in transit to this hellhole, the platoon reacts without thought. The guys around me open up with their las-guns, a torrent of light pulsing through the darkness. I find the shattered casing of a solar boiler and use its twisted panes to get some cover from the shells knocking chunks off the plascrete wall of the outhouse. Little did my boys know, but the shuttles wouldn't hang around forever, and I've still got every intention of warming my behind on one of those seats.

There's a shouted greeting and the remnants of another squad joins us, two of the Guardsmen carrying grenade launchers. They start fiddling with their sights to get the correct trajectory but by this time there's more incoming fire as the snipers behind the ridge get reinforcements. I snatch one of the launchers, select a frag round and send the charge sailing through the air. I grin madly, along with others I note, as three bodies are tossed into view by the explosion. Casting the launcher back to the Guardsman, I draw the concealed knife from my right boot and charge. Not too far now.

As I leap over a mound of bodies, I see the rest of the platoon on either side of me, pouring over the ridge. Stunned by the sudden attack the traitors are soon hacked down in a storm of lasgun fire and slashing bayonets. I gut two of the rebel swine myself. From there it's just a matter of half a minute's jogging to the forward trench line. As the others set off I turn on my heel and start heading back to the second line, which now would hopefully be empty. I see the grox-breath lieutenant to my right. He sees me too. But before he can say anything, him and his command squad are knocked off their feet in a bloody cloud by a hail of fire. I see shadows moving up on the left, cutting me off from my route to the shuttles – for now at least.

As I splash down in the front-line trench, I hear the sergeants crying out the roll-call. Lots of names get no reply and I guess they've lost about three-quarters of the men. The others are gonna die as soon as the rebels counter-attack, and I'm gonna make damn sure I'm not around to suffer a similar fate. Suddenly I notice everyone's looking at me, expectation in their eyes.

'What the frag is this? What're you looking at, for Emperor's sake?' I snarl at them. It's the oldest one of my guards who makes the plea.

'Lieutenant Martinez is dead! The command squad are all dead!' he says, high-pitched voice wobbling with fright.

'And?' I ask.

'And you saw to Commissar Caeditz!' he replies.

'Yeah, and?' I ask again. I don't like the sound of this at all. I dare not believe it, but I have a feeling something bad is happening.

'We're stuck here until another command squad gets sent up,' he explains. 'There's no one in command. Well, except you. You said you were a lieutenant.'

'Yeah, of a fraggin' penal legion platoon!' I spit out. 'That don't mean nothing in the real world.'

'You got us this far,' pipes up another nuisance, his face streaked with rain and blood, his lips swollen and bruised.

'Look, no offence, but the last thing I need right now is a bunch of wet-backed brainless fraggers like you weighing me down,' I explain to them. 'I got me this far. You guys have just tagged along for the ride. There's a seat on one of those stellar transports with my name on it, and I fully intend to sit in it. Do you understand?'

'But you can't just leave us!' comes the call from someone at the back.

The pitiful misery in their eyes is truly galling. There's no chance in creation I'm gonna lumber myself with this thankless task. I set about rummaging through the packs they've dumped in the trench to see if I can scrag some rations. I feel a faint tremor in the ground and look up. I see movement in the darkness, and as the wind subtly changes direction it brings the faint smell of oil smoke. Out in the rainswept darkness of the night I can make out the silhouette of a rebel Demolisher siege tank rumbling forwards. By its course I can tell the crew haven't seen us yet, but as soon as they pass a clump of twisted concrete columns to our right, we'll be easy targets. Bad news, bad news indeed.

'Listen up!' I call out, getting their attention. 'I am not in command! I am going to leave you to your fate! Make no bones, but there's a Demolisher on the prowl out there and he's gonna blow me to little pieces with that big gun of his if you give him the chance.'

I'm thinking really hard now. Maybe this would give me the chance I need to get away. I've survived for years on my wits, and I'm not going to give up that easily now. Being alive is a hobby of mine, and I don't feel like giving it up right now.

'Do exactly what I say and I may just get out of this with my skin,' I say to them, brain working overtime.

They listen intently, staring up at me with expectant eyes as I detail the plan. I check they understand and as they all nod I send them on their way. As the Demolisher rumbles forward someone switches on the turret's searchlight. The tank's hull glistens with rain and the steady sheet of water pouring from the sky reflects along the beam's length. Damn! I hadn't thought of that! Still, it's too late now, the plan's in motion and to shout now would be asking for death. I signal my bunch of guys to hunker down more as the others move out into position. I watch the Demolisher constantly as it slowly grinds its way through piles of bones, smashing aside small walls, its bulldozer blade creating a furrow in the deep mud. The searchlight is swinging left and right, but we're slightly behind it now and the commander isn't checking every angle. If he spots us, that turret is going to turn round on us, slow as he likes and drop one of those massive Demolisher shells right on top of my head!

Suddenly the searchlight is swinging my way, sweeping over the ground and harshly illuminating the piled bodies of the dead, ours and theirs. It swings onwards and I find myself holding my breath, but a few heartbeats before it's shining in my face it swings back the other way, moving fast. Looking down the beam – the tank's about forty strides from where I'm crouched – I see the other attack party standing rigid. I feel like screaming 'Run, don't stand there!' but when it comes down the line, if I shout I'll be dead just as surely as them. And as I say, I ain't ready to die for a long, long time.

As I had predicted, the turret turns with a slow grinding and the huge Demolisher cannon, wide enough for a man to crawl inside, tilts upwards. With a blossom of flame and a wreath of smoke the tank fires. A moment later the searchlight is outshone by the explosion of the shell. I fancy I see bodies flung into the air, but it's unlikely since Demolisher shells don't usually leave enough of you to be thrown about. As the flames flicker down, the searchlight roves left and right and the heavy bolter in the hull opens up with a flash from its muzzle. In the searchlight beam I see the survivors being kicked from their feet by the attack, blood spraying from exit wounds as the explosive bolts punch through skin, muscle and bone as if they were paper.

I snap back to the job in hand. Raising my fist I signal the charge. We run silently towards the tank, no battle cries, no shouts of defiance, just nice and quiet. However, the first guys are still about twenty strides from the tank when the sponson gunner on our side wakes up and opens fire with his heavy flamer. A raging inferno pours out from the side of the tank, turning men into charred hunks of flesh and quickly silencing their screams.

The searchlight swivels around towards us, but I level my lasgun and open up on the run, sending two shots into the wide lens and shattering it. I hear a faint cry of alarm as I dodge behind the tank. Its tracks churn wildly as the driver tries to turn it round to bring its weapons to bear.

As those huge steel tracks rumble round, so close to my face I could reach out and touch them, I leap up, grabbing onto the engine cover. I pull myself onto the tank's hull and wrench the panel loose to expose the oily, roaring mass of the engine. As the other survivors pile on board, blasting into the engine compartment with their lasguns, I make a jump for the turret.

The commander's shocked expression makes me laugh as I smash the butt of my gun into his chin, breaking his neck. I fire a couple of shots into the hatch and jump inside. The crew look at me in horror: daubed as I am in blood and mud I must seem like some hideous alien come for their hearts. And I have. My knife tears into them, I've always prided myself on my knife-fighting skills, and in a matter of a few breaths it's over.

Suddenly somebody's shouting down the hatch to get out.

I WATCH IN satisfaction from the trench as the charges go up, turning the siege tank into a storm of whirling metal debris and tangled wreckage. Right, now the coast is clear, time to head for those evacu-ation landing bays. Someone grabs my shoulder as I turn to head back across no-man's land. It's someone I don't know, a long scratch across his face and his left side and leg smouldering from a close encounter with a heavy flamer.

'You can't go, Kage – I mean, sir!' he begs. 'We need you, and you need us!'

'Need you? *Need you?*' I'm almost screaming in frustration. 'Look, I'm heading back. Any of you dumb fraggers tries to follow me and I'm gonna start shooting. I don't need you, you're all liabilities. Is that perfectly clear?'

There's silence. I think a couple of them are gonna start crying, their lips quiver so much. Well tough luck, it doesn't work on Kage, not one bit. I turn and start climbing up the back wall of the trench, towards our own lines. Someone says, 'Give you a hand up, soldier?'

I grab the proffered hand without thinking and get hauled out of the trench by strong arms. As I kneel there in the mud my spine tin-gles with horror as my mind catches up with events. I look up. Blazing back at me are two pits of coldness, ripping into my soul. The Colonel stands there, bolt pistol pointed directly between my eyes!

'Deserting scum!' he snarls. 'You had your last chance. It is time to pay for your crimes!'

Just then he looks away and my fuddled brain suddenly identifies a rush of clicks and whine of power cells. Glancing over my shoulder I see the platoon, the whole sorry, bedraggled mess of them, all with their weapons trained on the Colonel, a wall of lasgun barrels, plasma gun muzzles and even the tube of a grenade launcher. I fight down the hysterical urge to laugh. Some of them are shaking with fear; others are rock-hard and steady. Each one of them is staring at the Colonel with a silent ferocity. It's a scary feeling, like a herd-beast suddenly sprouting fangs. Rations Boy braves the Colonel's wrath with words.

'I–I'm sorry, sir, but Kage doesn't deserve that,' he tells Schaeffer. 'If you shoot, we will too.'

'Yes, sir,' someone else chips in their two-cred worth, his lasgun cra-dled over the ragged, bloodied mess of a broken arm. 'We'd all be dead three times over if it wasn't for him. We're not going to let you kill him!'

They're all focused now. Their guns are steady, and I can see their eyes filled with bloodlust. The adrenalin is pumping and they're so hyped up they could kill just about anyone right now. Flushed with victory, I heard someone call it once. I can see it, and the Colonel can too. For what seems like an eternity he just stands there, turning that icy stare of his onto them. Each one in turn takes the full force of the Colonel's look, but not one of them breaks off, and that's saying something! Still, the Colonel is the Colonel and he just sneers.

'This wretched piece of slime is not worth your time,' he barks at them. 'I recommend you use your ammunition on something more worthwhile.'

No one moves and the sneer disappears. 'Very well. You have proved your point, Guardsmen,' the Colonel almost spits the words out.

The bristling guns are as steady as ever.

The Colonel's voice drops to a whisper, a menacing tone that even us in the Last Chancers dread to hear. 'I am ordering you. To lower. Your weapons.'

Still no movement.

'Have it your way,' he says finally. 'You will all be mine soon enough.'

It's several more long, deep breaths before the first of them lifts his gun away, finally convinced by the Colonel's sincere look. For me, I still think he's gonna blow my brains out.

'On your feet, Kage!' the Colonel snaps. I stand up slowly, not daring to breathe. 'Get that uniform off this instant – you do not deserve to wear it!'

As I begin unfastening the tunic, Colonel Schaeffer turns me around so I'm looking at Coritanorum, the heart of the rebel army. Even before the traitors had turned against the Emperor, the stronghold had a reputation for being nigh-on impregnable. Wall upon wall stretch into the hills, gun ports blazing as the artillery barrages a point in the line a few kilometres west of us. Searchlights roam across the open ground before the fort, showing the rows of razor-wire, the mass of plasma and frag minefields, the tank traps, death pits, snares and other weapons of defence. As I watch, a massive armoured gate opens and a column of four Leman Russ tanks spills from a drawbridge across the acid moat, heading south.

'What happens now, sir?' I ask quietly.

The Colonel points towards the inner keep and whispers in my ear.

'That is what happens now, Kage. Because that is where we are heading.'

Oh frag.

THE MAN'S RAGGED breathing echoed off the condensation-covered pipes that ran along both corridor walls, his exhalations producing a small cloud of mist around his head. A dismal, solitary yellow glow-strip illuminated his freshly shaven face from the ceiling, bathing it in a sickly light. He glanced back nervously, bent double catching his breath, hands resting on his knees. A flicker of movement in the distant shadows caught his attention and he gritted his teeth and started running again, pulling a stubby pistol from inside his blue coveralls. The clatter of something hard on metal rang along the corridor floor after him, accompanied by a scratching noise like rough leather being drawn along the corroded steel of the piping.

'Emperor's blood, the hunter has become the hunted,' he hissed, looking back again.

There was a blur of movement under the glow strip, an impression of bluish black and purple dashing along the corridor towards him. He raised the pistol and pulled the trigger, the muzzle flash almost blinding in the dim confines of the passageway, the whine of bullets passed into the dim distance. With preternatural speed the fast-approaching shape leapt aside, bone-coloured claws sinking into the rusted metal to pull itself out of the line of fire. The pipes rang with the sound of scraping on metal as the monster continued its relentless advance, its chase moving effortlessly onto the wall.

The man broke into a sprint again, his legs and arms pumped rapidly as he sped down the passage. His eyes scanned the walls and

ceiling as he ran down the twisting corridor, desperately seeking
some avenue of escape. He had run another thirty metres, the creature bearing down on him all the while, when he noticed an opening
to his right. Jumping through the doorway, his eyes fell on the lock-
down switch, which he slammed his fist into. With a hiss the blast
door began to descend rapidly, but a second later it was only halfway
down when his inhuman hunter slipped under it. It pulled itself up
to its full height right next to him, its dark, alien eyes regarding him
menacingly.

He blasted randomly at the monstrosity with the pistol as he dived
back underneath the door, rolling under its bottom edge and to his
feet on the other side. Half a second later the door slammed shut,
sealing him off from the voracious predator. Breathing a deep sigh of
relief, he could hear the sound of powerful limbs battering at the
other side of the portal, broken by the screech of long claws shredding metal. The noise of the futile assault ceased after a few seconds,
replaced by the clicking of claws disappearing along the side tunnel.

'Emperor willing, I'll catch you yet,' he said with a wry smile to the
entity on the other side of the doorway, before he turned and carried
on running down the corridor.

SEVEN
NEW SUN

+++ *Commencing Operation New Sun.* +++

+++ *I look forward to seeing you.* +++

THE COLONEL AND I approach a sizeable bunker complex, four or five large modules connected by enclosed walkways. The hatchway he leads me to is flanked by two of the Commissariat provosts, the black plates of their carapace armour slick in the continuing rain. Their look of disgust bites more than the cold wind and bitter rain on my bare flesh, making me fully aware of the pitiful state I'm in. My teeth are chattering with the cold, my naked body chilled with the rain, my feet numb from walking through the puddles and mud barefoot. Half my face is covered in grime from where I slipped over a while ago, and there are scratches along my lower legs from stumbling into a half-buried coil of razorwire. I've got my arms clasped tightly across my chest, shivering, trying to keep myself a little bit warmer. Their stares follow me as the Colonel opens the door lock and the hatchway cycles open, and he waves me inside. A few metres down a short corridor is another door to my left, and at a gesture from the Colonel I open it and step inside.

Within the small bunk room on the other side of the door are the rest of the Last Chancers: Linskrug, Lorii, Loron and Kronin. The Colonel told me on the way here that just after they left me Gappo managed to find a plasma charge minefield, the hard way, and was scattered liberally over a wide area. That was a blow to hear, though I suspect Gappo would be glad that his death warned the others of danger.

They look at me with astonished gazes. They've seen me nude before, every day on the ship during daily post-exercise ablutions in fact, but my bedraggled state must be pretty extraordinary.

'And Saint Phistinius went unto the enemy unarmed and unarmoured,' jokes Kronin and they all burst out laughing. I stand there humiliated for a moment before I find myself joining in with the laugh, realising that I must make for a particularly pathetic spectacle.

'Not that unarmed,' I quip back, glancing meaningfully down past my bare stomach, getting another laugh from them.

'More of a sidearm than artillery...' Lorii sighs with mock wistfulness, eliciting another round of raucous cackles from us all. As we subside into childish sniggers I hear someone come in behind me and turn to see the Colonel. He's carrying folded combat fatigues, shirt and flak jacket and dumps them on one of the bunks. Behind him a provost carries in a pair of boots and a standard issue anti-frag helmet, which he adds to the pile.

'It's bad luck not to put new boots on the floor,' I say to the provost as he leaves, but I can't tell his reaction past the dark visor of his helmet.

'Be quiet, Kage,' the Colonel tells me, nodding with his head to a door leading off the bunkroom. 'Clean up through there and get in uniform.' Inside the small cubicle beyond the door is a small showering unit. I find a hard-bristled brush and a misshapen lump of infirmary-smelling soap in a little alcove and set to scrubbing myself clean under the desultory trickle of cold water that dribbles from the showerhead when I work the pump a few times.

Cold, but clean and invigorated, I towel myself off back in the bunkroom and get dressed, feeling more human than I've done in the past day and a half since I made my bid for freedom. The Colonel's gone again and the others sit around with their own thoughts as I ready myself.

'I knew you weren't dead,' Linskrug says as I'm finishing, 'but I figured out what you were up to. Sorry it didn't work out.'

'Thanks, anyway,' I reply with a shrug. 'How the hell did the Colonel know, though?'

'When we got here, there were some odd reports floating around,' Loron says, sitting on the edge of one of the bunks and kicking his feet against the floor. 'The provosts told the Colonel that a storm trooper patrol found an enemy infiltration squad dead in their camp, about three kilometres past the front trenchline. Nobody was supposed to be in that area, and the Colonel said that you were the only one stupid enough to be out there. He left us here and headed off to look for you.'

'Did you kill that squad, Kage?' the Colonel asks from the doorway, causing us all to glance towards him in surprise.

'Yes, sir,' I tell him, sitting down on the floor to lace up my boots. 'I'm glad I did, even though it helped you catch me. This whole place might be swarming with rebels otherwise.' He just nods and grunts in a non-committal fashion.

'I have someone new for you all to meet,' he says after another moment, standing to one side and waving somebody through the door. The man who steps through is swathed in a dark purple robe, a skull and cog emblem embroidered in silver onto the top of the hood over his head, instantly identifying him as a tech-priest of the Cult Mechanicus.

'This is Adept Gudmanz, lately from the forgeworld of Fractrix,' the Colonel introduces him. 'To save tiresome speculation on your part, I will tell you now that he is with us for supplying Imperial armaments to pirates raiding Navy convoys. A most extreme abuse of his position, I am sure you will agree.'

Gudmanz shuffles over towards us, pulling back his hood to reveal a tired, withered face. His scalp is bald, puckered scars across his head show where implants have been recently removed. His eyes are rheumy and as he looks at us listlessly, I can hear his breath is ragged and strained.

'Make him feel welcome,' the Colonel adds. 'I will be back shortly.'

With the Colonel gone, we get down to the serious business of questioning our latest 'recruit'.

'Bit of a bad deal for you,' says Linskrug, slouched nonchalantly along a bed at the far end of the long bunkroom.

'Better than the alternative,' Gudmanz replies with a grimace, easing himself cautiously down onto one of the other bunks, his voice a grating, laboured whisper.

'You look completely done in,' I say, looking at his tired, frail form.

'I am two hundred and eighty-six,' he wheezes back sadly, head hung low. 'They took my enhancements away and without regular doses of anti-agapic oils I'll suffer increasing dysfunctions within the next month owing to lack of maintenance.'

We sit there absorbing this information for a moment before Loron breaks our contemplation.

'I think I'd prefer just to be hanged and get it over and done with,' he says, shaking his head in amazement.

'They would not have hanged me, young man,' the tech-priest tells him, eyes suddenly sharp and aware as he looks at each of us in turn. 'My masters would have had me altered to be a servitor. I would have my memory scrubbed. My biological components would be permanently interfaced into some menial control system or similar. I would be cogitating but not alive, simply existing. I would know in my subconscious that I am a living, breathing thing, but also denied the ultimate synthesis with the Machine God. Not truly alive and not truly dead. That is the usual punishment for betraying the great Adeptus Mechanicus. Your Colonel must have some good influence to deny the Cult Mechanicus its vengeance.'

'Don't I know it,' Linskrug says bitterly. Further questions are interrupted by the Colonel's reappearance, accompanied by the scribe I'd seen several times in his chamber aboard the *Pride of Lothus*, Clericus Amadiel. Amadiel is carrying a bundle of scrolls, which I immediately recognise as the pardons the Colonel had shown me before.

'And now you all learn what I really intend for you,' says the Colonel gravely, taking the pardons and placing them on the bunk next to Loron, everybody's eyes locked to him as he walks across the room back to the door. 'This is the time when your careers in the Last Chancers will soon be over, one way or another.'

There's a tangible change to the atmosphere inside the bunkroom as everybody draws their breath in at the same time. If I'm hearing right, and the reaction of the other Last Chancers suggests I am, the Colonel has just told us we can get out of the 13th Penal Legion.

'Those,' the Colonel continues, jabbing a finger towards the pile of parchments, 'are Imperial pardons for each and every one of you. I will sign and seal them once we have completed our final mission. You can refuse, in which case the provosts will take you to another penal legion.'

'And the Heretic Priests of Eidoline came forth, bringing false images for the praise of the lost people,' Kronin says, frowning hard.

'What?' says the Colonel, taken aback by the madman's statement.

'He means this is far too simple,' translates Lorii. I know what she means, the offer seems too good to be true. And then I understand that it isn't, that I know what the Colonel has in mind.

'You were serious when you said we're going into Coritanorum,' I say slowly, making sure the other Last Chancers understand the statement.

'Of course I was serious, Kage,' the Colonel answers brusquely. 'Why would I not be serious?'

'Well,' puts in Linskrug, leaning forward, 'there is the small matter that Coritanorum is the most impregnable citadel in the sector, the most unassailable fortress for a month's warp travel in every direction.'

'No citadel is impregnable,' the Colonel replies, radiating self-confidence and sincerity.

'The fact that five hundred thousand Imperial Guard, backed up by the Imperial Navy, haven't been able to take the place doesn't vex you?' blurts out Linskrug, highly perturbed by what the Colonel is proposing.

'We shall not be storming Coritanorum, that would be ridiculous,' the Colonel tells us in an irritated voice. 'We shall be infiltrating the complex and rendering it inoperable from the inside.'

'Assuming you can get us inside – which is a hell of an assumption – there's about three million people living in that city,' I say, brow knitted as I try to work out what the Colonel's whole plan is. 'We're bound to be discovered. Frag, I couldn't even hide among people on my own side, on my own.'

'Then we shall have to endeavour to do better than your recent exploits,' the Colonel replies curtly, obviously getting impatient with our reluctance. 'Make your decisions now. Are you coming with me, or do I transfer you?'

'Count me out,' says Linskrug emphatically, shaking his head vehemently. When he continues he looks at each of us in turn, forcing himself to speak slowly and surely. 'This is so insane, so reckless, it's unbelievable. It's sheer suicide trying to attack Coritanorum with seven people. I am going to survive this and get my barony back, and marching into the middle of a strongly held rebel fortress is not going to help me do that. Do what you will, I'm not going along with this suicide squad deal.'

'Very well,' the Colonel says calmly, strolling over to the bed with the pardons on. He sorts through them for a moment, finds Linskrug's and holds it up for all to see. Then, slowly and deliberately, he begins to tear it up. He tears it lengthways down the middle and then puts the two halves together and tears it across its width. He does this a couple more times until sixteen ragged pieces nestle in his hand. With the same deliberation he tips his hand over, the scraps of parchment fluttering to the floor around his boots. He treads on the pieces, twisting his foot on top of them to scrunch them up and tear them even more. We watch this in horrified silence, and to me it's like he's torn up and scuffed out Linskrug.

He bends over and picks up another pardon, holding it up for us to see. I read *my* name across the top and my heart flutters. Linskrug has got a good point: the whole idea of going into Coritanorum is suicidal. I have a philosophy about staying alive, and that's to do it for as long as possible. Going into the enemy fort isn't going to help that at all. But for all this, that's my life the Colonel has gripped between finger and thumb. If I say yes, and I survive this ridiculous mission, then I'll be free. I'll be able to do whatever I want. Stay in the Guard possibly, make a home for myself here on Typhos Prime, or perhaps be able to work my way back to where I was born on Olympas.

If I survive…

The Colonel looks at me with those ice-shards he has for eyes, an expectant expression on his face. I think about all the pain, misery and danger I've been through in the past three years, and consider the whole of my life being like that. I can tell that this is the only chance I've got to get out of the penal legions. If I'm transferred, I'm dead, sooner or later. That'll be the whole of my fate, for perhaps another three years if I'm lucky; just more wars and death and wondering when that bullet or las-bolt will finally get me. Perhaps I'll end up like Kronin, head snapped with the enormity of his destiny. And will there be someone around to watch my back the same way I look out for Kronin? Maybe, maybe not, but do I want to risk it? One choice, almost certain death, but the chance for freedom. The other choice, death almost as certainly, and no escape. I had my best bid for getting out the easy way here on Typhos Prime, and that wasn't good enough, and besides, do I really want to spend the rest of my life wondering if I could have done it the proper way?

All these thoughts are whirling round my head at the speed of a las-bolt, everyone else seems to be caught in some kind of stasis loop around me, the universe pausing in its slow life to let me make my decision. And through it all there's a recurring voice at the back of my head. You're an Imperial Guardsman, it says. This is the chance to prove yourself, it tells me. This is where you show them all that you're worth something. This is where the Colonel sees what kind of man you are. A man, it repeats, not a criminal scumbag.

'I'm in, Colonel,' I hear myself saying, my mind feeling like it's floating around a hand's breadth above my head, letting some other part of me take control for the moment. The others give their answers but I don't register what they actually say, my mind is still racing around and around, trying to catch up with itself. I hear Gudmanz muttering how dying in Coritanorum will be a release for him. Then, with a slamming sensation in my consciousness it hits home.

If I survive this, I'm free to walk away.

I have no doubt that the Colonel will keep his promise. All I need to do is survive one more mission, one more battle. Okay, it's Coritanorum, but I've been through some real crap lately and I'm still here. Who knows, this could be easy in comparison, if the Colonel's got it figured right.

With this realisation seeping into my thoughts I manage to turn my attention to the others. There's still only one torn-up parchment on the floor, so that must mean all the others accepted as well. They're looking at me, including the Colonel, and I realise that someone was speaking to me but I hadn't heard them, my mind was so engrossed in its own thoughts.

'What?' I say, forcing myself to try to think straight. It's going to be essential to think clearly if I'm going to get to see that pardon again.

'We said that we were going with you, not the Colonel,' repeats Lorii, looking encouragingly at me.

'What?' I snap, angry because I'm confused. 'What the hell does that mean?'

'It means that if you think we can make it, we're willing to try,' Loron explains, his pale face a picture of sincerity.

'Okay then, Guardsmen,' the Colonel says. 'We move out at nightfall. You have two hours to prepare yourselves.'

THE STORM SEEMS to be passing, the thunder rumbling away to be replaced by the roar of distant artillery batteries. We're sitting on a rocky hillock, about eight hundred metres past the current Imperial trenchline, as far as I can tell. A plain stretches out for a few kilometres in front of us, swarming with rebels. It seems to be a kind of staging area, the open ground buzzing with activity. In the distance I can just about make out a sally port of Coritanorum. Two gatehouses flank a big armoured portal dug into an outcrop of rock from the mountain into which most of the citadel is dug. It's that mountain that makes it so easy to defend, rendering it impervious to all but the most sustained and concentrated orbital bombardment. Who knows how deep its lowest levels go? The parts that are above ground are rings of concentric curtain walls, each metres thick and constructed of bonded plasteel and rock-crete, making it hard to damage with shells and energy weapons, their slanted shape designed to deflect attacks towards the dead ground between them. That open space is a killing ground too, left clear and smooth to give no cover for any foe fortunate enough to get over one of the walls. I can see why half a million Guardsmen have thrown themselves against this bastion of defiance with no effect.

I'm distracted as a cluster of starshells soar into the air over to the west, to our left, exploding in a blast of yellow blossoms.

'That is the signal we have been awaiting,' the Colonel says from where he's stood on the lip of an abandoned rebel trench.

The fighting's moved away from this area now, and the communications trench along this ridgeline gives us perfect cover from the scrutiny of Coritanorum's defenders. The forces being assembled before us are probably for a push along the southern flank of the Imperial line, hoping perhaps to turn the end of the line and pin a large part of the Emperor's troops between this sally and the walls of Coritanorum.

'The diversionary attack will have begun,' the Colonel informs us, clicking shut the case of a gold chronometer that he procured from the commissariat, before we left the relay outpost where he'd given us our ultimatum. Placing the timer into a deep pocket of his great-coat, he looks around, seemingly at ease. Very at ease, actually, considering this is the most important and riskiest mission we've ever been involved in.

The sound of small stones skittering over the rocks above us gets everybody swinging round with weapons raised – except the Colonel, who's still stood there gazing towards Coritanorum.

'Good evening, Lieutenant Striden,' the Colonel says without looking, and we see a young man scrabbling down from the ridgeline, his thin face split with a wide grin.

'Good to see you, Colonel Schaeffer,' the man says pleasantly, nodding politely in greeting to each of us as well. He's swathed head to foot in an elaborate camouflage cape, patterned to blend in almost perfectly with the grey-brown rocks of the hills around Coritanorum. He jumps over the narrow trench to stand next to the Colonel, the cape fluttering around him.

'Now, Colonel Schaeffer?' Striden asks excitedly.

'When you are ready, Lieutenant Striden,' the Colonel affirms with a nod.

'What's happening, sir?' Lorii asks, looking suspiciously at Striden.

'Lieutenant Striden is going to call down some fire on these rebels, to clear a path to the sally port,' the Colonel replies, dropping down into the trench.

'You're going to need some big guns to shift that lot,' I say to the lieutenant. He turns his permanent grin towards me.

'Oh, we have some very large ordnance, Mr Kage,' he says, pulling a complex-looking device from beneath his cape. He squats down and opens up a shutter in the fist-sized box, holding it up to his eye. His fingers travel back and forth along a row of knobs down the side of what is evidently a range-finder or something, making small adjustments. Pulling the box away from his face, Striden looks down and I see a series of numbers and letters displayed on a digi-panel. He nods with a satisfied look and then looks upwards into the cloud-filled night sky.

'Wind's sou' sou' west, wouldn't you say, Mr Kage?' he says suddenly.

'Wind?' I blurt back, taken completely by surprise at this unusual question.

'Yes,' he says, glancing at me with a smile, 'and it looks as if there is a counter-cyclic at about six thousand metres.'

'Your guns must lob their shells a hell of a long way up for that to matter,' comments Loron from the other side of the lieutenant.

'Oh no, they don't go up at all, they just come down,' he replies amiably, pressing a stud on the bottom of the gadget and holding it up above his head.

'Doesn't go up…' murmurs Gudmanz. 'This is coming from orbit?'

'That's right,' Striden affirms with a nod. 'I'm ground observation officer for the battleship *Emperor's Benevolence*. She'll be opening fire shortly.'

'A battleship?' I ask incredulously. My mind fills with memories of the cruiser that was with us in the Kragmeer system, and the rows of massive guns along her broadside. Emperor knows how much firepower this battleship has!

'Here it comes,' Striden says happily, directing our eyes upwards with his own gaze.

The sky above Coritanorum begins to brighten and a moment later I can see the fiery trails of ten missiles streaking groundwards. As they approach, movement on the ground attracts my attention as the rebels begin to scurry around in panic when they realise what's happening. With a vast, thunderous roar the torpedo warheads impact into the plain, and `a ripple of explosions, each at least fifty metres across, tears through the assembled traitors, tossing tanks thirty or more metres into the air with great balls of fire. I don't see any bodies flung around, and I assume the men are completely incinerated. The ground is engulfed in a raging inferno, and then the blast wave hits us, from a kilometre away, causing the Navy officer's cape to flutter madly as the blast of hot air sweeps over my face, stinging my eyes. The air itself seems to burn for a few seconds, blossoms of secondary explosions filling the skies. Striden taps me on the arm and nods upwards and I can just make out a series of streaks in the air, reflecting the light of the flames around Coritanorum. The Colonel climbs out of the trench to watch, his eyes glittering red from the burning plain.

The shells' impacts are even more devastating than the torpedo fire as they explode in four parallel lines towards us, each one ripping up great gouts of earth and hurling men and machines in all directions. The roar of the detonations drowns out their screams and the screech of sheared metal. The blasts from the shells extinguish the murderous fires from the plasma warheads; a black pall of smoke drifts into the night sky, silhouetted against the twinkling lights of distant windows in Coritanorum. The salvo continues, numerous explosions creeping closer towards us across the plain. For a full minute the shells impact nearer and nearer and I start to worry that I'll go deaf with the intense, continuous pounding in my ears.

This is replaced by a more urgent fear as the bombardment carries on into a second minute, and it seems as if the battleship is going to go too far. When shells start exploding at the bottom of the ridgeline and keep coming, panic grips us, and everybody starts hurling themselves into the trench. As the bombardment continues I begin to fear for my life. I wouldn't trust ground artillery to shell that close to me, never mind a battleship more than a hundred kilometres above my head! The Colonel jumps in after us, a concerned look on his face, but Striden just stands there on the lip, gazing in raptured awe as the devastation approaches. Rock splinters are hurled into the sky by an explosion no more than fifty metres away and in the bright glare of the detonation, I see Striden raising his arms above his head and just make out shrill laughter over the tumult of the barrage. His cape is almost being ripped from his shoulders by the successive blast waves, but he stands there as solid as a rock.

Then everything goes silent and dark, my ears and eyes useless for a few seconds as they adjust to the sudden lack of violent stimuli. Striden's still laughing like a madman, and the Colonel gives a scowl and brushes down his coat before climbing out of the trench. The Navy lieutenant drops his hands to his sides and looks back over his shoulder, his eyes wide with excitement.

'Emperor help me, it doesn't matter how many times I see that, Mr Kage, I still get a tingle watching it!' he exclaims passionately, bright teeth showing in the darkness.

'That was a little fraggin' close!' I shout at him, pulling myself up over the rim of the trench and striding over to him.

'Orders, I'm afraid,' he says apologetically. 'Usually we'd bracket a target first to make sure of our positioning, but we weren't allowed to do that this time. This time, we're here, so we don't want anything unfriendly dropping on us, do we? And we were requested to miss the gatehouses too, which is a bit strange, but orders is orders. There's no need to worry, though: we've had quite a lot of practice at this.'

'I guess we won't be able to get in if the gate is fused into a molten lump,' says Lorii, vaulting gracefully over the top few rungs of the ladder out of the trench. I survey the scene as it is now, not even five minutes have passed since the starshells went up. The plains are pockmarked with hundreds of craters, at a rough guess, and from here, with my eyes still reeling, I can just about make out tangled heaps of wreckage scattered around. For about six kilometres in every direction, the plain has been bodily ripped up and dumped back down again. A haze of smoke floats a metre or so above the ground, dispersing slowly in the sluggish wind. The tang of burnt shell powder is almost asphyxiating, the air is thick with it. Nothing could have survived that, nothing that ever walked, crawled or was driven across the face of a world, at least.

'Going inside?' says Striden suddenly, Lorii's words filtering into his over-excited mind. 'Emperor's throne, that sounds damned exciting. More exciting than standing here waiting for my next target orders. Mind if I join you?'

'What?' I exclaim. 'Have you totally lost it?'

He gives me a pleasant smile and then looks towards Coritanorum, eyes staring with fascination.

'He can come,' I hear the Colonel say heavily from where he stands, further down the ridge, looking at the devastation wrought by the *Emperor's Benevolence*. I can tell that even he's impressed by the magnitude of the slaughter – there must have been near on ten thousand men down there a few minutes ago, and upwards of a hundred tanks. Now there's nothing. 'I do not think we could stop him, in fact,' says the Colonel meaningfully. I understand what he's saying – Striden'll follow us anyway and short of killing him, which the Navy won't appreciate one little bit, there's nothing we can do.

PICKING OUR WAY across the ruined landscape is a time-consuming process. We need to move quickly, but the route to Coritanorum is littered with burning tanks and mounds of corpses, not to mention the fact that the ground has been torn up and in places the rims of the shellholes are six metres high and fifty metres across. As we get nearer, within a few hundred metres of the gate, a thick layer of ash carpets the ground, in places piled up in drifts which go knee-deep. I remember that this is where the plasma torpedoes impacted.

'Do you know what happens to someone who gets caught in the noval centre of a plasma warhead explosion?' Gudmanz asks nobody in particular as he hauls himself up the slope of another impact crater, his robes covered with flecks of grey ash. We all shrug or shake our heads. Gudmanz bends down and grabs a handful of the dusty grey ash and lets it trickle through his fingers with a cruel, rasping laugh.

'You don't mean…' starts Lorii and then she groans with distaste when Gudmanz nods.

'Emperor, I swallowed some of that!' curses Loron, spitting repeatedly to clear his mouth.

'Silence, all of you!' barks the Colonel. 'We are almost at the gates.'

I STEP THROUGH the small portal into the left watchtower with lasgun ready. When I'm inside I understand how the Colonel could lead us through the gate with such confidence. Inside the tower men and women are strewn haphazardly across the floor and up the spiral stairs, their faces blue, contorted by the paroxysms of death.

'Airborne toxin, I suspect,' mutters Gudmanz, peering closely at one of the bodies, a young woman perhaps twenty years old, dressed in a Typhos sergeant's uniform.

'From where?' Striden voices the question that had just popped into my head.

'Keep moving,' the Colonel orders from further up the stairwell. When we reach the top, the whole upper level is a single chamber. There are gunslits all around, and a few emplaced autocannons, their crews lying dead beside their guns.

'Gudmanz,' the Colonel attracts the tech-priest's attention and nods towards a terminal in the inner wall, facing away from the gate. The tech-priest lurches over and leans against the wall. He reaches up and pulls something from behind his ear. It's like a small plug, the size of a thumbnail, and as he pulls it further I see a glistening wire stretching between it and Gudmanz's head. Punching a few runes on the terminal he inserts the plug into a recess in the middle of the contraption and closes his eyes. The display screen flickers into life, throwing a green glow onto the ageing tech-priest's craggy features. A succession of images flickers across the screen, too quick to see each one individually but giving an overall impression of a map or blueprints. Then a lot of numbers scroll up, again too fast to read, a succession of digits that barely appear before they are replaced by new data. With a grunt, Gudmanz steps back, the plug being ejected from the port and whipping back into his skull.

'Just as well that I checked,' he tells the Colonel. 'They have changed some of the security protocols in the inner areas and remapped the plasma chamber access passages.'

'You have a map of this place?' asks Lorii in amazement. 'How can you remember all that information? This place is over forty kilometres across!'

'Subcutaneous cerebral memograph,' Gudmanz replies, tapping an area of his skull just above his right ear. 'They did not take all of my implants.'

'I'm not going to even pretend I understood a word of that,' I butt in, 'but I take it you have an exact copy of the latest schematics in your head now?'

'That is correct,' he affirms with a single nod before pulling his hood up over his head. I turn to the Colonel.

'He mentioned plasma chambers, Colonel,' I say to him. 'What are we actually going to do here?'

'Coritanorum is run by three plasma reactors,' he explains as everyone else gathers around. 'We will get into the primary generators and disable them. Every system, every defence screen and sited energy weapon, as well as many of the major bombardment turrets, are linked into that power system.'

'I can see that,' agrees Lorii. 'But how do we get in?'

The Colonel simply points to the nearest body.

'GETTING INTO THE next circle is going to be harder,' Gudmanz warns the Colonel.

With our stolen uniforms, chosen to fit us better than my scrappy attempt with the Mordian outfit, getting around hasn't been too difficult. Everybody seems to take it for granted when an officer and a bunch of Guardsmen, accompanied by a tech-priest, walk past. They've been on a war footing for two years now, I suspect the security is a little bit lax. After all, nobody would be stupid enough to come in here without an army. Except us, of course.

With their extraordinary hair concealed beneath Typhon Guard helmets, and their faces partially obscured by the high collars of the blue jackets, even Lorii and Loron have gone unnoticed. I'm not sure what uniform the Colonel procured for himself, but it seems to be one that makes the Typhons look the other way lest they attract his attention. It's black, without any decoration at all, and I wonder if it isn't some local branch of the commissariat. Even in stolen clothes he's managed to come up as someone everyone else is scared stiff of. Typical. With his camo-cape discarded, Striden is revealed as a skinny young man of about twenty, almost painful in his lankiness, though he doesn't walk with the gawkiness you might reasonably expect.

I'm beginning to understand even more now about how impossible it would be to take Coritanorum by open attack. Even if a sizeable enough force could gain access, the layout of the lower levels is roughly circular, a series of four concentric rings according to Gudmanz. Each is only linked to the next by a single access tunnel, which are on opposite sides of each ring so that to get from one to the next you have to get around half the circumference of the ring. The builders even made the air ducts and power conduits circular, so there's no quick route through there either. It's taken us a day and a half just to get around the outer circle. We grabbed a few hours sleep in an empty barracks block during the morning, and it's about midday now, and we're in a small chamber leading off from the passageway that goes to the next security gate.

'What do we need to do?' asks Schaeffer, dragging a chair from behind a chrome desk and sitting down. The plain, white room is bare except for the desk and chair, obviously disused now.

'We have to get one of the security officers – a senior one, I mean,' Gudmanz tells us. The Colonel looks over at me where I'm lounging against the wall.

'Kage, take Lorii and get me a senior security officer,' he says, as calmly as if asking me to pop out and get him some fresh boot polish or something. Lorii and I exchange glances and head out of the door. The corridor smells faintly of disinfectant and gleams brightly from a recent cleaning. The main tunnel is quite high and wide, its rhombic cross-section five metres tall and ten metres wide at the base with gradually sloping walls. Every surface is sheathed in shining metal panels, like steel planks, riveted into the naked rock. A few people go this way and that, paying us almost no attention at all. Most of them are Guardsmen, but the odd Administratum scribe goes past now and then. Lorii and I wander along the corridor a bit until we come to a junction, much narrower and leading off in a curve to our right. We lean against the wall and start chatting, eyes looking over each other's shoulders for a sign of someone who might be the sort of man we're looking for. To everyone else, we just look like we're loafing, merely off-duty Guardsmen passing the time.

'Do you think we can pull this off?' Lorii asks, keeping her voice low, a gentle purr in fact.

'If anyone can, it's us,' I assure her, scratching at an itch on my thigh caused by the coarse material of the white Typhon trousers.

'It's still not going to be easy taking this place, even with the power down,' she says with a wry look.

'I've been thinking about that, and I don't reckon there'll be anything to take after we've done,' I reply, voicing a suspicion that's been growing in my mind since the Colonel outlined his plan.

'I don't get you,' she says with a little frown creasing her thin white eyebrows.

'This idea about getting to the plasma chambers and shutting them down…' I start but fall silent when she gives me an urgent glance and then flicks her gaze over my shoulder along the main corridor behind me. I push myself off the wall and glance back. Walking towards us are three men, two of them in security uniforms that we've seen before – deep blue jump-suits, metal batons hanging off leather belts, peaked caps instead of helmets. The man between the two security officials wears a similar outfit, but with red piping running the length of his sleeves and legs. He carries a short cane under one arm, like a drill sergeant I guess, and his stern demeanour shows that he's nobody to mess with. As they walk past we fall in a few metres behind them. I slip a short-bladed knife into my hand, procured from a kitchen we raided for food last night, and we quicken our step. Looking around to check we're alone, we make our move.

The security man on the right, in front of me, hears our footsteps and turns. Lorii and I pounce at the same time, my knife slamming into the left eye of the one who's looking back at us. Lorii wraps her arms around the head and neck of the other like a snake and with one violent twist and a hideous cracking noise, snaps his neck in two. The officer reacts quickly, lashing out at me with his cane. It just brushes my left arm but must be charged or something, because it sends a shock of pain up to my shoulder. Lorii's in too fast for him to get a second blow, bringing her knee up into the elbow of his out-stretched arm and chopping down on his wrist with her right hand, breaking his arm and sending the cane clanging to the floor. His gives a shout of agony and Lorii brings her left arm sharply back, slam-ming the outside edge of her hand across his nose, snapping his head back. His legs buckle as blood streams down his face and she lashes out with a kick that connects with his chin and poleaxes him to the ground, completely out of it.

We're just recovering our breath, wondering what to do next, when from the next side corridor appears a clericus, staring intently at an opened scroll in his hands.

'Frag!' I spit, and he looks up, eyes widening comically as he sees the two of us crouched over what looks like three dead security men. I go to leap after him but my whole left side is going numb with the shock from the cane and I slump to one side. The adept gives a shriek, drops the parchment and turns to run, but Lorii's up and after him, five strides from her long, slim legs propelling her right up to him. She leaps into the air, her right foot striking out, smashing perfectly into the base of his skull and pitching him onto his face as she lands lightly on her feet. She grabs his head in both hands, and as with the security guard, breaks his spine as if wringing the neck of some fowl for dinner.

Luckily for us nobody else comes along and we find an empty ter-minal room behind the first door we open. Piling the dead men inside, I shut the door and then ram the blade of my knife into the lock on the door, snapping it off with a twist of my wrist.

'Hopefully nobody'll be too bothered about getting in there,' I say as we grab an arm each of the officer and start dragging him along the corridor.

'Those were some pretty special moves you had there,' I comment as we get to the junction, and Lorii peeks around the corner.

'Special training,' she replies, waving me on.

'What *was* your unit before you were sent to the penal battalion?' I ask, realising that everything we knew about the twins starts from after they were discharged.

'It was a special infiltration force. Fifty of us,' she tells me, return-ing to pick up her end of the unconscious Typhon officer. 'I can't really talk about it.'

'Were you… special in that outfit?' I ask, picking my words carefully considering Loron's earlier warning about remarks concerning their outlandish appearance.

'Oh no,' she says, glancing at me with a smile. 'We were all like that. It was part of our unique, erm, preparation and training.'

The feeling is returning to my left arm now and I heft the unconscious rebel over my shoulders and we run for it. We get to the door where the others are waiting and I knock on it with my foot.

'Yes?' I hear the Colonel saying from inside.

'It's us, you stupid fraggers, let us in!' I snap tersely through the gap between the door and the frame, my face resting against the cold metal of the door, my shoulder beginning to ache from its oblivious burden. The door opens a crack and I barge it open, throwing Striden to the floor, a pistol in his hand. I unceremoniously dump the security officer at Gudmanz's feet with vocal relief, as Lorii kicks the door shut behind us.

'This one do?' I ask Gudmanz. 'Cos if it don't, you can fraggin' well get your own one next time!'

'He is alive?' the Colonel asks as a groan escapes our prisoner's lips and he begins to move sluggishly.

'Oh, that's not necessary,' Gudmanz assures us, laboriously kneeling down beside the prone traitor, his fingers doing something to the man's neck that I can't quite see. When the tech-priest has finished, our captive has become a corpse, his face flushed red with blood.

'What did you do then?' asks Striden bending for a closer look, curiosity and excitement flashing across his face.

'I merely manipulated the flow of blood in his carotid artery and jugular vein to create a haemorrhaging effect in his brain,' the tech-priest explains, in the same matter-of-fact tone I can imagine him using to describe how to operate a comm-link frequency dial. I give an involuntarily shudder and step away.

'What do we do with him now?' asks the Colonel, still sitting where he was when we left a few minutes ago. Gudmanz looks at me as he pushes himself to his feet, joints cracking loudly in protest at this harsh treatment.

'We need a saw of some kind,' he says, looking expectantly at me, withered head cocked to one side.

'Oh, bugger off,' I reply miserably.

* * *

CONSIDERING THE TROUBLE we had to go through to get everything Gudmanz wanted in the end, it might have been easier just to single-handedly storm the accessway. As we march purposefully up the main access corridor towards the two guards stationed by the portal to the next ring, I offer a silent prayer to the Emperor that this ridiculous scheme works. In the end we decided it would be best to break into an infirmary to get all the items on Gudmanz's list. The Colonel, Loron, Striden and me back-tracked to a traumarium a couple of kilometres back the way we came. We knew it'd be impossible to find any medical facility in the citadel that wasn't crammed with war wounded, and decided just to go for the nearest one. So it was that Striden was dragged by us, kicking and screaming enough to be heard across the system, into the infirmary, clasping his hands over his face.

'Plasma blindness,' the Colonel said curtly as the medicos clustered around.

I dropped Striden and made my way into the next room, where there's about fifty wounded soldiers, some of them in beds, most on rough pallets strewn across the floor. The ward stinks of blood and infection, tinged with the bitter smell of old hygienic fluids. Back in the other room, Loron covered the door into the medical centre. I didn't see what happened next, but the Colonel strode into the ward, a bunch of brass keys in his hand. He detailed me to dispose of the bodies while he fetched the surgical tools Gudmanz needed. I went back into the other room and saw Loron and Striden looking strangely at each other. I glanced down at the two dead medicos and see that their faces are contorted as if shouting but can't find any other mark on them. I asked the other two what the Colonel did, but they refused, saying some things were best forgotten.

And that's how we get here, the Colonel dressed up in the security officer's uniform, boldly walking towards the two guards. They straighten up as they see us approach, exchanging a quick glance with each other. Neither of them says a word as the Colonel and Gudmanz step up to a red glass panel set into the wall on the right side of the door. Gudmanz is standing between the guards and Schaeffer, hands held innocently behind his back, so that they can't see what I can.

The Colonel pulls the security officer's severed hand from the darkness of Gudmanz's sleeve and deftly fits the tube projecting from its sutured wrist into the intravenum Gudmanz inserted into his arm earlier. With his own pulse stimulating a fake heartbeat in the dead hand, the Colonel places it against the screen and a beam of yellow light plays between the fingertips, apparently reading the pattern on the end of the fingers. The screen changes to green and a tone sounds from a speaker set in the ceiling. As expertly as he attached it, the Colonel disconnects the hand from himself and passes it back to Gudmanz.

The two security men salute as we walk through the opening gates, standing to attention with their laser carbines along the seams of their right leg, their faces staring obediently into the middle distance. It's a position I learnt well when on garrison duty.

'Hurry up,' hisses the Colonel between tight lips when we're a few metres further down the tunnel. Walking next to him, I look over with a puzzled look. He notices my stare and glances down at his right hand before fixing his look ahead of him again. I surreptitiously look down and a lump appears in my throat when I realise an occasional droplet of blood is running down his wrist, gathering on his fingers and sporadically dripping to the floor. I glance back over my shoulder and luckily the two guards are still in their parade ground position, but it won't be long before one of them looks our way and sees the faint trail of blood on the metal flooring. We take the next quiet turning, the first couple had some people in them, and break into a run, sending Lorii ahead to check it out first. She comes back and guides us along a deserted route until we find an empty hab-complex. The floor is patterned with red and white triangular tiles, I guess the Typhons must really like triangles. The underground houses show signs of being in use, but no one seems to be around at the moment. Loron starts checking the twenty or so glass-panelled doors around the circular communal area at the centre of the little complex, and the third one he tries is unlocked.

'I remember the days when you could leave your door unlocked without fear,' jokes Lorii.

Hurrying through, we find ourselves in a dining chamber, a small kitchen area at one end. There's more tiling on the floors and walls, in two different shades of blue. The Colonel rips the intravenum from his arm and flings it into a waste grinder beside the small cooking stove.

'I thought these were supposed to seal up without the tube inserted!' the Colonel barks loudly at Gudmanz, who flinches from Schaeffer's anger.

'There must have been some flow-back from the rebel's hand,' he explains with his hands raised slightly in a placating gesture.

'They were not designed for this kind of procedure, please remember.'

The Colonel calms down slightly and we nose around the hab-pen. There are two small bedrooms off the living space, and they have their own ablutions area, complete with a basin and bathtub.

'Lucky bastards,' I say to Striden as he splashes cold water over his face. 'My barracks were never like this.'

'These are not barracks, Kage,' I hear the Colonel correct me from the front chamber. 'The second and third rings are the factory areas. This is where the civilians live.'

'Civilians?' says Lorii, popping her head round one of the bedroom doors, a dark red floppy felt hat on her head.

'Yes, civilians,' repeats the Colonel. 'This is the capital city of Typhos Prime, it is not just a fortress. And take that stupid thing off!'

Lorii disappears again, muttering something about the hat suiting her. Loron, who's by the front door keeping watch, gives an urgent hiss.

'Someone's coming!' he whispers, backing away from the glass panel.

When a figure appears right outside the door, we bundle into one of the bedrooms, while the Colonel peers out through the living space. I can hear the front door opening and closing and the Colonel ducks back inside, face screwed up in consternation. It's strange to note how much more alive he seems to have become since we got inside Coritanorum. It's like this is the only thing he lives for. Perhaps it is.

The door to the bedroom opens and a plump, middle-aged woman steps in. Quick as a flash, Kronin grabs her from behind the door, clamping a bony hand across her mouth.

'And the Emperor sayeth that the meek and silent shall be rewarded,' he whispers gently into her ear. Her eyes are rolling left and right, looking at the strangers in her bedroom, terror in her mad glances.

'What the frag do we do with her?' I ask the Colonel, as Kronin leads her over to the bed. He puts a finger to his lips and she nods understanding, and he lets her go. She gives a fearful whimper but doesn't scream.

'We can't take her with us, and she'll be discovered if we leave her here,' says Lorii, eyeing our captive with a frown.

'You can't just kill her!' Striden exclaims, stepping protectively between the Colonel and the woman.

'She's already dead,' Gudmanz says quietly in his grating voice. The Colonel looks at me and gives a slight nod. With his attention fixed on the Colonel, Striden doesn't see me cross to the side of the bed. The woman is also staring at the Colonel, probably wondering why a security officer is in her home.

I lean across the bed and before the woman knows what's happening I grab her throat in both hands. She gives a stifled cry, and lashes out blindly, her fingernails clawing at my face. She writhes and squirms as I squeeze tighter, her eyes locking on mine, alternating looks of pleading and anger. I feel someone grabbing at my shoulders, Striden shouting something in my ear, but my whole universe is just me and the woman. Her thrashing grows sluggish and her arms drop to the bedclothes, which have been rucked up around her with her struggling. With a final effort I squeeze the life out of her, her dead eyes looking at me with a mixture of confusion and accusation. I feel someone dragging the Navy lieutenant off my back, and I let go of her throat slowly. I look down at her pleasant face, purple from the choking now, and I don't feel anything. No guilt or remorse.

Inside, another human part of me seems to die.

'That was too extreme,' Loron says with a doubtful look, as I pull myself off the bed.

'Like Gudmanz said, she's already dead,' I tell them. 'They're all dead if we succeed, all three million of them.'

'What?' asks Lorii, walking over to the bed and closing the dead woman's eyes with her fingertips.

'We're not going to shut down the plasma reactors, are we, Colonel?' I say, turning to face Schaeffer.

'No,' he says simply, shaking his head.

'I'm not a tech-priest, but the hive I'm from ran on plasma reactors,' I tell them, flopping down onto a plastic chair in front of what looks to be a dressing table. 'Once they start, you don't shut them down, it's a self-fuelling process. But you can make them overload.'

'We're going to overload one of the plasma reactors?' asks Loron, turning on Gudmanz and the Colonel, who are standing by the door.

'All three of them, actually,' replies Gudmanz. 'They are omaphagically linked, if one of them fails, they all fail.'

'Call me stupid,' says Lorii, sitting on the edge of the bed, 'but I still don't see where this is going. We kill the power by overloading the reactors, not shutting them down, so what?'

Gudmanz sighs heavily and lowers himself onto the bed next to Lorii, weariness in every movement.

'Let me try to explain in terms you might understand,' he says, looking at all of us in turn. 'A plasma reactor is, in essence, a minia-ture star captured inside graviometric and electromagnetic force walls. If you remove the Machine God's blessing from those shields, the star goes into a chain reaction, resulting ultimately in detonation. Three plasma reactors fuelling each other's chain reactions will create an explosion roughly sixty kilometres in every direction.'

'Nothing but ash will be left,' adds the Colonel, 'and at the heart, not even the ash will survive.'

'Sounds like an extreme way to win a war,' offers Striden, who's not calmed down at all.

'It has to be done this way. I will not tell you any more,' the Colonel says insistently. 'We must get moving, I want to find another termi-nal, so that Gudmanz can check what the security teams are doing. I expect at least one body has been found by now, and I want to know if they suspect any kind of enemy infiltration. We will have to pro-ceed even more carefully.'

ABOUT HALF AN hour later and we're walking along what appears to be a main thoroughfare across the factory area. Massive shuttered gateways fill one wall, indicating closed sites, to provide workers for the munitions works, I suspect. The ceiling and walls here are brick-lined rather than metal, but the now-familiar Typhon fondness for different colours in geometric patterns can be seen in a huge mosaic that covers the floor of the twenty-metre wide passageway. Apart from Gudmanz who wears his robe as normal, tech-priests are a fre-quent sight around here by the look of it, we're dressed in civilian garb looted from the hab-pens where I strangled the woman. Lorii has a rather fetching light blue dress, and the hat she was so fond of, while her brother, Striden and myself are dressed in dun-coloured worker's coveralls.

The Colonel, rot his soul, managed to find what might have been a wedding suit or something, tight black breeches and a long-tailed dark blue coat. It's not as out of place as you might think, it seems the sort of outfit the higher-ranking civilians wear around here. Kro-nin found a rough-spun jerkin and some leggings that fitted his short, wiry frame and from the tools we found in that home, I guess they used to belong to a spanner-boy. We used to have them back on Olympas, well they still do I guess. Their job is to crawl into the bow-els of machinery and tighten up gears and chains. It's a dangerous job, because you can't afford to stop the machines running, and you can easily lose a limb or your head to some whirling arm or pumping piston. One of the cruellest things I saw was to send in a couple of other spanner-boys to remove a body that was clogging up a transmission mechanism. Of course, during a full trade war, their job is the opposite – they sneak into the enemy factories for a bit of sabotage.

We're almost unarmed, we ditched our captured guns into a waste grinder in the hab complex. I've got a knife secreted in my coveralls though, I'm not totally defenceless. There's a lot more people around here at the moment. I think it must be a shift change, a klaxon sounded a few minutes ago and the streets, well I call them streets but they're just wide corridors really, are packed with the throng. I feel more at home here, underground. When I've been in other towns I always have the strange sensation that someone's stolen the roof. Being brought up on a hive makes you like that, I guess. We've split up a bit so as not to attract too much attention, after Gudmanz told us to keep heading anti-clockwise around the second ring.

Gudmanz found another terminal to plug into, and says that the security forces have been wildly sending reports around. Some smart officer has realised there's a connection between the flurry of murders in the outer ring and the bloodstains found near the gate to the next circle. There's also the question of the dead troopers at the gatehouse, and they've tightened up security on the third ring, the one we've got to get into next. Gudmanz assures us that there's a lot more through-traffic between the second and third circles, as they are both civilian areas, but if the guards are getting itchy, there could be all kinds of problems.

Strolling along with Striden, who's been in a silent, tetchy mood since I had to kill the woman, I catch snippets of conversations from the people around. Most of them are chatting about usual stuff – how the boss is having an affair with some wench from the factory floor, what the plans for the wedding will be, how the food in the factory kitchens has been getting worse lately. Day-to-day life that denies the raging conflict only a short distance away.

But they do talk about the war a bit, and that's what's started confusing me. They keep talking about the 'damned rebels' and 'traitor army' camped outside their walls. These people seem to think that we're the rebels, not them. They accuse the rebels, I mean the Imperium actually, of starting the war, of attacking without provocation. I'd ask the Colonel about it if I thought there was any point, but I don't reckon he'd give me a straight answer.

As the people around disperse a bit more, I catch a glimpse of Kronin ahead of us, looking like he's having an argument with a couple of the locals. He must have got separated from Loron, who was supposed to be looking after the headcase. Cursing to myself I hurry forward.

'Just asking for an apology, I am, ' one of the factory workers is saying angrily, hands on hips. His face is pitted with burn scars and his head is beginning to go bald. Kronin's not a tall man, but he's still a couple of centimetres taller than this tiny fellow.

'And all were blessed in the sight of the Emperor,' says Kronin, getting worked up, frustrated that he can't make himself understood.

'Stop saying that stuff,' the other worker snarls. 'You a preacher or something, you think?'

'Why don't we all settle down!' calls Striden as we jog up to them.

'Who the hell, off-worlder, are you?' demands the first, turning to confront us. His friend steps up next to him, offering support with his threatening posture. He's more my height, and his thick biceps and solid forearms show he's no stranger to heavy manual labour. He looks like he can handle himself, but then again so can I.

'Bad news for you, if you don't frag off this instant!' I hiss at them, squaring up to the pair of them.

'You're all the same, coming down here, to tell us how to run them factories!' the second one says, pointing an accusing finger at me. 'Treats us like we just fell outta the sky, you do. 'Bout time somebody's put in their place, ask me.'

I just laugh, I can't stop myself. It's so ridiculous, the irony is outstanding. I've fought in a dozen wars and now I'm about to get in a fight with a couple of factory workers because I talk with an off-world accent. There's a manic edge to my laugh that makes them stare closely at me, suddenly wary.

'All mad, you are!' spits the first one, throwing his arms up in disgust. 'All of you off-worlders.'

'Mad enough,' I say, putting every ounce of menace I can into those two words. The tall one realises the threat isn't empty and grabs his friend by the shoulders, pulling him away. The short one keeps looking back at us, hurling abuse back at us, causing some of the passers-by to look.

'You!' I snarl at Kronin, grabbing the front of his coveralls and dragging him up to his toes. 'You keep next to me and don't say nothing!'

Pushing the two other Last Chancers ahead of me, I cast one final look around. There's a security team, three men, walking further along the corridor, and I see a young woman hurrying over towards them. I start to walk faster, trying to hurry but be inconspicuous at the same time, which is some feat I'll tell you. I hear a shout to stop from behind.

'Frag!' I curse, breaking into a run and grabbing the other two as I run between them. 'Get your legs moving, we're in trouble!'

THE PAST TWO hours have been the worst in my life. I've seen neither hide nor hair of the Colonel, Loron, Lorii or Gudmanz, and the three of us have been ducking and diving like mad as security teams poured into the factory area. At one point we rounded a corner and walked slap-bang straight into five of them. Luckily, Kronin and me were quicker on the uptake and took them down with only a short fight. These ones were armed as well, which was a first, carrying heavy automatic pistols, which the three of us relieved their unconscious bodies of. Which all leads up to where I am now, crouching with a pistol in each hand at the top of a ladder while Striden and Kronin are behind me trying to prise the grille off a ventilation duct. It was a stroke of pure luck that we took the turning that led here, a district of abandoned factories. Another fortunate twist brought us to this air filtration plant, and from there it was an easy choice to decide to get off the streets for a while. We're not totally alone though, I can hear security men shouting to each other in the distance. I've got no idea what's happening outside, but I can see nobody's entered the building yet.

There's a clang as they drop the grille to the floor and I wince, wondering if anyone else heard it. Turning, I see Striden grinning back at me.

'You two in first, go left and keep heading that way, don't turn off at all until we can work out some kind of plan,' I tell them, peering down the ladder again to check no one's nearby. The rockcrete-floored plant is as deserted as it was a moment before. Satisfied that it's safe, I push myself up through the grille and follow the other two.

'FRAG IT!' I shout, slamming my fist against the metal lining of the conduit. 'For Emperor's sake, give me a break!'

I slump to the ground, teeth gritted with frustration. For half an hour we've crawled along this duct, and when it widened out I thought we were getting somewhere. I was wrong. About twenty metres ahead of us, a massive fan is spinning, blocking any route forward. Crawling around in the darkness, never sure if you're going to pitch down some hole in the blackness, my nerves have started to jangle. And this is all I need, to have to backtrack a couple of hundred metres or so to the last turning.

Pulling myself together I stand up and walk closer to the extraction fan. It isn't going that fast, too fast to jump past though, and beyond its blades I can see an area that looks like the communal foyer of a hab area. Like most of Coritanorum, the area is tiled with different colours and shapes, a stark contrast to the grimy, dull metal of the hive factories where I'm from. I can see two children sitting in the middle of the open area, playing some kind of game with their hands. All in all, it doesn't look like an unpleasant place to be brought up, even with a war raging outside the walls. Studying the fan itself, it seems to be made of some kind of ceramic, about twice as wide as my outstretched arms. There's a thin metal mesh on the far side, clogged up in places with bits of dirt and stuff, so I guess it's there to stop the fan being jammed.

'Back up a bit,' I tell the others as I pace back from the fan, drawing the pistols from where they're rammed into the belt of my coveralls.

'What are you doing?' asks Striden, looking at the pistols.

'Taking the initiative,' I tell him, aiming both pistols down the duct. The muzzle flare is blinding as it reflects off the metal of the air shaft and the conduit rings with the roar of firing. As I hoped the fan shatters into shards which fly in all directions. With my ears recovering, I hear shouts from the end of the duct. I push myself forwards past the wreckage of the fan drive system. There's about two dozen people clustered into the communal area now, all looking up at me standing at the end of the duct, pistol in each hand. I kick out the grille, forcing some of them to jump back as it clatters to the ground.

'Anyone moves, I kill them,' I tell them, keeping my voice calm and steady. I mean it as well. I look down at their dumbfounded faces, and all I can see in my mind's eye are little piles of ashes. They're all dead if we succeed. They're walking corpses. Kronin and Striden crowd in behind me and I lower myself the couple of metres down the wall, whipping round with the pistols to make sure nobody gets too close. The two children are clinging to their mother, a slim young woman dressed in red coveralls, their eyes wide with fear. But they're not two children really, just two tiny, pathetic piles of ash. I hear the other two dropping behind me and Kronin steps up next to me, a pistol in his hand.

As we walk forward, the crowd parts around us, everybody's attention fixed with grim fascination on the strange men who have dropped into their lives so violently and unexpectedly. We've almost reached the corridor leading off from the hab-pens when some idiot hero makes a lunge for Kronin's gun. The pistols in my hand spit death, flinging his ragged corpse into the crowd, who immediately break into hysterical screaming, fleeing towards the safety of their homes. Breaking into a run of our own, we hurry off. I don't even spare a second thought for the dead man in the plaza.

DITCHING THE GUNS into a waste shaft – they'd be no use really and are far too conspicuous – we make our way towards the next gate. Well, as far as I can tell, my sense of direction is somewhat turned on its head by the time spent in the air ducts. We come across some kind of market place, a huge open space full of stalls, many of which seemed to be closed down. I guess there isn't too much to sell really, as Coritanorum is under siege. An immense bronze statue, of Macharius I think, dominates the centre of the plaza, stood upon a marble pedestal a clear three metres taller than me. The place is quite busy though, and gives us plenty of cover to avoid the few guards prowling around, ducking into the crowds if they get too close. Most of the people around are women and young children, I assume the older children and men are working hard in the factories and struggling to maintain this huge citadel as the noose of the Imperial forces outside tightens even more. I wonder what the hell has happened to the rest of the Last Chancers, and I'd happily let them go off and finish the mission while we hole up somewhere. That isn't an option, though – unless I fancy being fried by a plasma explosion.

We manage to get back onto the main corridor eventually, running in a wide circle around the second ring. From there it's easy to get my bearings and we hurry as much as possible. I've got no idea what we'll do once we get to the accessway, or how we're going to link up with the Colonel, but I decide that we need to worry about one thing at a time for the moment. An increase in the frequency of the guards warns when we start getting close to the linking tunnel, and we walk straight past it, getting a glance at how well manned it is. I can't stop and count without arousing too much suspicion, but I reckon on a dozen men at least. We walk about another hundred metres down the corridor when we come across what looks like a guardhouse, the symbol of the security forces blazoned onto the solid double doors. No one is around, not even a security team, and I saunter closer for a better look, the other two trailing dumbly behind me, quite content just to follow my lead. Realising that there's nothing to be done here, I turn to walk away. At that moment I hear the doors grinding open behind me and a shiver runs down my back as I hear someone walking out.

I hear the Colonel's voice behind me. 'Get in here, you idiot!'

TWENTY DEAD SECURITY guards lie inside the station, which doesn't appear to be anything more than a terminal room, with a few cells to one side. Once more, there's a mosaic, this time a representation of some battle from the past rather than abstract shapes. I can't tell what it is, the bodies of the dead security men obscure too much of it. Their bloated faces match those of the Guardsmen in the gate tower, reminding me that we're not the only ones fighting against the rebels from within.

'You took your time,' Loron says as we stroll in.

'What happened here?' Striden asks, looking at all the corpses.

'Dead when we arrived,' answers Lorii with a shrug. 'I guess our invisible helper from the gatehouse is still watching over us.'

'Have you been deliberately trying to get caught, Kage?' demands Schaeffer, closing the doors behind us. He gestures towards Gudmanz, who is sitting at the largest terminal, plugged in again. 'We have access to the whole security network from here and have been monitoring the comm-channels. We have been tracking reports of your whereabouts for the past four hours. Luckily for you, Gudmanz managed to conjure up some false reports and a fake fire emergency to lead them off the trail.'

'So how do we get past the next gate?' asks Striden. 'They'll be extra cautious now.'

'We will just walk through, as we did last time,' the Colonel tells us, gesturing to the uniformed men lying around us. 'Security teams have been going through each way for the past two hours, one more will not arouse any undue attention.'

Everyone's attention is drawn to Gudmanz when he gives a gasp, and as I look at him the neural plug whips back into his head and he slumps further into the chair.

'What is it?' asks the Colonel, going over to lean on the back of the chair and stare at the half dozen screens on the terminal face.

'I cannot use the terminal network any more,' he tells us slowly, recovering from some kind of shock. 'They realised what I was doing and other tech-priests started scanning the network for me. I manage to eject just before they found me, but only because I have had more practice at this type of thing over the past two days. They will find me straight away if I go in again.'

'What was the last thing you found out?' asks Schaeffer, turning his head from the screens to look at the tech-priest.

'There has been nothing to suggest that they know we are heading for the plasma reactors,' he reassures us. 'They suspect we might be trying to get to one of the turret clusters in the central keep. They have no idea that we are here for something far more unpleasant than disabling a few cannons.'

'Good, then we will press on,' the Colonel says, standing up and passing an eye over the dead security men in the room. 'We should be able to get to the last access tunnel before night, the third ring is not very big at all.'

'And then what?' Loron asks, crouching down to strip the coveralls from a likely sized guard.

'We finish our mission,' the Colonel replies grimly.

'I'VE BEEN THINKING about our mysterious guardian,' says Lorii as we walk down a flight of steps that take us away from the main corridor in the third circle. 'Why didn't they blow up the reactors?'

'It is a very complex process, to curse a containment field of the type we are talking about,' explains Gudmanz as he hobbles down the rockcrete steps in front of us. 'The bulk of a plasma reactor is dedicated to creating wards and heligrams to make sure the Machine God's blessing remains. Many fail-safes will stop you, you cannot just touch a rune and say a few canticles to turn them off. It takes one of my order to do it.'

'And I can see why you couldn't be sent in alone,' adds Loron from above, referring to the tech-priest's increasing frailty. It's as if he's ageing a year every hour, he's slowed down that much since we met him three days ago. He said he would last a month, but looking at his current condition, I can't imagine him seeing the end of the day after next. The Colonel's gone tight-lipped on us again, obviously tensing up the closer we get to our goal. He was almost human for a while, but has reverted to man-machine mode now.

The third ring is similar to the second, terraces of factories interspersed with mazes of hab-pens. There's the strange mix of metal panelling, brickwork and tiling that can be found in the outer rings. Trying to imagine the pattern of different styles in my head, with what little I know of Coritanorum's layout, it seems to me that originally this area was in fact several different citadels, which over time have slowly been joined together, with the central access tunnels constructed to link them all together at some later point.

As nightfall approaches outside, things start to get a lot quieter. We see fewer people, many of them security guards who we swap salutes with before hurrying on. As we approach the final accessway, the sprawling rooms become more military looking, with lots of terminal chambers, and what appear to be barracks. I can feel everyone getting more nervous as we march along the twisting corridors, and I try to distract the other Last Chancers to stop them getting too jumpy.

'I wonder how Linskrug is doing?' I ask in general.

'Glad he isn't here, I bet,' Lorii ventures, casting an edgy glance down a side tunnel.

'He's dead,' the Colonel informs us quietly from where he's walking ahead of us.

'How can you possibly know that?' asks Loron.

'Because the penal legion he was sent to was the one ordered to make the diversionary attack when we came in through the sally port,' he explains, not looking at us.

'And turning from the flames Saint Baxter leapt from the cliffs,' says Kronin, half to himself.

'He might still have survived,' Loron says, grasping at a shred of hope for our departed comrade.

'No,' the Colonel tells us. 'I personally gave Commissar Handel strict instructions that they were to fight to the last man. He will have carried out his orders to the letter.'

We walk on in silence for another couple of minutes, pondering this turn of events.

'What would you have done if we all refused this mission?' asks Loron as the Colonel takes us down a left turn, leading us across a gantry that passes over what looks to be a metalworks, the furnaces dead at the moment. 'You'd be fragged if at least half of us had turned you down.'

'I admit that I did not expect Linskrug to refuse,' says the Colonel, still facing forward. 'I thought that none of you would turn down the opportunity I presented you with. Linskrug had less character than I credited him with.'

'Why so certain that we'd come along?' Loron persists, hurrying forward to fall into step beside Schaeffer.

'Because that is why you are still here,' he replies. 'You have a lust for life that defies the odds. I knew that if I offered you the chance for freedom you would take it.'

'But Linskrug didn't accept,' crows Loron victoriously. We fall silent for a minute as we reach the end of the gantry and turn into another metal-walled corridor, a couple of scribes coming towards us, giving us suspicious looks as we pass them by.

'That must have rattled you,' Lorii says when the Typhons have disappeared from view. 'You must have been a bit shaken up when Linskrug said no.'

The Colonel stops abruptly, turning on his heel to face us.

'I did not choose to have Linskrug in the Last Chancers, he was forced upon me,' he snarls at us. 'The rest of you, I personally recruited. I studied your files, watched you in battle, and weighed your personalities. I did not wage war on a dozen worlds over three years for no reason. I had to be sure of you.'

With that he turns and stalks away. We exchange stunned glances for a couple of seconds before hurrying after Schaeffer.

'You mean you've known this is what we'd be doing all along?' I ask, amazed at the concept.

'Yes,' is all he replies.

'You mustered four thousand men, when you knew that only a handful would be able to get into this place?' I press on relentlessly.

'Yes,' is all he says again, and I can feel the anger radiating from his body.

'Why?' I demand. 'Why the hell do all that?'

'Because we needed the best, Kage,' he says through gritted teeth. 'Like it or not, the Last Chancers produce the best fighters and survivors in this part of the galaxy. You have all shown the combat skills and qualities of personality needed for this mission. I have tested you to destruction, but I have not been able to destroy you.'

'Tested?' I almost scream at him, curbing my anger at the last moment in case it attracts unwanted attention. It's easy to forget we're in the middle of an enemy stronghold. The off-white lighting of the glowstrips set into the ceiling flickers as we pass into another area, and the corridor seems dimmer than the others. Problems with energy distribution, I reckon. If we're successful, the Typhons' power supply problems are going to get a lot worse.

'It is true,' the Colonel admits, pinching the bridge of his nose like he's got a headache or something. 'Many of the events over the past three years have been chosen or engineered to focus on different

parts of your military ability and personality traits. They have tested
your initiative and resourcefulness. They have examined your determination, sense of duty, discipline and responses to fear. I admit it is
not a precise process, but I think you will agree that I have managed
to turn all the situations to my advantage, and along the way we have
helped win a few wars. Is that so bad?'

'Not a precise process?' I spit angrily. 'I guess the Heart of the Jungle was a little bit unexpected, wasn't it? And what about the eldar
attack on the transport? Inconvenient was it? And the shuttle crashing in Hypernol?'

He doesn't reply, simply keeps marching resolutely along the corridor. Then my brain catches up with the rest of me as his earlier
words sink in.

'You said engineered,' I say, surprised that I can get even angrier at
what this man has done to us.

'Yes,' he admits, glancing back over his shoulder at me. 'Mostly I
chose situations that would provoke the required conditions, but
some had to be set up deliberately. The shuttle crash was one of those
situations. You cannot just hope for that sort of thing to happen, can
you?'

That's the final twist, something inside me snaps. I jump forward
and lay a hand on Schaeffer's shoulder and spin him around. Before
I can do anything else, he slaps me backhanded across the face,
almost knocking me from my feet. I'm stunned by the act as much as
by the pain – I've never before seen him hit a Last Chancer who
didn't attack him first.

'Maintain discipline, Lieutenant Kage,' he says coldly, staring at me
with those glitters of ice he has for eyes. 'I will no longer tolerate this
insubordination.'

I'm half-shocked and half-not by this news. Our suspicion had
been growing over the past few months in particular, but the extent
to which the Colonel has created and manipulated events is almost
unbelievable. I begin to wonder how often he's done this before.
How many times has he killed thousands of soldiers to see who were
the best, the greatest survivors? How many times more would he do
it? It seems such a merciless, uncaring thing to do, but part of me can
see his reasoning. It's a merciless, uncaring galaxy we live in, and if
other missions were as important as this one, to save whole worlds,
I could just about forgive him. Just about. It still doesn't explain why
he was still so secretive about the mission goals. Did he really think
we'd back down when we realised what was at stake? Does he think

so little of us he doesn't believe we have at least that much decency and courage we'd be willing to fight for the sake of a world of people, for the hundreds of thousands of Guardsmen and Navy personnel who'd lose their lives trying to take the place by force?

We walk on in resentful silence.

FINDING WHAT LOOKS to be a deserted archive room, we hide out and formulate the next part of our plan. Rows and rows of parchments, dataslabs and crystal disks surround us on endless shelves. Hidden among the teetering mass of information, we cluster around a battered wooden table, looking intently at a copy of Coritanorum's innermost layout, brought forth like magic from one of Gudmanz's voluminous sleeves.

'Our benefactor have anything lined up for this one?' asks Loron, leaning across the schematic at the far end of the table.

'We will have to work this out ourselves,' the Colonel replies, shaking his head. All eyes turn to Gudmanz.

'This will not be easy,' he says heavily, taking a deep sigh. 'To open the gate requires a retinal scan.'

'A what?' asks Lorii, looking across from where she's perched on the edge of the table, bent over the map.

'Remember at the first gate, the scanner read the skin indentations of the security officer's fingertips?' he asks, and we all nod in agreement. Who could forget that macabre episode? 'Well, this portal has a device that can map the blood vessels within your eyeball.'

'An eye?' exclaims Striden, looking thoroughly disconsolate. He had been starting to cheer up again, getting over the grisly episode with the woman, I guess. 'That's going to be even trickier than getting a hand!'

'Forget about eyeballs,' says the Colonel quietly and we turn to look at him, sat a little away from the table in a padded armchair, right elbow resting on the arm, fingers cradling his chin. 'We will do this the easy way.'

NOW, I WOULDN'T say that the Colonel's way was going to be easy, but it's certainly a lot more straightforward. There's two Guardsmen stood outside the armoury as we approach, lasguns held at the ready. They ease up slightly as they see the Colonel, in his senior security officer's uniform, but are obviously on their toes. The Colonel walks up to the opticon eye set next to the armoured portal in the weapons store.

'State your business,' a disembodied voice says from a speaker grill just above the opticon.

'Permission to enter?' asks the Colonel, in a near-perfect imitation of the burr of a Typhon accent.

'We've orders to let no one in,' says the Guardsman from inside.

'I've got written confirmation,' replies the Colonel, waving a bunch of important-looking films that we scrounged from the data library. We wait for about half a minute, exchanging nonchalant shrugs with the two Guardsmen as we wait for the other man's decision.

'Them orders – let's see them,' he says finally and there's a loud clank as a lock-bar drops away from the door and it swings open on powered hinges. The Colonel strides purposefully in and the door whines shut behind him.

Striden's almost hopping from foot to foot with nerves and I give him a stern glare, hoping he'll calm down before the Guardsmen get suspicious. I feel a trickle of sweat running down my right side and have to fight my own unease, hoping it doesn't show.

'Taking his time, isn't he?' comments one of the Guardsmen, glancing back over his shoulder at the heavily constructed door. I just murmur and nod in agreement, not trusting my linguistic ability to impersonate a Typhon. It was probably a smart move to leave Loron, Lorii and Gudmanz in the archive chamber. These Guardsmen seem to be keyed up at the moment, and they're bound to have been told to be on the lookout for any pale-skinned strangers with a tech-priest. I suspect the Colonel's plan is the best one now; the chances of pulling off a fancy subterfuge at the last access tunnel have passed us by.

The awkward silence is broken by the portal hissing open again. The Colonel stands there with a compact stub gun in his right hand, a bulky silencer screwed on to the end of the barrel. The talkative Guardsman looks back and his eyes widen in surprise a moment before the first bullet smashes his head to a pulp, spraying blood and brains across the floor just to my right. The other Guardsman turns quickly, but his lasgun is only half-raised when the next shot punches into his chest, hurling him back against the wall.

'Grab them and drag them inside,' orders the Colonel, taking a step out of the armoury. 'I have signalled the others in the archive room from inside, they will be here shortly. And find something to clear up that mess.'

* * *

'TIME TO GET serious,' Lorii says as we walk together between the high-stacked crates of power cells and ammunition.

'Let's just hope nobody else drops in for fresh supplies,' comments Loron from behind me.

'We want something with a bit more firepower than lasguns,' the Colonel tells us from up ahead, as he scans the rows of boxes and racks of guns. 'We need one-hit kills if we are going to challenge their numbers.'

We search around for a few more minutes before Gudmanz uncovers a shelf of fifteen bolters. Freshly cleaned, they gleam in the bright, white light of the armoury, in my eye as beautiful as they are deadly.

'Ammunition is in those bins overhead,' says Gudmanz, pointing to a row of black containers hung over the bolters. Lorii grabs one and pulls it down, letting it drop to the floor. Inside are dozens of bolter magazines, loaded and ready to go. She and Loron start transferring the ammo to the heavy work trolley pushed by Striden.

'I want something with a better rate of fire,' I mutter to myself, looking around for a more suitable weapon.

'And the Emperor's rewards are bountiful for those who labour in His name,' says Kronin with a smile, using a crowbar to lift the lid off a wooden crate, revealing rows of frag grenades within. He starts tossing them to Striden, who places them on the trolley next to the bolters.

'Is this what you would like?' Gudmanz asks, holding up a long rifle. It's finished in black enamel, oozing menace and lethality.

'Ooh, that looks mean,' I say appreciatively, walking closer. 'What is it?'

'Fractrix pattern assault laser,' he says with a smile, running a gnarled hand lovingly along its length. It's the first time he's looked happy since I met him. 'Five shots per second, twin power pack capable of fifteen seconds' continuous fire. Multiple target designation range-finder. I used to be overseer on one of the manufacturing lines,' he adds, glancing at me.

'Reliability?' I ask, knowing that there's always a catch, otherwise everyone would have them.

'Oh, it is very reliable,' he assures me. 'The only drawback is that the focus prism needs to be changed every one thousand shots, and that requires a tech-adept. Not practical for extended battle conditions, but perfect for our task.'

I take the gun from him and heft it to my shoulder, closing my left eye to look through the sight along its length. I can't see anything at all and give a confused glance towards the tech-priest.

'You must disengage the safety link before the optical array is powered up,' he tells me, pointing towards a fingernail-sized stud just above the trigger guard. I give it a push and the assault laser gives a little hum as the power cells warm up. Sighting again, I look back towards the others. In the small circle of the gunsight, each is surrounded by a thin light blue glow, outlining their silhouette.

'It can detect heat patterns as well,' Gudmanz tells me proudly. 'You might not be able to see the person, but you will be able to see their outline.'

I grin to myself, swinging the laser so that it is pointing at the Colonel. One squeeze of the trigger and a storm of las-bolts will tear him into little pieces. I ask myself why I shouldn't do it. Why shouldn't I pull the trigger? But I know the answer really. For a start, I'm beginning to realise that the Colonel wouldn't have done to us what he did, if he thought there was any alternative. He has his own reasons, and to him they justify any act, including killing three million people. I have an idea what it might be, but I'm not sure. Second, he's the only one who has the vaguest chance of getting us out of Coritanorum alive. He has the mysterious contact on the inside, and he's been studying this place longer than any of us, and probably knows more about it even than Gudmanz. I think he's spent the best part of the past three years planning this operation, and I'm sure that includes getting out again in one piece. He might not be planning on bringing us along, who knows, but if I stick close to him then I've got the best chance there is. I press the safety stud again and the small circle goes black.

'Flak jackets and helmets are along the next aisle,' the Colonel says, pointing over to the left. He turns and sees me with the gun pointing towards him. He calmly meets my gaze.

'It suits you,' he says and then turns away, completely unconcerned. He knew he wasn't in any danger. Bastard.

'Right,' I declare, slinging the assault laser over my shoulder by its strap, 'now I need some really good knives.'

'REMEMBER WE NEED one alive,' Gudmanz reminds us as we push the trolley of guns and ammo, concealed under a bundle of camouflage netting, towards the accessway. It must be almost midnight outside, though the glow tubes are shining just as brightly down here as ever. Everybody's sleeping, or at least that's what we hope. According to the schematic, the nearest plasma chamber is only around eight hundred metres from the access portal, so the plan is to hit the enemy hard and fast. We get the guards on the door, using a live one to bypass the eye-scanner, and then leg it as quick as possible, storming the plasma reactor room and then holding off the Typhons while Gudmanz does his thing. The tech-priest thinks it will take a couple of hours to deactivate all the wards on the plasma chambers, hence the gratuitous amount of ammunition on the trolley being pushed beside me by Striden. Six people fighting off an entire city? I fragging hope the Emperor is backing us on this one. Once that happens, we've got roughly a couple of hours to get clear.

We round the corner into the accessway and don't even need the order to open fire. I fire the assault laser from the hip, spraying dozens of red energy bolts into the Typhons by the gateway, pitching men off their feet, scouring burn marks along the walls. Loron and Lorii open up with their bolters, the explosive rounds detonating in a ripple of fiery blossoms, blowing fist-sized holes in the Typhons' chests and tearing off limbs. I see a Guardsman's head blown apart by a direct hit from the Colonel's bolt pistol. One of them manages to return fire, the snap of his lasgun just about heard in breaks between the roar of the bolters. A las-bolt zips off the wall and catches Lorii across the shoulder, spinning her to the ground. Striden brings up his shotgun, the half-random blast shredding the remaining Guardsman, scattering a mist of blood across the passageway. And then, as suddenly as it started, the fight is over. A few seconds of concentrated bloodshed and the job's done.

The Colonel dashes forward and starts picking his way through the mangled remains of the Typhons while we reload. Loron is bent over his twin sister, an anguished look on his face.

'Is she all right?' I ask, walking over.

'I'm fine,' Lorii replies, pushing herself to her feet, blood streaming down her left arm in a red swathe. Loron tears a strip from a dead Guardsman's tunic as Lorii strips off her flak jacket and shirt. Leaving Loron to bandage her, I check on Striden and Kronin, who are at the main corridor end of the accessway, checking nobody is going to stumble upon us. I hear the Colonel give a satisfied grunt and turn to see him dragging one of the Typhons towards the eye-scanning reticule beside the gate. He pushes the man's face into it and a moment later the doors begin to slide open.

'We are in,' says the Colonel, placing his bolt pistol under the Guardsman's chin and blowing his brains out, scattering bits of skull over the scanner and wall. We stand there for a second, staring at the strange scene of the Colonel cradling the headless corpse.

'Get moving!' he shouts, dropping the body with a thump, and we jump to it, Kronin and Striden grab the trolley and run forward, the Colonel and Gudmanz up front, me and the twins covering the back. When we're all through the gateway, I hit the lever that closes it, and as the doors grind back into place, I ram a grenade into the power cabling leading to the locking bar. As I run off, I hear the crump of the grenade detonating and glance back, noting with satisfaction the twisted mess of wires left by the explosion.

My attention is drawn to the front by the sound of the Colonel's bolt pistol and I hurry forward, assault laser ready. Some Guardsmen are up ahead, just around a bend in the main tunnel, using the side corridors for cover. Las-bolts spit down the passage towards me, zinging off the walls and floor, leaving faint scorch marks. The Colonel's crouched down inside an opened door, poking out now and then to fire off a shot, the bolts tearing chunks of metal from the walls.

I leap forward, rolling across the floor as a ragged lasgun volley flares towards us, slamming through a doorway on the left of the passage. As I steady myself and come up to a crouch, I aim my gun at the nearest Typhon, about twenty metres down on the same side of the corridor. In the laser's sight, his head and shoulders are brought into sharp focus as he leans round the corner for another shot, and I squeeze the trigger gently. Half a dozen red bolts flash into his upper body, a couple of them punching straight through and dissipating further down the tunnel. Another fusillade of laser fire forces me to duck back into the room.

This is gonna take forever, I tell myself, realising that the longer we're pinned down here, the more troops are going to come pouring into the area.

'Grenades!' I bellow, pulling one from my belt. As I hurl it down the passageway, three more clatter along the floor next to it, thrown by the others. One brave Guardsman dashes from cover to grab them and toss them back, but a shot from either Loron or Lorii punches through his leg, the impact of the bolt severing it at the knee. His screams echo down the passage for about a second before the grenades explode, flinging him into the air. Even as the blast dissipates, I'm charging down the corridor, assault laser at my shoulder, using the sight to pick off the Typhons through the smoke and haze.

I must have missed one down a sidetunnel, because as I'm pounding forward I feel something slam into the right side of my head, making my ears ring and my knees buckle. Turning, I see the Typhon, a middle-aged man, his uniform slightly too tight for him. I see his eyes narrow as he lines up his next shot, the muzzle of his lasgun pointing directly at my face. Something smashes into me, hurling me down the passageway, and the only thing that registers is the smell of Lorii on top of me. The las-bolt flashes above us as we roll across the metal floor. Sliding to a halt, Lorii's back on her feet in an instant, a laspistol in her hand. Her first shot is a bit low, the energy blast ripping into the Guardsman's thigh, sending his next shot into the ceiling as he falls sideways. Her next is straight and true, punching into his plump face with a small fountain of blood and shattered teeth, hurling him backwards.

'You're either a hero or an idiot,' she says with a smile as she helps me to my feet. 'Lucky for you, I'm just as brave or stupid.'

In the stillness, I hear a man groaning, quickly silenced by a round from Striden's shotgun. I pull off my helmet and look at it, still a bit dazed from the hit. There's a charred gouge just where my right ear would be, almost burnt through. I poke at it with my finger and I'm shocked when my fingertip passes straight through. The las-bolt had been within the thickness of a piece of parchment from actually getting through! Thanking the Emperor for his protection, I stick my helmet back on and pick up the assault laser.

The roar of Loron's bolter echoes along the corridor from behind; more Typhons must be advancing on us. The Colonel comes dashing around the bend, virtually dragging Gudmanz with him, Kronin charging along beside him with the metal trolley, madly wobbling left and right as its wheels skitter in all directions at once.

'Get him to the plasma chamber,' the Colonel yells, pushing Gudmanz towards me and Lorii. Grabbing the aged tech-priest between us, we head off up the tunnel with Gudmanz. I can hear the shouts of the others and the ring of shots on the corridor walls and ceiling. The steady thump of Striden's shotgun punctuates the near-constant thundering of Loron's bolter and Schaeffer's bolt pistol, and I can see the flicker of intense muzzle flash throwing their hazy shadows against the wall.

Gudmanz is panting badly, barely able to stand up as we haul him by the arms along the passageway.

'How much further?' asks Lorii between gritted teeth.

'Just another… another two hundred metres perhaps,' gasps the tech-priest, face pale, eyes showing the pain wracking his rapidly ageing body.

Just then, a round object about the size of my fist bounces off the ceiling and drops to the floor just in front of us.

'Grenade!' hisses Lorii, dropping Gudmanz and leaping forward. With a powerful kick she sends the grenade back the way it came and there's a shout of alarm a moment later, followed swiftly by the explosion. I dump Gudmanz against the wall and ready the assault laser, even as Lorii throws herself prone and swings the bolter round from where it was hanging across her back.

'About a dozen of them,' she tells me before opening fire, spent cases cascading from the bolter's ejection vent and piling up next to her.

'Door to my left…" I hear Gudmanz wheezing from behind me.

'What?' I snap, firing blindly along the passageway as I look back at him.

'Door to my left… leads through… five bunkrooms,' he explains between ragged gasps for breath. 'Get you… behind them.'

'Keep them occupied!' I tell Lorii as I plunge through the door.

'Will do!" I hear her reply.

As Gudmanz said, I'm in one of a line of linked bunkrooms, each about a dozen metres long, three-tiered beds lining the left wall, kit lockers on my right. I can see into the next couple, but then the sharper curve of Coritanorum's innermost ring puts the others out of sight. I can't believe they wouldn't cover this approach and I drop down to a crouch. I have to keep the element of surprise as long as possible, and I dump the assault laser onto one of the bunks as I sneak past, drawing one of the six combat knives I've got strapped across my chest and to my thighs.

It feels good to have a knife in my hand, I'm a bladesman at heart, always have been. I don't mind admitting that I prefer the personal touch you get when you stab someone – shooting them from a distance seems a bit of an insult. Still, if some sump-sucker's shooting at me, I'll return the compliment as quick as I can, and I'm not going to risk my neck for the sake of the slightly greater satisfaction of sliding a blade between someone's ribs.

I duck back quickly when I catch a first glimpse of a Guardsman up ahead. There's enough space for me under the bottom bed of the bunk tiers and I crawl under it. Pushing myself forward on my stomach, I can see the Guardsman's boots, stepping back and forth as he keeps looking behind him to check that no one's got through the other way. I realise I'm holding my breath and pause for a moment to let it out. I don't have to be too quiet, I can hear the snap of las-fire and the cracks of the bolter rounds exploding from the tunnel, masking any noise I might accidentally make. I slide forward a few metres more, taking me just past the Typhon.

I wait again for a few seconds, trying to figure out the best way to take down the Guardsman. Looking up, I see that the actual bed pallet isn't fixed to the frame, it's just laid on top of a couple of struts. I manage to roll onto my back, so that my feet are pointing towards the Typhon. With a grunt I push up with all my strength, flinging the mattress over and on top of him. There's a flash of light as his finger tightens on his lasgun trigger, sending an energy bolt searing into one of the lockers. Before he can recover, I leap on top of him, and I hear his breath rushing out as he's winded. Without even looking I slash and stab a dozen times under the bed pallet, feeling the knife cutting into flesh and scraping along bone. He stops struggling and a crimson pool begins to spread out around me, soaking into the tattered grey bedclothes.

Rolling back to my feet, I can see another Guardsman, kneeling in a doorway in the next room, his attention fixed outside as he fires his lasgun down the main corridor. He doesn't notice me until the last moment, a startled cry spilling from his lips a moment before the knifepoint drives up into the soft part under his chin. I tug at the knife to get it free, but it's stuck in the top of his jaw and I let it go and pull another one from the bandoleer. It's then that I look up and see another Typhon just across the corridor, ten metres from me. He notices me too and as he brings his lasgun up to fire, I force myself back, rolling the dead Guardsman on top of me. I lie there for a second or two as las-bolts thud into the corpse, feeling it rocking from the impacts. Teeth gritted and eyes screwed up from the closeness of the shots, I fumble with my free hand for the dead man's lasrifle. More energy bolts sear into the body and I feel one pluck the material of my trousers, scorching the hairs and skin of my left calf. My hand closes around the trigger guard of the discarded lasgun and I swing it towards the corridor, finger pumping on the trigger, blasting randomly for a good five seconds.

I wait a moment for more return fire, but none comes, and I risk a peek over the now-ragged body. The doorway where the Guardsman was is empty, except for a foot poking around the frame from inside, a smear of blood on the gleaming tiles. Letting out my breath slowly,

I lie there, waiting for my heart to stop its frenzied battering against my ribs.

Someone stands over me and they grab my shoulders, hauling me to my feet. It's Schaeffer, Gudmanz behind him leaning gratefully against the bunks, hand mopping sweat from his face, handing me the assault rifle with the other

'We do not have time for you to lie around, Kage,' says the Colonel, leaning out of the doorway with bolt pistol ready, checking the way ahead. 'We take the next turning to the left and at the end are the doors to the plasma chamber.'

Loron and Lorii come along the corridor cautiously, relaxing as soon as they see my ugly face.

'Wondered if you made it or not,' says Lorii, her eyes checking me over for signs of injury. I'm covered in blood and little scraps of charred flesh, but none of it's mine in any appreciable amount.

'Kronin, Striden,' says the Colonel as the two of them jog up through the bunk rooms pushing the trolley. Schaeffer grabs the trolley from Striden, pushing it out through the door. 'You two cover the main passageway until we gain access to the plasma chamber.'

As a group we hurry to the turning that leads to the reactor, guns ready but not needed. Kronin and the Navy lieutenant take position either side of the side tunnel, checking both approaches, while the rest of us dash for the huge armoured door at the far end.

'Any smart ideas how we get in?' Loron asks when we're stood in front of it. You can tell just by looking at it that the blast door is solidly built.

'Seems I've spent my whole life trying to get through fragging doors lately,' bitches Lorii, looking over the welded metal plates with a scowl.

'We have melta-bombs,' Gudmanz points out, pulling a cylindrical canister from the now much smaller heap of ammo belts and energy packs on the trolley. Twisting off the top, he up-ends the tube and ten discs, each about the size of your palm, clatter to the floor.

'How many do we need?' Schaeffer asks the tech-priest, picking one up and turning it over in his hand. It's four centimetres thick, split into two halves around its edge. On the top is a bright orange button, set into a small well.

'Do I look like a demolitions expert, Colonel Schaeffer?' Gudmanz rasps back, slumping to sit against the wall. 'Almost all of my memo-pads were removed, remember?' he adds with a sour look at the Colonel.

'Frag it, let's use the whole lot,' Lorii decides for us, grabbing a couple of the melta-bombs, at Gudmanz's prompting twisting the two halves in opposite directions to activate the magnetic clamp. We each grab a handful and start slapping them onto the door, putting most of them at the edges around the huge hinges.

'Better save some, just in case,' Loron suggests as I grab the fourth and last canister. I toss it back and look expectantly at the door.

'You need to activate the charges,' Gudmanz tells us with a heavy sigh, forcing himself to his feet, using the wall as a support. 'Press the red activator, it sets a five-second delay. Then clear away quickly, because although most of the melta-blast is directed towards the door, there is a slight backwash.'

'Kage and I will set the charges,' the Colonel says, thrusting the trolley away.

Just then there's the distinctive zing of a las-bolt against metal and Kronin gives a startled cry and pitches back from the end of the corridor, smoke rising from the scorch mark on his flak jacket, just above his heart.

'Hurry!' hisses Striden, swivelling on his haunches and firing his shotgun down the corridor. The Colonel and I glance at each other and then start stabbing at the fuse buttons. We've done just about half of them when the Colonel grabs my collar and hauls me backwards, sending us both diving to the floor. There's a wash of hot air over my back and a deafening clang as the armoured door crashes to the floor. Looking back, I see the doorway is now a ragged hole, a thin cloud of smoke hanging in the air, the walls spattered with droplets of cooling steel.

'Go!' barks the Colonel, jumping to his feet and pulling his bolt pistol free. He leaps back a moment later as a hail of las-bolts ping off the walls around us. I can hear Striden shouting something but can't make out the words over the boom of his shotgun. Loron comes running up to us, dragging the unconscious Kronin with him.

'How many behind us?' asks the Colonel, firing blind into the plasma chamber with his bolt pistol.

'Most of them, I think,' he tells us with a worried look. I check over my shoulder and see Lorii's taken up position where Kronin was, her pale face given a yellow tinge by the flare of her bolter as she fires along the main corridor.

I edge out from what's left of the bulkhead around the ruined doorway, and I can just about make out the dozen or so Typhons stationed inside the reactor chamber, taking cover behind data terminals and coils of pipes which snake in every direction. The chamber's big, vaguely circular, or hexagonal maybe, it's hard to see the walls because of the clutter of machinery. A huge datascreen is set on to the wall at the far side, scrolling with numbers. I can't see any other doors at first glance. A fusillade of las-bolts screams towards me and I duck back quickly.

'We have to get inside,' Gudmanz wheezes.

'Suggestions welcome,' I snarl back, unslinging the assault laser and unleashing a storm of lasblasts towards a head poking around a buttress jutting from a wall to my right. Peering through the door again, I see someone walk into the chamber along a metal gantry hanging five metres or so off the floor. He's dressed in the worker coveralls that seem to be so common around here, and I can see that he's got two autopistols, one in each hand, more ammo clips thrust into his belt. I give a gasp of shock as he opens fire with the pistols, spraying bullets into the back of the Typhons, cutting down half of them in the first hail of fire. As they turn and look up at this new threat, I push myself forward firing wildly with the assault laser. I can hear the Colonel's bolt pistol thundering just behind me as he follows. Lasbolts ricochet off the metal mesh of the gantry and the stranger vaults over the rail, still firing with his free hand. Caught between the attack on two fronts, the Guardsmen are dead in a matter of seconds.

'Everybody in here!' Schaeffer calls out, and I look down the corridor to see Striden and Lorii running back. A Typhon appears at the far end but is sent scurrying back by a salvo of bolts from Loron.

'Our mysterious accomplice, I presume,' Lorii says, inspecting the newcomer where he stands looking down the corridor, reloading the autopistols.

'Last Chancers,' the Colonel says, waving a hand towards the stranger, 'may I introduce the man we are currently fighting for: Inquisitor Oriel.'

'THEY SEEM TO be holding back,' calls Loron from the gaping hole of the doorway into the plasma chamber.

'Their officers are probably cursing the architects of Coritanorum at the moment,' says Inquisitor Oriel, pushing the autopistols into the belt of his coveralls. He is clean shaven, with a narrow face, and thin black hair. He exudes an aura of calm, tinged with a hint of menace. 'The whole inner circle is designed to be a final bastion of defence, which works in our favour now, not theirs. It's what makes this whole mission possible.'

I can see his point. The plasma chamber is octagonal, about twenty metres from wall to wall. There are a few free-standing display panels, still littered with dead Typhons, and power coils snaking from apertures in the walls to a central terminal in the wall opposite the entrance, shielded from view by a huge datascreen. The access way is four, maybe five metres wide, almost impossible to come down more than four abreast, and thirty metres long at least, a real killing zone.

'The Inquisition?' says Lorii, still dumbfounded. She's crouched next to Kronin, who's slouched against the wall, still out of it. He's barely alive, the lasblast caught him full in the chest.

'Makes sense,' I say. 'Who else would have the resources or authority to destroy a sector base?'

'It will not be long before they try another attack,' the Colonel tells us, calling us back to the matter in hand. 'Gudmanz, link in and start the overload. Revered inquisitor, how many ways into this chamber are there?'

'Just the main gate and the maintenance duct I came through,' he says, pointing to the gantry above our heads. 'That's why we can hold them off with just a handful of men.'

'What about the duct?' I ask, casting a cautious glance upwards.

'I left a little surprise just outside for anyone who tries to come in that way,' he reassures me with a grim smile.

'You've changed,' says the Colonel, glancing at the inquisitor, taking us all a bit aback. I'm surprised they've seen each other before, but then again I guess I shouldn't be. Between the inquisitor and the captain of the twins' penal battalion, I suspect the Colonel has been out and about a lot more than we realise.

'Mmm? Oh, the beard? I required a change of identity once the command staff learned who I was,' he tells us. 'It was the easiest way. That and a suitable alter-ego as a maintenance worker.'

'Something's happening,' calls Loron, drawing our attention to the corridor outside. I can see some movement at the far end, heads popping into sight to check what's going on.

'Mass attack?' Lorii asks, taking up a firing position next to the gateway, the bulky bolter held across her chest.

'There are no other options, it seems,' the Colonel agrees.

'Should we be building a barricade or something?' suggests Striden, thumbing more shells into the breech of his shotgun.

'One way in, one way out,' Lorii points out, jabbing a thumb back down the access corridor. 'When it's time to go, we'll need to get out fast.'

'I never even thought about getting out,' Striden admits, running a hand through his sweat-slicked hair. 'Getting in seemed ridiculous enough.'

'You don't even have to be here!' I snap at him. 'So quit complaining.'

The attack is heralded by a storm of fire along one side of the corridor, las-fire in a deadly hail that rips along the wall, impacts into the doorway and comes flaring into the plasma chamber. As we're pinned back by the covering fire, a squad of Guardsmen charges up the other side of the accessway, bellowing some kind of warcry.

The Colonel and I toss a couple of frag grenades through the doorway and the warcry turns to shouts of panic. Bits of shrapnel scythe through the door as the blast fills the passage, and as the smoke clears, I look around the edge of the doorway and see the Typhons in a pile of twisted corpses, caught full by the blast as some of them tried to turn back and ran into the others behind them.

'Score one to the Last Chancers!' laughs Lorii, peeking above my shoulder for a look.

'How many do we need to win?' I ask her and she shrugs.

'Of the three and a half million people left in Coritanorum,' the inquisitor tells us from the other side of the doorway, 'seven hundred thousand are fully trained Guardsmen. That's how many we need to score.'

'Seven fraggin' hundred thousand?' I spit. 'How the frag are we supposed to get out?'

'When the plasma reactors go to overload, getting out is going to be the matter on everyone's mind, Kage,' the Colonel answers me from beside Oriel. 'They will not be too keen to stand and fight when that happens.'

'Good point, well made,' agrees Loron. 'The only fighting we'll be doing is over seats on the shuttle!'

'Another attack is being launched by Imperial forces on the northern walls,' the inquisitor adds. 'They have two fronts to fight on.'

'What happens to our men when this place goes boom?' asks Loron.

Our banter is cut short by a succession of distinctive 'whump' noises, and five fist-sized shapes come bouncing into the plasma room.

'Fragging grenade launchers!' Lorii cries out, pushing me flat and then throwing herself across Kronin. The grenades explode, shrapnel clanging off the walls, a small piece imbedding itself in my left forearm. Another volley comes clattering in and I roll sideways, putting as much distance as I can between me and the entrance. More detonations boom in my ears and debris rings across the equipment around us.

'Are you trying to blow up the reactor?' Oriel bellows down the corridor.

There's a pause in the firing and the inquisitor looks at us and smiles.

'Well, they don't know that's what we're trying to do anyway,' he chuckles. 'They'll be wary of any heavy weapons fire from now on.'

IN THE NEXT half hour, they tried five more attacks. The bodies of more than a hundred men are piled up in the corridor now, each successive wave being slowed by the tangles of corpses to clamber across. A muffled explosion from above, just before the last attack, indicated someone trying to come in through the maintenance duct and running into the inquisitor's booby trap.

It's been quiet for the past fifteen minutes or so. Gudmanz is still plugged into the plasma reactor, face waxy and almost deathlike. He's sat there in a trance; I did wonder if he had died, but Lorii checked him and he's still breathing. Who knows what sort of private battle he's fighting with the other tech-priests inside the terminal network. We're running low on ammo, I've had to ditch the assault laser, which stopped working during the fourth assault. I must have used up my thousand shots. I've got one of the spare bolters now, a big lump of metal that weighs heavily in my hands, a complete contrast to the lightweight lasgun that I'm used to.

'I can't see what they can try next,' says Loron.

'Oh frag,' I mutter when I realise one of the options open to them.

'What now?' the Colonel demands, casting a venomous glance at me.

'Gas,' I say shortly. 'No damage to the reactor, but we'll be dead, or asleep and defenceless.'

'They can't use normal gas weapons,' Oriel informs us. 'The ventilation of each circle is sealed to prevent an agent being introduced from the outside, but it also means that any gas will be dispersed into the surrounding corridors. It's another of the defence features working against them.'

'I've heard of short-life viruses,' Striden points out. 'We had a few warheads on the Emperor's Benevolence. They're only deadly for a few seconds. A base the size of Coritanorum might have something like that.'

'Yes they did,' Inquisitor Oriel confirms with a grin. 'Unfortunately their stockpile seems to have been used up by someone.'

'The watchtower and the security room...' Lorii makes the conclusion. 'Very neat.'

'I thought so,' the inquisitor replies, scratching an ear.

Just then, someone shouts to us along the corridor.

'Surrender your weapons and you'll be dealt with fairly!' the anonymous voice calls out. 'Plead for the Emperor's forgiveness and your deaths will be swift and painless!'

'I bet...' mutters Loron in reply.

'You're the damned rebels!' Lorii shouts back. 'Ask for *our* forgiveness!'

'That'll stir them up a bit,' Oriel comments. 'Only the command staff are the real rebels.'

'So why's everyone fighting us?' I ask. 'If they're still loyal, they could overpower the commanders easily.'

'Why should they?' he retorts, shrugging lightly.

'Because it's what someone loyal to the Emperor would do,' I reply. It seems obvious to me.

'I don't get it,' Striden adds. 'I can see Kage's point of view.'

'Why do you think they are rebels?' asks Oriel, gazing around at us.

'Well, you, the Colonel, everyone says they are,' answers Loron, nodding towards the inquisitor and Schaeffer.

'My point, exactly,' agrees Oriel with a wry smile. 'You know they are rebels because you have been told they are rebels.'

'And the Typhons have been told that we are the traitors,' I add, realising what Oriel is saying. 'For all we know, they could be right, but we trust the Colonel. We don't decide who the enemy is; we just follow orders and kill who we've been told to kill–'

'And so do they,' finishes Oriel, glancing back down the access tunnel.

'So that's the reason why this rebellion at the sector command is so dangerous and must be dealt with,' Loron follows on. 'If they wanted to, the command staff could convince admirals and colonels across the sector that anyone they say is the enemy. The command staff could say that any force that moved against them was rebelling against the Emperor.'

'It is one of the reasons, yes,' confirms the Colonel.

Our thoughts on the perils of the chain of command are interrupted by more las-bolts flashing through the door.

'Some of them have sneaked up through the bodies,' the Colonel tells us after a look outside. 'More are moving forward.'

'Cunning bastards,' curses Lorii, kneeling beside me, bolter ready.

'Return fire!' orders the Colonel, levelling his bolt pistol through the door and firing off a couple of shots.

THE FIREFIGHT CONTINUED sporadically for the best part of another hour. There's no telling how many Typhons worked their way along the tunnel, skulking among the mounds of dead, almost perfectly camouflaged by the piles of uniformed corpses. I haven't fired a shot in quite a while. We're beginning to get seriously concerned about the ammunition supplies, and every bolt or las-shot has to count. The Typhons, on the other hand, are quite happy to blaze away at the first sign of one of us poking a head or gun into view.

I'm lying prone on the right hand side of the doorway, Lorii crouched over me. On the far side are the Colonel and Loron, while Oriel and Striden are sheltering behind a panel of controls and dials almost directly opposite the entrance. A shuddering gasp from Gudmanz attracts our attention and I look back to see him staggering away from his terminal at the further side of the chamber, the neural plug whipping back into his skull.

'Have you done it?' demands the Colonel.

'Do you hear any warning klaxons, Colonel Schaeffer?' he rasps back irritably. 'I've set up blocks and traps so that the overload process can only be rectified from this room, not from another terminal.'

'So how much longer?' I shout over to him.

'Not long now, but I will need some help,' he replies. The Colonel gives a nod to Striden, who rises from his hiding place, shotgun roaring. A moment after he's jumped clear the Typhons' return volley slams into the data panel, sending pieces of metal spinning in every direction. Gudmanz grabs Striden and pushes him out of sight behind the screen. My attention is snapped back to the corridor by the thump of booted feet.

'They're charging!' snaps Loron, his bolter exploding into life, the small flickers of the bolt propellant flaring into the tunnel. To my left I glimpse Oriel rolling out from behind the panel, autopistol in each hand, firing into the tunnel while he rolls. As his roll takes him to his feet, he drops the pistol in his left hand and sweeps the Colonel's power sword out of its scabbard. With a yell he leaps straight at the attacking Typhons, the blue glare of the power sword reflecting off the corridor walls.

Meeting the charge head on, the inquisitor drives the blade through the stomach of the first Typhon, a spin and a backhand slash opens up the throat of the next. The inquisitor ducks beneath a wild thrust of a bayonet, lopping off the Typhon's leg halfway up the thigh, arterial blood splashing across his coveralls. In a detached part of my brain I watch Oriel fighting, contrasting the fluid, dance-like quality of his movements to the precise, mechanical fighting style of the Colonel. The autopistol chatters in his right hand as he blasts another Typhon full in the face, the power sword sweeping up to parry a lasgun being wielded as a club, its glowing edge shearing the weapon in two. Oriel bellows something that I can't quite catch over the scream of dying men and the noise of the autopistol, his face contorted with rage.

I see a Typhon rising out of a mound of corpses behind Oriel, left arm missing below the elbow, his remaining hand clutching a bayonet. Without even thinking, I pull the trigger of the bolter and a moment later the Guardsman's lower back explodes, his legs crumpling under him, his spine shattered. The Typhons turn and flee from the inquisitor's wrath, the slowest pitched to the floor in two halves as Oriel strikes out once more. Las-bolts flare from the far end, kicking the corpses into jerky life again. One seems to strike Oriel full in the chest and a blinding flash of light burns my eyes. As I blink to clear the purple spots, I see Oriel still there, diving for cover over a pile of dead Typhons.

'He has the Emperor's protection,' Lorii says in an awed whisper.

'Witchery!' cries Striden, eyes wide with horror.

'Or technology,' Loron adds, sounding just as scared.

'Conversion force field,' the Colonel tells us calmly as he clicks fresh bolter rounds into an empty magazine. We exchange bemused glances, none of us sure what he's talking about. Everything goes quiet again as Oriel crawls back to the door, and I can hear Gudmanz chanting a sonorous liturgy from behind me.

'And the fourth seal shall be raised, glory be to the Machine God,' he intones, voice echoing off the metal walls. 'And the departure of the fourth seal shall be heralded by the tone of the Machine God's joy. Now, if you please, Lieutenant Striden.'

There's a clang of something ringing against metal and a hiss from a panel to my left. From somewhere above us, a high-pitched wail blares out three times.

'How much longer?' the Colonel shouts as Oriel hands him back the power sword, the blade a dull grey now that the energy flow is switched off.

'Four of the seven seals have been lifted, Colonel Schaeffer,' Striden calls back. 'Not long now, I gather.'

'Here they come again, they're getting desperate!' Loron draws our attention back to the corridor. The narrow tunnel seems choked with Typhons pouring towards us, their faces masks of desperation and terror. I guess they've found out what we're doing, if they hadn't already guessed. They'll fight even harder now, battling to save their homes, friends and families. After all, like us, they've got nothing to lose. If they fail, they're just as dead.

I'd find the pointless slaughter sickening if it wasn't for the image of the pardon that lingers in the back of my head. That, and the piles of ash which is what the men and women running towards me really are. All because some commanders have decided to dare the Emperor's wrath and fight for their glory and not his. I don't see any of them down here throwing themselves headlong at a wall of firepower for their ideals.

This isn't combat, they stand no chance at all. Switching the bolter to semi-auto, I send a hail of tiny rockets exploding down the accessway, punching Typhons from their feet, gouging chunks in those already dead. The Guardsmen fire madly back at us, more las-shots zinging off the walls than coming through the doorway. They keep coming, hurdling over the dead and the dying. They're all shouting, at us or themselves, I can't tell.

It's only when the bolter starts clicking that I register its magazine is empty, I feel that detached from what's going on. My body is working on its own, without any conscious effort from my brain. Lorii drops one of her magazines next to me and I pull the empty out and slam the new one home. The attack is faltering by the weight of fire concentrated into the corridor, the Typhons can't physically get any further forward.

I fire: an arm goes spinning into the ceiling. Another shot: a man is thrown backwards, his intestines pouring from the gaping hole in his gut. Another shot: half a man's head disappears in a cloud of blood. Another shot; a lasgun explodes under the impact. Another shot: a helmeted head snaps backwards. Another shot: a woman hurls herself sideways, clutching the stump of her left wrist, hair matted with the blood of her comrades. This isn't a battle, it's a firing range with living targets.

Most of the Typhons turn and run, and I fire into their fleeing backs, knocking them from their feet, each roar of the boltgun followed by a man or woman losing a life. Someone's shaking my shoulders, screaming something in my ear, but I can't hear over the whine of the siren. My brain filters the information slowly and I feel like I'm surfacing from a dream. Yes, there's a siren ringing around, its screeching tones echoing off the walls and floor.

'We've done it!' Lorii is shouting in my ear. 'They're running for it! We've done it!'

'Kronin's dead,' I hear Striden say, and everybody turns to look at him, leaning against the wall over Kronin.

'Dead?' Loron asks, clearly shocked. I'm surprised too, I hadn't spared a thought for the wounded madman while I was battling for my life. I feel a touch of sadness that he died alone and unnoticed. He was alone when he was still alive, it seems disrespectful that none of us saw him die. I offer a prayer for his departing, tortured soul, hoping it isn't too late.

'Internal bleeding probably,' Oriel proclaims, snapping me from my thoughts. 'Now it is time for me to depart as well.'

'WE HAVE NOT succeeded,' Gudmanz whispers heavily. We're just a short way from the nearest shuttle terminal, on our way to life and freedom, but a few Typhons have decided that they're going to take us with them, forcing us to take temporary cover in a terminal alcove along the main corridor. Oriel went in the opposite direction, who knows where he was headed. A few minutes ago the blaring alarms stopped, which was a great relief to my ears and nerves. I don't need any reminders that in a short while this whole city is going to be non-existent.

'What do you mean?' demands Schaeffer, grabbing the front of the tech-priest's robe.

'The warning siren should not stop sounding,' Gudmanz says, brushing away the Colonel's arm and pointing to the terminal. 'Let me go, and I will find out.'

Everyone is staring at the tech-priest as he deftly manipulates runes and dials on the terminal. His shoulders seem to sag even more and he turns to look at us, face a picture of despondency.

'I am sorry, I have failed,' he says, slumping to the floor. 'I failed to find a hidden failsafe. The reactors will not overload.'

'Oh frag,' I mutter, dropping to my knees.

'Is there nothing we can do?' the Colonel demands, visibly shaking with anger.

'The coolant failsafe is located not far from here. It may be possible to dismantle it,' Gudmanz replies, though obviously without much hope.

'Which way?' snarls Schaeffer, hauling the tech-priest to his feet.

'Back towards the plasma chamber, corridor to the left marked "energy distribution",' he tells us. 'I did not think it was important.'

'You fragging idiot!' Loron swears, grabbing Gudmanz and slamming his back into the wall. 'You useless old man!'

'Let's just get out of here!' I tell them. 'This is the only chance of getting out of this city alive.'

'Damn right,' agrees Lorii, staring at the Colonel.

'Enough of this!' snaps the Colonel, dragging Loron away from the tech-priest. 'We get to this failsafe and deactivate it. We must hurry before the Typhon guards and security realise they are in no danger. Otherwise, they will throw everything they have at us. The panic at the moment is the only thing in our favour.'

'The mission's failed,' I tell the Colonel, looking him squarely in the face. 'We have to get out of here.'

'The mission cannot fail,' the Colonel replies, pushing Loron away, staring straight back at me.

'Why not?' demands Lorii hotly stepping towards the Colonel. 'Because you say so?'

'Don't try to stop us,' warns Loron, raising the bolter in his hands so that it's pointed at the Colonel.

'You would not dare,' Schaeffer hisses at the white-skinned trooper, staring straight at him.

'We are leaving!' Loron replies emphatically, his eyes just as hard.

'Coritanorum must be destroyed!' Schaeffer exclaims, and for the first time ever I notice a hint, just a hint, of desperation in his voice. I push Loron's gun away slightly and turn back to the Colonel.

'Okay, tell us,' I say to him quietly, standing between the Colonel and the others, trying to calm things down. If some fool shoots the Colonel, by accident or on purpose, we'll never get out of here. 'Why? Why can't this mission fail?'

'We do not have time for explanations,' the Colonel says between gritted teeth. I lean closer, still meeting his icy gaze.

'You have to tell us,' I whisper in his ear, drawing his eyes to mine. He gives a sigh.

'If we fail, all Typhos Sector will be destroyed,' he tells us. He looks at our disbelieving expressions and continues. 'I do not know all of the details, only Inquisitor Oriel has those.' He pauses as we hear a door slam shut further up the corridor. The Typhons are doing a room by room search for us.

'In brief,' he says casting an eye at the door. 'The command staff of Coritanorum has fallen under an alien influence. A genestealer in fact.'

'A genestealer?' I say, confused. 'You mean, one of those tyranid bastards we fought on Ichar IV? They're just shock troops. Sure, they're deadly, fast and able to rip a man to pieces in a heartbeat, but there'd have to be an army of them to stand against seven hundred thousand guard. What's the problem?'

'As I said, I do not fully understand this,' the Colonel continues, talking quickly. 'They are not just efficient killers, they are infiltrators too. Genestealers have some way of controlling others, some kind of mesmerism I believe. It creates an element within the society it has infected that is sympathetic to it. They protect it, allow it to control others, building up a power base from within. This can lead to revolt, rebellion and other insurgencies, as it has here. More to the point, as the power of this influenced cult grows, it begins to send a sort of psychic beacon, so I am told, as an astropath might project a message across the warp. Tyranid hive fleets can detect this signal and follow it. Hive Fleet Dagon appears to have located Typhos Prime and is on its way here now.'

'This still doesn't add up,' butts in Lorii. 'This all still seems very extreme, especially if the tyranids are already on their way. If we were recapturing Coritanorum to restore it as a command and control base, I could understand it, but we're not. What difference does it make if it's lost to this genestealer infection or destroyed?'

'The loss of Coritanorum as an Imperial base would indeed be grievous,' the Colonel agrees, still speaking rapidly. 'But not as terrible as its secrets falling into the hands of the tyranids. The Navy is endeavouring to stop Hive Fleet Dagon, but we have to assume it will fail. When the hive fleet arrives here, the tyranids will assimilate all of the data from the base and its corrupted personnel, learning the innermost secrets about the Imperial forces in the sector. They will find out where Navy bases are, where worlds ready for raising Imperial Guard regiments can be found, our strategies and capabilities. Without Coritanorum, the fight will be deadly enough, but if the tyranids possess such information they will overrun the sector much more easily. In fact, it is impossible to believe how they could be resisted at all.'

'Five hundred billion people,' I breathe quietly. 'It's a fair trade, you think? The death of Coritanorum and its three and a half million buys a better chance for the other five hundred billion people living in the sector.'

'People can be replaced,' the Colonel says grimly, giving us each a stern look. 'Habitable planets can not. Worlds stripped by the tyranids can never be recovered or repopulated.'

Another door slams shut, nearer this time.

'Do you think your lives are worth that?' he says with sudden scorn. 'Is that worthy of your sacrifice? Was I wrong in giving gutterfilth like you the chance to make a difference? Are you really the worthless criminals everyone thinks you are?'

I exchange looks with the other Last Chancers, volumes spoken in that brief moment of eye contact. It's not about pardons, or even saving the sector. It's about doing our duty, doing what we swore to do when we joined the Imperial Guard. We took an oath to protect the Emperor, His Imperium and His servants. We may not have chosen to be Last Chancers, but we chose to put ourselves in danger, to be willing to sacrifice our lives in the course of our duty.

'Move out!' barks the Colonel, shouldering open the door and leaping into the corridor, bolt pistol blazing in his hand. We jump out after him and set off at a run, Typhon lasfire screaming around us. Gudmanz gives a yell and pitches forward, a ragged, charred hole in the back of his robe. Striden stops to pick up the tech-priest but I grab the lieutenant's arm and pull him forward.

'He's dead,' I tell the Navy officer when he struggles. 'And so is everything else on over fifty worlds unless we get to that failsafe.'

LUCKILY FOR US, the Typhons aren't expecting us to double-back, probably they assumed we would cut and run. Can't blame them, only their commanders understand what's at stake, if any of them really know. They're totally disorganised now: an unexpected attack from within, thrown into disarray by the alarms, scattered to the shuttle ports, assaulted from outside by the Imperial army. The Typhon officers must be tearing their hair out by now.

Gudmanz's information was accurate. We come across a sign to 'Energy Distribution' and the side-tunnel leads us into a chamber looking a lot like the plasma room, although quite a bit smaller, barely four metres across. It's filled with lots of pipes, tanks and cables, with dozens of gauges, their needles flickering, red lights spread across panels on every surface.

'What can we do without Gudmanz?' asks Striden, looking meaningfully at me. We all look at each other for inspiration.

'Oh great,' says Loron, hands flopping to his side dejectedly. 'We're all ready to do the right thing, and now because that decrepit tech-priest got himself killed, there's nothing we can do about it.'

'There must be something,' argues Striden, looking around the room.

'We're Last Chancers,' I say to them with a grin. 'If in doubt, shoot it!'

As I open fire on the snaking cables and pipes with the bolter, the others join in, firing at everything in sight, sparks cascading as equipment banks explode. We keep the attack up for a few seconds, a few wisps of smoke and steam hissing around us, but it doesn't seem to be having much effect, lots of our fire ricochets harmlessly off the reinforced conduits.

'Hey!' Lorii calls out, pulling something off her belt. It's the last cylinder of melta-bombs. 'These might come in useful!'

'You're beautiful,' I tell her as she hands them out. I decide to put mine on a pipe that passes up from the floor and out through the ceiling, wider than I could wrap my arms around. Pushing the triggers, I take a couple of steps back. The pipe begins to glow white and a second later explodes into a shower of vaporised metal and plastic. I hear similar detonations, thick oily smoke floods the room, panels explode with multi-coloured sparks and suddenly the air is filled with a deafening scream as the alarms start sounding again. Striden gives a delighted laugh and Loron is punching me on the shoulder, grinning like a fool.

'Time to go,' the Colonel orders, heading for the door.

Loron jogs out first, the rest of us following close behind. Just a short hike to the shuttle bays and we're clear. Loron glances back and smiles, but when he steps out into the main corridor his head explodes, splashing blood across Lorii who's right next to him.

She gives a strangled scream, the droplets of blood on her face so dark against her alabaster skin, her searing blue eyes looking like they'll pop out of their sockets. I grab her and pull her back as more las-bolts slam into the wall nearby, but she turns and claws at my face, her nails gouging a trail across my forehead. I grimly hold on to her as she fights to get free, but she brings her knee up with unbelievable strength and my groin explodes with pain, making me instinctively let go of her and collapse to the ground clutching myself. Striden makes a lunge for her but a right cross to the chin sends him flying back. Stooping to grab her brother's bolter, she plunges forward, firing both guns as she charges into the corridor.

'She's going the wrong way!' I cry out, seeing her racing left, away from the shuttle pad.

'She will buy us extra time,' the Colonel says coldly, turning right at the corridor. I can still hear the roar of the bolter to my left, but there's no sign of Lorii. I hesitate for a moment then push myself to my feet, about to go after her. Striden steps in front of me, and puts a hand against my chest.

'She doesn't want to live, Kage,' he says, face sombre. 'Getting yourself killed is not going to save her.'

I'm about to push him aside when I hear a high-pitched scream resounding along the corridor. I can hear the Colonel striding away behind me, his boots thudding on the metal floor. Striden steps away and walks past, hurrying after the Colonel. I stand there alone, straining my ears for the sound of another bolter shot. There's nothing. I realise with a start that I'm the only Last Chancer left. I feel empty, hollow. Alone in my soul as well as physically. Lorii's death seems to sum it all up. Ultimately pointless and futile. Why did I want this? Do I really think any of this will make a difference, a year from now, ten years, a century? There aren't any heroes these days, not like Macharius or Dolan, just countless millions of men and women dying lonely deaths, unnoticed by most, unremembered by history. I feel like falling to my knees and giving up just then. The will to live that has carried me through three years of hell just ebbs out of me. The bolter in my hand feels heavier than ever, weighted down with countless deaths.

I taste blood in my mouth and realise I've been biting my lip, biting so hard that it's bleeding. The taste brings me back to my senses. I'm still alive, and I owe it to them as much as to myself to survive, so that this is remembered, that whatever happens, this sacrifice and misery doesn't die with us. I turn on my heel gripping the bolter tight once more, filled with purpose again, and start jogging after Striden.

'IT's DOWN HERE!' Striden argues, taking the turning to the left.

'Straight on,' counters the Colonel, pointing along the main corridor.

'I remember the map,' the Navy officer insists, walking on without looking back at us. Somewhere behind us I hear another emergency bulkhead slamming down. I guess it must be an automatic response, I can't imagine any of the Typhons hanging around long enough to close all the blast doors. Not that it'll do any good either, as far as I can tell. Another clang makes me look around and

I see the last tunnel behind us to the right is sealed off now. The Colonel plunges after Striden and grabs him by his collar. A moment later and the bulkhead closes, a wall of metal sliding down from the corridor ceiling, cutting me off from the pair of them. I stand there dazed for a moment, not quite believing they've gone.

The sudden pounding of boots tears my attention back down the corridor and I watch seven Guardsmen come running into view. None of them look in my direction as they sprint away from me. I guess the shuttles are that way, and run after them. The constant sound of the siren is making my ears ache, a shrill tone that cuts straight into your brain. I almost run head first into a pair of Typhons as they come barrelling out of a door to my left. I smash one of them, a young man with a long nose, across the jaw with the bolter. The other glances at me in confusion before I pull the trigger, the bolt tearing into his chest, the recoil almost wrenching off my arm. His round face stares at me horrified for a moment before he slumps back against the door. I grind the heel of my boot into the face of the first one, crushing his head against the floor with the sound of crunching bone.

The distraction means that I've lost the men I was chasing, and I pause for a moment, listening out for them. Walking along for a couple of minutes, I think I can catch the sound of their running from the next corridor to my left. Hurrying forward, I suddenly notice something moving out of the opposite tunnel. As I look over, my fingers go numb and the bolter clatters to the floor. Staring straight back at me is the genestealer. Just like the ones on Ichar IV. Its black eyes, set in its veined, wide dome of a skull, meet mine, and there's death in that gaze. It stalks quickly towards me on its long double-jointed legs, slightly hunched over. Its four upper limbs are held out for balance, one pair tipped with bony, dagger-like claws, the lower with more hand-like talons that slowly unclench as it approaches.

My eyes are drawn back to its alien gaze and I feel all the life leeching out of my body. They're like two pits of blackness and I feel as if I'm falling into them. I dimly note that it's standing right in front of me now. But that seems unimportant, all that really registers are those eyes, those pits of shadow.

It opens its long jaw, revealing a mass of razor-sharp teeth. So this is how I die, I dimly think to myself. It leans even closer and I notice its tongue extending out towards me, some kind of opening on the end widening. It's strangely beautiful, this killer. There's a sleekness about the deep blue plates of chitin over its sinewy purple flesh. There's a perfection of purpose in the claws and fangs which I can admire.

Heart of the Jungle.

The thought just pops into the back of my head, and it stirs something within me. It's like another voice, prompting me to remember feelings of alien influence. Memories of helplessness. Fighting for control of myself.

Ichar IV.

This time the memory is more vivid. Piles of bodies, torn apart by the same kind of creature in front of me now. Forests stripped to bare rock, even the dirt consumed by the tyranid swarms. A massive bio-titan strides across the ruins of a water recycling facility, crushing buildings underfoot, horrendous weapons unleashing sprays of bio-acid and hails of flesh-eating grubs.

Typhon Sector.

In an instant my brain multiplies the horrors of Ichar IV by fifty. This is what will happen.

I snap out of the hypnotic trance just as the genestealer's tongue brushes my throat.

'Frag you!' I snarl, acting on instinct alone, lashing out with my fist, the knuckles of my right hand crashing against its jaw in a perfect uppercut. Taken completely by surprise by the blow, the genestealer stumbles backwards, clawed feet skidding on the hard metal floor, scrabbling for purchase before it topples over. It stays down for just a moment, before springing to its feet, muscles tensing to lunge at me with the killing attack. I'm strangely calm.

The wall beside us explodes in a shower of metal and the genestealer turns and leaps away. More detonations ripple along the floor just behind it as it dashes for safety and then disappears with a flick of its tail through an air vent.

'Thanks, Colonel,' I say without turning around.

'Not this time,' Inquisitor Oriel replies, walking past me, a smoking bolt pistol in his right hand. 'I stopped the abomination getting out of the city, but it eluded me yet again. I almost had it this time.'

I'm still dazed, and the inquisitor picks up my bolter and places it into my unfeeling hands.

'This will be as sure as I get,' Oriel is saying, more to himself than me, I think. 'I will not let it get away from me again. It dies in Coritanorum.'

I just nod, my body quivering with aftershock. A genestealer was two metres from me and I'm still alive. Still alive. Oriel has forgotten me, walking up the corridor towards the shattered vent muttering to himself.

The sound of nearby engines rumbling into life draws my attention back into the real world and I start stumbling towards the shuttle pad. About a hundred metres further down the corridor I hear the whine of jets to my right. Following the noise, I come across a huge set of double doors and stumble through them. Inside are twenty or so Typhons, fighting with each other as they try to scramble up an access ladder to one of the two shuttles still left in the hangar. Those at the top are trying to push the others back so they can open the hatch. The rest of the vast open space is filled with scattered barrels and crates, hastily tossed out of cargo holds to make room, by the looks of it. The air shimmers from the heat haze and smoke left by the departed shuttles. No one is paying me any attention whatsoever.

'That's my shuttle,' I say to myself, pulling the last of the frag grenades from my belt and tossing it to the top of the boarding steps. The explosion hurls men into the air, sending them tumbling down to the gridded metal flooring, some of them raining down in blood-ied pieces. The bolter roars in my hand, shells punching into the survivors, pitching them over the handrails, tearing off body parts. None of them is armed and the execution takes a matter of seconds.

Racing up the steps, wounded men groaning as I step on them, I'm filled with fresh vigour. Only a few minutes from freedom now. Only a short journey to the rest of my life. I plunge through the hatchway and head into the cockpit. The shuttle pilot turns in his seat and shouts at me to get out. He gives a cry of alarm when I pull one of the knives from the sheaths across my chest, and flails madly for a moment, unable to fight properly within the confines of his gravity harness. His hands and arms are torn to ribbons by the blade as he tries to protect himself, a constant shriek coming from his throat. The shriek turns to a wet gurgling when I manage to find an opening and plunge the knife in.

Ditching the bolter and knife onto the floor, I sit down in the co-pilot's seat. I look over the controls and a doubt starts nagging at me. How the frag do you fly a shuttle? Well, I can work it out, it can't be worse than driving a Chimera, surely? If my freedom relies on work-ing this out just enough to fly a few kilometres, I can do it. I owe myself that much. I start chuckling at the irony of it. It was stowing away on a shuttle that brought me to the Colonel and the Last

Chancers in the first place, and now stealing one is going to get me out of it. Through the cockpit viewports, I see a handful of Typhons come running into the hangar, firing back through the entrance. It must be the Colonel down there, but that's his problem. There's another shuttle, he can get out on that. Those Typhons might decide to try to snatch this one off me, and I don't know if I can stop them. Nope, I'm damned sure I'm not waiting for the Colonel. He promised me my pardon and my freedom, and I'm going to get it.

A sudden realisation hits me like a sniper's bullet. The pardon's worth frag all without the Colonel's signature and seal on it. Just a piece of paper with meaningless words in High Gothic written on it. Oh, what the hell, I think. Everybody's going to be running around like headless sump spiders after all this. Nobody's going to notice me, one Guardsman among a million. Maybe the Colonel will hunt me down if he gets out, but then maybe not. He might think I'm dead, or he might give me my pardon anyway. He doesn't know I'm sat here, deciding whether to help him. Would he blame me?

No he wouldn't, and that's the problem. Running out on him is what he'd expect me to do. That nasty thought, the one that's been bugging me ever since I got to this planet, rises again. Man or criminal? Worthwhile or worthless? I glance back outside, and I see one of the Typhons kneeling, a plasma gun held to his shoulder. The ball of energy roars out of sight and I make my decision.

Picking up the bolter and heading back to the ladder, I discover there's only four rounds left in the magazine, and I've got no more spares. Five Guardsmen, four rounds. Why can't the Emperor cut me a fragging break and give me a full magazine? Cursing, I jump down the steps three at a time.

One of the Typhons catches sight of me as I dash across the open hangar, and I veer left, diving for the cover of some metal cases as las-bolts scream towards me. Four rounds, five Guardsmen. Raising the bolter to my shoulder, I look over the top of the crates. A las-blast sears just past my left ear and I pull the trigger, seeing the fiery trail of the bolt as it speeds across the hangar in a split second, tearing through one Typhon's shoulder, spinning him to the decking. The next goes down to a shot to the head, but the third is only caught a glancing hit on the arm. The three survivors are looking rapidly between me and the entrance when one of them is pitched off his feet by a blast to his chest. I fire the last round as they turn on the Colonel, who's charging into the hangar, power sword gleaming. Striden follows him, bolt pistol held in both hands as he snaps off another shot, the Typhon thrown half a dozen metres as the bolt catches him high in the chest. The last one seems to give up the fight, shoulders drooping as the Colonel rams a metre of powered blade through his midriff.

I burst from cover and give a shout. Striden almost shoots me but pulls himself short just before firing.

'Kage?' says the Colonel, noticing me as I leg it across towards them. 'I thought it was Inquisitor Oriel helping us.'

'Never keep a good man down,' I tell him.

As he turns to look at me, I'm shocked to see his left arm stops just above the elbow, the end a charred mess. I've never seen the Colonel hurt in battle before. Not even the tiniest scratch, and now he's missing an arm. That scares me, and I'm not sure why. I guess I thought he was invincible. I think I'm more bothered by it than he is, as his icy gaze flicks around the chamber, checking for enemies. He doesn't seem to have noticed he's got an arm missing. A devil in a man's body, I once called Schaeffer. I'm reminded of that fact looking at him, standing there with one arm, as alert and poised as ever.

'Plasma blast,' he explains, following my gaze.

We clamber hurriedly up the boarding ladder of the nearest shuttle. I'm about to get in after the other two when I hear a shout from behind. Turning, I see Inquisitor Oriel racing across the hangar towards us.

'She's all ready to go,' Striden calls out from inside.

Oriel bounds up the steps but I step into his path as he ducks to get into the shuttle.

'What is the meaning of this, lieutenant?' he demands, straightening up.

'How did a genestealer get here, months or years of travel from the nearest hive fleet?' I ask him, all the pieces beginning to fall into place in my head.

'I am an agent of the Emperor's Holy Orders of the Inquisition,' he snarls at me. 'I could kill you for this obstruction.'

'You didn't answer my question,' I tell him, folding my arms. I'm right, and this man has a lot to answer for.

'Stand aside!' he bellows, making a lunge for me. I side-step and smash my knee into his stomach, forcing him to his knees. He looks up at me, aghast, surprised I've got the guts to strike him. Lucky he wasn't expecting it; I don't think I could've laid a finger on him otherwise.

'You said you couldn't let it get away from you again,' I say to him as he kneels there wheezing. 'You let it escape didn't you? Frag, you might have brought it here, for all I know.'

'You don't understand,' he gasps, forcing himself to his feet. 'It was unfortunate, that is all.'

He makes a grab at the holster hanging from his belt, but finds it empty.

'Looking for this?' I ask, holding up the bolt pistol which I grabbed when I kneed him in the guts. 'Four thousand dead Last Chancers. Unfortunate. Three and a half million dead Typhons. Unfortunate. A million Guardsmen from across the sector. Unfortunate. Risking fifty worlds. *Unfortunate?*'

'You could never understand,' he snaps, stepping back a pace. 'To defeat the tyranids, we must study them. There's more than a few million people at stake here. More than fifty worlds. The whole of the Imperium of mankind could be wiped out by these beasts. They must be stopped at any cost. Any cost.'

'I guess this is pretty unfortunate too', I add, ramming the grip of the pistol into his chin, tumbling him down the steps. I step backwards through the hatch and pull it shut, cycling the lock wheel.

'Let's go!' I call out to Striden. As I strap myself in next to the Colonel, the engines flare into life, lifting us off the ground. I'm slammed back into the bench as Striden hits the thrusters onto full, the shuttle speeding from the dock like a bullet from a gun. We pass through a short tunnel, jarring against the wall occasionally under Striden's inexpert piloting, before screaming into the bright daylight, blinding after the glowstrips of the past few days. I look back and see Coritanorum stretched beneath me, built into the mountains almost fifty kilometres across.

A ball of orange begins to spread out behind us, a raging maelstrom of energy surrounded by flickering arcs of electricity. Two others erupt just after, forming a triangle until their blasts merge. The immense plasma ball expands rapidly, hurling stone and metal into the sky before incinerating it. For a moment I think I see a black fleck racing before the plasma storm, but it might be my imagination. Then again, there was another shuttle in the bay. Mountains topple under the blast and all I can think of is the pile of ash that'll be left. A pile of ash worth three and a half million lives because someone made a mistake. My thoughts are drawn back to my own survival as I see a howling gale hurling rock and dust towards us.

'Faster!' I bellow to Striden as the shockwave crashes through the air. The ground's being ripped up by the invisible force, rock splintering into fragments, the high walls exploding into millions of shards. With a final convulsive spasm the plasma engulfs everything. The light sears my eyes, the boom of the explosion reaches my ears just as the shuttle is lifted up bodily by the shockwave, hurled towards the clouds. The hull rattles deafeningly from debris impacts, the metal shrieking under the torment of the unnatural storm, bouncing us up and down in our seats. I hear Striden laughing in his high-pitched way from up front, but I'm more concerned with my heaving guts as we're spun and pitched and rolled around by the blast.

As it passes, and the passage begins to smooth, I hear this strange noise and turn to look at the Colonel.

He's laughing, a deep chuckle. He's sat there, one arm ending in a ragged stump, dishevelled and covered in the blood and guts of others, and he's laughing. He looks at me, his ice eyes glinting.

'How does it feel to be a hero, Kage?' he asks.

EPILOGUE

THE COLONEL WAVES away the orderly fussing over his arm with an irritated gesture. I stand there impatiently, waiting to get my hands on the pardon. We're back in the Commissariat relay post where we were told about our final mission. The door behind me creaks open and Schaeffer's personal scribe, Clericus Amadiel, walks in, the hem of his brown robes flowing across the floor. There's someone else with him, a young man, his face tattooed with the skull and cog of the Adeptus Mechanicus. Amadiel has the bundle of pardons in his arms, while the tech-adept is carrying some piece of bizarre equipment that looks like a cross between a laspistol and a spider.

'Here are the documents, Colonel,' Amadiel says slowly, placing them one at a time on the bare wooden desk in front of Schaeffer.

I restrain myself, wanting to grab the whole bunch and find mine. The Colonel, deliberately making his point, signs the pardons of the others – Franx, Kronin, Lorii, Loron and Gudmanz. Pardons for dead people, keeping the alive waiting. He works slowly and methodically, the clericus holding the parchments for him while he signs them with his good arm. Amadiel passes him a lighted red candle, and with the same infuriating slowness, dribbles a blob of wax onto the parchments, which the Colonel then seals with a stamp produced from the scribe's sleeve. Eventually, perhaps a lifetime later, the Colonel pulls mine forward.

'There are a number of conditions attached to the continuing application of this pardon, Kage,' he tells me sternly, finally looking up at me.

'Yes?' I ask, suspicious of what the Colonel might say next. I didn't think he was the type of person who would try to wriggle out of something. He has some honour, that much I'm sure.

'First, you are to discuss no details of the Last Chancers' activities in Coritanorum with anyone unless specifically ordered by myself or a member of his Holy Emperor's Inquisitorial Orders,' he says gravely, counting the point off with a raised finger.

'Forget this ever happened, right sir?' I confirm.

'That is correct,' he replies with a nod. 'We were never here, a malfunction in Coritanorum's reactors caused the citadel's destruction. An Act of the Emperor.'

'Understood,' I assure him. I'd been expecting something like this ever since the shuttle landed and we were bundled into another one of those black-painted Commissariat armoured cars.

'Second,' he says raising another finger, 'you are on parole. The pardon is revoked if ever you transgress any Imperial law or, should you remain with the Imperial Guard, any article of the Imperial Guard Code and Laws of Conduct,' he says, as if reading it out from a script inside his head.

'I'll keep my nose clean, sir,' I tell him with a sincere nod.

'I doubt that,' he says suddenly with a lopsided smirk, mentally throwing me off balance. That was almost a joke! 'Just make sure you do not get caught doing anything too serious.'

'Don't fret, Colonel,' I tell him with feeling. 'As much as I've enjoyed your company, I never want to see your face again.'

'Those are the conditions,' he concludes, scribbling his signature on the scroll and whacking down the seal. With a casual gesture, he offers it to me. I reach out cautiously, still half-suspecting him to pull it away at the last moment, laughing cruelly.

I'm afraid to say that I snatch it from his grasp, eagerly reading the words: *freedom... pardoned of all crimes.* Freedom!

'What will you do now, Kage?' the Colonel asks, leaning back in the rickety wooden chair, making the back creak under the weight.

'Stay in the Guard, sir,' I tell him instantly. I'd been thinking about it on the bumpy half-hour shuttle run. More to take my mind off Striden's poor flying than anything else. We had to ditch eventually, when another storm broke. He raises a questioning eyebrow and I explain. 'I joined the Imperial Guard to fight for the Emperor. I swore an oath to defend His realms. I aim to keep that oath.'

'Very well,' the Colonel says with an approving nod, 'your final rank of lieutenant will be transferred to whatever regiment you end up joining. There are quite a few here to choose from. But I recommend you stay away from the Mordians.'

'I will,' I say emphatically. 'I kinda like the uniforms of the Trobaran Rangers, so perhaps I'll see if they take me.'

'Notify Clericus Amadiel as soon as you have made your choice. He will ensure any necessary paperwork is in order,' the Colonel says, nodding in the scribe's direction. Amadiel looks at me with his fixed, blank expression.

'There is one other thing,' the Colonel adds as I'm about to turn to the door. He beckons the tech-adept forward with a finger.

'I can remove your penal legion tattoo,' the adept says, raising the peculiar gadget as if in explanation.

I roll up my sleeve and look at my shoulder, barely making out the skull and crossed swords emblem. Above the badge you can just make out '13th Penal Legion', and underneath I know is written '14-3889: Kage, N.', though you can't see it now past the white scar tissue.

'I'll keep it,' I announce, letting my shirt sleeve drop down again.

'Keep it?' stutters Amadiel, unable to stop himself.

'To remember,' I add, and the Colonel nods in understanding. The memory of four thousand dead is etched into my brain. It makes a strange kind of sense that it's tattooed into my skin as well.

We don't exchange another word as I salute, turn on my heel and march out, hand gripping the pardon so tightly my knuckles are going white. Outside the bunker, the two provosts click their heels to attention as I walk between them, and I studiously ignore them. A day ago, they would have shot me given the slightest chance or reason.

As I pick my way across the shellhole-pocked mud, I glance back and see the Colonel emerge. A sudden whine of engines and a downblast of air heralds the arrival of some kind of stratocraft – long, sleek, jet-black, no insignia at all. A door hisses open in the side and three men jump out, swathed in dark red cloaks that flap madly in the downwash of the craft's engines, and the Colonel nods in greeting. The four of them climb back in again and with a whoosh it accelerates back into the clouds again in less than ten seconds. That's the last I'll see of him, he's probably already planning the first suicide mission for the next bunch of poor bastards to be called the Last Chancers.

THE EMPTY BOTTLE smashes as I casually drop it to the floor, the shards of pottery mixing with the glass and ceramic of the four other bottles that proceeded it. I'm drunk. Very drunk. I hadn't had a drink in three years and the first glass went straight to my head. The second went to my legs, and the rest has gone, well, Emperor knows where! That's how it's been for the past two months, every night in the officers' mess, crawling back to my bunk when they throw me out.

I'm out on Glacis Formundus, back on garrison duty again, with the Trobarans and Typhons for company. I still don't really know anyone, I've spent every night here drinking my pay away, trying to forget the past three years, but it isn't easy. Parades and drills are so dull, my mind wanders back. To Deliverance, to Promixima Finalis, to False Hope and all the other places I fought and my comrades died in their hundreds. I swill the Typhon wine around the silver goblet for a while, pretending I can smell its delicate bouquet through the smoke of the ragweed cigar jammed into the corner of my mouth. Gazing up at the thousands of candles hanging from the dozen vast chandeliers that light the marble hall with their flickering glow, I wonder if there's a candle there for each dead Last Chancer.

The mess seems filled with Typhons today, giving me surly looks like they know something, but they can't, I'm sure of that. We won a great victory at Coritanorum, we won the war and preparations have begun to receive Hive Fleet Dagon, which is why we're stuck out here for the moment. A great victory, but nobody else seems like celebrating. Everybody in the mess is sombre. I don't know what they've got to be so unhappy about, having to eat fine meat, dining on fresh vegetables, drinking, whoring, gambling and wasting their lives instead of fighting. I guess that's why I haven't fitted in, because I've begun to miss combat. Shouting orders at a bunch of uniformed trolls as they march up and down the parade ground is no substitute for crawling about in the mud and blood, kill or be killed situations that bring you to life. Miserable bastards, don't they know we've just won a war?

Everyone else's grim mood has brought me further down. I think about the other Last Chancers. The dead ones. The ones who got their pardon too late. Three thousand nine hundred and ninety-nine of them. All dead. Except me. I start to wonder why I'm alive and they're not. What makes me special? Was I just lucky? Have I been set aside from harm by the Emperor? I'm tempted to think the latter, which is why I joined up again, to pay him back for watching over me these past three years. Emperor, I wish these Typhons would cheer up, the miserable fraggers.

'What did you say?' a man demands from over towards the bar, three metres to my right. He's decked out in blue and white, the

Typhon colours, gold braiding hangs across his left breast, a cupboard full of medals adorning the right. A colonel I reckon. I must have spoken out loud.

'Wha?' I mumble back, unable to recall what I was thinking, trying to drag my brain out of the drink-fuelled murk.

'You called me a miserable fragger,' he accuses, stepping through the haze of ragweed smoke to stand on the other side of the small round table. I sit back, letting my elbows slide off the table and peer back at him.

'We've just saved the fraggin' sector, and everyone's moping around like their sister's died,' I say as two more Typhons, both majors or captains by the uniforms, step up behind him.

'I had to leave my wife and go to some bastard slime pit in the middle of nowhere,' the one on the left stabs a finger at me, some froth from his ale still stuck to his huge, drooping moustaches. 'What's to be happy about?'

'Welcome to the fraggin' Imperial Guard,' I say, shrugging my shoulders and knocking back the last glass of wine.

I try to get up but the first one, a bald, middle-aged man, thrusts me back onto the bench with a gnarled hand on my shoulder. As I thud back into place, one of them pulls my pardon from where it's been jolted out of one of the chest pockets on my jacket. I always keep it there, a good luck talisman. The stub of the cigar drops into my lap and I brush it to the floor.

'What's this? Penal legion scum!' he hisses, looking at what's written on the parchment.

'Not any more. I'm a proper officer now,' I tell them, still half-baked with the wine. 'Look, I'm sitting around on my fat arse doing nothing, shouting at the troopers and trying to jump a lass from the local town, I must be an officer.'

'You should've been hanged!' Big Moustache adds, looking over his comrade's shoulder. 'You're a disgrace to the Imperial Guard.'

'You'd all be dead if it wasn't for us,' I mumble back. 'Should thank me, ungrateful bastards.'

'You think so?' the third one demands, his piggy nose thrust into my face. 'You're nothing! You're scum!'

'You should all be killed!' Baldy declares, face a bright red now.

'We were!' I snarl back, sickened by their attitude. 'They were fraggin' heroes. You part-time soldiers don't even deserve to lick their boots!'

'You traitorous filth,' Pig Nose bellows, pulling an ornate sword from its scabbard and waving it at me. Something inside me snaps, looking at these prissy, pompous, spoilt, officer-class weevil-brained snobs. A feeling I haven't felt since Coritanorum surges through me, a feeling of energy and vitality, of being alive, infusing me with strength and power.

'I'm a man, a soldier!' I scream back at them, hauling myself to my feet. 'They were all soldiers, real men and women! Not scum!'

Pig Nose makes a clumsy swipe with the sword, but he's too close and I easily grab his wrist. I trap the basket hilt in my left hand and twist, wrenching it easily from his grasp, as easy as taking sweetmeats from a babe.

'You want it rough?' I shriek, slamming the hilt into his pig nose, causing blood to cascade over the white breast of his tunic. They begin to back away. I hear murmurs from around the room. 'You're Guard, can't you fight me? What did you get those medals for? Polishing? Shouting? Fight me, damn you!'

I take another step forward, lashing out with the hilt into Big Moustache's stomach, doubling him over. They stumble away again, eyes darting around looking for the trooper that's going to fight for them.

'No one else to fight this battle,' I snarl. 'You'll have to get bloody and dirty now.'

There's a clamour all around as people scramble for the doors. Chairs and tables are overturned as people back off from the madman screaming and waving a sword around. This is the closest half of them have ever been to a fight. The alcohol mixes with my anger to fuel me with blood lust, a red mist descends in front of my eyes and I keep seeing little piles of ashes, faceless strangers clawing at me from my dreams, men cut down and blown apart. My head whirls with it and I feel dizzy. It's like four thousand voices are crying out for blood in my head, four thousand men and women crying to be remembered, asking for vengeance.

'This is for Franx!' I shout, plunging the sword into Pig Nose's guts. The others try to grab me, but I lunge back at them, slashing and hacking with the sword.

'For Poal! Poliwicz! Gudmanz! Gappo! Kyle! Aliss! Densel! Harlon! Loron! Jorett! Mallory! Donalson! Fredricks! Broker! Roiseland! Slavini! Kronin! Linskrug!' The litany of names spills from my lips as I carve the three arrogant Typhons to pieces, hacking into their inert bodies, blood splashing across the light blue carpet to create a purple puddle. With each stroke, I picture a death. All the ones I saw die, they're stored up there in my head and it seems like they want to rush out. 'For fraggin' all of 'em! For Lorii!' I finish, leaving the sabre jutting from the chest of Pig Nose.

People are shouting and grabbing at me, someone's throwing up to my right, the coward, but I push them away, remembering at the last second to turn back and snatch the pardon from Baldy's dead fingers. I stumble out of the door and start running off into the streets, the rain cascading off my bloodied hands as I stuff the pardon back into my pocket.

I WAKE WITH a banging in my head loud enough to be all the forges on Mars. My throat feels as if several small mammals have nested in it for a year and my limbs feel weak. With hazy recollection the events of the night before come back to me. I can feel the Typhons' dried blood caked on my hands. I really should try to control my temper. My next instinct is to check that I have my pardon. I fumble in my pocket and my heart leaps into my throat when I find it empty.

Just then I hear a tearing noise and force my eyes open. Someone's stood over me where I'm collapsed against an alley wall. The sun reflects off a window behind him, so he's hidden in shadow. Squinting into the light, all I can see are two pinpricks of glittering blue. Two pieces of flashing ice. He drops something and I see my pardon, torn in two, fluttering to the wet ground. He pulls a bolt pistol from his belt and points it at my face.

The first thing that pops into my head is, 'What the hell is he doing here?'

The second is, 'How in all that's holy did he get his arm back?'

'I knew you would come back to me, Kage,' the Colonel purrs savagely. 'You are one of mine. You always will be. I can kill you now, or I can give you one more Last Chance.'

Oh frag.

LIBERTY

Prison guard Serpival Lance suppressed a yawn and withdrew into the sentry alcove a little further to get out of the driving wind and dust. The permanent tempest howled around the roof of the tower, all but obscuring the ruddy lights that shone from the edge of the landing pad only a dozen metres away. He had been on duty for three hours and still had three to go, and he glanced enviously at the light shining beneath the door of the guardhouse to his left. Here he was, wrapped up in his heavy weather coat, hood pulled tight around his face, while the others laughed and played cards inside. It wasn't right for a man of his age. He had served the Emperor on this prison planet for thirty years, and still he was stuck out here on Emperor-forsaken nights like this.

His misanthropic musings were interrupted when the internal comm speaker squawked behind him. He pressed the receiver rune and bent his aching back to listen closely.

'He's come back. Due to land in a few minutes,' the guard captain's voice crackled over the comm-set. Serpival grunted an acknowledgement and cast his eye into the cloud-covered skies. It wasn't long before the landing beacon sprung to life, a guiding low energy laser piercing the gloom from the centre of the landing pad. Shortly after, answering lights could be seen glimmering in the darkness as the shuttle descended, the howl of its engines growing clearer and clearer as they drew closer and blotted out the noise of the wind.

With a clang of metal landing feet on the mesh surface of the roof, the shuttle settled, its engines at a roar which kicked up the dust into even more violent swirls before cutting out. An erratically wobbling entry gantry extended out from the docking area and connected with the shuttle's hatchway. The door opened and banged against the shuttle fuselage and a tall uniformed figure stepped out. The three guards in the tower spilled out and stood to attention by the doorway into the interior. The Imperial Guard officer said something to them and pointed inside the shuttle. The guards saluted and hurried past to emerge a moment later carrying a heavy bundle.

Curious, and knowing that it was a breach of regulations but unable to stop himself, Serpival ducked out of the sentry post and hurried across the rooftop to the others. They were carrying a man, slumped unconscious in their arms, dressed in full combat fatigues and camouflaged in black and dark blues. As they bundled him into the room, his head lolled towards Serpival and the guard suppressed a shudder at the sight of the man's face. It was horrifically scarred, criss-crossed by weals and cuts, bullet grazes and burns.

'The governor has all of the official notification. Lock him up with the rest,' the officer said curtly before turning on his heel and walking back towards the shuttle.

At that moment the new prisoner groaned and came round, shaking his head. The others lowered him to the floor, glancing at the retreating back of the officer. Groggily, the Imperial Guardsman stood up, blinking his eyes to clear them.

'Where the frag?' he asked, still slightly disorientated.

'Ghovul vincularum,' Serpival told him.

'A prison planet?' the man asked for confirmation, his eyes suddenly focussing on Serpival, all dizziness gone, making the guard squirm as if he were looking down the barrel of a lasgun.

'Yes, a prison,' the prison guard repeated himself, nervous under the evil stare of the newcomer.

It was then that the prisoner followed the gaze of the others. The officer was just climbing through the hatchway.

'Come back here, you bastard! Schaeffer, you sump-sucking piece of crap!' the newly arrived inmate screamed, roughly shoving Serpival aside and taking a step out onto the docking gantry. The officer turned, looked once and then slammed the hatch shut without a word. The prisoner broke into a run, yelling incoherently, and the other guards sprinted after him.

It was Shrank who caught him first, grappling the man's left arm. The prisoner stumbled, recovered his footing and then smashed the extended fingers of his right hand into Shrank's face, who fell away screaming, clutching at his eyes. Frentz swung a right-handed punch, but the guardsman easily swayed to his left, delivering a short kick to the prison officer's knee that made it snap the wrong way, tumbling him to the ground with shrieks of agony.

The shuttle engines roared back into full life, bathing the rooftop in their white glare, the prisoner silhouetted against them, his fist raised, his words of hatred drowned out by the noise. Serpival and the remaining guard, Jannsen, drew their heavy pistols and took aim at the prisoner, who stood there, fist still raised, watching the departing shuttle.

'Try any more of that and I'll plug you, you vicious scumbag!' Jannsen called out.

The prisoner turned around slowly, his face lit by the lights of the landing pad, bathing his scarred features in a hellish red glow. Slowly the man walked back towards them, and Serpival had to fight to remain calm and his grip on his pistol steady as the stranger slowly strode towards them, murderous intent on his face. He stopped a couple of metres away.

'Just take me to my fraggin' cell before I take that pistol off you,' the man growled, nodding towards the gun in Jannsen's shaking grip.

'The prisoner will lie face down and do as he is told,' Jannsen said, without much confidence.

'Kage,' the prisoner replied, glancing at each of them in turn and then stepping easily between them, looking back over his shoulder at Serpival. 'Call me Kage.'

I'M STANDING THERE wishing this repetitive, idiotic man would just shut the hell up. The prison governor is a sour, hatchet-faced man, crouched like a malevolent rodent behind his massive desk. That desk says volumes on its own – three metres wide, two metres deep, an Imperial eagle burnt into the surface but otherwise empty. He sits there behind it, elbows resting on the deep red wood, his chin resting on the knuckles of his clasped hands as he drones on and on and on. Behind him are two guards with shotguns, and I know there are two more behind me, similarly armed. They really don't trust me in here with their commander.

'...Which is why you will adhere by these rules at all times,' Governor Skandlegrist is saying, peering at me over a pair of half-moon glasses. He is dressed in layered robes of black and deep red, strangely matching the desk in colour. 'Punishment for infractions will vary depending on the severity of the offence. I have had special instructions from Colonel Schaeffer to keep an eye on you, Kage, and I will do so. I will be watching you like a hawk, and if you step out of line the full force of my authority here will fall upon you. Be warned, you are under close observation, so don't think you can get away with anything, anything at all.'

'Right, I get the picture,' I butt in desperately, taking a step forward which causes the guards to pull up their shotguns. At least they're paying attention, which is more than I am. 'Can I just get to my cell now?'

'Your disrespect for a commanding officer is shocking, Kage, as is your disregard for the laws and regulations of the Imperial Guard,' Skandlegrist replies. 'You are a bad seed, Kage, and I have no idea why Colonel Schaeffer wants you to be detained at this facility instead of being on the gallows like you should be, no idea at all. But, unlike you, I have my orders and I follow them, and follow them I will, mark my words. Yes, I'll be watching you, Kage, very closely, very closely indeed.'

With a gesture from thin, crabby fingers he orders the guards to escort me out. We're near the top of the tower, maybe just a couple of floors down from the landing pad on the roof. The whole tower is a broad cylinder, with just a single elevator shaft linking all the floors at the circle's centre. We stand there while the lift cranks and rattles up from the depths of the tower, the guards still nervous and agitated.

When the conveyor arrives, one of the guards opens the doors, which squeal on rusting hinges with an ear-grinding shriek. A shot-gun butt in my back propels me into the interior of the open ironwork cage, and they follow me in, not standing too close, guns lowered at my belly. One of them pulls the lever, to the eighteenth storey I note, and we start to judder our way down the shaft.

'Shrank was my friend, you piece of filth,' one of the guards hisses in my ear over the sound of grinding gears. 'I'm gonna make you pay for blinding him, one of these days.'

I turn and look at him with a patronising smile.

'You try anything, I'll rip your arm off and shove it down that big mouth of yours,' I tell him, meeting his gaze and causing him to flinch.

'I bet,' he says, recovering well. Before I realise what he's doing, he slams the shotgun in his hands straight into my chin, smacking my head against the iron grillwork of the elevator cage. Another one steps up and puts a boot into my gut, winding me badly, while the first jabs the shotgun into my face again, bruising my right cheek. Another three or four blows rain down on me. I take the brunt of it on my shoulders, before they step back, panting.

I crouch there for a moment before straightening up, feeling my right eye begin to swell and close. I roll my neck with an audible clicking and look at each of them in turn through my good eye. I take a good look at them, memorising the names on the tags on their uniforms.

'I'm gonna kill all of you meatheads, and I'm gonna do it slowly,' I warn them, meaning every word of it.

As I STEP into the cell, the door clangs behind me. There's a rough ironwork bunk on either side of the room; the left one has an occupant. He snorts and wakes, sitting up. He's a huge bear of a man. As the crudely spun woollen blanket falls from his torso, it reveals a mass of hair across his broad chest, shoulders and back. He looks at me in the dim light of the glow globe set behind a grille in the ceiling, his dark eyes almost invisible under a bushy brow. His hair is cropped short on top, as is his full beard, and over his right eye he has a tattoo of a pair of dice, mirrored on his left cheek. He gives a wheezing grunt and swivels further around.

'Welcome to Ghovul,' he says, his voice a hoarse whisper. I ignore him for the moment, sitting myself down on the other bed, nursing the growing bruises on my chest and ribs.

'Guards don't like you then, man,' my cellmate comments, and I look up at him.

'Nobody likes me,' I say quietly. 'I prefer it that way. Puts everybody in the same place. Me and everyone else. Frag, even I don't like me.'

'Thor's teeth, man, I can see you're gonna cheer me up with your witty banter,' the other man grumbles, his fat lips twisted into a sour grimace. 'Name's Marn.'

'Kage,' I say, offering him my hand to shake. As he leans forward, I see he really is hairy pretty much all over. He takes my hand in his massive paw, giving it a firm squeeze which I return. We sit there for a couple of seconds, measuring each other up.

'You're not gonna give me any trouble, man, are you?' he asks, letting go. 'I keep myself to myself, and if you do the same then we'll get along fine.'

'I'm not much for gabbling and gossip,' I reassure him. 'In fact, if these are the last words we say to each other, that wouldn't bother me for a moment.'

'Well,' he replies, rubbing his hand across his head and lying back down again. 'You don't have to go that far, man, but we're cellmates, not friends.'

'Damn right,' I reply, unlacing my boots and placing them neatly under the bed. 'All my friends are long dead.'

I strip off my socks and shirt, slide under the blanket and close my eyes. I'm weary as a poor infantry footslogger after a week's marching, but sleep won't come. My mind is whirling with recent events. After the Colonel picked me up again, I've been in a holding cell aboard the *Pride of Lothos*. Must have been several weeks travelling, crossed quite a few systems I reckon. I didn't see hide nor hair of the Colonel until I got here, and he was leaving me to rot in this cell.

Emperor knows what he's got in store for me. After all, the last words I heard him say were, 'I can shoot you right now, or I can give you one more Last Chance.' I bloody said yes of course, considering he was pointing a pistol at me at the time. But that's all I know. I've got one more Last Chance. I figure that's another spell in the Colonel's suicide squad, the 13th Penal Legion. Another suicide mission or two, another chance to get my arse blown off and back again on some hellhole or other, fighting some poxy aliens or heretics who should know better than to try their luck fighting the Emperor's armies. Maybe I'll be blowing up another city, who can tell?

All I know is that if the Colonel wanted me to just rot in a cell, he would have left to rot on that prison planet he first picked me up from. And if he wanted me dead, well then he would have just pulled the trigger and blown my head to bits. He's got something in store, I'm certain of that. But I don't really plan on hanging around for it to happen.

With that in mind, and the droning noise of Marn's snoring, I begin to drift asleep.

THE CLATTER OF bowls and plates fills the mess halls as the inmates sit down with their food. I'm sat on a bench at a long wooden table, twenty of us to each side, the bowl of soup, the hunk of dark bread and the plate of what may once have been meat but now resembles boot leather in front of me. We sit there patiently, waiting. It's about half a minute before Preacher Cleator starts his sermon. He keeps it short, which he normally does, Emperor bless the doddering old fart, and mumbles something about the bounties of faith and the punishments of sin. Just like he has done for the last sixteen days I've been here. He finishes.

'Praise the Emperor,' we all intone solemnly before grabbing up our knives and spoons and tucking in with gusto. The food tastes like crap, but when you only get cold gruel for breakfast and this sump filth twelve hours later, you'll eat whatever they dump in front of you. It's quite varied, to tell the truth. Sometimes the unidentifiable carcass is seared beyond recognition into charcoal, other times it's so bloody and raw I'd swear the fragging thing is probably still breathing. Never somewhere in between though, never nicely cooked. And the thin, watery spew that passes for soup, well, it probably came out the same animal is all I can say. Doesn't stop me soaking up every last drop with the fist-sized hunk of mud that passes for bread. Better than going hungry, as I learnt from two years of protein chunks on my last tour out with the Last Chancers.

Marn is sat opposite me, wolfing his food down. Thor's blood, but he eats fast. Not an ounce wasted though, it all gets crammed into that maw of his with ruthless efficiency. It's like watching a well-oiled machine at work, both hands working simultaneously, his jaws chewing constantly, barely pausing for split second for him to open his lips and shove another quivering spoonful into his mouth. Thirty seconds and he's done, while I'm barely halfway through the soup, which is piping hot if nothing else. Emperor knows how he stays so big on such meagre rations, because he must weigh at least half as much again as I do.

We all eat in silence; nobody really has anything to say. It's odd, comparing this prison with life on the *Pride of Lothos*. There was upward of two hundred of us in each of those converted holds, and we pretty much hated each others' guts. But we were a fighting unit, we were in squads and platoons, and had some kind of unity from that. We all had our only little groups which we kept to, who we talked to stop ourselves going mental and slashing our own throats or blowing our brains out the next time we went into battle. Well, after a while, I remember when we first got to Ichar IV, the first warzone we were deployed on, there was a good eighty, ninety soldiers topped themselves in the first week. I don't know if that was the effect of fighting the tyranids, or the realisation that they were gonna be stuck in one long war until they died, with no respite and not pardons. Well, no pardons back then, at least.

Here, it's every man for himself. There's you, and a vague bond with your cellmate, and that's it. It's driving me nuts, and no mistaking. I wake up at first light, well, when the glow globes on the landing outside the cells come on anyway. I never have been a heavy sleeper, I'll wake up at a gnat's cough. I lie there for maybe three hours before breakfast call. Then we're roused out, herded to the hose rooms to get washed down, then we come down here, to the mess hall at the bottom of the tower. It takes forever, only a handful of prisoners and twice as many guards in the lift at one time. It's a really inefficient system for moving large numbers of prisoners around. Perhaps I'll make a complaint to the governor. Anyway, it takes the best part of an hour to get the two hundred or so prisoners into the hall and then we all queue up again for our slop. We sit there while the guards hand out the knives and spoons and the Preacher totters about, waving incense around in the rusty old burner that usually hangs from his belt, staining his white robes browny-orange down his left leg. Then it's five minutes to eat up, another wait while they count the knives back in, and gather up the spoons and dishes. Then back in groups of twenty up in the exercise hall on one of the middle levels, for two hours. After that, back to Marn's quiet company for nine hours until the whole meal ordeal is repeated for dinner. Then it's lock up and shut up.

Deacis's holy arse, but I'm bored out of my wits. All my bitching about suicide missions and getting my face blown off aside, I'd much rather be out there with the Colonel doing whatever insane thing it is he's doing, than stuck in here slowly getting older, with my brain dribbling out of my ears. My resolve hardens. Another month here and I'm going to be smashing my grey matter out on the walls of that cell, standing over Marn's ragged corpse, screaming and damning Schaeffer's name to the Abyssal Chaos and back. I have to get out of this fragging tower.

DAY EIGHTEEN, AND my desperation is beginning to grow. Last night, Marn's snoring was driving me insane. I can't sleep as it is, even pushing myself to the limits in the two hours of exercise I'm allowed is nowhere near enough to tire me out. I feel so lethargic and tired, this inactivity is slowly killing me. If the Colonel does come back for me, which I'm starting to doubt more and more with each passing day, I'll be a flabby, useless piece of filth, rather than the fit, lean soldier I was when he brought me in here. Surely he wouldn't let such a good fighter go to waste like that. Anyway, Marn's snoring like a fire klaxon, his wheezing breaths echoing off the walls, driving through my ears right into my brain. I got up, and my fingers were within centimetres of his throat. Hell, he wouldn't have known a thing, my thumbs would've crushed his windpipe before he even woke up. I'd probably be doing him a favour. I must have been stood over him like that for over an hour, resisting that murderous urge.

I work out what anger I can on the sand-filled punch bag, pounding my bare fists into the poorly tanned leather, alternating between imagining Marn's hairy face there and the Colonel's chiselled features. There's just me and them, and I work and work, throwing jabs and crosses, bone-breaking uppercuts, organ splitting body blows, kicks that would burst men's intestines and shatter ribs into dozens of pieces. I picture all this in my mind, and it's easy, because I've done it to real men and see then effects. I imagine the blood flooding from Marn's nostrils as I drive my elbow into what would be the bridge of his nose. I imagine the Colonel collapsing breathless as the middle knuckle of my left hand slams into his abdomen. Over and over, punishing them with my fists and feet, until even my callused knuckles are raw and bleeding, the thick skin scraped off on the clumsily made punchbag. Sweat pours off me in rivulets, I can feel it rolling down my back, splashing all around me as I wallop Marn with a right roundhouse to his bushy eyebrow. My heart's hammering in my chest, the blood coursing through my body, fuelling the destruction of these two hated men.

Suddenly I'm aware of someone stood behind me. I spin on my right heel, fists raised. There's another prisoner there, I've seen him here every day, obviously, but I don't know his name. Marn's the only person here who's name I know. He's a little taller than me, with muscles bulging out of his ragged vest like boulders. He looks like he was carved rather than grown. His bald head is tattooed with blue flames, as are his massive chest muscles and biceps.

'You've been on that for ages. My turn, trooper,' he says, nodding towards the bloodied punch bag. 'I think it realises you don't like it.'

'I'm not finished yet,' I tell him, turning away and taking up my stance again.

'I wasn't asking,' he barks, shoving me to one side, almost knocking me off my feet.

'Frag off, or I'll kill you,' I warn him, squaring up.

'Go play with the others, pretty boy,' he laughs.

He stops laughing when the extended fingers of my right hand slam into his throat. He reels back and I follow up immediately, slamming a left hook into his jaw, his face already reddening from choking, and then catching him under the chin with the heel of my right hand. I hear shouting and chanting start up around me, but don't listen, focussing on this bastard in front of me instead. He flails madly, forcing me to duck, and as I rise, my right fist drives straight into his nose, ripping open a nostril and crunching cartilage. He stumbles back against the bare stone wall and I feel rather than see the other prisoners and the guards forming up around us. Their noise is blocked out by the roar of blood in my ears.

A spinning kick to his midriff hurls him back against the wall as he rebounds towards me, and I get my whole body weight behind the next punch, driving it between his eyes and smashing his head back against the unforgiving stone, leaving a bloody stain as he slumps to one side.

'That's enough,' I hear someone shout and a guard's gloved hand closes around my right wrist. With a simple twist of my hands, I snap his arm at the elbow, not even turning around, and drive the heel of my left boot into the other prisoner's face again, crushing his jaw and cheek and pounding his head against the wall once more. He flops to the ground and I stamp on his neck for good measure, feeling the crack of his spine snapping like a twig. Then something hard smacks across the back of my neck, stunning me and forcing me to my knees. I see the baton swing across my face and feel a sharp pain across my forehead before I fall unconscious.

I'M STOOD TO attention in the governor's office again, nursing a bump on my head the size of Terra and still feeling groggy. There's six armsmen in here with me this time, I figure that the governor's not one to take chances.

'I am sure I don't have to tell you that this kind of behaviour is wholly inappropriate, wholly inappropriate to a military facility, whether it be a garrison or a prison,' he tells me. 'I understand well the pressures placed upon our inmates, and that occasionally tempers will flare. In fact, given our population, I expect instances of this kind now and then. We have highly trained, aggressive soldiers penned up here, and fuses can be short on occasion with no outlet for that professional aggression. In most cases, I am lenient and understanding.'

'That's very broad-minded of you, sir,' I say, resisting the urge to rub the bruise on my forehead.

'However,' Skandlegrist continues, with a scowl of annoyance, 'I cannot tolerate the death of another prisoner at your hands. Fighting and brawling I consider an unpleasant but necessary evil of running a vincularum. Murder I do not. Murder, cold-blooded or otherwise, is not an option, and an example will be made of you.'

'That's ridiculous,' I snort, earning another stare from the governor. 'I've been trained to kill. That's what I do. What do you expect? It's the whole point of fighting, isn't it?'

'You are trained to fight and kill under orders, Kage,' snaps the prison governor, standing up, his expression hard. 'You were trained to be a disciplined killer, to exterminate the enemies of the Emperor as ordered by your superior officers. You were not trained to kill every man or woman who happens to disagree with you. You are so far out of line, Kage, and you do not even see it. If I cannot convince you, perhaps the whip can. As the authority of the Imperial Commissariat on this world, I sentence you to two dozen lashes, to be carried out before breakfast tomorrow in front of the other inmates. I could, and would, normally order you executed for this heinous, malicious act, but given the specific orders I received from Colonel Schaeffer that is not an option available to me. Take him away!'

He spins on his heel and clasps his hands behind him, ignoring me as the armsmen grab me by the arms and roughly bundle me out of the room.

'Costaz should get the honour,' one of them says to the others. I remember that name; it was the guard who attacked me in the elevator.

The solemn beat of a drum echoes around the exercise hall, whose walls are lined with the assembled prisoners and guards. At one end, a wooden slab with two chains hanging from thick rings is propped up against the wall, the governor stood next to it. Two guards walk in front of me, with four others behind, my punishment escort. At a slow march, we pace across the hall in time to the drum. I look at the sea of faces, recognising none of them, they're just a blur of different coloured flesh all wrapped up in the same drab grey prison fatigues.

'Prisoner and escort, halt!' commands the governor, his voice surprisingly loud and strong. We all halt, our boots clashing in unity on the bare boards of the floor.

'Prisoner, advance!' the governor orders me forward and I step out sharply, my chin high, looking at the chains on the wooden board. I spread eagle myself against the board, and two guards step forward and clasp the manacles around my wrists, before pulling the chains up, stretching me out, and fastening them to bolts screwed into the top edge of the slab. One of them offers me a leather strap, and I open my mouth and he places it between my teeth. This isn't the first time I've taken a whipping. I know the routine. I bite down hard, vaguely wondering who else's mouth the leather bit has been in.

I hear the clump of the guards' boots as they withdraw and focus my attention on the grain of the wood in front of me. The wood is quite pale, but dark red stains the grooves between the planks, and the deeper areas of grain. There's no mistaking that it's blood, the blood of those who've been punished like this. There are a few score marks above my right shoulder, though I can't think what could have caused them.

It's then that I realise the governor is talking again.

'...in accordance with Imperial Guard regulations,' I hear him finish.

There's a hiss behind me and a short crack a moment before searing pain tears across my shoulder blades as the whip's end opens up a furrow in my skin. I bite harder on the leather, my eyes going wide as agony wracks my back. There'll be no blood trickling down yet, it'll be five or six more before the weals split into cuts and gashes. Another hiss and crack and more pain, this time further down, across the small of my back. It's fleshier down there and the pain seems to spread further around to my sides. I block it out, it's easy at the moment. It was more painful when a tyranid warrior stuck its bonesword through my thigh on Deliverance. It was a hell of a lot more painful when a spore mine exploded in my face, hideously scarring me for the rest of my life and making one side of my face almost totally numb. Another hiss and crack, and pain explodes across my shoulders again. I don't know if it is the guard who attacked me holding the whip, but whoever he is, he knows his stuff. Four more times the lash rips across my spine before I can feel the trickle of my blood oozing out of the lacerated flesh.

I close my eyes until they water as he carries on, methodically, relentless tearing strips of skin and fat from my back. I lose count and open my eyes again, staring deep into the wood, pretending I'm elsewhere as hot pain burns across the whole of my body. In the short pause between blows, I glance up and see blood leaking out of my clenched fists and on to the chain, from where I'm clenching my hands so hard my nails have broken the skin. I relax them, only to tighten my grip even more when the next lash strikes me.

And that's how it goes on until the sentence is carried out. My eyes are watering, my throat is constricted and my heart is hammering in my chest, but not once do I cry out. I take the pain, and I take it deep inside. Storing it away, using it as fuel for myself. My life has been built on pain, pain that I'll throw at my enemies. Pain and agony that I'm saving up for the Colonel. As the guards unfasten the manacles, I give a grunt, the only noise to have passed my lips. It's a grunt of satisfaction, because deep inside that pain is boiling around, and it'll come out one day. One day when the Colonel's throat is in my grip. This is just another episode of pain and hate in the life he's created for me, and I'll pay every second of it back to him. Every second.

IT'S FOUR DAYS of agony before I can even start thinking straight again, laid up in the tower's infirmary, my back swathed in saltwater-soaked bandages. It hurts like a bastard, but the salt will help my tattered back knit itself together. The prison surgeon, some inmate called Stroniberg, had to put a few stitches into the worst of the cuts, but my back was so numb by then I didn't feel a thing. The day after I'm out of the infirmary, I begin to plot my escape.

There's only one way out of the tower, and that's the roof. If I can get up there, perhaps with a rope or something, I'll be able to scale the outside wall and get to safety. There's one problem. The only way up to the roof is the elevator. I have to find some way of gaining control of the elevator long enough to reach the top. I'm not sure yet how to do that, but I know a weapon of some kind will be needed. I have to work out a way of making a weapon, easily concealed but deadly.

The answer comes to me during dinner the next day. As they've always done, the guards clear away the knives first, keeping careful count of them. I'd never get away with one of them. However, the spoons on the other hand are just cleared away with the rest of the dishes, without too much attention paid to them. At breakfast the day after, I make my move.

Everybody's finishing their gruel, well everybody except my glutto-nous cellmate who wolfs his down without taking a breath. Next to me is a slim man, with tawny hair and a drawn face. To be honest I've never noticed him before, I've always sat fixated watching the eating machine on the opposite side of the bench from me. Today, however, he becomes the object of my attention.

I rise to my feet with a roar, smashing his dishes and mine across him.

'What did you say about my mother?' I bellow at him, grabbing him by the collar of his prison vest. He snarls wordlessly at me, and swings a punch which I put my head down into so his fist cracks against the hard part of my brow. I heave him upwards and slam him down onto the table, scattering more bowls and spoons and cold gruel over those nearby. The prisoner opposite and to my right lunges at me across the table, but I drag the skinny guy upward, so the other inmate's punch slams squarely across his face. Letting go of him, I turn to the man on my left, seeing out of the corner of my eye that Marn is starting to lay into the guy who tried to attack me.

Pretty soon, there's seven or eight of them brawling around me. One of them punches me on the chin and I roll with the blow, hurling myself over the bench and rolling under the table. Quickly, I snatch up one of the discarded spoons and shove it into my boot, pulling my fatigues out of them to hide the long handle. I shelter there for about half a minute more, and then emerge as the guards break up the fight. One of them grabs me and pushes me to one side.

'Clear this mess up, troublemaker,' he growls at me, pointing to the broken dishes and scattered cutlery.

'Of course, sir, sorry about that,' I mumble, dropping to my knees and picking up the pieces of cracked pottery and gathering up the spoons. I stand there holding the jumbled mess until another guard turns up with a metal basin and tells me to drop it all in.

'No dinner tonight, Kage,' the guard with the basin tells me. 'If you can't eat without acting like an animal, then you can't eat.'

'Sorry, sir,' I apologise again. 'I'll watch my temper in future.' Inside I'm grinning like a fool. The plan's starting to work.

It takes three nights of furtive labour to file the edge of the spoon's bowl into a sharper blade. The scraping hidden by Marn's snoring, I spend my night hours rasping the spoon back and forth across the bricks of the wall, under my bed so a casual inspection won't see the score marks. Another four days of rubbing, my hands cramping on occasion with holding the thin handle of the spoon, allows me to sharpen the end of the handle into a point. Perfect for piercing throats, lungs and windpipes. With my weapon sorted out, albeit a bit of a crude one, I turn my attention to what I have to do next.

The elevator only stops at a floor when it's time for meals, ablutions or exercise period, and at those times, there's always a bunch of guards and other prisoners around. Certainly too many people for an efficient escape attempt. I need to think of some way to get the guards to make a special visit, only one or two of them preferably, and somehow get them to open the cell door at the same time.

IT'S TWO SLEEPLESS nights listening to Marn's incessant droning snore before the answer comes to me. It brings an ironic smile to my face when I think about it. I rise up in the dim glow through the vision slit in the door and pull my pillow clear from my bed. I stand over Marn, considering my options, and decide this is the best one. I lean down and place the pillow over his face, pushing ever so slightly harder and harder so as not to startle him. He wakes up briefly, eyes staring wide at me in accusation, but lack of breath pushes him into unconsciousness a few seconds later. I pull the pillow off, and check that he's still breathing, but only shallowly. I don't want him dead yet. Taking my makeshift knife from where it's concealed under my mattress, I roll Marn onto his side. I count down his ribs and probe the sharp end of the spoon between the fifth and sixth one, almost effortlessly sliding the point back, puncturing his lung. I let him flop back and then sit on my bed and wait.

It's several minutes before his breathing gets more and more laboured, and then flecks of blood start appearing on his lips. Soon, more is bubbling up into his mouth and I decide it's time to act.

Running to the door I shout through the grille at the guard stationed a few doors down.

'Quick!' I call to him. 'Something's wrong with Marn. I think he's got a pox or something, lungrot maybe.'

The guard stride over towards me, his expression full of suspicion.

'Look for yourself,' I say, backing away from the door. He shines a handlamp through the grille onto Marn, the small circle of light settling on his face and the trickle of crimson from the corner of his mouth. The guard swears and I hear him pound off across the landing. A couple of minutes pass before the clank of the elevator sounds from the shaft, followed by the rusty creaking of the guard opening the doors. It's another tense three or four minutes before the elevator returns.

'Back into the far corner, Kage,' I hear the guard order me, and I do as he says, my hands behind my back concealing the sharpened spoon.

There's a rattle of keys and the door opens. There are three guards stood there, and between them a medical orderly. He's dressed as a trustee, one of the sycophantic inmates who's got extra responsibilities by behaving himself and toadying to the governor or guards.

They step inside, and the orderly bends over Marn, checking his breathing. I wait, poised to act, until the guards are looking at my dying cellmate.

Three steps and I've crossed the cell, slashing the blade across the jugular of the guard closest to me, blood fountaining through the gloom. I kick the next guard hard in the chest, hurling him against the wall, and wrap my arm around the startled trustee's throat, the point of the spoon hovering next to his right eyeball. The third freezes where he is, hand hovering over the pistol at his belt.

'One wrong move and he dies,' I snarl as the winded guard clambers to his feet, his face aghast under a thick mop of black hair.

'What the hell are you doing, Kage?' he asks quietly, his eyes straying to the corpse of his comrade.

'Back out onto the landing, meatheads,' I tell them, tightening my grip on the orderly, who squeals on cue.

'You can't go anywhere,' the dark-haired guard continues, trying to circle to my right, but I swivel on my heel, dragging the trustee with me, to keep him in view.

'I said to stay still!' I snap, ramming the spoon into the orderly's eye, who screeches briefly before collapsing. I hurl the body at the circling guard and dive at the other, who pulls his pistol free a moment before my hands close on his wrist and snap upwards, cracking open the bones in his arm. I snatch the gun from him as he collapses backwards cradling his arm and round on the remaining warden.

'Don't,' I warn him, the muzzle of the pistol aimed squarely between his eyes.

'Drop your weapons,' I say, and he does as he's told, unbuckling his belt and letting it clatter to the ground. 'Now out through the door.' I wave him on his way, darting a glance at the guard with the broken arm, but he's slumped on the floor, whimpering. Hooking his weapons belt over my shoulder, I follow the guard on to the landing.

We make our way over to the elevator and I push him inside before swinging the doors closed behind us. Switching the pistol to my left hand to keep him covered, I crank the lever fully to the right, and the conveyor begins to rumble into motion. Floor by agonising floor we slowly crawl our way up the centre of the tower, the progress of the elevator marked out by an illuminated dial set above the door way. We're twenty floors short when a klaxon starts to sound out, an escape warning.

'They're onto you,' the guard says with satisfaction. 'They've got orders to kill you if you resist. Give yourself up or you'll die.'

'You won't see it,' I tell him, pulling the trigger of the pistol and blowing half his face away. As the gunshot's retort still echoes around me, the elevator creaks to a halt, and then begins to descend again. I try the lever desperately, but there must be some kind of external override. I glance around the conveyor and notice the maintenance access panel in the roof.

Ramming the pistol into my belt, I jump up and smash the panel open. Leaping again, I get a grip on the edge and pull myself on to the elevator roof. Above me, dimly lit by sparsely placed glow globes, the shaft stretches upwards out of sight. I see the doors to other levels passing me, and walking to the edge, I look down and see light pouring from several entrances not far below me, where the guards have forced the doors open. I can't stay where I am, too much of an easy target.

There's a ladder running the length of the elevator shaft, up the wall just across a small gap. It's no big matter to grab one rung as I slowly descend, and pull myself on to it. Dragging the pistol free, I aim at the receding shape of the elevator's braking block and fire two shots. There's a hiss of hydraulic fluid spraying into the gloom, and the elevator picks up pace, accelerating down the shaft. I've been climbing for several seconds before there's an ear-shattering crash from below as the lift hits the bottom of the shaft. I haul myself upwards as fast as I can, more light pours into the shaft from opened doors above and below me. Something ricochets off the wall next to me, accompanied by the sharp crack of a pistol. Soon more bullets are flying, tracers amongst them, some of them passing close by, others way off. The guards can't really see me. They're aiming blind. I pull myself up a few more floors, the fire pinging and screaming around me, and then pause for breath. At that moment, the door on the opposite side swings open, and I hang there face to face with two trustees and a couple of guards.

I react first, bringing up the pistol and emptying the clip into them, punching them off their feet in a hail of bullets. The shots at me intensify from above, and I swing off the ladder into a small maintenance alcove just to my left. Crouched there, I discard the empty pistol and pull the other free from the belt, throwing that down the shaft as well.

I crouch at the edge of the alcove, and fire a few shots upwards, aiming for the rectangles of light that indicate the open doors above me. There's a scream and a guard comes toppling out, falling past me. Realising that it's only a matter of time before they get me if I stay here, I jump back on to the ladder and carry on climbing.

My shoulders and arms burn as I drag myself up rung by rung, the wounds in my back opening again and causing blood to trickle down onto my fatigues and soaking my vest. I pause occasionally to fire at the shapes of guards I see peering and shooting from the open doors above, and by keeping their heads down in this way make good progress.

I've climbed perhaps two dozen floors when the elevator chain begins to grind into action once more, so I figure the crash didn't take it out of commission permanently. I redouble my efforts, pulling myself up rung by rung, trying to outrun the approaching lift whilst also firing up at the opening above me.

More shots flare around me from below, and I glance down and see firing through the open work elevator roof, about ten storeys below me. I fire back down at them, trapped in a horrid crossfire. Swinging desperately from the ladder, I wait until the elevator is just a few floors below, before jumping off the ladder, firing down as I leap on to the roof. I land with a clang of boots and roll automatically, falling through the open maintenance hatch into the midst of the guards inside.

I fire the pistol point blank into the gut of one and twist, bringing the butt of the pistol smashing across the face of another. I punch a third in the throat, crippling his breathing. Another already lies on the floor, holes stitched across his chest. I stand there panting as the lift grinds its way upward, taking me to the top of the tower.

Just before I reach the last level, I ram the lever into the halt position and the brakes squeal in protest before the elevator comes to a stop. Climbing out on to the lift's roof once more, I pull myself up to the doors to the roof. Now with two more pistols claimed from the guards lying dead and unconscious in the lift, I brace myself on the inside of the door, trying to detect any movement on the far side. I hear and see nothing.

I crash my shoulder against the doors and they fly open, a guard on the far side giving a startled yelp as one of them smashes into him. I roll through the opening, arms crossed, firing the pistols to either side of me, before coming to my feet and spinning around, the guns blazing in my hands. Three more corpses litter the floor behind me as I sprint out onto the roof.

There's a massive storm raging, lightning flickers all around and thunder rolls. The wind howls across the tower, stinging my flesh and whipping up a cloud of dust and grit. Behind me I hear more shouts, and realise that there are more wardens spilling from the guard-house. I pay no heed, and run for the edge. I'll climb down by hand if I have to.

I JUMP UP onto the parapet that runs around the tower roof and stop. In the light of the storm, I look out over Ghovul. Far below me, the tower stretches down onto a rocky mesa. Beyond that is a flat, fea-tureless plain. Everything is grey and rocky, with no shelter from the elements, no cover to hide in, nothing to drink from, nothing to eat, just barren rock and gravel. As far as the eye can see. Distant lightning shows me that the plain stretches on far into the distance. There are no hills, no mountains, nothing, just a massive expanse of desola-tion.

There's nowhere to go.

I hear shouts from behind me and shots whine past. I raise my hands above my head and let the pistols fall from my fingertips, feel-ing numb.

Nowhere to go, nothing to do except wait here for the Colonel.

The Colonel. As I think about him, the pain flares up inside me, the burning anger builds in my gut and chest. I clench my fists above me as the guards close in, and scream into the storm.

'Schaeffer!' I shriek. 'Come back here, you bastard!'

KILL TEAM

ONE
PROLOGUE

THE AIR WAS filled with swirling grey dust, whipped up into a storm by a wind that shrieked across the hard, black granite of the tower. The bleak edifice soared into the turbulent skies, windowless but studded with hundreds of blazing lights whose yellow beams were swallowed quickly by the dust storm. For three hundred metres the tower climbed into the raging skies of Ghovul's third moon, an almost perfect cylinder of unbroken and unforgiving rock, hewn from the infertile mesa on which the gulag stood.

A narrow-beamed red laser sprang into life from its summit, penetrating the gloom of the cloud-shrouded night. A moment later it was answered by a triangle of white glares as a shuttle descended towards the landing pad. In the bathing glow of the landing lights, technicians scurried back and forth across the pad, protected against the violent climate with bulky work suits made from a fine metal mesh, their hands covered with heavy gloves, thick-soled boots upon their feet.

With a whine of engines cutting back, the shuttle's three feet touched down with a loud clang on the metal decking of the landing area. A moment later a portal in the side swung open and a docking ramp jerkily extended itself on hissing hydraulics to meet with the hatchway. A tall figure ducked through the low opening and stepped out on to the walkway. He stood there for a moment, his heavy dress coat whipping around him, a gloved hand clamping the officer's cap to his head. With his back as straight as a rod despite the horrendous conditions, the new arrival strode across the docking gantry with a purposeful gait, never once breaking his gaze from directly ahead of him.

Inside, a black-clad guard saluted the man and without a word gestured for him to proceed into the open work iron elevator just inside the landing pad building. With a creak of rusty hinges the warden swung the doors shut and jerked a lever to start the conveyance descending with a rattling of chains and grinding of gears.

'Which level is the prisoner on?' the officer asked, speaking for the first time since his arrival. His voice was deep and quiet, the authoritative tone of a man used to being obeyed without question.

'Level sixteen, sir,' the guard replied, not meeting the piercing blue gaze of the officer. 'One of the isolation floors,' he added hesitantly. The visitor did not reply but merely nodded.

The lift rattled on for a couple of minutes, passing slowly down through floor after floor, an illuminated dial marking their descent. When it reached seventeen the guard hauled back on the lever and a moment later the shaft echoed with a screech of badly oiled brakes. The elevator shuddered to a halt a few seconds later.

The officer glanced up at the floor indicator, which now was shining through number sixteen.

'The tech-priests promised to look at it, sir, but say they are too busy,' the warden answered apologetically at the officer's questioning glance. The prison guard was old and haggard, with thinning tobacco-stained white hair and an ill-fitting uniform. Coughing self-consciously the guard flung open the doors with more screeching and stepped out of the way.

The level onto which the tall man stepped was as round as the tower itself, heavy armoured doors spaced evenly around its wall. Everything was the colour of ageing whitewash, a pale grey stained in places with patches of reddish-brown.

'It's this one, sir,' the guard said, walking around to the right of the elevator door when he realised the officer was waiting for directions. Another guard, younger and sturdier than the one who had been waiting at the landing pad, was standing by one of the doors, dressed in the same plain black uniform, a heavy cudgel hanging from his belt. The first guard led the officer over to the door and flipped down a small viewing window. The smell of stale sweat swept out of the small grille, but the officer's face remained impassive as he gazed through the narrow slit. Inside, the cell was as bare as the hall outside, painted in the same drab colour. Only a few metres square, the room was illuminated by a single glow globe set into the ceiling behind a wire mesh. Its lacklustre yellow light cast a jaundiced tinge across the room's occupant.

He was stretched out on the far wall, wrists manacled to the corners of the ceiling with heavy-linked chains. His feet were similarly restrained to the floor. His head hung down against his chest, his features hidden by a long, bedraggled mane of unkempt hair. He was clad in nothing but a rag about his waist, the dim light showing up his taut, sinewy muscles. His chest was crisscrossed with scars, some new, others years old. His arms were similarly disfigured, a particularly prominent slash across his upper right arm obscuring what was left of a tattoo. His left thigh was marked on both sides by large puncture scars from a wound that had obviously passed completely through his leg.

'Why was he moved here?' the officer asked quietly, his voice causing the prisoner to stir slightly.

'In the first month he was here, he killed seven wardens and five other prisoners and almost escaped, sir,' the older guard explained, casting a nervous glance through the slit and exchanging a look with the other guard. 'The commandant has had him confined to isolation for the last five months for the safety of the other inmates and the guards, sir.'

The officer nodded and for a fleeting second the warden thought he saw what looked like a satisfied smile pass across his lips.

'And his mental condition?' the man asked, moving his gaze from the warden back into the cell.

'The chirurgeon has examined him twice and has declared him psychopathic, sir,' the guard replied after a moment. 'He seems to hate everyone. He refuses to eat anything except protein gruel. The only time he allows us near him is when we take him down to the exercise hall. We can't allow him in there with other prisoners though, and no one is allowed to carry anything that might be turned into a weapon in his presence. We learnt that when he tried to escape.'

The officer turned back, an eyebrow raised in query.

'Nobody thought to count the spoons in the mess hall,' the warden replied, ashen-faced.

The man turned his attention back to the cell once more.

'Perfect,' he whispered to himself. 'Open the door,' he ordered the younger of the two guards, before stepping back and to one side.

As the sullen, dark-haired warden did as he was told, the door screeching open, the prisoner looked up for the first time. Like the rest of his body, his face was a mass of scars. A long beard hung down over his chest. The warden's look was returned by a venomous stare, hatred burning in the dark eyes of the inmate, a feral intensity shining in them. The second guard took up position on the other side of the prisoner, dragging his heavy club free and holding it easily in his right hand.

'Now the manacles,' the officer prompted.

'I don't think that's a good idea, sir,' the ageing guard replied with a startled look. The prisoner's eyes hadn't moved, continuing to burn straight through the warden.

'S-s-sir?' the younger prison official replied with a horrified stare. 'Did you hear what he told you about this animal?'

'He is not an animal,' the officer snapped back. 'The manacles.'

Visibly shaking, the white-haired warden crept forward and fumbled with his ring of keys. The other guard followed him, dragging his cudgel free from his belt. Hesitantly the crouching guard unlocked the left leg first, flinching nervously, expecting the foot to lash out at him. A bit more confident, he unlocked the other leg. He glanced up at the prisoner's face, but the inmate's gaze had not left the face of the other security man. Quickly he undid the wristlocks and took a few hurried steps back, ready to bolt.

The prisoner took a step forward, rubbing his arms to revive the circulation. Then, without a word, the inmate stepped to his left, his right hand lashing out, sending the maul spinning from the younger warden's grasp, who yelped and clutched his broken wrist. The other guard stepped forward, but the prisoner was quicker, twisting on his heel to deliver a spinning kick to his midriff, hurling him back against the wall with a thud and a hoarse cry of pain. The guard with the mangled wrist had recovered now, but the prisoner turned his attention back to him, smashing rigid fingers into his throat then wrapping his arm around the guard's neck in a headlock. There was an audible crack as the guard's neck snapped, and the prisoner gave a satisfied grunt as he let the body slump to the ground. He took a step towards the surviving warden and was about to repeat the move when the officer stepped into the room.

'That is enough, I think,' the visitor said quietly, and the prisoner looked round, a wolfish grin of savage joy splitting his scarred face.

'I'm fraggin' happy to see you, Colonel,' the prisoner said, laughing hoarsely. 'Do you need me again?'

'Yes, I need you again, Kage,' the Colonel replied.

TWO
VINCULARUM

+++The playing pieces are being assembled, the strategy is in motion+++

+++Time to prepare for the opening moves+++

IT IS WITH a mixture of relief and dread that I look at the Colonel. On the one hand, the fact that he's here means an end to six months of misery and boredom. On the other, his presence means I could be dead any time soon. I've been hoping for and dreading this moment for half a year, torn between expectation and apprehension. All in all, I'm pleased to see him though, because I'd rather take my chances with the Colonel than rot in this damn cell for the rest of my life. He just stands there, looking exactly the same as he did the last time I saw him, as if he'd just come back in after a moment, rather than having abandoned me for nearly two hundred days to stare at four bare walls.

'Get him cleaned up then bring him to the audience chamber,' Schaeffer tells the guard curtly, giving me a final glance before turning and striding back out of the door.

'You heard the officer,' the warden prods me into life as I stand there staring at the Colonel's retreating back. He casts a nervous glance at the corpse in the corner of the cell and takes a step away from me, his eyes wary, hand hovering close to the pistol at his belt.

I follow him to the lift, and wait there in silence for a few minutes while the elevator takes the Colonel back to the top of the tower. My mind is racing. What does the Colonel have in store for me? What's the mission this time? Commander of the 13th Penal Legion, known commonly as the Last Chancers, Colonel Schaeffer led me and nearly four thousand others in bloody suicide missions across a dozen worlds last time around, and all to whittle us down to a few survivors. Would it be the same again? Was I going to spend the next two years being shipped from battlezone to battlezone, wondering every time if this was the fight that would be my last? To be honest, I don't care one bit. If my time in this stinking prison has taught me anything, it's that life on the battlefield, fighting for your life, is far more desirable to sitting on your arse for nine-tenths of the day.

I knew he would come back for me, though. He didn't say anything when he left, but I remember his words when we first met, just over three years ago. 'Just my kind of scum,' he had called me. Shortly before knocking me out, I might add, but these days I wouldn't hold that against him. He's done a lot worse, to me and others.

With a shuddering clank the conveyor arrives and the warden ushers me inside. We rattle up a couple of floors to the wardens' level where the washrooms are. I've never come this way before, for the last five months my washing routine has consisted of being hosed down with cold water every other day. I follow the guard without much thought, my mind still occupied with the Colonel's arrival. It guarantees nothing but bloodshed and battle, but then that's all the Colonel has ever represented. That and an unbending, uncompromising faith in the Emperor and unswerving loyalty to the Imperium.

I've always had plenty of faith, but it wasn't until the Last Chancers that I realised my part in the grand scheme of things. I'm a murdering, cold-hearted bastard, I don't mind admitting. But now, I'm one of the Emperor's murdering, cold-hearted bastards and He has a use for me again. It gives me some small measure of satisfaction that although all I know how to do now is to cripple and kill and maim, I have a sense of purpose I never had before. It's a cruel, hard galaxy out there, and if you're going to survive you have to learn some cruel, hard lessons. I learnt them while four thousand other Last Chancers didn't, and I'm still here. I figured all the time I was in that cell, remembering every battle, every gunshot and stab, that the Emperor and the Colonel weren't finished with me just yet. I reckon neither will ever be finished with me, not even after I'm dead, I'm sure.

I pull off the rag and step into the showering cubicle. The guard turns the water on from outside and a scathing jet of hot water cascades down on to me from the grille in the ceiling. He tosses in a gritty bar of soap and I start scrubbing and scraping.

'I need to shave,' I call out over the splashing of water. The guard mumbles something back that I don't hear over the water drumming off my head. 'I said get me a blade, I need to get rid of this fraggin' hair and beard!'

'You're not allowed sharp implements, Kage,' the guard calls back. 'I'm under orders.'

'For Emperor's sake, you sack of crap, I can't go in front of the Colonel looking like a sodding beggar,' I argue with him, stepping out of the cubicle. He retreats quickly. I point to the pistol and then the knife in his belt.

'If I wanted to kill you, you'd already be a cooling body,' I tell him with a smile. 'Give me your damn knife before I come and take it off you.'

He unbuckles the sheath and tosses it over to me, looking ready to bolt at any point. The look of fear in his eyes sends a shiver of pleasure through me. What I would have done to have had a reputation like this a few years ago back on Olympas. It would have made things a lot easier for me growing up, that kind of terror.

I step back under the stream of water and lather the soap across my face and head, then pull the knife out and throw the sheath back out on to the tiled floor. I start with hacking off the hair as close to my skin as I can get it, dropping the ends in tufted lumps to swirl down and block the plughole in the floor. I then shave the beard off, scraping the knife across my cheeks and chin, removing a layer of skin at the same time. It stings more than a las-bolt wound, but I don't mind. I rub my hand across the smooth skin, enjoying the sensation of cleanliness for the first time in ages.

My hair is a bit more difficult, but I eventually manage to cut all that off as well, leaving a few nicks and cuts across the back of my scalp where the angle was awkward. Hey, my face was ripped apart and put back together again years ago, so I'm never going to win any medals for looks anyway.

Satisfied that I'm as presentable as I'm going to get, I dry myself down with the coarse, scratchy towel proffered by the guard while he goes to fetch me something suitable to wear. He returns a short while later with standard prison fatigues – badly made grey, baggy trousers and shirt woven from raw linen, and a pair of ill-fitting laceless boots. I feel like a right idiot wearing these clothes, like a small kid who's dressed up in his older brother's gear. I follow the guard back up in the elevator for my talk.

The guard knocks at the door and the Colonel calls me in. Unlike the rest of the prison tower, the circular hall is decorated with a bright mural that runs continuously around its walls, depicting some Ecclesiarchy scene as far as I can tell. Some saint's martyrdom judging by the final images which portray a man with a glowing halo being torn apart by greenskinned monsters which I take to be fanciful interpretations of orks. I've fought real orks, and in the flesh they're even scarier than the grotesque parodies painted around the hall.

The Colonel is sat to one side behind a plain desk of dark, almost black, wood. A simple matching chair is placed across from him. The desktop is piled high with papers in mouldering brown sleeves tied with red cord and stamped with various official seals.

'Kage,' the Colonel says, looking up from the sheaf of parchments in his hand. 'Sit down.'

I walk across and lower myself into the chair, which makes squeaking protests from its legs as I settle into it. The Colonel has turned his attention back to studying the documents he is holding. I wait there patiently. Locked up in that cell, patience was something I learned quite a bit about. The sort of patience I imagine a hunter has, waiting for his prey, sitting or lying there immobile for hours on end. The sort of patience that tests your sanity, the slow drifting of the hours and days threatening to unravel your mind. But I learnt. I learnt how to settle my thoughts, focussing them inwards: counting my heartbeats; counting my breaths; mentally going over a hundred rituals of weapons preparation and maintenance; fighting armed and unarmed combats with different opponents in the confines of my own head while my arms and legs were chained to the wall.

I realise I've drifted into the well-practiced trance state when the Colonel coughs purposefully, and I blink and focus on him. He hasn't changed a bit, though I didn't really expect he would have. Still that strong, clean shaven jaw, sharp cheek bones and the piercing glare of his ice-blue eyes. Eyes that can bore into your soul and burn through you sharper than a las-cutter.

'There is another mission,' he begins, sitting back and crossing his arms.

'I figured as much,' I reply, keeping my back straight, my expression attentive.

'There is not much time, relatively speaking,' he continues, his gaze constant. 'You will assemble and train a team to assassinate an alien military commander.'

This surprises me. Last time out, he was very defensive about revealing the mission objectives. I guess things are different this time.

'As you are probably expecting, the selection process will be more directed and focussed than last time,' he says, as if he can read my mind. 'I cannot afford the luxury of the time required to repeat the procedure you underwent before.'

I bet, I think to myself. It took four thousand soldiers and two and a half years to 'select' the Last Chancers when the Colonel last led me in battle.

Other than the Colonel himself, I was the only survivor.

'This prison contains some of the most specialised soldiers in this sector of the Imperium. I have had them incarcerated here for just this purpose, gathered here in one place where I have easy access to them rather than scattered across the stars. It makes assembling a team much more straightforward, with the additional benefit that few people know they are here, and I can maintain absolute secrecy,' he tells me, indicating the records on the desk with a sweep of his hand. 'You will go through these files and choose those you deem most appropriate for the mission. You will then train them in the skills they do not possess while I prepare the final details of the mission itself. I will then lead the Last Chancers on that mission. Is that understood?'

'Perfectly, sir,' I answer carefully, mulling his words over in my head. 'If I'm gonna choose, I'll need to know a little more about what you're planning.'

'For the moment you do not. I would rather you choose men and women whose skills you value regardless of the exact situation we might face,' he says with a shake of his head. 'Our choice of personnel will, to some degree, inform the plan of attack that I will devise. Flexibility will be the key to success.'

'I think I get you,' I tell him, leaning forward and resting my hands on the desk. 'Pick a team that'll be able to do what we need, whatever that is.'

'Once again, your ability to grasp complex issues astounds me,' the Colonel replies sarcastically. 'That is what I said, is it not?'

'Almost,' I answer with a grin. Something then occurs to me. 'Colonel, why use penal troops? I mean, I'm pretty sure you could have your pick of Guard regiments across the segmentum.'

'You yourself once told me the answer to that, if you can remember,' Schaeffer replies after a moment's thought. 'I can bark orders, I can make men do what I want, but for my missions that is not enough.'

'I remember now,' I say when the Colonel pauses. 'You want a team that has nothing else to live for except succeeding in the mission. It was in Deliverance, wasn't it? Yeah, I remember: give men nothing except life itself to fight for and they'll be the best fighters ever.'

'You learnt that well,' Schaeffer says pointedly.

'Well, I'm still here,' I reply with a bitter smile.

THERE ARE TWO hundred and seventy-six military personnel in the prison. It takes me just over a week to go through their records, sitting down with one of the vincularum scribes to read me out their details. I never did learn my letters, there wasn't really any need for it. I see the Colonel once in that time, to tell me that I've got three more days to make my choices. To begin with, I didn't know where to start. The Colonel's briefing was so vague, I found it difficult to picture what we could be doing. I spent the first day just sitting and thinking, something I've had plenty of opportunity to do in recent months. I figure that about ten or so good fighters will be enough. My experience from Coritanorum tells me that on the Colonel's missions, if you can't do it with a few well-trained men, then an army isn't going to help.

So I go through all the records with the adept, trying to make some more sense by dividing them up by expertise, previous combat experience and, almost as important, why they're in this prison. There's all kinds of dregs in here, but all of them are ex-military. That's not too surprising, considering the Colonel's purpose in life. But there's something particular about this bunch of convicts. They're all specialists of one kind or another. There's pilots, snipers, infiltration experts, saboteurs, engineers, jungle fighters and cityfighters, tank crews, artillery men, storm troopers, pioneers and drop troops. Like the Colonel said, he's gathered together some of the best soldiers from across the segmentum, and they're all here for me to choose from. So what am I looking for? How do you pick a team of expert soldiers when I've got a whole company of them to choose from? What could I look for that would set some of them apart from the others?

With only two days left to decide, my frustration is beginning to build. I need an angle, some way of picking out the best of the best.

I begin to appreciate more why the Colonel did what he did for the last mission. I start to understand that perhaps dragging four thousand men and women through hell and back and seeing who survives is the only way you can really find out who has that warrior instinct; who the fighters and survivors are, and which ones are just cannon fodder, destined for a bullet to save the life of a better soldier. Perhaps I should just get them to fight it out, pit them against each other and see who walks out.

Then I have a flash of inspiration from the Emperor. Perhaps I can't put them through a few battles to see who comes out on top, but I don't have to physically eliminate the weak links. It's halfway through the night when I send the guards to rouse the adept. I pull on my new uniform, kindly supplied by the Colonel. I slip into the plain olive shirt and dark green trousers, pulling the belt nice and tight then step into my boots. I can't tell you how good it feels to wear tight, solid combat boots on my feet after months of being barefoot. It makes me feel like a soldier again, not a prisoner.

I make my way to where the Colonel outlined my task and wait for the adept. A few minutes pass before he gets brought into the audience chamber, sleepy and confused.

'We're going to talk to all of the prisoners,' I tell him, grabbing the first couple of dozen folders from the desk and thrusting the pile of records into his arms.

'All of them?' he asks wearily, eyes bleary, suppressing a yawn.

'Yes, all of them,' I snap back, pushing him tottering towards the door. 'Who's first?'

Juggling awkwardly with the shifting pile of paperwork, he looks at the name on the top folder.

'Prisoner 1242, Aphren,' he tells me as we wait for the elevator. 'Cell thirteen-twelve.'

THE GUARD IS asleep on his feet when we step out of the lift onto the thirteenth floor, leaning against the wall. I give him a push and he falls to the ground, a startled yelp escaping his lips as he bangs his head on the floor.

'Wake up, warden!' I shout at him, dragging him to his feet.

'What's going on?' he asks dizzily, rubbing his eyes.

'Open cell twelve,' I tell him, grabbing his collar and dragging him towards the cell door. 'And you will address me as lieutenant or sir, I am an officer!'

'Sorry, sir,' he mumbles, the keys jangling in his shaking hand as he puts them in the lock. As he swings the door open I push him to one side.

'You, in here,' I snarl at the clericus as I step into the cell. He follows cautiously. The room is just like all the others, cramped and bare with a pallet on the ground along the wall opposite the door. The man inside is already on his feet, fists balled and raised. If ever a man could be described as big, it's this guy. He's easily half my height again, with shoulders like an ogryn's and biceps bigger than most men's thighs. He's wearing just his prison trousers and muscles ripple across his chest as he clenches and unclenches his hands. He's got a broad face and small eyes that are too close together under a heavy brow. I doubt he could count to ten, even using his fingers.

'You gonna try and hit me?' I ask casually, closing the door behind me and leaning back against it with my arms crossed.

'Where did you just drop out of the warp?' Aphren snarls back, taking a step forward. The adept makes a panicked squeak and backs into the corner. 'You can't just barge in here, I'm entitled to six hours sleep a night. Prison regulations say so.'

'Prison regulations say I'm not allowed to kill anyone here as well, but that didn't stop me,' I tell him in the same off-hand tone.'

'You're Kage, aren't you?' he asks, suddenly less sure of himself. 'I heard about you, you're fragged in the head.'

'I am Lieutenant Kage of the 13th Penal Legion, the Last Chancers, and you better remember that when you address me, soldier,' I remind him. The Colonel told me he had reinstated my rank when he gave me the uniform, which was kind of nice of him.

'Do you expect me to salute?' the prisoner replies with a sneer.

'Read it,' I say to the clericus, ignoring Aphren. The adept visibly pulls himself together and clears his throat in a pompous manner.

'Kolan Aphren, ex-drill sergeant of the 12th Jericho Rangers,' he begins in a monotonous drone. 'Seven years' service. Three campaigns. Arrested and court-martialled for brutality of recruits. Sentenced to dishonourable discharge and five years' hard labour. Sentence converted to life imprisonment, order of Colonel Schaeffer, 13th Penal Legion.'

'A drill sergeant? I could've guessed,' I say to him, meeting his angry gaze with a cold stare of my own. 'Like beating up on the new guys, eh? You're no good to me, I need a real soldier, not some training camp bully. Someone who's fought in a battle.'

'Why you little runt!' he bellows, hurling himself headlong at me. I side-step his clumsy charge and ram his face into the metal cell door. He drops like a stone. I pluck the record from the adept's grip, smiling inwardly at the look of horror on his face, and toss it onto the bed. 'You can pick that up later when we're done,' I tell him, rolling the unconscious Aphren out of the way with my foot and opening the door. 'One down, two hundred and seventy-five to go.'

'ERIK KORLBEN,' THE clericus reads out in his monotone voice. 'Ex-master sergeant, 4th Asgardian regiment. Three years' service. One campaign. Arrested and court-martialled for insubordination on the field of battle. Sentenced to thirty-five lashes, dishonourable discharge and ten years' imprisonment. Sentence extended to life imprisonment by order of Colonel Schaeffer, 13th Penal Legion.'

Korlben is short and stocky, with a thick mop of red hair and bushy eyebrows. He sits on the edge of his bed, gazing blankly at the floor, hands in his lap. Everything about him says dejected and broken, but I give him a chance to prove himself useful.

'So you don't like taking orders, Korlben?' I say, scratching my head. 'Bit of an odd choice, joining the Imperial Guard.'

'I didn't ask to join,' he mumbles back, not looking up.

'Oh, a draftee,' I reply slowly. 'I bet you must be plenty fragged then. Dragged into an army you don't want to fight in. Then slammed up in here to rot for the rest of your life. I guess the Emperor really doesn't like you, Korlben.'

'I guess he doesn't,' he agrees, meeting my gaze for the first time with a bitter smile.

'How'd you like to get out of here, maybe even go back to what you did before?' I offer, studying his reaction. 'It'll mean following more orders though.'

'I would like that a lot,' he nods slowly. 'I don't mind following orders – unless it's on a suicide charge to storm an enemy bunker.'

'Well, Korlben, that was the wrong answer,' I tell him viciously, slapping his record out of the adept's hands. 'You won't be seeing me again.'

'GAVRIUS TENAAN,' THE adept mumbles sleepily, barely able to keep his eyes open. We've been at it solid for the last thirty-six hours straight, going back to the Colonel's audience chamber and picking up more records when we run out, stopping only twice in that time to grab something to eat and drink. He's swaying on his feet, on his last reserves of energy. Weakling. Just like most of the inmates here.

Only about half a dozen or so have impressed me so far, the rest have got serious discipline problems, or are cowards, or would probably kill me as soon as look at me. 'Ex-marksman, Tobrian Consuls. Thirteen years… service. Six campaigns. Arrested and court-martialled for firing on Imperial citizens without orders. Sentenced to hanging. Sentence… sentence overturned to life imprisonment by order… order of Colonel Schaeffer, 13th Penal Legion.'

Tenaan is a wiry man, in his early forties I'd guess. He has a grizzled, thin face and a cold, distant edge to his eyes, like he's not really looking at me. He's sloppily stood to attention, fingers fidgeting with the seam of his fatigues.

'You like the killing don't you?' I say to him, cocking my head to one side and giving him the once over. 'I bet you used to be a hunter, before joining up.'

'That I was, sir,' he drawls back. 'Used to hunt deer an' such in the mountains. Then they came an' said that I could shoot orks if I wanted to, and that seemed like a good offer.'

'So how come you shot non-combatants?' I ask, wanting to hear the story in his own words.

'They was in my way, sir,' he replies in a matter-of-fact tone and a slight shrug. 'They shouldn't a been there.'

'How many?' I prompt, knowing the answer was in the records, but wanting to keep him talking. This guy had some potential.

'I don't remember exactly, sir,' he replies slowly. 'I think that time it was a dozen or so, I think.'

'That time?' I ask, surprised at this admission. 'How many civilians have you shot?'

'About fifty odd, by my reckoning, sir, mebbe a few more,' he nods, inwardly confirming this tally.

'Fifty?' I say incredulously. Okay, so my bodycount makes that look like spit in the sea, but at least I was under orders. 'You're too trigger happy, even for me.'

'Sorry to hear that, sir,' he apologises and gives another slight shrug.

With a grateful sigh, the adept drops the file and stumbles out of the cell and I follow him out.

'How many does that leave us with?' I ask him as we walk back to the elevator. He glances down at the small sheaf of papers left in his hands.

'Eight, lieutenant, there's eight you haven't rejected,' he tells me wearily, handing the documents to me.

'You'll be needing those,' I tell him, tossing the records back as I step into the lift. 'Have them mustered in the audience room tomorrow after breakfast, and inform Colonel Schaeffer that I will meet him there. I'm off for some sleep.'

MY EIGHT 'RECRUITS' are lined up in the chamber, standing at ease, each of them with their eyes fixed on me. All of them are curious, it didn't take long for the rumour to spread that psycho Kage was talking to everyone and offering a way to get out of prison. But other than that, they don't have a clue what's going on. One or two of them shuffle nervously under my gaze. The door swings open and the Colonel strides in, wearing his full dress uniform as always.

'Attention!' I bark and they respond sharply enough. It's one of the reasons they're here, they've still got some measure of discipline left in them.

'What have you got for me, Kage?' the Colonel asks, walking slowly up the line and eyeing each of them in turn.

We start at the left of the line, with Moerck. He's tall, well proportioned, handsome and smart. His blond hair is cropped short, his face clean-shaven, his eyes bright. He stands rigidly to attention, not a single muscle twitching, his gaze levelled straight ahead.

'Ex-Commissar Moerck, sir,' I introduce the Colonel and he nods, as if remembering something. 'An odd one, I'm sure you'll agree. Commissar to a storm trooper company, Moerck here has an exemplary history. He left the Schola Progenium with a perfect record. He has been cited for acts of bravery ten times. After five campaigns, he spent three years on attachment to the Schola Progenium training commissar cadets before being granted his request to return to battlefield duty. He has been wounded in action seven times; on three occasions he refused the offer for honourable discharge and a return to training duties. In short, sir, he is a genuine hero.'

'Then remind me why he is in a military prison, lieutenant,' Schaeffer says sourly.

'The commissar and his storm trooper company were participating in a night drop attack, as part of an anti-insurrection operation on Seperia,' I tell the Colonel, dredging back the details I spent most of last night committing to memory. 'The attack was a complete success: the enemy camp was destroyed, all foes eliminated with no prisoners, as ordered. The problem was, they had the wrong target. Some

departmento map maker had mixed up his co-ordinates and our
hero here led his men on an attack into the command camp of the
25th Hoplites. They wiped out their entire general staff. Without loss,
I should point out,' I smile at Moerck, who has remained dispas-
sionate throughout the sorry tale. 'To cover their own hides, the
departmento charged the entire company with failing to carry out
orders, and they were drafted into the penal legions. That's when you
came in and transferred the hero here. A genuine mistake, and probably the only innocent man in this whole prison.'

'You must hate him then, Kage,' the Colonel says, giving me an
intent stare.

'Of course, sir,' I reply, tight-lipped.

'So why have you chosen him?' he asks, turning his attention to the
ex-commissar. 'Some measure of revenge, perhaps?'

'Not at all, Colonel,' I reply with all honesty. 'This man will follow
your orders to the letter, with no questions. He has almost
unmatched combat experience, discipline and faith. He is entirely
dedicated to the Emperor's cause and will do everything to ensure
our mission is a success. I personally can't stand him, sir, you're right.
But if I want someone watching my back, our hero here is the best
for it.'

The Colonel just grunts and steps up to the next in line. He's short
and wiry, bald as a cannonball but with a bushy beard so that you
could be mistaken for thinking someone turned his face upside
down.

'Hans Iyle,' I tell the Colonel, looking down on the little man's
shiny scalp, puckered by a jagged scar just above his left ear. 'Formerly served in a recon platoon for eight years, Iyle here is the best
scout I could find. He has actual combat experience in desert, forest,
jungle and urban warzones. I think he likes the wilderness a bit too
much though. He deserted whilst fighting on Tabrak II, slipping away
while on picket duty. He survived out in the plains for eighteen
weeks before the advance of the rest of the army caught up with him
and he was captured. He's resourceful and has proven he can act on
his initiative.'

'Any other reasons for choosing him?' Schaeffer asks, a slight scowl
creasing his brows. 'I do not want another desertion halfway through
a mission,' he adds pointedly, referring to my numerous escape
attempts during the last tour of duty.

'Well, sir, because he hates being locked up in a cell even more than
I do, and will do anything to get out of here,' I explain. I do have a

slight doubt, but I think that Iyle would be more willing to see the mission out to the end than try to go it alone again. Of course, I don't say this to the Colonel. Schaeffer gives the man another hard stare before moving on.

'This is Paulo Regis,' I indicate the next man in line. He's about my height and build, a bit flabby around the waist and face, with pallid skin and a crooked nose. He's the most nervous of the bunch, his eyes flicking between me and the Colonel, fear mixed with flashes of hatred in them.

'A gunnery sergeant for seven years, our friend Paulo has extensive siege and bombardment experience,' I continue as the Colonel turns his ice-blue eyes on Regis. 'Our greedy gunnery sergeant was caught looting in the ruins of Bathsheman hive on Flander's World, against explicit orders from his captain.'

'A looter?' the Colonel exclaims with a grimace, eyes still fixed on Regis.

'One who was sentenced to hang for it, until your intervention, Colonel,' I point out. 'Not only that, there was a great deal of suspicion that looting wasn't all he did. Some might call it outright pillage or worse, but there was no way to prove it. He's unadulterated scum, sir, but I think he has learnt the importance of following orders.' Regis gives a grunt and a nod, and a look of irritation passes across Schaeffer's face.

'Did I say you could move, Regis?' I bellow at the prisoner in response.

'N-no, sir,' he stutters back, a panicked look in his eyes.

'Then you don't move!' I snarl, annoyed at being shown up like this in front of the Colonel. If it gets screwed up now, we'll all be enjoying the hospitality of this tower for the rest of our lives. That's something I definitely don't want. I glance at the Colonel to see his reaction, but he's now concentrating on the next soldier.

'Sniper first class, Tanya Stradinsk,' I announce as the Colonel looks her up and down, his face a mask. Tanya's not bad to look at, though I wouldn't go so far as to say she's pretty either. She has short cut, raven hair and soft brown eyes, full-lipped with prominent cheek bones. She's a few inches shorter than me, with the well-muscled build you'd expect a soldier to have.

'Without a doubt, she's the best shot in this prison, probably in the sector. Four hundred and fifty-six confirmed kills over nine years of service. Has won thirty-eight regimental and inter-regiment shooting medals, also awarded three medals for acts beyond the call of duty.

She's in here for refusing to fire on the enemy, something which she did four times before being court-martialled. She was involved in an unfortunate incident that left the royal nurseries of Minos a flaming ruin and killed twenty children, including the Imperial commander's heir. She was exonerated of all blame by an investigation conducted by the Inquisition, but has since been unable to shoot except on a firing range. Don't let that fool you into thinking she's had it tough. There is a suspicion that she fired on that nursery on purpose.'

'You have brought me a sniper who refuses to shoot?' the Colonel asks doubtfully, one eyebrow raised. 'I fail to see your reasoning, Kage.'

'Well, sir, you must have thought she might be some use when you had her sent here for your collection,' I point out, my inescapable logic earning a scowl from Schaeffer. 'If nothing else, she knows more about shooting than either of us and has training experience. Anyway,' I add, giving Tanya my hardest stare, 'I will get her to shoot again.'

Colonel Schaeffer's expression remains doubtful, his eyes lingering on me for a few seconds. I hold up under his close scrutiny, meeting his gaze evenly. The expressionless mask the Colonel usually wears for a face drops back into place again and he moves along another place to Lowdon Strelli.

If ever a man looked shifty and untrustworthy, it's Strelli. Slim built and long-limbed, it's like he was stretched as a baby or something. Even his face is long, with a pointed chin and high forehead, separated by an arrowhead of a nose. He looks at me with narrowed eyes and clenched jaw, assessing me, trying to gauge what sort of man I am.

'Strelli here is the team's shuttle pilot, should we need one,' I explain to the Colonel. 'Originally a pirate from the Sanbastian mining asteroids, Pilot Strelli saw the error of his ways when orks invaded that system eight years ago. Until his court-martial, he served as a shuttle pilot, and then later on Thunderbolt interceptors. It was during this time, and despite becoming a widely-known and respected fighter ace, that he took the rivalry between the guard and navy a little too far by strafing an armoured infantry column belonging to the Fighting First of Tethis. The colonel of the Tethis First demanded that the navy turn Strelli over to them and be subject to their justice and he was duly convicted and sentenced to death by hanging. Your intervention saved him.'

This time the Colonel says nothing, staring long and hard at Strelli, as if trying to pin him to the wall with his stare. The pilot shifts uncomfortably under the unremitting icy gaze and I notice his long fingers beginning to tap nervously on his thighs. As the Colonel's harsh scrutiny continues, Strelli's eyes begin looking towards the door and I think he's going to bolt. At that moment the Colonel turns his attention away and steps on. Strelli darts a quizzical look at me, his earlier cockiness gone. I ignore him.

'Next we have Trooper Quidlon, formerly of the New Bastion 18th regiment, who is here because of his inability to curb his curiosity and pay attention to the warnings of his superiors.' The first thing that springs to mind when looking at Quidlon is 'square'. He's short, has broad, straight shoulders, a lantern jaw and a flat head. Even his ears are almost square. Standing to attention, perfectly immobile, you might think he was a sculpture by an apprentice who hasn't worked out the finer points of the human form yet.

'It seems he can't stop messing about with machinery,' I continue hastily at the Colonel's prompting stare, pulling my thoughts away from the young soldier's strange appearance. 'Following several complaints from servants of the Adeptus Mechanicus and despite reprimands from his senior officers, Quidlon here continued to make unauthorised alterations to the weapons and vehicles of his tank platoon. Fed up with him, and wisely not wanting to start a feud with the tech-priests, his superiors eventually charged him with insubordination.'

'Why did you not heed the warnings you were given?' the Colonel asks Quidlon, the first time he's spoken directly to any of the prisoners since he came in.

'I like to know how things work, sir, and the changes I made didn't do any harm, they made the engines and guns work better,' the trooper replies quickly, the words coming out in tumbled bursts, like a stubber firing on semi-auto.

'And why do you think you are here, trooper?' the Colonel continues his questioning.

'Here, now, in this line with the others and you and the lieutenant, or here in this prison, sir?' I was amazed by the speed of his talking when we first met, but I soon realised it was because his brain works that fast. It does have the unfortunate effect of making a very smart man sound very stupid though, and I can imagine why his talents have been overlooked by others who might not have realised this.

'In this chamber now,' the Colonel confirms, 'with these other prisoners.'

'Well, sir, I don't know for sure why I'm here but I might hazard a
guess, considering everything I've heard so far, and my conversation
with the lieutenant yesterday, that perhaps I might be useful to you,
sir, because I know how to fix things,' Quidlon blurts back, looking
up at Schaeffer.

'You might be,' agrees the Colonel with a nod before taking a couple more paces along the line.

'I've no idea what rock you turned over to find this next one,' I say,
looking at him. The man appears unremarkable in every way. Average height, average build, dark brown hair, grey eyes, plain-looking
face with no distinguishing features. His record was strangely short as
well, and those bits that were in it were vague. But what was there
made interesting reading. Well, interesting listening as it turned out,
but that's not the point.

'Oynas Trost, a former expert in sabotage and terrorism,' I
announce to Schaeffer.

'I'm still an expert,' Trost growls beside me.

'Did I tell you to open your mouth?' I snarl back, face inches from
his. His eyes meet mine and a shiver runs down my spine. They're
dead. I mean absolutely emotionless, flat like they're painted on. It's
a look that tells me I could be on fire or bleeding to death and he
would just walk past without a second glance.

'Try me. I'll show you what cold-blooded is,' I whisper in his ear,
regaining my composure.

'I remember this one,' the Colonel says, pushing me to one side
and squaring off against Trost. 'I remember this one very well. Trost,
covert agent of the Officio Sabatorum. He has probably killed more
people than everyone in this tower put together, including you and
me, Kage. I remember that he made a mistake and ended up poisoning three admirals and their families.'

Trost is still trying to stare me down, but I'm not giving him an
inch. If I show weakness now, he'll know it and I'll have a hard time
imposing my authority later if I need to.

'Who is this final one?' the Colonel asks, pointing to the last man
in the line.

'This is Pieter Stroniberg, field surgeon of the 21st Coporan
Armoured Cavalry, sir,' I tell Schaeffer, tearing my eyes away from
Trost. The chirurgeon is gaunt, dark-skinned with thinning black hair
and a nervous tic in his right eye. He looks at the Colonel with tired,

bloodshot eyes. 'While on campaign in Filius Sekunda, he became addicted to a strange cocktail of stimms and pain suppressants of his own making. Not only did this affect his performance, losing five times more patients than he saved by the end of the campaign, he began to distribute this substance to the troopers in return for favours and money.'

'And you think that his medical expertise will prove useful on this mission?' the Colonel says derisively. 'He looks dead on his feet, I would not trust him to open a pill bottle, and would never consider letting him near me with a cauteriser.'

'He's been here three years, Colonel, and cannot sleep more than four hours a night due to his long-term addiction,' I explain. 'However, he has acted as prison doctor for the last year to the satisfaction of the governor.'

'Hmm, we will see about that,' the Colonel grunts, darting a glance back at me.

The Colonel clasps his hands behind his back and turns on the spot, striding to stand in the middle of the room in front of the 'recruits'. I walk over to stand just behind and to his left. He looks up and down the line a couple more times, weighing up the merits of each of them in his head. I'm not sure whether it's them he's judging, or me for choosing them.

'They all seem satisfactory, Kage,' he says quietly to me, not turning around. 'But we must see which of them passes the final test and which will fail.'

'Final test, sir?' I ask worriedly. I can't think what the Colonel has in mind, I thought I'd covered every angle.

'My name is Colonel Schaeffer,' he barks out, his strong voice filling the chamber. 'I am the commanding officer of the 13th Penal Legion,' he glances towards me for a second, 'which some of you may have heard being called the Last Chancers. It was I who brought you all to this prison, and I now stand before you to offer you a choice. I need soldiers, fighters like you, to take part in a dangerous mission. It is likely that many of you, perhaps even all of you, will not survive this mission. You will be subjected to the most ruthless training that Lieutenant Kage here can devise, and I will expect total obedience. In return for your dedication to this duty, I offer you a full pardon for the crimes for which you have been convicted. Survive my mission and you will be free to pursue whatever lives you can. If you do not survive, then you will be pardoned posthumously, so that your souls may be cleansed of your sins and ascend to join the Emperor.

Remember that a life not spent in the service of the Emperor is a life doubly wasted, in this world and the next. I also remind you that you all swore oaths of loyalty and service to the Emperor and the Imperium that serves him, and I again offer you the opportunity to fulfil those oaths.'

I look at the Colonel. He's stood there, ramrod straight, hands held easily in the small of his back. I can't see his face, but I remember the last time he gave that speech, to me and nearly four thousand others over three years ago. It wasn't exactly the same speech, but I recall his face. It radiates confidence and sincerity, those blue eyes shining with pride. He truly believes he is here to save our souls from damnation. And maybe he is. My old friend, Franx, certainly believed so, and after what I went through in the Last Chancers I'm damn sure I earnt myself some redemption.

'Moerck,' he says, looking towards the ex-commissar. 'Do you volunteer for this duty?'

'I do, sir!' he booms back, and I can picture him now, striding through the bullets and las-bolts, his voice like a clarion call to the soldiers around him. 'It will be an honour and a privilege to serve the Emperor again.'

'Iyle,' the Colonel calls out. 'Do you volunteer for this duty?'

'If it means staying out of that cell, then yes I do,' the recon man replies with an emphatic nod of the head.

'Regis, do you volunteer for this duty?' the Colonel asks the gunnery sergeant. Regis hesitates, glancing along the line to his left and right, and then back at the Colonel.

'I don't want to die,' he mumbles, eyes cast downwards as he says it. 'I would rather stay here, sir.'

I see the Colonel stiffen, as if Regis just insulted his mother or something.

'I offer you one last chance, Regis,' Schaeffer says, his voice dropping low, a sure sign that he's angry. 'Do you volunteer for this duty?'

'You fraggers can go to hell,' answers Regis, his sadness suddenly replaced by rage, lunging towards the bolt pistol hanging from the Colonel's belt. 'I'm not going anywhere with you madmen, I'll kill the fragging lot of you!'

Schaeffer steps into his rush, brings the heel of his hand into Regis's jaw and hurls him backwards to the ground with a single blow. He scrabbles to his feet and takes a swing at the Colonel, but I get there first, smacking a solid punch across his nose, spraying blood everywhere and spinning him to the floor again.

'I am truly sorry to hear that,' the Colonel replies solemnly, unmoved by the attack. 'By failing to volunteer you have proven to me and the Emperor that you are no longer a faithful and useful servant. Your presence in this facility is no longer warranted. By the authority invested in me as a commanding officer of the Emperor's judiciary, your sentence of life imprisonment is revoked,' the Colonel continues. A smile creeps across Regis's face. When the Colonel unbuckles the flap on his bolt pistol holster, the smile fades, replaced with a look of horror. 'I hereby sentence you to death, to be carried out immediately. Lieutenant Kage, do your duty.'

He pulls out his bolt pistol and holds it out for me to take. It feels heavy in my hands, smelling of fresh gun oil. It's the first time I've held a gun in months and its weight is reassuring.

'Don't move, and it'll be quick,' I tell Regis, aiming the pistol at his head. Regis ignores me and leaps to his feet, sprinting towards the chamber door. I head after him, but Trost intervenes, tackling him to the ground. The two roll across the floor, scuffling and exchanging short punches with each other as Regis tries to break free. I catch up with them and bring the butt of the pistol across Regis's forehead, stunning him. Pushing Trost aside, I place a booted foot across Regis's throat, pinning him in place. He tries to struggle a moment longer, hurling threats at me before going limp. Tears stream down his face, a dark patch spreading from the crotch of his grey fatigues.

'Take your punishment like a soldier,' I hiss at him, sickened, levelling the bolt pistol at his left eye. One smooth pull of the trigger is all it takes, the crack of the bolt's detonation ringing off the walls as the explosive round blows Regis's skull apart, spattering my legs with blood and shards of bone. I step back, the pistol smoking slightly, and look at the others. Quidlon looks aghast; Strelli wears a savage grin; Moerck is still standing to attention, eyes fixed straight ahead. The others look at me with blank expressions. Death is no stranger to them. Good, because before this mission is out, I'm sure they'll see plenty more.

I return the Colonel's pistol to him and shout at the others to fall in line again. Schaeffer continues as if there had been no distraction at all, asking each in turn if they volunteer for the duty he has for them.

They all say yes.

THE CRACKLING FLAMES in the grate blazed with a shower of sparks as the room's occupant dropped another log onto the fire. Rubbing his hands together, he returned to the low, leather covered armchair at one side of the fireplace. He was lean, with hooded eyes, his dark hair slicked back, a perfectly groomed goatee beard adorning his chin. He was wearing a heavy shirt of dark blue wool, tied at the collarless neck with golden cord, with which he fidgeted as he sat waiting. His long legs were stretched out in front of him, clad in tight trousers made from the same material as the shirt. He gazed interestedly around the room: at the red lacquered panelling on the walls, and the ceiling-high bookshelf that stretched several metres along the entire length of one wall. A clock stood upon the mantle, apparently carved from ivory or bone, ticking methodically above the sound of the fire. Turning his attention back to the bookshelf, the man stood and slowly walked over to study the assembled volumes. He ran his fingers along their spines, head cocked to one side to read their titles.

At that moment the door behind him opened with the clicking of a latch. Turning, he greeted his host with a smile. The other man was much older, his face creased like a crumpled parchment, but his eyes were bright and clear. A few wisps of white were all that remained of his hair and he leant heavily on a walking cane.

'Gestimor, it is so long since we last met,' the younger man said stepping forward and laying an affectionate hand on the old man's shoulder.

'It is,' Gestimor replied shortly, his voice firm and strong. 'I fear that both of us pay more attention to our duties than to our friendship.'

'It cannot be any other way,' the visitor said matter-of-factly, helping the ageing man to the chair. 'Come, sit and we will talk.'

The younger man took a straight-backed chair from in front of the study's desk and sat opposite Gestimor, leaning forward with his arms on his knees, hands clasped together.

'You look even older than I imagined,' he said sadly.

'Yes, Lucius, I am old,' Gestimor agreed, nodding his head slowly. 'But I still have a few more years of grace left to me, and my mind is as sharp as ever.' He tapped at his temple in illustration.

'Why do you submit yourself to this? You know there are ways to remedy your ageing,' asked Lucius.

'To be human is to be mortal,' the ageing man replied philosophically. 'To deny that is to invite thoughts of immortality, which is the province of the blessed Emperor alone. That or the gift of the Dark Powers we must thwart. To deny my mortality is to deny my humanity and all that I have fought hard to protect in others.'

The two sat in silence for a few minutes, the comfortable silence allowed by many years of familiarity. It was Gestimor who spoke next, turning his gaze from the flames in the grate to look at Lucius.

'You didn't travel across seven sectors to inquire after my health,' he pointed out, his face serious.

'You received the data I sent?' Lucius asked, sitting back, his expression businesslike.

'I did, and I say you are playing with fire,' Gestimor answered sternly. 'But you will have whatever aid you need from me.'

'It is advice that I need more than anything, old friend,' Lucius explained. 'You are right, the endeavour is risky, but the potential rewards are well worth the hazards. For all that, I would prefer some more surety than I currently have. I may need to act swiftly and strongly and decisively, and I am not sure that the men I have are equal to the demand.'

'Ach, that is simple,' Gestimor dismissed his comrade's worries with a wave of his veiny hand. 'Invoke the old oaths, rouse the brotherhood to duty once more.'

'Such things should not be done lightly,' Lucius replied with caution. 'The brotherhood is intended for use in extreme cases. Besides which, subterfuge and stealth are my weapons, as ever.'

'If you need their intervention, then the time for deception and intrigue will have long passed,' Gestimor countered, rubbing a hand over his bald head. 'Take just a single brother. For surety, as you said.'

'I will consider your advice,' Lucius said thoughtfully, looking into the flames and remembering the battles of the past.

THREE
LAURELS OF GLORY

+++The target is ignorant and proceeding without thought. We have their total trust+++

+++Beware of underestimating them. They must remain unaware of our plans+++

'YOUR ADDITIONAL TRAINING begins immediately,' announces the Colonel as we board the shuttle, the wind whipping across the landing pad while we make our way across the gantry. 'Lieutenant Kage has my full authority when I am not present. You will do exactly as he tells you. Your lives will depend on you maintaining discipline and learning everything you and he have to teach each other.'

The interior of the shuttle is better furnished than those I'm used to. In place of long wooden benches, the main compartment has individual seats, six rows of three each side of a central aisle. Upholstered with black padded leather, pillow-like headrests, hung with thick safety restraints with gilded buckles and clasps, the luxurious seats are obviously for the comfort of more important Imperial servants than us. Still, it's ours for the moment, and I settle into one of the seats near the back, enjoying the sensation after five months of being manacled to a wall. To my surprise, the Colonel comes and sits next to me.

'You do understand your position, Kage?' he asks, strapping himself into the harness.

'I think so, sir,' I answer after a moment's thought. 'I have to turn this bunch of misfits into a fighting team.'

'I mean, that I only offer one last chance,' Schaeffer says. 'You have already squandered that. There is no pardon for you this time.'

I had suspected as much, though it's still a blow hearing it stated so bluntly. So, this is it. There is no pardon, no end to the fighting except death.

I'm surprised by my own feelings, I find myself strangely calm. I get the weirdest sense of detachment, of someone else taking control of my life. It's an odd feeling, hard to explain. My whole life I've fought against everything. I fought to get out of the hives on Olympas. I fought boredom on the world of Stygies, and ended up in the Last Chancers. I fought for two and a half years to escape the Colonel and the death I was sure he had waiting for me. I fought against the guilt and depression of being the only survivor from Coritanorum and failed. And for the last six months I fought to get out of prison, and against the growing madness that all the fighting had been building in my head.

I realise that, as last time, even if I was free, I would still be fighting. I don't know how to do anything else. Call it my destiny, my fate, if you like. Perhaps it's some part of the Emperor's scheme for me to fight until I die. Maybe that's all I have to offer Him.

It's then that I'm struck by a revelation, astounded that it didn't occur to me earlier. That's why I am here, why the Colonel has chosen me, and why I survived when thousands of others died. I fight. It's what I *do*. Perhaps I might have been able to change given the chance, but the Colonel made sure that never happened, with two and a half years of constant bloodshed and battle. I have become his creature. Now I really am his type of scum.

'I understand, sir,' I tell Schaeffer, looking at him sat next to me. Oh yes, I understand exactly what he's done to me, what he's turned me into. Like I said, given a chance I might have changed, but my last chance was just to keep on living, not to have a normal life. This existence is the only one that's left for me now, thanks to Schaeffer.

'Good,' he replies shortly, leaning his head back.

'There's one other thing, Colonel,' I say through gritted teeth. He looks over at me out of the corner of his eye. 'I hate you for what you've done to me. And one day I'll kill you for it.'

'But not today, Kage,' he replies with a grim smile. 'Not today.'

'No, sir, not today,' I agree, leaning my head back too. I close my eyes and picture my hands around his throat, as I drift off into a contented sleep.

THE DAY CYCLE begins with the glowstrips in my room flickering to life. I push myself out of my bunk and dress quickly, pulling on my new uniform. Stepping through the door that links my chamber to the team's dormitory, I see that most of them are still asleep; only Stroniberg looks in my direction as I walk in.

'Wake up you lazy, fat, useless sacks of sump filth!' I bellow at them, walking along the room and kicking at their beds. 'You are supposed to be soldiers, not babies!'

'Drop dead, soldier-boy,' snarls Strelli, swinging out from his bunk and landing on his feet in front of me. 'You may think you're the man in charge because the Colonel says so, but you push me and I'll kick the living hell out of you.'

I hear Trost step up behind me and I turn slightly and take a step back to keep both him and the pilot in view.

'I'm with the navy man on this one,' Trost says hoarsely, his dead eyes meeting my gaze. 'You know how many people I've killed. Adding you to the list won't even make me blink.'

I say nothing, keeping my face impassive. I look at the others. Moerck is ignoring me, pulling on his prison fatigues, his back to me. Tanya sits on the edge of her bunk, swinging her feet, not joining in but certainly not leaping to my defence. Quidlon looks a bit confused, his eyes shifting between me, Strelli and Trost, trying to judge which side to be on. If he has any sense, it'll be my side. Iyle is still lying on his bunk, arms behind his head, looking blankly up at the ceiling and pretending nothing is happening.

Finally, I look back at Strelli.

'I think a little discipline is needed around here,' I say to him, crossing my arms.

'What are you going to do?' he taunts me. 'Put us in explosive collars?'

'I don't need to,' I tell him quietly. He smirks, just a moment before my fist thunders into his face, smashing a tooth free and slamming him into one of the metal bed posts. Quick as lightning I spin on Trost, who's stood with a dumbfounded expression, which turns to one of intense agony as I drive my boot up into his groin, crumpling him to the floor.

'You could have done this the easy way,' I say to all of them as Trost squirms about on the floor and Strelli pushes himself upright, keeping his distance. 'You're Last Chancers now. That means that you're the lowest scum in the galaxy. That means that you're going to wish that you were dead. It also means that if you go up against me, I will break you into little pieces and shove the leftovers out of an airlock. And if any of you think you can take me out, then please, have a go. But make sure you do it right, because if I survive, you won't.'

'WHAT IS THIS?' I ask Stroniberg, holding my knife up in front of his face. It's the first day of real training, aboard the ship *Laurels of Glory*. A fine vessel, and no mistaking. Purpose built for storm troopers, the Colonel informs me, the *Laurels of Glory* has got just about everything you might want. Right now, we're stood in one of the combat bays. The ship has fourteen, each of them rigged out to represent all sorts of warzones and maintained by a veritable army of tech-priests. There's a jungle bay, a city bay, a desert bay, a nightworld bay, shooting ranges, drill quadrants, even a beach in one of them. I've not actually seen any of them yet, so I'm kind of curious to see how you can make a jungle on a spaceship. Trees made out of planks, perhaps? The best thing is that there's an armoury you could overthrow a hive city with, housing all kinds of lethal kit that I'm just itching to get my hands on. But that's for later; for now we start with the basics.

'It's a knife,' he replies bluntly, a dumb look on his face.

'Do I have a rank, Trooper Stroniberg?' I rasp at him.

'You're a lieutenant,' he answers quickly. 'I mean, you're a lieutenant, sir.'

'That's better,' I say, stepping back, brandishing the knife towards him. 'What is this?'

'It's a knife, sir!' he replies sharply.

'Wrong!' I bark back. 'What is this?'

'I don't understand, sir…' he answers hesitantly, looking at the others gathered around me. This bay is just an exercise hall, a wide open space for running, close combat training, rope climbing and such. We're stood in the middle of the chamber, the others forming a circle around me. I hold the knife up above my head, and turn around slowly, looking at each of them.

'Can any of you tell me what this is?' I ask them, spinning the knife between my fingers.

'It's a Cervates pattern general issue combat knife, sir,' answers Quidlon. 'Standard close combat armament for many Imperial Guard regiments, originating from the Cervates forge world.'

'Is that a fact, brains?' I ask, looking at the knife in mock amazement. 'I suspect you could tell me all sorts of interesting things about this knife, couldn't you?'

'That knife in particular, sir, or that kind of knife?' he asks innocently.

'What?' I reply, startled. 'Emperor's blood, you think too much, Quidlon.'

I take a moment to gather my thoughts again, closing my eyes and trying to put Quidlon out of my mind. Taking a deep breath I open my eyes and look around the circle once more. A couple of them are exchanging glances with each other. Trost looks bored, standing with his arms crossed, his gaze on the ceiling.

'This is not a knife that I hold,' I bark at them, my voice ringing off the distant bulkheads of the training bay. 'I hold a weapon in my hand. The only purpose of a weapon is to inflict injury and death. This is a man's death.'

They look at me with more interest now, intrigued to know where my speech is going.

'Hey, Trost, what is the purpose of a weapon?' I snap at the saboteur, who is still looking around the hall.

'Mmm?' he glances at me. 'The purpose of a weapon is to inflict injury and death. Sir.' His voice is flat, emotionless, his expression vague.

'What is so fraggin' interesting that you think you can ignore me, Trooper Trost?' I shout at him, dropping the knife and striding up to him.

'Am I boring you, Trost?'

'I was working out how many thermal charges would be needed to blast through one of these bulkheads,' he replies, meeting my gaze finally.

'A real demolition man, aren't you?' I say, squaring up to Trost. He smirks at me. My fist smashes into his jaw before he realises I'm even swinging at him, knocking him to his knees. He tries to fend off my next blow with a waved arm so I grab his left wrist in both hands, twisting it forward and pitching him face first into the floor. Putting one foot on his shoulder, I wrench on his arm and the joint pops like a cork, Trost spitting through gritted teeth. 'Your thermal charges didn't help much then, did they demolition man? Try setting one of your bombs now.'

I step back, letting his dislocated arm drop to the floor. He pushes himself to his knees with his good arm, groaning and darting murderous looks at me.

'Stroniberg, fix that,' I tell the surgeon, pointing to where Trost is knelt cradling his injured shoulder, gasping, his face twisted with pain.

'This'll hurt,' the medico warns Trost, taking a tight grip of his arm and twisting it back into place with an audible click, making him cry out.

'Right, everyone will pay attention to what I have to say, is that understood?' I ask them, daring them with my stare. Stroniberg helps Trost to his feet before taking his place in the circle again. 'I don't give a frag whether any of you live or die, you can be sure of that. I do care whether I live or die, and that means I have to rely on scum like you. Make no bones about it, if the Colonel thinks any of us are not shaping up, the chances are he'll put a bolt into all of us and start afresh, so you best start acting like you care. Listen to me, and we'll all live. Ignore me, and we're all fraggin' shafted.'

Iyle raises a hand and I give him the nod to speak.

'Who the hell are you, sir?' he asks.

'I am the man the Colonel visited a dozen kinds of hell upon and survived,' I reply slowly, gesturing for the others to gather in front of me so I don't have to keep turning around to look at them all. 'I am the man who helped the Colonel kill three million people. I am the only man to survive when four thousand others died on the battlefield. I have killed men in their sleep. I have shot them. I have stabbed them. I have strangled them. I've even beaten them to death with my hands and fists. I've fought tyranids and orks, I've marched across searing deserts and frozen wastelands. I've nearly died six times. My own men have tried to kill me on more than one occasion. I've fought things you don't even know exist. And I killed them.'

Every word of it is true as well, and they can tell it by the look in my eye, even Trost, who shows the first sign of any feelings at all, a glimmer of respect.

'But none of that matters,' I carry on, walking up and down in front of them, looking at each of them in turn. 'I am Lieutenant Kage, your training officer. I will do what the hell I like, to who the hell I like, when and where the hell I like, and there's nothing in the Emperor's wide galaxy you can do or say to stop me. And it will be the worst, the very worst, time of your life. But, as the Colonel said, if you want that pardon and live to hold it, hold it in your hand and walk free, then you will listen to what I say, and do exactly what I tell you to do. If just one of you messes up, I will frag you all.'

I leave them with that thought for a while, picking up the knife as I walk to the far end of the training hall. I smile to myself. I once said I'd be a great training instructor if it wasn't for my lousy temper. Now I'm here, I figure my lousy temper is the best weapon in my arsenal. That and the knowledge that my own life depends on these bone-heads shaping up to the Colonel's satisfaction.

I look back at them and can hear them talking amongst themselves. They're a long way from becoming a fighting team, but their mutual hatred of me will bring them together. That's the way I plan it, anyway. It worked for me. My loathing of the Colonel and everything he stands for gave me the determination to survive. I'll dare them to die on me, prove to me how weak they really are. I'll break them and put them back together, and to be honest, I'll enjoy every minute of it. Why? Because other than actual battle, it's the only thing left in my life to take pleasure in.

I toy with the knife in my hands, standing there looking at them. They're all veterans, they all think they're special. It's an illusion. I've seen first-timers walk through a battle with honours, while old campaigners got blown to bits or broke down and cried. Time served means nothing to me, I don't care how good they think they are, what they think they are capable of. I've seen men pushed to their limits of sanity and endurance. I was one of them. The Colonel tells me I've got about two months to work on them. Two months to turn them into a fighting force he's willing to lead into battle.

And there's an odd thing. Why is the Colonel leaving this to me? Why did he leave me in the vincularum with the others, to be dragged out again later, like an old sword handed down from father to son? It's a trend that started when he put me in charge last time around, just before False Hope and the horrors of the god-plant. Even back then, did he have something like this in mind? I'm certain he knew I'd be fighting for him again if I survived Coritanorum. The fact that he caught up with me so quickly proved that.

I give myself a mental slap. All this thinking and pondering is a symptom of the prison we've left behind. I don't have time to stand around and think. I have work to do. I realise that I'm going to have to train myself too. Six months in that cell may have sharpened my philosophy skills, but they've blunted my battle readiness. Idly tossing the knife from hand to hand, I walk back to the group.

'What is the purpose of a soldier?' I call out to them as I approach. They answer with shrugs and shaking heads.

'To follow orders and fight for the Emperor, sir?' suggests Iyle, hand half-raised like a child.

'Pretty close,' I agree, looking at the knife before turning my gaze on them. 'The purpose of a soldier is to kill for the Emperor. Any fool can fight, but a true soldier kills. He kills whoever he's told to kill, whenever he's told to. Battles are not won by fighting, they are won by killing. An enemy who can fight you is not a problem. An enemy who can kill you, there you have a threat. Which of you claims to be a soldier?'

'I've killed more men than can be counted. Sir.' Trost steps forward. 'By your reckoning, that makes me a soldier.'

'How did you kill them?' I ask, setting the knife spinning on its pommel on the tip of my index finger. 'Did you stab any of them?'

'No, I've never had to stab a man,' he admits. 'I use explosives, gas and poison. If I had to fight man-to-man that meant I'd been discovered, which meant my mission had failed. I never failed a mission.'

'I'm sure those three admirals thought highly of you as they died,' I sneer.

'The mission was still completed. Normally a few additional deaths are allowed,' he states coldly. I focus my attention on Strelli and point the knife at him.

'Are you a soldier, flyboy?' I ask him. He opens his mouth to reply, but at that moment I whip round and hurl the knife into Trost's left foot, pinning it to the floor. He shrieks and keels over. Pulling the knife free with both hands, he lets it clatter to the floor in a bloody puddle. 'You forget to call me "sir" one more time, demolition man, and I will do a whole lot worse to you!' I growl at Trost.

'Well, Strelli?' I ask, turning back to the pilot. 'Are you a soldier?'

'Not by your definition, sir,' he tells me, glancing at Trost squirming on the floor, hands clutched around his bleeding foot. 'I flew shuttles and fighters, I've never fought face-to-face with an enemy.'

'Do you want to become a soldier now, flyboy?' I challenge him.

'Not with you, sir,' he smiles back cockily. 'You'll cut me to pieces.'

'Yes, I will,' I assure him with a grim smile.

'Sir?' I hear Stroniberg ask from my right. I don't turn around, I already know what he's going to ask.

'Nobody gets treatment until I say so,' I tell him, still looking at Strelli. I hear a grunt and the thud of feet and spin to my left. Trost plunges the knife down at my face, but I catch the blade on the outside of my left forearm and deflect it away. Even as he tumbles off balance, my right foot connects with the outside of his left knee, buckling his leg and pitching him into the floor.

'I'd wait until I've taught you how to use a knife properly before doing that again,' I tell him, pulling the blade from his blood-coated fingers. The others are all staring at me. At my arm to be precise. Blood is dripping from my finger tips onto the clean wooden planks of the floor. I check out the wound. It isn't severe, not much more than a layer of skin taken off.

'If this is the most blood you see in the next couple of months, I'm going too easy on you,' I tell them with a grin. 'Enough of the theory for today. I'm going to show you how to use this knife like a soldier.'

I SPEND THE rest of the week teaching them knife-fighting. Proper knife-fighting, hive fashion, including every dirty trick I've learnt over the hard years. We all get a few more cuts and bruises, but I allow no one to go to the infirmary until the end of the day. Each morning after breakfast, I give them a sermon on what it means to be a soldier. One day it is about following orders. The next it's on the nature of victory. I tell them about teamwork and trust. Other times I regale them on the uses of fear as a weapon.

There's no pattern to my teachings, just stuff that's come to me the night before as I lie on my small cot in the officer's room adjacent to the dormitory they share with each other. It's all stuff that I know in my heart is true, but finding the words to explain it to them is difficult. How can I teach them something which I just know inside me?

I have no doubt that what I have to say is just as important as knife-fighting, marksmanship, wilderness survival, camouflage techniques, field navigation and all the other stuff they can fill your head with, but I can't quite figure it out just yet. I sit on my bunk at the end of the first week trying to get it all straight, trying to work out exactly what it is they need to know if they're going to survive. On my own in that small room, with just a bunk and a small locker, I feel like I've just swapped one cell for another. I hear a laugh through the connecting door, and my heart sinks. I'm not one of them this time around. I'm the officer in more than just title. I can't sit in there and swap stories with them. They are not my friends.

I slouch there wishing more than ever that Gappo or Franx were still alive. Even better, that Lorii wasn't a scattering of ash on Typhos Prime. It all seems unreal to me, like it was all a dream or something and I've just woken up in this bed, half-remembering it. Why was I the only one who survived? What is it about me that I can pass on to these others, so that perhaps they'll live as well?

It's with a start that the answer comes to me, and I almost bang my head back against the wall as I sit up. It was more than plain determination, more than just skill and luck. You can leave destiny hanging for all I care, I've been thinking about this the wrong way around. It's not why I survived, it's why the others didn't. They didn't really want to. Not as much as I did. Never once did I truly think that I was going to die. I never really believed anyone could kill me. Except perhaps the tyranids, but even they didn't manage it.

The Emperor helps those who help themselves, one of the old sayings tells us. Everything I've been struggling to understand starts to come together. This isn't about building a team, training soldiers, passing on skills. It's about giving each of them the same indestructible belief in themselves that I have. Tonight's the night for realisations I guess, because it's then that I see how the Colonel can walk through the bloodiest battles in the galaxy without a scratch. He's got even more belief in himself than I have. It protects him almost like a shield. The only problem left is how do I get the others to create their own shields, to think they're invincible?

A plan begins to form in my mind.

THE NEXT MORNING I appear in the mess room with a pile of grey and black uniforms in my arms. While the others settled into bed last night, I took a trip to the store rooms with a special request. The hall itself is about thirty metres long, fifteen wide, with six wide tables arrayed in two rows along the length. The bare, unpainted metal of the walls is polished and pristine, the result of the team's labours yesterday before I allowed them their evening meal.

Well, discipline isn't just about being calm under fire, or following orders, it's also about being able to do the dull, lousy jobs and still stay sharp. Like sentry duty, or cleaning the mess hall.

'Form up!' I shout and they push themselves to their feet, standing at ease behind their places at the long bench.

'This morning I have something different to show you,' I announce, placing the uniforms at the end of the table. 'You will not become true soldiers until you think like true soldiers. You will not think like true soldiers until you understand what it means to be true soldiers. You will not understand what it means to be true soldiers while you think you are something else. The logical conclusion of this is that while you think you are something else you will never be true soldiers.'

They look at me with dumbfounded expressions. I don't expect them to understand, it only became clear to me last night. I look at the name tag sewn on to the breast pocket of the first uniform.

'Who are you?' I ask, pointing at Stradinsk.

'Tanya Stradinsk, sir!' she replies, standing to attention.

'No you are not,' I tell her with a shake of my head, picking up the top uniform. 'Who are you?' She thinks for a moment before replying.

'Trooper Stradinsk, 13th Penal Legion, the Last Chancers, sir!' she answers with a look of triumph.

'Nice try, but still not right,' I say, looking at all of them. 'A true soldier does not know who they are because of their name. You,' I say, pointing at Moerck. 'How does a true soldier know who they are?'

'I do not know the answer to that, sir!' he barks back, snapping to attention as well.

'Can anyone here tell me how a true soldier knows who they are?' I cast my gaze around as I'm speaking.

'By knowing his purpose in the eyes of the Emperor, Lieutenant Kage!' a voice bellows like a thunderclap behind me, causing us all to jump to attention. The Colonel strides up and stands beside me, glancing down over my shoulder at the uniforms. 'Am I correct, Lieutenant Kage?'

'Yes, Colonel, you are,' I say. His eyes meet mine and his ice-blue stare holds me for a second. He gives an approving nod.

'Carry on, Lieutenant Kage,' he tells me, stepping back a couple of paces. I try to block his presence from my mind, replaying the last minute or so in my head to catch up with where I had got to in the little mental script I devised for myself instead of sleeping last night.

'A true soldier does not know himself by his name, where he is from, even who he fights for,' I tell them, the words coming back to me. I can feel the Colonel's eyes on me and my throat goes dry. I cover my discomfort by beckoning Tanya over with a finger, before continuing. 'A true soldier knows himself by what he does.'

I turn to Stradinsk, and hand her the uniform.

'You are not Tanya Stradinsk, you are not Trooper Stradinsk,' I tell her. 'Who are you?'

'I still don't know, sir,' she says apologetically, glancing at the others for help, or maybe just support.

'What does your name badge say?' I ask softly, indicating the uniform in her hands.

'It says "Sharpshooter", sir,' she replies after glancing down.

'Who are you?' I ask her again, my voice firm.

'Sharpshooter, sir?' she answers hesitantly.

'Why are you asking me?' I say, voice dripping with scorn. 'Do I know you better than you know yourself?'

She stands there for a few heartbeats, looking at me, then the uniform, then back at me. Her jaw sets tight and her eyes go hard as she realises the full truth.

'I am Sharpshooter, sir!' Her voice can't hide the bitterness she feels, her new name a constant reminder of the guilt she feels.

'Return to your position, Sharpshooter!' I command her, picking up the next uniform. One by one I call them over, give them their fatigues and send them back. When they're all back in line again, each holding their uniforms in front of them, I walk to the opposite side of the table. Out of the corner of my eye I can still see the Colonel, watching everything, studying me and the other Last Chancers.

'Sound off!' I bark, looking at Strelli at the left of the line.

'Flyboy, sir!' he shouts.

'Demolition Man, sir!' Trost calls out next.

'Sharpshooter, sir,' Stradinsk tells me again.

'Hero, sir!' comes Moerck's parade ground bellow.

'Brains, sir!' Quidlon replies.

'Eyes, sir!' shouts Iyle.

'Stitcher, sir!' Stroniberg finishes the roll call.

'From now on, those are your names,' I tell them harshly. 'You will use those names all the time. Every time your name is spoken, you will hear it well and know who you are. Anyone forgets this rule, and you'll all be punished. Is that clear?'

'Yes, sir!' they chorus.

I'm about to dismiss them to get ready for the morning's training when the Colonel interrupts.

'What is your name?' he asks.

'My... My name, sir?' I ask, taken aback. I turn and look directly at him. 'I hadn't thought of a name for myself.' He seems to think for a moment, before the corner of his lip turns up into the slightest of smiles.

'You are Last Chance,' he says with a nod. As he strides out of the mess hall, he looks back over his shoulder at me. 'I expect to see you in uniform in the future.'

* * *

THE TRAINING CONTINUES steadily for another two weeks, as I work on the Last Chancers' fitness and marksmanship. It almost settles into a routine, so halfway through the second week, I speak to the ship's officers and arrange for the day/night lighting cycle to be adjusted in our quarters. Sometimes we'll have the equivalent to a twenty hour day, followed by just a few hours' sleep, other times I let them rest for half a day before rousing them. I'm still worried about their alertness, though; I need them to be as sharp as knives when we arrive at wherever we're going. So I organise a little exercise to test them.

It's midway through the twenty-first night, and I creep into their dorm. The room is filled with heavy breathing and gentle snores, the Last Chancers worn out from a day of training wearing heavy packs the whole time. In my hand I have some small slips of parchment used for identifying corpses, that I had a scribe write on, 'You were killed in your sleep'. The first bunk is Trost's, curled up with his face to the wall, hands holding his blanket tight around him. Barely breathing, I lean over him and place the first piece of paper on the pillow next to him. On the bed above Stroniberg lies stretched out on his back, his blanket down to his waist, mouth open, his breathing punctuated by a nasal whistling. I lay the parchment slip across his throat. I continue like this around the dormitory, easing myself from one bunk to the next in the dim night lighting. There's only Moerck left, the most likely to wake up, when a murmuring causes me to freeze. I stay like that, breath held, for a few seconds trying to identify where the noise is coming from. It's to my left, and I cautiously follow the mumbling to its source. It's Stradinsk, talking in her sleep. She's restless, plagued by her dreams.

Satisfied she's asleep, I creep back to Moerck's bunk and slide the parchment under his blanket. I then sit myself down by the door to my room, back against the wall, and wait for the morning.

It was far too easy for me, and that's worrying. I have to work out how to punish them so that they'll learn never to be so complacent again. I can't be too hard on them though, who would think they have to set a watch aboard a friendly starship? Something short and sharp should do the trick. If they don't learn this time, I'll have to come up with something more serious.

I sit there watching them. So quiet. So vulnerable. Two and a half years sharing a hall-sized cell with hundreds of murderers, thieves and rapists taught me how to sleep lightly. I listen to their slow breathing, imagining the blood bubbling into their lungs if I'd been a real enemy. I hear Stradinsk give a short gasp before rolling over. I filter out the noises: the breathing, Tanya's mumbling, Stroniberg's light snoring, and listen to the sounds of the ship around me. The walls hum slightly; energy conduits coursing with plasma run underneath the floor. I can hear a faint clank-clank-clank of heavy machinery operating in the distance. There's the sound of the armsmen patrolling the corridor outside, their boots clumping along the metal decking. The calm is a long way from the thunder of shells, the crack of lasguns and the boom of grenades that I'm more used to. I concentrate on the sounds, picking out different ones in the music being played out by the ship, to keep myself awake.

It's Stroniberg who wakes first, his withdrawal-induced sleeplessness rousing him only a couple of hours after midnight. I watch him from the darkness, sitting up in bed, startled by the fluttering paper that drops to his lap. He picks it up and turns it to the faint light from the dimmed glowglobes above, trying to see what it is. He slides his feet out of bed and sits on the edge. I don't move a muscle, I just look at him. He must have noticed me out of the corner of his eye, because he twists sharply to look at me, alarm on his face. I raise my finger to my lips to keep him silent and then point at his bed. He gets the message, lying back down again, the parchment crumpled in one hand.

The others rouse themselves when the lights flicker into daytime brightness at the end of the eight-hour sleep cycle. One by one they wake, making confused exclamations or just scratching their heads upon finding their mortuary tags.

'Form up!' I shout, pushing myself to my feet. They fall and scramble out of their beds, standing to attention in front of their bunks.

'So now I'm leading a squad of corpses,' I tell them scornfully, walking the length of the dormitory. 'Well, that's the mission fragged good and proper, isn't it?'

None of them reply, they all look straight ahead, not meeting my gaze as I walk past them. I walk back again slowly, deliberately, teasing out the suspense, aggravating their anxieties. Stopping at my door again, I spin on the spot to face them, hands behind my back.

'Next time I shall use a knife,' I warn them, meaning every word of it. 'And I won't think twice about cutting you. As for your embarrassing performance last night, I have this to say: you are all corpses, and as we all know, corpses don't eat, so there will be no meals today and battlefield water rations only. Do any of you have a question?'

Tanya steps forward, concern on her face.

'Yes, Sharpshooter?' I say.

'You were in here last night, Last Chance?' she asks worriedly.

'Almost the whole night, Sharpshooter,' I tell her with a smile. 'Does that worry you? Don't you trust your training lieutenant, Sharpshooter?'

'I trust my training lieutenant, Last Chance!' she replies quickly.

'Then you're an idiot, Sharpshooter,' I snarl at her, striding down the room towards her. She flinches as I stop in front of her. 'There's not one person in the Emperor's dark galaxy that I would trust, least of all me. I am not here to be nice to you, Sharpshooter. I am not here to look after you.' I round on the rest of them and bellow at them. 'I am here to make sure that when the time comes you can look after yourself, and me, and the rest of your squad!' I whirl on her again. 'I'll break you in half on a whim, Sharpshooter, so don't ever trust me unless I tell you to. Is that clear?'

'No, Last Chance, it isn't,' Quidlon replies, stepping forward. 'If we can't trust you, then how are we supposed to trust you when you say that we can, given that you may be lying to us about trusting you?'

'Exactly my point, Brains,' I tell him with a grin. 'Now, all of you get cleaned up. Breakfast time will be spent in the armoury doing weapons maintenance drill. I will join you at the normal time for today's new adventure. In the meantime, I believe there is still some fresh meat left in the officers' kitchen, which I shall be enjoying.'

They break ranks and busy themselves with getting ready. I turn to walk out when something occurs to me.

'Oh, one more thing,' I say to them, causing them to pause in their preparations. 'If any of you can tag me with one of those, you all earn one day's rest and recuperation. However, if any of you try and fail, then it'll be another day without food. That sounds fair, doesn't it?'

'Yes, Last Chance!' they reply in unison.

'Good. I'll be seeing you shortly,' I tell them, whistling a jaunty tune that my dead comrade Pohl taught me a couple of years ago. I won't bore you with the bawdy lyrics, but suffice to say it's called the Hangman's Five Daughters.

THE NEXT DAY, and the day after that, they all look exhausted. None of them have got any sleep as far as I can tell. I suspect they're having disturbing dreams of me sneaking around with my knife. Good, that was the point. I overheard them this morning discussing a watch rota. That should be interesting to see in action, considering the variable length of the nights that I've requested. I've decided to give them another week before I try anything again. That'll show whether they can keep their guard up night after night, or whether they lapse into a false sense of security again.

I think it's time to start doing some squad-based training now. After breakfast on day twenty-four I lead them to training bay six. We're kitted out with full equipment; we'll be spending the next several days in there without coming out. I've issued everyone with lasguns, the standard Imperial Guard armament, as well as knives, ammunition for a hundred shots each, rations, water canteens, bedrolls and everything else. I also gave them new uniforms, with a common brown and green camo scheme. They don't have name badges to remind them who they are now. Not one of them has slipped up so far on that front, but I'm waiting for it. They're starting to get tired. Weary from irregular sleep and day after day of me bawling them out, pushing them hard, relentlessly driving them on.

It's for their own good. If they can't take the training, how in the Emperor's name are they going to fare in real combat? Like I said, their pasts mean nothing to me, all of their previous achievements count for nothing. Here, and on the mission, is where they'll prove themselves to the Colonel. And prove themselves to me, as well. I'm spending a lot of energy myself, doing this for them.

It's been tiring work for me too. Somehow, I doubt they appreciate the effort I've put in on their behalf.

When it comes down to it, I'm starting to feel responsible for them, like I've never felt responsible for anyone else before. I tell myself that if they get themselves killed, if they foul up and the mission goes up like a photon flash flare, ultimately it'll be their own fault. But inside, I know that isn't one hundred per cent true. I know that if I miss something out, if I take anything for granted, if I go easy on them for just a moment, I will have failed them, and through them the Colonel.

Anyway, we're all decked out in battledress and heading into the training bay. We pass through a couple of airlocks monitored by white-robed tech-priests, whose job it is to maintain the stable environments inside each of the bays. At the end of it a large double-doored portal rolls open.

It's amazing. On one side of the door is metal mesh decking. On the other side steps lead down into rolling hills and fields. I can see a small pre-fabricated farmhouse a few hundred metres to my left, smoke drifting lazily out of its chimney. We walk down the wide stairwell on to the grass, gazing around us like first-timers in a brothel. With a clang, the doors slam closed behind us.

I assume the walls have some kind of image painted on to them, because the agri-world landscape stretches as far as the eye can see. Above our heads, small puffy clouds dot a deep blue sky. I blink in disbelief as I notice the clouds are drifting across the ceiling.

'Last Chance...' Iyle whispers in awe. 'Sorceries of the machine god.'

He's looking behind me and I turn to see what he's staring at. The doors have disappeared, as have the steps. As in every other direction, the hills stretch as far as the horizon. In the far distance I can just make out the purple slopes of a mountain range, topped with snow. The others are murmuring suspiciously, shrinking back from the open sky above.

'Yes, magic, the most powerful techno-magic,' I say quietly in agreement, awed and afraid at the nature of our surroundings.

'This is unbelievable...' gasps Quidlon, dropping to his knees and running his fingers through the grass. 'It feels real, and even smells real.'

I notice that he's right. It smells like an agri-world. There's even a faint breeze blowing from our left. Fresh air, on a ship where the air gets constantly cycled through great big refiners, breathed millions and millions of times before until it's almost thick with age. I was expecting something pretty special, after the Colonel told me there were only a couple of dozen of these ships in the entire navy, but nothing as extravagant as this. His powerful contacts have been working hard for him again.

'It is real,' I say ominously, a sudden shiver of unnatural fear coursing through me. 'I think it's been grown here by the tech-priests.'

This is wrong, a voice at the back of my mind tells me. Ships don't have woods and meadows on board them. They have engines, and guns, and they're built out of metal, not dirt. At that point a voice blares out, seemingly from the air itself, shattering the illusion.

'This is Warrant Officer Campbell,' the heavenly voice tells us. 'Tech-priest Almarex will be monitoring you in training bay six. If you need to contact him, adjust your comm-sets to shipboard frequency seventy-three. When you wish to leave, return to this point and transmit a signal on shipboard frequency seventy-four and the doors will open. Oh, and a word of warning. Our climate regulators predict rainfall for most of the night, so set up a good camp. Good luck with your training.'

'Rainfall?' Tanya laughs nervously. 'We're going to get rained on aboard a starship? There's a first.'

'No fauna though,' Quidlon continues, looking around.

'No what, Brains?' asks Trost, who's sat on his pack, tossing a grenade from hand to hand.

'No fauna,' Quidlon repeats himself, squinting up into the sky.

'What Brains means is there aren't any animals here,' Stroniberg explains, squatting down next to the ex-Officio Sabatorum agent. 'No birds, no animals, no insects. Only vegetation.'

'Why didn't he just say that!' complains Trost, ripping up a handful of grass and letting it scatter between his fingers.

'Okay everyone, daydreams in paradise time is over!' I snap at them. 'We are here to work, not rest. Flyboy, you have the map, find out where we are.'

Strelli pulls off his pack and starts to rummage through it, looking for the chart one of the tech-priests handed to me as we passed through the bay entryway.

'Emperor's blood, Flyboy,' Iyle swears at Strelli, pulling the pack from him and tipping its contents on to the ground. He finds the chart and waves it angrily under the pilot's nose. 'What in hell's use is a map that you can't find?'

'Well, you take care of the map then, Eyes,' Strelli snaps back, gathering together his stuff and piling it back into his backpack.

'Flyboy keeps the map,' I tell them, snatching it off Iyle and handing it to Strelli.

'Why, Last Chance?' asks Iyle. 'I was in recon, remember. I can find places with my eyes closed.'

'That's why you don't need to learn how to use a map, you stupid son-of-an-ork!' I shout at him, pushing him onto his backside. I glare at the others.' And that's why Flyboy here is in charge of the map! When Eyes gets killed, who else is going to know what to do?'

'Don't you mean if *I* get killed, Last Chance?' says Iyle defensively. I round on him and kick him in the chest, flattening him again.

'The way you're going, Eyes, it's most definitely "when", not "if",' I spit at him. 'When everyone has finished arguing, we might carry on. Right, our mission for today is to take and attempt to hold that farmstead.' I point at the clutch of buildings about half a kilometre away.

'This whole area is to be considered hostile. We're expecting the place to be reinforced at dusk, so we have to be in by then. There will be targets appearing during the course of the day, and our progress will be monitored by the tech-priests. This evening we will set camp and have a full debriefing. Now, Flyboy, show me that map.'

The others gather round as I spread the chart onto the grass. It shows that the farm is in the cleft of a shallow valley between two hills. We have no way of knowing how accurate the map is though, but there appears to be a road or track of some kind, leading in from what I reckon to be the north.

'How would you attack, Demolition Man?' I prod Trost in the arm.

'Wait for cover of darkness, then sneak in, Last Chance,' he tells me. 'I could rig something up with the squad's grenades, blow the whole thing to tinder.'

'Great, then we get to defend a pile of sticks,' Strelli points out. 'Listen to the orders, fraghead. Take and hold, not level the place.'

'Well, the orders are stupid,' Trost huffs, stepping away from the group.

'Flyboy's right, Demolition Man,' I say, standing up and dragging him back to the map. 'When we find out whatever it is we've got to do, there'll be a plan, and everybody has to stick to the plan. You may be used to working on your own, but unless you want a bolt pistol pointed between your eyes, you better start learning to share.'

'So what would you do, Last Chance?' Stradinsk asks, squatting down and looking at the map again before turning her eyes on me.

'I want to hear what you meatheads come up with first, and then you get a chance to shoot holes in my plan,' I tell them, pulling my pack off and sitting down on it. 'Come on, Sharpshooter, let's hear what you've got to say.'

So we spend an hour or so discussing different ways of taking that farm. We go over frontal assaults, flank attacks, diversionary feints, fusillade and half a dozen other ways of kicking a potential enemy out. As the time passes, I let them get on with it more and more, and soon they're discussing the good points and the pitfalls without any intervention or prompting from me.

I let them think that they're going to have their say, although I decided straight away what we're going to do. It's best to let them get it out of their system first before I start giving them orders. Hopefully, they'll learn a thing or two, including following the man in charge. One of them distracts me from my thoughts. 'What was that?' I ask, looking around. 'Someone say something?'

'I asked what type of support we can expect, Last Chance,' Quidlon tells me. 'You know, air support, artillery, tanks, that sort of thing.'

I just laugh. I laugh until I'm red in the face. They look at me like I've gone insane, which to them probably isn't too far from the truth.

'You got sod all, Brains,' I say, grinning like a fool. 'This is it. No planes. No tanks. No artillery. Just the eight of us, with our lasguns and frag grenades and our heads switched on.' I rein myself in and get serious. 'I'm training you for a real mission, when all we're gonna have is us. Forget about support and what you don't have, that's how dead men think. True soldiers think about themselves and what they can do, without help from anyone else. So, have you agreed on a plan yet?'

'We think we have one that will work, Last Chance,' Stroniberg informs me solemnly.

'Good, now forget it,' I tell them. My statement is answered with objections and confusion, and they start to try and tell me anyway, arguing that it'll work. Trost hurls abuse and stomps away angrily.

'I don't give a frag about your plan, I'm in charge,' I tell them harshly, slapping away Stroniberg's hand, which he laid on my arm when he was arguing with me. 'I never said we'd use your plan for the actual attack, I just asked how you would do it. Now, shut the frag up, and listen to what I'm going to tell you. If we don't take this farmstead, nobody eats tonight and we try again tomorrow, is that clear?'

They answer sullenly, like children who've been told that they can't play. Tough.

'This is the plan. Any of you fail to follow orders, it'll be bad for all of you,' I tell them. They gather around the map while I point out the various locations.

'Demolition Man, Eyes, Hero and myself will infiltrate the farm and sneak into this building,' I point to a barn-like structure within the compound, about twenty metres from the main house. 'If we encounter any resistance we take them out quickly and silently, using knives only.'

I glare at them to make my point. If this was a real fight, any noise would probably bring down all kinds of crap onto us before we even got started.

'Sharpshooter and Stitcher will take up positions on this ridge,' I point to the slope to the east of the objective. 'Find some good cover with flexible firing positions. Your job is to bring fire down onto the farmhouse before our assault begins, and to cover our backs when we go in. We die, it's your fault.'

The pair of them nod seriously, understanding the importance of their role. The only way to take that building is to get someone actually in there and clear it room by room. However, that would be worthless if reinforcements came in behind us or surrounded us before the others could bolster any defence we might muster.

'You two,' I say, looking at Strelli and Quidlon, 'will move into position once the others begin their fusillade. Get on to the roof of this outhouse,' I indicate a large building just behind and to the left of the one we plan to assault from, 'and provide covering fire on the target as we move in. Once we're inside, take over our position ready to follow us in quick when I give the shout.'

Quidlon is studying the map intently, a slight frown creasing his flat forehead.

'You have something to say, Brains?' I ask, turning my gaze on him.

'The attack is all centred on the south and east, Last Chance,' he points out, drawing an arc around the farm with his finger. 'You've got nothing to protect you from the north and west.'

'We can't spread ourselves too thin,' I reply patiently. 'Any less in the assault team and we risk getting kicked out straight away. One person on the ridge won't be enough to keep any enemy heads down before we go, and won't be able to cover their own back. The same goes for you two inside the compound with us. The main road comes in from the southwest.' I trace the point of my dagger along its length on the map. 'So we'll have run into anything along there. The objective itself will shield us from any counter-attack from the opposite direction, 'cos the enemy will have to either enter from the opposite side of the building, which puts them in front of us, or circle round to where we go in and get caught in a crossfire by you guys and the team on the hill.'

'You talk about enemy moving round and encircling, but aren't these just pop-up targets like on the shooting ranges, Last Chance?' asks Trost.

'I've got two answers to that,' I snap at him. 'First, this whole area is littered with those targets and the tech-priests in control can raise and lower them in sequence to simulate movement. Second, and more importantly, this is a battle. Don't think of this as an exercise, something to pass the time. When we're on the mission, we'll be fighting real bastards who will want to kill us, and I don't want any of you getting into a routine where the enemy stays in one place. A soldier who sits still too long is a dead soldier, and useless to me and the Emperor, or an easy target if he's fighting for the other side.'

'That's true,' agrees Stradinsk. 'First rule of the sniper is to take a shot and then move on.'

'Well, thanks for your support, Sharpshooter,' I say sourly before getting back to the attack. 'This has to be timed right, everyone needs to act when and how I tell you. Eyes goes in first and scouts around, and reports back to me. We'll make any changes then, and after that you follow your orders no matter what happens. Is that understood?'

They all nod, although Quidlon and Trost seem doubtful.

'Once we have a clear route, Stitcher and Sharpshooter get into position on the ridge,' I continue, 'I'll give you half an hour to make your way there. You can see the whole thing from where you'll be, or you should be able to if you get in the right place. Sharpshooter, once you're up there point out a few good places for Stitcher to settle.'

'I'll pick a couple of good spots, Last Chance, don't worry,' she assures me with a tight-lipped smile.

'I bet you will,' I agree, remembering her lethal record. 'When you see everyone else in position, open fire on the building. The covering team in the compound,' I look at Strelli and Quidlon, 'will open fire only when the assault teams fire. Direct your shots at other parts of the building to the ones we're firing at. When we get inside, get off the roof, don't waste any time at all, and then get into where we were. Don't anyone even think about firing into the farm once we've gone in, you're there to keep the grounds clear. Anyone shoots me, I'll come back and haunt you for the rest of your fraggin' lives and make you even more miserable than you are now.'

'No firing on the building once you are inside, I can remember that,' says Quidlon with a nervous nod.

'Relax, Brains,' I tell him. 'I've been through more blood and guts fighting than you could imagine, and I know what I'm doing. Now, everyone tell me what the plan is.'

I make them repeat it to me three times each, first all of the attack in the order I explained it. I then get them to tell me their own parts, pointing at them each in turn, then doing the same again but picking on them randomly. Satisfied they understand what's expected of them I wave them away to get their kit together.

We move out some time in what I guess to be mid-afternoon. I forgot to ask how long the 'day' was supposed to last in here. That said, I don't know how much information we'll have on the actual mission so some flexibility and adaptation won't be out of order. I mean, the Colonel and Inquisitor Oriel had been planning Coritanorum for years and we still had to make it up as we went along at some points. For all I know, we might just get dropped into a big mess and be forced to improvise the whole thing from the start. It's too much to expect this bunch to be able to do that at the moment, though. I'd rather they learnt how to follow orders to the exact letter, and can get their heads around a plan without it taking hours to explain.

Everyone is lined up with their kit on, and I shoulder my own pack and join them.

'Right, we'll move out in single file, ten paces apart, Eyes goes on point thirty paces ahead,' I tell them, waving the recon specialist on with my lasgun. 'Everyone keeps their eyes and ears open and their mouths shut, I don't know what surprises this place has got in store for us. You see the enemy, hit the dirt and wave everyone else down. Don't fire until I give you the order. I want this to be disciplined and calm, no mad firefights unless I say so.'

'Yes, Last Chance!' they chorus back.

'Right, let's move out,' I give the order, and we set off across the field.

MARCHING ACROSS THE fields of the training bay brings back some memories. Memories I'm not sure I want. While half my brain scans the surrounding grasslands, the other begins to wander, remembering the faces of all those comrades left broken and bleeding on a dozen battlefields. I look at the others in front of me, fanning out to sweep a track ahead, and wonder how many of them are going to die. And then I get to wondering how much of it will be my fault if they do. I picked them. I plucked them out of their cells and held the gun to their heads, so to speak. I'm also the one who's training them, teaching them what they'll need to know to survive. If I fail them, if they die, then some of it must be down to me, mustn't it? All those other bodies, all those dead faces that haunt my dreams, they weren't my fault, I'm sure of that. I wasn't the one who put them there, I wasn't the one who was responsible for them. But these Last Chancers, these are my team. Chosen by me, trained by me, and I suppose led by me when the time comes.

The weight of that dawns on me and my hands begin to tremble. I've faced horrors blade to blade and gun to gun that you wouldn't dream of in your worst nightmares and not given it a second thought, and here I am shaking like a new recruit in their first firefight. I drop back a bit so that the others won't notice, pulling the map out of my leg pocket to make out I'm checking something. The paper shakes in my hand and I feel my heart flutter. There's something wrong. This doesn't happen to me, I've killed more people then most have met. So why am I getting a massive attack of the jitters in an Emperor-damned training bay?

'Okay, rest up for a few minutes while I check something,' I call to the others just as the first of them, Iyle, reaches a hedgeline across our advance.

They drop into the grass and I walk off a little ways, down into a shallow hollow, and dump my gun on the ground. Spots start dancing in front of my eyes and my whole body is trembling now. I sit down heavily, my legs pretty much buckling under me. The straps of my pack are tightening across my chest and I wrench them off and let it fall behind me. Every muscle in my body seems to be in spasm at once. I can't stop clenching and unclenching my fists.

This isn't just nerves! I scream at myself. This is some kind of pox I've caught, perhaps in that Emperor-forsaken prison. My breathing is ragged, my head swimming. A shadowy figure wavers in front of me and I can just about hear what they're saying over the hissing and pounding in my ears. I wonder vaguely why the sky's behind them.

'Are you okay, sir?' I dimly recognise Tanya's voice.

'Name's Last Chance,' I slur back, trying to focus on her face, which sways from side to side. 'No rations for anyone this evening.'

I feel someone grabbing my shoulders firmly and a face leers into mine, making me recoil with surprise.

'Hold him still,' snaps Stroniberg and hands clamp on my legs and arms, pinning me down in the grass. I taste something metallic in my mouth and gag.

There's an explosion to my left, and I hear screaming. It sounds like Quidlon, or maybe Franx. It's all a bit unclear. My eyes are playing up: one moment I'm lying there on the grass in the field, the next I'm in some kind of ruined building, bullets tearing the place up around me. I get dizzier, and a surge of frustration fuels my anger, threatening to rip me apart from the inside.

'Open your mouth, Kage, open your mouth!' Stroniberg shouts at me, and I feel his fingers on my jaw, and realise my teeth are welded together. 'Dolan's blood, somebody take that knife off him before he does any more damage!' he snaps to the others, who I can just about see around me in between flickers of the dark, ruined city. One of them pulls it from the cramped fingers of my right hand. I didn't even realise I was holding one. Something wet is dribbling down my throat and chest, and I try to reach up to touch it, but my arm is held firm.

'What the frag is he screaming about?' I hear Strelli asking.

I don't know who he's talking about, I can't hear any screaming. I try to sit up and look around to find out who it is. For Emperor's sake, we're supposed to be in the middle of a battle here, if someone's making that much racket, they'll have hell to pay when I'm feeling a bit better.

I feel a sharp stinging pain in my face that brings tears to my eyes and makes my ears ring.

'This is just getting better and better!' I hear Trost shouting. What's he talking about? I'm just feeling a bit ill, that's all. If they'd just give me some room, I'll be alright. I try to wave them away, to give me some air. Something heavy lands on my chest, pinning me down. I try to heave it off, but a stabbing pain in my leg distracts me.

Suddenly all the strength leaves me. I can feel it seeping out, starting at my fingers and toes and spreading up my body. A wave of panic hits me as I can no longer feel my heart beat and a moment later everything goes black.

WHEN I OPEN my eyes, it's to a vision of insanity. Right in front of my face are dozens of glass lenses, clicking in and out of an arrangement of tubes, a bright light shining through, almost blinding me. Tiny chains and gears spin back and forth rhythmically, accompanied by a low humming. Little cantilevers wobble erratically, pumping a dark green fluid through a maze of transparent tubes. My nostrils catch a mix of oil and soap, along with the distinctive smell of blood.

I try to turn my head, but I can't. I feel something hard and cold around my face, like bars running across my chin and forehead and down my cheeks to a block under my jaw. As sensation slowly returns I can feel more restraints. Glancing down past my chin, I can see heavy metal clamps across my chest and legs, held in place with serious-looking padlocks. I can feel things in my arms and throat, piercing the flesh in half a dozen places. I turn my attention back to the apparatus around my head, my eyes tracing cords and cables that disappear into the mass of the machinery. My ears catch the squeaking of a badly-oiled wheel somewhere in the mechanism.

I open my mouth to say something, but my jaw can't move and it just ends up as a cross between a growl and a moan. The lights in the machine flicker and go off, leaving me bathed in a lambent yellow glow. With a whirr the apparatus pulls back from my face, its lenses and levers folding in on themselves, retracting into a small cube that disappears from view above my head. I can see the ceiling and far wall: brick painted in a light grey.

I hear a door latch and then the sound of a door closing to my right, and a tech-priest enters my field of vision. He wears light green robes, spattered with dark patches of what looks like blood. A heavy cog-and-skull sigil hangs from a silver chain about his neck. His face is old and lined, creased heavily like a discarded shirt. A variety of tubes and wires sprout from his neck and head, lost from view over his shoulders. In his hands he carries what looks like a gun with a needle instead of a barrel.

'Am I audible to you?' he asks, his voice a hoarse whisper. 'Blink your eyes for an affirmative.'

It takes me a moment to realise he wants to know if I can hear him. I blink once for yes.

'Am I visible to you?' he asks next, moving to the left side of the bed I'm bound to.

Another blink. I hear the door opening and closing again, and I see Stroniberg walk to the other side of me. He exchanges a look with the tech-priest, who nods once and then turns his attention back to me, his dark brown eyes regarding me clinically.

'So it is mental, not physical,' Stroniberg says, as much to himself as me and the tech-priest. He still hasn't looked at me, busying himself instead with a sheaf of papers hanging from a hook at the foot of the bed.

I lie there, helpless as a new-born, my mind starting to race as I recover my wits. What the hell has happened to me? What did Stroniberg mean by 'mental, not physical'? Surely I've just caught a dose of something? All I did was get a bit shaky and dizzy, nothing too serious about that.

I want to ask him what the frag is going on, but as before it just comes out as a meaningless mumble between my teeth. It attracts his attention though and he comes and stands by my left arm.

'There's no point trying to speak, Kage,' he tells me, not unkindly. 'You're in a restraint harness for your own safety. And ours. You really are a good fighter, aren't you.'

One blink. Yes I am.

'No one on board fully understands what happened to you. We don't have anyone who has done much more than a cursory study of this area of madness,' he continues, turning and pulling a chair to the bedside before sitting down. I can just about still see him out of the corner of my eye. 'You are suffering from some kind of battle-induced vapours leading to a self-destructive trauma. Do you understand what I'm saying, Kage?'

No blink. He could be speaking in foul ork speak for all I know what he's on about. He chews his lip for a moment, obviously in thought, choosing his words.

'Okay, I'll start with the basics,' he says with a sigh. 'You are insane, Kage.'

I try to laugh, but the jaw restraint constricts my throat, making me cough instead. When I recover, I direct à vicious frown at Stroniberg.

'Your years of intense fighting have allowed dangerous amounts of ill vapours to build up in certain parts of your brain, affecting your mental state,' he carries on explaining, patiently and slowly. 'Something that happened in the training bay triggered another release of these vapours, which have begun eroding your senses of judgement, conscience and self-preservation. Are you following me?'

No blink. I never did know much about medicine, and all this mad talk of vapours eating my brain sounds like grox crap. I mean, I'd feel it if my brain was melting.

'The symptoms you displayed in the training bay all point towards a serious battle-psychosis developing, hence your suicide attempt,' he tells me.

Suicide attempt? What the frag is he talking about? I've never even thought about killing myself, not in all those long months and years of fighting and locked alone in that cell. Suicide is for the weak, the ones who have nothing useful left to offer. I'd never kill myself! Emperor, what kind of soldier does he take me for?

'You tried to slit your own throat,' he confirms, seeing the disbelief in my eyes. 'Luckily, the madness vapours had also affected your ability to control your muscles so you just ended up slashing your jaw. You severed a tendon, which is why we've had to bind your jaw shut until the muscles knit together again.'

In a flash of memory, I recall the metallic taste of blood in my mouth during the seizure, and my teeth locking in place.

'I think we caught this before too much damage could be done to your brain, and Biologis Alanthrax,' he indicates the other man, who is still regarding me dispassionately, much as he might look at an interesting specimen, 'was able to perform the surgery and release the vapours before they became fatal.'

Surgery? What in the Emperor's name have these blood fiends done to me? I guess my expression must show what's passing through my mind, as Stroniberg lays a hand on my arm, to try and comfort me I guess. I flick it irritably away with my fingers, one of the few parts of me that I can actually move.

'It is a fairly standard practice, though not common,' he tries to reassure me. 'Biologis Alanthrax has performed it several times before, with almost fifty per cent of his charges making full recoveries. It is a simple matter of temporarily removing a portion of your skull, making an incision into the affected area to release the vapours and then bone-welding the cranium back in place.'

You stuck a knife in my brain! I want to scream at him. For Emperor's sake, you bastard, you stuck a knife in my brain! I'd rather take my chance with the madness than have these sawbones chopping me to bits. I try to push myself up, but there's no give in the restraints at all. Pain shoots through my face as I clench my teeth and snarl at Stroniberg. Emperor damn it, I didn't go through hell and back with the Colonel to die on some damn surgery table under the knife of a jumped-up tech-priest who's got more in common with the knife in his hand than me.

How could the Colonel let them do this to me? He can't believe in all this garbled nonsense. What the hell does he think he's doing, putting me under the knife? Mother of Dolan, I've seen as many men die at the hands of cretins like these as from bullets and blades. I've seen men dying in agony from rotting wounds, cut into them by these sadistic bloodmongers.

'You need to remain calm, Kage,' Stroniberg tells me, standing up, concern written all across his face. 'You need to allow your body to heal.' He glances across at Alanthrax, who steps forward with the gun-like needle. I try to spit a curse at the Emperor-damned pair of them as he pushes it into my forearm and squeezes down on the trigger. As before, sleep washes gently over me.

I SPEND ANOTHER week in the infirmary, locked down on to that table. To make matters worse, we must have dropped into the warp because my nightmares start again. Pumped up on Alanthrax's witches' brew, my dreams are plagued by the dead from my past, just like last time. Men and women missing limbs, their heads sheared in half, entrails open to the world, wandering aimlessly around my bed, staring at me with accusing eyes. I feel like I'm in a waking nightmare, strapped up tight with those creatures circling around and around me. All the time, the two small children I saw in Coritanorum stand at the foot of the bed and just stare at me. Their eyes say it all. You killed us, they say. You burnt us.

I want to scream at them to leave me alone, that I was just following orders, it was them or me, but the lock on my jaw stops me. Not once does the Colonel visit me. Not while I'm awake, at least.

For that whole week it seems like I've died and gone to hell.

THERE'S SUSPICION AND fear in the eyes of the team when I next meet them. It's just before lights-down; they're sprawled in their bunks chatting when I walk in to the dormitory. None of them says a thing and I stand there, feeling their eyes upon me. I look at Stroniberg, who meets my hard gaze without a trace of guilt.

I feel like an invader, such is their hostility.

'Training will resume tomorrow,' I tell them. None of them replies. I don't blame them, I wouldn't know what to say either. I turn and take a step towards the door to my chamber.

'Excuse me, Last Chance,' I hear Quidlon blurt from behind me. 'Colonel Schaeffer said we were to assemble in the briefing room after breakfast tomorrow.'

'The Colonel?' I ask, turning around.

'He carried on with the training while you were…' Iyle leaves it unsaid. Strapped to a bed in case you turned into a raving lunatic and tried to kill yourself or someone else, is what he doesn't say.

'And what did Colonel Schaeffer have to say about me?' I ask, suddenly worried. What's to become of me, if the Colonel is taking direct control of the training again? I feel the horrid sensation of failure begin to well up inside me. He can't have me shipped back to vincularum, not now we're in the warp and underway I don't think. But there's bound to be a brig aboard the *Laurels of Glory* and he could just as easily have me banged up in there for the duration. Or perhaps he'll just finish it, put a bolt through my head as an example to the others. They shake their heads or shrug in response.

'Nothing, Last Chance,' Tanya tells me. 'He said nothing about you.'

'Very well,' I reply, keeping my voice level. 'I want you all looking sharp tomorrow morning, now is the time we have to stay focussed and disciplined.'

I walk out and into my room. I hear them start to chatter again and I'm about to close the door when a random thought occurs to me. I stick my head around the doorframe.

'Does Schaeffer have a name?' I ask them. 'Like the ones I gave you?' They exchange glances, half-smiles on their lips.

'Yes, Last Chance, he does,' Quidlon tells me. 'He said he is Colonel.'

Figures, I think to myself, nodding and closing the door. As I do so, I catch a snippet of what Trost says next.

'We set a double watch tonight,' he says to the others. 'That psycho's not coming anywhere near me while I'm asleep.'

At first I'm tempted to wrench the door open and pound the mouthy meathead into the deck for saying that, but I stop short. I sit down on my bunk and I can't stop a smile creeping across my face. That's one lesson they'll never forget, I reckon. I lie down on my bunk and close my eyes, waiting for sleep and the nightmares to come again.

THE NEXT MORNING, the Colonel sends an armsman to wake me up early. I dress hurriedly and follow him up to Schaeffer's chamber. He's there waiting for me, immaculately dressed despite the early hour, clean shaven and bright-eyed. The armsman closes the door behind me without a further word.

The Colonel looks at me for a long, long time, his eyes unwavering, stripping away layer after layer of my soul. I begin to fidget under his gaze. The circular scar on the side of my head itches like mad and it's all I can do to keep myself standing at attention and not scratch at it.

'One more mistake, Kage,' he says slowly, 'and I am finished with you.'

I say nothing. There's nothing to say.

'I am watching you more closely than ever,' he warns me, eyes not moving. 'I will not tolerate the slightest slip-up on your part, nor the merest hint that your treatment was unsuccessful. Do I make myself clear, Kage?'

'Perfectly, sir,' I answer quietly, dread knotting my stomach. Now the pressure's really on.

THE BRIEFING ROOM is shaped like half an amphitheatre. Thirty metres across, it has a hundred stepped benches descending to a semicircular floor with a similarly shaped dais on it. There's a table on the dais, a lumped cloth covering whatever is on it. The Colonel seems to fill the room with his presence as we enter, all of us focussing our attention on him as we walk down the steps to the lowest benches. The others stand to attention in front of their places, me to one side. The Colonel waves us to sit down and begins to pace up and down.

'So far you have been training blind,' he tells us, scanning his ice-cold eyes along the line. 'Now we begin to prepare for the mission in earnest. It is our task to assassinate an alien commander who has been causing the Emperor's servants considerable pain, and his own rulers at the same time. With their collaboration we will infiltrate his base and kill him.'

He pulls the cloth back off the table to reveal a scale model of a bizarre looking building. I've never seen anything so odd in my life. If I guess the scale correctly from the size of details like doors and windows, it's a massive dome, probably big enough to house a small town. The Colonel removes the dome and places it to one side, revealing an open plan of the interior, divided into numerous large chambers, and beckons us over to look inside. The chambers look remarkably similar to the training bays. Some of them have small model jungle trees inside, one has a little replica of a beach, another what looks to be the outskirts of an Imperial city.

'This is the target area,' the Colonel explains. 'The alien we are hunting is from a race who call themselves the tau. He has some unpronounceable heathen name, which I am assured by a lexist translates to something equivalent to Commander Brightsword. Now, this Brightsword virtually rules one of the tau worlds only a few weeks' travel from the Sarcassa system that falls within the Emperor's dominions. Over several years, Brightsword has been very aggressively sending colonising fleets into the wilderness space surrounding Sarcassa. We believe it is his intent to invade this system within the next two to three months. His superiors, the rulers of the so-called Tau Empire, very wisely wish to avoid a bloody and costly war with our forces and have agreed to this co-operative strike.'

He pauses to let the full weight of this settle in. These aliens, these tau, are helping us to kill one of their own commanders. Either they must be really scared of what we'll do to their little empire if Brightsword goes ahead with his mad plan, or they really don't have much sense of loyalty to their own people.

'Excuse me, Colonel?' Quidlon raises his hand slightly. 'Why are the tau engaging in this mission with us, rather than simply removing Commander Brightsword from office, or perhaps covertly removing him themselves by other means?'

The Colonel waits a moment, probably while his brain catches up with Quidlon's quickfire way of speaking.

'Unlike our own great Imperium, the tau have no great Emperor to bind them together,' the Colonel explains, lip curled in distaste. 'They are godless, as far as we can tell, and have this strange concept which the tau call the "greater good". Their empire supposedly sustains itself through harmony between all of its subjects, rather than by making the supreme sacrifices the Emperor asks of us.

'As you might understand, with no such guiding hand, their empire is very fragile. Any hint that there are those not working towards this fictitious greater good undermines the whole basis for their society. They cannot admit to their citizens that one of their commanders is, in essence, a renegade. Similarly, they cannot risk being uncovered trying to assassinate that commander, for the same reasons. Thus, we have constructed a subterfuge that allows us, as outsiders, to kill Brightsword, posing as renegades rather than Imperial servants. We can show them official records and provide witnesses if necessary that will show that you are all military criminals.

'That is another reason why I am using scum like you. A half-truth is always better than an outright lie. All of this means there will be no call for a response against our forces. No blame will be traceable to either the tau government nor the Emperor's loyal subjects.'

'Very neat,' I mutter, not realising I've spoken out loud until the Colonel darts me an evil glare.

'You have something to say, Last Chance?' he asks scornfully, hands on his hips.

'Yes, Colonel,' I tell him, standing up straight and looking him in the eye. 'Aliens killing aliens I can live with. Us killing aliens, I can live with. Aliens helping us to kill aliens makes me suspicious. Besides, Colonel, this whole thing reminds me of Coritanorum too much. All this infighting, I mean.'

'Believe me when I say that this whole mission has been examined from every angle, by myself and others,' he retorts, looking around at all of us. 'We would be fools to trust the tau, you can be sure of that. However, the opportunity presented to end the threat posed by Brightsword, whom we believe is fully intent on and capable of taking Sarcassa, is too good to pass up. Therefore we will proceed, but with caution.'

He directs his attention back to the miniature building on the table and we close in again.

'This is a barracks and training area, what the tau refer to as a battle dome,' he informs us, leaning forward with his hands on the table. 'It also serves as the headquarters of Commander Brightsword. Currently he is reviewing his forces on the newly colonised worlds around Sarcassa but he will be performing an inspection of his troops at this battle dome before he leaves to rejoin his fleet for the invasion. Before and after the parade he will be beyond the reach of both us and our tau allies, so we will strike when he arrives to perform the inspection.'

I, and a couple of the others, nod approvingly. Any kind of hit like this, and believe me I did a few back on Olympas during the trade wars, relies on surprise. I don't know how paranoid and security conscious these tau are, but if we have people on the inside it shouldn't be too difficult.

'What are all these different areas, Colonel?' asks Tanya, pointing at the various chambers.

'The battle dome is a training facility, Sharpshooter,' he replies. 'Just as on this ship, each of these training areas represents a different type of locale, and can be modified to represent specific targets and objectives for an upcoming campaign. After our first diplomatic envoys to the tau reported on the efficiency of their tactics, we sent agents to observe their military facilities. On this vessel, and her sister ships, we have replicated the more laudable and practical aspects of their training methods. The tau have a somewhat lax attitude to the perils presented by over-reliance on technology, so the Adeptus Mechanicus have been unable to duplicate the more arcane and blasphemous systems employed by the tau. However, these ships represent the best training facilities we have currently at our disposal. Our tech-priests are currently reconstructing three of the training bays to represent the battle zone where we are planning to trap and kill Brightsword.'

He points towards an area at the centre of the battle dome which seems to be some kind of power system terminal surrounded by a wide concourse, perhaps a parade ground or embarkation level.

'When the new training bay is complete, we will begin operational training,' he continues, standing up straight. 'Until then, we will go over the exact particulars of the mission using this scale representation of the combat zone and continue with your general training. Now, pay attention to the plan.'

FLASH FLARES AND detonations explode across the pale yellow floors and walls, blinding in their intensity and billowing a cloud of acrid black smoke through the doorway where I'm crouched, an autogun gripped in my hands. As I've done a dozen times before over the last two weeks, I dive forward into the gloom, rolling through the smoke to the other side of the corridor.

I ripple off a burst of fire down the smoke-filled tunnel, covering for Quidlon and Stradinsk as they dive after me, heading for the gateway a few metres behind me. I work my way towards them crouched on my haunches, emptying the rest of the magazine with short bursts of fire at the silhouettes of possible targets moving backwards and forwards through the smoke. Sheltering in the gateway, I pull out the mag and toss it away, smoothly pulling another from my weapons belt and slamming it home.

I begin to count in my head. After I reach twenty, I give the nod to Quidlon, who pulls a las-cutter from his pack and begins to burn his way through the armoured gate. Sparks dance around the gate alcove, falling onto my left arm and leg and spilling onto the floor. Rivulets of molten metal pour down the doorway and pool on the floor, cooling with a cloud of steam. I count to another twenty before leaning out of my cover and firing off on semi-auto for another five counts. I watch as Trost emerges from a doorway in front of me and dashes past, throwing himself in behind Tanya.

'The door is open,' Quidlon informs us, stepping back and delivering a sharp kick, knocking out a section of metal and leaving a space just high and wide enough to crawl through. Trost pokes his head through and then wriggles out of sight.

'Clear on the other side,' he calls back after a few seconds. I fire another burst down the corridor while Quidlon, then Tanya, follow the bomb expert, before turning and diving through myself. Pulling myself up on the other side, I glance around to check the concourse is clear of targets.

'Cover smoke, Demolition Man!' I snap to Trost, who pulls a grenade from the bandoleer across his chest, primes it with a thumb and then hurls it into the centre of the parade ground. It clatters to a stop almost exactly halfway between our position and the door to the control chamber of the travel station. A moment later bluish smoke gouts forth, quickly spilling across the wide area and obscuring visibility in every direction.

'Let's move,' I say to Tanya and Quidlon, dashing out from the gateway, the others pounding across the floor behind me. Trost stays behind to cover the hole in the gate.

'Movement, get down!' screams Tanya, diving to the floor beside me. I drop and roll, noticing something moving in the smoke out of the corner of my eye. I hear the sharp crack of Stradinsk's marksman's rifle, followed by a scream of agony.

'What the frag?' I hear Trost shout.

'Since when do targets scream?' asks Quidlon from behind me. I get to my feet and dash over, keeping low, Quidlon just behind me. As I run through the smoke, I see something lying on the ground, a lumpen shape. As I get closer, I see it's Stroniberg, laid flat out, legs and arms splayed wide. A puddle of blood oozes from under him. Bending over him, I see the bullet hole in his left cheek. I roll his head to the side and half his skull comes away in fragments. I feel something pluck weakly at my arm. He's still alive!

'H... hel... help me...' pleads Stroniberg, eyes wide, tears streaming down his face and mixing with the blood seeping from his cheek. He coughs and spits, pieces of shattered tooth spraying bloodily onto his tunic.

Quidlon is on his knees, fumbling for the medi-pak strapped to Stroniberg's left thigh.

'It'll be okay, Stitcher, it'll be okay,' Quidlon says, pulling his knife out and cutting the medi-pak strap and tugging the bulky pouch free.

I look at the side of Stroniberg's face, or more precisely the gory, ragged remnants of it, and wonder what was going through his mind as he stood and watched that damn tech-priest digging around in my brain with a scalpel. Almost transfixed by the bubbling fluid spilling from the wound, I reach forward tentatively with a finger, and I'm about to prod the grey and crimson mess when Trost appears and grabs my wrist, pulling me away.

'What the frag are you doing, Last Chance?' he snarls at me, hate in his eyes. 'You are seriously cracking up. You need to be put out of your misery!'

I slap his hand away and push him back, snapping out of the trance. I turn back to Stroniberg and crouch over him.

'What should we do? Tell me what to do, Stitcher,' Quidlon asks desperately, spilling bandages, needles, tourniquets and stimms from the medi-pak across the floor. 'Stitcher, you have to tell me what to do, I don't know what any of this stuff is for.'

'G... green phial,' the chirurgeon replies, blood leaking from the corner of his mouth. 'Need to... to drink it...'

Quidlon finds the phial and pulls the stopper out, pouring the contents into Stroniberg's gaping mouth. The physician gags and chokes before swallowing it, frothy blood now leaking from his nose as well.

'Pad... and bandage,' Stroniberg gasps next, his hand flapping through the pile of stuff on the floor, using his touch to identify what he's after.

'We don't have time for this,' I say suddenly, standing up and pulling Quidlon with me.

'What do you mean?' Trost snarls hoarsely, a hand on my shoulder twisting me to face him.

'We only have roughly five minutes before the target will appear,' I tell him calmly. 'Quidlon needs to lock down the rail carriage and Tanya needs to be in the observation tower for her shot.'

'Stitcher will die if we leave him,' moans Quidlon, looking back at Stroniberg who is staring up at me with a glazed expression.

'You can't save him,' I say, staring back at him. 'Let the butcher die.'

Quidlon stands there stunned; Trost looks like I shot Stroniberg myself.

'We have to call off the exercise,' he growls.

'Oh right,' I snarl back. 'Like we'd call off the attack if this happens on the real mission. Don't be so fraggin' stupid. Now, get back to covering that gateway before I put a bullet through your head! And get Sharpshooter to shift her arse over her, we need to get moving. You,' I turn to Quidlon. 'Get into that control room and shut down the transport power.'

They all stand there like statues.

'Emperor damn it,' I curse, punching Trost square across the jaw and buckling him at the knees. 'Emperor so help me if you don't get moving now I will break every bone in your fraggin' bodies!'

He stumbles away, cursing like a navy rating, and Quidlon hovers for a moment before seeing the look in my eye. He grabs his gun from the floor and sprints over towards the entranceway. The smoke is beginning to thin and I see Trost bent over, talking to Stradinsk, who's sat on the ground by the looks of it. I run over to them and catch the end of what Trost is saying.

'...will kill you if you don't get moving,' he's telling her, shaking her by the shoulder. He sees me approaching and legs it for the gateway, unslinging his gun from his shoulder as he runs through the smoke.

Tanya is sat cross-legged on the hard floor, staring straight ahead, her gun lying next to her.

'On your feet, Sharpshooter,' I shout at her. 'Grab your weapon and come with me.'

She doesn't move a muscle, doesn't even blink. I snatch up her rifle and thrust it towards her, but it just falls out of her limp hands into her lap. Snarling, I grab a handful of tunic and drag her to her feet, where she stands swaying slightly, eyes still unfocussed.

'Pick up your rifle, Sharpshooter,' I say to her slowly and deliberately. 'That is an order, soldier!'

She doesn't move. I stare down at her, right in the eye, my face nearly touching hers. There's nothing there at all, her eyes staring through me at something in the distance I suspect only she can see.

'Never mind about me,' I say to her softly, calming myself down at the same time. 'If the Colonel sees this, we will both get shot. Don't you understand? You have to pick up your rifle.'

I grab the weapon and slowly ease it into her unresisting hands, before closing her fingers around the stock. She stands there doing nothing, absolutely out of touch with everything around her. The gun clatters to the ground again as I let go of her hand.

'Emperor damn you, snap out of it!' I scream at her, smashing the back of my hand across her face, splitting her top lip. She sways and staggers for a second before righting herself. I see a glimmer of life in her eyes then, a moment too late as her boot smashes up between my thighs and knocks me to the ground.

'Bastard!' she screams, kicking me in the midriff as I roll around the floor. I think I feel a rib crack under the blow. 'I don't want to shoot anyone again. Don't you understand? I'm not a killer, I'm not this true soldier you keep talking about. I'm never picking up a gun again. You can't turn me into a murderer!'

I sit up, clutching my ribs and wincing. Slowly I push myself to my feet. I stare at Stradinsk for a long, long time, my face expressionless. With a deliberate slowness, I reach down and pick up her sniper rifle. She eyes it with disgust, barely able to bring herself to look at it. I pull the slide and eject the spent casing.

'Why didn't you say we had live ammunition?' she asks quietly, looking at the cartridge on the floor.

'What did you expect?' I answer calmly. 'This is not some kind of game we're playing here. We're not doing this for fun, Sharpshooter.'

'Don't call me that!' she snaps, recoiling away from me. 'I hate that name.'

'It's who you are,' I tell her viciously. 'That or a corpse, like Stroniberg.'

'Don't you mean Stitcher?' she replies sourly.

'When he was alive, and he was useful, he was Stitcher,' I say, glancing over my shoulder at his cooling corpse. 'Now he's just a useless dead lump of meat.'

'I'm not Sharpshooter, my name is Tanya Stradinsk,' she argues. 'Do what you like to me, I'm not firing a gun again.'

I toss the rifle at her and she catches it easily. Her grip is loose and sure, used to handling the weapon without thinking. She looks down at it and then drops it to the ground with a clatter. I pull the short stub gun out from the belt of my fatigues and cock it in front of her face. I point it at her, right between the eyes and move my finger onto the trigger.

'Pick up your gun, Sharpshooter,' I warn her. She shakes her head. 'Pick it up, damn you, I don't want to kill you!'

'I'd rather be dead,' she tells me defiantly.

'Is that right?' I ask, uncocking the stubber and thrusting it back into my belt. I grab Tanya and drag her across the concourse to where Stroniberg lies in a pool of deep red.

'That's what you'll look like, that's all you'll be,' I snarl at her. She tries to look away, tears in her eyes. I grab her by the hair and push her to her knees next to Stroniberg. She gives a whimper as I pull out the stubber again and place it to the back of her head. 'Is this really what you want?' I demand.

'I can't fire a gun again,' she pleads, looking up over her shoulder at me, her cheeks streaked with tears.

'I'm not asking you to fire it, Tanya,' I say softly, lifting the gun away. 'I just need you to pick it up.'

She hesitates for a moment, wiping the back of her hand across her face, and then gets to her feet. She glances at me and I nod towards the rifle. I follow her as she walks over to it. She bends down, her hand hovering above it.

'Just pick it up,' I prompt her, my voice level. Her hand closes around the barrel and she pulls it to her. She stands there for a second, holding it away from her like it's a poisonous snake or something.

With an anguished cry, she falls to her knees, cradling the rifle to her chest.

'What have I done?' she asks between sobs.

'You killed a man,' I answer bluntly, turning away from her. The sight of her sickens me to the pit of my stomach. I'm gonna have hell to pay with the Colonel over this whole fragged up mess. 'You killed a man,' I say again. 'It's what we do.'

As I EXPECTED, the Colonel is less than happy with the day's events. I'm in his cabin, which looks surprisingly familiar to the one he had aboard the *Pride of Lothos*. I guess he has his own furniture or something and brings it with him. The walls are panelled in a deep red wood, behind him is a glass-fronted bookshelf with a handful of books on the top shelf. His plain desk and chair sit in the middle of the room, a pile of papers neatly stacked in one corner. Schaeffer himself is pacing up and down behind the desk, his hands balled into fists behind his back.

'This was a simple training exercise, Kage,' he growls at me, not even looking in my direction but pouring his scorn onto the universe in general. 'Now my team has a dead medic and a sniper who can barely bring herself to hold a gun.'

He rounds on me at that point, and I can see that he is really, really angry. His eyes are like shards of glittering ice, his jaw is tight and his whole body tensed.

'Stroniberg I can live without,' he admits angrily. 'But Stradinsk? The whole plan we have devised relies on her making that shot. She will only get one chance at it, one chance. You promised me you could get her to fire that shot. And you? Collapsing in the middle of an exercise and trying to kill yourself! What happened to the Kage that was with me on Ichar IV? Where's the hardened killer that watched my back on False Hope? Where's the good soldier that was with me in Coritanorum? Now, only weeks away, am I going to have to inform my superiors that the whole mission has to be abandoned?'

He stops in his tirade and takes a deep breath, turning away from me. I just stand there at attention, waiting for it to start again. My mind is reeling, I've got no idea what he's going to do next. Is he really going to call off the assassination? Is it his decision, or someone else's? If he does, what happens to me and the Last Chancers? What happens to him? As these thoughts fly through my head, he turns back to me.

'I am very disappointed in you, Kage,' he says solemnly, shaking his head. 'Very disappointed indeed.'

His words cut me more than any knife can, and all I can do is hang my head in shame, because he's right to be disappointed. I've failed.

'Climb faster!' I bellow at Stradinsk, standing at the bottom of the travel terminal's command tower in the mock-up battle dome. She's hauling herself up the side of the building on a rope, painfully slowly in my eyes. 'You've got thirty seconds to reach the top, from start to finish. Climb faster!'

She glances back down over her shoulder at me before renewing her efforts, her tired arms dragging her slowly, metre by metre up towards the observation chamber.

'I can't see why this is so necessary, Last Chance, considering there are stairways inside the tower,' Quidlon says, standing next to me and looking up. 'Is this supposed to be some kind of punishment, perhaps?'

'No, this isn't a punishment, Brains,' I reply, keeping my eyes on Tanya. 'This is called playing it safe. If something goes wrong and you can't open the doors to the terminal for some reason, I want there to be a back-up plan. Sharpshooter has to be in position for that kill, whatever happens to the rest of us.'

Tanya's only a couple of metres from the top now, but slowing badly. All it needs is one final effort and she'll be up, but she just hangs there, exhausted. Okay, this is the tenth time she's made that climb in the last hour, but she needs to build up the right muscles.

Moerck is standing beside me on the other side, intently looking at the climbing figure.

'She'll fall,' he says simply, glancing at me out of the corner of her eye. 'I think losing our sniper now would be a bad thing.'

He's right, the rope is swaying badly, and it looks as if she can only just about hang on, never mind climb any further.

'Motivate her,' I tell Moerck, crossing my arms. He pulls out his laspistol and readies it, the gun emitting a short, high-pitched whine as the power cell warms up.

'Sharpshooter, listen to me!' he bellows, deafening me. His voice could carry through an artillery barrage in a thunderstorm. 'I am going to count to three and then I'm going to shoot you if you're still hanging on that rope!'

She glances back again and sees him turn side on and raise his pistol towards her, assuming a duelling stance and sighting down the length of his arm. He stands as still as a rock, attention fixed on the struggling woman.

'One!' he shouts out. Tanya begins to haul herself up once more, reaching deep into her reserves of energy, dragging herself painfully up the rope.

'Two!' he continues, not moving a muscle except to adjust his aim higher. Tanya gets a hand to the rim around the top of the building, then the other. She pulls herself up onto the edge and then rolls over, disappearing from view. I turn to Moerck and nod appreciatively. Tanya pops her head back over and hurls abuse down at us, waving an angry fist.

'And you all think I'm a cruel training officer,' I comment to Quidlon, shouldering my autogun and heading off towards the tower door.

'The difference is, I wouldn't have fired,' Moerck calls out as I walk away. 'You would have.'

I stop and turn back towards them, looking at Quidlon then Moerck. 'That's true,' I agree with a nonchalant shrug.

STRELLI LUNGES AT me with the knife, making a jab towards my midriff. The attack is low and fast, but I manage to step back, using the outside of my right arm to deflect his hand away before stepping back in and driving my fingers towards his throat. He sways back, the blow falling just short, and tries to chop down on my wrist with his left hand. I roll my wrist over his and grab his arm, dragging him forward onto my knee, but he jumps at the last second, performing a forward tumble and rolling to his feet.

We stand there panting for a few seconds, eyeing each other warily.

'Okay, that's good,' I tell him, stepping away and wiping sweat from my forehead with the sleeve of my tunic. 'Quidlon and Iyle, you're next.'

The two of them circle each other, blades held back, away from the enemy until they're ready to strike. Iyle feints to the left and slips round to the right, but Quidlon's not fooled and meets the move, dropping low and driving his foot into Iyle's left knee. The scout stumbles but recovers quickly enough to leap aside as Quidlon lunges for him. Iyle rams his fist into the small of Quidlon's back, knocking him forward, but Quidlon turns the blow into a roll, rising up and spinning on the spot with an easy motion, a grimace on his face. The mechanic tosses the knife into his left hand and makes a slash at Iyle, who is forced to dance back a couple of steps. Quidlon follows up immediately, switching hands again. Iyle tries to take the initiative back and makes a sloppy stab. Quidlon easily avoids it, trapping Iyle's knife arm against his body and dragging him forward onto his own blade. Iyle gives a startled cry and flops sideways, pulling the blade out of Quidlon's hand. He sits there on the mat, legs out in front of him, blood pouring down his stomach and pooling in his lap.

'Good blow, Brains, now finish him,' I say, my voice quiet. Quidlon glances back at me, a confused look on his face. Iyle pulls the knife free and lets it drops through blood-slicked fingers.

'Last Chance?' Quidlon asks, taking a step towards me. I toss him my own knife, which he catches easily, and point at Iyle.

'Finish him,' I say with a shallow nod towards the wounded man.

Iyle stares up at me with a look of fear, still holding his guts. He tries to say something, but just croaks hoarsely, glancing between me and Quidlon. I see understanding dawn on him, and a look of determination crosses his face.

'Do it, Brains,' hisses Trost from my left, eager for blood.

'Leave him be!' Tanya argues from the other side, darting a murderous look at me. 'Don't do it, Brains!'

'He won't,' I hear Strelli mutter, standing to one side, arms casually crossed. 'He hasn't got the instinct for it.'

Quidlon's still looking at me, a shallow frown creasing his brow. He looks back at Iyle and then at me. I just nod. He turns away and takes a step towards Iyle.

'I'll make you eat the fragging thing!' Iyle gasps, trying to push himself to his feet. It's a good attempt, I'll give him that, but with that wound he'll get nowhere. Quidlon takes a running step and kicks Iyle square in the face, smashing him to his back. He leaps on top of him, driving a blocky fist into the scout's nose. Winded and concussed, Iyle can do nothing as Quidlon forces his head to the ground and pushes the knife point up under his chin. Quidlon closes his eyes and thrusts, sliding the blade up through Iyle's mouth and into his brain. Just as slowly, he pulls it out and stands up, facing away from me, the bloodied dagger in his hand.

'I can't believe he actually did it,' exclaims Strelli in astonishment. 'Maybe brains aren't all you've got.'

I look at Iyle's corpse and nod to myself. He died like a soldier. He died fighting for his life, not begging for it. I can respect that.

'You just murdered Eyes, you scum!' Tanya shrieks at Quidlon, turning away in disgust.

'No,' Quidlon replies slowly, turning around to face us, a splash of blood across his face. His voice is flat, his expression blank. 'I was just following orders.'

'Welcome to be being a true soldier, Brains,' I say to him, stepping forward and clapping him on the shoulder.

'This seems like a damn fool way to get a lot of men killed, if you excuse my plain speaking, lord,' the Imperial Guard captain proclaimed. He was standing with the robed inquisitor in the shuttle bay of the Imperial transport *Pride of Lothos*. His bullet-head and broad shoulders gave him a brutal look, but his soft spoken burr and quick eyes betrayed the fact that he was far smarter than he looked. Dressed in a simple uniform of black and grey camouflage, Captain Destrien was a tall, imposing figure. Yet the elderly man with whom he was speaking seemed to command much more attention. The black robes that he wore were a mark of the Adeptus Terra, the priesthood of Earth, yet Destrien was not fooled. This was no Administratum bureaucrat.

No adept of Terra carried themselves with such authority and confidence, yet with no hint of pompousness or pride.

No, though he chose to act as something else, the captain knew full well that he spoke to a member of the Inquisition, and the inquisitor knew it too.

'I agree that your orders are highly irregular, captain; one might even say unorthodox,' the inquisitor said with a smile, leaning heavily on his cane. 'Be that as it may, they are your orders and have been countersigned by your superiors, including Warmaster Bane himself.'

Destrien stiffened at the mention of Bane, Warmaster and overall commander of the Imperial forces in the Sarcassa region. This inquisitor wasn't playing around. He had organised this thoroughly, from the top down.

'You're right, those are my orders, and I'll follow 'em, but don't expect me to like it,' complained Destrien, knowing that any argument was useless, but wishing to make his protest all the same. 'We'll be here for another week at least, while we resupply.'

'I believe there are several lighters currently waiting to dock as we speak,' the inquisitor countered, still with the same polite smile on his face. 'I thought it would be necessary to resolve this matter as expeditiously as possible, and brought some of my... influence to bear on the Departmento Munitorum on your behalf. I believe the new uniforms and equipment specified in your orders are aboard. See that they are issued to your men in due course.'

'I just bet you could nail a fog cloud to a wall, couldn't you, lord?' Destrien answered grumpily. He was well and truly cornered here. He'd been hoping to use the week to get in contact with Warmaster Bane and try to get this assignment shoved onto someone else, but the inquisitor was one step ahead of him all the way.

'Yes, and tiptoe along the threads of a spider web as well, captain,' the inquisitor replied, his voice suddenly harsh and ominous, no trace of the previous smile. He pointed his cane at Destrien. 'Remember that you are not to speak of the detail of your orders to anyone, anyone at all, until you are en route to the target. Once there, you will open the second set of sealed orders and follow them to the letter. Is that absolutely clear?'

'To the letter, lord,' Destrien parroted heavily.

'Good.' The inquisitor's smile had returned as easily as it had disappeared. 'Now, I must be on my way. I wish you Emperor's speed and good luck, captain.'

FOUR
RETURN

+++The signs are clear, the Blade inverted is revealed+++

+++It is imperative that he arrive. He is the key+++

THE COLONEL WATCHES us impassively as we file into the briefing auditorium, standing behind the model of the tau battle dome, arms crossed. We stand to attention by the lowest bench and wait for him. With a nod he directs us to sit down and begins to pace back and forth across the dais, hands behind his back.

'As you are no doubt aware, we left warp space yesterday,' he announces, glancing at us from time to time as he strides to and fro. I had noticed that my warp dreams didn't come last night, and I'd guessed that was the reason. 'We are here to rendezvous with the vessel that will take us into tau-controlled space. This vessel is a tau warship, and under the guise of a diplomatic mission we will enter the Tau Empire and make contact with our allies in the tau government. Whilst aboard the tau ship we must, at all times, be on our guard. The crew of the ship are not privy to our scheme and must totally believe our subterfuge. If they become suspicious of our motives, then the whole mission is placed in jeopardy. I will give you each individual briefings as to your assumed identities before we embark the shuttle for transfer.'

He pauses for a moment, scratching his ear with a thoughtful expression and looking at us sternly.

'The tau will be watching us closely,' he warns us. 'Firstly, even if they believe everything they have been told, I am sure they will be under standing orders to study and observe us at every opportunity. Secondly, the growing tension around Sarcassa, and the rebellion of another renegade called Farsight, mean that the tau are very much on their guard at the moment. They are expecting an escalation of hostilities between their empire and the Emperor's servants soon, but we must do nothing to precipitate that. You will be on your best behaviour and act according to your roles as members of a peaceful delegation.'

I smile inwardly at the irony of this statement. I've spent the last few months training these people to be the hardest, most ruthless killers they can be, and now we have to try and hide that from the tau. It won't be easy. I've done a fair amount of this sneaking around in the past, and the Colonel's right. One slip up and your days are numbered. The fact that it's a tau ship picking us up is also an eye-opener. It shows that our accomplices within the Tau Empire must be pretty important. I don't know whether that's good or bad. On the plus side, they should have the muscle to make sure we can get everything done. On the down side, I've never known such people to fire straight. There's always a hidden motive somewhere.

The whole deal smells a little too clean for my liking. I'll be keeping my eyes and ears open, make no mistake. So will the Colonel, I'd happily bet. He's no stranger to this type of thing either. I mean, the whole Coritanorum mission was us fighting for the Inquisition, and a more slippery, manipulative and untrustworthy bunch doesn't exist. That said, I'd rather have them on our side, all things considered.

'Kage, I will be speaking to you first. Report at the start of the next watch,' the Colonel tells me, interrupting my thoughts. I guess he wants to give me the low-down on the others, as well as my own story.

I KNOCK AT the door and hear Schaeffer call me in. As I step inside, I'm surprised to see two armsmen flanking the Colonel's desk. Eyeing them suspiciously, I step inside and close the door behind me. They look like standard armsmen, carrying shotguns and wearing their black uniforms and dark-visored helmets. I have no idea why they are here though. The Colonel seems to read my thoughts.

'They are here to make sure you do not do anything rash,' he explains, glancing to his left then right and then looking back directly at me.

'Why would I do that, Colonel?' I ask hesitantly, totally confused.

'You are not going on the mission, Kage,' he tells me bluntly.

'Not... not going?' I stammer, my mind whirling. 'I don't understand, sir.'

'It is obvious that you are no longer mentally capable of performing in the mission I have planned,' he states coldly. 'Another episode like the one in the training bay would destroy any cover story we may be travelling under. You are too much of a risk.'

'No, this isn't right,' I say back to him. 'I can do this, better than any of the rest. You can't just get rid of me!'

'I can and I will,' he says calmly. 'The penal colony Destitution lies in the system where we are meeting the tau. You will be transferred by shuttle to an intrasystem vessel and be incarcerated there until such time as I need you again.'

'You can't do this!' I scream at him, taking a step forward. The armsmen take a protective step towards me, raising their shotguns and I back off. 'You can't lock me up again! If I've got problems in my head, it's because of what you've done to me! You're the one who's been fraggin' with my brains for the last three years. I don't deserve this, I've worked fraggin' hard whipping that bunch out there into shape. Emperor damn it, you know I can do this, and you know what going back to a cell will do to me!'

'I have made my decision, Kage,' he says sternly, standing up. 'Either you accompany these armsmen to the shuttle bay, or I will have them shoot you right here and now. Which is it to be, lieutenant?'

I stand there, my emotions swaying between murderous anger and crushing sorrow. How could he do this to me? How long has he intended this to happen? A thought strikes me, making the blood boil in my veins.

'You organised the meeting with the tau in a penal colony system,' I snarl at the Colonel, pointing an accusing finger at him. 'You planned this all along. Drag me along for the training and then dump me. You ungrateful bastard, don't you care at all?'

'I never once said that you were going to participate in the actual mission,' the Colonel replies evenly, like that's all the justification he needs.

'I bet you didn't,' I hiss.

'Now, Kage, do you walk out of that door, or do these men open fire?' he says, locking his gaze to mine. Without a word I spin on my heel and slam open the door. I turn back just before I'm outside.

'This mission will fail,' I tell him slowly. 'It will fail because I'm not there to pull you out of the fire, and not one of the scum that'll be with you gives a damn.'

The armsmen swiftly follow me out as I stalk down the corridor. The anger is welling up inside me, I want to lash out. I want to hit someone, something. What I really want is the Colonel's throat in my grip as I squeeze the last breath out of him. The desire to kill burns through me; I'm actually gnashing my teeth in frustration. It's all I can think about, every muscle in my body is tensed. Six months I was in that cell. Another three months I've been on this ship, sweating blood to train that team. And for what? To rot in another jail somewhere? To slowly go mad with it, to know that I was almost there, fighting again, doing my part for the Emperor. And Schaeffer just snatches it away from me, just takes it away like he had planned all along.

He said he needed me, but that was just a lie, wasn't it? He didn't need me, I was just useful. I just saved him the hard work. Now that's done, he doesn't give a damn, doesn't care a bit that I'm gonna end up clawing my own eyes out or smashing my brains out on a cell wall, cursing his name with my final breath. And all the while, he's off on the mission getting the glory that should be mine.

I can't let him get away with this, it just isn't right. I stop, panting heavily and balling my hands into fists.

'Keep moving, Kage,' one of the armsmen tells me, his voice muffled by his helmet. I round on him, ready to punch his lights out, but the other reacts quickly, smashing the butt of the shotgun into my midriff. His second blow smashes across my forehead and I spin dizzily to the floor.

'Said we shoulda done this straight off,' the other says, clubbing me in the back of the neck.

I COME TO my senses inside the shuttle. Not the plush shuttle we were on earlier, but a standard transport with wooden benches and canvas harnesses lashed to the ceiling. My wrists are manacled together by a length of chain, which passes through an eyebolt obviously recently welded to the decking. My legs are secured the same way, the heavy locks weighing down my ankles. The safety harness is strapped across me as well, pulled painfully tight across my shoulders, groin and stomach. My head pounds and my gut is sore, and I can feel dried blood just above my right eye. Sitting opposite me are the two arms-men, their shotguns held across their laps. They've got their helmets off and are chatting quietly. The one on the left is quite old, his short cropped brown hair greying at the temples, his face lined by the hard years in the navy. He'll be the tough bastard who knocked me out. The other is younger, perhaps in his mid-twenties, with the same short crop style to his blond hair, and clean shaven cheeks. His blue eyes dart back and forth between me and his shipmate, and it's him who notices I'm awake. He gives a nod to the other guy who looks over at me.

'Awake now, prison boy?' the older one says with a gruff laugh. 'Shoulda come quietly, boy.'

I just stare sullenly at him and he shrugs. I sit there in silence while they continue talking about their stupid little lives, my mind begin-ning to tick over. There's absolutely no way I'm going back to prison. It really would be the death of me, and I'd rather die trying to get out than spend another day alone in a cell.

But even if I could somehow escape, and that's a bloody big if, where would I go, what would I do? I'm stuck on a shuttle heading for another ship which is heading to a penal colony. Somehow I think freedom would be short lived down that route. And even if that wasn't the case, and I could go anywhere I wanted to, I still don't know what I would do. Go to an agri-world and raise crops or grox herds? I don't think so. Become a preacher in the Ecclesiarchy like my dead comrade Gappo? I reckon a month of listening to the monoto-nous dronings of some fat cardinal would be enough to make me want to crack some heads.

I could hire myself out as a bodyguard, join some pirates perhaps, or become a mercenary. That wouldn't be so bad, in itself, but what would be the point? Hijacking freighters and kidnapping are low, even for me, especially since I should be on a mission that's vitally important to the defence of the Emperor's realm. Emperor damn it, I saved an entire sector, I'm a fragging war hero by all rights, and now the Colonel is just shipping me off and forgetting about me.

My anger starts to rise again, thinking about the cold-heartedness of it all. The Colonel betrayed me, good and simple. But there's a part of me, a part that's growing bigger the more I think about it, that says I should prove the Colonel wrong. It's the same part that made me go back for him in Coritanorum. I've never told him that I was just seconds away from leaving him to roast in that fireball, but he must've guessed as much, he's a shrewd character. What thanks do I get for it? None at all. But it's not about getting thanks, is it? I knew he wouldn't be grateful when I did it, but I still did. And it's not about being a hero. I'll leave that to the likes of Macharius and Yarrick and Stugen Deathwalker. I'm not a hero, I'm just a soldier.

That's the whole point, though, isn't it? I'm just a soldier, and the Colonel isn't even giving me that. Well, damn it, I'll show him the kind of soldier he's created. A resolution begins to build inside me, a cool determination that's totally different from the burning anger I felt earlier. I'm going to prove to the Colonel just how good a soldier I am, and just how valuable I am to him.

A plan begins to form in my mind.

I'VE BEEN AWAKE for a couple of hours when the opportunity presents itself. I've spent all that time going over what I have to do in my mind. Using the techniques I learnt in that cell, I focus my thoughts on every part of the plan in turn, analysing it, trying to see what will go wrong, coming up with answers to questions that crop up in my mental dry run. There's still a few details which I'll have to improvise, but I figure if I can take over the shuttle and get it back to the *Laurels of Glory* and demand that the Colonel takes me on the mission, he can't fail to see how good I am.

So when the younger of the two armsmen pulls off his restraints and leaves the room, I put my plan into action. It'll be easier this way round, I reckon, so at least that's a break to start with.

'Hey, navy boy!' I say to the older guy left. 'Your company so dull, you're driving your shipmates away?'

'Shut your mouth, guardsman,' he mutters back, trying to ignore me.

'You know, I once gutted an ork who looked a bit like you,' I carry on with a laugh. 'Except the ork was better looking and smarter. Smelled better too, I reckon.'

'You talk a lot for a boy strapped to a bench, soldier,' the armsman says threateningly. 'Perhaps I should just push your teeth in right now.'

'Nah,' I sneer back. 'You better wait for your friend to get back first. You'll need his help like you did back on the ship. I would have kicked your face in so far you'd be able to see out your arse.'

That gets the best reaction yet, his face going a livid red.

'Unless you want to be eating soup for the rest of your short, sorry life, you shut your damn mouth, boy!' he shouts at me.

'I've heard about you navy boys,' I carry on relentless, smiling like an ethershark. 'You couldn't break wind, let alone my face. The only reason you made armsman is that you enjoy slapping other men around. Happens a lot, I hear.'

'Why you…' He's speechless now and rises to the bait like a dream. He puts the shotgun to one side and unstraps himself, before snatching it up again and stomping over in front of me. He pulls back for a swing, but as it comes in, I sway to my left, avoiding it thanks to spending the last hour gradually loosening my harness. It clangs against the bulkhead behind me and jars his arms. There's enough play in the chain around my legs to get a good kick in behind his left knee, causing him to buckle. As he stumbles forward, I grab the shotgun in both hands and ram it back into his face, smashing his nose to a pulp and loosening his grip on it. A quick twist crashes the butt into his cheek and sends him tumbling to the deck. I stamp my foot on his neck to trap him there and wedge the barrel of the shotgun between my legs, up against the side of his face. Now all I have to do is wait.

'What's your name?' I ask him conversationally, trying to avoid thinking too much about how hopeless this whole situation probably is. I keep the shotgun pressed to his face with one hand while I unstrap my harness.

'Frag you,' he curses out of the corner of his mouth.

'Listen,' I tell him. 'I don't really want to blow your brains out, and if you're smart you'll just do what you're told and you'll live to tell your shipmates about how the psycho Kage hijacked a shuttle you were on. You can leave out the part that has me overpowering you while chained down, if you like.'

'You're a really funny guy, do you know that?' he replies sarcastically. 'No way are you gonna take over this shuttle, there's another six armsmen on board, plus the pilot and co-pilot.'

'You don't think I can do it?' I say, giving him a prod with the shotgun. 'If you behave yourself, you might live to eat those words rather than a mouthful of shotgun shell.'

'Killing me won't help you escape,' he says defiantly.

'Not yet, but it would make me feel a hell of a lot better about myself,' I laugh back.

'Just where do you think you're gonna go with the shuttle, even if you do pull this off?' he asks. I reckon he's talking to try and keep me distracted, so I humour him.

'Well, I figured on going back to the Colonel and giving him another chance,' I tell him in all seriousness.

Gav Thorpe

'Hah!' he sneers. 'Schaeffer's gonna have you shot as soon as he sets eyes on you. You're a hell of a lot dumber than even I thought.'

'So dumb I'm the one sitting here with the gun pointed at you, instead of the other way round,' I point out, pressing down on his neck with my foot and making him wince. 'I guess that really puts you far down on the brain scale.'

'You got lucky, that's all,' he replies, meaning it.

'Funny, the more fights I get into, the luckier I get,' I laugh, bending forward and patting him on the head in a patronising fashion. 'You'd have thought it'd have run out by now.'

'It's about to…' the armsman crows as the clump of boots resounds from the adjoining corridor. I sit back and look towards the doorway. A moment later, the young armsman enters, and the astonished look on his face is so funny I grin.

'Back so soon?' I ask pleasantly. He glances at me, then his shotgun lying on the bench opposite, a good five or six strides from where he is. 'Even the Emperor's vengeance doesn't act that fast,' I warn him.

'Wh… what do you want?' he asks, taking a step back.

'First off, you're gonna take two steps towards me away from that door,' I tell him flatly. 'Then you're going to take the keys off your belt and toss them over to me.'

'What if I don't?' he asks, one eye on the corridor behind him.

'First I shoot this fella here,' I give the armsman under my boot a nudge with my foot. 'Then I shoot you.'

'You wouldn't kill him just like that!' his voice rings with disbelief.

'He bloody well will!' my hostage spits out hurriedly. 'Just do what he bloody well says, Langsturm, just do what he says!'

'You heard your friend, Langsturm, shift yourself,' I tell the younger guy, gesturing him into the room with my head. He takes two hesitant steps in, eyes flickering between me and the other man.

'Now the keys, nice and slowly,' I order him, keeping my voice calm and even, though my heart is actually racing. This looks like it might just work. Might. He unhooks the ring of keys from his belt and holds them up for me to see. Then he gets stupid.

He tosses the keys full speed towards my face. My finger tightens on the trigger and something wet splashes up my leg. I bring the shotgun up and pump another shell into the chamber as he makes a dive for his gun, my ears ringing from the first shot. He grabs the gun and blasts one-handed at me, sending splinters from the bulkhead spinning into my left shoulder. My return shot catches him low in the right leg, blowing the limb off below the knee and sending him spinning, the shotgun whirling from his grasp as he pirouettes to the ground, the stump spraying crimson across the decking. Gunsmoke drifts up my nostrils, an acrid stench mixing with the tang of fresh blood.

'You… you shot my leg off, you idiot!' he screams at me, making me laugh out loud.

'Looks like I did,' I agree, still chuckling. 'I did warn you.'

'But… But… You shot my leg off, you bastard!' he yells at me, seeming more angry than in pain. I put it down to shock. The body does a wonderful job of shutting off anything too nasty for your head to sort out. Like the burning pain in my shoulder. I check out the wound: it's not too bad, slivers of metal imbedded in the muscle but not bleeding too badly. I'll live, that's for sure. Langsturm sits up on the deck, leaning back against the bench, looking at the shattered end of his leg in disbelief.

'Hey, a navy boy with a pegleg, who'd have thought it, eh?' I joke to him, but he doesn't smile. He keeps staring at the gunshot wound. I look around for the keys, but they're out of reach, a metre to my left. I try dragging them closer with the shotgun but no matter how much I stretch and wriggle I can't quite get far enough over. I have to act quick, if the dead guy was telling the truth and there are more armsmen aboard. They must have heard the shots, I suspect they're trying to decide what to do. Am I dead? Am I free and coming for them right now? It won't take them long to get their act together though, and if I'm still sat here like a firing range target when they arrive, I can pretty much kiss my life farewell.

'Langsturm,' I say to the wounded armsman. He glances up at me vacantly and I point the shotgun at him. 'That was a really stupid thing to do, so do something clever now and toss me those keys.'

'Forget that,' he spits back, his voice growing weaker.

'You're losing blood. I can sort that for you if I can get out of these chains,' I promise, giving him an earnest look. 'Otherwise I'll blow your other leg to bits,' I add in an offhand manner.

He looks at the spreading pool of blood he's sitting in and then at the keys. With a grimace he flops forward and drags himself across the decking. With his arm at full stretch he knocks the ring of keys close enough for me to bend down and pick them up. As I fumble through them someone shouts from outside the door.

'What in the Emperor's name is going on in there?' a deep voice calls out.

'You got a dead man and one on his way,' I shout back. 'You so much as stick your head through that door and you're gonna lose it!'

With my left hand I try the keys on my ankle locks, keeping the shotgun trained on the corridor, quickly swapping my attention back and forth between the two. I find the key to my left foot and the manacle drops away. The next key opens the lock on my right wrist, allowing me to drag the chain through the eye hole and stand up.

'I'll let one unarmed man in to get the wounded guy,' I shout to them, releasing the other locks and dropping the chains to the floor. I work my way along the bench towards the door, keeping my eye on Langsturm at the same time.

'What promises do we have?' their impromptu negotiator calls back.

'None!' I spit, rounding the doorway and blasting off a shot before ducking back. I didn't see if I hit anything, but that doesn't matter, they get the message. I hear Langsturm behind me grunt in pain and turn to see him swinging the discarded shotgun up towards me. I dive to my left and the shot slams into the bulkhead where I was standing.

I roll to a crouch and pump another round into the chamber, firing low, catching the armsman in the guts and hurling him backwards. At that moment someone else bursts through the doorway, firing on full with an autogun, wildly spraying bullets at the far end of the room. I react without thinking, leaping at him and smashing the barrel of the shotgun into his face. Stupid idiot had his visor up. I let go with one hand and rip the autogun from his grip before driving an elbow into his throat. He drops, gasping madly, hands clasped to his throat. Using the sling on the autogun, I hang it over my shoulder and with my free hand grab the collar of the guy's dark suit and drag him further from the door.

'Thanks for the new hostage and spare gun!' I call out, answered by an assortment of harsh curses involving my immediate ancestry.

I stand there, shotgun in one hand, dazed armsman in the other, and assess the situation. It's not going as well as could be hoped, but it's salvageable. They'll be trigger happy by now, as soon as they see me so much as put a toe outside this room I'm going to get filled with bullets. That's when a thought occurs to me. They won't if they think I'm already dead. My blood's pumping fast, my brain working at full speed. I look down at the armsman half-unconscious next to me, noticing his uniform, including that dark-visored helmet. The earlier thought begins to develop into a plan, all I need is for the others to leave me alone for a while.

I pull the helmet off the armsman and he looks up at me groggily before I smack his head back against the bulkhead, knocking him out cold. Stripping off his uniform is tricky, using one hand only as I cover the doorway with the shotgun, but after much wrestling with his inert form I have his clothes piled behind me. My uniform, complete with the Last Chance nametag, is next. I struggle to pull on his jump-suit and eventually have to leave the shotgun propped up against the wall, within easy reach, while I get dressed. I bundle his inert form into my uniform, a task as laborious as getting him out of his own clothes, one eye on the corridor all the while just in case. I finish by putting on his helmet, turning Kage the escaped prisoner into Kage the faceless armsman. I heft the guy up, a hand under each armpit, and then slam him hard against the wall, shouting incoherently as I do so. Holding him against the wall in one hand, I snatch up the autogun and put it against his chest. I pull the trigger for a quick burst as I let go, the bullets' impacts sending the ragged corpse flying out across the doorway.

'He's down!' I yell out, trying to disguise my voice and hoping the helmet muffles it enough to convince them. Apparently they buy it as three pound into the room. I fire high, spraying bullets into their helmeted heads, kicking all three off their feet in a single quick salvo. Without pausing I leap into the corridor, slap bang into the next one. He gives a startled yell as my fist drives into his unarmoured gut. As he doubles over I see another one behind him bringing up a shotgun and I drop and roll, pulling the armsman down with me. He kicks as the shotgun blast hits him in the back and vomits blood over me. One-handed, I fire the autogun down the corridor and hear a cry of pain. Glancing over the armsman's corpse, I see the other guy leant back against the wall, red holes stitched across his chest and abdomen.

I flick the autogun to single shot and walk up to him, casually putting a bullet through his facemask as I walk past. The corridor's short, about five metres, ending in the entry bay, the walls to either side of me unbroken, the engine housings behind them. The entry bay door is open and I can't see any movement beyond it.

As far as I remember, across the docking hall is another room like the one I've just been in, with a doorway through to the cockpit. This is where it's going to get really tricky. I need to get into the cockpit without getting killed and leaving either the pilot or his co-pilot alive. And there's another armsman or two somewhere, I feel pretty sure of that. I have to be on my toes, my whole body ready to react in an instant. The rush is great, I can tell you; there's no feeling like real combat. I take a step down the corridor and suddenly there's a stabbing pain right inside my head. I whirl round, trying to see if I've been hit, but I don't remember hearing a shot. The pain intensifies, making me cry out despite every effort not to, and dropping me to my knees. It's like a red hot coal has been driven into my left eye and it's smouldering through my brain.

Kneeling on the decking, my vision swims madly. The shuttle disappears and I'm suddenly swept up by the feeling that there's someone standing over me. It's like there's a massive shadowy figure towering above me, intent on killing me. All around me are gunshots and explosions, battering my swirling senses. My heart hammers in my chest, needles of pain shooting through my head and eyes. I feel like vomiting, my stomach churning as the attack begins to subside, until I'm back on the shuttle, my whole body wracked with pain.

I kneel there for a few seconds, teeth clenched against the agony, trying to keep my eyes focussed along the corridor, but my vision spins again for a moment. Then, as suddenly as it came, the pain disappears. Not even a dull ache left. Panic envelops me. What the hell is happening to me? Just what did those butchers do to my head while I was asleep?

Blinking away the tears of pain from my eyes I haul myself to my feet and stalk towards the landing bay. I pull off the helmet. I can't hear anything with it on and I need all my senses operating at full. I pause a couple of metres short of the doorway and listen, blocking out the sound of my own heavy breathing, the rush of blood in my ears and the hammering of my heart in my chest. There's no sign of movement, but just to be sure, I toss the helmet through first. It clatters noisily across the mesh decking of the stowed boarding ramps, but other than that nothing happens.

I edge out cautiously into the loading bay. It's about ten metres square, heavy exterior airlock gates to either side, the door to the far room shut. No cover at all and no other way through except that door, which they're bound to be covering. As I stand there pondering my options an unwelcome thought occurs to me. I have no idea how long this shuttle run is supposed to take. For all I know we could be just minutes away from the penal ship and getting ready to dock. I have to take charge now, because once we're onboard the other ship, there's going to be no way out. But how to do it? How can I get through this door and out the other side in one piece? Even if they don't blast me straight off, I have to enter the far chamber some way or another to get to the pilots.

I'm at a complete loss. I try to remember what I'd figured out earlier if this happened, but my mind has gone hazy. A throbbing pain has started in my head as well, not like the sharp stabbing agony of earlier, but in the same place, making it difficult to think straight. I sit myself down against the wall opposite the door, autogun in my lap and ready to go, but I can't wait them out. I toy with the idea of opening up the tech-priest access panels and messing with one of the engines but dismiss the idea almost straight away. For a start it's as good a way as any to get myself fried, poking about with things I've got no clue about. Secondly, there's no guarantee that whatever I did would be fixable, and we'd all be left drifting out here, waiting for the air to run out. I've almost gone that way before and I've no desire to repeat the experience.

A wave of depression hits me as I sit there. There's no way they're going to let me just give myself up now. Not with a handful of dead armsmen. Besides, I just can't go back to a cell, not yet, not without a fight. It's too much like giving up. Again, I feel so alone, so cut off from everything that's happened. As usual, it's me against the galaxy with no one on my side to back me up. How in all that's holy did I get into this situation? The Emperor must surely have it in for me, the amount of utter crap he's put me through these past few years. Is it some kind of test? I must have proved my faith countless times in my life, from when I first saw one of my family die to right now, fighting for the right to go on some completely mad suicide mission. Just what in hell am I doing? Do I really miss the fighting that much?

The truth is, I do. I'm beginning to calm down from killing my guards, but it was such a good feeling, being right there in the thick of it. The sheer sense of achievement I felt as I pulled the trigger and watched them die instead of me. Emperor, it was exciting! I never feel like that any other time, only when the bullets are flying and my life is in the lap of the Emperor.

Which is why I've got to keep fighting, why I have to take over this shuttle, turn it round and get back to the Colonel before he leaves the *Laurels of Glory*. I push myself to my feet and try to get my brain working at full speed again, ignoring the dull ache inside my head. I look around the loading chamber, seeking inspiration. There's a ventilation grille in the ceiling, but far too small for me to get through. There are a couple of panels set into the far wall. Weapons lockers perhaps? I step over to the one opposite to investigate. It's flush with the wall with no handle to open it, and there's a keyhole, so I figure it's locked. I try to open it with a finger but there's no give in it. Perhaps one of the armsmen was carrying a knife…

I go back to the bodies to check this, but come up empty-handed. In total, I have three shotguns and four autoguns, with about twenty shotgun shells and a hundred rounds of autogun ammo. I could try firing blind through the other door and hope I hit something, but it's quite thick. And even then, there's nothing to stop them trying the same against me as soon as I open fire. No, brains rather than guns are going to sort this one out. I look around for anything else I might be able to use, and notice the safety harnesses with their metal buckles. If I rip them out, there's a makeshift rope there. What can I use a rope for? Well, opening the other door from a distance, for a start. So, I start thinking it through one step at a time. I can get the door open without getting shot on the spot. So, I have a fire corridor if I need it. There's no point starting a firefight through the door, they can just keep out of the way and wait to dock before calling in some help. For all I know, they've already called ahead to report something's wrong and there's a welcome committee all ready and waiting for me.

So I need something that will allow me to attack. I could just rush them, take them by surprise and hope I shoot them first. That's too much like fifty-fifty odds for my liking. They could be waiting for that. So, a distraction of some kind perhaps? A fake hostage maybe, I think, looking at the scattering of bodies around me. They'd be suspicious though, and there's no telling whether they'd give a damn anyway.

Is there some other way I could trick them? I doubt it. If I was them I wouldn't be trusting anything right about now. And this fella, or fellas, is the smart one, he stayed out of trouble when the others dashed in. Maybe he's a coward, then? Maybe I can cut a deal – tell him to come quietly before he gets the same as his friends.

No, all this thinking about tricks and cunning ploys is getting me nowhere. I need to come up with a way that's going to take out whoever's in that room, once and for all. All I need are some bullets that fire round corners, I joke bitterly with myself. My wry smile disappears as I carry on thinking. Maybe I do have some bullets that fire around corners. I could rig up something with the magazines and shotgun shells. Something that'd go off like a grenade if I shot it. Yeah, a few magazines tied together, with cartridges wedged in for good measure. Open the door with a rope, toss the thing in and then set it off with a burst of semi-auto. While they're still reeling, assuming they're still standing at all, I rush in and finish the job. It's a one-shot plan, because it'll use most of my ammo to get a nice big bomb. What the hell, I tell myself, one shot's better than no shot, which is the alternative.

I set to work with a vengeance, conscious of every second ticking past bringing me closer and closer to the penal ship and swift execution. Straining every muscle, I manage to pull out one of the harnesses, and laboriously saw my way through some of the stitching with a jagged key left by Langsturm. With one strap I bind three magazines to each other in a kind of triangle, poking eight shells into the gaps left. A further refinement occurs to me and I strip off one of the buckles and put it into the pocket of the armsman fatigues I'm still wearing. I carry my hand-made grenade back into the docking area and place it carefully on the floor within easy reach. The door is on a latch and I gently turn the handle until it clicks off, pulling the door open by a fraction. I loop another strap around the handle, ready to tug it open. Using the butt of a shotgun, I smash open the ventilation grille. As I suspected, there's a conduit running back and forward towards the tail and nose of the shuttle.

With the door rope in one hand, and my grenade close by, I take the harness buckle out of my pocket and toss it through the opening, listening to it clatter towards the front of the craft. With a single motion, I yank the door open and sweep up the bomb, leaping past the open doorway and hurling the explosive inside. I drop to my belly and roll back to the doorway, autogun at the ready. I wait for a couple of seconds to see if anyone tries to pick up the grenade, then open fire. With a series of cracking detonations, the shotgun shells explode, shattering the magazines which go up half a second later, showering the room with small pieces of shrapnel, some of it clattering around me. I roll forward, and fire blindly to the left and right and then dive for the cover of the central bench. There's no return fire and the silence is almost deafening after the bomb explosion. I strain my ears but can't hear a thing. I move up to a crouch and glance around.

The room's totally empty.

All of that for no fragging reason at all. I'm actually disappointed for a moment.

I stand up slowly, scratching my head. Was the armsman lying, or are there more in the cockpit? I'm starting to get fed up with this messing about. At that moment the comm panel set into the wall next to the cockpit door crackles into life, and a tinny voice reverberates around the chamber.

'Was that an explosion we heard?' it asks. I stride across the room and press down on the reply switch.

'Yes, the prisoner rigged up some kind of bomb which went off,' I tell them, smiling to myself. 'I need some help out here clearing up this mess.'

'Who am I talking to?' the man on the other end asks, suspicious.

'He's still alive, I think,' I answer hurriedly. 'Give me a hand and stop asking stupid questions. He'll blow us all up, he's mad enough to do it.'

'Right,' the guy replies, the comm unit not masking the concern in his voice.

A second or two later, the door wheel to the cockpit spins and it opens into the room hesitantly. I grab the edge and wrench it open, barrelling through, ramming into the armsman on the other side and smashing him to the deck. I smack him across the head with the butt of the autogun and look up. The pilot and his co-pilot are looking round at me over the backs of their seats, horrified. I point the gun casually at them.

'Change of plan,' I tell them, stepping over the unconscious armsman towards them. 'Do exactly what I say and everything will be fine.'

'What are you going to do?' the co-pilot asks, eyes fearful.

'I'm not gonna do anything,' I say with a grin. 'But you're gonna turn this shuttle around and head back to the *Laurels of Glory* right now.'

'But we're locked into our landing approach,' argues the pilot, pointing out of the window. I look through the cockpit screen and see the penal ship, pretty close now. It's long and grey and almost featureless. Just like you'd expect a prison ship to look.

'Now, that's not the sort of answer I'm looking for here,' I warn them, the smile disappearing. 'Abort the landing and turn around.'

'If we break from the landing pattern they'll know something is wrong,' the co-pilot informs me. 'They'll open fire.'

'Well, give them a reason for turning around then,' I reply in exasperation. 'Tell him one of the engines is in danger of going critical or something.'

'They already know you've broken free,' the pilot admits heavily. 'We called that in over the comm a few minutes ago. If they think you've taken over the shuttle they'll assume we're dead too and blast us all to pieces.'

'Then you better save your own hides too,' I say menacingly, waving the gun at them to prove my point. 'Because if you try and land on that ship I'll kill you both where you're sitting.'

The pilot looks at me and then at his co-pilot. He sags in his seat a little more and turns back to the flight controls. He throws a few switches, and then nods to the co-pilot, who does the same on his end of the panel. There's a shrill tone sounding from a grille in the ceiling and a yellow light begins to flash. The pilot glances at my annoyed expression and punches a few more keys, turning off the alarm. Another light begins to pulse in the middle of the controls.

'That's the comm,' the co-pilot explains, leaning forward and pulling free a handset which he holds up to his ear. 'They're asking why we've disengaged the landing tracker.'

'Sod 'em,' I say harshly. 'Turn this crate around and hit the throttle, I'm going back to see the Colonel.'

'They will shoot us,' the pilot warns me earnestly. 'You have to believe me.'

'Then you better start praying that this shuttle can dodge and weave like a fighter,' I answer matter-of-factly. He scowls at me and then grabs the control column. The co-pilot makes some adjustments and my ears catch a change in the sound of the engines vibrating through the whole shuttle. The pilot banks us to the left, the prison vessel sliding out of view and then settles us on a new course.

The co-pilot ramps up the engines again, and the floor starts juddering underneath my boots.

'They're telling us to turn back to our original heading or they'll open fire,' wails the co-pilot, hand clamping the comm set to his ear.

I stand there saying nothing. A few seconds pass without a comment from either of them.

'Here it comes,' mutters the co-pilot, dropping the handset and gripping the arms of his seat tightly.

Something streaks past my field of vision, a tiny yellow spark, that erupts into a massive plume of red a moment later. The pilot dives the shuttle underneath the plasma burst, swearing under his breath. Thrown backwards, I curse as my body smashes into the door wheel.

'They missed,' says the co-pilot, relief and disbelief fighting within him.

'Just a warning shot across the bows, you idiot,' I say to him and he withers under my glare. 'Pay attention to flying this thing.'

More detonations soon follow, and I fix my attention on the pilot as he smoothly moves the controls from side to side and up and down, erratically pulling corkscrews and climbs, dives and spins. Suddenly the shuttle lurches and begins to shake. Half a dozen red lights spring into life along a display at the same time as a klaxon begins sounding.

'Shut the door! We've got a hull breach!' snaps the pilot, and I turn and slam the cockpit door shut with a clang, dropping the autogun so I can spin the wheel on it until it's locked tight. Just as I turn back, the co-pilot launches himself at me, but I swing into the attack, driving my fist hard into his right eye, hurling him from his feet.

'Don't be a hero,' I warn him, leaning over and punching him again, this time splitting his lip. 'If you promise to behave, I'll stop hitting you,' I add, smacking him between the eyes and breaking his nose. He whimpers and tries to roll away from me, but a boot to the stomach stops him. I drag him up and dump him back in his chair, where he sits stunned.

'Just do what you're told in future,' I hiss at him, but he's too dazed to hear me.

'You're going to have to help me,' the pilot says ominously. 'He's in no condition to.'

'Yeah, like I know how,' I reply sarcastically, looking at the pilot with a doubtful expression.

'Just do what I say, and we'll be fine,' the pilot assures me, his words given meaning by another detonation close by clanging along the length of the hull. I push the co-pilot back to the floor.

'Any red light, just flick the switch beneath it, okay?' the pilot instructs me, glancing across at me before concentrating ahead of him again.

'Okay,' I answer calmly, working my way along the display and flicking all the switches beneath the red lights. This isn't too difficult.

'There's three red levers just to your right,' the pilot continues, not looking at me. I can see them, right next to each other. 'They're the engine controls. From your left to right, they are larboard, main and starboard engines. Got that?'

'Larboard, main, starboard,' I repeat, touching each one in turn. 'Got it.'

'Adjust the throttles when I tell…' His last words are lost as an explosion bursts into life right in front of us, showering fragments of shell over the shuttle. A crack appears on the main window, causing a knot of fear to tighten in my chest. I don't want to get sucked out into space. That's a really grim way of dying. Not that dying any other way isn't pretty grim to me either.

'Pull all three back to seventy-five per cent power, at the same time,' the pilot instructs me.

I lean over and grip all three levers in my hand and pull them slowly towards me. They lock into place next to a notch with a label that reads 75%, and I leave them there.

'Now move the main engine back up to full,' the pilot says slowly, making sure I don't misunderstand him. I follow his instructions, pushing the lever back up.

'That's it, we're cruising now, soon be out of range,' the pilot sighs, leaning back.

'This isn't so bad after all,' I chuckle to myself, looking at the other controls. 'I thought flying a shuttle was difficult.'

'It's easier without a gun pointing at your head,' the pilot replies sourly.

'What's this one do?' I ask, pointing at a dial set above my head, its needle wavering about in a red section. The pilot glances over.

'Emperor's mother!' he curses, leaning forward for a closer look. 'We're leaking plasma from the main engine. Shut it down and eject the core before the whole shuttle explodes!'

'Like I know how to do that,' I snap back. The pilot unbuckles himself and pushes me out of the way, sitting down in the co-pilot's seat. His hands move quickly over the controls, finishing by stabbing a finger into a red-flashing rune near the top of the panel. The hull shivers with the sound of four successive detonations, there's a pause for a couple of seconds and then a final explosion which sets my ears ringing. The pilot gives me a relieved look and takes his own place. I hear a groan from the co-pilot, and look at him. He's recovering his senses, so I grab a handful of hair and ram his forehead down into the decking, knocking him out cold. I can't be bothered with him any more, he's obviously not that essential.

MOST OF THE flight passes without event, the pilot seeming content to do what he's told. I have to knock out the armsman in the cockpit again when he starts to come round after about an hour, but apart from that, I just sit in the co-pilot's chair, asking what the different controls mean. You never know, it might come in handy one day.

That all changes when we get back within comms range of the *Laurels of Glory*. I hear a buzzing from the handset, still hanging from its cord from the panel, and lift it to my ear.

'*Alphranon*, this is *Laurels of Glory*, what is your situation?' the voice asks. 'Repeat, shuttle *Alphranon*, please report your condition.'

I press down on the transmit stud.

'*Laurels of Glory*, this is Lieutenant Kage of the 13th Penal Legion,' I report, a grin creeping across my face. 'Requesting permission to land.'

'Who the hell?' the comms officer on the other end exclaims. 'What is going on?'

'Ah, *Laurels of Glory*, this is Lieutenant Kage of the 13th Penal Legion,' I repeat. 'I've, er, commandeered this shuttle for important military reasons. Please contact my commanding officer, Colonel Schaeffer.'

'Someone get Schaeffer up here at the double!' I hear the officer calling off the link, before he talks back to me directly.

'Who is piloting that shuttle?' he asks me hesitantly. I look over towards the pilot.

'What's your name?' I ask him, realising I don't know it yet.

'Karandon, Lucas Karandon,' he answers, looking confused.

'Pilot Karandon is in control, with my assistance,' I report back, giving the pilot a wink. 'We've suffered some damage, had to jettison the main engine.'

I glance over at Lucas, letting go of the transmit switch.

'Anything else they should know about?' I ask, waving the link at him in explanation.

'Ah, tell them we have a possible hull breach as well,' he tells me after a moment's thought.

'We also have a hull breach, not sure where,' I pass the message on, holding the link back up to my mouth.

'Kage, just what do you think you are doing!' the Colonel barks back at me, making me almost drop the comm set. I start to reply but fall silent, confused suddenly. What *am* I doing? It all seemed perfectly clear a couple of hours ago, but in all the excitement I've kind of forgotten.

'Give me one good reason not to order the crew to destroy you and that shuttle,' Schaeffer continues, and I can hear the anger in his voice. Perhaps this wasn't such a good idea, I begin to think. Maybe I was being a little optimistic.

'Well, I've got three good reasons here in the cockpit with me,' I reply, trying to keep the doubt from my voice, a little unsuccessfully. 'Plus there may be some others left alive.'

'Allowing their shuttle to be taken over does not particularly endear them to me, Kage,' he says heavily.

'Don't send me back to prison, Colonel,' I suddenly blurt out. 'Take me with you! At least let us land and I'll explain everything.'

'I will get you permission to land, but no other promises,' he tells me, and I hear the comm link click off.

The next half an hour is a nerve-wracking affair for me. I sit there, making the few adjustments Lucas suggests, as I try to sort out my thoughts. The Colonel doesn't sound too pleased, to put it lightly, and is going to take some convincing. Plus, what's to say he won't shoot me on the spot as soon as I step off board? Actually, that's more likely than anything else. Still, I've got three hostages. Despite what the Colonel says, that must give me some leverage. Well, if the navy have anything to say about it, at least. If it was just up to the Colonel, he'd sooner see them all dead than bargain with me, I reckon.

It's with a trembling heart that I stand in the docking bay and pull the lever that lowers the door ramp. I've got Lucas with me, shaking like a leaf. Not surprising, I'm holding him in front of me, arm round his throat, the autogun pressed to the back of his head. The shuttle's a complete mess. I did a quick inspection after we landed. There's a hole you could crawl through in the rear chamber, the benches are all ripped up and there's no sign of the other armsmen, I guess they got blown out into space.

With a clang the ramp touches down on the deck and I look out.

There's a line of twenty or more armsmen, all with shotguns. At their centre stands the Colonel and a couple of naval officers. I stand at the top of the ramp and stare back at them.

'Give yourself up, Kage,' bellows the Colonel. 'Otherwise I will have you shot where you stand.'

'I just want to talk to you, Colonel,' I call back. 'Just listen to what I have to say.'

'No deals, Kage,' he answers curtly. 'Unhand that man and step out of the shuttle, otherwise I will give the order to fire.'

The two Navy guys exchange glances at that, but don't say anything.

The Colonel's stare is fixed on me, unwavering and hard as steel. I stand there and stare back at him.

'Aim!' he commands, and the armsmen follow the order, bringing up their weapons.

'Oh frag!' I curse, pushing Lucas forward and diving clear just as the Colonel shouts the order. Lucas's ragged body is flung back across the bay as I scramble into the aft seating chamber.

'For Emperor's sake, Colonel!' I shout out, cradling the autogun to my chest. 'I'll kill all of them if you come in after me, I swear!'

'You're not going to kill anyone else, Lieutenant Kage,' calls out a voice that sends a shiver down my spine. 'Step out where I can see you.'

It's the voice of a man I thought dead for the past year and a half. A man I left to die in a fireball that wiped out an entire city. A man who has absolutely no reasons to want me still breathing. It's the voice of Inquisitor Oriel.

I resist the urge to call back, but something in his voice nags at my mind and makes me stand up and walk back to the loading ramp. I stand there for a moment before throwing the gun away.

I was right, it is Oriel. He's stood next to the Colonel now, dressed in a long blue coat, trimmed with gold thread. He's grown a short-cropped goatee beard, making him look even more sinister than he did last time. He stands there casually, arms crossed, looking at me.

With a gesture he gets the armsmen to lower their weapons and strides towards me.

'Surprised, Lieutenant Kage?' he asks, walking up the ramp and stopping a couple of paces in front of me.

'I guess I shouldn't be. There was a second shuttle, after all,' I reply slowly, looking over his shoulder at the Colonel. 'And you've pulled the Colonel's strings before.'

'Yes, there was a second shuttle,' he smiles coldly, ignoring my other comment. 'Tell me why you've come back here, Kage.'

'I need to go on the mission,' I explain, speaking slowly, emphasising the words. 'It'll kill me if I have to go back to prison.'

'Coming back may kill you as well,' he answers after a moment. 'Going on the mission might kill you.'

'I'm prepared to risk it,' I reply evenly, finally looking into his dark eyes. 'I'd rather take my chances here or with the tau than in a prison cell rotting away.'

'Yes, you would, wouldn't you,' he says, eyes narrowing.

We both stand there facing each other for what seems like an eternity, Oriel slowly sizing me up. I'm convinced he's going to walk away and give the order to open fire, but he just stands there, watching me with those wise eyes of his, weighing his options. I say nothing, realising now that there is nothing I could actually say. It's up to this man, and this man alone, what happens to me next. This man who I pretty much tried to kill. A feeling of dread fills me.

'I'm impressed by your resilience, Kage. You refuse to die, don't you?' he says suddenly, breaking the heavy silence.

'I'll never die easily, that's for sure,' I tell him, feeling hope beginning to grow in my chest, like the first sparks of a fire.

'Very well,' he nods. 'You come with us on the mission. You give me any reason to doubt you, though, and I will have you killed.'

My reply is a sigh of relief and a wide grin.

'You won't have any need for that,' I say, feeling very tired all of a sudden. 'I'll do whatever's necessary, whatever you ask me to do.'

ORIEL SAT IN front of the low desk, a single candle guttering on a silver stand over his right shoulder. He pulled the deck of Imperial tarot cards from a small drawer concealed within the desk itself, and fanned them across the table. Each crystalline sliver glittered in the candlelight, making the holographic images impregnated into them dance and judder. Scooping them back together, he cut the deck into three piles, and then into six, before gathering the cards back together, following the proscribed ritual. He performed this twice more, muttering a prayer to the Emperor as he did so.

He closed his eyes for a moment, focussing his thoughts and prayers on to the cards. Opening his eyes again, he placed the top card in front of him. Above that he placed the next, and then two more cards at right angles between them.

He turned the top card over, end-to-end away from himself and looked at it. A stylised grim reaper, complete with skull face and black robes, swiped its long scythe at him.

'Death,' he said aloud.

He then turned the right card over, revealing a swirling, gaping maw. 'The Abyss,' he stated to the galaxy in general, another important part of the ritual.

The left card turned out to be a many-tentacled beast, with eyes on stalks that wobbled around within the hologram.

'The Fiend.'

Lastly, with just the briefest of hesitations, Oriel slowly revealed the card nearest to him. It was upside down, and the holo-picture was of an ornate looking sabre, slicked with blood.

'The Blade, inverted.'

Oriel stroked his chin and looked at the cards, his eyebrows coming together in a slight frown of concern.

'Always Death and the Blade inverted,' he muttered to himself, picking up the Blade card and examining it closely. 'I was right about you, Kage. I was right.'

FIVE
ME'LEK

+++Contact made+++

+++The fly approaches the web+++

THE OTHERS STEER clear of me while we wait for the tau ship, which is due to arrive soon. They're not sure what my role is now, and to be honest, neither am I. The Colonel hasn't spoken to me since I came back, he just stalked off angrily when Inquisitor Oriel told him I was coming along. It's Oriel who summons me a little while later, after I've had a chance to clean myself up from the fighting during my hijack. He's taken up office in one of the state rooms aboard the *Laurels of Glory*, and I'm escorted there by a sullen armsman. I probably killed some of his friends, for all I know. Not that I care. There's nothing anyone can tell me about losing comrades in battle, because I've lost them all. It's one of the reasons I feel I have to carry on with life, so that someone remembers them and the sacrifices they made so that others would be safe. They'll never be commemorated, never be heroes except as I remember them. I can see their faces as I walk along the corridor behind the armsman. Good memories. That might seem strange, and I never would have considered it at the time, but there's not a bunch of people I would rather go through hell with than them. But they're not here this time, so it's just up to me now.

Oriel calls me after I knock, and I step into the state room. It's richly furnished, with five deep leather armchairs, a few low tables and cabinets neatly arranged along the walls. Oriel is sitting in the chair furthest from the door, and he beckons me over to the chair opposite with a wave.

'Sit down Kage,' he prompts me. 'You have some catching up to do.'

I do as he says, sitting on the edge of the chair, feeling uncomfortable under his gaze.

'Colonel Schaeffer has briefly explained the situation, I believe,' he carries on when he's decided I'm settled.

'Yeah, there's a tau ship coming to pick us up,' I say, trying to recall what the Colonel said earlier. It seems unbelievable that it was only a few hours ago; it seems like days. 'We pretend to be a diplomatic mission while on board, go to some tau world and meet up with the guys on the inside who are helping us out.'

'Yes, it's something like that,' agrees Oriel, leaning forward and resting his arms across his knees. 'I will be masquerading as an Imperial commander of one of the worlds close by the tau territories. You and the others are supposedly my counsellors, my advisors as it were.'

'That should be fun,' I say impulsively and he gives me a quizzical look. 'Giving advice to an inquisitor, I mean.'

'Well, you forget all of that as of now,' he says sternly. 'Even our contacts do not realise who I truly am, they believe in my part of the subterfuge. If they even get a sniff that the Inquisition is involved, they'll get scared off. They don't know too much about us, but they've heard enough stories to make them suspicious of anything that involves the Inquisition.'

I can't think why, I say to myself. Not that I think they're a bunch of underhand, murderous, double-dealing torturers and witch hunters, you understand. Or that my previous experiences with Oriel have left me with the certain knowledge that they consider everyone expendable to their cause, including themselves. Now, I don't mind that so much, after all I've sacrificed a few bodies for my own ends myself, but at least I don't claim the Emperor gives me the right to do it.

'Now, I and Colonel Schaeffer will do any talking when necessary,' he continues, not noticing my distraction. 'If you are asked any direct questions by anyone, then simply reply that you don't know the answer, or that you're not in a position to comment.'

'Play dumb, you mean?' I summarise in my own charming style.

'Yes, play dumb,' agrees Oriel patiently, tapping his fingers together slowly, as if counting something. 'Remember to refer to me as either "sire" or "Imperial commander", and don't call Schaeffer "Colonel" or "sir", none of us are supposedly military rank. Obviously, the tau don't believe that for a moment, but we have to play the game called diplomacy, which means at least pretending we're not on a military mission to spy on them. That's exactly what they're expecting us to be doing, and they will also be continuously trying to get what information they can from us.'

'Excuse me, but why exactly would we be sending diplomats to an alien world?' I ask, a thought occurring to me. 'And why are we bothering with the mission at all? Why not just assemble a war fleet and blast this traitor commander back under the stone he crawled out from.'

'Let me explain it in simple terms,' the inquisitor replies calmly, no hint of annoyance or impatience over my interruption. He's a cool character, and no mistaking. 'Our relationship with the tau is delicately balanced. At the present time, their empire is slowly expanding into the Emperor's domains, and contest for worlds has occurred. However, they are not overtly hostile to mankind, they merely see us as being in the way. Unlike, for example, the tyranids, who would wipe us out. In fact, with the massive tyranid threat posed by their latest hive fleets, in this area of the galaxy we cannot afford to start a long and costly war with the tau without weakening our defences in other sectors. Therefore, for the moment we try to keep our approach as peaceful as possible. Soon, some time in the future, the tau will need dealing with. But not yet. The Emperor has ruled the galaxy for ten thousand years; there's no need to be hasty.'

I sit there nodding, absorbing this piece of information. So what he's saying is there's no point starting a fight we don't need, not when there's plenty of other battles to win first. I can see the sense in that, after all only an idiot picks to fight more than one guy at a time. And, like he says, there'll be plenty of time later to sort out the tau, once we've dealt with the tyranids.

He spends the next hour or so explaining the various details of the cover stories, emphasising again and again how important it is that we don't raise any suspicions amongst the tau. He lays it on pretty thick, but this is his mission so I guess he has the right to. I take it all in, the name of the world we're from, why we're supposedly visiting the tau, what to keep my eyes out for, what we can learn about these aliens for the future, as well as completing the mission itself.

As I said, I'll do what I'm told. I'm just a soldier, and I'll follow my orders, I'm not really worried about the reasons. That kind of thinking is for those who might question their orders, and I've got no time

for them. I broke my oath once, and look where it got me. This time
out I'm doing things the right way, even though the Colonel tried to
stop me. When he finishes, Oriel asks if I have any questions.

'How come you didn't back up the Colonel?' I say.

'Why didn't you just have me shot?'

'Because any man desperate enough to take over a shuttle and fly
back to take part in a suicide mission is desperate enough to do
whatever's necessary,' he answers with a smile. 'I know from your past
that I can rely on you, Kage. So does Colonel Schaeffer, but he can't
be seen to bargain with you, he can't allow the others to think that
there's some kind of weakness in him. And to be honest, there isn't.
I can be more flexible. I don't need to maintain my authority; I have
absolute authority.'

'Guess being an inquisitor answers that question, eh?' I reply,
matching Oriel's smile. His fades.

'I have a sacred duty, just as Colonel Schaeffer has,' he tells me
sternly. 'I have absolute authority because I have absolute responsibility. All means are at my disposal, but all threats to the Emperor
and his servants are mine to combat. I'm allowing you on this mission because I think you'll contribute and help me in my cause. I will
use you any way I please and as soon as I stop finding you useful,
Colonel Schaeffer can do what he likes with you. Is that clear?'

'Perfectly,' I answer quietly, feeling like I've been slapped in my face.
'But I'm not a tool, I'm a weapon, and they can go off in your hand.'

'Yes they can,' laughs Oriel. 'Just don't self destruct on me until the
mission is over.'

He dismisses me with a wave of his hand, and I feel his eyes on me
as I leave the room. The armsman takes me back through the ship to
our quarters, leaving me outside the door to my room. I watch him
walk away before opening the door and stepping inside.

SOMETHING SMASHES INTO my face, dropping me to my knees.
Through watery eyes I look up and see Moerck standing over me, the
others behind him. I put an arm out to push myself up and Trost
steps forward and kicks me in the ribs, knocking the wind out of me.

'Just stay there and listen for a moment, Kage,' Strelli says, walking
up and pushing me over with his foot on my wounded shoulder.

'The Colonel wasn't too impressed with you coming back, Kage,'
Trost snarls. 'You're like a gun with a hangfire, could go off at any
moment. We're keeping an eye on you. You so much as breathe out
of turn, we're going to enjoy putting you in a bodybag.'

Quick as a sump snake, I roll over, wrapping my arm around Strelli's leg and wrenching him to the ground, twisting his knee viciously. Trost tries to kick me but I sweep his legs out from underneath him with a kick to his knee. Moerck throws a strong punch at me, but I turn and take it on my shoulder, rolling to my feet in one move. Strelli launches himself up at me from the floor, but I bring my knee up and smash it into his face as he tries to wrap his arms around my waist and bear me down. His momentum knocks me back a step, and Moerck wraps an arm around my throat, squeezing tight. I ram an elbow back into his ribs and he grunts, but doesn't let go. Trost has recovered and pushes himself to his feet as I try to wriggle free, slamming my elbow repeatedly into Moerck's body, weakening his grip enough that I burst free and drive my fist straight into Trost's face, spinning him down to the ground.

Moerck kicks me in the guts and then grabs me by the throat, heaving me off my feet and hurling me backwards into the wall, smashing my head against the bulkhead. Stunned, I just manage to dodge as he thunders a right hand at me, but duck into Strelli's fist, which catches me on the right cheek, stinging like mad. My vision whirls, and I see the others standing there watching impassively as Moerck drives one of his massive fists into my guts again and again, bruising the ribs and knocking all of the breath out of me.

'This is just so you don't forget, Kage,' he says, no trace of anger in his voice. Like a machine he grabs my throat in his left hands and holds me back against the wall before delivering a short jab with his right that crashes my head back, pain flaring through my brain at the impact. He lets go and I drop to the floor, gasping for breath and bleeding from my mouth and nose.

Trost makes to lay into me some more, but Moerck steps in and shoves him away.

'I think he's got the message,' the ex-commissar says, holding Trost back.

I dart them all a murderous look as I lie there, every part of me aching painfully. They file out through the door connecting my room to their dorm, contempt in their eyes. My ribs are really sore and pain flashes through me as I push myself to my feet. I reckon one of them's bruised, or maybe even cracked. My bottom lip is beginning to swell and dried blood is clogging up my nose as I slump down on my bed with a groan.

I've taught them well, I think. They're the sort of soldiers the Colonel needs, the ones who understand about fighting and power, and how to use it. I start to chuckle but stop abruptly as my ribs send stabs of pain through me again. I lie there looking at the ceiling, feeling the bruises growing across me. They've proved they have what it takes, that they'll kill when they need to. They're my true soldiers, alright. I close my eyes and let sleep take away the pain.

IT'S THREE MORE days of training in the firing range, on the combat mats and in the mock-up of the tau battle dome before the Colonel informs us that contact has been made with the alien vessel. We assemble in the briefing auditorium, where the Colonel issues us with clothes chests with our disguises. We lug them back to the rooms and prepare for the shuttle. In my trunk are four brown robes, typical of an Administratum flunky. I understand the choice when I put it on and pull the hood up – it hides my face in complete shadow, obscuring the tapestry of scars that covers my face and head. I'll be Brother Kage then, I tell myself with a bitter smile. Probably the only scribe who can't read or write in the Imperium.

There are amused looks from the others as we assemble in the docking bay. Oriel is dressed in a very grandiose and over the top dress uniform, hung with gold cording and medals. The red jacket is almost painfully bright, crossed by a garish yellow sash. Just the sort of pompous and totally meaningless display of opulence you might expect from one of the Imperium's ruling elite. The Colonel wears a severe black suit, with a long-tailed coat draped over one arm. Tanya wears a long dress of deep blue, tight at the waist and high at the neck, her hair cropped really short. Oriel explained that she's posing as a member of the Sisters Famulous, a branch of the Ecclesiarchy that provides housekeepers and chatelaines to the Imperial nobility. Trost, Strelli and Quidlon wear less extravagant versions of Oriel's uniform, while Moerck is dressed in plain white leggings and a white shirt with a soft leather jerkin over the top, looking every bit the gentleman. Oriel walks over to us and gives us each the once over.

'Will you all relax and try not to look like soldiers?' he says with an annoyed scowl. 'This isn't going to work if you keep standing at ease like that and quick march everywhere. Remember, you're civilians!'

We look at each other, and I see that it's true. I try to purposefully slouch a bit more, as do the others. I cross my arms and hide my hands in the sleeves of my robes, as I've seen various Departmento Munitorum scribes and their like do over the years. It's kind of uncomfortable really, and I walk back and forth a bit, trying to get it to feel natural. I feel horribly vulnerable without my arms free and the hood obscuring most of my arc of vision.

'Take shorter strides, Kage, you are not on a cross-country march!' the Colonel calls out to me, from where he's stood at the ramp to the shuttle. I look over at him and he nods, gesturing for me to try it out. I pace the length of the shuttle bay, some two hundred metres each way, keeping my steps half what I'm used to, and I feel like I'm tottering about like a small child. I bend my back a bit more, leaning my chin down into my chest and try it again and it feels a bit more natural, my gait more like the image I have in my head of Clericus Amadiel, the Colonel's scribe on the last mission.

When Oriel is satisfied that we don't stand out like a squad of highly trained soldiers pretending to be diplomats, we get all of our kit on board the shuttle and settle in for the ride. The mood is tense and nervous. None of us have any weapons. If the tau take a disliking to us, there's not a thing we can do to stop them killing us out of hand. I can understand why, though: if this is a peaceful delegation, it'll raise a few eyebrows if we turn up with a small arsenal. That's if the tau have eyebrows, I suddenly think to myself, making myself smile. We've not seen a single picture of them. They could be big bags of gas or tentacled squidgy blobs for all I know. I guess from the fake battle dome that they can't be too different from us, physically I mean. The doors were sort of human sized, the steps built for just two legs, so I guess that rules out floating gasbags. I let my mind wander with thoughts like these, preferring to put any thought of the upcoming mission out of my mind.

A couple of the others seem worried and I tell them to relax. There's no sense worrying now. The plan is in motion and it'll lead us wherever the Emperor cares. Personally, I try not to worry about anything. There's two things people worry about. There's things they have no control of and they're worried how it'll affect them. Then there's the things they worry about doing or not doing. Either way, it's a waste of time. If it's something you can't do anything about, then all of the worrying in the galaxy isn't going to change what will happen one bit. And if you can do something about it, then do something, don't just sit around and worry, take your destiny in your hands. It's that kind of thinking that's kept me alive and sane all these years.

Sane. I'm beginning to have my doubts about that, which I guess proves that I'm not mad yet, at least I don't think so. Do you have to be sane to wonder if you are; do lunatics just assume they are sane and not question it? I know what the others think, Oriel included, despite his choice to bring me along. They think my mind's more twisted than a rock drill head. I don't see it that way, it's not bent at all. In fact, it's so straight, so focussed on what I am that it might seem mad to other people. They like to clutter themselves up with all sorts of little illusions about who they are, what they're here for. Not me. I worked it all out in the stinking prison cell.

As I said to Oriel, I'm a weapon, nothing more. Point me at the enemy, and let me go. That sort of clarity is more comforting than worrying about if I'm doing the right thing, wasting time and energy agonising with my conscience and my morals. My conscience is the orders I'm given; my morals are the ones I'm told to have. Somebody else can have that responsibility, someone like the Colonel or Oriel. I just don't care any more.

We've been travelling for a couple of hours when the Colonel enters from the adjacent room.

'Here is your chance to get a first look at the enemy,' he tells us, pointing towards one of the wide viewing windows. I unbuckle myself along with the others, and we gather around the thick pane and look out into the stars. It's out there, the tau ship, and we get a good view of it as the shuttle circles, losing momentum to start its landing pattern. It's long and sleek, almost pure white. The main hull is like a slightly flattened cylinder, with a cluster of pods at the back, glowing faintly, so I guess they're the engines. The front end gets flatter and wider, a bit like a subtly squared-off snake's head. There are several outlandish Tau symbols emblazoned in massive lettering along the side, but I can't make out any sign of ports, docking entries or any other openings. I can't see any gun decks either.

'Is this a warship?' I ask Schaeffer.

'I believe it is non-military in its normal duties,' the Colonel replies.

As we approach, a section of the hull disappears from view, revealing the interior in a blaze of yellow light. It's not like a door slid back or opened, the section of ship seemed to roll out of the way, leaving a perfectly circular opening. We return to our seats and buckle down for landing, the blast shutters grinding up over the windows. It's a few more minutes, which pass with tortuous slowness as we sit there not knowing what's going to happen, until I feel and hear the shuttle landing. With a whine the engines power down, and the Colonel tells us to get to our feet.

'First impressions last,' he tells us ominously. 'From the second we step off this craft we'll be under close scrutiny. Right from this moment, you have to think and act exactly like the people you're supposed to be. We'll try to keep ourselves out of the way as much as possible, but there will be a number of official engagements on board while we are in transit, which good manners dictate we will have to attend. Be on your guard at all times, though. The tau will give us a certain amount of leeway, I hope; after all, we are placing a lot of trust in them not to hold us hostage. Now, move out and act casual!'

We troop after him and the Colonel as they make their way along to the docking chamber. We stand there, Oriel in front, us lined up behind him, and wait for the ramp to lower. My first view of the tau is like nothing I've seen before.

The shuttle bay is flooded with light, and the air is dry and warm, much hotter than I'm used to aboard ship. As we walk down the ramp, I look around, trying hard not to stare. The chamber is like a large oval shape, the floors and ceilings melding with the walls in a continuous line. Everything is a cool pale yellow colour. There's no sign of any hard edges anywhere, no supporting beams, no criss-cross of girders and cranes for manoeuvring shuttles into position. The space is cavernous in its emptiness and I feel swallowed up by it and yet horribly exposed at the same time.

A small delegation waits for us at the bottom of the ramp. There's no guards, no guns in sight. They either really trust us, or they have some other way of dealing with us if we start to cause trouble. Three tau dressed in thin, pale robes stand patiently as we gaze around, studying us with interest.

I was right, they're basically humanoid. All three are at least a head shorter than me, and they have delicate, thin limbs. Their greyish-blue skin seems to glisten with some kind of oil, and as the middle one steps forward and bows to one knee in greeting, I catch a sweet scent. I look at his flat face and bald head, noting the yellow eyes and slit-like nose, noticing his lipless mouth and rounded teeth. He stands and opens his arms in greeting, revealing a flap of skin that stretches from his waist to his upper arm, like deformed wings. I suppress a shudder. Nobody mentioned these... these things might be able to fly!

The one to the leader's right steps forward then, mouth curling in a poor imitation of a human smile.

'Welcome to this vessel, one of our newest, the *Sha'korar Aslo*,' he greets us, beckoning us down with a long-fingered hand. His voice blurs the words together slightly, his pronunciation tinted by a husky accent. 'We extend the hand of friendship to our human allies.'

Oriel replies in stilted gibberish, which I reckon to be some kind of formal greeting he's learned for the occasion. This seems to please the tau, who look at each other and nod.

'This is Kor'el'kais'savon, who you may simply address as captain or El'savon if you wish,' the interpreter continues, indicating the tau who had bowed earlier.

'I do not speak well your words,' the captain explains apologetically, bowing his head slightly but keeping his gaze on Oriel.

'This is Kor'vre'anuk,' the tau nods a head towards the third member of the delegation, who stands watching us impassively. 'I am Por'la'kunas, and will be your voice while on board the *Sha'korar Aslo*.'

'Please tell Captain El'savon that his hospitality does him credit,' Oriel replies with an officious manner. 'I and my advisors would appreciate some time to rest from our journey before conducting a tour of this fine vessel.'

Por'la'kunas says something to the captain in Tau, who replies with a single word and a glance at Oriel. All this gibbering in Tau is making me nervous. It doesn't seem like Oriel's command of the language is particularly great, and I haven't got a clue what they're saying. They could all be plotting against us, laughing right in our faces, for all I know. Just another factor of this mission that makes my spine crawl.

'Of course, we have rooms prepared for you,' the translator assures us. 'If you would follow me, please.'

Without a further word, he turns and begins to walk away from the shuttle. Looking ahead, I can see no sign of a door out, the wall continues unbroken all round us. When we're a few metres from the wall, a swirl of small lines appears, making a series of spirals which swiftly expand as a portal opens up in front of us, vanishing seemingly into the fabric of the wall. I glance over at Oriel, but he's maintaining an air of disinterest, gazing about him in a bored fashion.

The others shuffle about nervously, and I can understand their unease. The whole ship stinks of technology gone wild. I glance at the doorway as I walk through and see that the wall is in fact hollow and the segments of the iris-door have simply slipped between the two bulkheads. Still, it's not that reassuring.

The corridor outside is just as featureless as the docking bay, and as empty of people. As with the shuttle chamber, small curved corners seamlessly connect the walls with the floor and ceiling, the pale yellow surrounding us without any other decoration. Or source of light, for that matter. I haven't seen a single glow globe or lighting strip. The more I think about it, the more disconcerting I find the sensation. How can they create light in the air itself? It's not even as if the walls are glowing, it's like the air is charged with light. Just what kind of creatures are we dealing with here? How in the Emperor's name can we trust them on a mission like this?

With a start I realise I've almost broken into a parade ground stride whilst I was thinking about other things. I glance at the others, who walk along in silence, subdued by our strange surroundings. I suspect they're just as nervous as me, even Oriel and the Colonel. I focus my attention back on myself, shortening my step, pulling my head further back into the hood. The air is dry and warm as well, making my throat and nose tight. I turn and look back, and the loading bay has disappeared, the door shutting silently behind us. I feel isolated and vulnerable, stuck on this alien ship with no weapons other than my bare hands.

We follow our interpreter along the corridor and I notice something else. Or rather, it's something I don't notice. The whole ship seems to be still: there's no vibration, no noise, nothing. The ship was most definitely moving when we docked, I saw that as we came in to land. Inside, though, we could be in an underground bunker somewhere.

Walking further along the corridor, my disorientation grows. There's not a single door to either side, though a few side corridors branch off along the way, melding seamlessly with the one we're walking along. Our guide has remained speechless since leaving the shuttle area, walking ahead of us with effortless steps. I take some time to look at him. He doesn't have the membranes under his arms that the captain has, and is even more slightly built. His robes are light and airy, wafting around him as he walks, like a breeze given shape. Like the rest of the ship, he is surrounded by an air of calm and stillness. Every movement is slight and efficient, he barely swings his arms as he walks, his face set straight ahead without a moment's distraction.

I try to work out what the ship is made from, but it's impossible. There's no welding that might indicate metal; the coloration seems to be part of the material itself, no brushstrokes or drips from paint. I wander along one wall and let my hand briefly brush along it, feeling a slight sensation of warmth from the wall itself.

I watch the others from within the folds of my hood, which is beginning to get uncomfortably hot. I have to resist the temptation to pull it back for some fresher air. That makes me realise that there are no air currents, no artificial winds from cooling vents and air purifier ducts. But the air doesn't taste stale, it's just hot and has no moisture to it. Oriel strolls along behind Por'la'kunas with a languid, rolling gait, the Colonel stepping beside him with a more stiff stride, his attention focussed on the tau in front. Quidlon keeps looking around him, staring intently at the walls and floor, probably trying to figure out how this all works. It could be witchcraft for all I know, like the accursed eldar technology. That gives me a sudden bout of anxiety. These tau are obviously decadent enough to blatantly use such strange technology – perhaps they put up with psykers as well? Maybe this guide is not what he seems, maybe he can read minds. This could all be some elaborate ruse to lull us into a false sense of security. I try to think like a scribe, just in case, but my thoughts soon begin to wander.

I wonder if they'll torture us for information, trying to find out the full extent of our plot. What will be their reaction when they find out we're collaborating with their own kind? Or perhaps they'll just kill us out of hand. I know nothing about these tau, nothing useful. I can't work out how they think, how they'll react, what their motivation really is. How predictable are they in combat? How disciplined?

All of these thoughts fill my brain as we carry on walking down this Emperor-forsaken corridor that seems to stretch on forever, unending and unbroken. If they get suspicious there's absolutely nothing we could do, nothing at all. We're in the middle of their ship with no weapons whatsoever. And Oriel said they would be wary. They're probably watching our every move even now, waiting for us to slip up, ready to pounce on any opportunity to unmask us and interrogate us for everything we know about the Emperor's domains and armies. For all I know, this could be some elaborate plot by them, manipulating Oriel so that he's brought us all here, some of the finest soldiers in the Imperial Guard, just so that they can get their hands on what we know.

I start to feel tense, and the pain behind my eyes returns. I begin to sweat even more heavily, glad my discomfort is concealed by the heavy robes. That's just the sort of nervousness that they'll be looking for. If I have another attack here, we're all dead. Perhaps the Colonel was right, perhaps I am too much of a liability.

My mouth gets even drier as the pain in my head increases. I think I can hear the others talking, slightly panicked themselves, but I pay them no heed, concentrating on my own private agony as my heart starts to beat faster.

It must be obvious by now. I feel as if I'm panting like a dog, clenching and unclenching my fists inside the folds of my sleeves. If the translator turns and looks at me now, he'll see something's wrong. He'll either guess we're up to no good, or he'll fetch medical help. Then they'll be able to separate us, get me on my own and go to work on me. Will it be torturers or mind-readers?

I blink heavily as I catch up with someone. Biting my tongue in panic, I glance up. It's the Colonel, who looks across at me, his face expressionless, except for a slight tightness to his cheeks which I know means he's either angry or slightly worried.

'Control yourself, Kage,' he whispers harshly at me. 'Try to relax. The tau expect us to be a bit tense and uneasy, but you look more guilty than a man with a smoking gun standing over a corpse. Remember to breathe in through your nose, it'll help calm you down.'

With that, he quickens his pace again to catch up with Oriel, who glances at him and receives a nod of reassurance in return. I wish I was as confident. I try to distract myself by looking at the others again, but that brings little comfort. Strelli, normally so cocky and confident, gnaws on the nail of his left thumb, darting glances at the interpreter every now and then. Tanya walks along with her head bowed, staring resolutely at her feet, not meeting anyone's gaze. Moerck is the most obvious, in my opinion. He just strides along, his disgust barely concealed as he scowls at the back of our guide. I see his fingers twitch spasmodically, like he's itching to get a hold of Por'la'kunas's neck and squeeze the life out of him.

Por'la'kunas takes us down a right turn, then a left, and then two more turns which I would swear took us around in circles but there's no way of telling. He then stops abruptly and faces the wall to the right. He reaches out his frail-looking hand and touches the wall and a moment later another of the strange portals opens up, revealing a room beyond where moments before there had been nothing. I look at the wall closely and see that there's actually some discoloration there, almost like runes or switches manufactured into the material of the wall itself.

'These are your quarters,' our interpreter says, indicating the room with his hand. At that moment, another tau steps from an unseen side corridor and walks up to us. He doesn't say a word, simply stands next to the door, back to the wall, his face set. This one is dressed in more workmanlike clothes, a tight-fitting blue bodysuit that is ribbed across the waist and joints, his hands and feet bare, the suit drawn tightly around his neck. As he moves there appears to be no wrinkling or gathering, as if the material is stretching and contracting around him.

'If you require anything at all, please inform me at once,' Por'la'kunas tells us, stepping inside the room, and we follow him in. We are in what appears to be the main living space, a rounded square about ten metres across. A low circular cushion seems to be the only furniture, set into a hollow in the centre of the room and taking up most of the space. Thankfully the adjoining rooms are reached through curved arches rather than the odd disc-doors. There are ten of them: in eight I can see low, broad beds, without any kind of sheets or blankets, which is strange. From what I can see, the other two rooms appear to be washing areas of some kind, I can just make out a basin-like fixture through the arches.

'Some refreshments, if you please,' Oriel says, not looking at the interpreter but strolling through into one of the bedrooms.

'How do we contact you?' the Colonel asks, leaning forward towards the short alien.

'If you say my name, the ship will inform me,' he replies, taking a couple of quick paces back from the imposing figure of Schaeffer.

'The ship will inform you?' Quidlon says, obviously intrigued by this magic. Out of the corner of my eye I see Moerck make a protective gesture, the sign of the eagle, with his hands. It's the first time I've seen him do anything like that. I suspect it's not part of his commissariat training. I wonder if he's holding up that well. He's not mentally prepared for this kind of action. He's an officer and a leader. His place is in the midst of the bullets and las-bolts, shouting speeches, shooting deserters and leading the glorious charge.

'Yes, of course,' Por'la'kunas replies with a little surprise, totally oblivious to my thoughts on Moerck. 'I will be able to attend to your needs immediately.'

Quidlon looks as if he's going to ask something else but Schaeffer waves him away irritably.

'Is that a guard on our door?' the Colonel asks gruffly, pointing towards the corridor.

'We have found that humans sometimes become lost on our vessels and he is there to ensure that should you wish to leave the room you will have an appropriate escort,' the tau replies smoothly. 'You are, of course, our guests, not our prisoners. While on the ship you may roam almost where you wish, We ask that you only enter certain areas with an escort as they may present a danger or disturb the crew in delicate duties. A full tour will be provided for you when you are rested.'

The Colonel just grunts and darts a look at me. I stand there dumb for a couple of seconds until I remember that I'm supposed to be the menial. I shuffle forward, trying not to walk with too much swagger.

'Bring food and drink, please,' I say, as politely as I can manage, the words almost catching in my dry throat. 'And, is there any way you can make it cooler in here, it's like a bl... like a desert.' I stop myself swearing just in time, and avoid the tau's gaze.

'Of course, forgive my inattention,' Por'la'kunas apologises. 'I shall endeavour to make the environment within your chambers closer to your normal climate.' The tau nods to the Colonel and leaves, the door swirling back into place behind him.

'Isn't this place amazing?' blurts out Quidlon as soon as the door is closed. 'Can you imagine what sorts of things these people are capable of, considering just what we've seen so far about their ship, about the way they conduct themselves. It's so fascinating.'

'They're not people, they're aliens, don't forget it,' Trost grumbles, lowering himself cautiously onto the cushion, as if expecting it to swallow him up.

'I could do with some freshening up,' says Strelli, wandering over to one of the rooms I'd identified earlier as an ablution chamber. He walks in and then comes out a moment later, scratching his head in confusion. 'There's no pipes, no taps, nothing. How does any of this stuff work?'

'It senses your presence,' Oriel says, appearing at the doorway to his room. 'I've made sure we can talk freely here in these rooms, but once we step outside the door, guard your tongues.'

'What makes you so sure?' Tanya asks. We all fall silent as the door opens soundlessly and our guide returns. Behind him hover five trays, bobbing along on their own as if they were alive. I hear an involuntary hiss escape Trost, who springs to his feet. The tau seems to be bemused at this reaction, and I realise we're all staring at the food with wide eyes.

'The food is not to your liking?' he asks innocently, what I take to be concern on his face.

We exchange incredulous looks, and it's Quidlon who recovers first.

'Ah no, the food will be fine, we were not expecting it to be delivered so, um, swiftly,' he says quickly, a brief smile flashing across his lips. 'If you would like to, um, leave the food with us we have some matters we wish to, um, discuss amongst ourselves, if that would not be impolite of us.'

'Of course, I understand,' the tau replies evenly with a bow of his head. 'Please take as long as you require.'

He bows again as he leaves, the trays floating across the room to hover about knee height over the communal cushion. Moerck leans over and peers underneath one of the floating trays, scowling like a cudbear with a sore head.

'How does it stay up?' he asks, straightening stiffly and looking at Oriel.

'I should have expected this,' he sighs, rubbing at his forehead and walking further into the room. 'The tau employ a great many of these things, which I believe are called drones. I've never seen one working before. It must be some kind of anti-gravity technology. You'll have to get used to them, apparently they're all over the place on the tau planets, running errands, taking messages and such. Think of them as odd looking servo-skulls, mindless but capable of following simple orders and performing basic tasks. Of course, these are merely constructs, they have never had a soul like a servo-skull. One reason the tau must halt their expansion into our space. Who could tell what mad, heretical notions might grip the populace if they heard of such abominations?'

A growl in my stomach reminds me that I've not eaten yet today and I walk over to the food and plonk myself down onto the cushion. The nearest servitor-plate appears to be carrying some kind of fruit, a garish yellow thing that smells sweet. I take a small bite and its juice runs down my chin. It's like honey, with a tang of something else I can't identify. The others stare at me, waiting to see if I keel over and go blue or something. I nod to them and point to the trays.

'Tastes pretty good, tuck in,' I tell them, picking up a star-shaped green thing and giving it a nibble. It's smoky, with a bitter aftertaste like hot caff or chocolate. There's some dishes of blue-coloured rice. The only utensils provided for eating are some spindly paddles which appear to be no use at all as far as I can tell, so I use my fingers instead. The others settle down as well, and we compare the various foodstuffs, passing our own judgements on the fruits and vegetables on offer.

As I chew on a bread-like stick the size of my finger, a thought occurs to me.

'None of this is meat,' I say to the others and they agree after a moment's thought.

'The tau do not eat flesh apparently,' confirms Oriel. 'I don't know if it's a biological thing, or maybe religious. There's not much data on that aspect of their culture.'

'I think it's time you tell us some more,' Strelli says to Oriel. 'What other surprises are there?'

'Are you sure it is safe to talk here?' the Colonel asks, eyes narrowed as he looks around the room.

'Perfectly sure,' confirms the inquisitor leaning back on one elbow, his other hand clasping a shallow dish of grape-like juice. 'Alright, I'll give you a broad overview of what we've found out in the last couple of hundred years. For a start, the Tau race is lucky to be here at all. Extensive research into some of our oldest records has recently shown that several thousand years ago, we almost wiped them out. Luckily for them, warp storms prevented the colonisation fleet reaching their home world. In the last six thousand years they've grown into the civilisation we will be seeing shortly.'

He downs the rest of his drink and places the glass back on the nearest tray, which drifts off towards Tanya with its load.

'As you have already seen, they have no respect at all for the limitations of technology,' he continues, using a fingertip to wipe some food debris from his beard. 'As far as we know they are utterly heathen, with no kind of formal religion. The closest they have are the ethereals, their ruling class. The ethereals are in charge of everything supposedly, but it's the other castes who do all the work. The air caste, for example, are our hosts at the moment. They run the ships. Then there's the water caste, like our friend Por'la'kunas, who do all the diplomacy and bureaucracy. We'll being seeing more of them when we arrive on Me'lek.'

'Sorry, Me'lek?' I interrupt. 'What's a Me'lek?'

'Me'lek is the tau name for the Kobold system, where they have a colony on one of the worlds,' explains Oriel. 'That is where we are heading.'

'That's where this Brightsword fella is?' asks Strelli, stretched out on the far side of the cushion-seat.

'No, he is on Es'tau, one of their more recent outposts, where we will be going once arrangements have been made with our contacts,'

Oriel answers slowly. 'It's a lot less developed, only a single city, if my information is correct. We are going to Me'lek first so that I can update my intelligence with the contact I have inside the water caste. Speaking of Commander Brightsword, he is a high-ranking member of the fire caste, who are the fighters of the Tau empire. You've seen what the battle domes are like, and now you've got some idea of the technology we're up against, so you can understand why we wish to avoid a widespread conflict with the tau if possible. In the main, the fire caste are still kept in check by the ethereals though, even if some like Brightsword and the renegade Farsight are straining at the leash.'

'I would guess the other caste is the earth caste, since you've talked about the fire, water and air castes. It seems their society is based around the elements,' says Quidlon, who's sat cross-legged listening attentively to everything Oriel has to say.

'Yes, the workers of the earth caste are the last ones,' confirms Oriel. 'They are the builders, the farmers, the engineers and the like.'

'Sounds like they get the rough end of the deal,' I say. 'I mean, the others get to be warriors and pilots and such, they do all the labouring.'

'The tau don't see it that way at all,' counters Oriel, leaning over and dragging one of the food trays closer, making its engines whine in protest for a moment before it complies and glides next to him. 'This notion of the greater good which they believe in binds them together. It teaches them from birth that everyone has their place, and that the survival of the Tau empire is more important than any individual.'

'That's not too different from the oaths we swore when we joined up,' comments Tanya.

'This is nothing like dedication to the Emperor,' Moerck argues angrily. 'Mankind would never survive without the Emperor to protect us, no matter how many sacrifices were made. These tau are heathen creatures, devoid of any spiritual guidance. They will fall prey to their own selfishness and base desires in time.'

'Yes, in time they may well do that,' agrees Oriel, plucking another starfruit from the tray. 'There are already indications that the further they expand and the more contact they have with other races, the more stretched this ideal of the greater good becomes. We need only look at what is happening with Brightsword and his kind.

'At the present they are expanding rapidly, dominating whatever races they meet and incorporating them into their empire or expelling them. Yet, when they run into serious opposition, it remains to be seen how much sacrifice the castes are willing to make for the greater good. And we will do what we can to hasten that day. Until then, however, they are a highly motivated, united society which presents a significant problem in this area of the galaxy, and we should not underestimate them just because their society is spiritually and philosophically flawed.'

'So why are we helping them with their Brightsword problem?' I ask, swilling down another mouthful of fruit juice to try and ease the dryness in my throat. 'Surely it would be better to wait for him to attack and then crush him. That would give them far more to think about, a real display of our strength that would make them think twice.'

'Do you not listen at all, Kage?' snaps the Colonel. 'We do not have any strength in the Sarcassa system to display. If Commander Brightsword is allowed to attack, he will be victorious if all things remain as they are. We will not be able to respond, and this will further bolster the tau's courage and resolve, believing us to be weak.'

'As the Colonel says, it is better to strike now and prevent a war than try to win it,' Oriel says sternly. 'Rest assured, by the time we have finished, the tau will be in no doubt the foe they face is equal to what they might throw at us. We will be teaching them a singular lesson in interplanetary manners, make no mistake.'

'Well, I wouldn't mind giving that jumped-up interpreter a slap, that's for sure,' laughs Strelli.'

'You will do nothing of the kind,' snarls Schaeffer angrily. 'We will do nothing to provoke the tau, or that might indicate we are anything other than what we appear to be.'

'I was only joking,' grumbles Strelli. 'Do you think I'm stupid?'

'Do you really want an answer to that?' I butt in before the Colonel can reply.

'Shut your damn mouth!' Strelli snaps back at me, clambering to his feet.

'Behave, all of you!' snarls the Colonel. 'I will not tolerate any kind of bickering or lack of discipline, no matter how unfamiliar and unsettling our surroundings. When we are in the battle dome, there will be no time for this kind of behaviour.'

Strelli shrugs expansively, darting a look at me and I give him a slight nod of apology.

'I think it is time we saw some more of this vessel,' announces Oriel, standing up and walking carefully across the soft floor. He

looks around and then up at the ceiling before giving a shrug.
'Por'la'kunas? I would like to have a tour now, if you please.'

We all stand up and wait there, wondering if this is some kind of
alien joke. However, a couple of minutes pass and then the door
opens, revealing Por'la'kunas standing there. As soon as the tau
enters, I can feel everyone stiffen slightly, on their guard again. I don't
know why we're so nervous just because he's actually here – after all
we only have Oriel's word for it that the tau haven't been listening in
to everything we've being saying whilst in the room. Still, Oriel is an
inquisitor and should know what he's talking about, and on top of
that he does seem to have a naturally persuasive manner.

'I hope that everything was to your satisfaction,' the tau guide says,
stepping lightly into the room.

'It was,' Oriel replies shortly, strolling out past the interpreter, who
remains unflustered at this arrogant display.

We file out into the corridor after our guide, and I note that our
guard is still standing there, I could swear he hasn't moved a muscle
since we entered. Perhaps he hasn't. Perhaps he's a different one; they
all look pretty much the same to me. Por'la'kunas leads us back to
the main corridor we came along before and then through a door
into a high-ceilinged chamber, which rather oddly has a set of steps
in the middle leading up to nowhere. It all becomes clear though
when a portal opens to our left and a long, silvery, bullet-shaped
vehicle glides into view and stops next to the steps.

'If you would follow me on to the transport, please,' our guide says,
walking slowly up the steps.

We follow him cautiously – there are no hand rails on the narrow steps – eyeing the vehicle with suspicion. At our approach, the
vehicle changes, like it's sloughing its skin, revealing a door which
opens upwards and over the transport. A row of large windows
shifts into view as plates rearrange themselves underneath the
vehicle, and a ramp silently extends down from the door to meet
perfectly with the small landing at the top of the steps. Por'la'kunas bows and extends a hand to invite us to enter first and we
troop in, looking at each other hesitantly and gazing around us
like children.

The interior is a crisp white, like the outside of the ship itself. The
seats are arranged down the middle, with an aisle either side, in rows
of four. They look to be made of some kind of hard material, but as
I sit down, the seat shifts underneath me and moulds to my backside.
It's a rather unpleasant sensation, actually, making me want to

squirm and fidget but I force myself to sit still and gaze out of the windows at the blank wall beyond.

When everyone's settled in – I note there's no kind of safety harnesses – Por'la'kunas stands up at the front of the carriage. I take a tight grip of the arm rests either side of the seat.

'The captain is pleased you wish to view his ship and has allowed me to take you wherever you wish,' he announces. 'Is there any part of the vessel in particular that you wish to view first?'

'Not really,' replies Oriel with a vacuous smile. His persona as the Imperial commander is so different from the intense, serious inquisitor, it makes me wonder if that isn't just an act as well. I doubt we'll ever know what he's really like or really thinking. 'If anything occurs to me, I'll be sure to let you know.'

'Very well,' Por'la'kunas replies unperturbed. 'In which case, we shall start with the power plant and move forward to conclude at the control bridge.'

The tau touches a panel on the wall behind him, revealing a screen. He touches his finger to one of the boxes on the screen and then turns back to us. Without any warning, and as silently as it arrived, the carriage begins to rapidly accelerate. My grip on the arm rests tightens more, and my stomach begins to shrink and tie itself in knots. We flash through an opening in the wall into a dark tunnel, although the inside of the transport remains lit, again with no sign of any light source that I can make out. It's only about half a minute before we emerge back into open space again, the vehicle smoothly decelerating to a halt next to another set of steps. I realise my fingernails are dug into the slightly soft covering of the chair, leaving crescent-shaped indents. The Colonel's right, I have to try and relax more.

We disembark on slightly wobbly legs, and stumble down the steps into a room that looks exactly like the one we boarded in. Por'la'kunas shows us through another hidden door, into a truly enormous chamber. It rises in a dome about forty, fifty metres above our heads. The centre of the chamber is dominated by a large structure which stretches from floor to ceiling, roughly cylindrical but with outcrops and radial spars that link it to the walls at regular intervals. I can see various panels cut into its otherwise unbroken surface, and as with the rest of the ship there's no evidence of welding joins, bolts, rivets or any other means of construction. For the first time since boarding, I can detect the slightest hint of noise. It's a deep humming that obviously emanates from the power plant in the middle of the room,

making the floor vibrate just enough to feel. A group of half a dozen
tau are gathered around the base of the engine, inspecting flickering
green windows, which I assume to be display screens of some kind.

This is like no engine I've ever seen before. Where are the cables
and pipes? There seem to be no moving parts at all, no pistons, no
cams or gears, nothing to indicate the roaring energies this thing
must have to produce to keep a ship this size functioning. The calm-
ness of the ship is very unsettling, when you're used to the bangs,
grinding noises, rattles and hums of an Imperial starship.

'Here is our primary power plant,' Por'la'kunas announces with just
a hint of pride. 'There are two sub-stations on the lower levels in case
of emergency or battle, but this plant provides enough power for normal usage.'

'Battle?' the Colonel asks, too quickly to be entirely casual.

'As your own Imperial Navy is no doubt aware, this area of space is
plagued by roaming bands of pirates,' the translator replies smoothly.
'Of course, such considerations are not an issue within our own
empire.'

I bet, I think bitterly. These tau think they're so clever, I'm going to
enjoy knocking off one of their top leaders.

Oriel wanders closer and looks over the shoulder of one of the
tau, who's dressed in a similar tight-fitting garment as our guard
back at the living quarters, except his is dark grey. The tau bows his
head and steps aside for us to crowd around the screen. Only, it
isn't a screen as far as I can tell, it really is a window. I gaze into the
green glow, my eyes adjusting to the brightness, and realise I'm
looking into the heart of the reactor itself. It's full of something like
a gas or fluid, with strange eddies and currents merging and breaking apart in a constant flow. It's quite entrancing actually, looking
at the ever-shifting shapes coalesce and disappear. Bright, star-like
points dip and weave in the energy currents, like tiny suns caught
in a storm.

'What is it?' Quidlon asks in a hushed tone.

'We call it sho'aun'or'es, I am not sure there is a human word or
phrase which would equate,' explains Por'la'kunas apologetically. 'I
would hazard that it translates simply as "source of power" which I
am afraid is not very helpful. The fio'vre would perhaps be able to
explain better, but I am afraid that their expertise is not in lan-
guages.'

'The fio'vre?' asks Oriel suddenly interested, though whether genuinely or part of his act, I'm not sure.

'Ah, yes, I am sorry,' the interpreter apologises again with a bow of his head. He indicates the other tau with a sweep of his arm. 'The fio'vre attend to the smooth operation of the power plant.'

'Just the six of them?' Trost suddenly speaks up. 'What if something goes wrong?'

'I am afraid I do not understand,' Por'la'kunas replies, turning his attention to Trost. 'The monitoring is merely a sensible precaution. There have been no incidents concerning a power plant of this type for hundreds of years. It is quite safe and stable.'

Trost looks doubtful and turns to peer back through the viewing window. I can just imagine what he's thinking. He's wondering how much it would take to shatter one of those panes and unleash the raging energy contained within the reactor. It's the sort of thing he thinks about too much. I also suspect, from what I've seen of the tau so far, that it would take a direct hit from some pretty heavy weaponry to so much as chip that screen, never mind break it open. I wouldn't say the tau are afraid, but they are certainly cautious and in control at all times. That could prove a useful piece of knowledge later. Sometimes our rashness and emotion is what makes us strong. I don't know if the tau are genuinely passionless or if it's driven out of them and suppressed by their dedication to their ideal of a greater good, but either way it makes them more predictable.

We move back to the transport and the tour continues for another hour or so. Everywhere is pretty much the same – large chambers, mostly empty except for a few panels or viewscreens, very few of the tau around. We see more of the drones in other parts of the ship, flitting around on their various errands. It's all very strange, but a little underwhelming really. Everything is the same, there's little decoration or individuality. In a few places there are some symbols on the walls, which appear to be strange writing, but other than that there's nothing. No paintings, no patterns, it's all rather bland. It just makes the ship feel even more impersonal, and makes me feel even more like an unwanted visitor.

As I follow the others silently around, keeping to my role as the unimportant scribe, I start to realise just how different the tau are. They look a bit like us but they certainly don't think like us. They don't have any individuality as far as I can tell. They're so wrapped up in their greater good that they've pushed out any scope for individual achievement.

That's the big difference between their beliefs and ours. I've been to over a dozen worlds in the Imperium, and they've all been different in some way or another. We've changed and adapted to live on ice worlds, in the depths of jungles, on airless moons and on board space stations, yet everyone is still human in some deep down way. The tau on the other hand are just repeating themselves, trying to turn the galaxy into their vision. That's what will kill them off in the end, I reckon. Life will throw all sorts of different challenges your way, and sometimes you have to go around them, while I think the tau will just try to ride straight through it all, driven on by their stupid idea that the greater good will see them through.

We finally end up at the front end of the ship and enter the bridge. This is a bit more familiar, or at least more like I imagine a ship's bridge to be since I've never actually been on one. Like the rest of the ship, the room is a broad dome, though less high than the other chambers. An elliptical viewing screen dominates the front of the chamber, and arrayed around the floor in a circular pattern are various consoles and displays, each with a tau air caste member standing at them. Seeing this brings home something else as well. Through the engine room, the gun decks – very disappointing, identical sealed-in modules, not a sign of anything gun-looking in the slightest – the surveyor arrays and all the other places we've been, I don't recall seeing a normal seat anywhere. They all seem to stand up on the job, as it were. Even the captain, who's standing in the centre of the room watching everything carefully, is dressed in a similar outfit to the others. Obviously the robe he wore earlier was purely for the welcome ceremonial rather than his regular uniform.

He turns to us as we walk in and the iris-like door closes, and says something in Tau.

'El'savon welcomes you to the control centre of his vessel,' translates Por'la'kunas with a slight bow of the head. 'If you have any questions, please do not hesitate in directing them to me and I shall inquire on your behalf.'

WE WATCH AS a small opening appears in the floor and a drone drifts up into sight, the aperture closing behind it. It hovers over to the captain and warbles something in Tau before disappearing back the way it came. He turns to our interpreter and says something long-winded, looking occasionally at us as he does so. Por'la'kunas replies in length, also looking at us, and the captain nods in agreement.

'It appears you have arrived on the bridge at a fortuitous time,' he tells us with a slight nod. 'Shortly we will undergo the transition into vash'aun'an, which I believe you call "warp space".

He directs our attention to the large screen, which pans across the stars before settling on a reddish blob. As the ship powers closer, the blob expands into a spiral pattern erratically expanding and contracting in on itself. It shifts colour too, and sometimes disappears from sight altogether. The captain explains something to Por'la'kunas.

'Ahead is the sho'kara,' the water caste tau informs us with due grandeur. 'Which you might called the lens or window, perhaps. We will pass through the sho'kara into warp space and ride the currents within.'

'You have to use these warp holes, or lenses or whatever, to enter the warp?' asks Oriel, feigning only slight interest.

'The fio have yet to find a successful method of creating an artificial sho'kara,' admits Por'la'kunas sheepishly. However, he rallies well. 'It will only be a matter of time before the problems they have so far encountered are resolved.'

'And when inside the warp, you navigate how?' Schaeffer asks.

'I am unsure of the details, I will confer with El'savon,' he answers slowly, obviously a little put out by this sudden line of questioning. I guess warp travel isn't one of the things they've mastered yet, not that anyone can really master it if you ask me. However, it's obvious from Por'la'kunas's reaction that he'd rather not discuss this shortcoming. After a long discussion with the captain, during which the interpreter does most of the talking, Por'la'kunas turns back to us. He pauses for a couple of seconds, obviously collecting his thoughts and working out what to say.

'The captain informs me that the ship navigates along an extensive network of pre-designated pathways,' he announces, not quite hiding his faltering confidence. He glances back at the captain once before continuing. 'El'savon says that powerful beacons allow him to travel between our planetary systems with great speed and accuracy. For instance, we shall be arriving at Me'lek, our destination, within six rot'aa. From what I know of your time partitioning, that will be approximately four of your human days.'

'And these beacons allow you to talk to the other worlds whilst travelling perhaps?' the Colonel presses on. 'I only ask so that Imperial Commander Oriel's arrival be properly announced and anticipated.'

Sly bastard, I think to myself. Por'la'kunas is in a really difficult position now. He either has to tell us whether they can communicate whilst in warp space, a handy piece of information to know, or risk offending his honoured guest by not answering. In the end, after another brief talk with El'savon, he opts to answer, though whether truthfully or not I can't tell.

'A kor'vesa-piloted vessel is used for communication between ships in transit and our worlds, and also for the sending of messages to the widespread outposts of our sizeable empire,' Por'la'kunas duly informs us, using the opportunity to try and scare us away by talking about the size of the Tau Empire. I remain unimpressed though. Given time and no distractions, I haven't got a doubt that, should the Emperor will it, we could snuff out this jumped up species. They're just lucky we have to deal with the tyranids. I suspect their empire would be swarming with Navy warships and Imperial Guard regiments otherwise. Enjoy your lives while they last, I think to myself, glad that in some small way I might be playing my part in their downfall. It also shows up how little they know about the Imperium if they think they can threaten us by talking about numbers. I bet there's more of us on a single hive world than they've got in their whole empire.

As I ponder this, I watch the warp hole growing larger on the screen and I have to admit it starts to worry me. The warp's an uncontrollable beast, which can tear ships apart or fling them off route to wander lost between the stars. The idea of diving in through this opening and drifting along the currents of the immaterium doesn't fill me with joy. I don't even like the idea of a ship with proper warp engines and navigators on board, and all this reliance on spiritless technology, in a place where souls can be given form, makes me shudder. The others are fidgeting a bit as well, attention fixed on the screen. I spare them only the briefest of glances as I concentrate on the whorl of power that's sucking us into the dimension of nightmares and Abyssal Chaos.

The small warp tempest swirls ever closer and closer, distorting the appearance of the stars behind it, twisting them and stretching them into swirls and lines of light. I feel like we're going faster and faster, being relentlessly sucked in, and a brief panic begins to grip me until I realise that we're just approaching at the same pace and it was all my mind playing tricks on me. I'm glad for the heavy cowl concealing my face as my nerves fray just a little bit more.

Another minute or so passes until the warp hole is filling the entire screen, and its outer edges disappear from view. The shifting colours are dizzying to watch as is the rhythmic pulsing that can now be made out at its centre.

I actually feel sick looking at it, the mesmerising effect of the sight combining with my nervousness to make my stomach lurch a couple of times. I'm glad when the screen goes blank for a moment, the nauseating view replaced by a schematic of obscure symbols and ever-changing Tau writing. An alien standing at a panel to our left calls something out and the captain nods once.

'We are entering the sho'kara now,' Por'la'kunas announces, totally at ease again now that we've stopped bugging him with questions.

I would have expected some hectic activity, messages being sent from different parts of the ship, officers bustling around busily. It's not like that at all. The tau stand at their posts in silence, monitoring their positions without a word being spoken. Everything is conducted in the same calm, ordered manner the tau seem to employ in everything they do. They've obviously done this many times before, and such is their faith in their machines, however misplaced that may be, they have no thoughts of failure.

Another tau speaks up next, and the captain says something to our guide, bowing his head in Oriel's direction.

'El'savon wishes to inform you that we have safely navigated the sho'kara and now that his duties are complete for the day he would be honoured for you to be guests at his dining table this evening,' Por'la'kunas translates for us.

Oriel nods to Schaeffer, who turns and looks at the captain.

'Please convey Imperial Commander Oriel's thanks for El'savon's gracious invitation, which he will of course accept,' the Colonel says, addressing the captain directly. Por'la'kunas repeats the fanciful acceptance speech in Tau and the captain nods again before turning and leaving through a side door.

'I shall escort you back to your quarters now, if that is acceptable to the Imperial commander,' Por'la'kunas says stiffly, keeping his gaze on Oriel. There's something going on here, some petty etiquette or diplomatic statement being made which I'm not aware of. Oriel just nods and starts to walk out, forcing Por'la'kunas to hurry forward to keep pace with him. The Colonel watches us all file past, and I hang back and fall into step beside him before I realise I'm almost marching alongside. I shorten my paces like I'd practised and hope nobody noticed.

'What was that about?' I ask the Colonel in a hushed voice, not turning my head towards him.

'Word games,' he says curtly, glancing across at me. 'The kind of banter that rulers and politicians seem to crave. Imperial Commander Oriel has demonstrated that he too can talk through an intermediary.'

'So what does that mean?' I say, still keeping my voice low.

'It means nothing, except that our translator is more confused about his honoured guest than he was when we arrived on board,' the Colonel explains. 'There are rules governing how to behave in certain situations like this, and I suspect the tau take them very seriously. At least tau from the water caste like Por'la'kunas. Imperial Commander Oriel is trying to break a few of them to see what happens.'

Hearing the Colonel's rough pronunciation of the tau's name makes me smile, luckily concealed within my hood. It makes me wonder about all those scribes I've seen before, busily doing their jobs, probably secretly smirking at us and pulling faces all the time, unseen by everyone else.

'If everything goes to plan, this verbal fencing will be the only combat we will see before the mission starts,' the Colonel adds.

'I've never been on a mission when everything went to plan,' I reply, serious again.

'Neither have I,' Schaeffer admits ominously.

Por'la'kunas leaves us saying that he will return when it is time for us to join the captain. Our kit has been transferred from the shuttle and we pick our rooms. I notice the rooms are cooler than they were before, verging on being cold now, rather than hot.

We sort out an order to use the ablution rooms, and while we scrub up in pairs the rest of us congregate on the floor-cushion again. I must admit, it takes some getting used to, but it is actually quite comfortable and forces us either to sit together or spend our time isolated in our rooms. It is also a great leveller, since no one can look too dignified slouching about on the floor, and as it's circular there's a kind of equality because nobody can sit higher or further towards the head of the table. Something tells me the tau don't need seating orders and bigger chairs to indicate who's in charge; they just know it.

'We have to be careful what we say while outside this room,' Oriel reminds us sternly, pulling off his boots and settling on to the cushion. 'The captain for sure speaks Low Gothic, and I suspect more of the crew than Por'la'kunas says also understand us.'

'How can you know that?' Trost asks. The inquisitor is about to reply when a shriek from Tanya in one of the washing rooms makes us all jump. Moerck is on his feet and dashes to the door, asking if everything is all right.

We gather behind him and peer into the room. At the far end is a shallow bowl-like depression, filled with water that quickly drains away through a small hole at its centre. Tanya is backed up against the wall looking at the floor in horror, arms hugging herself across her bare chest. Her legs are trembling and she glances up at us with a start as we enter. Seeing her naked is nothing new for any of us after the communal washrooms aboard the *Laurels of Glory*.

'What's the matter?' demands Oriel, pushing to the front and darting a look around the room.

'I'm sorry, it st-startled me,' Tanya replies, clearly put out, her teeth chattering.

'What startled you?' the Colonel asks, peering suspiciously around the room as well. We all look around too, backing towards the door again. All I can see is the sink and the bare walls.

'Watch,' she tells us, and steps gingerly into the depression, shoulders hunched. Water begins to spray down from the ceiling, and I see that tiny holes have appeared where there weren't any before.

'And it's cold!' she adds, prancing back out again, causing the downpour to stop immediately. 'And there's nothing to dry myself on, and the hole in the floor just opened up underneath me. I just wasn't expecting it,' she finishes lamely, recovering from the shock and now beginning to feel embarrassed.

Quidlon takes a couple of steps towards the showering area and then quickly backtracks as a panel appears at waist height in the wall next to him and slides out of view into the ceiling. As he moves away, the panel reappears and then slots back into place, leaving only the faintest of lines, so thin you wouldn't see them if you didn't know they were there. He takes another cautious step forward and the alcove reappears.

'Be careful,' Moerck warns him, stepping away from Quidlon.

'I hardly think there will be anything too dangerous in a bathroom,' the Colonel says crossly. 'What is inside?'

Quidlon bends down and looks into the hole before laughing nervously.

'It's a garderobe,' he says, chuckling to himself, turning to us with a relieved expression on his face. 'Everything must be activated by proximity detectors. Just back yourself up against it and… Well, I don't have to explain the details, I guess. There might be some other things around here. Let's investigate.'

We look totally ridiculous for the next minute or so as we cautiously wander back and forth across the room, waving our hands at the walls and floor, seeing what else appears. If you look closely, you can see faint panel lines and the same kind of discoloration that activate the doors. Trost gets subjected to a blast of hot air from a hidden nozzle just to the right of the sink, next to the showering receptacle, while Oriel works out that the sink is activated just by putting your hands inside.

'Right, do you think we can leave Tanya to finish her ablutions without supervision?' Oriel says bitterly, drying his hands under the blower before herding us outside. 'If you're all going to react like this every time something odd happens, this is going to be a very irritating and short-lived mission.'

We exchange nervous glances as everyone drifts back to the communal seat. I never thought having a wash could be such a frightening and interesting experience, and I have a moment's trepidation when I think what other strangeness we might encounter on this trip.

The more I learn about the tau, the more I'm glad to be human. I never thought I'd ever appreciate the simplicity of taps and towels, but the episode with the shower room brings home to me just how lucky we are that the tech-priests keep control of the wild excesses of techno-magic.

'As I was saying before our little excursion,' Oriel says harshly, focussing our attention on him, 'we must not assume that the tau who are with us cannot understand what we are saying.'

'How can you be so sure it's safe to talk here?' Strelli asks, looking meaningfully around the open room.

'You'll just have to trust me on that,' Oriel answers with a tight-lipped, humourless smile. 'Now, it has become obvious to me that the tau are willing to share most of what they know with us. In fact, I haven't learnt anything so far that I did not know before from other sources. Also, they are still slightly suspicious of our motives, especially Por'la'kunas. At this formal engagement with the captain, we must be a bit more free and easy, it's all been far too tense and official so far. Have a drink, enjoy the food, but don't let your tongues wag too much. Ask any questions you wish, and if you're asked anything that won't directly show up our real plans then answer them honestly.'

At that moment, Tanya exits the bathroom and gives me a nod, since I'm up next. I miss the next part of the conversation as I hurriedly duck under the chill waterfall. I look around for soap, but realise there's actually some kind of cleanser in the water itself. Shivering, I step out in front of the dryer mechanism, which blasts me from head to toe with warm air, a matter of a few seconds. I pad through to my bedroom and pull a clean robe from my chest, tossing the dirty one haphazardly over the bed. I feel slightly more refreshed for a little while, but by the time I return to the others, the constant heat of my thick garments has sweat prickling all over my body again, making the heavy robe chafe painfully in places.

'We may not actually be a genuine diplomatic mission,' Oriel is saying, 'but that doesn't mean we can't cause a serious mess if we do things wrong. That said, the tau already look down on us, so they'll forgive most of our indiscretions, and the more they believe we're a stupid and short-sighted race, the more they'll underestimate us in the future, so don't hide your ignorance under a bushel.'

'Shouldn't be too difficult for you, Demolition Man,' Strelli jokes, without thinking what he's saying. I cringe, because I know what's going to happen next.

'What did you call him?' snaps Oriel, jumping to his feet and glaring at Strelli.

'I, ah, it's his name,' Strelli replies lamely, looking over at me. I glance horrified at the Colonel.

'It is part of Lieutenant Kage's training regime,' Schaeffer explains to Oriel. 'One which I fully authorised.'

'So you've all got jolly nicknames?' Oriel's voice drips with scorn. 'Emperor protect us! A slip like that in front of the tau will raise all kinds of questions. What did you think you were doing?'

'I was training soldiers for a military mission,' I butt in quickly, my anger rising. 'You wanted trained soldiers, and that's what I've given you. You want spies to be sneaking around pretending to be people they aren't, you can sort it out yourself.'

'Did it not occur to you that a degree of subterfuge would be involved?' Oriel replies testily. 'Or did you not think at all?'

'If I'd been told you wanted a bunch of brain-dead nobility for the mission, I might have done things different,' I snarl back, rising to my feet, my hands balling into fists by my side. 'What you've got is a squad of the best-trained soldiers the Imperial Guard can provide, and when we get down to the meat of this mission, you'll be thanking me you have, because these mind-games aren't what we're here for.'

Oriel stares at me angrily, gritting his teeth.

I knew it wouldn't be long before he showed his true colours. That he's out to get me one way or another. I match his venomous stare, daring him to carry on. He takes a deep breath and looks around at the others, visibly calming down.

'Thank you, Kage,' he says finally. 'We are all on edge here, understandably so, so your aggression will be overlooked this time. It was also an oversight on my part, I realise now. I should have briefed Colonel Schaeffer more fully. You are right, we must not lose sight of our true mission here. Your focus on the military aspects is commendable. Now, if you would like to tell your men that the next one who so much as thinks about using one of your names will be shot by me.'

He stalks from the room, leaving us looking at each other.

'What other "oversights" has he made?' Trost growls, scratching his stubbled chin and looking at the Colonel.

'Keep your opinion to yourself, Trost,' Schaeffer tells him coldly, walking off into his own room.

'Did you mean that?' asks Tanya when the Colonel's disappeared. 'About us being the best the Imperial Guard can provide.'

I look at her and the others, who are watching me like hawks.

'Yes I did,' I tell them, pulling up the hood of my robe and walking out.

AFTER ORIEL'S WARNING, we're all a bit jittery at the captain's dinner. We were escorted here by Por'la'kunas as usual, and brought into a wide, oval room not far from the bridge. Well, I think we're not far from the bridge, I still haven't got myself fully orientated, but I think I've managed to work out which way is the prow and which way is aft. The ceiling is quite low and flat, compared to the high, dome-like structures of the other rooms. The main chamber is the dining area. To one side are rows of shelves, the first I've seen, being laden down with food by a small army of drones that glide back and forth through a hatchway in the opposite wall. I watch in horror as one floats up to the shelf, a tray on its upper surface. The tray then rises up, a flickering blue mist around it, and is deposited on the shelf. How can food be surrounded by something like that and not be contaminated? Emperor knows what pollutants could be leaking out of those drones! And these tau expect us to eat this stuff after they've been messing with it? Not only that, they could have put Emperor-knows-what in there. Narcs to drug us to get us to tell the truth, perhaps? Then I remember the Colonel's words and calm myself down a little. If the tau wanted to do anything like that, there's nothing we could do to prevent them.

At the centre of the room is a large round table surrounded by backless stools, which seem to be moulded up from the floor itself. As I look closely at the floor, I see a slight patterning there. It's very subtle indeed, almost unnoticeable, but actually in the spread of white are different hues of green and blue.

Por'la'kunas notices my gaze and detaches himself from the Colonel and Oriel and walks over.

'Is it not beautiful?' he says, looking across the floor himself. I squirm uncomfortably inside my heavy robes, not happy that I have his undivided attention for the first time.

'But you can hardly see it,' I say, shifting my weight slightly so that I'm further away from the alien.

'It is a particularly celebrated school of art within our empire,' the guide explains. 'It demands that one pay attention to it and examine it carefully. It aids contemplation and is calming to the nerves.'

It's not calming my bloody nerves, I think to myself, darting a pleading glance behind Por'la'kunas's back at Oriel and the Colonel. The inquisitor gives a brief frown before calling the interpreter's name. The tau gives me a slight bow and then heads back to talk to the pair of them. I breathe a sigh of relief and smile my thanks to them.

'I don't trust that creepy bastard one bit,' Trost whispers to me, standing with his back turned slightly towards me, keeping his eye on the tau.

'Me neither,' I agree. 'Don't start anything, just keep your mouth shut and your ears open.'

'Nothing in the Emperor's galaxy could get me to talk to these freaks willingly,' he tells me with feeling.

A chime sounds from nowhere, startling everyone except Por'la'kunas. The door cycles open, and El'savon, the captain, appears with four other tau. They are dressed in similar flowing garments to the ones they wore at the welcoming ceremony. Por'la'kunas makes the introduction – more bizarre, unpronounceable names – and we all sit down at the table, in no particular order.

Por'la'kunas translates a few pleasantries from the captain, who informs us the journey through the warp is progressing to schedule, and that a drone-controlled pod has been despatched to Me'lek to ensure our arrival is anticipated. He asks if the conditions of our quarters are satisfactory, and so on. As he speaks, one of the other tau gets up and strolls over to the food, and begins filling up an oval plate with various fruits. We all give him a surly look.

'Is something amiss?' Por'la'kunas asks, noticing our displeasure.

'We were expecting something a little more, well, formal,' Tanya says, remembering that she's supposed to be the chatelaine of the group. 'The Imperial commander is not used to inferiors dining before him.'

The interpreter looks at us blankly for a moment, and El'savon speaks in Tau to him. An alien conversation ensues, and they talk right over us, almost forgetting we're here in the room with them. They all give a start when the Colonel pointedly clears his throat.

'Would you mind explaining what you are talking about?' he asks, no hint of aggression in his voice.

'My apologies,' the interpreter says, apparently sincere, turning his attention back to Oriel. 'No disrespect was intended. We are all equal in our labours for the greater good. Such enforcement of hierarchy is unnecessary within our society. We were just discussing how to resolve this situation. As I'm sure you understand, this is El'savon's vessel and therefore he has greatest authority amongst us, yet you are a planetary ruler and so may see yourself as his superior. We are unsure how to proceed. Perhaps you could advise us?'

Oriel seems momentarily taken aback by the tau's candour, but rallies quickly.

'Well, when on Terra, do as the Terrans do, as we say,' he says casually, waving a hand towards the shelf. The gathered tau look at Por'la'kunas and he translates. They look quizzically at each other and then at Oriel.

'We shall follow your example,' Tanya explains after a surreptitious gesture from the Colonel. 'For, we are as united and equal in our dedication to the great Emperor of the Galaxy as you are to your cause.'

Nicely done, I think to myself, catching her eye and giving her a wink. Let's not allow them to forget who they're dealing with here. Por'la'kunas has been a condescending little scumbag since we arrived, it's about time these upstarts were put in their place. I suppress the urge to remind them that they're only around now because a warp storm stopped us wiping them out in their racial infancy. Anyway, the reply seems to satisfy everyone. Oriel smiles at Tanya; the tau nod approvingly. I feel someone kick me under the table, and glance to my right to see Strelli looking at me.

'I believe it would be a fitting gesture for our scribe, as the lowest and most humble Imperial servant present, to demonstrate our willingness to embrace this wonderfully liberal ideal,' he says smoothly.

All eyes turn to me when Por'la'kunas translates, and I stand up, my flesh prickling under their scrutiny.

'You're dead,' I silently mouth to Strelli from the confines of my hood, darting him a murderous glance as I walk past him. The tau standing by the shelves gives me a pleasant nod. I hesitantly take a plate he proffers towards me, and walk up and down the shelves, looking at the trays of food. There's forty dishes on the four shelves, and I glance at the tau's plate to see what he's taken, trying to identify the same foodstuffs on the loaded platters in front of me. They come from different shelves, all over the place, so I guess there's no formal order to what should be eaten when, as far as I can tell anyway.

I load up my plate, grabbing different fruits and vegetables at random, a couple from each shelf, spooning various hot sauces over the top. There's what sounds like amused muttering from behind me and I turn around. The tau are looking at me, slightly incredulous expressions on their faces. Por'la'kunas says something sternly to them, and they avert their gazes, before saying something at length to the tau standing next to me. He gently, but firmly, takes my plate from me and says something in Tau. A drone glides into the room through the hatchway and extends its green mists, plucking the plate from the tau's hands before drifting off again. The tau says something to me, and then points towards the shelves, and his plate, indicating each food in turn. It's only when he does this that it becomes clear he has taken from every eighth dish. With this in mind, I realise one of the things that's been nagging at me all day, and it's hammered home when the tau passes me a fresh plate. They only have one thumb and three fingers on each hand. Of course they would count in eights, and it makes some sense. If you're a fragged up alien that is.

I look at the food for a short while before grabbing a couple of the starfruit I had earlier, since I know they're quite tasty. I then count eight along. I look at the tau and he nods approvingly, moving away from me back to the table. I spoon a small pile of dark blue grains onto my plate, then count along again, arriving at a deep bowl with a brown gravy-like substance in it. I ladle some over my food, wondering why I'm putting gravy on fruit, and then get to the final plate. This is more familiar, it looks like bread, although there are striations of different colours – greens and greys – running through the loaf.

There's a small device next to the plate and I pick it up. Somebody appears next to me, and another tau is there, along with the Colonel.

I ignore him and examine the device, seeing a small stud, which I press. A blade extends outwards, thankfully away from me, I could have slit my wrist by accident. It begins to shimmer. In fact, judging by the feel of it, it's vibrating rapidly. I use the knife to slice some bread for myself, and then press the stud again, turning the vibro-knife off. My hands are shaking and I hurry back to the table.

I sit down and then realise that I can't eat this with my fingers, not with gravy all over it. I look at the tau who started before me and see he's got some of the paddle-like utensils we found in our quarters. He has a pair in each hand, deftly using them to slice up the food, using one pair to hold it in place and the other to cut, before spooning the food into his lipless mouth. I look around for the utensils and Tanya catches my eye. She reaches under the table, pulls some out and waves them at me with a patronising smile. I look down, and see that there are small drawers in the outside of the table, with finger holes for handles. The tau have slender hands and only my little finger fits in the hole.

I pull the drawer out and find eight of the eating paddles, along with a silky, napkin-like cloth and a covered bowl of white crystals. I tentatively dab a finger into the bowl, using the long sleeves of my robe to conceal the action, and then cautiously taste it. I'm surprised to find it's just salt. Good old, familiar salt. I take some in my fingers and sprinkle it on my dish, before sorting myself out with the utensils.

It all takes some getting used to, and we spill quite a lot of the food on the table. Strelli almost takes Trost's eye out when he accidentally catapults a hot round piece of potato-like vegetable across the table, causing Tanya to stifle a laugh and the Colonel to scowl at him. Every now and then a drone buzzes in, extends its mist-field and clears up.

The tau don't seem to mind our amateurish attempts, one or two of them circling round the table, giving us some help with the positioning of our less articulate fingers. One of them says something and the others give little nods and make a tittering noise which I guess is laughter. Oriel raises an inquisitive eyebrow and asks what is funny, affecting a slightly offended tone.

'A joke, Imperial commander, which intended no insult,' Por'la'kunas responds good-naturedly.

'Perhaps you'd care to share it with us?' Strelli asks, sitting back and forgetting there's no chair back, so he has to lean forward hurriedly to stop himself falling off his stool. I give him a sneer which no one else can see thanks to my hood. Once again, I wonder just what all those adepts we see around the place are really up to when we're not looking at them.

'The Emperor loves you so much, he has gifted you with extra fingers,' the interpreter explains, nodding in amusement. He stops and looks slightly put out by our blank reaction. 'In the Tau tongue, it is quite a humorous play on words,' he assures us. 'Perhaps it does not translate very well.'

Por'la'kunas barely has time to eat, as the conversation begins again, with Quidlon plying the various tau with questions about their technology, the drones in particular, although the answers seem to baffle him even more. Moerck and Trost are steadfastly silent, only picking at their food and trying to ignore the tau as much as possible. Tanya asks about the various foodstuffs, and like Quidlon gets more and more confused by the explanations given to her.

Another drone swooshes gracefully through the hatch after about fifteen minutes or so, carrying a tray of drinks in long, slender goblets of pale blue ceramic. Por'la'kunas explains that it's a fine tau drink. Like wine, I suppose. We all take a glass, and Oriel stands up and raises his.

'I wish to toast El'savon,' he declares, looking at the captain. Both he and Por'la'kunas look shocked.

'You wish to do *what*, Imperial commander?' Por'la'kunas asks quickly.

'I propose a toast,' he repeats, turning his attention to the translator.

'You wish to immolate El'savon?' Por'la'kunas asks, horrified.

'I... What?' Oriel answers, glancing around the table, realising the misunderstanding. 'No, no! A toast is, ah, an act of appreciation.' He looks at the rest of us for support and we all stand and raise our glasses too. The tau chatter to each other for a second before copying us.

'To El'savon, may he live a long and healthy life,' declares Oriel, and we repeat it, drinking from our glasses. The wine isn't really wine at all, it tastes almost salty rather than fruity, and is a bit sour. I take only the smallest of sips and put the goblet down again. Por'la'kunas translates and the tau mimic us in their own language, taking deep draughts of the drink. El'savon speaks up, and the process is then repeated in reverse, with El'savon toasting Imperial Commander Oriel, and I'm forced to drink some more of the tau alcohol.

With no formal courses to follow, the meal drags on for what seems like hours and hours. Both sides are wary of making too many

more social mistakes, and the conversation dies away to the odd
question about the food, and polite inquiries regarding our destination, Me'lek. It seems the world is fairly well established, although
not as old as much of the Tau Empire. Oriel deftly avoids some questions about his reasons for visiting and we finish eating in silence.
Finally, after a short lifetime of worry and discomfort, El'savon bids
us goodnight and the tau leave, except for Por'la'kunas who shows us
back to our quarters.

Nobody says a word as we go to our beds, all too tired and
wrapped up in our own perturbed thoughts for conversation.

WE PRETTY MUCH keep a low profile after that as the ship ploughs
through the warp towards Me'lek. Back in the warp, my nightmares
return, my nights filled with the living dead from my past. Combined
with being constantly on my guard around the tau, the sleeplessness
leaves me exhausted and feeling ancient. The others are just as
ragged, and several times, there's close calls, when one or other of us
almost trip up and blow our cover stories.

Oriel is withdrawn, the Colonel his usual uncommunicative self,
so that leaves me to deal with the other Last Chancers. I gather them
all together to go over the plan again, mentally praying to the
Emperor that Oriel was right in saying we could talk freely inside
our own chambers. If not, the tau will know exactly what we're up
to. And perhaps that's their plan. To lull us into a false sense of security so that we'll open up and tell them everything they need to
know.

But I can't just leave the Last Chancers alone, I have to get them
doing something, and focussing them back on the mission seems
like the perfect distraction from our unsettling surroundings.

The one sticking point is Tanya. When we reach the stage when it's
time for her to make the shot she says the words, but there's no conviction in her eyes, no belief. I corner her the next morning as she
wakes up.

'You realise this is all for nothing if you don't pull the trigger?' I
quietly say to her, blocking her into the room by standing in the
doorway.

'It's not that difficult a shot. You could make it, so could Hero,' she
replies, not meeting my gaze.

'Possibly, but you're Sharpshooter, you make the shot,' I tell her,
taking a step forward.

'I know, Last Chance,' she sighs, sitting back on the bed.

'You'll have to do better than that!' I snap at her, advancing across the room.

'What do you want me to say?' she replies hotly. 'That I don't want to take that shot, that I can't kill another person?'

'I'm not talking about a person, I'm talking about the target,' I snap back. 'It's just an alien, like an ork or an eldar or a hrud. It's not like I'm even asking you to kill a real person.'

'I don't think the tau will see it that way,' she counters, gazing at the floor.

'What's this crap?' I hiss, my voice dropping low. 'Feeling sorry for aliens? You disgust me, Tanya. How can you sit there and compare one of these stinking tau to a person, how can you pretend they're more important to you than me, or the Colonel, or your squad mates?'

She looks up at me then, brow knotted in confusion.

'I never said that,' she protests.

'It's what you were thinking, even if you didn't realise it,' I continue harshly, not letting up for a second. 'If you don't make that shot, this Brightsword scumbag is going to invade Sarcassa and butcher thousands of humans. They'll die because you think some damned alien has got more right to be alive than they have.'

'I don't think that at all!' she stands up, pushing me away. 'I don't want this mission! Why does it have to be me? Why do they have to rely on me?'

'Because you swore an oath to protect the Emperor and his domains,' I reply quietly, trying to calm things down. 'Look at it another way – why didn't you just turn down the Colonel back at the prison, and take a bolt to the head? You must have known you would be asked to kill someone.'

'I didn't think about it,' she says, shaking her head.

'I just didn't want to die.'

'So you're just a selfish bitch, is that it?' I'm getting angry again, I can feel my blood heating up inside me. I jab a finger into her chest. 'As long as you're still alive, all those innocent people on Sarcassa can just go to hell, murdered at the hands of the creature you refuse to kill?'

'I don't want that to happen!' she snaps back, slapping my hand away and giving me a shove. 'Get out of my face, Last Chance.'

'Not until you promise me you'll make that shot, not until you've thought long and hard about what it means if you don't pull the trigger,' I reply, stepping back in front of her again, glaring down at her.

'Yeah, well maybe it'll be you in the crosshairs straight after Brightsword,' she threatens me.

'If that's the way it's gotta be, I'm happy,' I admit, taking a pace back and giving her some room. 'If you want to see me in the crosshairs when you pull that trigger, that's just fine by me. Do whatever you like, as long as you nail that bastard dead.'

I look at her then, and she glares back at me, hatred in her eyes. Good. She'll make that shot, I'm pretty sure.

OUR RECEPTION ON Me'lek is more grandiose than the one on the ship. As the ramp touches down on the landing concourse, some kind of band strikes up, mostly composed of different drums, with a few tootling pipes thrown in seemingly just to add to the discordant noise. It's totally unlike the well-paced, rhythmic hymns and marches I'm used to, and starts to grate on my ears after just a couple of seconds. Two lines of large walking machines flank the route towards the space port building in front of us, which rears from the ground like a stylised mushroom, a broad dome atop a spindly-looking tower.

The machines are about three and a half, maybe four metres tall, and broadly humanoid in shape. Judging by their shape, and assuming they actually have pilots, I'd say the driver sits in the main body, the flat, many-lensed head atop the broad form just some kind of remote link. The arms are stocky and heavyset, and armoured plates cover the shoulders and thighs. The lower legs are actually made of open struts, though everything else is encased in heavy-looking, gently faceted armour. Each machine also has an extended back pack from which protrude rows of nozzles, possibly some kind of jet device. They're obviously war machines of some sort; the devices mounted on their arms are unmistakably weapons of different designs. Several of the battle suits also have weapons mounted on one shoulder, long-barrelled guns and rocket pods in the same efficient clutterless design of all the tau machines I've seen so far. Several of them have drones hovering around them, which flicker with some kind of energy field.

Both the battle suits and drones are coloured in a jagged camouflage pattern of grey and orange, with Tau lettering and symbols written across them in various places. Possibly squad markings, maybe the pilot's name.

As one, accompanied by a whine of servo-motors, the twenty machines raise their right arms in a salute, forming an incomplete arch for us to walk through. If these are what the tau use to fight, I can suddenly understand why we need to stop them invading Sarcassa. They look unstoppable to me, walking tanks rather than heavy armour, from what I can tell. Almost like the massive Space Marine dreadnoughts that I heard about on Ichar IV. I glance over at Oriel, who's standing just to my right, taking it all in.

'If we do this right, we won't have to fight against battle suits,' he whispers, giving me a meaningful look which says if we do this wrong, that's exactly what we'll be facing.

Oriel starts off down the ramp and we follow a respectful distance behind, masquerading as the dutiful entourage. As we walk down the aisle of battle suits, I'm even more intimidated by them up close. They tower over us, hulking things that could probably pound us to bloody pulps with their artificial muscles and impressive-looking weaponry. Each lowers its arm behind us as we pass, making me feel even more hemmed in and panicky.

At the end of the row is a small cluster of tau dignitaries, dressed in ceremonial robes similar to those worn by the captain and Por'la'kunas when we arrived on the tau ship. Behind them are ranked up another few dozen warriors, not in battle suits, but still well armed and armoured. Their uniforms are made from a light, billowing material, over which they've got plated carapace armour on their chest and thighs, and thick shoulder guards protecting their upper arms. All of them are wearing helmets, fully enclosed with a small cluster of different sized lenses instead of a proper visor. They too sport the grey and orange camo scheme, except for their helmeted heads which are different shades of blue, yellow and red, possibly to identify individual squads.

If this is supposed to be a show of strength, it's working on me. I certainly wouldn't want to face this lot. They're armed with long rifles, about two-thirds my height. I suspect those guns have got enough punch to put a hole in the back of a battle tank. I mentally kick myself then. I will be facing this lot, I tell myself, not long from now. Well, not this bunch exactly, but others like them. I pull myself together, telling myself that healthy respect for the enemy is one thing, but actually they're not so scary as say an ork or a tyranid. I'm almost convinced by my own arguments. Almost.

The band stops its banging and screeching and the tau in the centre of the group steps forward, bowing politely to Oriel, before addressing us all.

'Welcome, one and all, to the tau world of Me'lek,' he begins, his speech almost perfect, with no trace of the slurring and accent that

Por'la'kunas had. 'I am called Por'o-Bork'an-Aloh-Sha'is. You may address me as Liaison Ambassador Coldwind if you so wish, or simply as ambassador; I will take no offence.'

His tone is pleasant and his eyes active, looking at each of us briefly as he speaks, making sure he has eye contact with us. There's a voice in my head that tells me he's our contact. I don't know how I can tell, perhaps just something about the way he looks at us, but I'm sure of it. He introduces the others, representatives from the water and earth castes whose names are just a jumble of meaningless sounds to me.

'May I add that it is an honour and a pleasure for me to welcome you to Me'lek,' he concludes. 'You are the first official visitors from His Holiness, the Emperor of Mankind to visit us, and I wish your stay to be pleasant and constructive.'

Once more, Oriel gives a stuttering speech in Tau, probably to say how happy we are to be here and all that, while I direct my gaze around the space port. The other buildings are a series of low, flat-topped domes linked by covered walkways along the ground and a few metres in the air. Most of the buildings are white, and like the ship everything is almost painfully bright. Also, the air is dry and the sun is warm on my back, which is pretty much how the tau like it, judging by conditions on the alien ship. When the formalities are over, Ambassador Coldwind tells us that he has a vehicle waiting to take us to our temporary quarters.

He leads us through the space port terminal, a white-walled building with high arches linking the domed chambers. It's here that we start to see just how many drones the tau have. They buzz about everywhere, some of them carrying boxes and bags, others without any visible purpose, although Coldwind informs us that many of them are messengers. For a busy space port, there seem to be relatively few of the actual tau themselves: there's the odd fire caste warrior, dressed like the others outside, standing at some of the doorways, stubby carbines in their hands. One or two of the robed water caste pass us by, giving respectful bows to Coldwind and Oriel as they walk past. Through a distant archway I catch a glimpse of a group of air caste, or so I assume since they seem to be wearing the same tight-fitting outfits the ships crew wore.

As we pass through a massive sliding glass door at the front of the terminal, we get to see the city proper. The space port is located on a hill overlooking the rest of the settlement, and the clear day allows us to see for many kilometres in every direction. Broad boulevards radiate out from the space port in every direction, lined by high-sided buildings of every shape you could imagine. Some are domes, others needle-like towers, while many have flat facades facing the streets which curve gently into spherical shapes or pyramids with rounded edges.

Most of the buildings are white, with the odd pale grey, yellow or blue mixed in at fairly regular intervals. It all gives the sense that everything has been put in its place quite deliberately. Numerous walkways and elevated roads criss-cross between the buildings, giving the city a busy appearance, although there's a feeling of space and calm I've never experienced in any Imperial town. The air above is a pale blue, with just a scattering of fluffy clouds drifting past, the Me'lek star a large, bright orb just below its zenith. Coldwind has the presence of mind to allow us to stand there for a few minutes, looking at the vista.

It then comes home to me. If we were hung out on a limb on the tau ship, we're right up to our necks in the sump water now. This is a fraggin' tau planet, for Emperor's sake! There's just a small group of us, and there's a massive army here. I suspect that even the detachment paraded at our reception would be enough to wipe us out several times over. If we thought we had to be careful aboard the ship, we're gonna have to be perfectly behaved here. The more it goes on, the less and less I like this whole mission. This sneaking around just reminds me of those spine-chilling moments in Coritanorum when we were almost caught. And of course, those innocent people we had to kill simply because there was a danger of them giving our position away.

Then again, that won't be a problem here, these are only aliens after all. The galaxy certainly won't miss them, and I'll miss them even less.

'They like to spread out a bit, don't they?' comments Strelli, shielding his eyes against the glare.

'Don't you find it all a bit soulless?' I ask the others, keeping my voice low enough for Coldwind not to hear.

'I don't get you,' says Tanya, turning towards me.

'It's all the same, wherever you look,' I complain, waving a hand to encompass the whole city. 'It hasn't grown, or changed, or anything. It's probably exactly how they intend it to look. There's nothing personal here, no distinctions between the different districts.'

'And I suppose you're used to that are you?' butts in Trost. 'You're just hive scum, what do you know about building cities?'

'At least in the hive you could tell where you were,' I answer him with a smile, remembering the dank, claustrophobic corridors and tunnels of my youth. 'Everywhere had a different light, a different smell. You could tell which of the levels were older, which of the hab-zones belonged to which of the clans. There was graffiti and totems to mark territory, and gang symbols painted on the floors and walls. It had a life to it. This place is dead.'

'I understand what you mean,' Moerck agrees with me, much to my surprise. 'I don't think the tau have any sense of history, or tradition. They seem so concerned with the greater good and building the empire, they ignore their past.'

'Perhaps they have reasons to forget,' Tanya muses, looking back over the city. 'Perhaps this is all a new beginning for them.'

Oriel coughs to attract our attention and with a nod of his head directs us towards a wide, shallow ramp leading down from the plaza where we're standing. We follow him and Coldwind down towards the street, where our vehicle is waiting for us. It's similar to the transport on the ship, in that it hovers above the ground, although only about half a metre up. It's made from the same silvery material, but is a lot less broad. Its blunt nose is rounded at the corners, the front curving up and blending seamlessly with a transparent windshield which extends another metre above the seating inside. The back end is open to the elements, a roughly oval cavity lined at the edges with padded seating, which we duly haul ourselves into when a section of the side drops to the ground to form a ramp.

Once we're settled, Coldwind seats himself as well, near the front, and then says something out loud in Tau. The vehicle rises up another half a metre and slowly accelerates. I glance towards the front, but can't see any driver. Quidlon asks the obvious question. You can always trust him to do that.

'Erm, excuse me ambassador, but how is the vehicle steered, I mean who is controlling it?' he says hesitantly, torn between looking at Coldwind and gaping at the buildings we go past.

'Thank you for asking that,' Coldwind replies with a slight nod, which I'm beginning to realise is actually not so much a sign of respect but one of pleasure, like a smile. 'This ground car, as you might call it, has a small artificial brain inside, much like the drones you have seen. It is not really sentient as such, but does know the layout of Me'lek City and can respond to simple verbal commands.'

'You just have to tell it where to go, and it takes you there?' Tanya checks, shifting uncomfortably in her seat. They are a little low, making you hunch up slightly. I guess they're more comfortable for the water caste members, who are shorter than us, and the fire warriors we saw at the space port. I then realise that it isn't the seat making her uncomfortable, it's the idea of some alien brain-device driving us around the city, taking us who knows where.

'That is correct,' confirms Coldwind. 'Rest assured that it is perfectly safe. In fact, I suspect it is safer than a vehicle driven by a sentient pilot. It cannot be distracted, nor does its mind wander and daydream. Its sensors are far more accurate and cover a much wider range of the spectrum than any living creature's.'

'Could you tell us a little about these buildings?' the Colonel asks after Oriel whispers something to him.

'Most certainly, chief advisor,' Coldwind replies, looking at the Colonel with his dark eyes. 'We have just left Me'lek space port, one of two such facilities on the planet. The geodesic structure approaching on our right,' he points to a faceted silver dome that reflects the light in a hundred different ways, creating a dappling sheen across its neighbours, 'contains the surface housing for members of the kor, whom you refer to as the air caste. Only a few of them can live planetside nowadays due to the depreciation of their muscles and skeletons caused by prolonged space flight over successive generations. The conditions inside are maintained at a lesser gravity than the rest of the city.'

'You're very forthcoming, ambassador,' comments Oriel, sitting forward suddenly. 'Any particular reason why?'

'There are two reasons, Imperial commander,' Coldwind replies smoothly. 'Firstly, I am of the highest rank of the por, the water caste in your tongue, and as such it is my duty to co-operate fully with such an important and honoured visitor. Secondly, I will be furnishing you and your team with much more confidential information before we depart for Es'tau.'

So he is our contact, I think triumphantly. None of the others seem surprised, least of all Oriel. It's good to have it said though.

'I assume that we can talk safely here?' Oriel asks, looking steadily at Coldwind.

'This vehicle has been secured against any kind of surveillance,' Coldwind assures him earnestly.

'Are you absolutely sure?' the inquisitor presses the matter.

'I would certainly not be engaging in this discussion if I did not believe that to be the case, Imperial commander,' Coldwind points out.

'Hmm, I suppose not,' Oriel concedes, leaning back again and relaxing slightly. 'Have you any update on Commander Brightsword's movements?'

'O'var, as we often refer to him, returned to Es'tau almost a kai'ro-taa ago,' the ambassador replies without hesitation. He sees our confused looks. 'Sorry, that is almost two Terran months. He is expected to remain there for several more weeks, I believe. He is currently assembling sufficient transports and escorting warships for his army to move on the world you call Sarcassa.'

'What can you tell us about Brightsword himself?' the Colonel asks, leaning forward and resting one elbow on his knee, cupping his chin in his hand. His eyes are fixed on Coldwind, and the ambassador seems momentarily put out by his icy, penetrating gaze. I can't blame the tau; everybody I've met feels uncomfortable when they have Schaeffer's full attention. Even aliens, apparently.

With a look at Oriel, who nods in agreement, the tau delicately clears his throat before speaking.

'He is Shas'o-Tash'var-Ol'nan-B'kak,' he tells us, the Tau syllables almost blending into one long word. 'That is, he is a fire caste commander, from the world of Tash'var, who has earnt the honorary titles of Brightsword and Sandherder.'

'Sandherder?' laughs Trost. He has one arm hooked over the edge of the car and slaps his hand against the outside in amusement. 'What sort of name is that?'

'One of great value,' Coldwind replies, ignoring Trost's rudeness. 'It is a traditional title that dates back many generations. As a tau I find its origins intensely interesting, but I suspect that as outsiders the explanation may tax your powers of attention.'

'Yes, it will,' the Colonel says heavily, glaring at Trost for the interruption. 'Please continue telling us about O'var.'

'Like all members of the shas caste, O'var was born to be a warrior,' Coldwind tells us, looking at each of us rather than focussing his attention on one person. He's certainly used to speaking to groups, that's obvious, and his command of our language is better than most humans I've met. 'During his most formative years, the period sometimes referred to by the shas as 'on the line', O'var fought for the great military hero O'shovah for several years. During this time, O'shovah was impressed by O'var's skill at arms and tactical forethought and they conducted the ta'lissera together. This allowed O'var to join O'shovah's hunter cadre, as we know our military formations.'

'This ta'lissera is some kind of bonding ceremony isn't it?' Oriel interrupts. 'It's supposed to be a very grave undertaking.'

'Indeed it is, Imperial commander,' Coldwind answers, giving no hint of surprise that Oriel should know this. 'It is one of the most profound commitments that we can make to achieving the tau'va; the aim in life for all of our people, a complex concept which your translators interpret merely as the greater good. O'shovah became O'var's mentor, and taught him many battle skills and the intricacies of the art of war. In time, O'var rose to a position of authority which meant he could no longer remain in O'shovah's cadre. It was supposedly an emotional parting for both of them. It was also at this time that the seeds of dissent were sown in O'var, as the fio might say. O'shovah, once a brilliant and highly respected leader of our armies, has since turned his back on the greater good and shunned our ways. O'var, no doubt inspired by his mentor, has become an aggressive and headstrong leader. Although he still swears to uphold the ideals of the tau'va, his militaristic approach is increasingly becoming counter to our non-aggressive policies of colonisation.'

'You mean he's a gun that could go off any time,' Strelli states humourlessly. 'That must be a real headache for you.'

'What an evocative analogy,' Coldwind replies, again with that tiny nod of amusement.

'Sorry,' Tanya butts in. 'These names are confusing me, could you go over them again.'

Myself and Moerck both nod in agreement. The Tau syllables are all mixed up in my head, along with the translations.

'There's only one we need worry about,' Oriel replies. 'That is O'var. We call him Commander Brightsword. The other is O'shovah. That translates as Farsight. Farsight was Brightsword's commander in his early military career, that is all you need know about him. Please try to pay attention and keep up.'

'Well, I was getting confused,' snaps Tanya, crossing her arms. 'After all, I am supposed to kill this guy, I'd like to know I got his name right in my head when I pull the trigger.'

We all glance sharply at her.

'I would prefer you weren't so specific about our mission, especially out here in an open-topped car,' Oriel snarls at her. He turns his attention back to Coldwind. 'Not that I do not trust your assurances, ambassador. Now, about Brightsword?'

'He has, as you point out, become something of a problem, although not as much as O'shovah,' the tau diplomat continues. 'But

as you say, O'shovah is not our concern for now. O'var's expansion-
ist aggression will, if allowed to continue unchecked, inevitably lead
to conflict with your people. Much more widespread conflict than
the relatively small skirmishes that have so far been fought. And, of
course, ignoring your somewhat premature and abortive crusade
through the area you call the Damocles Gulf.'

'We're not here to rake over history or make a critique of the
Imperium's military policy, Coldwind,' Oriel says sourly. None of us
have a clue what they're talking about, I've never heard of any Damocles Gulf crusade. In fact, up until a couple of seconds ago, I'd never
heard of the Damocles Gulf, wherever that may be.

'We, of course, wish to avoid all conflict where possible,' Coldwind
smoothes over the tension. 'It is unproductive and counter to the
needs of the greater good. Your officials,' he looks at Oriel then, 'also
realise the folly of a war between our two states and wish to avoid
conflict. Thus, we arrive here, conspiring together to rid us both of a
problem.'

'So why can't you just depose him or something?' asks Tanya. 'Pro-
mote somebody else in his place?'

'I am afraid that would be contrary to the tau'va,' the ambassador
explains. 'On appearances, O'var is doing nothing wrong. He is
expanding our domains so that the tau'va may be spread to other
races across the galaxy.'

'So why get us to kill him, why not do the dirty work yourselves?'
Trost argues back. Oriel darts him another warning look about speaking too openly and the demolitions expert gives a surly grunt and
folds his arms. I'm momentarily distracted as we pass by a huge
sphere supported on stilts, linked to the ground by spiralling moving
stairways. I snap out of it and listen to what Coldwind is saying.

'The thought of killing another tau is absolutely horrific to us,
except for certain shas ritual combats,' Coldwind is actually physically repelled at the thought, his skin blanching a paler blue. 'Even if
such an individual could be found to perform the act, the risks are
far too great. If it were ever discovered that we had done such a deed,
it would cast doubt on the tau'va. Surely you understand that.'

'We don't really need to go into the whys, do we?' I say to the
Colonel and Oriel, trying to keep the conversation relevant. 'What we
need to know are the details of how, where and when.'

'Yes, of course,' Coldwind replies, glancing ahead of the car. 'Unfortunately, we have arrived at your residence for the evening and will
be in company with others in a moment. Tonight there is a dinner in

your honour, and we will not be able to talk then. Tomorrow morning I will be conducting you on a tour of the city, during which there will be periods when we can converse properly.'

The ground car slows to a halt outside a rearing edifice like an inverted cone, its levels splaying further and further outwards as it reaches into the sky. I have no idea how it could stand up, it seems supported only by the linkways and bridges that connect it to the overhead roads and nearby buildings.

'If you would follow my aide, Vre'doran, he will show you to your chambers,' Coldwind says, indicating a shorter, skinny-looking tau waiting patiently by the flower-like doorway to the building. As we clamber out, he bows deeply and steps aside, allowing us to precede him as the 'petals' of the door open into the building to allow us access. I glance back and see the car disappearing back down the street, taking our ally with it.

OUR QUARTERS ARE a slightly more grandiose version of those aboard the ship. As before, there's a central chamber, this time with a large central cushion and three smaller ones in a triangle around it. There are ten bedrooms connected to the main living area, each with its own showering room. We barely have time to wash and refresh ourselves before a chiming noise attracts our attention to the door. Vre'doran is waiting for us on the landing outside, and he asks us to accompany him to the upper floor where the state dinner is being held.

'Are all the rooms like ours?' asks Tanya, though whether out of curiosity or just trying to play her role, I'm not sure. 'Are these normal quarters, or those specially prepared for offworld visitors?' I think she almost said 'aliens' then, but realised that they're still the aliens, even if we are on their world.

'They are similar in design to our own habitations,' Vre'doran informs us, leading us along a hallway which is coloured a very pale blue, decorated by a thin frieze of Tau lettering at about head height. 'If they are not suitable, I can arrange for rooms to be specially prepared that are more suitable. We are not fully aware of all human needs.'

Tanya glances at Oriel, who shrugs.

'The quarters we have will be sufficient, thank you,' she tells the tau graciously.

We follow the alien onto the moving ramp that serves instead of a staircase, gently revolving around a central pillar that runs the height of the building. The inside is hollow; the twelve floors have circular landings with bridges that reach out from the conveyor, the rooms radiating outwards from there. The central column itself is startling – glass or some other transparent substance that contains an ever shifting mix of coloured liquids that gently rise and fall along its length.

Like all of the stairwells I've seen, the mobile ramp has no handrails, and we crowd into the centre near the column for fear of plummeting to our deaths. It's obvious the tau don't lose their footing very easily. I can see why, they seem a very leisurely race, I've not seen anything except the drones hurrying around. Like everything to do with the tau their pace of life is calm and sedate as well.

We reach the final landing and are led into the banqueting hall. It runs the entire circumference of the building, as far as I can tell, its outside wall a continuous window allowing a magnificent view of the city in every direction. Low, wide circular tables are arranged along the centre of the room, disappearing to the left and right, each surrounded by the now familiar seating cushions. Me'lek's star is just setting, and as we wait for the other guests to arrive, we stand at the window and look out over the settlement, bathed in the rosy glow of the coming twilight.

For the first time since we arrived, the city starts to come alive as darkness descends. The sunset casts a warm tint across the harsh white buildings, softening the glare, and lights from thousands of windows spring into life in the space of a few seconds. Strips of luminescence run the length of the roadways and bridges, adding to the spectacle, and as the star rapidly dips beneath the horizon, I'm amazed at the glorious array of twinkling starlight and iridescent rainbows that replace the severe whiteness of the city in daylight.

A steady stream of yellow and blue lights moves along the roadways as the vehicles build in number, soon forming an almost constant stream.

Looking to my right I can see the space port atop the hill, blazing with beacons and landing guides, geometric shapes shining in red, green, blue and white making an almost dizzying pattern from this angle. The bright landing jets of some starship erupt into life as it lifts off and I watch the white sparks ascend into the clouds, underlit by the last rays of the day.

'That's pretty impressive,' Strelli says casually. 'Can you imagine how much power it takes to run all of those lights?'

'Pretty lights and baubles,' snorts Moerck, turning away. 'Glittering decorations that impudently seek to outmatch the stars. Only a race so blind to the obscenities of technology would try and rival the beauty of the Emperor's heavens.'

'Beats living in the dark,' Tanya says pragmatically, gazing at the bright array blazoned across the land as far as we can see.

'No light can hide the darkness in an alien's soul,' Moerck sneers from behind us.

We turn as we hear others entering. Four fire warriors, fully armoured and armed, precede a young-looking tau wearing a robe of several differently coloured layers. In his hand he carries a short rod, a glittering gem at its tip. They pay no attention to us, but move out of sight around the bend. Ambassador Coldwind follows soon after and directs us towards a table a little way from the door, with a view of the space port out of the window. He follows our gazes outside.

'Magnificent, is it not?' he says, bobbing his head slightly. 'We adore the night, you see. When our ancestors were still young, we lived in the dry and arid heat of T'au, and spent much of the hot day sheltering. At night, that is when we prefer to live our lives.'

'You're a nocturnal race?' Quidlon asks quickly.

'Only culturally,' replies Coldwind. 'Biologically we are like humans, capable of diurnal and nocturnal activity. Our traditions place great regard on the night, and the pleasures she brings.'

'Who was the tau who came in before you?' Oriel asks, sitting down at the table and motioning for the rest of us to join him. I keep forgetting he is supposed to be the guest of honour.

'That was Aun'la-Shi'va-Run'al,' he replies curtly.

'A member of the ethereals?' Oriel says with sudden interest, glancing along the room in the direction the mysterious tau went.

'Yes,' Coldwind confirms, obviously not too eager to discuss the matter.

'Why so suddenly quiet?' I ask him, leaning my elbows on the table. The Colonel gives me a harsh glare and I snatch them back, realising my sleeves have flopped back, showing the scars and weals around my wrists from the time I was in prison. I don't know if the tau would understand where they're from, but I guess it's better to avoid questions.

'We do not discuss matters concerning the aun with outsiders, even those who are our allies,' the ambassador replies sternly.

'Is he not here to welcome me?' Oriel asks in surprise.

'He shares the same room, that is sufficient to honour the arrival of an outsider,' Coldwind tells Oriel without any sign of embarrassment. The ambassador looks up and nods to an approaching tau, taller than the others we've seen and quite broad. He carries himself like a warrior, I tell myself, noting the slight swagger to his walk and the hard stare he gives us as he stops next to the table.

'This is Shas'el-Vior'la-M'yenshi-Elan,' Coldwind introduces the newcomer. 'May I present Imperial Commander Oriel of his Most Holy Majesty the Emperor of Terra.'

I go to stand, but note that Coldwind remains seated. Obviously, it's not a sign of respect here. I should have remembered that from the captain's dinner aboard the starship.

'Welcome to Me'lek. Address me as Shas'elan, Commander Oriel,' the fire warrior says, dipping his head a fraction in deference. His voice is much deeper than that of the other tau I've met, his accent far more pronounced. Now, I'm not exactly an expert on tau body language yet, but he doesn't look too pleased to be here. He seats himself at the opposite side of the table, pushing his way between Quidlon and Tanya.

'Shas'elan is an old friend of mine and a high-ranking officer in the shas here on Me'lek,' explains Coldwind, either oblivious to his friend's discomfort or simply ignoring it.

We sit there in a slightly uncomfortable silence for a minute or so, before the Colonel speaks up.

'Forgive my ignorance, Shas'elan, but I know little of the structure of your military,' he says quietly, the most polite I've heard him be with anyone. Ever. 'You have the rank of shas'el, is that right?'

'I am shas'el,' he answers proudly.

'How many warriors do you command?' the Colonel continues, scratching his ear in a nonchalant fashion.

'I command one… one…' he glances across to Coldwind for help, who answers in Tau. 'I command one cadre of warriors. At present, they number fifty-six.'

'And your superior is?' Oriel interrupts, still affecting his assumed indifference.

'Shas'o-Vior'la-Mont'yr-Shi'mont'ka,' Shas'elan replies after a moment's thought. 'Shas'o controlling all shas on Me'lek.'

We digest this for a while, waiting for the food to arrive. When it does, it's a bewildering assortment of dishes carried by drones, laden down with vegetables, fruits, fragrant rice and thick-crusted pastries, more of the crunchy biscuity things I took a liking for on the ship, plus jugs of honey-coloured and deep purple juices. A few of them I recognise from the captain's dinner, but most of them are new to us.

Unlike the shelf arrangement on the ship, there seems to be no formal order, and we all tuck in, Coldwind and Shas'elan included. Both the tau seem to lighten up as we begin to eat, recommending various foods, commenting to each other in Tau, with Coldwind occasionally translating for us and Shas'elan.

A couple of times I have to remind myself that Shas'elan is not in on the conspiracy, and stop myself saying something that would give away my military training. I can tell the Colonel is also eager to get what information we can about tau fighting from the fire warrior leader, but is holding back. Despite the unnatural but vaguely pleasant surroundings, I lose my appetite quickly, and I'm soon just picking at small titbits out of politeness.

As we eat, I watch Me'lek's twin moons rise across the night sky, and in the moonlight the city changes again. Most of the lights dim, leaving just the buildings glowing in a variety of colours, some looking silver or gold, others with a kind of pearly hue, yet others still dappled with glowing blues and purples.

'Our cities are planned and built so that they interact with the movement of the celestial bodies, taking their mood from the changing positions of the moons and stars,' Coldwind tells us, noticing the direction of my gaze. 'Do you have such spectacles on your worlds?'

I glance at the Colonel, who gives a shrug and a nod. I decide I can tell them the truth, there's no way Shas'elan could guess I wasn't a scribe just because of where I'm from.

'I come from a city that stretches three kilometres into the skies of Olympas,' I tell the tau, trying to make it sound as impressive as I can. There's no point letting them think they're the only ones who can build a fancy city. 'The lower levels are delved a similar distance into the rock. A billion humans live in that one city, and there are thirteen such cities on my world.'

'That cannot be,' argues Shas'elan. 'That is more humans on one world than there are tau in this sept!'

'We call them hive worlds, from the busy nests of insects,' explains Quidlon. 'There are many hive worlds in the Imperium, and other kinds of worlds too.'

'Many worlds with this many humans?' Shas'elan looks shocked and glares accusingly at Coldwind, muttering something in Tau. Coldwind answers back in a sharp fashion, as far as I can tell anyhow. The rest of the meal is eaten in uncomfortable silence.

* * *

IT IS COLDWIND who meets us the next morning. The day is already beginning to warm up as the ground car glides up onto one of the high aerial roads. I pay more attention to the journey this time, watching as other vehicles pass us in the opposite direction: floating cars like the ones we are in, long articulated transports, small pod-like conveyors carrying a single tau. I notice how many drones there are as well. They seem to be everywhere, flitting along the roads, skimming in and out of the buildings, weaving their way up through the bridges and walkways.

'We must leave tonight,' Coldwind says suddenly, drawing my attention back inside the vehicle. 'I have received word that O'var will be departing Es'tau very shortly. If we do not move as soon as possible, the opportunity may be missed.'

'You say "we", does that mean you are coming with us?' I ask, glancing at the Colonel.

'I shall meet you there,' he replies evenly. 'O'var is assembling many mercenaries to supplement his own fire warriors, and in the guise of mercenaries you will arrive on Es'tau and enter the employ of O'var. I have made this possible, and must travel to O'var to ensure that all of the necessary records are completed in a fashion that does not link you to me in any way.'

'Covering your back then?' Trost laughs. 'You seem to trust us not to give away your secret.'

'If you were to reveal the connection, the records will support my argument that such an arrangement did not exist,' the ambassador answers smoothly, not put out in the least. 'Also, you have nothing to gain from such a revelation, as popular opinion would be far more concerned with eliciting recompense from the Imperium than questioning my role in the affair.'

'Nobody is going to reveal anything to anyone,' Oriel says sternly, giving us each a hard look before turning to Coldwind. 'Has our starship arrived yet?'

'Several days ago, the vessel you described to me achieved orbit,' the ambassador confirms with a nod. 'I have also arranged for you to be conveyed by lifter to the outer regions of the system so that you may engage your warp engines as soon as possible.'

'What do you mean, conveyed?' Schaeffer asks suspiciously.

'Do not be alarmed, it is a standard procedure,' Coldwind assures us. 'Often when dealing with alien vessels, we use the superior acceleration capabilities of our own ships to give them a boost, as you would say.'

'So how long do you expect it will take us to reach Es'tau?' Strelli asks from the back end of the ground car.

'It is a short journey, relatively speaking. I would estimate three, perhaps four rot'aa,' he replies after a moment's thought.

'That's just over two days?' Oriel says, glancing over to Coldwind for confirmation, who gives a nod. 'Not long at all. We'll use the time to make our final preparations.'

'Good, I believe everything is in order then,' the ambassador seems pleased.

We spend the rest of the day going over the next part of the plan. The ambassador briefs us more as he escorts us around various local places of interest. We pass close to the palace of the ethereals, a towering edifice with dozens of skyways webbing out from the central spire, and have our first look at a real fire warrior battle dome, a huge building that can train thousands of warriors under its arching roof. Coldwind becomes particularly animated during our tour through the water caste district, going on at length about the dozens of domes and towers full of administrators collating information from all across the planet and the nearby worlds.

The stop-start nature of our conversations means we have to backtrack a lot so that we're all clear about what's going on, but I think I get it all in the end. There's a decommissioned ex-navy transport in orbit, a small vessel barely capable of warp travel, which will take us to Es'-tau and Brightsword. We will land, sign up for Brightsword's army and then keep out of trouble until it is time to strike. When the tau commander makes his final pre-invasion inspection, we hit hard and fast, shoot the bastard in the head and then leg it as quick as we can.

Coldwind assures us that in the mayhem and confusion we should be able to get away and into orbit without too much difficulty. I have my doubts. It was the same problem with Coritanorum – getting in was difficult enough, but it was getting out that nearly killed me. Midway through the afternoon, Coldwind returns us to our quarters and says that we have a few hours to make any final preparations before departing.

That evening just as the sun is dipping behind the tall domed buildings, Coldwind turns up yet again with the floating car to take us back to the space port.

'I've just had a thought,' Tanya says as we smoothly overtake a long tanker of some kind. 'What happens to you, Coldwind, when all this goes off? I mean, you won't be able to entirely deny any involvement with us.'

'Our story is that you are renegades, acting without authority,' the tau ambassador replies calmly. 'In the unfortunate event that I am somehow implicated I will of course support this story. Rather foolishly, I have trusted the evil humans, and O'var has paid the price.'

'So, you'll just look incompetent rather than treacherous?' I laugh harshly. 'That won't do your career much good.'

'If that comes to pass, it is almost certain that I will lose much prestige and rank,' Coldwind agrees with a nod, still seemingly at ease with the thought.

'However, my personal circumstances and career are secondary to the needs of the tau'va.'

'You would risk having your life ruined for this?' Tanya asks, leaning forward. 'This tau'va must be pretty important.'

'I certainly risk much for the tau'va, it is true,' answers Coldwind slowly. 'However, ask yourself this. Why do you all risk even more than I do, for your distant Emperor?'

Nobody replies, as we ponder this. I have the quick answer, though some would say it's avoiding the issue. I risk everything for the Emperor and mankind because it's better than any of the other options. I remember a preacher once, he came to the hive factories, and held a great mass. He wanted to bring together the different houses through the worship of the Emperor. It didn't work, the mass turned into a riot, then a battle, than a full scale trade war. I think he got shot by accident, though nobody wished him any harm really. Anyway, this preacher was extolling us to work for the Emperor, and to fight for the Emperor. He quoted from the Litanies of Faith, or perhaps some other holy book, I can't really remember, I was very young at the time. He said there were two types of people. There were those who worked and fought for mankind and the Emperor. They were the ones who dedicated themselves to an ideal bigger than them. They were the ones who would be gloried in the afterlife when the Emperor took them. Then there were the others, the leeches he called them, sucking life and blood from the rest of us. They had no purpose beyond themselves, and when they died there was only the Abyssal Chaos to greet them. It must have had an impression on me, though I didn't realise that until I was in the 13th Legion.

WE'RE ALL SHOCKED out of our thoughts when the front right-hand side of the groundcar explodes, sending silvery metal spinning in all directions and causing the vehicle to plough into the roadway, nearly spinning over and tossing us in all directions. I don't remember seeing a blast or missile, but I guess someone must have shot at us.

'What the frag?' I shout, jumping to my feet. I hear the ting of small arms fire rattling off the transport, and we all spill out of the carrying compartment to shelter behind the bulk of the ground car. I check out everyone to see if they're alright, but the padded seats and floor mean that none of us will have worse than bruises in a few hours.

'Where's it coming from?' shouts Tanya, scanning the buildings around us. There's a spire-like tower we were just passing, standing alone amongst the elegant tangle of roads and bridges. Behind us is a complex of interlocked domes around a central spherical hub, but with no visible windows. Further along the road is another building still being assembled. Grav-cranes hover over it, winching in large slabs of whatever material it is that the tau use.

'The construction site!' I snap, just as Tanya says the same, and I point. It's about three hundred metres away, with plenty of cover, yet open routes of escape in every direction. I hurl myself to my feet again and I'm about to start towards the building when Oriel grabs my robe and flings me bodily to the floor.

'You're a scribe, you stupid idiot!' he hisses. 'Not a bloody Space Marine!'

'Sorry, I forgot...' I apologise as more bullets rattle into the roadway. I glance around, nobody seems to have been hit. My heart is pounding; the suddenness of the attack galvanising my body into action. I have to fight hard against the urge to get myself a weapon and go on the offensive.

'Who do you think is attacking us?' the Colonel bellows at Coldwind.

'There are some fundamentalists who believe we are too tolerant of other species, particularly humans,' Coldwind replies, cowering underneath the shattered remnants of the ground car. 'The shas hunt them down when they can, but there are always one or two who refuse to see the wisdom of our policies.'

It's at this point that the shas, the fire warriors, choose to make their entrance. Judging by the speed they've got here, I guess they've been following us around all day. Not that unexpected considering Oriel is supposed to be a very important dignitary. I don't know where they come from, but suddenly five battle suits are landing on the roadway in front of us, screaming groundwards on their jetpacks. As they land, their feet gouge holes into the surface of the road, their knee joints and lower leg structure compacting smoothly to absorb the landing impact. No sooner have they arrived on their feet than they open fire. As the hovering cranes lift themselves out of the line of fire, salvoes of missiles erupt from shoulder-mounted pods on two of the suits. The other three leap forwards, powering away into the air with hissing bounds, their multiple weapons spitting bullets and plasma bolts into the half-built dome. Something erupts over our heads and a massive blast of energy sails between the advancing battle suits, its detonation sending a massive fountain of debris into the air. A shadow passes over us and I glance up.

It's a tau tank, gliding above the roadway, passing overhead. It's big, bigger than any grav-vehicle I've ever seen, though that's not many to be fair. Like the space ship we travelled on, it flattens and widens at the front, almost like a hammer head. The expanded front houses two weapons pods, one on each side just forward of what looks to be a cockpit, fitted with the same multi-barrelled cannons that I noticed on the battle suits. The guns track left and right, seeking targets. The back end, flanked by heavy engines which are tilted slightly downwards at the moment to push the whole thing slowly forwards, is much blockier, topped by a turret with an offset cannon. The gun itself is huge, easily three or four metres long, and blocky. As it passes us by, the whine of its engines making my ears ring, the tank opens fire again, spitting a ball of energy into the target zone, its aim slightly adjusted from the previous shot.

'I think we should get out of here,' mumbles Strelli, glancing back along the road. Traffic from behind us has slowly started to snarl up, and many of the vehicles have settled on to the ground, out of the way of the advancing tank, providing cover for us to escape. I see tau abandoning their vehicles and fleeing away from the fight.

I look around and see the air caste dome nearby, and the shape of a craft lifting up into the air a short distance away.

'We're within walking distance of the space port. We should just head for the shuttle!' I say to the others, and Oriel nods.

'Yes, once we're there, Coldwind can get us clearance to leave and we can get out of here with the minimum of fuss,' the inquisitor agrees.

'Yes, they will send another vehicle for you soon,' Coldwind agrees. 'It may be wiser to avoid any escalation of the situation. Close scrutiny of your presence here would be undesirable.

'We can't carry all of our gear,' Strelli points out, nodding to the pile of bags and chests now spilled from the storage compartment of the wrecked groundcar.

'We don't need it any more,' I argue. 'Once we're out of here, our cover story changes and we have to dump it all anyway.'

'Very well, double back. The less official attention we get, the better,' Oriel says quickly, running past us in a stooped stance, keeping the smouldering wreck of the ground car between him and any attackers. We follow swiftly, and within a couple of minutes are out of the area and on our own, hidden in the shadows under a taut, blue awning that extends for several hundred metres from the side of one of the nearby domes.

'I must apologise for this attack,' Coldwind says to us as we catch our breath, his composure regained. 'I hope this does not compromise the mission any more than necessary.'

'Just get us to the space port and to our ship,' snaps Oriel, stalking away.

WE HEAD TO the shuttle, on foot this time, heading down fairly empty backstreets after Coldwind. The few tau we see give us odd looks, but we try to look as if we're out for a stroll rather than fleeing for our lives, and most of them only give us a glance before going past. Coldwind uses his position of authority to get us past the fire warrior security at the space port without any questions, but it's only once we're on the shuttle heading for orbit that we begin to relax a little.

Coldwind isn't with us; he'll be meeting us again at Es'tau. The ambassador is travelling on his own vessel, as it would appear very strange if he were to arrive there on a mercenary transport, so we're completely free to talk about him while he's not here.

'Well, the tau didn't take their time rescuing us,' Strelli says, slouching comfortably in his padded leather seat.

'I would like to know how they knew where we would be,' Moerck says, looking at Oriel. 'And if they knew that, what else might they have found out?'

'Imperial Commander Oriel has been under fire warrior protection since he first landed,' the Colonel says scornfully. 'If you had paid more attention, you would have noticed the transport craft that was shadowing us for the last two days, a few hundred metres up and about a kilometre behind us. But you were all too busy looking at the buildings and the tau.'

'I have never heard of tau dissidents before,' states Oriel, deep in thought. 'If such radicals did exist, then the whole subterfuge with Brightsword would be entirely unnecessary. No, Coldwind was lying to us about that, I could sense it. I also think Coldwind was anticipating the attack. He didn't seem to be as scared about it as you'd expect a non-combatant to be.'

'Perhaps he's just brave for his caste?' suggests Tanya, earning herself a withering look from Oriel.

'No, there's more going on here than we bargained for,' the inquisitor says slowly. 'The car was hit with the first shot, but in such a way that none of us were injured. After that, the shooting was pretty poor. If it was a shot at all. Did anyone see a muzzle flash before we were hit, or a rocket or shell?'

We all shake our heads.

'No, this seems to be orchestrated to me,' the inquisitor continues. 'He either thinks we are more stupid than we are, which I don't believe for a moment, or he's playing some kind of game which I don't quite understand yet.'

'Maybe it's part of his own cover story, so that he can explain why we left in such a hurry,' muses Tanya, and we all look at her in amazement. Her explanation does make some sense. 'Well, I know all about distractions, lures and false trails, so don't give me that funny look. There's more to being a sniper than just aiming straight,' she says petulantly, turning her head away to look out of the shuttle window.

'Well, whether it was for our benefit or his, I don't know what Coldwind is playing at, or what purpose the attack serves,' Oriel says, unbuckling his safety harness and standing up, 'but from now on, keep a close eye on our friendly ambassador.'

The inquisitor walks out into the front chamber, followed by the Colonel.

'I wouldn't trust the slimy cretin as far as I could throw him,' agrees Trost with a sneer.

'There is no such thing as a trustworthy alien,' Moerck says emphatically. We all nod in agreement.

THE CLUTTERED HOLD rumbled and rattled in time with the pulsing engines located nearby. A light strip flickered into life with an erratic buzzing, shedding a yellow glow across the stacked crates and metal boxes. Oriel strode through the open doorway, glancing back into the corridor briefly before closing the door. He walked quickly through the maze of piled cargo before entering a more open space near the centre of the hold.

'Where are you?' he asked, his voice low.

'I am in prayer, inquisitor,' a deep voice rumbled back from the gloom.

'This will be my last chance to talk to you. Come out where I can see you,' he told the hidden figure.

'Have you no respect for my traditions, inquisitor?' the deep voice answered.

'You have done little else but pray on this journey, Dionis, I am sure the Emperor will forgive this short interruption,' Oriel responded evenly, sitting down on a smaller carton.

A tall, broad figure emerged from the shadows, swathed in an armless, open-fronted robe, a hooded cowl over his face. The man was very large and towered over the inquisitor. His exposed arms and shoulders were corded with thick muscle, rope-like veins pulsing beneath his deeply tanned skin. Across his expansive chest muscles were numerous scar lines which cut across an ornate tattoo of a double-headed eagle with its wings spread. The face inside the cowl was similarly broad and square-jawed, the lips set in a hard line.

'What else have you to tell me, inquisitor?' the man asked, no hint of deference in his voice.

'We are underway again, heading for Es'tau and the final stage of the mission,' Oriel told him, looking up at the giant.

'This much I have already observed, inquisitor,' he answered curtly.

'I thought you would have,' Oriel replied quietly. 'I want to check one last time that everything is understood.'

'Rest at ease, inquisitor,' Dionis told Oriel, crossing his thick arms across his chest. 'I know that I am to act only when called upon by you. I know that I am to remain covert until that time, or until we return to the Emperor's realms if my prowess is not needed. I also know that it is a dangerous game that you play, and more likely than not I will be called upon to fight.'

'I understand this is not the dignified and glorious methods of battle you are familiar with, and I thank you for your patience, Dionis,' Oriel said smoothly. 'You understand why I wish it to be this way.'

'I understood that well when I swore my oaths of obedience,' acknowledged Dionis. 'I will start my battle-prayers and the rites of honour. I shall also pray for you, inquisitor, that you do not have need of me even as I pray for the battle I have been born to fight.'

'Pray for us all, Dionis,' Oriel whispered, turning his gaze away. 'Pray for us all.'

SIX
ES'TAU

+++The playing pieces are ready for the end game+++

+++Then let us make our final moves+++

LOOKING OUT OF the shuttle window as we descend towards Es'tau, I see that the planet is mostly desert. Ochre-coloured sands stretch as far as the eye can see once we're below the cloud layer. I see a blob of buildings far below us and guess that must be where we're heading, but it's still indistinct when the Colonel calls over the internal comm for us to unstrap and get our kit together. I cast one last glance out of the opposite port, wondering if this will be the last world I'll ever see.

Our reception on Es'tau is certainly not as ceremonial as the one on Me'lek, but no less military. That's to be expected, since we're now just another band of Imperial renegade mercenaries to them, rather than visiting officials. Fire warriors are everywhere, carrying their carbines and rifles and obviously not just for show. These ones wear a dark blue and grey camouflaged uniform, with red identification markings on their chests.

'Sarcassa is a night world,' Schaeffer murmurs to me as we pass by a squad. 'They are obviously almost ready to depart.'

Indeed, several tau craft sit on the landing apron, squads of fire warriors marching on board. I see three of the tanks, Hammerheads the Colonel calls them, gliding slowly on to a massive transport ship. The tau don't seem to pay us any more attention than anyone else around, so obviously our first appearances are convincing.

We're dressed in a ragtag collection of old uniforms, armed with a variety of different weapons. I've got an autogun and an old revolver, Tanya has her sniper rifle, Oriel and the Colonel carry stub pistols and chainswords, while the rest have lasguns. We've got an assortment of other bits and pieces like a few frag and smoke grenades, plus Trost has a pack full of demolition charges and fuses. A tau warrior sees us and holds up a hand to stop us.

'Warriors?' he asks, face hidden behind the viewing lenses of his helm, his strangely-accented voice emitted through a hidden speaker.

'Yes,' Oriel replies. 'Is there a problem, shas'vre?'

'All warriors checked,' the shas fighter replies, pointing to a temporary-looking dome beside the main space port complex.

'We have to go in there?' the Colonel asks, looking over towards the checking centre.

'Yes. All warriors checked,' the shas'vre repeats, more angrily this time, thrusting his finger towards the building.

'Alright, we're going,' Oriel placates him, giving us the nod to change course.

'What's going on?' I ask the Colonel as we make our way across the black-surfaced landing pad.

'I am not sure,' he replies, glancing around at all the fire warriors in the area. 'Maybe Brightsword has got wind of something, I do not know.'

As we make our way to the building the fire warrior indicated, I can see another group entering just in front of us. The mercenaries are a mix of races, mostly humans but with a couple of lanky, blue-skinned creatures with high crests over their heads and ridges down the centre of their faces. Inside the building is fairly open, with just a couple of archways to other rooms and a single door out on the opposite side.

Oriel tells us to wait and makes his way over to a small table to one side, behind which is sat a tau. Judging from his build and robes I'd say he was water caste, an observation which is proved correct when he pulls a sheaf of transparent sheets from a bag beside the table and begins writing.

He talks to the other sellswords first for a few minutes before directing them through into one of the side rooms, and then turns his attention to Oriel, who speaks at some length with him, the pair of them occasionally looking over in our direction.

I fidget nervously as we wait, keeping my gaze on the floor, trying not to catch the eye of the fire warriors passing through and stationed at the archways. I guess we're signing on for Brightsword's army. I hope Oriel's cover story is good, and that Coldwind has helped us out behind the scenes. I can't imagine Brightsword being too trusting at the moment, after all he's about to launch a major invasion and he must have some idea that not everyone in the Tau Empire is giving him their full support.

I snap out of my thoughts when Oriel comes back to us.

'Well, we've joined up,' he tells us with a grim smile. 'Coldwind's references smoothed the whole thing admirably. We should get out of here though and keep a low profile.'

As we turn to the exit we see three smaller figures standing close to the doorway.

'What the hell is this?' growls Trost uneasily.

'Psykers,' Oriel replies quietly, teeth gritted. 'Stay calm, we'll be fine.'

As we get closer I see that the figures are small aliens, nearly naked but for short skirts, grey-skinned with wide yellow eyes and completely devoid of hair. They look at us as we approach. I eye them back evilly.

'Think of something simple, something easy to remember,' I hear Oriel say. 'Like an old nursery rhyme, or a gun drill, or a marching chant. Repeat that in your head, just keep thinking it over and over again.'

As we pass between the aliens my skin crawls. I probably imagine it, but I swear I can feel something poking around in my head, like clawed hands turning my mind over and having a look. The sickening feeling carries on.

'Don't think about them, it will make it easier for them to read your mind,' warns Oriel. I try to remember the house anthem, but only get part way through the third verse, so I start again. That's when events catch up with me and I have to try hard not to stop dead in my tracks. It sounded just like Oriel was whispering in my ear, both times he spoke, but he's at least five paces ahead of me, in front of the others. He's a thaumist, just like these aliens!

'Keep singing that anthem, Kage,' Oriel's mind-voice tells me. 'I'll explain later, just don't think about me!'

I try to put all thoughts of Oriel and psykers from my mind and go over the lasgun maintenance drill I was taught back when I joined up. I used to pass hours going over and over that drill when I was in prison. I reckon I could do it with my eyes closed now. As I pass through the doorway, I try hard not to glance over my shoulder. Just ahead, Trost growls at one of the aliens, making it flinch, bringing a wolfish smile to his face. Gone is the cold-blooded mass murderer, now I think he enjoys it more than he's ever done. I'm not sure which one I find scarier.

Once we're outside, I see that this city is much less developed than the Me'lek capital. There are no sky-roads, no soaring towers, just many more low domes and spheres, all in a very regular radial pattern around the space port. Planned by a more military mind, is my first impression.

Oriel leads us left along the road outside the starship terminal, taking us towards one of the boulevards stretching outwards from the central hub created by the space port. None of us say anything as we walk for a couple of minutes, all of us wary of the mind-reading aliens we've just left behind.

'Okay, we're far enough away now,' Oriel tells us, glancing around to make sure there are no tau close by. He stops us at a junction with one of the radial roads, which is deserted at the moment.

The city seems very quiet, but perhaps that's just because there aren't many tau here who aren't fire caste, and they're all busy preparing for their invasion, I reckon. 'We need to contact Coldwind as soon as we can, and make a final survey of the battle dome to see if anything has changed.'

'Don't try and avoid the fact that you're a damned witch,' I snarl at the inquisitor. 'You've been messing with my head, haven't you?'

'I wouldn't know where to start,' he sneers back.

'What's this?' Tanya asks, and the others look accusingly at Oriel, except the Colonel who glares at me.

'He's a fraggin' psyker, that's what,' I hiss, pointing at the inquisitor. 'I bet he's been inside all of our heads.'

'This is none of your concern,' Oriel says sternly. 'You are in no position to judge me. Especially you, Kage, of everyone here. Others far more worthy have done so and declared me pure and strong. Do not forget that I am an agent of the Emperor's Holy Orders of Inquisition, and not answerable to the likes of you. If I have gifts that are useful to my vocation, I will use them. How do you think I knew El'savon could speak Gothic? How do you think I ensured our privacy aboard his ship? How do you think I know Coldwind was expecting us to be attacked, or that he's been hiding something ever since we met? If it wasn't for the protection I just gave you all, we would have never got past the telepaths. I am not prepared to discuss this matter.'

We look at each other and then back at Oriel, defiance in our eyes.

'We're on a Tau world, in Tau space,' Trost points out. 'All your authority counts for nothing here. What's to stop us just walking over to the next tau and turning you over to them. Damn, we could just as well be real mercenaries.'

'How dare you consider such a thing!' barks Moerck, stepping over to stand beside the Colonel. 'Any more talk like that, soldier, and I will kill you myself.'

'Looks like five against three, not too good odds,' Strelli laughs coldly.

'Four against four, actually,' I tell them, squaring off against Trost. 'I don't care much for mind-fraggers like Oriel, in fact I'd rather they were all dead. But I came here to kill an enemy of the Emperor and that's what we're gonna do. Any one of you want to dispute that with me, they're quite welcome to step up right now and give it their best shot.

'Any of you think you can take down Last Chance? What about you, Flyboy? Come on, Demolition Man, you've been wanting to do this ever since I put you on your backside that first day of training.'

No one moves. It's a stand-off, neither side ready to back down. We glare at each other, the tension thick enough to cut with a bayonet. It's the Colonel who breaks the deadlock.

'We should move on,' he says looking around. 'If the tau get suspicious we will all end up dead. Remember, we are just a mercenary company, and we need to act like it. Anything out of the ordinary might get noticed, and Brightsword doesn't seem to be taking any chances, so be careful.'

Reminded that we're in up to our necks together on this one, we grudgingly put aside our differences, warily stepping away from each other.

'What next then?' I ask.

'All the mercenaries can be found in the alien quarter,' the Colonel replies.

'Well, let's get something to eat,' suggests Tanya. 'And see what the locals are like.'

WE FIND THE alien quarter easily enough. It's the one with all the aliens in it. Oriel seems to know the layout of the area and it was only a few minutes' walk from the space port.

I've never seen so many freaky things in my life, and I've been around a bit. There are tall ones, short ones, fat ones, hairy ones, spiky little guys, things with more arms and eyes than is entirely necessary for any kind of lifeform. And all of them living together in the same part of the city. Since we're not far from the space port, I guess all the off-worlders have been gathering in this place over a few years, making it a real home from home.

The buildings are still tau construction, but heavily adapted, decorated and adorned by the local population. Banners and streamers flutter from food shop fronts, religious-looking icons on tall poles are stuck into the ground in front of other buildings. As we pass one in particular there's an unpleasant charnel house smell. We look at the building and see it's daubed in savage-looking alien runes and hurry on, not wanting to know what goes on inside. Fire smoke from different types of wood fills the air with a mix of sweet and acrid scents, which blend into each other to create a disturbing stench. There's sand and dust everywhere as well, blown in from the surrounding desert, and combined with the noise, smell and heat makes me feel sick.

There are market stalls selling anything and everything from clothes to guns and grenades. We take a look at one of the arms traders, a small green guy with a scaly skin and pale yellow eyes, who deftly picks through his wares with three-fingered hands.

'Interested in guns, yes?' he asks us as we stop next to his stand. His voice is kind of scratchy, more of a hiss than anything else. 'Lots of guns for brave fighters.'

He's right, there are lots of guns, and most of them seem to be Imperial in origin. There's lasguns, autoguns, a couple of bolters, some knives, a few grenades, plus what was once obviously an officer's power sword. I pick it up, and read the inscription on the hilt.

'Colonel Verand, 21st Hadrian Guard,' I tell the others, putting the sword down again. 'I guess he ran into some bad luck.'

'What's this one?' Quidlon asks, pointing at a bizarre pistol-shaped armament which looks more like it was grown than built. It's green and veiny, shining slickly in the bright light.

'Kathap pistol, you like?' the store owner says, picking it up and offering it to Quidlon. He reaches out for it, but Moerck's hand clamps down around his wrist.

'You do not want to touch that,' he warns the short man, dragging his arm away. 'It is not consecrated by the machine god. Its taint will spread to your other weapons. Best to leave it be.'

'Aah, machine god is it?' the gun-runner butts in. 'You humans all same. You idea that there be machine god, you make bad weapons.'

'You don't seem to be shy of a few,' Strelli argues, indicating the assorted Imperial weapons.

'That because only cheap humans buy bad work like this,' the dealer smiles. 'Proper fighters want proper weapons.'

'I'll give you proper fighters,' I snarl, taking a step towards the merchant, who hisses in fear and turns to scurry away.

'Leave him alone, Last Chance,' the Colonel says sternly, and I back off.

Nobody comments that we're using our mission names again. It seems natural now that we're allowed to be soldiers once more. That's good, it was why I did it. We may be undercover here, but we're a lot more natural when it comes to being fighters than we are at being an Imperial commander and his entourage. It'll hopefully make things easier than it was back on the ship and on Me'lek.

'Where's a good place to drink?' Oriel asks the arms dealer, proffering a small coin delved from one of his pockets.

'Two streets on, look for the skulls,' the green alien replies, hesitantly taking the money, glancing up at me as it does so. He points to show us the way and then impatiently waves us away.

THE DRINKING HOLE isn't hard to find. Like the dealer said, just look for the skulls. It's a small tau dome with the front of the bottom level missing, open to the street. Arranged over this is a line of spikes with skulls impaled on them, of different species. I recognise human, ork, a couple of tyranid creatures, a slender one that I guess to be eldar, plus four others which aren't familiar.

'Nice place,' mutters Tanya, eyeing the skulls.

'We need to maintain the masquerade. If we start acting suspiciously, someone may notice. If this is where mercenaries drink, it's where we'll drink,' Oriel tells us quietly before stepping into the shade inside.

There's a small counter just off the street with a burly-looking creature sat behind it. It's squat, its head sunk deep beneath its broad shoulders, its three beady eyes peering at us from beneath a heavy brow. Thick-fingered alien hands beckon us over.

'No weapons inside,' the alien growls, standing up and dragging a crate from a pile behind it. 'In here till you leave.'

'You all seem to speak Gothic quite well,' Strelli remarks, placing his lasgun carefully in the crate.

'You humans speak nothing else, and humans are troublemakers,' the security thing grunts back as we hand over our guns and knives.

'Nice to know we're welcome,' Tanya says sarcastically as we enter the main room.

The bar is quite dark, the few red lamps around the wall do little to light the circular room. A round bar in the centre, similarly lit, appears like a red island in a sea of smoky darkness. There are tables and chairs filling the rest of the space, of assorted shapes and heights. Most of them are occupied. Many sets of eyes, not all of them in the regular pair, regard us as we walk in. I see more of the same species as the door warden gathered around a circular table to my right, arguing heavily with each other in guttural grunts. Most of the other aliens I don't recognise.

'What are they?' Trost whispers to Oriel, looking over at a pair of diminutive creatures swathed in rags in one of the darkest areas. Small, clawed hands clasp their drinks tightly, long snouts twitching in our direction. I catch the hint of a tail whipping nervously under their table.

'Hrud,' the inquisitor replies. 'Scavengers and tunnel-dwellers for the most part, you'll find them all over the galaxy, though never in large numbers. They're pretty much parasites, if you ask me.'

'What about those?' I ask next, indicating three multi-limbed creatures splayed on a bench along one side of the bar. They have no heads, but clusters of eye-like organs wave towards us, like grass in a breeze. They have no arms or legs, just a set of six tentacle limbs which I guess must serve them for both purposes.

Oriel thinks for a moment before replying.

'I've never seen one before, but they match the description of galgs,' he tells me as we stop by the drinks counter. 'I think their world was conquered by the tau a few centuries ago. They're not particularly warlike as far as I remember, and not too advanced technically either.'

'Emperor on his holy throne!' curses Tanya quietly. We all look at her with surprise and she surreptitiously nods towards the far side of the room. There, as unmistakable as my own face, sits a group of bloody orks. Five of them in fact, the burly greenskins ignoring us, concentrating instead on two of their number who are having some kind of contest. Born warriors, I've fought orks on a couple of occasions, and barely lived to tell the tale. They're big, though not massive, with powerful muscles and an ability to soak up injury and pain like nothing else I've seen.

The two orks have their hands locked behind each other's thick necks, and are grunting to each other in their crude language. It's like they're counting or something. When they reach three, they smash their heads together, with a crack I can hear across the room. They all burst into raucous laughter, grabbing jugs of thick-looking drink from the table and taking large swigs.

'Weak or strong drink?' says the bartender, dragging our attention away from the head-butting contest.

The owner is a gangly alien, with dark blue skin and no fat at all, just wiry sinews and taut muscle. Its face is pretty much one big mouth, with a single vertical slit for a nose and tiny white eyes.

Oriel replies in some gibberish language that sounds like coughs and splutters, gesturing for us to sit down at a nearby table. He joins us after a short conversation with the barkeep.

'We can have rooms here on the upper level,' he tells us. 'I don't want to stay on the shuttle if we have to go through a mind screen every time we go in and out of the space port.'

'Where did you learn to talk like that?' Trost asks, looking at the bartender. Oriel just gives him a patronising look, but Trost still doesn't get it.

'He's an inquisitor,' Tanya explains slowly, keeping her voice low. Trost gives a grunt, not entirely satisfied, and slouches back further in his chair.

The alien barman bring us over our drinks, eight large glasses of frothing blackness. I take a cautious sip first, the others waiting to see if I drop dead on the spot. I give them the all clear with a grin.

'It's just like ale, really,' I tell them, taking another mouthful. It's actually quite refreshing after the heat outside. The others start on their drinks, Quidlon giving an appreciative nod, Strelli drinking half of his in one long draught.

'Hey,' I say to the others when I realise what's just happened. 'How come I've become the official food tester? Why doesn't one of you eat or drink something before me for a change?'

'Because if you die, we don't have to change the mission plan,' Strelli points out. 'All of us have specific jobs to do. You're just hanging around to provide a bit of firepower.'

I'm about to give him an angry reply but stop short. He's got a point. We have Flyboy, Demolition Man, Sharpshooter, Brains. I'm just Last Chance; all I do is survive.

'So what do we do between now and the mission?' Tanya asks, wiping some froth from her top lip.

'Keep quiet, and don't attract any attention, strictly low profile activity,' Oriel answers, toying with his glass. 'This is the part that has the greatest chance of going wrong. I don't know how Coldwind is going to contact me. I don't know when Brightsword is going to do his inspection, or if he's done it already and left. I don't know exactly how tight security is going to be while he's back. The last thing we need is any trouble, so keep your lips tight and your eyes and ears open.'

With this in mind, we hunker down and try to look the other way as the orks leave their table and stride past. They dart us a few glances, joking with each other in their own guttural tongue, but nothing else happens. I breathe a bit easier knowing that they've left.

'You said the tau conquered these galg things?' asks Tanya, looking over at the blobby aliens.

'Conquered is not really the right word,' Oriel replies thoughtfully. 'Coerced them might be a bit better. You see, the tau'va, the greater good, isn't really a religious thing just for them. They believe it's a common destiny across the galaxy, and includes everyone. The tau would much rather prefer other races as allies, or really servants to be honest, than enemies. You see, they're not fighting a war against anyone really, but there are lots of races in their way that they need to deal with.'

'Sending an invasion fleet seems to be an odd way of not fighting a war,' says Strelli, and I nod in agreement.

'Well, for a start, that's Brightsword being overzealous,' counters Oriel, taking another sip of his drink. 'We sometimes have the same problem with Imperial commanders taking it on themselves to pick a fight with some other world which we don't need to fight just yet. Unlike the tau, we can remove them without worrying that it damages our beliefs. After all, the Emperor is infallible, not his servants.'

'Does that include inquisitors?' Trost asks slyly.

Oriel glares at him. 'We were talking about the tau, though, not mankind. The tau arrive at your world, with a fleet, tanks, attack craft, fire warriors and battle suits, and they ask if you want to join in their quest to achieve the greater good. Well, that's the way I think it happened with the galgs. The galgs were clever enough to say yes, but there are some records that show what happens to those worlds who say no. Sooner or later they either say yes, with their cities burning and their soldiers rotting in their open graves, or are in no position to say anything at all.'

'I guess there must be a lot of resentment then, all those conquered races, the tau obviously in charge, not everyone's going to be happy with that,' suggests Quidlon, looking around the tavern.

'Unfortunately, that isn't usually the case,' Oriel replies with a shake of his head. 'The tau are very magnanimous in victory. Those races that become a part of the Tau Empire aren't slaves, although they certainly aren't in charge either, as you say. The tau find out what they are able to do and then put them to good use. They don't always colonise the worlds they've conquered either, sometimes they just want to remove a strategic threat. As you've probably noticed, they favour very hot, dry worlds and there's usually not much competition in that regard.'

'Until they ran into mankind,' adds the Colonel. 'We can live on tau worlds just as well as they can, and occasionally the explorators will investigate a world at the same time as the tau colony fleet arrives. It does not always end in bloodshed, but frequently does.'

I'm about to add something when Moerck's look distracts me. I have my back to the door, sitting opposite him, and turn around to see what he is staring at. There is a small group at the door, humanoid in shape, talking with the guard.

'What's up?' I ask the ex-commissar.

'Traitors,' he says grimly, nodding back towards the outside. I look again and see that it's true: the newcomers are humans. As they enter, I can make them out better. Like us, they are wearing an assortment of different clothes, some of them obviously alien-made, and each of them wears a band of white, either as a bandanna, armband or around their waists. I've seen their kind before, professional mercenaries who'll sell to the highest bidder regardless of what they look like or who they have to fight. I've fought against them and I've fought alongside them, and I didn't like it either way.

They give us nods as they walk past into the bar, but there's an angry murmuring from our left. Looking that way, I see a group of tarellians walking in our direction. I saw tarellians on Epsion Octarius. Well, their corpses at least. Narrow-waisted and broad shouldered, the tarellians are a bit shorter than most people, with long canine-like faces, which is why we call them dog soldiers. There's six of them, and they growl to each other menacingly.

One of them steps forward from the group and snarls something at us in Tarellian. We look at Oriel, who shrugs and looks over at the bartender, saying something in the language he used earlier.

The barkeeper points at us, replying quickly, and then at the door. Oriel says something back, and the owner shakes his head.

'The tarellians say that we have to leave. They don't like us drinking here,' Oriel translates.

'I heard him,' says one of the mercenaries, who have stopped next to our table and are glaring at the tarellians. He makes a kind of barking noise at the aliens, adding emphasis by tapping himself on the chest. This doesn't please the tarellians, who snarl and bark something back.

'Oh, frag this,' I say, getting to my feet and walking over to the tarellian leader. I hear Oriel call my name but ignore him. The aliens gather round me, snapping their jaws, but I ignore the rest and focus on the spokesman. 'If you want to be able to ever drink again, leave now,' I say to the soldier, smiling. He looks over at the bartender, who gives a quick translation. The tarellian peers up at me, showing his long teeth. One way or another, these tarellians have got a real problem with us and I don't figure on them letting us just walk out of here.

If I remember my legends correctly, we virus-bombed a few of their worlds back when the Emperor was leading the Great Crusade. Guess they still haven't got over that after ten thousand years. The tarellian is snarling something to the barkeeper still, jabbing a clawed finger into my chest as he does so.

By the Emperor, this is the slowest-starting bar brawl I've ever been in and it's a while since I had a good fight, so I ball my fist and smash the stupid alien straight across the jaw, knocking him backwards into a table. 'One for the Emperor!' I spit, spinning on the spot and driving my boot into the stomach of another dog soldier.

As the tarellians jump on me, the other Last Chancers pile in, as well as the human mercenaries. The rest of the bar seems against us, though, as all manner of things crawl and jump out of the darkness. A tarellian tries to grab my throat but I sway back out of reach. As it steps forward, I take a stride as well, driving my knee into its ribs. I get it into a headlock, but something hits me in the back of my neck, causing me to lose my grip. Turning, I see one of the galgs launch itself at me, flailing with its limbs at my face. I react just in time, grabbing it in mid jump and spinning, hurling it across the room.

A tarellian tries to take my head off with a chair, but I duck, seeing Moerck hurling another of the dog soldiers bodily across the bar counter. Grinning like a fool, I drive my elbow into the tarellian's face and kick the chair out of its hands. It lunges at me, jaw snapping, and I jump to one side, rolling across a table. I land on my feet the other side, just as the galg recovers and propels itself towards me. I snatch up a stool and swing it, connecting heavily with the galg and sending it hurtling back again. A glass crashes across the back of my head, stunning me for a second. A green-scaled alien with a frog face and long arms swings at me, backhanding me across the chest and knocking the breath out of my lungs. I block the next attack with my arm, grabbing the thing's wrist and tossing it over my hip on to the table. I drive my fist towards its face but it rolls out of the way and my knuckles crash painfully into the unvarnished wood.

A tarellian kicks a chair at me, which I jump over, landing awkwardly as I bang my hip against the table. The tarellian snarls something and tries to grab my throat, but I bat its hand away and step back. It makes another lunge and I duck, spinning on my heel to deliver a sweeping kick to the tarellian's right knee and knocking it from its feet. There's no time to follow up though, as the frog-face is back on its feet, its webbed hands grabbing my arm and swinging me into an upturned bench, crashing me to the ground. I kick out hard, feeling my boot connect with something soft, and the creature staggers back, howling like mad. I take the quick break in fighting to look around.

Moerck is bashing a tarellian repeatedly against the wall, a galg latched onto his back, trying to wrap its tentacles around his throat. I see the Colonel deliver a neck-breaking punch to another greenie, smashing it into a back flip. Oriel is struggling with another tarellian: he has its neck in a lock, and is trying to smash its head against the bar. Tanya and a spiny-headed thing roll across the floor, each other's throats in their hands. I can't see Trost or Strelli, the press of bodies is too tight. One of the mercenaries is clubbing a tarellian on the floor with a stool, shouting something I can't understand. A second lies draped over a table, blood dribbling from a cut to his forehead. The two hrud are hiding in the shadows, hissing at each other in their strange language and pointing in my direction. It's then that I realise just how outnumbered we are. It's pretty much us against the whole bar.

The tarellian on the floor springs to its feet and charges me, driving its shoulder into my gut and slamming us both to the ground. I defend myself with my arms as it flails at my head with its fists, and then head butt it on the end of the snout, causing the dog soldier to recoil in pain. I drive my fist into its face, cracking it just below the right eye and forcing it back far enough to give me space to get to my feet.

Something lands on the bar, screeching like a bird of prey. Crouched on the counter, I can see that it's long-limbed and rangy. Its skin is a greenish-grey hue, patterned with body paint in zigzags and jagged lines. It doesn't appear to be wearing clothes as such, just a tight harness with various pouches and trinkets attached. Its face is beak-like and orange and red spines splay angrily from the back of its head. It puts its head back and shrieks across the bar, a piercing noise which causes everyone to pause for a moment. Unleashing the power of its whipcord muscles, the alien pounces a good five metres across the room, landing on the back of the creature strangling Tanya.

More of them appear, bounding swiftly from table to table, their long arms swinging as they join the fight. Their speed is amazing, and the way they hurl themselves around, you'd think they were built out of springs. One leaps long and high, rebounding off the wall and spearing into a tarellian. I see the first one wind up for a punch, its long arm swinging around in a wide arc before catching another tarellian full across the head and hurling it through the air to crash down through a table.

I redouble my own efforts, grabbing the face of one of the scaly green things and driving my knee up into its gut and then again into its chest. Dropping the frog-thing to the floor with a thud, I sprint across the bar, picking up the splintered remnants of a chair and bringing it full force onto one of the tarellians, smashing it clear of the human mercenary. The others are fighting back hard as well.

Put off by our surprise reinforcements, the tarellians and other aliens break off, heading for the door. Some of them stop on the threshold and turn to face us, calling out taunts and jibes in whatever language they're speaking. The quill-headed aliens all put their heads back and begin screeching, the sound filling the room and deafening to hear, putting the others to flight.

I stand there panting, leaning on my knees, and one of the aliens walks over to me in a low, sloping stoop.

'Well, that was fun,' I say to myself, standing up straight and meeting the gaze of the approaching creature.

'Yes, it was,' it replies to my amazement, in strangely good Gothic for something that looks so feral. 'But there's no profit in it.'

OUR UNLOOKED-FOR allies are kroot, an entire race of sellswords, most of them working for the tau. There are several hundred of them on

Es'tau, in the employ of Commander Brightsword. They're organised into family groups which Oriel calls kindreds, and the one that came to our rescue is led by a kroot called Orak. There are thirty or so of them, and Orak invites us back to their camp after the fight in the bar. Oriel accepts, obviously he thinks that a refusal might displease our new-found allies and attract more unwanted attention, and we follow the tall, gangly aliens through the streets of the city.

On our way out we picked up our weapons, and I note the long rifles and power cartridge bandoleers that all the kroot carry. Although they look like guns, the longrifles also have lengthy stocks carved into vicious-looking blades, and curved bayonet-like attachments under the barrels.

The kroot walk easily and confidently through the throng in the streets, their rangy legs carrying them along quickly and effortlessly until I'm panting in the heat to keep up. They chatter to each other with clicks and whistles, and the crowds part before them to get out of their way.

A hrud bustles up to Orak and tries to sell him a jar of something. The kroot isn't interested, and as the exchange continues it seems to get more heated. Orak's quills quiver more and more, and with a final angry hiss, they stand out like spikes, a fearsome crest which sends the hrud scurrying into the gathering gloom.

'Problem?' I ask the kroot leader, who looks at me, his quills lowering again.

'Bad haggling,' Orak replies, clicking his beak, laughing I suspect. 'It was new here, it will learn.'

'So how long have you been a mercenary?' I ask as I half-jog alongside the tall alien, puffing to keep up, the arid air turning my mouth dry.

'All my life, of course,' Orak answers. 'I did not fight until I came of age, but always have been a fighter for the Tau empire. How long have you been fighting?'

'All my life as well,' I reply after a moment's thought. 'But for myself, never for anyone else.'

'Not even for family?' the Kroot asks, quills shaking in surprise.

'Not for a long time,' I tell him quietly. We carry on walking through the street as the sun dips towards the horizon, turning into a large, deep red disk just above the domes.

'You will be fighting for O'var?' Orak says after a while.

'When he's in battle, I'll be fighting for sure,' I reply, trying to think how to change the subject. 'Is your camp far?'

'No,' Orak answers abruptly. 'Why did you start the fight in the bar?'

'Someone was going to,' I tell him with a lopsided grin. 'I figured it'd be better if one of us did, than one of them. Always pays to get the jump on the other guy.'

'That makes sense,' Orak agrees. 'Still, it was a brave or stupid thing to do. If we had not come to your aid, they might have killed you.'

'It was just a bar fight. It would never have got that serious,' I say with a shake of my head.

'You forget, humans are despised by most races here,' the kroot disagrees, turning down a smaller street leading off the main thoroughfare. 'Nobody would have missed you.'

'Why such bad feeling?' I ask, wondering what we could have done that is so upsetting.

'You humans are everywhere, you spread across the stars like a swarm,' Orak tells me, with no hint of embarrassment. 'You invade worlds which are not yours, you are governed by fear and superstition.'

'We are led by a god, we have a divine right to conquer the galaxy,' I protest, earning more clicking laughter from the kroot leader. 'It is mankind's destiny to rule the stars, the Emperor has told us so.'

'Driven by fear and superstition, even worse than the tau and the tau'va,' the kroot says, his voice suggesting good humour rather than distaste.

'So what do you believe in?' I ask, wondering what makes the kroot think he's got all the answers.

'Change,' he says, looking at me with his piercing dark eyes. 'As we learn from our ancestors, we change and adapt. We learn from our prey and grow stronger. The future is uncertain, to stagnate is to die.'

'You worship change?' I ask incredulously.

'No, human,' he says, showing signs of irritation again. 'Unlike your kind, we simply accept it.'

As the stars begin to appear in the sky, the flames of the bonfire stretch higher into the air. We're seated outside a half-finished dome with Orak and his kindred, and I watch the flames crackling on the great pyre. Huge steaming chunks of meat on sharpened poles hiss and spit within the fire, bringing the smell of cooking flesh and smouldering fat.

I'm seated next to Oriel, who has been watching the kroot closely since our encounter.

'What do you know of these guys?' I ask him when we've got a bit of space to talk privately.

'Not too much, except that they are exceptional close combat fighters, but you know that already,' he tells me with a grim smile. 'The kroot have been hiring themselves out as mercenaries to other races for hundreds of years, the majority of them to the tau. They'll fight with or against anyone as long as the pay is right.'

'They don't look too rich to me,' I comment. 'They don't really wear ostentatious clothes, they don't have palaces or anything else like that. What do they take as pay?'

'It's rather grisly,' Oriel warns me with a distasteful look. 'They fight for technology, arms and ammunition, but also for the bodies of the slain.'

'What do they want them for?' I ask, intrigued at this somewhat morbid form of payment.

'They eat them,' the inquisitor replies curtly. 'They believe that by consuming slain foes, they can take the prowess and skills of their enemy. They also eat their own kind, supposedly to preserve their souls or something. It's a bit complicated really, but some magi amongst the tech-priests believe that the kroot may be actually capable of absorbing information from their food, and passing it on to future generations. I don't understand the details, and it seems highly implausible to me, but the kroot certainly believe it.'

'They're cannibals?' I say, gazing around with new found horror at the aliens around us. 'That's pretty sick.'

'To you or I, certainly,' Oriel agrees with a nod. 'To them it is perfectly natural.'

At that point Orak rejoins us, still with his rifle slung over his shoulder.

'The feasting shall begin soon,' he tells us with relish, his eyes reflecting the firelight.

'Is this some kind of celebration?' Tanya asks as drums and whistles begin to play somewhere in the darkness.

'Yes, it is,' affirms Orak, standing tall above us, looking proudly over his kindred. 'Tomorrow we go to fight once more. Some of us will not return. Some of us will kill many foes and take their essence and grow strong. Either way is unimportant as long as the kroot survive, and the dead are not allowed to waste their treasures.'

'Do you look forward to battle?' Strelli asks. 'Is it an honour and glory thing for you?'

'It is a necessity of evolution,' Orak says strangely, turning away and calling out something to the other kroot. Two of them appear carrying a rack of meat between them. It smells somewhat odd, but not unappetising. There are no plates, and the kroot just tuck in, using their sharp beaks to tear away strips of flesh, gulping them down with relish. I pull out my knife and hack off some meat for myself. I bite hard, but it is surprisingly tender, the hot juices running from the corner of my mouth down my chin. The others cut off chunks for themselves too, cradling the hot meat gingerly in their hands as they eat.

'We took these carcasses in our last campaign, and have preserved them for tonight, to bring luck to the coming battles,' Orak informs us, his thick tongue wiping solidifying fat from his beak. 'Hopefully we will feast on this sweet gift again during the coming war.'

'I thought that O'var was waging a war against humans?' Schaeffer says uneasily, looking hard at Orak.

'Yes, that is so,' the kroot confirms. I get a sick feeling in the pit of my stomach, and bile rises in my throat as I look at the cooling flesh in my hands. I remember Oriel's words.

Cannibals. The kroot are cannibals. It doesn't mean anything to them to eat their own kind. I look at the others, who are coming to the same conclusion. Trost's hands are trembling; Tanya clamps a hand over her mouth; Strelli hurls the hunk of meat away from him, earning him a puzzled look from some of the surrounding kroot. With a choke, Quidlon turns away and vomits onto the dusty ground, his retching punctuated by sobs.

'Is something wrong?' Orak asks, his quills rising slightly. Trost is about to say something but the Colonel cuts him off.

'I think perhaps the excitement of the brawl earlier has unsettled our stomachs,' Schaeffer says hurriedly, darting a venomous glare at all of us to contradict him.

'I understand,' the kroot accepts Schaeffer's explanation and his quills subside again. 'Perhaps the dish of honour will be more comfortable for you.'

He stands up and gestures to one of the other kroot, who disappears for a minute before bringing back a covered tray. I can't help but notice the distinctly Imperial look of the silver platter, probably looted from some noble's house.

'Together we share this morsel,' Orak tells us sincerely. 'Your kindred and mine will be linked, for we shall share the same essence of the foe. In eating together, we shall become a wider kindred. Never before have I allowed this with a human, but your actions impress me. You fight as brave warriors, and you sit with pride at the feast. Join me now.'

He lifts off the lid with his four-fingered hand to reveal what is unmistakably a raw brain. A human brain, by the look of it. In the firelight, the grey mass shines orange, and I can still see a piece of spinal cord dangling from it. I want to gag. Orak picks it up reverently in both hands and holds it above his head and declares something in his own tongue.

'Not for this feast the quick gorging of battle,' he tells us. 'With pride we eat the most precious of all flesh. This warrior was a great leader, he and his soldiers battled well against us. I have been saving this gift for only the most worthy to share with me, and now I offer it to you.'

He lowers the wobbling brain and his beak snaps forward, nimbly stripping away some of the rubbery flesh. He turns towards us and offers the brain forward. We just sit there dumbfounded and nauseous, looking at the quivering pile in Orak's hands.

'Who among you will share this treat with me?' he asks, looking at each of us. None of us move except to swap horrified glances. Even the Colonel looks pale.

'Who among you will share this treat with me?' the kroot leader asks again, his quills beginning to tremble. 'This is a great honour, and I do not offer it lightly.'

When none of us react, clicks and quiet squawks begin to sound around us, and the kroot I see are getting to their feet, their quills extending in anger. I look at Orak, who still holds the brain towards us like a medal. Fighting back the sickness threatening to swamp me, I stand up.

'I will share this treat with you,' I reply hoarsely, and I hear a hiss of breath from the other Last Chancers. I gulp hard. I can hardly believe I'm going to do this. If I don't though, it could be my brain on the platter next time. The kroot don't seem too pleased with us at the moment.

'Very well,' Orak says, proffering the human brain towards me. I take it gingerly, my hands trembling madly. The touch of it makes me want to hurl up the contents of my guts. It's soft and seems to slither around in my grasp as I lift it up above my head for the assembled kroot to see.

My body shaking, I slowly lower it again and look at the organ in my hands. I try not to think about the man this once belonged to. I try to pretend it's something else like grox brain which I've eaten before. It doesn't work. It's like it has eyes that stare accusingly at me.

Gulping again, I lift the brain to my lips and glance at Orak. He gives me a casual wave to proceed, leaning towards me eagerly.

My mouth is very dry and my throat feels like someone is choking me. I close my eyes and bite down on the brain. It doesn't come away easily, I have to gnaw a portion off. My gut rebels, but I choke back the bile in my throat. I swallow hard, not daring to chew, and that almost makes me vomit as well. Opening my eyes, I hand the rest back quickly. Orak lifts it up once more for all to see and we're surrounded by a sudden clamour of birdlike shrieks and stomping feet. I guess I passed the test, but I feel like fainting. I don't think I'll ever forget the taste.

Orak passes the honour dish to another kroot and gestures for me to accompany him slightly outside the circle.

'That was well done,' he tells me, bending down to talk quietly in my ear.

'Uh, thanks,' I reply, desperately trying to forget the last half minute of my life.

'I understand how difficult that was,' he confides in me, his black eyes gazing into mine.

'You do?' I ask, surprised at this comment.

'I am not stupid, human,' Orak assures me, laying a long-fingered hand on my shoulder. 'I know that you do not share our same beliefs and abilities.'

'You knew how disgusting I thought that was?' I say angrily, remembering at the last moment to keep my voice a whisper. 'Why the fraggin' hell did you do it then?'

'To see if you would,' Orak replies evenly. 'To see what kind of humans I would be fighting alongside. We go to fight against your own kind. What you have just done proves to me that when the fighting becomes fierce, you will not stay your hand. Now, return to your friends, and I will have you brought food that you will find more agreeable.'

I stumble back into the firelight and sit down heavily with the others.

'It was damn test,' I hiss to them. 'All along it was a damn test.'

'Well, we seem to have weathered that little storm at least,' Oriel says, lying back with his arms behind his head.

'Yeah,' I reply sourly. 'Next time you can eat the brains though.'

* * *

WE DECIDE NOT to return to the skull-laden bar and our rooms, after the trouble we caused our re-appearance might not be appreciated. Instead we make a rough camp not far from Orak's kindred. As we watch their fire dying a couple of hundred paces away, Oriel calls us all together.

'Orak said that they are leaving tomorrow,' he says. 'That doesn't give us much time I suspect. If they are leaving, Brightsword will be making his inspection soon. I still haven't been able to make contact with Coldwind, so we might have to play this by ear for a while. Wake up bright and early tomorrow, we could be forced to move at any moment.'

The night passes fitfully for me, close as we are to fighting the final part of the mission, and mixed with scattered nightmares of horrific feasts with the kroot. In one dream, I imagine devouring Brightsword's brains, even as the others point at me and hurl abuse. I wake just before dawn, caked in sweat and dust, and push myself tiredly to my feet. I see that the Colonel is awake already, standing looking at the coming sunrise with his hands behind his back.

'Do you think it will be today, sir?' I ask him, and he turns and glances at me across his shoulder. It's not often we talk, but sometimes we do, and sometimes it even makes me feel better.

'Perhaps not today,' he says, looking into the distance again. 'But if not today, then certainly tomorrow.'

'What if we can't talk to Coldwind? What do we do then?' I say, a slight doubt nagging at me.

'We will do what we can,' Schaeffer replies quietly. He spins on his heel suddenly and turns his ice-blue stare on me full force. 'Will Tanya make the killing shot?'

'Of course she will,' I answer hurriedly, taken aback by the surprise question.

'If she does not pull the trigger when needed,' the Colonel warns me, 'you will certainly not live to regret it.'

'If she doesn't pull the trigger,' I reply grimly, 'none of us will live to regret it.'

Oriel stood in the pre-dawn glow out in the desert a few kilometres from the city and watched the lightening sky. The wind, chill at the moment, whipped up small sand devils around him, and fluttered the long sand-coloured coat around his shoulders. He was sure he was alone; there was no sentient presence that he could detect. Removing a small wand-like object from a pocket inside his coat, he placed it in the ground, driving it into the sand with a thump. Fiddling with the instrument, he activated the beacon, which began to pulse with a dim red light, barely visible to him, but he knew the keen receptors of the craft it was intended for would pick it out as brightly as a searchlight.

It was not long before a streak of light began to descend through the sky like a shooting star. It arrowed down towards Oriel, and then veered a thousand metres up, swinging into a wide landing circle. As it grew closer, Oriel could make out the white-hot pinpricks from the shuttle's plasma engines, though the black hull was all but obscured from view by the darkness. Another minute passed as Oriel waited, and the small shuttle began to slow. With barely more than a whine, it descended, sophisticated anti-grav motors kicking in rather than loud and clumsy jets. The hull shimmered and rippled, the darkness around it distorted by an energy field which extended for several metres around it. Oriel gave a silent prayer to the machine god, hoping that the infernal tau surveyors had been fooled by the specially constructed stealth shield. The tech-priests had assured him this would be the case, but he was never one to rely heavily on the artifices of the Adeptus Mechanicus. Clawed landing feet extended from the hull and the shuttle touched down, taking a few seconds to settle into the soft sand. The whine of the engines died down almost immediately and a second later, the fore hatch opened with a short hiss of pressure.

The inquisitor watched impassively as Dionis walked down the ramp, the metal reverberating to his heavy tread, his helmet under one arm. As he stepped off the ramp, it hissed back into place and the shuttle shimmered, the cloaking field activating fully, causing the small craft to disappear from view. Within a few seconds the small transport, which was barely three metres high and five metres long, was invisible.

'Greetings, inquisitor,' the new arrival said, stopping in front of Oriel, his voice low but clearly audible.

'And greetings to you, brother,' Oriel responded formally, looking up into Dionis's broad face. 'You are prepared?'

'I am always prepared, inquisitor,' Dionis chided him slightly. 'Is it not my brotherhood's motto to stand ready at all times, to counter the threat when called upon?'

'So you have sung your battle hymns and made your offerings to the Emperor?' asked the inquisitor.

'I am ready to face the foe. My soul is pure and my weapons cleansed, inquisitor,' answered Dionis.

'May we not have need of them,' muttered Oriel, turning away.

'Praise the Emperor, inquisitor,' Dionis called out to Oriel as he plucked the portable beacon from its hole.

'Yes,' Oriel replied with feeling. 'Praise the Emperor indeed. Today, we may well copy his sacrifice for mankind.'

'It was what we were born for, inquisitor,' Dionis reminded him.

'Yes, sooner or later,' agreed Oriel with a grim smile to himself. 'Let's hope it's later though, there's lots more work to be done.'

SEVEN
ASSASSINS

+++Time to cast the final die+++

+++Fate and luck be with you+++

ORIEL WOKE UP not long after me and headed off without a word to either me or the Colonel. I guess he's gone looking for Coldwind. If Brightsword is making his inspection today, we could be fighting within hours. The thought that I'll be in battle again, real battle against enemies trying to kill me, sends a thrill through me. No more targets that don't shoot back. No endless drill and routine and theory. This is the real thing, and there's nothing like it.

As the sun begins to creep over the horizon, between two domes in the distance, I sit down and begin to strip down my autogun. My hands work automatically, allowing my mind to wander for a while. At first I run over the plan in my head, but that's so ingrained now, all of the possibilities looked at, that there's little diversion there.

I just want it to start. I want the bullets to start flying, the blood to pump through my veins, that feeling of life which I briefly grasped again during the shuttle hijack but which has otherwise been denied to me for over a year. I want to know if Tanya makes that shot, whether Trost will do his job properly, whether those months of hard training have been worthwhile. I want to know if I was right, and I deserve to be on this mission, or if the battle psychosis grips me again and the Colonel should have left me behind.

That part worries me more than anything else. I don't want to be the cause of the mission failing. It's odd, the mission for me isn't about stopping an alien commander invading a human world. The test has become much more personal, a challenge from the Colonel and Oriel. It's whether I picked and trained the team well enough to complete the mission. It's whether I can hold up under the pressure. For me, that'll be the victory, regardless of what the wider consequences are. This isn't a battle against the tau, it's a battle against Schaeffer and the inquisitor he serves.

'Thinking deep thoughts?' asks Tanya, standing behind where I'm sat and looking at the coming dawn.

'Yes,' I reply shortly, not feeling like sharing them with her. She's not my friend, there's nothing special between us. She's Sharp-shooter, and my only concern is that she makes that shot so we can get the hell out of the firestorm that'll follow.

'What are you thinking about?' she asks again, sitting down beside me.

'You first,' I say, turning my head to look at her, my fingers still working over the mechanisms of the autogun.

'Whether I'm going to see another dawn,' she admits, not looking back at me. 'But I'm not scared, not really. I'm just curious.'

'Like this isn't you, that it's happening to someone else's life?' I suggest, knowing the feeling.

'Yeah, it's something like that,' she agrees, looking at me for the first time, understanding in her eyes. 'Is that how you feel?'

'All the time,' I admit, snapping the magazine of the autogun back in place and cocking the firing mechanism with a loud click. 'When the time comes, it's almost like the rapture some preachers talk about. It's like the Emperor enters me, takes me over, like I become his weapon and nothing more.'

She looks at me with curious eyes and I meet her gaze. Suddenly the detachment is gone, and I don't see Sharp-shooter, I see Tanya Stradinsk. Possibly the last woman I'll ever see in this life. I stand up and look at the others, at Trost and Strelli, at Moerck and Quidlon.

For a moment I see them as people, looking past the names and labels I gave them. There's Tanya, strong and confident again, but still haunted by her guilt. Trost, a merciless killer who acknowledges the pleasure he has gained from his bloody work and now relishes it. Strelli, without a care about anyone or anything else, determined to survive. Like I was a couple of years ago, I suddenly realise. And Quid-lon, more restrained, more awed by the wondrous and horrifying galaxy we live in, his eyes opened to the perils he has to face, but still determined to examine it, to try and understand it. And then there's Moerck, sanctimonious, unforgiving, unrelenting in his beliefs and morals. He sees himself as a rock amongst the effluence of the stars. I couldn't hope for a better team. Then the moment passes, the grim reality of what we have to do returns and they become names and labels again. Sharpshooter, Flyboy, Demolition Man, Brains and Hero. All of them part of an intricate plan, like a finely tuned clockwork device, that must work together perfectly or the whole system breaks down and we all die. And of course there's me, Last Chance. Will I turn out to be the weak link?

'Is this going to be the last sunrise I see?' Tanya asks from behind me.

'That's up to you,' I reply coldly. 'It depends how much you want to see another one.'

'I still don't know if I can take that shot,' she says quietly, and I spin on her, ready to bawl her out. But she's sat there, cross-legged, watching Es'tau's star rising in the distance, bathing her in a red glow, lost from the world in her own thoughts. She wasn't telling me; she was asking herself.

'Of course you'll make that shot,' I assure her, whispering in her ear. 'If you make that shot, you get to see another sunset and another sunrise.'

'Is that a threat?' she asks calmly.

'No,' I say with a smile she can't see. 'It's my promise. If you make that shot, I'll make sure you see another sunrise.'

'You said to never trust you,' Tanya points out. 'How do I know you won't abandon me?'

I don't answer straight away. I don't understand myself why I said it, it just came out. I stand there, looking at her, and then at the others, and it comes to me.

'You're one of my Last Chancers,' I say after a short while. 'You're my team, not the Colonel's. You're my Sharpshooter, and I picked you because you're the best. I picked all of you because you're all the best at what you do. I want to see you get those pardons and walk free, to do that thing which I can never do again. I want you to enjoy your next sunset, knowing you can enjoy them for the rest of your life. Most of all, I have a head full of memories which are all that are left of the Last Chancers my first time around. I don't want to add any more. There's enough dead folks in my dreams.'

But Tanya isn't really listening to me, caught up in her own thoughts.

IT'S QUIDLON WHO wakes up next, and following my talk with Tanya, I decided to chat with him, to gauge how he's feeling. It's not some notion that I want to see he's okay, but rather trying to figure out how he's going to act if we do end up fighting today. Will he get over excited, will he be a coward, will he be focussed on the mission or is he distracted? Knowing those things, I can take them into account when the fighting starts.

'A bright and hot day,' I say to him conversationally as he drinks from a canteen.

'They all are, aren't they?' he replies. 'The Tau home world is dry like this, they settle more worlds like their own, so I guess it's always going to be a bright and hot day.'

'I've been in prison, aboard ship and on these hot worlds for almost a year now,' I tell him. 'I think I would like some rain. To feel it falling down on me.'

'I've never liked rain, it's cold, it's wet, and it makes people miserable,' argues Quidlon. 'Where I'm from it rains almost all the time, a constant, demoralising drizzle that goes on and on and on, and when it stops it's always cloudy. There's never any light, it's always grey and overcast.'

'Don't you miss that then?' I ask him as we walk together towards the shade offered by the looming dome between us and the sunrise. 'Would you like to see those cloudy skies again?'

'Not at all,' he says vehemently. 'I've been shown much more than I would've ever seen at home. There's so much in the galaxy I never knew about that I know about now. Every day has opened my eyes to something else. I've met soldiers and navy staff, I've talked to officers and commissars, I've seen sunrises on other worlds, and looked at different stars in the night skies, and none of that would have happened if I hadn't joined the Imperial Guard.'

'You realise that might all end today?' I say quietly as we enter the shade and sit down. I look around. A few kroot are walking past, one of them nods towards us and I wave back. The sounds of the city waking up begin to grow in volume, the clatter of stalls being set up, the alien traders' shouts increasing, the murmur of life building around us.

'I could be dead, that's true, but I'm not really thinking about it,' he replies.

'It doesn't worry you at all?' I probe, not believing him.

'I want to see more, but I've seen a hundred times the things most men see in a whole lifetime, more than I ever imagine existed when I was growing up,' he tells me earnestly. 'Who knows what'll happen when I'm dead? Perhaps that's the greatest thing of all, the experience of a lifetime so to speak.'

'Don't be too eager to enjoy it,' I warn him, remembering my own brushes with death. As I sit there, the pain behind my eyes starts again, a dull ache that spreads through my brain, not unbearable, but certainly uncomfortable. I get a glimpse in my mind's eye of bolts of lightning, and the stench of charred flesh. I try to ignore the thoughts and listen to Quidlon.

'Oh, Last Chance, I've got no intention of getting myself killed just to see what it's like,' he laughs back at me, not noticing my distraction. 'Like I said, there's so much more to see here in the mortal world before I pass over. I've met orks now, but I would like to see an eldar, to see if it's true that they walk without touching the ground, or perhaps to visit one of the great cathedrals, or make a pilgrimage to Holy Terra itself.'

'Is that what you'll do when you get your pardon?' I ask, pushing the strange vision out of my thoughts as much as possible.

'To travel more, oh certainly,' he tells me with a smile. 'I don't know how I'd do it. Perhaps I could continue working for Inquisitor Oriel, or maybe sign up as a crewman on a starship; after all I know a lot about mechanics.'

'I'd avoid the Navy if I were you,' I caution him. 'You don't seem to mix well with the Adeptus Mechanicus, and there's hundreds of tech-priests aboard every vessel. As for Oriel, the sooner you're shot of him and his devious ways, the better. He's a schemer, and his schemes can backfire horribly. And it'll be you in the firing line when it happens, not him, he's got a habit of escaping. Believe me, I know that, I tried to blow him up once and that didn't work.'

'I never realised you'd worked with Oriel before. What was it like? I mean you haven't said much about the last mission you were on,' he points out.

'That's because I'd rather not talk about it,' I tell him, looking away. 'Too many memories, too many people died who shouldn't have done. I did things I'd never thought I would be able to do, and now I'll do them without a second thought. It killed me, but also showed me exactly who I am.'

492   *Gav Thorpe*

'And who is that?' asks the Colonel, giving me a start. I see him standing behind me, watching me with those ice cold eyes of his.

'I'm Kage, lieutenant of the 13th Penal Legion Last Chancers,' I tell him, standing up. 'I'm Last Chance, like you said.'

'What does that mean?' he continues, gesturing Quidlon away with a flick of his head. The trooper gives me a glance and then walks off.

'It means I'm here to fight and die for the Emperor,' I explain bitterly, turning away from him and taking a step.

'Do not walk away from me, Kage,' he growls at me, and I turn back. 'What do you think you are doing, turning your back on an officer?'

'It's not like that any more,' I laugh coldly. 'It's all changed this time. I'm not just the lieutenant, you're not just the Colonel. This isn't about rank, this isn't about seniority. I've realised something. I've realised why you asked me to do the choosing and training. You can't do this on your own, can you? I know how much I've got bottled up inside me, all those memories, all that pain, all that blood on my hands. I can deal with it. You could deal with it as well, but how much more is there for you? I know you care, don't try to tell me you don't. It may only be for our souls, not our bodies, but you care, and you also give a damn about the mission, and you believe in the Emperor and everything else. You're not just a machine, you're a man just like me. Emperor knows, maybe you *were* me once, maybe you were just some poor grunt – or were you born to it? Were you raised on officer's milk as a babe?'

'You know nothing about me, Kage,' he says after a moment, his eyes boring into me. 'Yes, you are right, I needed your help. You showed something special in Coritanorum. I know you came back for me, and it was not just for some damned pardon in my pocket. You do understand some of what I am trying to do, but you don't have a clue about the wider picture. You do not know my past, and you do not know your future. I needed you, and I still need you, but that is all. I do not care about you, I made it clear that you only get one chance with me. You had that chance and you squandered it.'

'So why not just kill me now?' I dare him, holding up my hands like a hostage.

'Maybe I will,' he says, pulling his autopistol from its holster.

'Do it,' I snarl. 'Kill me, you don't need me for this mission, I'm just going to be babysitting Quidlon and Tanya, and they can take care of themselves. I've done my part. You could have had me killed any time over the last four years, any time at all. And you've had justification. You could have killed me after you caught up with me and the rookies on Typhos Prime, but you let them persuade you otherwise.'

'They were threatening to kill me if I did,' he tries to argue, but not too convincingly. The Colonel's never been too good at lying. Not telling the whole truth, he's got plenty of practice at that, but outright lies? No, he just can't pull it off.

'They wouldn't have, despite what they said,' I tell him, bringing my hands down and pointing accusingly at me. 'You could have killed me then, you could have left me for dead when we got lost in Coritanorum. You could have killed me after I murdered those Typhon officers and you found me drunk to the world, but no, you decided to wait until I woke up and then offer me another last chance, knowing I would take it.'

'What do you want me to say, Kage?' he asks, holstering the pistol. 'That I need you on this mission in case it all goes wrong? That is true, I do need you as my back-up. You are without doubt one of the best soldiers I have ever met. But that is not what you really need from me. You want me to carry on punishing you, because that is what you deserve. You know it is true. This is not about redemption, this is about punishment. You had your chance to get out of this forever, but you threw it away because you still feel guilty. You have felt guilty all of your life, Kage, and you want me to feel guilty for you. You want me to put you through hell so that you can hate me, so that you do not have to admit that everything you are trying to prove to me is in fact something you need to prove to yourself.'

'I'm a lying, cheating, murdering son of an ork,' I laugh at him. 'I was a bastard even before you got hold of me. What makes you think I feel guilty about anything I've done?'

'It is not what you have done that plagues you, it is what you did not do,' he says to me, striding up and standing full in my face. 'You are right, you do not give a damn about those people you have killed, you do not care about the misery you have brought others. But you do know that perhaps, if you had not been so selfish and obsessed with your own survival, more of the Last Chancers might have made it out of Coritanorum alive.'

'You never intended any of us to survive, you or Oriel,' I accuse him, stepping back from his intimidating presence.

'Where was your sacrifice when it was needed?' he continues relentlessly, stepping forward again, my personal judge and jury. 'Every night you ask yourself if you could have saved them. Do you think you could have saved Franx if you had not played dead in that air attack? Would you have steered Gappo away from that minefield if you had not been trying to desert? Why did you sweat blood on Krag-meer to save Franx? Was it because you felt he was better than you? Do you hate yourself because all of those people who died deserved to live more than you did? That is why you are Last Chance. That is why you need me to punish you, because yes, you are a loathsome, selfish, cowardly piece of filth who the Emperor should have killed. But for your life you do not know why he has not, and instead has taken away everyone you once knew, except me. I am the only thing you have left, Kage. I am not a memory and I am here to tell you that you do not walk away from me when I am talking to you. Nothing has changed, you are still scum and it is still my duty to save you from yourself.'

I just laugh out loud. A good hearty laugh from the gut, making my jaw ache. The Colonel stands there, looking at me with a quizzical stare, one eyebrow raised. I manage to get myself under control. A couple of the others start to come over, but when they see the Colonel, they back off again.

'Yes, Colonel,' I reply, saluting smartly, even as I try to stop smirk-ing. 'If you have finished being a sanctimonious son of a bitch, sir, I would like my squad to fall in for inspection.'

'Carry on, Lieutenant Kage,' he says with a nod, the formality restored. My thoughts are jumbled as I walk away, feeling his pierc-ing gaze on my back, but they soon clarify when I start shouting orders at the others.

ORIEL TURNS UP about midday and tells us to pack up and clear out. The mission is going ahead here and now. Without comment we get ready, do our last weapons checks, pack our ammo up and leave the rest. Having sleeping rolls and camp burners will only weigh us down, so we head off light. We exchange brief waves of farewell with the kroot, who are also getting ready to leave. Oriel leads us unerr-ingly through the streets, avoiding the worst crowds of the alien quarter, taking us up past the space port. He points to a tau ship standing on the apron, a gleaming white shuttle decorated with large tau symbols in red. That's Brightsword's transport; he's already headed to the battle dome for the inspection.

The inquisitor leads us away from the space port and we see another dome, out in the desert, linked to the city by a single gleaming silver rail. As we get closer, I see bullet-shaped carriages slipping back and forth along the rail and realise it is some kind of locomotive.

'That is how we will gain access to the battle dome,' he tells us, pointing as one of the transports zooms past. 'The training drill you performed on the *Laurels of Glory* represents the zone of action once we are inside the dome. Trost's demolitions will provide the distraction we will need to infiltrate the central complex where the power relays are situated. Once there, Quidlon, Tanya and Kage, rejoined by Trost, will cut the power to the outer entryways and the rail system, cutting the dome off from the outside. The Colonel, Moerck and I will sweep O'var out of hiding, into Tanya's sights. She kills the commander, and we exit again through the rail terminal. Strelli, there is a shuttle some five kilometres or so to the sunward of the dome, out in the desert, which you will go to.'

'When you activate this you should be able to see the shuttle.' The inquisitor passes Strelli a small cylinder with a brass rune etched into its base. 'Fly back to the dome to pick us up. Once we're on board, we will return to our ship in orbit. I have spoken to Coldwind and he assures us that the chain of command will be uncertain for a while following Brightsword's death, and he will do what he can to increase that confusion.'

'That's all well and good,' says Tanya, watching another transport bullet speed out of sight, 'but how do we get on one of the trains?'

QUIDLON CURSES GENTLY and continuously under his breath as we lower him down into the hole. Oriel assures us that the power relays for the travel rail are buried here, and Quidlon simply needs to temporarily cut the power, bringing one of the carriages to a halt. We take the train, switch the power on and ride it all the way inside the fortified dome. Sounds good on paper, but judging from Quidlon's swearing the practice is a little more difficult. It also took us the best part of an hour to find one of the power conduits, sneaking amongst the desert dunes in case a fire warrior saw us from one of the passing carriages and became suspicious. After a while, he emerges, blinking in the bright light after spending several minutes in the small opening we found after levering up a panel situated a couple of hundred metres from the rail.

'I think the power will shut down for several minutes,' he tells us, dusting himself off and putting some oddly-shaped tools back into his pack.

'You think?' Moerck barks at him.

'I don't know how tau timing systems work, they don't even use seconds and minutes, so I'm having to guess,' he moans back, obviously aggravated. 'I couldn't even read the labels on all the switches and terminals, so think yourself lucky I'm not a fried mess right about now.'

'So we manage to stop one of the carriages. What then?' asks Trost.

'I say we kill everybody on board,' I tell them, looking around for disagreement.

'Last Chance is right,' Trost agrees. 'Half of us each side, attacking from the front and back. We storm the place, shoot anything that moves and then wait for the power to come back on. These things don't have drivers, it'll take us right in there.'

'Demolition Man, Kage and Sharpshooter are with me,' the Colonel orders us quickly, glancing down the line towards the city where a dazzle of sun on metal indicates the next transport. 'The rest of you with Oriel. Keep low, shoot at chest height, that way we should avoid killing each other.'

'First in, with a grenade,' I suggest, pulling a frag charge from my belt. 'That'll take most of them out in such a tight space.'

The Colonel nods and Trost chucks one of his frag grenades to Oriel, who passes it to Strelli.

'Why do I get to go in first?' he whines, holding out the grenade for someone else to take.

'Because we can always walk out of there if we need to, Flyboy,' I tell him bluntly.

'Oh, gonna walk up to orbit are we?' he says bitterly, spitting on the ground and stalking away.

Oriel and the others cross the rail and wait on the other side a couple of hundred metres further up the route. We don't try to hide; as far as I know, there's nothing the tau on board the fast-approaching land shuttle can do to stop even if they did see us.

'You are in first, Demolition Man,' the Colonel says, pointing at Trost. 'Then Last Chance and myself. Sharpshooter, you stay here and take out any targets that present themselves at the windows.'

I can see the carriage approaching now, slowing down as it nears us, carried forward by momentum rather than power now that it has moved onto the section cut off from the energy grid. Like I said, it's bullet-shaped, about twenty metres long, with a row of narrow windows roughly two thirds of the way up the side. There are no obvious wheels, it glides soundlessly above the rail. It goes past us still moving quite quickly but slowing, and as we run after it, it settles down onto the track, its lower parts carving furrows into the sand, braking it even more quickly.

At the back of the carriage is a small triangle of steps leading down to either side. I point Trost to the right hand flight and he nods, hefting a grenade in his hand. Tanya peels off to our left, diving prone and taking up a firing position along a sand drift. The hatchway at the top of the steps opens and the door hisses upwards. A tau in a fire warrior's uniform sticks his head out and the Colonel fires, the bullets impacting into the alien and flinging him backwards.

With a skill born of years of practice, Trost lobs a grenade straight through the opening and there's panicked shouting from inside. The detonation blasts out the back five windows and hurls a body out of the door. About two seconds later an accompanying explosion takes out the front half of the train. Trost reaches the steps first and throws himself up, firing with his lasgun as he jumps inside. I go in next, firing the autogun to the right, one-handed, pulling myself through the hatch with my spare hand. Glass crunches under my feet and I see tau bodies strewn all over the benches that run the length of each side of the transport. One or two move and we fire into them, and I hear the Colonel jump up behind me, his autopistol at the ready.

The others burst in from the front and we stand there looking at each other and the three dozen or so corpses lying between us. A few more start to come round so we begin the grisly job of executing them all, pulling off their helmets and putting a round into every single head. Tanya joins us, but keeps her finger away from the trigger of her sniper rifle.

'Let's clear some space,' I hear Oriel say, as he grabs a corpse by its legs and begins to drag it towards the door. As I grab another under the arms and heft it up, a humming begins beneath my feet and I feel the train start lifting off the ground again. Hurrying, we grab bodies and push them out of the doors, watching them tumble helplessly into the dust and sand as the train picks up speed.

'Won't someone see them?' Tanya asks, putting her hands under the armpits of one of the fire warriors.

'We will be inside and the alarm raised by the time that happens, Emperor willing,' Moerck points out.

'How long until we get there?' asks Strelli, helping Tanya lift up the body.

'Ten, fifteen minutes at most, judging by our acceleration and the time it'll take us to brake to a stop,' Quidlon says, peering through one of the shattered windows.

'Forget the rest, get ready,' Oriel says, slamming a fresh clip into his pistol and cocking it. It reminds me of the first time I saw him, in the plasma chamber of Coritanorum, two smoking autopistols in his hands. He's assumed the same cockiness, the same confidence and air of control. There's no doubt at all he knows what he is doing – that if any of us will get out of this alive, it's him.

'When we start to slow down, jump for it,' the Colonel tells Strelli, pushing him towards the back doorway. 'Head for the shuttle but give us at least one hour before you deactivate the stealth field, because when you do the tau will know it is there. After that, get to us as quickly as you can.'

'Where's Coldwind?' the pilot asks, a bit of a strange question at a time like this.

'His part in the mission is over. He's not even going to be at the battle dome,' Oriel replies from up front, waving Strelli to get out. I stand at the top of the steps as he climbs down towards the speeding ground. I give him a thumbs up and he lets go, pushing himself off to one side with his legs. I see him land and roll. A moment later and he's on his feet.

He stands there and waves. As we carry on, I watch him, still standing there, making no effort that I can see to get to the shuttle.

The next few minutes pass in silence as we all watch the battle dome rise further and further out of the sands as we get closer. It's big, bigger than I imagined it would be when we were training back aboard the *Laurels of Glory*. I reckon it must be as least three, maybe four kilometres across at the base, dwarfing anything we saw back near the space port. Even the battle dome on Me'lek was only half the size, though I guess they had a lot more of them there.

I feel the locomotive decelerating quickly now. The dome's just a few hundred metres away, and I get ready, crouching down by one of the broken windows, the autogun warm in my hands, all thoughts of Me'lek put to the back of my mind. Trost jumps for it a hundred metres shy of the black hole that swallows up the rail, and heads off to the right, pulling charges from his pack. I check the autogun one last time and rest it on the sill of the window.

'Last Chance,' Quidlon says to me, a worried expression on his face. 'I've been thinking: we're about to take on a whole army, just the handful of us I mean. How are we supposed to beat a whole army?'

'Inquisitor?' I call out to Oriel at the front of the coach. 'How many are we gonna be facing?'

'Coldwind says it's just Brightsword's own hunter cadre and one other cadre left here,' he tells me, looking back down the carriage at us. 'About a hundred, maybe a hundred and twenty warriors.'

'Small change, Brains,' I say to Quidlon, grinning. 'Coritanorum, now that was a real army we took down, thousands of them.'

'How did you do it?' he asks, subdued for a change.

'Short answer or long one?' I say to him, peering out of the window. The opening in the side of the dome gets closer and closer. The white dome itself gleams in the strong light, dazzling against a pure blue sky.

'I think we've only got time for the short answer, Last Chance,' Tanya says from the opposite side of the aisle.

'Take them on in small lumps,' I laugh, feeling very calm. The throbbing in my head begins to subside as I settle down. It's like everything from the last few months focussing in to me, that out-of-body feeling I've had before. The rapture I told Tanya about earlier, the feeling that something else is inside my body.

Everything goes dim for a second as we pass inside the dome, but I realise it isn't really dark, the yellow lighting is simply nowhere near as bright as the harsh glare outside. In a moment we're through the gateway and entering the terminal. Long boarding platforms run the length of the track on each side, with wide archways at regular intervals. There are a few tau fire warriors stationed there and I can imagine their surprise as the train glides gently to a halt, its windows smashed.

We don't give them a chance to react.

I rise up slightly, still with the autogun on the window frame, and open fire with a short burst, gunning down the nearest tau, the bullets kicking across his stomach and chest, ripping chunks out of his armoured breastplate. The Colonel aims low at another, the row of bullet impacts from his pistol stitching a line along the wall before kneecapping the warrior. Oriel is jumping through the door, firing as he leaps, scoring a cluster of perfect hits on the helmet of a third warrior.

I propel myself out of the back door and roll left to the opposite of the now-stationary carriage, using its back end for cover. A fire warrior turns to run through one of the archways, but I get a bead on him first, the shots taking him high in the back and pitching him forward. He rolls and clambers to his feet, still alive and kicking, and returns fire with his bulky carbine, chewing a massive chunk out of the side of the train and forcing me to duck back.

Glancing out, I see Quidlon fire from inside, his fusillade of las-bolts slamming into the fire warrior and spinning him down again.

Just then, a dull boom sounds from our right, Trost's charges going up. A piercing wail fills the air as warning sirens screech into life.

'Make for the power complex!' the Colonel bellows, following Oriel and Moerck out of the other side of the station in search of Brightsword. They have to flush the commander out into the open so that Tanya can get her shot. I silently wish them the protection of the Emperor.

Quidlon and Tanya join me in the nearest archway. It all springs back to life, the hours and days and weeks spent on the *Laurels of Glory*. It's just how the training bay was set up. We go through this arch, take the next doorway on the left, three doors to the right down the corridor and across a jungle arena. On the other side are two more doors and then we're into the central plaza, the power facility and armoury entrance.

'Everyone knows the drill,' I say to the other two. 'Come on Last Chancers, time to die.'

With that I toss a smoke grenade through the arch, and follow it through a couple of seconds later. Shots detonate around me, too close for comfort, and I hit the ground, returning fire down the corridor. Tanya sprints across the tunnel and takes cover in the next door alcove, Quidlon following her, snapping off shots from the hip as he does so. I push myself to my feet, rattle off another burst of fire and follow them through. The magazine's empty so I pluck it out and discard it, slamming another one home with well-practiced ease. Another corridor and another smoke grenade, Quidlon firing back through the arch we just passed through, and I hear a shout of someone hit.

We get to a closed portal and I signal Quidlon to get it open. He searches around for an access panel and finds it just above the floor inside the archway.

'Come on, Brains, we haven't got all day,' I hiss at him, before firing at a glimpse of movement to my right. I glance back and see he has the panel open, an odd-looking instrument in his hands, like a pair of compasses made from crystal and wires. There's a hiss and the door slides open.

Tanya ducks through first and comes scurrying back a second later as explosions rock the room beyond.

'Grenades!' I tell them, and Quidlon tosses one through the doorway, followed a moment later by one from my belt. The twin detonations scatter shrapnel across a wide area, the smell of explosives hanging in the air. Another, much louder, explosion rocks the walls and I see debris pile up further down the tunnel. Trost comes bursting through the hole, firing blindly behind him with his lasgun.

I grab Tanya and force her forward, pushing her ahead of me until we reach the next alcove. The smoke, dust and yellow lighting makes everything look foggy and polluted, and it threatens to clog my mouth and nose. Tanya pulls out the lascutter and gets to work on the next door as we provide covering fire. Three more fire warriors go down further along the narrow corridor, and many more duck back out of sight. I can hear the hiss of the lasburner melting through the door, and a moment later Tanya calls out that she's through.

Crawling through the opening I find myself in the middle of a jungle, like I expected. The humidity and heat makes sweat jump out of my skin straight away, and it takes a while for my eyes to adjust to the relative darkness. Trost is rigging up a grenade and tripwire next to the opening as we take positions against the trunks of the trees, up to our waists in large fern leaves.

'Drones!' snaps Tanya, levelling her sniper rifle to the left.

I look that way, and half a dozen of the things come flitting down through the leaves. They're domed discs about a metre across, with thick aerials protruding from their curved tops, each underslung with a pair of linked guns that track and swivel as they scan the jungle for us. Tanya opens fire, plucking the closest out of the air with a single shot, its fractured casing spinning to the ground trailing sparks. Quidlon and I shoot next, a converging salvo of las-bolts and bullets that sends three more of the drones out of control, smashing into trees and plunging into the bushes.

The two that are left return fire and we duck for more cover as the shells smash fist-sized chunks from the tree trunks, hurling bark everywhere and spattering me with sweet-smelling sap. I roll sideways through the ferns, flattening leaves, and finish on my back, firing up. The shots ricochet off one of the drones, causing it to judder in its flight, but it recovers and dips down out of sight. Smart little beggar. A swathe of falling ferns is the only warning I get of the drone's shots and I roll to my feet and dive sideways, landing awkwardly behind a fallen log. The shells strip through the leaves at knee height, splintering along the log – the drone must be hovering just above the ground. One of them hits a more rotten patch of wood and passes straight through, scoring a bloody cut across the back of my right leg just below the knee, but missing the bone. I bite back the pain and fire back blindly, resting the autogun on the log and squeezing off the remainder of the magazine.

Banging more ammo home, I glance over the top of the fallen trunk, and see the drone gliding towards me, its guns tracking left and right, smoking gently. When it's just a couple of metres away, I burst out of my cover and leap at the thing, diving right on top of it.

It sways sideways trying to escape and I drop the autogun and grab its circular rim with both hands. My muscles strain against its anti-gravity motors as I turn it vertical, its guns spinning wildly, trying to point at me but instead just finding thin air. With a shout I break into a headlong run at the nearest tree, pushing the drone in front of me, and smash it against the trunk, gouging a strip from the bark and causing one of the guns to snap off its mounting. I smash it against the tree again four more times, until the motors die and it suddenly becomes heavy in my hands. I drop the drone to the ground, where it wobbles uncertainly for a few seconds before falling still. I go back and pick up my autogun and shout for the others.

Tanya appears first, her right cheek bloodied, splinters of wood imbedded in her face.

'Any closer, I would have lost my eye,' she tells me, sitting down against a tree and dabbing at the blood with her cuff. Quidlon and Trost appear together, apparently unharmed.

'I think it's this way, but I got turned around in the fight and it all looks the same, so maybe it isn't,' Quidlon says, pointing up a trail to our left.

'Check your direction-finder, idiot,' I tell Quidlon, and he pulls the magneto-compass from his belt, turning its dials to align properly. He gives it a shake and adjusts it again.

'It's no use,' he says, shaking his head. 'I think the tau have got some kind of interference generator, or perhaps just the structure of the dome is jamming the scanning beams.'

'If you hadn't stabbed Eyes, we would know for sure,' snarls Trost, inspecting the shot counter on his lasgun.

'Forget about the past, it's better to be moving than a sitting target for more drones, or worse,' I snap at the pair of them, slapping the compass from Quidlon's grasp. 'According to the set-up on the *Laurels of Glory* there should only be one other exit out of this area. We find that, we know where we are.'

'Oh, and the tau will just let us, will they, Last Chance?' spits Trost, pulling Tanya to her feet.

'No, but we can make them think twice about stopping us,' I tell them. 'Come on, less arguing, more moving.'

Progress through the jungle is slow, hampered by the undergrowth and the need to keep alert at all times. The arena is only a few hundred metres across, but we take our time, not wanting to run into the tau without expecting it. After about ten minutes, Trost hisses and hits the deck, the rest of us following suit.

'Movement, twenty, maybe thirty metres to the left,' he whispers. I rise to a crouch and see he's right, I make out fire warriors advancing cautiously between the trees. I'm not sure how many, maybe half a dozen, perhaps more. I point upwards and they all nod, understanding the plan. Keeping the trunks between us and the tau, we shin up into the lower branches and wait for the enemy to pass beneath us. The first few walk by without noticing, but a drone buzzes past just below me and then stops.

'Now!' I shout, dropping down, the gun blazing in my hands. At this range I can't miss and the drone explodes into a shower of flaming shrapnel. The tau turn, but I'm on them, swinging the butt of the autogun into the helmeted face of the closest, smashing the small cluster of lenses that are where his eyes should be. The next in line raises his rifle to blast me apart but I kick the muzzle aside and the shot tears through his comrade, nearly slicing him in half. I reverse the kick and power my boot into the tau's chest, smashing him on to his back, and then leap on him, driving the autogun under his chin and pulling the trigger. The top of his helmet explodes across the ferns in a bloody spray.

I look up to see Quidlon driving his knife up into the groin of another fire warrior while Trost smashes a rock over the head of another. The two remaining aliens turn and flee, but Quidlon snatches up his lasgun and cuts them down with an intense salvo of bolts before they get out of sight. I take a pause to catch my breath, looking at the mutilated bodies. Rather them than me.

We head off in the direction the tau came from, figuring they must have entered through the doorway we're looking for. Another hundred metres or so, and there's a stream across our path, cutting through a wide clearing. It looks like a killing zone to me, good lines of fire from all around the perimeter, the stream to splash about and slip around in. But we're up against the clock here, no time to look for a better spot up or downstream. The drone attack has put us behind schedule already, we need to get out of here fast and into the central chamber.

Movement across the clearing catches my eye and I instinctively bring up the autogun, ready to fire. I look harder, but all I can see are leaves and branches. Then to my right, there's more movement, and I focus on the area quickly, but still there's nothing to be seen. I peer out through the foliage, keeping my head down, trying to see what's moving out there. I catch a glimpse now and then of something, but nothing I could definitely identify as a tau. It's then that my attention is drawn to the large bole of a tree pretty much directly opposite from where I'm crouched. I look at the deep score lines in the bark running up and down, and they bend and twist slightly. The strange thing is, the pattern of the lines is almost a perfect humanoid shape.

'Sneaky bastards,' I whisper to myself, lining up a shot on what I take to be the head of the near-invisible warrior. I pull the trigger softly, sending a single round cracking out across the clearing, it impacts on something in front of the tree and it's then that I see a figure thrashing to the ground, the light somehow bending around it, making it near impossible to see. Then all hell breaks loose. There's muzzle flashes from all around us, just within the far tree-line. There's incoming fire from every direction, a massive fusillade of bullets that converge on our position, shredding leaves and branches and punching into the thick trunks of the trees spraying iron-hard splinters around us, forcing us to hurriedly duck further back into cover.

'How do we get past?' asks Trost, leaning back against a tree, glancing back over his shoulder nervously. 'I can't even see them.'

'One of us draws their fire, the others shoot on the muzzle flashes,' I say.

'Great. Who gets the job of target?' Trost says, obviously not volunteering himself.

'I'll do it,' Tanya says, and before I can stop her she's heading out towards the clearing. Trost and me follow quickly after her, scanning the trees for signs of movement. Tanya breaks from cover for a couple of seconds and then dashes out of sight again, but not before the tau open fire. I see a blaze of light just to my left and fire quickly, emptying half a clip, before turning my aim on more movement to my right, using up the rest of the magazine. I pull it out and slam another one in. Three reloads to go, and there's still plenty of fighting to be done.

'Rush 'em!' I shout, ducking my head down and dashing out, firing wildly from the hip, before diving down into the cover offered by the shallow lip of the stream. There's more return fire, which kicks up dozens of impact splashes in the water around me, and I quickly wriggle my legs out of the way and fire back, targeting a cluster of bushes where I saw three or four flashes of light. There's a crackle of sparks and something crashes out of the bushes, flattening the leaves underneath it. I hear fire from my right and see Trost targeting the same spot, and open fire again, guessing that there's more than one of them there.

Something buzzes past my head and carves a furrow in the bank behind me before exploding, showering me with dirt.

'Demolition Man, show me some fireworks!' I shout out to Trost, who's now just upstream from me. He gives me a thumbs up and pulls a large canister from his pack, about the size of my forearm. Pulling the pin, he hefts it towards the far tree-line. I watch it spin through the air.

'Don't look!' Trost shouts, but too late. I'm just twisting my head away when the bomb explodes and a sheet of white fire erupts in a circle, searing my vision and causing spots to dance in front of my eyes. I feel someone grab me by the shoulder and haul me to my feet.

'Follow me,' I hear Tanya pant in my ear and I stumble into a run as she guides me across the clearing. All I can smell is burning, and I can feel the charred earth crunching under my step. Blinking my eyes rapidly, my vision starts to return, first a blur of yellow and green, but after a few more seconds hazy shapes of bushes, and a grey blob I take to be Quidlon or Trost.

'Door's not far,' I hear Quidlon say, and rubbing at my eyes, I can see him much more clearly.

'You got any more of those incendiaries, Demolition Man?' Tanya asks.

'Just one more,' he replies.

'Better save it,' I tell him. 'Use ordinary grenades.'

We charge the exit, which isn't that well held, the ten tau taken down with three simultaneous explosions.

'I thought it would be harder getting out,' Tanya admits as we pound down the corridor towards the entrance to the power chamber.

'A lot of them came after me,' Trost tells us. 'I caused a hell of a bang, nearly took down half the dome, I reckon.'

'And there's the Colonel causing mayhem as well,' I remind them as Tanya goes to work with the las-cutter again. 'We have to keep the advantage of surprise. I don't know how quick they can respond, but something tells me the tau are good at getting organised very quickly.'

'I'm through,' Tanya informs us, snapping closed the cutter and hanging it on one of her pack straps.

'Remember the plan,' I say, readying a smoke grenade. 'Cover the ground to the tower and get inside. Demolition Man and me hold off any attackers while Brains cuts the power and locks down the doors. Sharpshooter gets to the top of the tower ready to fire. Any trouble, just shout out and I'll come running.'

'Got it, Last Chance,' Tanya says with a nod, pulling out one of her own smoke grenades. 'See you at the top of the tower.'

We roll the grenades through the opening cut by Tanya, and I glance after them to see thick blue smoke spilling everywhere.

'Go!' I slap Tanya on the backside and she jumps through the hole, followed by Quidlon. I hear a burst of gunfire and follow through quickly, Trost bringing up the rear. I hurl myself through the smoke, not bothering trying to fire as shots whine and whistle around us, and nearly slam face first into the wall of the tower. Something explodes above my head and showers me with debris from the tower wall.

'Get inside, right now!' I bark at the others, and they head off in the direction of the door. I see shadowy shapes to the left and right and sight along the barrel of the autogun, picking my shots. I loose off one burst to the left and see a figure drop, then another to the right is kicked off their feet by the volley. I take a few steps along the wall to change my position, and return fire begins to send splinters up from the floor and wall where I was standing. I fire back at the muzzle flares and hear a muffled scream as my shots hit home. A few more steps and I can see Trost in the doorway, waving frantically at me.

'What's the matter?' I ask, hurrying over to him.

'Quidlon's gone awol, disappeared out the other side of the tower,' he tells me, pointing over his shoulder with his thumb.

'Okay, hold position here, I'll drag the stupid fragger back,' I tell the saboteur.

The inside of the tower is wide open, a single spiral staircase winding up to the other floors around a central pole, small landings at regular intervals going up towards the ceiling. I glance up and see Tanya still running up the stairs, her rifle over her back as she steadies herself against the central column, with no handrail to guide her.

Pulling myself back to the task in hand, I look across the circular hallway to the door opposite, where the door is still open. I dart a look outside: there's no tau in sight, but there is a line of five empty battle suits standing on the concourse, in front of a pair of heavy armour doors, and I see Quidlon over by them. The suits stand open, the front part of the bodies hinged up, the thigh panels lowered, showing the cockpit inside. Glancing around again, I sprint over the open ground to Quidlon.

'Hey, Brains, what the frag are you doing?' I shout at him.

'Magnificent, aren't they?' he says, grinning like a fool. 'Think, if we had one of these, there'd be no stopping us, we'd cut through the fire warriors with no problems.'

'If we don't get a fraggin' move on now, then a bunch of tau bastards in these suits are gonna come for us, and we're not gonna stand a chance,' I bark at him, spinning him round by the shoulder. 'Now shut the damn power off before more reinforcements arrive along the grav-rail!'

'I'll just take a quick look in one of them,' he says, pulling himself away and stepping towards the nearest battle suit.

'We have not got time for this crap!' I yell at him, grabbing his arm. He twists suddenly and drives his fist into my gut, knocking me to my knees.

'Back off, Last Chance,' he snaps. 'I might die here, and I want to have a look at one of these machines before I go.'

He climbs up onto the battle suit, but I jump after him, dragging him back to the ground. He rolls easily out of my grasp and swings a kick at my groin, which I barely deflect with my thigh. I guess I taught him well. His fist hammers into my right eye, faster than anything he ever threw at me in training. I fall back on my arse, dazed, and he climbs back up again.

With the fronts of the thighs lowered down for access, I can see that there's a seat inside, surrounded by display panels and rows of illuminated buttons. Hooking his leg inside, Quidlon drops into the seat, and I notice how his legs drop into the thighs of the suit. Bracing clamps close with a hiss around his legs, locking him in place.

As I push myself to my feet, clutching my gut, he stabs at one of the controls. There's a high-pitched tone and a tau voice says something.

'Get out of there. You don't know what you're doing!' I yell at him.

'Back off, Last Chance!' he shouts at me, a wild, possessed look in his eye. His left hand settles on a stubby control column while his right punches a few more buttons. 'I think I've got it, the controls are actually really simple, all in the right places.'

The thigh panels flip back up into place, sealing shut with a clang, and then with a whining of motors the main canopy drops down. The last I see of Quidlon is his wide grin. The suit sits there motionless for a moment, and I wonder if he really has worked it all out.

Then the war machine begins to judder, shaking violently for a couple of seconds. With a hiss, the chest plate opens up again. The canopy hinges away to reveal a charred corpse in the seat, still smoking, burnt lips peeled back from grinning teeth. There's a few crackles of energy still playing around two rods inserted into either side of Quidlon's head. Silently, the rods withdraw back into the sides of the cockpit. The thighs peel downwards revealing his ravaged legs, pieces of material burnt onto the bone. The stench of burnt flesh fills my nostrils and I gag. I gulp heavily to stop myself throwing up.

'You stupid piece of sump filth!' I bellow at Quidlon's husk of a body. Losing my senses completely, I fire a few shots into the corpse, causing it to collapse into a pile of bones and ashes which spill out from the suit. I spit on the pile and then kick at it, scattering ashes and chunks of shattered bone around me. 'Stupid, fraggin', stupid, son of a bitch, stupid fragger!' I scream hoarsely, punctuating my shouting with kicks, before pulling myself together.

I stand there panting and look at the slightly smoking battle suit. I pull a grenade from my belt and toss it onto the seat, before stepping back. The explosion tears the cockpit apart, throwing out shattered glass and pieces of instrument panel that drop amongst Quidlon's burnt remains. Realising I haven't got too many grenades, I use my autogun on the other four, spraying short bursts of bullets into each one, my firing rewarded by sparks of electricity and small fires breaking out across the various control panels.

More gunfire draws my attention back to the tower, and I turn on my heel and leg it. Glancing to my left I see fire warriors coming into the surrounding chamber, and fire off a few bursts of shots, taking one of them down and forcing the others back out of sight. I reach the tower and Trost is there, firing from the other doorway. I look over his shoulder and see three more downed fire warriors sprawled halfway across the concourse.

'Keep it tight here, I'll check on Sharpshooter,' I tell him, before pounding up the steps two at a time, paying no heed to the fact that I could fall off and plummet to the ground below with a mis-step. It takes me some hard running to get to the top, passing rooms full of instruments and glowing control panels, but eventually I burst out onto an open platform.

Tanya is crouched behind the parapet, her sniper rifle clasped across her chest. Shots ring off the surrounding wall, and I duck and roll over to her.

'How's things?' I ask, pulling out the autogun magazine to check how many bullets are left. It's about half full.

'They know I'm up here. I can't prepare for a clean shot under this kind of fire,' she tells me with a grimace.

'Some hidden hunter you are,' I snap, worming my way forward as more shells kick chips off the edge of the parapet.

'They came in and started firing. They already knew I was here, they didn't see me,' she snarls back, giving me a sour look.

'We're gonna get surrounded pretty soon if we aren't careful,' I say, pushing the magazine back into the autogun.

I pop up out of the cover of the parapet and fire off three shots at a group of fire warriors crouched in one of the archways around the central chamber, causing them to duck back. Dropping back out of sight, I crawl across the platform to the opposite edge and peek a look over the top. Another seven fire warriors are closing in on our position from the other side. Again, I jump up, fire two quick bursts, catching one of the tau full on, before ducking down again.

Suddenly I hear someone bellowing in Tau, a much deeper voice than I've heard before. I scramble over to Tanya, and she nods. We both look down, and there we see a tall alien running amongst a group of fire warriors, wearing flowing red robes.

'That's Brightsword!' I hiss at her and she nods again, bringing her sniper rifle into position.

It's then that I hear another shout, this time in Gothic.

'He's heading for the armoury, stop him!' I hear Oriel's bellow, and see the inquisitor and the Colonel dashing into view from another archway, auto pistols spitting bullets, bloodied chainswords in their hands. Moerck follows them, firing shots at the fire warriors dashing across the chamber, taking a couple of them down. I join their fire for a couple of seconds, but can't get a clear shot on Brightsword. Another fire warrior squad intercepts Oriel and the others, cutting off their line of fire to the tau commander.

'Come on, Sharpshooter, take him down!' I snarl at Tanya, but she doesn't answer. As return fire makes me dive for cover again, I glance back at her. She's there, crouched over her rifle, taking aim. But she does nothing, she just slowly tracks him.

'Get a clear shot, Emperor damn you!' I snarl, but she ignores me. Then her hands begin to tremble, I see the muzzle of the rifle wobbling in her grip.

'Take it easy, relax, breathe, then plug the bastard,' I say, trying to keep myself calm. I crouch there staring at her, willing her to pull the trigger. *Now*, I try to mentally shout at her. *Now, damn it!* With a choked sob, she drops the rifle clattering to the platform and falls to the ground.

'Are you hit?' I yell at her, jumping over to her side. She balls herself up, arms over her head to protect herself, and I can hear her sobbing over the rattle of gunfire and the snap of lasguns.

'Tanya, are you hurt?' I demand, grabbing her shoulder. She's limp, and as I pull her arm away I see tears streaking down her face.

'I… I couldn't do it,' she sobs at me. 'I'm sorry, Kage.'

'Fraggin' stupid…' I lose the power of speech, I'm so incensed. I backhand her across the face. 'We are so dead now, you wouldn't believe it.'

'I'm sorry,' she apologises again, in between sobs and sniffs.

'It's too fraggin' late for that now,' I yell at her, dragging her up by the hair. 'Get your rifle, we have to get off this tower.'

She stands there dumbly for a second, staring blankly at me.

'Get your damn rifle, soldier, and move out!' I scream in her face. She seems to snap out of it, losing the glazed look in her eyes, and snatches up her rifle. She darts another look at me and then heads back towards the stairs. I take one last glance over the tower edge, just in time to see Brightsword and his bodyguard disappearing from view through the wide doorway just behind the damaged battle suits. I run after Tanya, changing the clip in the autogun, making an effort to slow myself as I dash down the treacherous spiral staircase. Tumbling down and breaking my neck would be such a stupid way to go. After all, I'm sure the tau are going to try pretty hard to kill me, I don't want to spoil their fun.

When I reach the bottom, Trost turns around to me.

'What's happening?' he asks, switching his attention back and forth between me and the fire warriors outside.

'Brightsword's escaped. We have to get out of here,' I say, heading for the other door. I see Oriel, Moerck and the Colonel fighting hand-to-hand with a squad of fire warriors. I'll say this, the tau have impressive guns, but they don't know the first thing about close combat. Schaeffer and the inquisitor easily cut them to bits with their chainswords and head our way.

More fire warriors appear behind them and I give them some covering fire, squeezing off just a few rounds at a time, knowing I've only got one magazine left. Moerck stops and turns, firing a few shots at the tau as well, driving them back into hiding again. Oriel's the first to reach the tower.

'Which way did he go?' the inquisitor demands, grabbing the collar of my camo shirt. I point at the doors, which have closed again now.

'He has got inside the armoury,' the Colonel says heavily, chest heaving from his recent exertions. 'That will make things more difficult.'

He and the inquisitor push past me, and Moerck jogs over, ejecting his lasgun's power pack.

'Sharpshooter failed us,' he says bitterly.

'Yep, she did,' I agree. 'Time for us to get the frag out.'

'The mission is not complete yet, Last Chance,' he says, sliding another power pack into place.

'In case you hadn't noticed, the mission has gone up like a demo charge, it's a fraggin' major catastrophe,' I snarl at him, trying to push past, but he grabs my arm. I wrench it free from his grip. 'It's over, we messed up, now it's time to cut and run!'

'Are you deserting, Lieutenant Kage?' he says ominously, the barrel of the lasgun swaying in my direction.

'Yes, I sodding well am deserting! You are not a commissar any more, Moerck!' I point out to him. 'You do not have to die here.'

'No, I am not a commissar,' he replies viciously. 'I am Hero. Do you remember that? *Hero*. Which is why I do not cut and run and I do not desert in the middle of the mission and that is why you are not going to take another step.'

'This is idiotic,' I snap back at him. 'Aren't there enough tau to fight without us gunning down each other? Today is a lost battle, but perhaps we've scared Brightsword enough that we'll win the war. Let's get on the shuttle and live to fight another day. Hell, I'm volunteering right now to join the defence of Sarcassa, but I am not staying here a second longer.'

'Hold your position, lieutenant,' I hear Schaeffer bark from inside. He steps through the doorway, and signals Moerck to get out of the way.

'Shoot me, cut me down, I really don't care any more!' I shout at the Colonel. 'I am getting out of here, and I'm not going to come back for you this time.'

The Colonel smiles then, a grim expression.

'Too late,' he replies simply, pointing over my shoulder. I look around. The armoury doors are sliding effortlessly open and I realise why Oriel was so confident that Brightsword would pass by Tanya's sniping position.

I FEEL THE ground tremble under my feet as the five battle suits advance, striding between the smoking wrecks of the ones in front of the doors. They pound straight towards us with their guns brought up. Brightsword's is easy to pick out: more decorated than the others, an intricate tau design on the front plate. A multi-barrelled cannon on his right arm swings in our direction, a missile pod mounted on his shoulder angling up towards the tower. On his left arm is a shield-like device which I can see crackling with energy. His bodyguard are armed with the same multi-barrelled guns, and a mix of other lethal-looking weaponry. I feel my legs buckle under me and I drop to my knees. Everything seems to slow down. I see the four barrels of Brightsword's gun begin to spin, building up speed, and then he opens fire with an explosive burst of light, the shells tearing into the wall just behind me.

I hear Schaeffer curse and dive back into the tower, and somebody calls my name, Moerck I think. Everything snaps back in my head, the roar of the guns is deafening and I dive to one side and roll, feeling the whip of bullets screaming around me. Something hot and painful catches my foot, sending me sprawling again, and I look down to see blood oozing out of a hole in my right boot. Biting back a shout of pain, I bring round my autogun and open fire, spraying bullets at Brightsword. They ricochet harmlessly off his battle suit in a random pattern of sparks, leaving tiny little dents but having no other effect. One of the bodyguards peels off towards me, and points what is unmistakably a flamer in my direction. I hurl myself to my feet, ignoring the searing pain from my foot, and dive into cover behind the tower a moment before a jet of flame crackles past, spilling burning fuel across the concourse. The heat washes over me, stinging my eyes.

To my right I see the others sprinting from the tower. A couple of seconds later, a series of explosions wrecks the tower from inside, flames billowing out of the doorways. I try to stand, but my leg gives way, slumping me against the wall of the tower. The battle suit with the flamer stomps around the corner, weapons tracking from side to side seeking a target. It aims at the fleeing Last Chancers, not noticing me, and I open fire with the few bullets left in my magazine, aiming for the canister of flamer fuel on its left arm. The canister explodes, setting fire to the left side of the armoured suit and hurling molten shrapnel across the floor. The suit's pilot ignores the damage, turning on me with the cannon. I take the only route open and dive between the battle suit's legs, just as the gun opens fire.

The battle suit swings laboriously around to face me, forcing me to dodge aside again. I break for the cover of the smouldering tower and jump inside just as Brightsword turns and fires, the bullets tearing up great chunks of the floor behind me. Inside, the tower is littered with rubble from the destroyed steps, dirty great cracks in the walls. My foot has gone numb and I sprint lopsidedly out of the other door, limping heavily. The others are sheltering in one of the door alcoves on the far side of the concourse, shooting ineffectually at the battle suits as they split up and round the tower from each direction.

My foot slips on debris as I run out of the exit, twisting my tortured foot and sending me head first into the floor with a cry of pain. I look up and see the grey and black armour of Brightsword looming over me, one foot raised to stamp on me. I roll sideways under the foot, which smashes down just centimetres away from my leg, cracking the solid material of the concourse.

As I drag myself to my feet, Brightsword swings quickly, pivoting on one foot, the barrel of his cannon smashing into my chest and hurling me against the tower wall. I feel something break inside me, a couple of ribs probably, and my breathing becomes tight and short. The tau commander brings his arm back for another punch and I drop to one side, the blow smashing chips from the wall and showering me with dust.

The others direct their fire on Brightsword as he looms over me, lasbolts and bullets pinging around us. I get the strangest sensation that I've been here before. I then realise this is like the waking nightmare I had on the shuttle. In fact it's almost exactly the same – the gunfight around me, the massive figure looming over me. He turns, raising his shield arm, and the shots ricochet off it wildly, causing small crackles of energy to leap from the disc. His shield still locked in place, he swings at me again, nearly taking my head off.

Strangely, I don't feel so scared now though. It's like I know somehow that he's not going to kill me. Then I hear a sharper crack over the zip of lasguns and rattle of autoguns. Something slams into the shield, causing it to detonate in a bright shower of blue sparks, falling to the ground in three shattered pieces. More shots ring out, armour-piercing shells punching neatly through the battle suit in a tight cluster at the centre of the main chestplate.

The tau commander forgets me and turns on the others, swinging the burst cannon around to a firing position. The next incoming shot hits one of the barrels end on, causing it to split, and as he fires, the gun ruptures, shearing off the whole arm, which spins past and clangs to the ground just to my right. More shots in rapid succession cut through the struts of his right lower leg, causing it to buckle under the weight of the suit and toppling him down to one side.

There's a hiss from the battle suit, and a moment later a section of the body is punched away on four small jets, hurling Brightsword from the crippled machine. The four bodyguards are leaping towards the Last Chancers, who are heading for the far end of the chamber, propelling their battle suits forward in long leaps on their jump jets. I look back at the escape pod and see the hatch swinging open. The others are cut off, the bodyguard in between them and Brightsword.

'I'm coming for you, you alien meathead,' I snarl, propelling myself across the concourse, the other battle suits oblivious to my presence, leaving blood red footprints behind me.

I reach the escape pod as Brightsword pulls himself clear, bleeding profusely from a wound in his arm. He slumps to the ground and looks up at me, anger in his eyes. He mutters something in Tau and takes a deep breath. I heft the autogun in both hands, and he makes no attempt to block me as I swing the butt at his head, cracking his skull and causing him to scream out in pain.

I hear a screech of metal on metal and look around to see the battle suited bodyguard turning quickly in my direction. Wasting no time, I dash Brightsword's brains out across the floor with another two blows and then start hobbling back towards the tower.

'Run!' bellows Oriel, sprinting my way. One of the battle suits pivots in his direction and fires, a ball of white-hot plasma screaming past just behind the inquisitor to explode in a blinding flash on the distant dome wall.

'I can't!' I snarl back at him through gritted teeth, as he reaches my position.

The bodyguard have split up, two of them pursuing the other Last Chancers, the other pair, including the one-armed suit I'd tangled with earlier, heading back towards us to exact some vengeance for their dead commander.

'We have to rendezvous with the others back at the transport terminal,' Oriel tells me, putting one shoulder under my arm and lifting me to my feet. He drags me through into the tower just as a plume of explosions outside heralds a rocket attack, the shockwave hurling both of us into the rubble.

'Can you walk?' he asks me, standing unsteadily on the shifting debris.

'I'll bloody walk out of here if I need to!' I tell him with feeling, grabbing his arm and pulling myself up.

'Damn, more fire warriors,' Oriel curses, glancing out of the opposite door. 'There's too much open ground to get across.'

'Make a dash for it, leave me here,' I say to him, but he just laughs.

'Leave the heroics to Moerck,' he tells me.

'Sod the heroics, I'm hoping you'll draw them off,' I snap back, not at all amused. 'Can't you use some magic on them or something?'

'And do what?' he snarls, exasperated. 'Persuade them to go away? I don't think that will work.'

'Well, I don't know,' I shout back, getting angry. 'It's your fraggin' power, not mine. Make 'em think we're dead or something, they'll go after the others then and we can make a break for it.'

A shadow looms in the doorway and we scuttle out of view as one of the tau thrusts through his burst cannon and lets rip, shredding the opposite wall and filling the air with dust and flying shards.

'Alright, I'll try it,' Oriel agrees. 'Lie down and play dead. At least if this doesn't work, we won't know about it.'

We sprawl ourselves on the rubble and wait. I try to make my breathing as shallow as possible. I feel the blood congealing in my boot, the dust settling in my mouth making me want to cough. I close my eyes so that I won't blink. Tau voices drift through the doorway behind us and I focus my attention on the sharp rubble under me, trying to act like I'm as dead as a stone. I can hear feet crunching, quite a few aliens by my judgement – inside now – and something prods at my back, the barrel of a rifle. There's more talking, and I hear the clump-clump of the heavy battle suits receding outside, followed by a burst of gunfire. The tau around us move out hurriedly, leaving us in peace. I lie there for a while longer.

'Sit tight, wait for them to leave the chamber,' I hear Oriel say, and then realise that he's inside my head again, rather than actually speaking. I count slowly to myself, picturing the tau running across the concourse after the others. When I've given them a couple of minutes to be well clear I sit up, and see Oriel is already by one of the doors, peering out.

'They've left a couple of guards at the far end,' he tells me, gesturing for me to look. I glance out and see two war drones hovering a hundred metres or so away.

'Guess you can't trick them Have to do it the traditional way,' I say, retrieving my autogun from where I'd discarded it on the floor.

'Take the one on the right, I'll take the left one,' Oriel says, moving over to the other doorway. 'On my count.'

I line up the shot, using the pitted and cracked edge of the door to help steady my aim. The drone is sat there, slowly rotating, using its artificial eyes and ears to keep watch on the tower and doorways on its side of the chamber.

'One… two…' Oriel counts down, and then stops. 'Someone's coming!' he hisses to me, ducking back inside.

'Who?' I whisper back, moving around to get a clear shot out of the doorway.

'A tau, no armour,' he tells me. 'Perhaps come for O'var.'

I look out and see the tau picking his way cautiously towards the tower, glancing around every couple of seconds. He's dressed in layers of light green and blue robes which waft around him as he quickly walks our way.

'It's Coldwind,' I say, relaxing as he gets closer. I gesture to get his attention and he spots me, startled. He quickens his pace and hurries over.

'The shas think you are dead,' he says, gazing at us with astonishment.

'That's what I wanted them to think,' Oriel confirms, not giving any details. 'What are you doing here?'

'The others are in a safe place for the moment, but I wanted to check up on the reports that you had been killed,' he tells us, regaining his composure. 'It is rare for our warriors to make such a mistake.'

'Can you take us to the others?' I ask, glancing at the drones outside.

'Yes, follow me after I have dismissed the battle drones,' he replies immediately.

I watch him walk out again and say something to the drones in Tau. They bob in acknowledgement and then turn and zip out of one of the doorways to our left, moving at some speed. He waves for us to come out of hiding.

'Where are the others?' Oriel asks, helping me limp across the concourse. 'And just what the hell are you doing here?'

'Close by, in one of the urban training areas,' Coldwind tells us, pointing us the right way. 'They have doubled back and are now behind the firesweep the shas are currently performing. I will lead you to them and then you should be able to reach your shuttle without a serious encounter. I am here because I thought it might be prudent should something go amiss. It seems it was a wise decision.'

Oriel stares at Coldwind, his eyes narrowed.

'You're still holding something back,' the inquisitor snarls, stopping in his tracks. 'Tell me!'

The ambassador hesitates for a moment, and then sighs.

'Your shuttle has been detected and intercept craft have been despatched from orbit to prevent your escape,' he tells us, urging us to keep moving with a wave of his hands. 'I cannot guarantee you will reach your starship safely.'

'Is that all?' I ask. 'I never expected to get an easy ride out of here anyway.'

We follow the ambassador out into a corridor, which curves gently away to the left. We pass several open doors, one or two containing the corpses of fire warriors. The walls are scarred with the signs of battle, cracked and pitted from bullets, las shots and plasma impacts.

'In here,' Coldwind tells us as we reach a wide double door. 'They are in the two-storey building just beyond this doorway.'

He opens the door for us, and we step inside a small Imperial town, swathed in darkness. Two- and three-storey buildings loom up into a fake night sky around us, illuminated by two dully glowing moons. I load my last magazine into the autogun as we cross the deserted street, listening for any sign of the others.

We stop, and hear whispered voices from a building dead ahead.

'Yes, in there,' Coldwind tells us, pointing for us to precede him. We scuttle through the shadows, and Oriel calls out.

'Last Chancers?' he hisses.

'Inquisitor?' I hear the Colonel reply. The door opens on creaking hinges and we step inside. I look back, and see that Coldwind has disappeared. At that moment, blazing light like a sun breaks out everywhere, bathing the building in a white glare. Squinting out of one of the windows, I can see the four battle suits standing in the square at the front of the building, searchlights springing from concealed lenses within their suits. I can also dimly make out other figures scurrying through the buildings, fire warriors hugging the plentiful cover.

'It's Brightsword's shas'vre. Coldwind has betrayed us,' snarls Oriel, ripping his pistol from its holster. He delves into a pocket in his coat and pulls out what looks to be a small globe. He whispers to it for a couple of seconds, before putting it away again.

I turn my attention back to the battle suits. With deliberate slowness, like a firing squad taking aim, the shas'vre angle their shoulder mounted rocket launchers at the building we're in.

'First rule of assassination. We should have realised,' I hear the Colonel say.

'What's that?' Tanya asks, loading large calibre bullets from her bandoleer into the sniper rifle in her hands.

'Kill the assassins,' I reply, cocking the autogun and taking aim at the lights.

'Your people will weep and your worlds will bleed!' a voice from one of the battle suits booms out, echoing off the surrounding buildings. 'You will not live to see the misery you have brought upon your people!'

This is it, we're all gonna die, I think to myself. Suddenly there's an explosion in one of the buildings to our right, and I see the bodies of tau warriors being hurled burning from the windows by the fireball. From out of the billowing smoke and flames strides a figure straight from legend. Something whispered about in military camps with awe. Something dreaded by all enemies of the Emperor. I feel goosebumps prickle across my body. An Angel of Death. A Space Marine.

'Emperor's blood,' curses Trost, eyes wide, his gun dropping from his fingers and clattering to the ground.

Even the Colonel darts a glance at Oriel, amazement in his eyes, before looking back at the advancing warrior.

Two and a half metres tall, and nearly a metre broad across the chest, the Space Marine towers over the burning bodies scattered around him. Clad head to foot in black power armour decoratively chased with metals that glint in the firelight, he advances on the battle suits. The red eyes of his helmet glow like a daemon's as he turns his head towards the aliens. He looks just like the pictures and woodcuts I've seen, only even more impressive in real life. I make out an Inquisition symbol on his left shoulder pad, an 'I' picked out in gleaming gold. In his left hand he carries a long power sword, gleaming blue in the darkness; in his right he raises a bolter and opens fire, the boom of the weapon resounding across the square.

I can just about make out the flickering trails of the bolts as they scream across the open ground, three of them impacting in quick succession on the closest of the battle suits, the one whose flamer I destroyed earlier, tearing great gouges out of the armour and knocking it backwards. Still advancing steadily, the Space Marine opens fire again, three more shots, three more perfect hits that set off a chain reaction in the suit, causing it to explode in a shower of shrapnel and burning body parts of the pilot.

The rest of the Last Chancers open fire on the tau furthest from the Space Marine, as the other two turn towards their attacker. Their cannon fire dims even the searchlights, and I see the shells converging on the Space Marine. Their impact would have shredded a normal man and hurled his bloody carcass a dozen metres, but the Space Marine is simply forced down on to one knee under the cannonade. Cracks and dents appear in his armour under the fusillade, and a shoulder pad goes spinning off, trailing sparks from its powered mounting. Unbelievably, the Space Marine pushes himself to his feet, ignoring the shells ripping up the ground around him and scoring across his breastplate, and returns fire, his bolts ripping through the burst cannon of one of the battle suits.

'For the Emperor!' I hear him bellow in a voice like a god's. He tosses away his bolter and grabs the power sword two-handed, breaking into a charge, his long strides covering over three metres every step, his boots cracking the concourse under his weight. The nearest battle suit, now one-armed, takes a step back, readying itself for a jump, but somehow the Space Marine gets there before the jets fire, swinging the sword in a crackling arc that severs one of the battle suit's legs and topples it to the ground. Without a pause, the Space Marine spins and delivers another blow, the glowing blade of his sword carving a massive rent in the body of the suit, shearing it wide open.

The battle suit the others are targeting launches itself into the air on a short trail of fire, its missile pod igniting as it does so, the salvo screaming towards us on smoky trails.

'Get down!' Moerck shouts and I hurl myself to the floor, hands clasped over my head. The front wall of the building implodes inwards in a shower of shattered bricks and mortar dust, lumps of debris landing heavily on my back. I glance up and see Tanya at one of the windows, kneeling on one leg, her sniper rifle tucked tight against her shoulder, aiming up into the air. Even as the dust settles around her, she fires a shot, ejects the spent casing, tracks further up and fires again. In all, she looses off five shots in the space of a few seconds.

Something heavy crashes into the floor above us, sending more rubble tumbling down the stairway that runs down the wall behind us. The floorboards above give an ominous creak and we scatter, seconds before the disabled tau battle suit comes plummeting down through the ceiling, trailing sparking wires and plaster. It lands with a heavy thump in a cloud of dust and twitches mechanically, one twisted leg juddering up and down, its rocket launcher erratically rotating left and right.

'I'm going after Coldwind,' I snarl, my blood up. Someone shouts for me to stay but I ignore them, running back out of the door, favouring my uninjured foot as the other drags along the ground slightly. I glance over my shoulder to see another battle suit lying blazing in the middle of the square, the other jetting away, firing salvoes of rockets at the Space Marine, who ducks down behind the cover of one of the ruined tau machines as explosions tear across the ground around him.

I scan the buildings left and right, illuminated by the burning battle suits, looking for some sign of Coldwind. Something tells me to move back the way we came in, and it's then that I hear a noise in the building to my left. I instinctively dive to the ground, a moment before a shot cracks out, the bullet punching cleanly through a wall just to my right. I roll onto my back and return fire, the autogun recoiling wildly in my hands as I blast at the dark windows. I half get to my feet and hurl myself bodily over the wall, slumping to the ground on the other side. I check to see what weapons I have. I've got about half a magazine left, one smoke grenade and two frag charges. What the hell was I thinking coming out here on my own?

I take a look over the wall, and can't see any movement in the darkened building. Something does catch my attention a little bit further away though, a wispy movement glimpsed down a narrow alley about thirty metres to my right. I head that way, keeping low behind the wall, ignoring the sharp stabs of pain from my foot every time I take a step. Getting to the end of the wall, about twenty metres from the alley, I vault over one-handed, the autogun in the other. Almost immediately, a ripple of fire from the building forces me into a sprint across the road, gritting my teeth to prevent a howl of pain escaping my lips. I slam into the wall of the alley and duck inside, panting heavily. It continues straight for another ten or twelve metres before turning sharply to the left around the back of a low building with a corrugated sheet metal roof.

I push myself onwards, burning with the desire to exact some revenge from Coldwind. My head is thumping, my leg feels like it's on fire, but the anger in my heart is fanned to new heights as I think about the slimy, double-crossing ambassador. All along, he intended for this to happen. Of course, I would have done the same, but I would have made sure of it. Now he's going to have to pay the price for his failure.

I stumble around the corner, almost running face first into a tau fire warrior emerging from a door to my left. I react quicker, smashing my autogun across his face, snapping his helmet backwards. His rifle tumbles from his grip and I snatch it up. Behind him are three more fire warriors, but startled, they fail to act, and I pull the trigger on the rifle. It has no kick to it at all, the heavy shell smashing straight through the closest tau and punching the next in line from his feet. The third brings up his rifle, but far too late. The next shot almost takes his head off completely, his body flopping messily to the ground. I step clumsily over the bodies and crash through the doorway.

Coldwind punches me across the chin, a weak blow that barely registers. I lash out with my good foot, kicking his legs from underneath him. He stares at me with no emotion. I place my boot on his chest and pin him down.

'You bit off more than you can chew this time, ambassador,' I say quietly, bringing the barrel of the rifle up to his face.

'I regret nothing,' he replies calmly, meeting my angry gaze with a passionless expression.

'That's good. Nobody should die with regrets on their mind,' I tell him. Sounds of sporadic gunfire outside attract my attention, but they soon quiet. 'Any other confessions to make, to clear your soul?'

'All that I have done, I have done for the tau'va,' he says evenly. 'I foresaw that I might die. I am not afraid. I have served the tau'va. We shall continue to grow.'

'But why the double-cross?' I ask, curious. 'Why risk this happening? Why sour the deal?'

'To teach you humans that your time is finished,' he says with a short nod of amusement. 'You are old and decrepit, like the crumbling mansions your rulers inhabit. Your time has passed, and yet you so jealously cling on to the remnants of what you once had. We are superior. The tau'va is far superior to your dead Emperor.'

'You might be superior, but we've had a lot more practice,' I grin at him, tossing the rifle to one side. 'I'm not going to shoot you.'

'You are not?' he replies, hope rising.

'No, I'm going to strangle you,' I tell him, my voice dropping to a cold whisper. I grab him by the throat and he tries to struggle, but his blows are feeble and undirected. I slam him against the wall, my fingers tightening around his neck. 'Your last sight is going to be of a human throttling the life from you. I hope you enjoy it!'

'You will all die. Victory will yet be mine,' he gasps, smiling, and I drop him to the floor.

'What do you mean?' I demand, dragging him back to his feet.

'It appears that your pilot took to the role of mercenary even better than you intended,' he says, hanging limply in my grip. 'You will never get off Es'tau alive.'

'Neither will you, alien,' I snarl, dashing his head against the wall, snapping his neck with a single blow. I drop him at the foot of the wall. I have to find the others, tell them about the change of plan. If they're heading to the pick-up point, chances are they'll be walking into a trap. Added to the fact that Quidlon got himself killed before shutting off the travel line power, this place could be swarming by now. Right about now I wonder if the Colonel's decision not to bring comm-links was a good idea. He'd been worried that any signals we made would be intercepted by the aliens.

But it's no use worrying about what you haven't got, I remind myself, just as I told the others back in training. I snatch up the tau rifle and head for the front of the building, passing by a charred staircase into a short entrance hall. Easing the door open, I peek outside, but there's no sign of the enemy. I haven't got a clue where I am; this wasn't part of the set-up in the training bay back aboard the *Laurels of Glory*. I decide to head back to the square and see if I can pick up some kind of trail from there. There's no way I'm getting off this planet alive if I try to go it alone.

I manage to get back to the square without running into any more trouble, and crouch in the devastated ruins of the building where I met the others, still smoking from the rocket bombardment. Flashes of light attract my attention, and I note the crackle of gunfire not far off. I work my way stealthily around the edge of the square, carefully checking each building and street. A main boulevard runs off opposite my position, and I can see flames burning in a building a couple of hundred metres down. Squinting against the light, I make out figures dashing across the wide road, their long, tapered helmets clearly marking them out as tau. Two of them are pitched off their feet by hits and I hear two reports of a rifle echo around the quiet town. Scanning the buildings, I try to make out Tanya's position, as I guess she's the one picking off the enemy with such precision, all scruples obviously gone.

I can't see her from here though, and decide to break across the square, pausing to take cover by the remnants of the two destroyed battle suits before running painfully to the far side. Moving slowly along the front wall of a building at the junction of the boulevard and square, I stop at the corner and look down the street. I can see a few tau, and the ominous shape of another battle suit stalking past the burning building.

In the firelight, I catch a movement in a doorway on the opposite side of the street, and watch as a long barrel extends out from the shadows.

There's a small flash and a bang, and one of the tau is spun to the ground by a clean hit to the chest. I see Tanya get up and move further down the street, hopping over an intervening wall and taking position on the wide steps leading up to the next building.

I sprint across the road, head down, and land in a heap on the far side, trying to push myself further into the wall. Gasping now, feeling my broken ribs rubbing against my lungs, I edge along the wall, closing in on Tanya. She fires again, and then moves back towards me, keeping low and out of sight. I hiss her name as she's about to duck into a side road about fifteen metres away, stopping her in her tracks.

'Last Chance?' she hisses back urgently. 'We thought you were dead.'

'Takes a lot to kill me,' I tell her, moving out of cover and joining her. 'Where are the others?'

'The entrance to this chamber is just a few hundred metres this way,' she says, pointing down the side street. 'The tau are blocking the way out though. I've been protecting their backs; more tau are coming through from the opposite side.'

'We have to get them to pull back,' I tell her. 'Strelli's sold out to the tau, there's no shuttle waiting for us.'

'Damn!' she curses, glancing over my shoulder towards the square. 'More battle suits!'

I look back and see it's true. Three more huge shapes stand over the ruins of their comrades' vehicles, weapons tracking the buildings around the square. A cluster of drones hover around them, glowing slightly.

'Let's get to the others,' she says, heading down the road. I can't believe the change in confidence in her. She seems calm, assured, almost enjoying herself.

'What made you finally take that shot?' I ask, struggling alongside her. She looks over me and hooks my right arm over her shoulders, pulling me more upright.

'I realised it was him or you,' she tells me, no hint of embarrassment.

'Never realised you cared,' I laugh back, which turns into a cough.

'I don't,' she replies harshly. 'But it made me realise that
Brightsword would have killed hundreds, thousands more. Just like
you said. So I shot him.'

'And?' I prompt her, feeling she has something more to say.

'I just thought of all those people. The rest was easy,' she admits. 'It
gave me satisfaction, shooting that monster.'

'It always gets easier, Tanya,' I agree with her, limping alongside the
sniper.

'My name's Sharpshooter,' she snaps back, turning us down a narrower street to the left. 'You taught me that. It's what I do.'

'I guess it is,' I say, nodding in agreement.

We run into Trost a couple of buildings further down the street. I
tell him there's a change of plan and he leads us to the Colonel and
Oriel.

Standing with them is the Space Marine. He's even more impressive this close, my head barely comes up to his chest. His armour is
scratched, pitted and cracked in dozens of places, but he doesn't
seem bothered in the least. He whips round as we enter, power sword
raised, throwing a blue glow across the smooth, rounded panels of
his black armour.

'Where the hell did he come from?' I ask Trost as I limp towards
Schaeffer.

'I guess you weren't the only ones I was creating a diversion for,' he
replies, glancing nervously at the massive figure.

'Colonel, it's worse than you think,' I gasp, my breath getting
shorter and shorter. I think blood's getting into my lungs, my own
life fluid slowly drowning me. I need medical attention and I need it
quick. 'Strelli cut a deal with Coldwind, he's not waiting for us.'

'What?' Oriel snaps, stepping away from a window on the far side
of the room.

'Coldwind admitted it before I killed him,' I explain. 'There'll be no
shuttle waiting for us at the transport terminal.'

'The tau will already have a heavy presence in the terminal,' the
Colonel says after a moment's thought. He turns to Oriel. 'What
other ways out of the dome are there, inquisitor?'

'None that won't be heavily guarded by now,' he sighs, closing
his eyes and rubbing the bridge of his nose as if he's got a
headache.

'They're attacking: three squads, two battle suits!' I hear Moerck call from another part of the building.

'Trost, can you blast us a new exit?' Oriel asks the ex-Officio Sabatorum agent.

'Get me to the exterior wall, and Demolition Man can make you a door!' he snarls back, patting his bag of explosives.

'Right, everyone pull out,' the Colonel barks. 'The wall to this chamber is only a hundred metres away. We will blast our way out of here into the next arena. On the other side of that is the outer dome.'

'The tau are coming in from every direction,' Tanya points out. 'They'll be after us like hounds at the chase.'

'I will hold the breach,' the Space Marine says, his voice deep, given a metallic ring by the external vocalisers of his helmet.

'No, Brother Dionis, you are needed to ensure the inquisitor is safe,' Moerck argues. 'Give me the spare ammunition, I'll hold off the tau.'

'Still Hero, eh?' I say, pushing past Moerck. 'You're welcome to it.'

'Inquisitor?' Dionis asks for confirmation, his helmeted head turning towards Oriel, red eyes glowing in the gloom. 'What are your orders?'

'We all leave this damned city, head for the open ground in the next arena,' he confirms, striding towards the door, chainsword in hand. 'Moerck can act as rearguard. Give him your spare magazines and power cells. We move fast, don't wait for stragglers.'

We file out of the building, looking around cautiously. I see squads of tau running parallel to us, down the other streets, closing in on our position. A plume of jets heralds the arrival of more battle suits as they land on the roof of a high building maybe a hundred metres to our right.

'Move out,' whispers the Colonel, waving us on.

Like shadows, we ghost down the dark streets, Dionis on point, his power sword dimmed for the moment. He moves swiftly, despite his bulky power armour. Tanya helps me along, her sniper rifle slung over her shoulder, not the best weapon for a close range firefight anyway. I grasp the alien weapon in both hands, ready to fire in an instant.

From building to building we flit, pausing at every corner, glancing behind us regularly. It takes a few minutes to reach the wall of the huge chamber, which stretches up into the fake night sky above us.

'Okay, Demolition Man, get us an opening,' I say, patting him on the back.

Meanwhile, the others pass their spare clips to Moerck, who gathers them in his pack, which he slings over one shoulder.

'Melta-bombs, step back,' I hear Trost say, and we move away from the wall a few paces. There's a rapid succession of bright glows, and a section of the wall falls away, just lower than head height. Light pours through from the other side, blinding after the false night of the mock Sarcassa town.

'Sorry big fella,' Trost says with a shrug as Dionis crouches down to look through the small hole.

'It is of no concern, trooper,' the Space Marine replies, straightening up again. He raises a booted foot bigger than my head and kicks at the wall. Twice more his heavy boot crashes against it, dislodging a cracked chunk of rubble which nearly doubles the height of the hole. Without a word, the Space Marine ducks through, his power sword glowing again.

A scream in the air attracts our attention, and I see the trails of half a dozen rockets arcing over the buildings towards us. Oriel and the Colonel dive through the hole next, followed by Tanya, Trost and then me. Moerck backs through the hole, firing now at targets we can't see.

'Something special for you,' I say, dropping an object into his pack. He grunts without turning round, and I set off after the others, who are running over the dusty dunes of the next training area. I crest the nearest hillock, and realise that we're in some kind of ash wastes, the grey expanse stretching out in every direction. It'll be a killing field, no real cover, if the tau catch us in here.

'Run for all you are worth!' shouts Oriel, scrabbling up the next dune. I hear muffled explosions, and look up. The ceiling high above our heads seems to shake, motes of dust start drifting down. I pay it no heed, preferring to concentrate on pushing myself through the sliding dust and ash of the battle ground. Another explosion, at ground level and behind us, heralds the detonation of the charge I placed in Moerck's ammo bag.

'What the hell was that?' Tanya asks, stopping and glancing back over her shoulder to see what I can see: a large portion of the wall shattering and collapsing, crushing tau and battle suits underneath the artificial avalanche.

'Insurance,' I tell her, dragging her back into a run. 'Moerck was never gonna hold them off for more than a heartbeat. Still, he did make for a good booby trap.'

'You're a cold bastard,' she snarls, letting go of me and hauling herself ahead.

'Actually,' I call after her, dropping to my hands and knees and crawling up the dune, it's quicker than trying to walk, 'I'm not cold. I enjoyed that.'

'So how much explosive to get through?' Oriel asks Trost, as the demolitions expert examines the wall.

'Thought I'd use everything I've got,' he replies, stepping back after placing the last of his explosives against the base of the wall.

We exchange bemused glances and begin to back away across the dunes, breaking into a run as Trost picks up speed and accelerates past us. Looking back out into the artificial ash waste, I see tau battle suits soaring into the air, about half a kilometre away and to our left.

'Do it now!' the Colonel yells, and we all dive to the ground except Dionis, who simply goes down on one knee and turns so that his remaining shoulder pad shields his head.

The detonation seems to build in volume as the secondary bombs go up, rising to a deafening crescendo that's joined by the screech of tortured metal. A blast wave passes over me, scorching the hairs on the back of my neck and fluttering my clothes around me. There's a dull rumble and I look back, seeing a crack splitting up the dome wall.

'Oh frag,' I mutter to myself, painfully getting to my feet.

'Run!' screams Trost, breaking into a sprint, and we race after him as the crack widens, showering chunks of the dome down into the grit and dust.

My legs burn with pain as I force myself through the clogging dunes, pieces of debris dropping around us. Gritting my teeth I urge myself on even faster, dragging my feet one in front of the other. I slip and start to slide down the dune, but someone grabs the back of my shirt. Dionis hauls me up in one hand as he runs past, ploughing through the dust like a tank, his arms and legs pumping ceaselessly accompanied by the whine of servos within his armour, carrying me as easily as I might carry a new born babe.

A massive triangular section of the dome begins to fall inwards, crashing down and sending up a billowing cloud of dust and ash which sweeps over us, engulfing us in a rolling wave of air that buffets me in the Space Marine's grip.

'Okay, put me down,' I yell at Dionis, who slides to a halt and dumps me in a heap on the ash, making me cough and splutter and sending a stab of pain from my broken ribs. We turn back and head for the gouge blown out of the wall, stretching some thirty metres

above our heads in a jagged wedge. The tau are closing in, shots
begin to send up plumes of dust around us as we scramble over the
shattered rubble, floundering through the newly created drifts of ash.

Just then something flashes inside, through the opening: a bolt of
light that catches one of the battle suits in mid-jump, turning it into
a fiery ball of slag.

'What the frag?' I exclaim, dragging myself over a jagged piece of
debris and looking out through the massive rent in the dome wall.

Outside is a warzone, and no mistake. Small tau buildings stretch
into the desert from this side of the dome, some of them reduced to
rubble, others burning. Explosions light up the sky all over the town-
scape, as Imperial drop ships plummet groundwards, bombs and
missiles heralding their approach, cratering the wide roads and
smashing the buildings to pieces. Imperial Guardsmen are running
everywhere, fighting with tau fire warriors and battle suits. A Ham-
merhead tau tank glides into view, its nose-mounted cannons
chattering wildly, mowing down a squad of guardsmen advancing
through the burning ruins of a tau building. I look over at Oriel as a
platoon of guardsmen run past dressed in mismatched uniforms, carrying all sorts of weapons. One of them sets up a lascannon,
steadying it on its tripod, before firing again at the tau, the bolt of
energy going wide this time. The tau are returning fire, explosions ripping along the ground towards us. We break into a run again and I
find myself next to the inquisitor.

'You know anything about this?' I ask him, knowing the answer
already.

'More forces I had in orbit in case Coldwind got a sudden rush of
intelligence,' he says with a smile, which changes to a wince as a
rocket explodes close by, showering us with dust and pieces of rock.
We're not safe yet, and the Colonel leads us through the breach.

We make it out into the open, but it's no safer here than inside,
there are aliens everywhere – squadrons of battle suits advancing
from the left, fire warriors piling out of the back of three hovering
APCs to our right.

'Make for open ground, more drop ships will be landing,' the
Colonel tells us, pointing to a gap between two shattered buildings
just ahead. We dash from cover to cover through the crossfire
between the two forces, in as much danger from friendly fire as from
the tau. We run into a squad setting up a communications unit in the
shell of a cracked tau dome, a small subsidiary building only seven
or eight metres high. I recognise the officer in charge, he's the leader

of the mercenaries we met in the bar, still wearing his white armband.

'Well, Emperor damn my soul,' he laughs, seeing us. 'I suggest you stick to starting bar room brawls in the future!'

'Captain Destrien, I presume,' Oriel says, nodding to the officer. 'I am Inquisitor Oriel of the Ordo Xenos. I believe you have been waiting for me.'

'When I got the signal to start the assault, I could hardly believe it,' he declares, serious now, folding his muscled arms across his chest. His jaw drops as Dionis strides in behind us. 'Well, if I ain't seen it all now.'

Out of a blasted doorway I can see the open desert surrounding the battle dome, now littered with drop ships as more troops land, dozens and dozens of men and women pouring down the gangways. Tank carriers land, their heavy ramps dropping quickly, Leman Russ rumble out of the holds, their battle cannons turning towards the tau force as soon as their tracks hit the sand.

There's a rush of air, and sand is billowed up from the ground only a dozen metres away as a drop ship lands close by, its jets kicking up a dust storm that swirls into the buildings. I turn my attention back to Oriel, who's just finished talking to the captain.

'We have had enough fighting for one day, and I need a rest,' he tells us all wearily, his shoulders sagging. 'We'll commandeer that drop ship and get back to orbit.'

'It'll be safer in orbit?' Tanya asks. 'I thought Brightsword had a fleet.'

'The fleet's already left, and we have forces boarding the two orbital stations as we speak,' Captain Destrien tells us, glancing at Oriel. 'Whoever came up with this plan certainly thought everything through.'

'I just want to know where that bastard Strelli is,' barks Trost, face screwed up in anger.

'Don't worry about that traitor,' Oriel assures us, his eyes hard. 'There's a tracker on his shuttle and we'll find him soon enough.'

The inquisitor smiles humourlessly at us for a second before striding towards the newly arrived shuttle. As we wait for the squad to disembark, another two drop ships land close by, and soon the air is filled with a choking, roiling dust cloud and the whine of engines powering down. I step on to the now empty ramp, following the others, and look around. The fight between the guard and the tau has mostly moved inside the battle dome. Turning away, I notice smoke rising from the main city in a dozen places, and look up to see the vapour trails of planes returning to orbit.

I get to the top of the ramp and look back, squinting through the light and swirling sand, my eyes tired, my head fuddled with fatigue and pain. I swear I see an illusion. Leading the squad out of the next drop ship along is a woman, with short-cropped, pure white hair, and pale skin, dressed in various shades of brown desert camo. She looks just like Lori – but Lori died in Coritanorum. She and her squad disappear from view behind another drop ship and I'm about to set off after her when the ramp begins to rise.

I turn and Oriel is stood there, watching the battle.

'Was that who I think it was?' I ask him as the door shuts with a clang and the drop ship begins to rumble with the build-up of power in the engines.

'I have no idea what you are talking about,' Oriel replies, meeting my gaze steadily.

'I just saw Lori,' I confess. 'Or, I think I did.'

'But you were the only survivor from Coritanorum,' he points out.

'That's true,' I agree, stumbling along the gangway to the main compartment. I flop down into the seat and begin to buckle myself in to the safety harness, stowing the tau rifle as a souvenir under the bench.

Oriel walks past and is just about to go through the other door when something occurs to me.

'I thought you died at Coritanorum as well,' I call out to him. 'You escaped on the second shuttle.'

'Yes, I did,' he answers curtly, before closing the door behind him.

THE NEXT DAY, back aboard ship and all patched up with a good night's sleep, I feel much better. Happy in fact. The bad guys got killed and the Last Chancers did the job. So it's with a sense of satisfaction that I make my way with the others to the officers' lounge for a debriefing by Oriel and the Colonel. We enter the wide, oval room, gawking at the splendour of the wood panelled walls, the thick red carpet underfoot and the low, velvet-covered chairs. Oriel is waiting for us, standing in front of a bookshelf, looking at the volumes. We settle into the seats as the Colonel walks in from another door and nods for us to do so. There's no sign of Dionis. He disappeared into the forward chamber of the shuttle without a word when we left Es'-tau, and none of us have seen him since.

Oriel turns, a smile on his face.

'Well, Last Chancers,' he addresses us, looking at each of us in turn. 'By my reckoning, a complete success.'

He paces away from the bookshelf and stands in the centre of the room.

'As you have probably guessed, you have been caught up in a game of sorts,' he tells us, becoming serious. 'It is a game that I and other members of the Inquisition must play on a daily basis. It is a deadly game, not just for us, but for others, like yourselves, who are ultimately the pieces we play with. Yesterday, we won the game, and that is important. For some of you, that will be the only time you are involved. For others,' he looks at the Colonel, then at me, 'you shall be asked to play it again perhaps.'

'Excuse me, inquisitor,' Trost asks, raising a hand. 'I like the fancy speech, but could you just tell me what the frag this was all about? This was more than just offing some rogue commander, wasn't it?'

The inquisitor doesn't answer straight away, but instead looks at us, lips pursed. He strokes his beard a couple of times, and then looks at us again, weighing us up. He glances at the Colonel before speaking again.

'You will all be sworn to secrecy anyway,' he tells us. 'You have done well, and I cannot see that it will do any harm for you to know a little more now. You are right, this was more than simply a matter of preventing O'var from invading the Sarcassa system, although that did provide me with a reason for instigating a much wider scheme and killing two birds with one bullet, so to speak.'

I notice that Oriel's smooth talking has returned, a contrast from the tired and anxious inquisitor who fled the battle dome with us, the shells as likely to take him out as anyone else.

'The tau are a threat to our future in this part of the galaxy,' he explains, pacing up and down. 'It is a threat that we are unable to deal with fully at this moment in time. Other pressing matters, such as the advance of tyranid Hive Fleet Kraken, draw away the military resources we would need to wage war on the Tau Empire. That much is true, as you have been told before. That the tau are not keen to start a serious military engagement with the Imperium either, that much is also true. However, they had the upper hand. They thought that we could not combat the spread of their empire in this sector, and without this intervention we could not. However, by their own complicity in the assassination of Commander Brightsword, they provided me with a golden opportunity to give them an object lesson in the nature of the foe they face. They think they are clever, learning tricks of manipulation from the eldar, but they are young. The Imperium may not be perfect, but it does have one thing they do not have. Experience. For countless generations, inquisitors such as myself have been fighting against the menace of alien expansion, and the invasion of our worlds. Over those long centuries and millennia, we have learned a trick or two. To put it bluntly, we're sneakier than they could hope to be, given the right conditions.'

'So what have we actually done, except start a war with them, something you say we can't afford to do?' asks Tanya, voicing my own thoughts.

'Es'tau is just an outpost, little more than a fire caste staging area for O'var and his warriors,' Oriel answers, picking his words carefully. 'The loss of Es'tau, which by the way should be called Skal's Breach as it is marked on our star charts until they took it from us, is not a major blow to the Tau Empire. Except in one regard. No longer can they feel they can encroach upon our territory without reproach. No longer will they be certain that we won't respond to their aggressive advances into our space. We cannot hold back the expansion of their empire with might and guns. Not in the straightforward sense. But we can make them pause and think. Perhaps to turn their attention elsewhere, to easier areas to colonise which do not belong to us yet. We have sent them a message that will give them pause for consideration. That was my larger purpose in this enterprise. I wanted Brightsword dead, make no mistake about that, but not to stop him invading Sarcassa. I wanted him dead so that the chain of command was broken, so that the tau were disrupted, so that their attention was focussed on the battle dome and not on the half a dozen Imperial transports in orbit, packed with guard masquerading as renegades and mercenaries. Even now, three thousand more troopers are landing on the surface, eliminating the resistance that remains.'

His smile returns and he gestures to the Colonel, who picks up two scrolls from a desk to one side of the room. Pardons; I recognise them from before.

'Truly have you earnt redemption in the eyes of the Emperor,' Oriel tells us, his smile broadening into a genuine grin. 'Truly have you earnt the right to live again as free servants of the Emperor. You did not assassinate an alien yesterday. You conquered a world!'

I watch detached as the Colonel hands out the parchments, clearing Trost and Tanya of all crimes. Just the two of them remain, from the eight I picked half a year ago. Those are the two survivors then. I smile to myself, glad that I kept the promise to Tanya to keep her alive. I hope she enjoys the next sunrise.

Then my heart goes heavy. It's all over again. I'll be going back to prison. No pardon for poor old Kage, N; 14-3889, 13th Penal Legion. Not that I give a damn about that, I wasn't expecting one. No, my mind's on something else.

I walk over to Oriel, where he's stood by the bookshelf again.

'When I accused you of being a witch, why did you say that of all people I should not judge you?' I ask.

'You're intelligent, Kage, you'll work it out for yourself,' he says, not looking at me.

'What does that mean?' I demand, making him turn around and look at me.

'When you're back in your cell, you'll have time to think about it,' is all he says, tapping the side of his head before walking off.

EPILOGUE

THE AIR WAS filled with swirling grey dust, whipped up into a storm by a wind that shrieked across the hard, black granite of the tower. The bleak edifice soared into the turbulent skies, windowless but studded with hundreds of blazing lights whose yellow beams were swallowed quickly by the dust storm. For three hundred metres the tower climbed into the raging skies of Ghovul's third moon, an almost perfect cylinder of unbroken and unforgiving rock, hewn from the infertile mesa on which the gulag stood. A narrow-beamed red laser sprang into life from its summit, penetrating the gloom of the cloud-shrouded night. A moment later it was answered by a triangle of white glares as a shuttle descended towards the landing pad. In the bathing glow of the landing lights, technicians scurried back and forth across the pad, protected against the violent climate with bulky work suits made from fine metal mesh, their hands covered with heavy gloves, thick-soled boots upon their feet.

With a whine of engines cutting back, the shuttle's three feet touched down with a loud clang on the metal decking of the landing area. A moment later a portal in the side swung open and a docking ramp jerkily extended itself on hissing hydraulics to meet with the hatchway. A tall figure ducked through the low opening and stepped out on to the walkway. He stood there for a moment, his heavy dress coat whipping around him, a gloved hand clamping his officer's cap to his head. With his back as straight as a rod despite the horrendous conditions, the new arrival strode across the docking gantry with a purposeful gait, never once breaking his gaze from straight ahead.

Behind him, another figure emerged from the shuttle, swathed in a ragged uniform, his head and face bared to the elements, seemingly oblivious to the searing dust storm. His face was pitted and scarred with a dozen cuts and fleshy craters, his scalp bearing a particularly horrendous weal just behind the left ear. He walked with a slight limp as he followed the officer more slowly, looking around him at his surroundings.

He caught up with the other man in the small elevator chamber, where a nervous guard stood. When the warden saw the scarred man his eyes widened in surprise and fear. He glanced at the officer in the heavy coat before fixing his gaze on the newly arrived prisoner. The guard gulped heavily, and shuffled nervously back a pace.

The prisoner turned and winked.

'Don't worry,' the man said, a savage grin wrinkling his many scars. 'I won't be here forever.'

ANNIHILATION SQUAD

ARMAGEDDON SECUNDUS

0   250   500

① Crash Site

④

③

②

Infernus H

KEY
1. Crash Site
2. Cerberus Base
3. Mouth of the Chaeron
4. Infernus Quay
5. Diabolus forge
6. Averneas forge
7. Acheron Hive

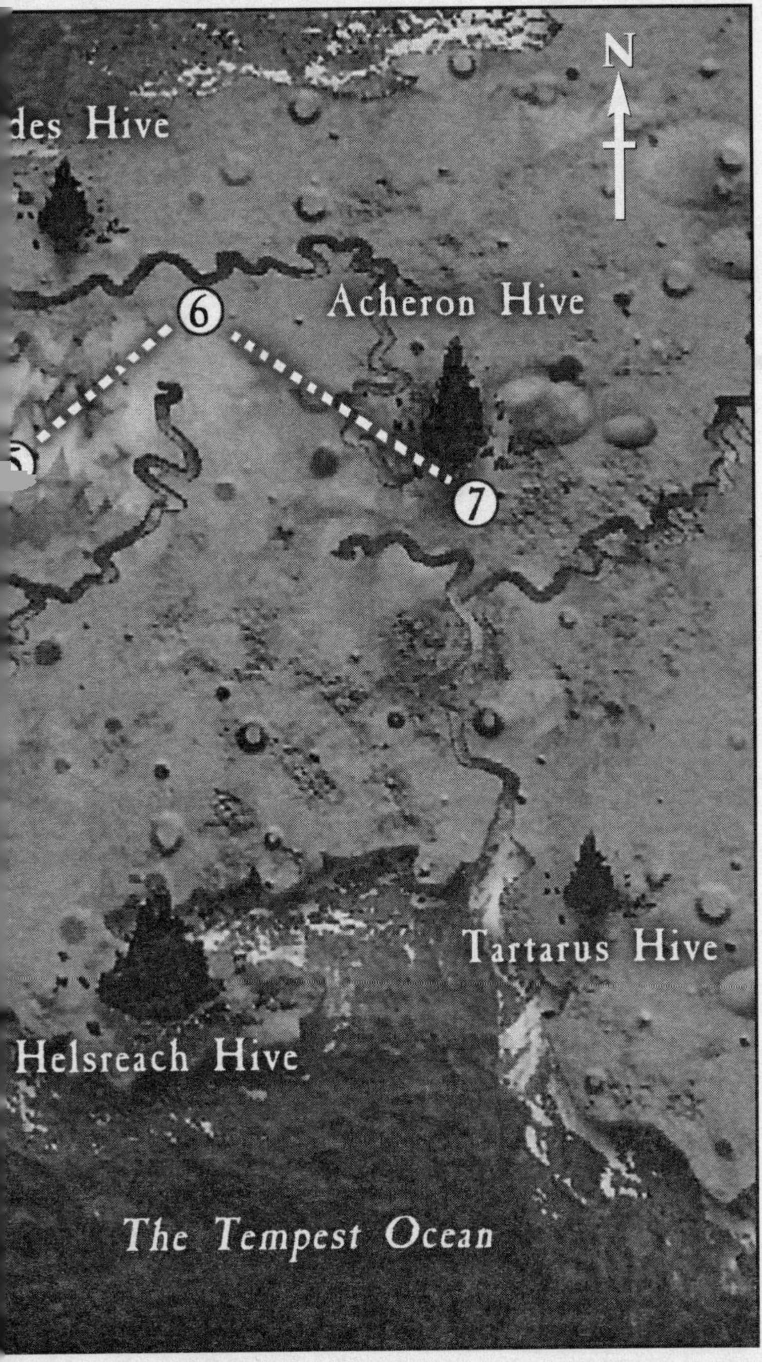
des Hive
N
6
Acheron Hive
7
Tartarus Hive
Helsreach Hive
The Tempest Ocean

ONE
PUNISHMENT

THE IMMATERIUM. WARP *space. It is a seething mass of roiling emotive energies, a kaleidoscope of colours and textures that reflect mankind's passions and fears. Sharp red waves of anger crash against blue whirlpools of despondency and soft purple clouds of passion. It is scattered with flickering pinpricks of white, a firmament of souls, the spirits of the living that resemble tiny stars of energy: miniscule, fleeting and soon forgotten. Here and there, like a candle in an insane wilderness of crashing colours, burns the soul of a psyker. The turmoil feeds its fire, giving it strength.*

Through the tempest of feelings surges a ship, its harsh lines obscured by a miasma of fluctuating forces. Its Geller Field pushes back the burning energies of the warp. Its eagle-beaked prow tears through hope and despair, the stubby wing shapes of its launch bays cut across love and hate, leaving wispy trails of rage and disappointment.

Behind the ship drifts a shadow, an empty tide of nothingness that consumes the disturbed energies, and feeds upon them. The cloud is more than a shadow; it is a shoal of emptiness made from thousands of warp-entities – daemonic sharks of the Immaterium that prey upon the energy of mortals. They gather around the ship, flickers of protective power flash along its length as they attempt to break through. But they are flung back by the psychic shield.

The Geller Field brightens and dims under the assault of the daemonic creatures; its power waxes and wanes. Around the vortices of its warp engines, a brief tear opens, and the energy of Chaos seeps in, a lone shadow flitting through the momentary break in the warding fields.

It passes effortlessly through the steel hull of the ship, seeking a host. It can feel its life-force dripping away, leeched from its invisible, incorporeal form now that it is cut off from the sustenance of warp space. It slips into a wide, low chamber, its unreal eyes spying the sleeping forms of humans. They look like grey, flat silhouettes. Their life force is weak, lacking in nourishment. A freezing black hole engulfs one of the rough pallets and the daemon veers away, terrified of the shadow that could consume it.

It then detects warmth, a glow of power, from further up the chamber. Drawn instinctively towards the source of energy, it speeds up, flitting back and forth, basking in the heat. Coiling around itself, it luxuriates in the sensation before dissolving itself into the energy until its whole being is fully encompassed.

WARP-DREAMS

It's a dream. A nightmare, in fact. I can tell, because I know I went to sleep on my bunk as normal, wrapped in a thin grey blanket, and there's no other way I could have ended up plummeting down a chasm into a roaring inferno. But it's not really a nightmare, because I'm calm about the whole thing. I should have been terrified as I plunged down into the fiery depths, falling through smoke, my skin burning from my flesh, the flesh blowing away from my bones as ash.

It's a warp-dream, horribly real in every sensation, more lifelike than life itself. Everything is sharper, clearer, more bright and focussed. Through eyeballs that have long since exploded into steam, I can see the cracks and crannies of the chasm wall, and small red eyes peering back at me through the fumes. The wind that screams into my cindered ears is sharp and loud. The flames that lick up from below, bursting forth from a river of boiling magma, are searing hot.

So why is there no pain? Why am I not afraid?

I don't feel as if I'm dying, just changing. I was once a clumsy, pain-ridden, emotional husk of a body, but now I am unfettered by its restrictions and my soul is allowed to burst free. Wings erupt from my back, and suddenly I'm soaring on the thermals, swooping and diving amongst the rising flames.

I laugh, though there is no sound. I delight in the freedom, the ease of movement as I climb upwards through the smoke and then kick my legs back and dive headfirst towards the inferno. The heat washes over me like a soft caress; the blistering heat is like the warm touch of a lover awakening me.

It feels beautiful, and I feel beautiful to be experiencing it.

And then something shudders within me. Something casts me free in the same way that I freed my own body. It takes my wings with it and soars up out of sight, leaving me falling towards the flames.

The terror starts then. It wells up from the pit of my stomach and a scream is wrenched from my lips. My horror bursts forth in a wordless screech as the heat blisters my entire being. Unimaginable pain infuses me; every fibre of my soul suffers vibrant agony.

Perhaps this is damnation. Maybe this is the Abyssal Chaos that I am doomed to be thrown into once my mortal life is ended. To know joy, liberty, and then have it taken away as I am damned for my sins – that is true torture.

I WAKE WITH sweat coating my body. With a shuddering gasp, I take in a lungful of the warm, stale ship's air. I hate warp-dreams. This one has been plaguing me for several weeks, although it's the first time I've had the sensation of fear. Usually it ends with me soaring majestically out of the chasm and disappearing into a halo of pure light.

Reality crashes into my senses, and for a moment I feel a disassociation with everything around me. For a split second it feels like I'm watching it from behind my own eyes. And then everything feels normal again.

The bunk throbs with the vibrations that come from the ship's deck. The air is filled with a steady humming from the machinery that keeps us alive in this hostile environment. The snores and heavy breathing of the other Last Chancers accompanies the relentless droning of the ship's systems, and I sit up and listen, trying to detect some oddity, some change in the eternal harmony that would have woken me. It all sounds normal though. I thought perhaps we might have dropped from warp, after all we must be somewhere near our destination.

We've been travelling for nearly a year now. A single, long, virtually impossible warp jump. I've never heard of such a thing before, I didn't even know it was possible. Usually a ship will jump into warp space for a short time, and then jump back into the real galaxy a week, or perhaps a month later. Ships that jump further get lost, or are destroyed. I've heard tales of ships that got caught in warp storms, only to emerge five hundred years later, their crews aged by just a few months. And I've also heard of ships that have disappeared for only a week or two, and are then found drifting, the crew nothing but ashes, the ships' logs showing that they died of old age.

Given a choice, I'd rather not travel in the warp. The strange dreams aside, it has got to be one of the most dangerous things a man can do.

But I don't have the choice, do I? I'm a soldier in the Last Chancers. Known as the 13th Penal Legion to everyone else. We're all here because we deserve to be. Each one of the thirty people sharing this chamber with me is being punished for their crimes. I murdered my sergeant because of a woman. Topasz, who lies to my left, is a thief who stole from the officers' mess of her regiment. Keiger, the bearded man to my right, hung his own squad for supposed insubordination. Looters, heretics, mass-murderers, rapists, thieves and all the other scum of the Imperial Guard end up here, doomed to spend their short lives fighting to their grisly deaths in battle.

Well, most of them are. We're different. We're Last Chancers. Our commander, the ice-hard Colonel Schaeffer, has other plans for us. We've got one mission, and that's it. It'll be tantamount to suicide, mark my words, and there are some here who'll wish that they'd chosen the firing squad or hangman's company before we see the thing through. Death is almost as certain this way as it is on the executioner's list.

But we're here because we're too good to waste. We're prime meat for the grinder that is the Emperor's wars. We're specialists, survivors, experts in our fields, and that means the Colonel has chosen to give us our Last Chance. If we finish the mission, we're free to go. Pardoned of all crimes, our souls absolved of our sins so that we might once again be part of the glorious Imperium of the Immortal Emperor of Terra.

Except me, of course. Even amongst these miscreants and frag-headed stains on humanity, I'm even more special.

I'm the Last Chancer who never got away. I'm too stubborn to die, but too mean to stay out of trouble. I'm useful for the Colonel to have around, for sure, and though I used to make his life hell and cause him no end of trouble, I've kind of got over that now. I'm just like the lifers in the other penal legions, except that by following the Colonel I'll see more fighting, more danger and more ways to end up dead than any long-serving veteran in other regiments. I had my Last Chance and I blew it. Now I have to live with it.

The lights flicker on to show that it's now morning, ship time. Obviously it's all artificial, and I swear the Colonel makes the days longer and longer so that we have to work harder. I know I did when he entrusted me with training the last squad. That didn't go so well in the end, and so although I'm still Lieutenant Kage, the rank is now more honorary than it ever was.

The others begin to wake. The chamber is filled with groaning, yawning, stretching and farting. Another day begins.

OUR DAYS START with the slop-spilling contest that passes for breakfast, and a compulsory punch-up between Kein and Glaberand over the seat nearest to the heaters. On the way out I count the cutlery, including the spoons, to make sure nobody's smuggled out anything that could be used as a weapon. It's bad enough that we give them guns to train with. Who knows what they'd do if they were let loose with a fork.

After we've all completed the cautious obstacle course that is a spin around the ablutionary block, it's back to the bunkrooms to see who's stolen what last night. Topasz has managed to acquire half a field rations pack – which nobody owns up to owning since we're not supposed to have any yet – a spare heel from a boot, two decks of playing cards and a small ball of string. After a year, everyone sleeps with their meagre valuables – the odd brooch, chain or ring – on their person or under their pillow. During the theft inspection, Goran and Venksin get into a fight, and Goran wins hands down because he's a big brute of a man. I send Venksin down to the med-bay to see if it's worth getting his ear stitched back on.

After this, and the odd argument, scuffle or backbiting comment, I lead the platoon down to the small stores room to gear up for training. Two commissariat provosts, even meaner and leaner than Navy arms men, guard the door to the armoury. They eye us through the black-tinted visors of their helms, shotguns held across the carapace armour on their chests. Anyone would think we were a bunch of criminals that might try and take over the ship. Nobody's had that idea since Walken got his head blown off by these two about six months ago. I give them a wave. No reaction.

Behind his worn counter sits Erasmus. His bespectacled eyes peer at us across his stores ledger, his quill-skull hovers over his left shoulder. He's not the fattest man I've seen, but there's a definite softness to him, like butter that's been left out too long and is starting to melt. His small, fidgety hands play with the corners of the ledger. I notice that his nails are caked in grease, and his fingertips smeared with red ink. He smiles at me as I walk in.

'Lieutenant Kage, how are you?' he says in his thin, stammering voice. 'Wh-what'll it be today? Close quarters? Knives and bayonets?

Or perhaps rifle drill? Or maybe heavy weapons training? I still have that Phassis-pattern grenade launcher for you to try out, but you're not interested in that, are you?'

Erasmus, or Munitorum Armourer-scribe Spooge as he is known officially, has a way of making every sentence a question. I have no idea how he does it, or if he's even aware of it, but it's impossible for him just to make a statement.

'Grenades and demolitions, dummies only,' I tell him and his smile turns to a pout.

'Dummies?' he says. 'No live charges? How will your men learn if they use decoys and dummies all the time? I mean, I know there was that poor business with Morgan the other week, but do you think the others will stop being so sloppy if they're using dummies?'

The 'poor business' he's referring to was the premature detonation of a faulty grenade Erasmus had supplied. Stephan Morgan, a first class soldier as far as I could tell, excepting his predilection for finding alcohol everywhere and anywhere and being drunk on watch, was blown into so many pieces it took four servitors to clean up the mess. I've got another scar on my ripped up face as a memorial to his bloody death. The only other thing that marks the occasion is a small entry into the ledger. I can't read much, but knowing the Departmento Munitorium, it probably says something like, 'Grenade, fragmentation Mk32, faulty, item unavailable for inspection.'

'Dummy charges and fake grenades,' I tell him again. He looks at me and nods, before whispering something to the quill-skull. It hovers over his shoulder, the polished bone gleaming in the yellow light of the storeroom, and a dripping pen extends from its whirring innards. The scuttlebutt maintains that the skull is actually from Spooge's father, who died in service to the Departmento, and Erasmus inherited the position. Along with his father's skull, of course, now refitted as an auto-scribe. At Erasmus's promptings, it scribbles squarely across the ledger, leaving dribbling blots as it goes. Little wisps of smoke bubble from its machinery-filled eyes. When it's finished, Erasmus gives it an affectionate pat. It returns to its position, hovering just above the armourer-scribe's shoulder.

'Please wait while your munitions are being prepared, if you don't mind?' says Spooge.

One of the provosts opens the armoury door and I see a servitor tottering away between the racks on six skeletal, artificial legs. Its arms have been replaced with a lifting hoist. Scraping and clanking, it works its way along the shelves, picking out crates and canisters. It loads them onto the flatbed back of another servitor, doubled up under a heavy plate. There are tracks where its legs were that grind across the grated floor. Its withered arms are bound across sagging breasts, life support tubes have been driven into its ribcage. The monotonous hissing of artificial lungs reverberates through the air. Drool hangs from its slack lips. The servitor's blank eyes look straight through us as it trundles out of the door, coming to a halt just in front of me.

'Load up,' I tell the squad, trying not to wonder who the servitor was before she was changed, or what affront against the Machine God she had committed to earn the wrath of the tech-priests.

Geared up, we make our way back along the ship, passing through humid, pipe-filled corridors above the engine rooms to the training deck. It was a loading bay once, but as it is the largest space on the cramped ship, it was turned to a more useful purpose. Seventy-five metres long and twenty-five metres wide, it's just about big enough to be a firing range, as well as a drill square. We ripped out most of the cranes and other machinery to make more space, dumping them before we jumped into warp space. With the help of the tech-priests we kept a couple rigged up for moving heavier objects around. They're useful for days like today.

'Get the tank ready,' I say, and the squad falls out to their assignments. A year in the warp, and drill every single day, they must have done this fifty times already. Still, no soldier is happy unless there's someone shouting at them, so the three sergeants, Blurse, Candlerick and Fiakir oblige, haranguing them for being slow and sloppy as they trot down to the far end of the chamber.

The 'tank' was devised by the Colonel. Made from welded-together packing crates and bits of old machinery, it's a blocky, square replica of a real tank, complete with turret and a gun made from old cable pipe. We moved a set of rails, which had previously run into one of the side chambers, so that they stretch for three-quarters the length of the training hall. Pulled along the rails by a loading winch, the tank can actually pick up a good speed for about twenty metres. We also have a dummy aeroplane, made of wood, thirty metres up in the overhanging gantries, which we can use to simulate an enemy strafing run.

The air in the chamber is sweaty and thick with grease as the platoon gets to work; hoisting the tank onto the rails and hitching up the winch. Almost half of the air filters on the ship have now broken down, and the air is becoming so stale it's difficult to breathe.

Schaeffer, typically, sees it as part of the training. 'Good for working at altitude,' he says. I don't mind it at all; in fact it's almost welcoming. It reminds me of the rank atmosphere of the hive factories from my home on Olympas. I grew up breathing oil and stinking of sweat.

With the tank rigged up to go, the platoon falls in again. They stand to attention, to varying degrees, as I walk along the length of the lines.

'Squad one, fall out for tank operation,' I order, stepping out in front of them. 'Squad two, demolitions detail, escarpment setting.'

The two nominated squads run to their positions, while the third strolls over to the wall to watch the proceedings. On the mesh floor, we've painted outlines of different terrains – in red there is a three-way junction in an urban area, in green a clearing in a forest, and in yellow a defile through a mountain valley. All perfect sites for infantry to ambush a tank.

Sergeant Candlerick stands by the winch, looking at me for the command, while Sergeant Blurse details his squad for the mock attack, positioning them behind the outlines of rocks and in small crevasses in the 'valley' walls. I like Blurse, he's a barrel-chested man with a thick moustache, and very much a traditionalist. I cause him a few problems though, because in his experience the Imperial Guard is run by NCOs like himself, while the officers are just around to make sure everything looks nice. In his regiment, the 38th Cordorian Light Infantry, he was used to the officers just giving him the nod and expecting him to sort everything out. Then he had to go too far, and anticipate the orders of his captain one time too many, leading an attack against a traitor camp. It would have been good if the captain had not already ordered an artillery strike a few minutes later, so that half of Blurse's platoon was blown apart by their own gunners' shells. Blurse was thrown in the brig. He carries a shrapnel scar across his chin. Despite that, he still retains an ingrained respect for the officer class. I simply don't fit into that mould. I'm vicious, dirty, cunning and I know exactly what I'm talking about. I've been in the Last Chancers for five years now. I'm perfect sergeant material as far as he's concerned, but the lieutenant's cap confuses him.

I give the signal and the winch grinds into life with a throaty growl, hauling the tank forward. Candlerick ups the gear and the tank lumbers forward quicker as it enters the 'defile' of the ambush site. Blurse gives a nod to his demo man, who rolls out in front of the tank with the dummy charge clasped against his chest. He waits for it to pass over. The magnetic charge clings to the underside of the tank as it continues, and I count for a five-second timer.

'Detonation!' I bellow and Candlerick kills the winch, bringing the tank to a halt. Within a second, the assault squad are out of their hiding places, leaping onto the immobilised tank. They tear open mock hatches and drop their fake grenades into the interior before jumping clear again.

'Emperor's teeth, what do you call that?' I shout at the squad as I stride down the hall towards them, stepping over the winch chain to march up to Blurse. 'Fall them in, sergeant!'

Blurse shouts them into line, and the ten of them stand there, looking straight ahead, avoiding my gaze. I can feel the smirks of the other two squads behind me. The bearable thing about being bawled out by an officer is watching it happen to someone else. Not me though. I turn to Fiakir's squad, lounging by the wall.

'Trooper Cardinal, what did squad two do wrong?' I ask. The man looks at me as if caught in a sniper scope; his thin smile turns to a look of horror, and sweat beads in his thinning hair.

'Sir?' he says, glancing left and right, seeking inspiration.

'Surely you realised that Trooper Dunmore exposed himself too early,' I say, referring to the Guardsman who had placed the charge.

'Yes, sir!' replies Cardinal, licking his lips nervously. 'The driver would have seen him and been able to take action, sir.'

'Don't lie to me, Cardinal!' I rage, storming back up the chamber towards him. 'Trooper Dunmore timed his attack perfectly. Suspended rations for you today, Trooper Cardinal. The rest of the squad piled in too soon. What did they forget, Fleschen?'

'I do not know, sir!' snaps the burly corporal, staring blankly ahead.

'Stupid, fat...' someone starts to mutter, but he or she falls silent as I pass my gaze along the line.

'That's a tank, in the Emperor's name, containing an engine and shells,' I say, and I see realisation dawn on the corporal.

'Secondary explosions, sir,' the corporal says. 'Squad two failed to wait and see if the charge set anything else off, sir.'

'That's right,' I say, turning and waving a finger to Blurse. 'Squad one on the winch, squad three ambushing in a town. Sergeant Fiakir, I want Trooper Cardinal on the demo charge, seeing as he's such an expert.'

* * *

AFTER FOUR MORE hours of training with the dummy tank, during which I suspend rations for another three of the platoon because they got into a fight with each other, we return the dummy charges and grenades and then retire back to the ablutions chamber to clean up for lunch. Responsibility for cooking is shared between the three squads, with Blurse's unit on food detail today. Not that it takes much, opening packets of dried rations, boiling them in water that's been reclaimed Emperor knows how many times in the last year.

I elbow my way into a space on the cramped bench with Candlerick's squad, who are tucking into the reconstituted slop with little vigour. I spoon the gruel in without ceremony, noting that it tastes of salt and not much else. The corporal, Festal Kin-Drugg, catches my eye and I give him the nod to speak.

'I can't see how this anti-tank training will be much use, sir,' he says, waving his spoon around.

'How so?' I ask.

'Infantry support,' Festal says, putting the spoon down. 'No tank commander's going to roll into a town or forest without infantry. We would never go in with just a tank.'

I look at him for a moment, and then at the rest of the squad.

'You were a drop trooper, right?' I say and he nods. He was one of the elite first company of the 33rd Kator Gravchute Regiment, in fact. He led an unauthorised landing to loot a town behind enemy lines, after it had been abandoned in advance of an ork attack. 'Used to operating behind the lines, then?'

'Yes, I'm trained as a pathfinder,' he says with a shrug. 'What of it?'

'So you're trained in sabotage, guerrilla activity and the like, then?' I ask, and he nods again. 'What do you think we're going to be doing?'

'I don't know,' Festal says with a shake of his head. 'The Colonel hasn't breathed a word about our mission.'

'That's right,' I say, finishing off the gruel and dropping the spoon into the bowl with a clatter. 'I don't know what we're up to either, but I'd bet my life it's something secretive. Not on the frontline, where tanks and infantry move together, but behind them, on tracks and roads, waylaying convoys and such.'

'You can't know that for sure,' says Gurter, another member of the squad. 'From what you've told us, we could be doing anything. For all we know, we could be on mine clearance or something.'

'Don't talk nonsense,' says Candlerick, slapping a meaty hand on the table. 'I'm not as sharp as some here, but I know that you don't ship thirty men across the stars like this just to clear a minefield! From what Lieutenant Kage has said, we'll be up to our necks in it, and no mistaking.'

'Have you not had anything from the Colonel, no hints at all, no mention of any particular type of training?' says Festal, leaning forward to talk quietly. I lean forward and whisper in his ear.

'Nothing,' I say, sitting back. He gives me a scowl and I smile at him. 'When the Colonel wants us to know where we're going, and why we're in such a hurry, he'll tell us. I've learned not to worry about it too much. It's all the same. One way or another, we're going to be up to out necks in cack and blood, and before it's over most of us'll be dead.'

They look at me for a long moment.

'What?' I say. 'Haven't you been listening to me? You're in the Last Chancers now, and when all's said and done, we don't have much of a chance.'

'There've been survivors,' says Gurter, glancing to the table to the left where Lorii is sitting with Blurse's squad. 'We might get through this. How long have you been following the Colonel, eh?'

I follow his gaze and then look back at him, resting my elbows on the table. I steeple my fingers against my chin.

'The difference being, Trooper Gurter, is that I'm invincible,' I say. 'What have you got going for you?'

He frowns and says nothing, turning his attention to the last few scraps of gruel in his bowl. The others glance at me as I stand up and step over the bench.

'Inspection in one hour,' I remind them. 'Full kit for the Colonel, right?'

They nod and mutter as I turn away. As I walk out into the central corridor, and turn left towards the wardroom where the Colonel's made his lair, I feel a twinge of pain in the back of my head. Knowing what's coming, I quickly make my way to the ablutions chambers, closing myself in one of the small cubicles there.

The pain extends forward, growing in intensity as it reaches my eyes. It feels like my brain is on fire. The off-white walls start to blur and dance in front of me, like pale flames. My ears are filled with the thunderous beating of my heart. I fall to my knees, my senses flaring with agony, and retch into the toilet bowl.

The roar of my heart turns into a drumbeat, before rising in volume to become like the deafening pounding of an artillery barrage in my ears. I go blind for a moment. Everything turns white. I find myself back on Typhus Prime, just outside Coritanorum. The ground is erupting around me from the orbital bombardment that paved our way into the rebel citadel. After a few seconds, I realise I'm no longer on the muddy fields of Typhus Prime, but in a grey desert, and the explosions are from bombs being dropped around me.

My whole body shudders. Part of me knows it isn't real, but my senses tell me that it's happening right now. The hallucination starts to fade, and I vomit the gruel over the floor and collapse sideways, slumping against the cubicle wall. A moment before my sight returns to normal, I see and hear something indescribable. It's a mess of confusing colours, clashing with each other amid a torrent of high-pitched screams.

I sit there for a few minutes, panting heavily. The pain subsides to a dull throb. It's happening more regularly, and it scares the hell out of me. In fact, I'm terrified of what the truth might be. The warp-dreams, Inquisitor Oriel's hints during the Brightsword assassination, the moments of instinct in combat when I seem to know what's going to happen a couple of seconds before it does. I have to face the awful fact.

I think I'm a psyker.

TWO
IRON DISCIPLINE

WHAT MAKES IT worse is that Oriel knows, and maybe the Colonel too. I can't understand why the Inquisitor has let me be, I always thought that rounding up untrained psykers like me was their reason for being. I don't know what worries me more: the thought that I might get turned in to the Inquisition for being a witch, or the idea that for some reason Oriel and Schaeffer are using me for something else. There's no way I can let the rest of the platoon find out. If they didn't kill me themselves, they'd be sure to make the Colonel take action. The problem is, with these seizures striking me more often, it's only a matter of time before the truth comes out.

Or perhaps I'm just going mad.

It's entirely possible, I suppose, given what I've been through. I instinctively touch the scar on the side of my head, a reminder of the operation I had. Some bastard drilled into my skull to release a dangerous build up of 'vapours', then dug around in my brain with a knife for good measure. I'm no medico, but surely messing around with someone's head like that can't be good for them? But the hallucinations had started before then, so who in hell knows what's happening up there.

Suitably calmed, I stand up and straighten my uniform. Opening the cubicle door, I glance around and find that the others are still in the mess. It's only been a minute, probably less, since the attack began. I open the storage cupboard and quickly mop up the floor before tidying everything away and leaving the ablutions chamber.

Just as I'm walking past the mess on my way to the Colonel's office to give my daily report, the others begin to file out on their way to the bunkroom. They've got an hour to prepare for the Colonel's inspection, and they're certainly good enough to be ready in half that, earning themselves a bit of leisure time. Lorii is one of the last to leave and looks at me questioningly.

'Are you alright, Kage?' she asks. 'You're looking pale.'

I laugh, perhaps slightly too hard. The thing is, Lorii is about as pale as you can get. Her skin is absolutely white, as is her short, cropped hair. Her pale blue eyes look into mine for a second, and I meet her stony gaze.

'Sorry,' I say glancing away for a heartbeat.

She doesn't say anything, but just stands there looking at me in that cool manner she has. Then she turns away and walks off without another word. I watch her. Any other man might have admired the swing of her hips, but I remember her gouging out the eye of a man who touched her, and so I can safely say I've got no interest in any kind of bunkroom tricks.

It was odd, meeting her again when I came on board. I thought she had been dead for the previous two years. The last time I had seen her before then, she had run off after her brother who had gotten his brains blown out while we were in Coritanorum. I'd heard gunfire and assumed she had died too. Turns out that Inquisitor Oriel, another person to have arisen like a ghost from the ashes of Coritanorum, had brought her out safely. She had worked for Oriel as a go-between for him and the Imperial Guard during the set-up for the Brightsword mission, and after talking to her, she confirmed that I really had seen her coming down the assault ramp of a lander after we'd killed the tau renegade.

Apparently, according to the Colonel, she requested to rejoin the Last Chancers. I think she has a death wish, perhaps because she lost Loron. Whatever it is, she's got a haunted look about her, and I haven't seen her smile once in the last year. She performs well in training, excellently in fact, but she's dead inside. I can tell from her eyes.

I felt a strange relief to find that another Last Chancer managed to get out of Coritanorum. It had been troubling me as to why I had survived when the rest of the team had ended up dead. I got over it of course, but, seeing her, I felt comforted that someone else was still alive who knew what we had done. Someone else knows about the three million men, women and children we killed. Someone else understands just what it is that the Last Chancers do, and why we have to do it.

I remember trying to explain it to the last squad, about how a soldier has to act, and learn to kill without thought or remorse. This time I haven't bothered to try. They'll either figure it out, or they'll die. Either way, I'm not thinking of them as my soldiers anymore. That was my mistake last time – thinking that the squad was mine. They never were; we're all the Colonel's meat for the grinder, and he doesn't think twice about any of us – not even me.

THE COLONEL LOOKS at me from behind his desk. His ice-shard eyes bore into me as I give my daily report. As usual, he's in his dress uniform, braids and everything. He sits erect in the high-backed chair, arms folded across his broad chest.

'And how about discipline, Kage?' he asks.

'Goran broke Topasz's nose last night for stealing his bootlaces,' I say, staring over the Colonel's left shoulder.

'His bootlaces?' asks the Colonel, leaning forward and resting his hands neatly on the desk.

'Topasz can't help herself,' I explain. 'Even when they've got nothing except their uniforms, she can't stop herself from taking something. And Goran is a bully, sir, through and through. He knows he's bigger than she is, all he had to do was ask for them back, but he asks with his fists.'

I meet Schaeffer's gaze. He's still staring at me intently.

'Nearly a year with them, and you cannot stop them stealing from each other, or fighting?' he says.

'Well, sir, if you had given me a stormtrooper regiment, I guess they'd be happy and smiling,' I say. 'As it is, they're the dregs of your gulag, and some of them won't be changed.'

'But every single day?' says the Colonel, showing his frustration. 'Five have been killed while they sleep; two in stand-up fights, and twice that number have spent a month or more in the apothecarium. It simply is not good enough, Kage.'

'They're stuck on the ship, in the middle of warp space, with absolutely nothing,' I say, trying to keep my voice even. 'Even if they weren't criminals, they would be slitting each other's throats or their own after all this time. There's nothing I can do about Topasz, short of cutting off her hands.'

'But you can deal with Goran,' says the Colonel, still staring straight at me.

His expression hasn't changed a bit, not outwardly, but his meaning is suddenly very clear.

'I've tried everything in the regulations detailed for the type of infractions committed, sir,' I say.

His stare doesn't waver for a second.

'Yes, sir,' I say with a vicious smile. 'Yes, I can deal with Goran, with your permission.'

'You have my full permission, Kage, to deal with the situation as you see fit,' the Colonel says, motioning me to leave with a flick of his head. 'I want to see a sharp improvement in discipline.'

I snap to attention and bring up the smartest salute I've done in a long time. I spin on my heel and march to the door.

'One thing, Kage,' says the Colonel, and I turn back. 'Bear in mind that the infirmary is not very well equipped, and the platoon is already at minimum strength after the incident with Morgan.'

'I'll bear that in mind, sir,' I say with a nod before opening the door and stepping out. As I turn and close the door, I catch a glimpse of the Colonel leaning the chair onto its back legs, a satisfied smile on his face.

IT'S TWO MORE days before Goran steps out of line again and gives me the opportunity to do what I've been wanting to do for the past six months. It's evening meal, and his squad, under Sergeant Candlerick, is up on dinner duty. He short-rations Brownie Dunmore's dish, and the heavy weapons man starts to complain. Although it's slush, it's the only thing we have, so I can see Brownie's point. Don't ask me why they call him Brownie, his real name is Brin. I should ask him sometime.

Anyway, things get a little heated over the counter, and Brownie ends up slapping his dish at Goran. Goran's a big guy, nearly a head taller than me. He looms over Brownie and takes a swing with his heavy ladle, smacking Brownie straight across the face. As Goran leaps over the counter, scattering pans and dishes everywhere, I make my move. I ghost up next to Dunmore, nobody noticing me.

Brownie's not seriously hurt, he's just smarting. Goran swings the ladle back for another attack. Goran, who once battered one of his squad mates to death over a game of cards, knows how to use his size well.

So do I.

Stepping forward, I drive the extended fingers of my right hand into Goran's windpipe, and he drops the ladle and clutches both hands to his throat. I drive my right boot into the side of his abdomen, low enough not to crack any ribs, winding him. My left hook catches him above the right eye. I don't break his jaw or nose, but the blow opens up a cut that bleeds down his face. Roaring, he takes a swing at me, which I duck. Then I turn the move into a leg sweep that crashes into the back of his right knee, sending him tumbling.

I let him get up and take a couple of swings at me. His face is contorted with anger. He's fast as well as big, and I have to stay on my toes, swaying back out of his long reach. Then I step inside his guard to hammer my right fist square onto his chin, driving his jawbone up into his face and stunning him. He swings another right at me, sluggishly this time, and I trap his wrist in my hands and twist. Pulling him towards me, I drive my left boot into his armpit and his shoulder pops like a cork.

A short strike to the back of his neck knocks him face down onto the metal decking. He lies there groaning, clutching his dislocated shoulder.

'Fix him up,' I say to Keiger, who's proved the most adept at blood work. 'Sergeant Candlerick, you will excuse Trooper Goran from heavy duties for the next two days.'

The platoon looks at me with a mixture of awe, shock and joy.

'It's time you all started acting like soldiers, not a pack of wild dogs,' I tell them, walking to the door. I pull out my small book of regs and tear it in half. I can't read it anyway; I always have to ask Lorii to find things for me. 'I'm the top dog, and anyone who steps out of line from now on answers to me. You were convicted under Imperial law, but now you're under Kage law, understand?'

They reply in murmurs, most of them are looking at the floor, avoiding my gaze.

'I'll think you'll find a sling in the infirmary,' I say to Keiger as I march smartly out of the room to the Colonel's office.

NEEDLESS TO SAY, the platoon is on its best behaviour for the next few days. Topasz manages not to steal anything, Goran gives me as wide a berth as possible, and I suspect that even Jueqna has stopped spitting in the gruel when he's on food detail.

Riding the mood, I give them solid drill for the next two days, marching them up and down the training chamber, and getting the sergeants to bellow out the orders. I never liked square-bashing myself when I was a trooper, but now I realise it's one of the best ways to show who's in charge. I say a word, a sergeant shouts a command, and they do whatever they've been told to do. In battle, unquestioning obedience is essential for survival. No pondering the rights and wrongs, no wondering whether I'm right. They do what they're told, because I'm in charge.

I exhaust them for the two days, drilling them until the sergeants are hoarse. I give them the next day as rest. Of course, with only half of them being able to bunk at any one time, they have to find their own diversions.

A lot of them sit in the mess, swapping stories. I remember doing that: telling the same old tales to the same people again and again, and listening to the same old tales from the same old people as if I'd never heard them. I listen to it all. I hear where they're from, what they did before joining up, their first love, their first battle, the wound that still gives them trouble whenever it's cold and wet. All of it is the same. I've met a lot of soldiers in my time, but underneath the skin, the uniform, they're all pretty much the same. Even these wretches.

In fact, I've come to believe that the Last Chancers are probably the ideal soldiers. I can understand why the Colonel finds us so useful. Every man or woman who joins the Imperial Guard knows that they can never go home. They are shipped for months to a war on a world they've probably never heard of. They might carry the memories of their home world and their family, but the reality is that they will never see either again. A regiment that serves well, does its time, fights its campaign, is often allowed to retire with honours. Some make their home where they have fought; others join an explorator fleet and conquer a new planet in the name of Holy Terra and the Emperor. Those are the ones that survive, of course.

Us Last Chancers get to live if we do well. It's as plain and simple as that. If we do poorly we'll die in battle, and that's the chance that every soldier takes. Our regiments aren't even our homes any more. I have no idea where the Olympas 24th Lifeguard is now. They might still be garrisoning that backwater hole called Stygies where I ran foul of my sergeant, causing me to be where I am now. Perhaps Stygies was invaded, perhaps not. Frankly, I don't give a damn.

All they have left is the Last Chancers, and the Colonel. No family, no friends, no home. Just comrades who would steal their teeth for a meal, or slice out their guts to look at the pretty colours. But they're the only comrades they've got, and so they tell stories.

The stories the Last Chancers tell always have a final chapter. It always ends with what they did wrong, and how they ended up with the Colonel. Take Brin Dunmore, for instance. His sin was pride. He's a top heavy weapons expert, trained as part of an engineer corps from Stralia. From heavy stubbers to lascannons and mortars, he can use them all. Problem is, he had to prove just how good he was. He took a bet that he couldn't use an anti-tank missile to shoot down an airplane. He proved he could, but unfortunately the plane he shot was an Imperial Interceptor returning from a sortie. They threw him in the lock house faster than the plane came down. I really should find out why he's called Brownie.

My musings are interrupted when klaxons begin to sound, reverberating off the metal walls. I leap to my feet and head out of the door towards the wardroom. The Colonel meets me halfway, his eyes dangerously narrowed.

'Send the platoon to the armoury,' he snaps. 'Meet me on the upper deck.'

I don't ask questions; I just turn and shout at the squad to move out to the armoury. I follow them down the spiral staircase to the deck below. Erasmus already has the doors open and is handing out lasguns and shotguns. I notice that the provosts are nowhere to be seen.

'Gear up, Last Chancers!' I shout, snatching a shotgun and a belt of shells from the back of the storeroom servitor. 'Time to die!'

I REACH THE upper deck at the head of the platoon and hear shots roaring out and ringing off the walls. We're halfway along the central access corridor that runs the length of the ship; it is about three hundred metres long. A few provosts stand at the far end, firing through the doors into the chamber beyond. There's a bright red flash and one of them comes flying backwards, trailing smoking innards. He crashes some twenty metres in front of us, screaming his head off.

'Keiger!' I snap, dashing past the stricken Commissariat trooper.

The Colonel emerges from a side chamber just before I reach the double doors at the end. With him is Vandikar Kelth, one of the ship's Navigators. He's tall and thin, with the distinctive bulbous skull of a Navigator. He wears a silk scarf tied tightly across his forehead. He swishes past me in a skin-tight green suit under a white robe, and looks down the corridor.

'What's happening, sir?' I ask over the shouts of the provosts and the cannonade of their shotguns.

'It is Forlang,' says Kelth, turning back to me. He is referring to the other surviving Navigator. The third that started with us, Bujurn

Adelph, went crazy and threw himself out of an airlock six months into the journey.

'Gone mad?' I ask, glancing at the Colonel.

'Worse,' Schaeffer replies.

Out of the corner of my eye, I catch a glimpse inside the far chamber, which is the landing that leads up to the tower where the Navigators stay, doing whatever it is that they do to steer a ship through warp space. There are two provosts on the ground, lying in a crumpled heap, blood leaking from their visored helmets. Three of the ship's crew are on the ground next to them, one of them a smouldering burnt husk, the other two missing limbs. I see Forlang standing at the foot of the steps. He's naked, except for a few tatters of bloodied white robes that hang from bony protrusions jutting from his flesh. His fingers have fused into long claws; there are scraps of flesh hanging from their tips.

A provost steps into the breech and fires his shotgun, obscuring my view. A moment later the sound of lots of bones snapping at the same time echoes down the hall and the provost collapses, crumpling in on himself.

'Possessed?' I say, horrified, turning to Kelth. 'How?'

'Take it down,' the Colonel says, ignoring my question.

'Squad one with me!' I shout, running down the corridor. 'Squad two, covering fire. Squad three, ready for reserve or rearguard.'

I hear Kelth shouting something after me, but I don't register what he says until I've burst into the room, the shotgun booming in my grasp.

'Don't look into his eye!' the Navigator warns.

'Don't what?' I ask, instinctively looking at the possessed Navigator's face.

His mouth is open in a grin; blood is streaming from toothless gums. His eyes are deep red, the colour of fresh blood. It's then I realised what Kelth had said. I always wondered what it was that navigators kept hidden under their scarves or bandanas. Now I know, and I wish I didn't. In the middle of Forlang's forehead is a swirling vortex, about the size of a normal eye, but it extends forever and into impossible depths.

To my right, Topasz screams. The sound echoes shrilly off the walls. There's the sound of a lasblast and parts of bloody matter spatter across my face and arm as she blows her own brains out. Just in front of me, Goran falls to his knees as Forlang turns towards him.

A blast of rippling energy leaps out of the possessed Navigator's third eye, enveloping Goran's chest. His ribs splay outwards, tearing through the skin and flinging ruptured organs across the floor.

Forlang turns his eye on me.

I look straight at it, into that swirling maelstrom. I feel a hot wind on my face, and hear the sound of crackling flames close by. The vortex turns red. Steam drifts out of the impossible orb.

I look away and bring up the shotgun. Forlang's face is twisted in a contortion of rage, which is replaced by a look of abject terror as I stare back at him.

'The fires await!' he screams at me, his voice unnaturally cracked and high-pitched. 'Damnation will burn your soul!'

I pull the shotgun trigger and the shell takes Forlang square in the chest, knocking him to the ground. He gets to one knee and looks up at me.

'It is not only the angel that ascends on wings!' he shrieks.

'Shut up!' I snarl, hoping that the others think he's raving.

I pump another round into the chamber and advance, shooting him in the chest again. Bone and muscle fly into the air, but still he's shouting at me. Three more shells, the last into his face, stop him moving. He's still not dead, though. I don't know how I can tell, perhaps just instinct, perhaps something more sinister.

The Colonel appears next to me, bolt pistol in hand, followed swiftly by Kelth, who sweeps past and runs up the steps into the Navigator's pilaster. He returns quickly with a black hood, which he pulls over the pulped remains of Forlang's head.

'He's not dead,' I say, and Forlang looks over his shoulder at me, his dark eyes glittering.

'Yes he is,' he says, standing up and taking a step towards us. 'But the thing still dwells in the carcass.'

'How do we destroy it?' the Colonel asks.

'We cannot, not here,' says the Navigator. 'I have a... a chamber, a special cell. I can keep it there until we jump back to the materium.'

'Do you need any assistance?' the Colonel asks, stepping towards the twitching corpse.

'No!' snaps Kelth, stepping in front of the Colonel and barring his way. 'I will deal with this, do not interfere.' The Colonel looks as if he's going to argue and then turns away.

'Notify me when you are done and I'll have the bodies cleared away,' Schaeffer says, looking at me as he walks out of the room.

'Clear out, platoon,' I say. 'Last squad ready for roll call is on gristle duty!'

THREE
UNHAPPY ARRIVAL

MORE THAN EVER, it's a blessed relief to jump out of warp space. Warp travel is the most dangerous thing a man can do, so I give an even longer prayer than usual to the Emperor for delivering me safe and sound into real space. We still have no idea where we are, and the Colonel's not forthcoming.

For another eight days we travel in-system, before the Colonel tells us to turn out for disembarking. We assemble in the docking bay, eager to find out where we are.

When the doors open, we walk across the threshold into a spacious airlock, and the ship's boarding gates close up behind us. The air that comes in is fresh and chill, a welcome relief for the others. After a long wait, the inner doors open and the Colonel leads us in. Waiting for us is a commissar, peaked cap low over his eyes, a data-slate in one hand. He talks quietly with the Colonel for a moment, before turning and walking down the corridor. We trail after him, exchanging questioning glances.

We're aboard an orbiting station of some sort, that's for certain. The corridors are of dull, unpolished metal, and here and there are signs of fighting, with blast and burn marks on the floor, walls and ceiling. There are old bloodstains in the grain of the floor, though everything else is polished clean. Some of the corridors are crudely barricaded, and the occasional blast door dropped across our path means that the commissar often has to take us on long loops around the blockages to get where we're going.

'Hull integrity breaches,' the commissar explains when he sees us looking at the blocked gangways.

I exchange knowing glances with the other members of the platoon, and we swap raised eyebrows and shrugs. It's no surprise really; we were expecting a war zone after all. Judging by the time it took us to get here after dropping from warp space, this is near the outer edge of the system – wherever that is.

I see jury-rigged generators attached to cabling that spills from broken ceiling tiles, and along one stretch, broken fans clank against internal ventilators through shattered grilles. After a few minutes, the commissar opens a large double door emblazoned with the Imperial eagle, and we step into a low auditorium.

The commissar makes his way to the pedestal at the front while the Colonel waves for us to sit down at the benches. When we're settled, Schaeffer joins the commissar.

'Armageddon,' the Colonel says, looking at each of us in turn. There are groans from some of the others. 'Even out on the Eastern Fringe, you have heard what is happening here. To bring us up-to-date with the facts, Commissar Greyt has compiled a briefing.'

The Colonel looks at Greyt and nods, before taking a seat on the front bench next to Candlerick's squad.

'Three Terran years ago, the orks returned to Armageddon,' the commissar says, glancing down at the data-slate. 'Led by the warlord Ghazghkull Mag Uruk Thraka, a large invasion force comprising hundreds of warbands entered the Armageddon system. Aboard hulks and smaller vessels, they swarmed in-system, and were engaged by Imperial Navy warships. However, we could not prevent a mass landing. Sporadic reinforcements have arrived over the years, some of them destroyed, but others get through. We do not know how, but orks from hundreds of days of journeying around Armageddon are being drawn to this world.'

The Colonel stands up at this point, and turns to face us.

'The surface of Armageddon is one large war zone,' he tells us, one hand resting on the hilt of his power sword. 'A hive world for several thousand years, Armageddon is a major manufacturing link in the sector, and its survival is paramount to neighbouring sectors. This is one of the largest military campaigns in recent history, and it is centred on this single system.'

He sits down again, and looks to Greyt to continue. The commissar pauses for a moment, to look at Schaeffer, before continuing.

'As well as this recent invasion, our forces on Armageddon must contend with indigenous feral ork populations that have remained since the first invasion fifty years ago,' he says, standing stock straight with his hands resting lightly on the lectern. 'Located in the equatorial jungles and the mountain ranges, these tribes have forayed forth in considerable numbers to engage our reserves, hamper logistics and generally stifle our efforts to destroy the ork landing sites. One hive has been destroyed, the others are heavily contested.'

He glances at the Colonel, who nods and stands up again.

'Armageddon is the most militarised planet you will have ever encountered,' Schaeffer says. 'The orks number in their millions, as do our own armies. In such an epic conflict, confusion and disorder are the norm, and we will be looking to our devices for the completion of our mission. The details of that mission will be related to you at an appropriate time, but I will tell you now that you are to minimise contact with the Imperial forces on Armageddon. Our presence is deemed secret, and any of you who divulge any information regarding our presence here will be executed immediately. The same applies to the contents of this briefing.'

Having given us this stern reminder of our duty, the Colonel sits down again and folds his arms. Greyt clears his throat, and continues.

'We thought Ghazghkull was dead after the first invasion, but we were wrong,' he says, his voice and gaze steady. 'We believe now that he retired to his stronghold in the Golgotha Sector, to recoup his losses and plot his return. As bold and huge as his first attack was, it was nothing compared to what was to come fifty-seven years later. There are some, myself and Colonel Schaeffer included, who think that his first invasion was merely to test our defences. It was nothing more than a reconnaissance, only performed on a planetary scale.'

He pauses to let this information sink in. Basically, this is no dumb ork we're dealing with here, but one who actually has the presence of mind to plan, to investigate and to scheme. I begin to wonder what we're here for, and I'm starting to get a good idea what it might be.

'Roughly thirty years ago, our base on Buca III was annihilated by missiles fired from an ork base hidden on an asteroid,' Greyt continues. 'The asteroid remained undetected before its attack, and we have now realised that this was the first test of what we now dub rock forts. They continue to play a pivotal role in this war, providing transport and fortification that can be landed on the surface.'

'I think we can skip to recent history,' says the Colonel. 'You only need understand that Ghazghkull, and a later warlord known as Naz-dreg, systematically tested their weapons and tactics against a variety of targets over several decades. Would you like to continue the brief-ing with the start of the invasion itself?'

'Of course,' says Greyt with a nod. He is possibly the politest com-missar I've ever met, but then again I've always been in the middle of a fight, one way or another, whenever I've met one before. 'After the near-loss of Armageddon during the first invasion, an investigation was launched to look at its defences, by all aspects of the Inquisition, the Departmento Munitorum, Imperial Guard, Imperial Navy and Adeptus Mechanicus. Given the importance of the system, it was rec-ommended that they be seriously improved. Sector naval command was transferred to the Armageddon System and the naval facility of Saint Jowen's Dock was rebuilt and expanded to accommodate all classes of interstellar warship. We established three monitor stations on the edge of the system, this is Mannheim and there were two oth-ers, Dante and Yarrick. Other orbital and ground munitions, bases and forces were substantially bolstered. In addition, a ruling council representing many Imperial organisations was convened to govern the planet. The previous Imperial commander, Herman von Strab, had disappeared at the end of the war.'

'It was believed at the time that von Strab may have fled to avoid the attention of the Inquisition regarding his less than loyal conduct during the invasion,' says the Colonel, stroking his chin. 'As it turns out, that was true, but he had also actually sided with Ghazghkull. Although his knowledge of the details of the system's defences was outdated, there is little doubt that his intelligence regarding our gen-eral strategic and military methods aided Ghazghkull in his planning.'

Schaeffer waves Greyt to continue, and the commissar scowls. It's only for a moment, but I notice it. It is the first sign of irritation at the Colonel's interruptions. I'd bet that the commissar doesn't even know what we're here for, or why he needs to act as schoolteacher to a bunch of penal legionnaires.

'It began, perversely enough and I suspect not entirely by coinci-dence, on the day of the Feast of the Emperor's Ascension,' Greyt says, his expression sour. 'Monitor station Dante transmitted a hur-ried message warning that over fifty ork cruisers and several hundred escort vessels had entered the system, before the trans-mission was cut. We despatched several battleships and their attendant task forces, and a series of naval engagements took place. Against overwhelming numbers of the orks, Admiral Parol's forces were gradually forced back, in order to preserve ships for an extended campaign. It was immediately evident that this was no simple raid though we did not realise at first that the beast had returned.'

Greyt rubs a hand over his face. Then he pulls a handkerchief from the pocket of his greatcoat and wipes away his sweat. Even with his training and experience, it's hard for him to stay focused. He was obviously there when the attack occurred.

'It took the orks six weeks of battle as they orbited Armageddon, bombarding Saint Jowen's Dock into uselessness while they were advancing,' Greyt continues. 'The landing itself happened after a three-day battle, but by then we were too late. It wasn't long before every hive was besieged. Our forces were battling merely to survive; there was no thought of any counter-offensive.'

'And so it has been for three years,' the Colonel concludes, standing up again, ignoring Greyt's irritated stare. 'The lines have moved back and forth, back and forth, but there has been little advance since the invasion was stifled in the first few weeks of fighting. We cannot afford to let up for a second, and the orks are never going to leave of their own accord. We are one of a number of strategies being employed to counter the orks or break the deadlock in the Imperium's favour. It is no exaggeration to say that our mission could decide the fate of Armageddon.'

AFTER GREYT IS dismissed and we're led back through Mannheim Station, we have a few hours in one of the bunkrooms before the Colonel pays us a visit. He tells us to get ready to embark. He leads down on to a different docking area, where we file on board an intrasystem transport, no roomier than our previous berths. But there is a bed apiece this time since there are no warp engines taking up half the length of the ship.

I bump into Erasmus Spooge as I head to the wardroom to see the Colonel.

'You're coming with us?' I say as the pudgy little man smiles up at me.

'Well, I'm responsible for your stores, aren't I?' he says. The servo-skull buzzes up from behind him, vibrating slightly. 'I have to stay with them until they're accounted for, don't I?'

'Is that alright?' I ask, looking at the quill-skull.

'Hmm?' says Spooge, glancing at the autoscribe with a look of concern. 'Oh yes, do you think I should have a tech-priest look at it before we leave?'

'Might be a good idea,' I say, stepping past him and continuing down the corridor.

I hear him tramp off as I knock on the door of the wardroom, hoping to get hold of the Colonel. Hearing a voice, I open the door to find the Colonel and the ship's captain inside.

'We have to wait for the escorts, Colonel,' the captain is saying. The Colonel looks up at me as I enter, a scowl on his face.

'Captain Hans Ligner, this is Lieutenant Kage,' Schaeffer says, nodding in my direction. I give them both a salute.

'All aboard and kit stowed, sir,' I say.

'Already?' says Captain Ligner.

'Lieutenant Kage has a way of motivating the troops,' says Schaeffer. 'As you have heard, we are now ready to depart, so what is the delay, captain?'

'The *Victorious* was having reactor trouble, Colonel,' Ligner explains. 'We will be departing at the end of the next watch.'

'Very well, captain,' says Schaeffer. 'Please inform me of any further news as soon as you can.'

'I will, Colonel Schaeffer,' the captain says before leaving. I turn to follow him but the Colonel calls me back.

'The system is still swarming with ork attack fleets,' he says to me. 'We're part of a ten-strong convoy that's gathered here to proceed to Armageddon, with a light cruiser, that is, the *Victorious*, and two frigates as escort. I want the platoon on standby status in case of trouble. I have authorised you to have direct access to a weapons locker. Familiarise yourself and the platoon with the ship's layout and drill for contingencies including boarding, counter-boarding, incendiary control and evacuation.'

He hands me a wad of schematics detailing the ship's decks, from engine rooms to bridge.

'Is it really that bad, sir?' I ask, taking the papers.

'It's about twenty days until we reach the fleet in Armageddon orbit,' the Colonel says. 'No harm in being prepared. Have the platoon ready for my inspection before we leave.'

'Yes, sir,' I reply, saluting and turning away. I stop and turn back to him again.

'Orks, sir,' I say. 'If they get aboard, I don't think we stand much chance at close quarters.'

'Then you best make sure they do not get aboard,' the Colonel replies.

I nod and leave, because there's nothing you can really say to that. As I close the door behind me, I catch a glimpse of a green robe further down the corridor.

'Kelth?' I call out. The figure turns, confirming that it's the Navigator. He waits for me to approach. 'Why're you here? This isn't a warp-capable ship.'

'There have been heavy casualties amongst the families aboard the fleet,' says Kelth, turning and walking down the corridor towards the steps leading to the bridge. 'There is an opportunity here for my House to assist in this shortage.'

'Very honourable, stepping into the breach and all that,' I say, falling into step beside him. He stops and gives me a hard stare.

'Honour has nothing to do with it, Lieutenant Kage,' he tells me. 'The standing of my House, and the assurance of future prosperity, is my only concern.'

'You want to make a quick credit?' I laugh. 'Millions are dying in space, and on the planets of this system, and you're concerned about profit.'

'Very laudable, lieutenant,' says Kelth with no trace of sincerity. 'The Imperium is a fragile thing, which does not bear too much scrutiny. It is nothing more than the sophisticated interplay of political dynamics, mutual need and self-interest. It survives because we need it, and we survive because it is there. The Houses of the Navigators are essential to its existence, and thus our dedication is duly rewarded.'

'But what is it you actually *do*?' I ask as Kelth starts walking again.

'We steer the ships through the Immaterium,' he says. 'You know this.'

'But how?' I ask, trying to keep up with his long strides.

'Think of a crystal of ice in an ocean,' he says, slowing his pace, his gaze drifting to the ceiling in thought. 'It bobs on the surface, gets drawn down by currents, and if it should melt, it would meld and become one with that ocean. That is how it is to navigate warp space.'

'I don't understand,' I say, my eyes straying to the scarf wrapped across his third eye. 'What is it that you can see?'

'Imagine a ship as a grain of sand,' Kelth says. 'When it drops into warp space, it is flung on to a huge desert. It is part of the desert, just like the untold billions of other grains of sand. But as the winds shift and change, those grains of sand also move, forming valleys and

drifts, hills and shallows. Imagine, if you will, how that grain of sand
would travel if it had a mind to steer itself into the winds it wished
to follow, and to avoid the swirls and gusts that would take it from
its path.'

'I still don't see what you mean,' I admit.

'That is my point, lieutenant,' he says. 'To explain the warp to one
who cannot see it, touch it, is like explaining light and sound to a
deaf, blind man. I have senses you cannot comprehend. Some call it
the third sight, but sight is such a basic sense in comparison. You
cannot imagine the sensation of seeing into the warp, of reading
motions born of desires, sensing the fragile flicker of souls. You cannot understand it, as much as I cannot understand why a man would
be a soldier.'

We're about to enter the bridge and he stops and looks at me.

'I'm wasting my time here,' he says. 'You have the soul of a soldier,
but you need the heart of a poet to understand the Immaterium.
Describing colours to blind men is child's play in comparison.'

I let him walk into the bridge, and try to work out what he was
telling me.

'Nope,' I mutter after some time. 'I still don't get it.'

THE CONVOY PROCEEDS as normal for eight more days, during which
we practise anti-conflagration drill, close quarters boarding combat
and all the other things that are essential to space combat. The
Colonel tells us that we're just passing Chosin, the fifth planet out
from the Armageddon star. We should reach Armageddon orbit in
the next twenty days.

Unfortunately for us, despite the stretched patrols of the Imperial
Navy, the orks are still very much active in the system, and a group of
them comes out of hiding over Chosin and comes after us. I put the
platoon on ready, and when I'm convinced, take a quick tour of the
ship. The bridge doors are open, and the crew seem busy, so I figure
nobody would mind if I slipped in to find out what's going on.

Captain Ligner and the Colonel are standing in the centre of the
small chamber, deep in discussion. Arrayed like a horseshoe, the
bridge is filled with panels and banks of screens and dials, attended
by various uniformed officers and dribbling servitors. There's no
other source of light, so the whole chamber is bathed in a multi-
coloured glow, creating an eerie scene.

Everything seems busy but calm at the moment. A static-broken
screen on the front wall displays the convoy's positions with blue

circles. Projected courses are outlined in dots. I guess the series of dark red runes far to the left of the screen are the ork raiders.

'Have we got relay from the *Victorious* yet?' the captain asks an officer stationed at a panel to his left, a set of comms-gear at his ear.

'Not yet, sir,' the lieutenant replies. 'Trying to work out whether it's transmission or reception that's at fault.'

'Perhaps they could route through the *Saint Kayle*?' suggests the captain, the comms officer nodding in agreement.

'That's the closest ship to us, sir,' the lieutenant says. 'I'll hail Captain Mendez.'

'Good,' says Ligner, turning back to the Colonel.

I hear someone stand next to me and turn to see Kelth, noticing the holstered laspistol at his belt.

'Can't comprehend what it is to be a soldier?' I say, looking pointedly at the sidearm. He glances down.

'Purely for self-protection,' he says, looking directly at me.

'Ever fired it before?' I ask, avoiding his deep gaze by looking back at the main screen.

'In duels, not in combat,' he replies, his voice soft.

'What's happening?' I say to change the subject. Only nobility has the pleasure of duelling, a form of combat as different from the dirty knife-fights of my youth as the coming space battle.

'The data on the screen is almost half an hour old,' Kelth tells me, crossing his arms and leaning up against a dormant panel behind us. 'The strategic information from the *Victorious* has been interrupted.'

'Damage from enemy fire?' I say, casting a glance at the Colonel, who is bent over a chart with Ligner, pointing and talking in a low voice.

'No, the fighting hasn't started yet,' Kelth says. 'The orks are coming in fast and straight, but it'll still be another hour before first contact, unless the escorts turn to meet them.'

'Will that work?' I ask, noticing for the first time a servitor wired into the wall beneath the screen. It's chanting something in a monotonous tone, too low for me to make out above the humming of the bridge equipment and throb of the engines that are powering into full life. Kelth notices the direction of my stare.

'It's a comms-servitor,' explains the Navigator. 'It relays and records all traffic received and transmitted across the convoy frequencies. And no, in answer to your question, the frigates and *Victorious* are not capable alone of preventing a flotilla of six ork raiders breaking through into the convoy.'

'Could they buy us time to get away?' I ask.

'Unlikely,' the Navigator replies. 'This ship is a little faster than the others, but there are a few ships in the convoy that would get run down within a few hours.'

'So what do you reckon they'll do?' I say.

My brow furrows as I look at Schaeffer arguing quietly with the captain. Perhaps he's advocating that we make a run for it and leave the rest of the convoy to its fate.

'The *Victorious* can outgun any one or two of the enemy,' Kelth says, stroking his chin. 'The frigates will try to ensure that they stay in support of her. Ork ships are generally not very manoeuvrable at speed. They'll have to attack in a series of passes. The frigates will try to herd them onto the light cruiser's guns one or two at a time.'

'And how easy is that to do?' I ask, feeling that I already know the answer.

'Commodore Griffin is experienced at convoy duty, or so I hear from the command crew,' Kelth tells me with a thin smile. 'The Emperor wills.'

'Yes, he does, doesn't he,' I mutter, turning my attention to the quiet hubbub of the bridge. I just wish he didn't will it against me all the time.

AFTER ANOTHER FIFTEEN minutes, the comms problems are overcome with some ingenuity and, I suspect, a lot of shouting and swearing by some poor bastard elsewhere in the fleet. The updated positionals appear on the screen, but I can't really make sense of them. I hear a low series of groans and sighs from the various members of the bridge crew.

'A problem?' I ask, turning to Kelth, but he's gone. He must have slipped away while I was distracted.

'I have a fleet communication from Commodore Griffin,' announces the comms lieutenant.

'Well, let's hear it then,' snaps Captain Ligner.

'There's actually a Navy task force, with the cruisers *Holy Wrath* and *Torch of Retribution*, about two days away,' the lieutenant says. 'We're to proceed to the enclosed position and meet up with them.'

'Two days?' I blurt out, and all eyes turn to me. The Colonel raises an eyebrow having noticed me for the first time.

'Why are you here, Kage?' he asks.

'I wanted to keep the platoon informed of the ongoing situation, sir,' I reply, thinking quickly.

The eyebrow rises even higher.

'I will pass on information as I see fit, Kage,' he says. I just look at him with a pleading expression, unable to come up with any better reason than because I'm curious. He gives me a long hard look and then shakes his head in irritation.

'Very well, you can stay for the moment,' he says eventually. 'But do not interfere again.'

'No sir, I won't, sir,' I say with a shake of my head.

'It's a mobile delaying action, then,' says Ligner. 'I hope the orks don't have any reinforcements close by.'

'Is that likely?' asks the Colonel.

'Not really,' says the ship's captain. 'Ork communications are unreliable, they tend to stay in close packs otherwise they end up scattered all over the place. It's when their ships are mobbed up in that fashion that they're at their most dangerous.'

The crew bustle around for a few more minutes and I start to lose interest until the captain glances up at the screen.

'Hold on,' he says, catching the Colonel's attention. 'The orks are making their first move.'

The blinking icons representing the ork attack ships start to move around to the top of the screen, attempting to flank the convoy to port. The frigates and light cruiser move to intercept, turning inside the ork ships.

'Which ship is that?' the Colonel asks, pointing at a solitary blue circle split off from the main cluster of the convoy ships.

'The *Spirit of Gathalamor*, sir,' replies one of the lieutenants from a position to the forward and right.

'Oldest bucket in the merchant flotilla,' mutters Ligner. 'Emperor knows how Izander keeps her going, she must be at least seven hundred years old by now.'

Another few minutes pass as we watch the escorts cut off the ork attack, one of them detaching to shepherd the *Spirit of Gathalamor* back into the main fleet. The orks slow and allow the convoy to get ahead of them, before cutting back and trying to cross the stern of the flotilla. Again, the *Victorious* and her companions head off the attack, interposing themselves between the attacking ships and the transports.

Kelth appears again and glances at me.

'Are all battles in space this dull?' I ask him and he shrugs.

'This is my first, I wouldn't know,' he says. 'I would rather it was dull than exciting though. I expect excitement in a space battle is pretty dangerous.'

I nod and turn my attention back to the screen. The orks, despite Ligner's words, have split into pairs, one for each of three ships. One continues to harass the starboard flank while the other drives straight for the rear of the convoy.

I look at Ligner, but he doesn't seem concerned in the least. He stands leaning over the back of his chair, glancing now and then at his comms officer.

The flickering icon of the *Victorious* breaks away from the frigates and heads towards the flanking group, steering ahead of them. The frigates keep their distance from the attacking group, staying with their broadsides to bear but are out of range.

'Aren't they the biggest threat?' I blurt out, earning a scowl from the Colonel. Ligner turns to look at me.

'Just watch,' the captain says with a confident smile. My attention is fixed to the screen when I hear the comms officer.

'*Victorious* has announced torpedoes launched,' the lieutenant says and a new icon appears on the screen, its projected line intersecting the starboard ork ships a few minutes from now. Her payload launched, the *Victorious* slows suddenly and almost turns around completely, powering up her engines to cut through the heart of the convoy towards the other ork squadron.

The ork ships slow and turn away to avoid the torpedoes and several minutes later they're falling behind. The frigates close in on the ork squadron as the *Victorious* approaches them from the other side.

'Cunning bastard,' I mutter, seeing the orks are in a classic crossfire, the light cruiser and frigates are attacking at right angles to each other, and the *Victorious's* course takes her across their vulnerable sterns.

'Frigates have opened fire,' announces the comms lieutenant. 'Report light damage to one ship, no hits on the others.'

The frigates close their range as the orks desperately try to turn towards them.

'Ork ships have most of their guns to the fronts,' explains Ligner. 'They should have stayed on course and come for us, now they're in a turning race they can't win.'

'Sir, *Victorious* is sending details of a new contact!' snaps the comms officer, making adjustments to the screen controls. A solitary icon appears in the middle of the transport flotilla.

'A ship can't just appear!' I say, looking at the lieutenant, who ignores me; he is intent on the information being relayed down his earpiece and through the comms servitor.

'Space goes up and down, as well as forward, backward, left and right,' says Kelth, shaking his head in a condescending manner.

'You mean they're above us?' I ask.

'Or below us,' he says looking down towards the decking.

'Give me an intercept time,' says Captain Ligner, moving across the bridge to another station where a fresh-faced young ensign is analysing incoming data.

'Thirty to thirty-five minutes, given current velocities,' the ensign replies, pointing to something on his panel. Ligner looks over his shoulder to the main screen.

'Enemy destroyed,' announces the comms lieutenant. A red icon disappears from the screen to the starboard of the light cruiser. 'Full broadside from *Victorious*.'

The *Victorious* is still engaged with the other two of the squadron, while the group of three ships to the flank has managed to pull out of its course away from the torpedoes. It swings round to the front of the convoy.

'If they get ahead of us…' I mutter, and Kelth gives me a worried glance. 'How come you've never been in a battle before?'

'The Emperor wills,' he replies. 'He has seen fit to guide me along the brightest trail.'

I say nothing. The Emperor has seen fit to have the Colonel drag me through five lifetimes' worth of blood, mud and filth.

The Colonel walks over to me. 'How prepared are we for boarding?' he asks.

'As ready as we'll ever be, sir,' I tell him. 'A platoon that is under strength isn't going to be much use against a ship full of orks, though.'

'Better than just a ship's complement,' he says. 'This is the only troop transport in the convoy.'

'Sir, I don't think this is our fight,' I say, looking straight at him. 'You've haven't told us what we're going to do on Armageddon yet. But I'm sure that if it's important enough to drag us across the galaxy, then it's important that we don't sacrifice ourselves for a few grain and mineral transports.'

He gives me a long hard look.

'Our duty is always to the Emperor,' he says slowly.

'That's not what happened on Kragmeer,' I remind him. The Colonel risked his reputation pulling us out of the front line against orks on the ice world, so that we could continue on to Typhos Prime and the attack on Coritanorum.

'That was different,' he says, returning my gaze.

'How so?' I ask, not flinching.

'There were many other Imperial forces to hold the line,' he tells me. 'Our presence, or lack of it, would have had no impact on the campaign. There is no other line of defence for the convoy.'

'Did you ever hear what happened in the end?' I ask, the thought suddenly occurring to me. I've been in a dozen war zones on various missions with the Colonel, but we rarely hang around long enough to find out who's won.

'The campaign is still progressing,' he tells me. 'Besides, we are just as at risk from attack if we separate from the convoy.'

'Not if we head for the rendezvous with the task force,' I point out.

'The orks will pounce on us if we isolate ourselves,' the Colonel says. 'The *Victorious* and the frigates are the only protection we have, and they will not abandon the convoy for us.'

I look away from him, admitting the logic of his argument.

'How many orks are there on one of those ships?' I ask, looking at the main screen and the flashing red icon of the newly arrived ork vessel.

'The crew probably numbers in its hundreds,' he says quietly.

'And we've got less than thirty men,' I say.

'More if you conscript non-essential crew, and the four surviving provosts under my command,' he says.

'That's still not much against hundreds of orks,' I say. 'If they attack in force, we'll be overrun in minutes.'

Captain Ligner joins us.

'What are you two conspiring?' he asks, switching his gaze back and forth between the two of us.

'Please place your ship to intercept the attack on the fleet,' the Colonel tells him. He is answered by the captain's doubtful look.

'I don't see what good that will do,' he says. He points to the main display. 'Our only chance is to manoeuvre for time and wait for the escorts. The commodore has despatched one of the frigates in our direction.'

'How many vessels are armed?' the Colonel asks.

'Every ship has close defence turrets, the *Yarrick* and the *Boncephalis* have a few bigger guns,' he tells us. 'It doesn't matter though, just a few salvoes from that ork ship would be enough to destroy any one of us.'

The Colonel looks thoughtful for a moment and then turns to Ligner.

'Is there a council channel to the rest of the fleet?' he asks.

'I can have one arranged, including the warships,' says Ligner.

'Then please do so, and inform me when it is ready,' says Schaeffer. The captain looks dubious for a moment but soon melts under the Colonel's glare. 'Kage, come with me. Captain, if you could join me in the wardroom when you are able.'

He marches off the bridge, leaving me trailing in his wake. Ligner directs an enquiring look at me, but all I can do is shrug.

IN THE WARDROOM, the Colonel outlines his plan to Captain Ligner and me. I stand there, speechless with incredulity.

'Well, do you think you can manage that?' he asks.

'That's the best way of getting yourself killed I've heard in a long time,' says Ligner, shaking his head.

'Welcome to my life,' I mutter, earning myself a scowl from the Colonel.

'Is it possible?' the Colonel says.

'You're asking for good close quarter steering,' says Ligner. 'The only other military crew in the fleet is aboard the *Yarrick*, the other ships just have mercantile companies. I can't vouch for their abilities.'

'But you agree that it is possible?' insists Schaeffer. The captain sighs.

'Yes, Colonel,' he says. 'I can't see how the others will agree though.'

'They will agree because Commodore Griffin is going to invoke certain clauses of the naval articles of war,' says the Colonel. 'However afraid the other captains are of the orks, I am sure that they would rather face them than a military execution.'

'I see,' says Ligner. 'We have about twenty minutes to arrange matters. I shall transmit your intention to the fleet.'

Schaeffer watches the captain's back for a moment as he walks out, and then turns his attention to me.

'You will need to be ready in ten minutes,' he says and I nod. 'You understand your mission?'

'Of course, sir,' I say heavily. 'Everyday duties for a Last Chancer, sir. You want me to lead an attack on an ork ship with forty men, disable its engines and then return, sir. Not a problem at all, sir.'

'Your enthusiasm is noted, Kage,' the Colonel says, dismissing me with a wave of his hand.

Great, I think as I head down the corridor at a trot. Now all I have to do is explain this to the platoon.

* * *

WE'RE ASSEMBLED on the docking platform when the provosts join us. Like us, they're geared up in vac-proof environment suits. Grey, bulky and hot, they'll be the only thing protecting us from the chill airlessness of space once we break through the hull of the ork ship.

'I have been ordered to report to you,' one of them says. I can hear the grudging tone in his voice, even through the visor.

'What's your name?' I ask, looking him up and down.

'Sergeant First Class Kayle,' he says.

'I think you'll find I'm a lieutenant, sergeant,' I say to him. 'Proper form of address and all that.'

He raises the visor on his helmet, revealing a craggy face with a long scar running from his left ear across his mouth to his chin. His dark eyes meet my gaze.

'I don't care if you're a trooper or a general,' he says between gritted teeth. 'You're penal legion scum to me, and that's the end of it. Don't push it.'

'I like a man with principles,' I say with a grin. 'I want you up front with me when we attack. I'm sure you'll watch my back, won't you sergeant?'

'I understand the objective, we'll do our part,' he says with a sneering smile.

'Just so that we understand each other, sergeant,' I say with a meaningful nod.

We eyeball each other for a few seconds until the Colonel strolls onto the deck. Sergeant Candlerick barks out the order and the platoon snaps to attention. I notice the holstered bolt pistol at the Colonel's belt, and his power sword hanging in its scabbard on the other side. Oh, and the fact that he's also wearing a vac-suit gives the game away.

'Joining us for this little jaunt, sir?' I ask.

'I will lead the attack,' he says, casting his eye over the platoon. Each is carrying a shotgun and a bandoler of ammo. Three men in each squad also have a sack of grenades, while the sergeants each have a demolition charge.

'So, we're still going do this, then?' I say with a sigh, stooping to pick up my vac-suit helmet.

'It is too late to alter the plan now,' the Colonel says. 'The *Yarrick* is moving into position as we speak.

'And how long before that frigate arrives?' I ask, knowing I won't like the answer.

'Twenty minutes at the earliest,' the Colonel says, still not looking at me. 'You seem unduly worried, Kage?'

'Unduly?' I laugh. 'We're about to use a ship as bait to lure an enemy ship in, then attack it with transports. Then you are going to lead a platoon to attack that same enemy ship in the hopes of disabling its engines. I think some worry is due, sir!'

'You expect us to fail?' the Colonel asks quietly.

'Not at all, sir,' I sigh. 'That's not the problem. We always succeed. The problem is, the more we push our luck, sooner it's going to run out. Perhaps we should be saving it for Armageddon.'

'You think some strange things, Kage,' the Colonel says. 'Luck has no part to play in your life. It is the will of the Emperor whether you live or die.'

I just wish He would make up His mind, I think.

A lieutenant appears. He walks up to Schaeffer and salutes.

'The captain reports that we are now simulating engine trouble, sir,' the Navy officer says. 'It appears the orks are taking the bait.'

'Thank you, lieutenant,' Schaeffer says before turning to me. 'Mount up the platoon, Kage.'

I shout the order and the sergeants hurry the men onto the shuttle. It's the only one the ship has, so I hope it stays in one piece otherwise this is going to be a one-way trip. A short one at that.

Once we're inside the shuttle, belted up and ready to go, the pilot appears at the door to the carriage compartment.

'We're ready to go in thirty seconds, Colonel,' he says and Schaeffer gives him the nod.

I watch the rest of the platoon as the engines power up. I can feel their apprehension, nervous excitement and fear. Dunmore is laughing with Cardinal, but I can hear the nervous edge to it. Candlerick has his head bowed in prayer, as do some of the others. Morin is checking the slide on his shotgun, for the tenth time I reckon. Radso is fidgeting with the bolt shell pendant he wears. Supposedly it's a good luck charm, since it hit him in the shoulder but failed to detonate. When it was extracted, he had an armourer disarm it for him, and now he wears it as a talisman.

Me, I sit there watching them, listening to the noise of the engines increasing in volume and pitch. With a lurch that pins me to the seat, we lift off, powering out of the open bay. The pilot then cuts the engines into reverse for a moment, and then off completely. We start to drift slowly away from the ship. The pilot's voice crackles out over the shuttle comms system.

'The captain's just told me that we're less than five minutes from contact,' he says.

I turn to the Colonel, who's sitting to my right.

'What if they just open fire?' I ask. 'Maybe they don't want to board.'

'They are raiders,' he replies. 'They want to capture the ship and its cargo, not destroy it. They will board.'

'But if they don't?' I insist.

'Then we can thank the Emperor that we are out here on a shuttle, rather than aboard the ship,' he says, and I laugh. He gives me a look and a chuckle dies in my throat when I realise he isn't joking. Of course he isn't, he never jokes.

It's a tense few minutes as we sit there in the shuttle, drifting through space as easy as a firing range target. If the orks spot us, which is unlikely I admit, we won't even survive long enough to know it.

I grab my helmet from under the seat and place it over my head. With a twist, I fit it into place and then turn to the Colonel, who's returned from the cockpit. I point to the sealing clamps. He fastens them for me, and then puts on his own helmet, and signals for me to fasten his clamps.

A thought crosses my mind briefly. If I just leave one of the clamps, just one of the four, a bit loose, it'll compromise the suit's integrity. Nobody would know what went wrong. Hell, these suits malfunction, break seals or just disintegrate one time in ten anyway.

I dismiss the thought and tighten all the clamps as far as I can. Killing the Colonel is just about the worst thing I could do at the moment. Oddly enough, he's the best chance I have of staying alive. Without him, there is no Last Chancers. And with no Last Chancers, I'm irredeemably corrupt and would be executed without hesitation. And there's that other bit, the one about me probably being a witch.

'Comms check,' the Colonel's voice echoes in my ear with a tinny note.

A series of affirmative replies come back from the platoon, and I add my own.

'Ready for disembarking,' the Colonel says and we all stand up and march clumsily to the rear doors. I'd cross my fingers but the suit won't let me.

Slipping the shotgun on its strap from my shoulder, I chamber a round and glance at the others. I see my face reflected in the black visor of one of Kayle's provosts, obscured by the condensation building up from my sweat inside the faceplate of my suit.

'Hey, provy, looking forward to your first real combat?' I ask. He swivels towards me, his shotgun levelled at my groin.

'I hope my finger doesn't slip with my inexperience,' he says, stepping forward. 'I'd hate to have a nasty accident on my first time out.'

He looks down and sees the tip of my gun angled up towards his chin.

'That would be terribly bad,' I say, easy as you like.

'Look, shit mouth, I fought on Danaa Secundus,' he says, swinging the shotgun away. 'I don't need to prove anything to you.'

I shut up. We never went to Danaa Secundus, but everything I've heard makes it sound like the Colonel would have loved it. More tyranids, a splinter of Hive Fleet Kraken after Ichar IV. Turned into a rout, only twenty thousand men out of a three million strong army got off alive. The number of non-combatants who escaped the three-month onslaught amounted to about a tenth of that. Three months is all it took for a world to die. Makes me glad that we won on Ichar IV.

'Hold on,' says the pilot over the internal speakers. 'Emperor's blood!'

I rush clumsily to the cockpit, heading through the door just a few steps behind the Colonel.

Looking out of the canopy, I see a slowly spinning field of stars. After a moment, the ork ship comes into view, its bulbous nose studded with cannons and jutting spars. A bright blue flare glows from its engines. It's several kilometres away, but I can see that, oddly enough, it seems to be painted red. What look like columns of flame are pouring from underneath the ship and as I watch, a series of detonations explode along its length. I look at the Colonel, and then the pilot.

'The *Yarrick* is reporting a previously unregistered energy spike,' the pilot informs us.

'What does that mean?' asks the Colonel, his voice in my comms-transmitter but distorting from the external speaker at the same time.

'Someone else was lying in wait, systems offline to avoid detection,' the pilot says. 'They were playing dead, basically.'

'Who?' I ask.

The pilot is listening to the fleet frequencies, his eyes widening with surprise.

'Space Marines,' he says, staring out of the shuttle canopy as another series of explosions tears the ork attack ship to pieces, its midsection breaking clean through. The two halves tumble away from each other, gouting gas and flames. 'Rapid strike vessel *Terminatum* of the Black Templars.'

The Colonel unbuckles his helmet and takes the comms-piece from the pilot, holding it up to his ear. He nods to himself as he absorbs what's going on, before turning to me.

'Stand the platoon down, Kage,' he says and I realise I've been holding my breath. I release it in a long sigh. Schaeffer looks at the pilot. 'Take us back to the ship.'

FOUR
WRATH OF GHAZGHKULL

It turns out that the Black Templars had been hunting this particular band of orks for the last few days. They knew they were lurking near Chosin but were unable to locate them. Hearing that the convoy was passing their way, they decided to lie in wait, thinking the orks would be unable to resist the lure of the transports. As well as the *Terminatum*, there were two more rapid strike vessels and a strike cruiser all within an hour's travel of our position.

With the Space Marines as an additional escort, it's an uneventful journey to the inner system. We rendezvous with another fleet at Saint Jowen's Dock before we press on to Armageddon itself. The buzz around the fleet is that a new ork hulk has arrived in the system in the last week or so, but nobody's found it yet.

It's a cautious approach to Armageddon orbit. Despite the fleet's victories, there are still hundreds of ork vessels unaccounted for, some of them large and dangerous. Added to that, it seems the orks have captured one of the rocket factories on the surface and have been randomly launching warheads into space, adding to the general fun.

We've just entered upper orbit and Captain Ligner informs the Colonel that a small, previously uncharted asteroid field lies across our line of descent. Schaeffer agrees to navigate the asteroid field, using it to cover our approach until we hit lower orbit. The hope is that the orks won't be aware of us until it's too late to launch any form of attack.

585

Playing it safe, Ligner orders the ship to be cleared and braced for combat, while he edges us into the asteroid field. I'm on the lower deck with Dunmore and Lorii, securing energy cells near the engine room. The rest of the platoon is on various other duties throughout the ship, under the supervision of the provosts. Lorii's just passing me a fuel canister when the deck trembles under my feet.

I look at the others and their bemused expressions confirm that they felt it too. We exchange glances as I cautiously lower the fuel cell to the deck. The ship shudders again, more violently this time, sending the cell spinning out of my hand and clattering across the deck. A second later, an alarm klaxon rings out across the ship, deafening us as it squalls from a speaker just overhead.

There's an explosion in the engine room behind us, a blast wave sweeps through the open doors along the corridor, hurling us from our feet. With the screeching twist of metal, part of the roof collapses and smoke starts to billow out of the ventilation system.

'The saviour pods!' I scream to the others, dragging myself to my feet. We're under attack, there's no mistake about that. I don't know how, and I don't care. It's obvious that we've already taken critical damage; we won't survive another five minutes. I race off up the corridor, with the other two following me. I vault up the stairs two at a time, until another impact causes me to lose my footing. I stumble, then fall backwards.

Brownie sticks out an arm and stops me. Flames in the ventilation ducts reflect off his bald head as he helps me to my feet, grinning.

'That one's for taking care of Goran,' he says, pushing me forward. I nod and start hauling myself up the steps again. Lorii's in front of me.

Reaching the mid deck, we're confronted by carnage and chaos. The walls are buckled, supporting rafters hang down from the ceiling, severed cables spewing sparks and oil, the air is filled with smoke. I can see at least half a dozen bodies crushed underneath the mess, pools of blood glinting as they spread across the decking. Their charred uniforms identify them as Last Chancers. I guess they won't be going any further, but there's no time to spare them a second thought. A smouldering pile of crates that has dropped from the storage bay above blocks our way forward.

'What now?' says Lorii, taking a step back as an oil hose ignites, sending a jet of flame scorching across the corridor just a few metres in front of her.

'Keep going up,' I say, pointing to the stairwell on the other side of the corridor.

Brownie forges ahead up the stairs, sweat dripping from him from the nearby flames. My shirt is sticking to my back as I feel the heat licking up the steps after us. Glancing over my shoulder, I see the flames spreading to the foot of the stairwell behind Lorii.

'Faster!' I yell, slapping Brownie on the back to urge him on.

The spiral staircase is littered with two more corpses, crew this time, which we have to jump over. Smoke is all around us as we burst onto the top deck.

The flashing red lights of the saviour pod doors stretch out in front of us. Most of them have already ejected. I see a green light a little further on, and lead the others to it, stepping over snaking wires and smouldering bodies. We're a couple of metres from the door when the Colonel appears, heading from the opposite direction. With him are Kelth, Kin-Drugg, Sergeant Candlerick and another Last Chancer called Oahebs, who joined the Last Chancers with Lorii.

The Colonel waves us into the saviour capsule with his bolt pistol, glancing over his shoulder. Two more figures appear out of the gloom, and as they emerge from the darkness and smoke I see that it's Corthrod, one of the Navy ratings. Behind him, cowering from the flames is Spooge, his servo-skull still obediently bobbing along behind him. The polished bone is tarnished with soot and oil now, and its anti-grav motors sputter and choke occasionally, causing it to dip alarmingly towards the floor.

I watch them all jump into the pod, and then duck inside just in front of the Colonel. We each slump down into one of the ten seats, laid out in a circle around the hull of the capsule. The main control panel juts down from the ceiling in the centre, while the retro rockets and parachute take up most of the floor space in between us.

It's cramped, but we manage to strap ourselves in as the Colonel cycles the door closed and sits down. Before pulling on his straps, he leans forward and activates the countdown launch sequence. He grunts and stares at the panel for the moment before looking up at me, and then Corthrod.

'There seems to be a problem with the electrics,' he says, prodding a few runes on the display.

Corthrod unbuckles himself and stands to have a look. He shakes his head a few times, muttering under his breath. My stomach starts to churn, I can see flickering hints of yellow through the small circular porthole in the pod door.

'The connection's broken,' Corthrod declares, spitting on the deck. 'There's a manual launch on the deck.'

'Kage, get to the manual launch and activate it,' says Schaeffer, not even looking at me.

'Why me?' I say, crossing my arms stubbornly. 'I always get this kind of shit. Send Corthrod, he knows what he's looking for.'

The Colonel doesn't even look up.

'Kage, get to the manual launch and activate it,' he says again. I notice the pistol in his hand is pointing straight at me from his lap. 'Before I shoot you.'

'For Emperor's sake, I always end up doing the hard work,' I say as I unstrap myself and cycle the door lock. 'Give me a fragging hand, Kage. Silence the fragging woman, Kage. Fragging eat the brains, Kage.'

I continue swearing as I step out onto the deck. The heat from the fire is nearly unbearable. I cough heartily from the smoke gathering in the corridor. I put my head back into the capsule.

'Where is it, then?' I ask Corthrod. He gestures back along the deck.

'It's about fifteen metres down. A red-trimmed panel, you can't miss it. Just pull the trip switch and get back here in thirty seconds. The door will close automatically and all the pods on this side will be fired off.'

'Right, thirty seconds,' I say, heading off at a trot.

Corthrod is right: the panel's easy to spot. Unfortunately, the piping that's collapsed from the ceiling ducts is in the way and takes some shifting, but after a few seconds of pushing and grunting, I clear the panel. I wrench it open and pull down on the lever. There's a warning siren, and a red light begins to blink just below the lever.

Just as I'm about to turn back to the capsule, a dark figure appears out of the smoke. I recognise Kayle, the provost sergeant. He's without his helmet, and his face is half-burned, his hair smouldering. He has his shotgun in his hands.

'What are you doing?' he demands, grabbing hold of me.

'Emergency launch!' I snap at him, throwing off his hand. 'You've got about twenty seconds to get in a capsule.'

He nods and shoulders his way past me, pushing me up against the wall. The metal is hot, and it sears my hands as I push myself upright. It's then that I realise he's heading to the open pod.

There's only one seat left, and it's mine.

A swift kick between the legs from behind connects with Kayle's prized possessions, toppling him forwards into a crumpled heap. I snatch the shotgun from his hands and ram the butt into his face, driving him to the deck. He makes a half-hearted grab for my ankle but I skip past, heading for the capsule door.

'Bastard!' he shouts after me and I give him a grin as I duck back through the door.

The Colonel looks at the shotgun in my hands, eyebrow raised.

Ignoring him, I hurl myself into the remaining seat and drag the harness over my shoulders, ramming the lock down into the seat socket between my legs. The door grinds shut and locks itself, while the ejection motors grumble into life below our feet. I see Kayle's twisted, shouting face appear at the door window for a second before the pod is launched upwards, punching out of its ejection tube into space. The force rams us all down into our seats and I grit my teeth against the pressure. The blood rushes to my legs, making me dizzy. Out of the corner of my eye I see Spooge collapsing inside his harness. He's blacked out. As the retro fires, we begin to circle slowly.

Free of the artificial grav of the ship, we tumble in weightlessness, straining the safety straps. After a few minutes I heave a massive sigh of relief.

'What the frag?' I finally say, looking at the Colonel. He doesn't reply for a while.

'The asteroid field was not safe,' he says eventually. 'Most of them were the rock forts that Commissar Greyt warned us of. They opened fire as soon as we were in range.'

Corthrod is busying himself with the short-range comms unit fitted to the saviour pod's control panel. I unharness myself and guide myself over to the viewing portal in the door. I can see the burning remnants of the ship, and it suddenly occurs to me that I never knew its name. There are other explosions and trails of fire as the orks launch attack craft to hunt down the saviour pods and open fire at random. Not so far away, I see the glinting reflection of another capsule, a moment before a missile detonation engulfs it.

All around us, missile trails zoom past, probably kilometres away but too close for comfort. Amongst the debris, I see charred bodies, clumped in groups as they are blown out of the ship by hull breaches. They slowly freeze together. Everything dwindles away as we drift away from the battle, and soon all I can see are the distant sparks of engines and the ominous shadows of the rock forts blotting out the views of the stars beyond. Minutes later, I can't even see them.

'We're going to die,' Corthrod says, his voice shrill. 'There are only two other capsules left. The orks are going to hunt us down!'

'Shut up,' snaps Lorii. She turns to her right, where Erasmus is unconscious, and tries to revive him. With no gravity field to support it, the quill-skull is nestled in the scribe's lap, buzzing erratically.

'Shut up?' says Corthrod. 'The beacon isn't working because the transmitter was fragged on launch. We're also getting pulled down into the gravity well. Even if the orks don't get us, and we manage to avoid burning up on entry to the atmosphere, we're going to crash Emperor-knows-where.'

'Stop whining,' I say, still staring out of the window. I can't see any fire that's directed in our area, or telltale flickers that might be closing attack craft. 'We'll be fine.'

'We are not going to be fine!' says Corthrod and I turn to see him sneering at us all. 'You don't understand. It's not a war zone down there. It's hell. We might get lucky and actually land on solid ground. Then all we have to worry about is perhaps freezing to death if we land near the poles. Or dehydration. Maybe we'll land in a radzone, or a chem-pit. Or we might get fortunate and just be killed by orks. We have no weapons, no survival gear, and no comms. Even if we landed near Imperial forces, there's no way of us knowing it, or of them finding us. We're as good as dead.'

'Kage, silence him,' snaps the Colonel.

The boom of the shotgun is unbearably loud in the confines of the pod. The recoil sends me crashing into the door and bouncing back. The remnants of Corthrod drift around in the air, globules of blood and brains spattering against my face and chest as I glide through the cloud of gore. Everyone's looking at me aghast, except the Colonel and Lorii.

'That's out of order!' roars Candlerick, but he falls silent as I steady myself and the muzzle of the shotgun swings in his direction. He glances at Schaeffer for a reaction.

'Our first priority is survival,' the Colonel says slowly. 'Doubt and fear compromise our chances of success. Everyone here is subject to summary execution for cowardice under military law. Once our immediate survival is no longer an issue, we will proceed with our mission to the best of our abilities.'

That's no surprise. Losing three quarters of our force is just a minor setback when you're with the Last Chancers.

FIVE
MORE BAD LANDINGS

THE NEXT HOUR was probably the most terrifying of my life. Though I've been through some of the most Emperor-awful stuff you can imagine – battlefields choked with the dead, and personal moments like the time a tyranid warrior sawed halfway through my leg at Deliverance – the utter helplessness of our predicament sets my nerves jangling.

Aided by Kelth, the Colonel manages to at least get the automated telemetry working so that the capsule will take us into the atmosphere at the correct angle, rather than bouncing off or burning us up. Well, in theory. The only way we'll know if they've really got it right is when we hit the upper atmosphere in about fifteen minutes.

I'm not the only one getting stressed out by the situation. Erasmus is quiet now, though he was gabbling nervously to himself a little while ago. He's just sitting there, cradling the servo-skull in his hands, and stroking it carefully, reverentially. Lorii is alert, her eyes continuously flicking from one of us to another, her jaw clenched tight. Candlerick fidgets with his buttons on his cuffs all the time, drawing little circles with his index finger on the dull brass hemispheres.

Kin-Drugg is pretending to be cool. He is sitting with his hands behind his head, eyes closed, but I see them half open occasionally, checking everything before closing again. He's a drop trooper, so I guess this situation isn't as alien to him as it is to the rest of us. But then again, there's a world of difference between plummeting into a savage war zone in an out-of-control saviour pod, and grav-chuting into a prepared DZ with a platoon of your comrades.

Brownie's humming to himself, and tapping out the beat of some regimental march on his knees. His eyes stare at the floor between his legs. As I watch him, he stops his little tune and pulls his combat knife from his belt. Immediately I'm tense and ready, and I see Lorii shift slightly in her seat, ready to act if he does anything stupid. Instead, he spits in his left hand and rubs it over his scalp and then, carefully and slowly, he scrapes the blade over his head, removing the tiny protrusions of stubble that have appeared since he shaved his head this morning.

He looks up at us, feeling our gazes on him. He lifts the blade away a little and shrugs, then turns his attention back to the floor as he continues to scrape the knife across his scalp.

Gideon Oahebs is directly opposite me but it's only by leaning slightly to one side that I can see him. I'm glad of that, because he absolutely freaks me out when I'm near him. I don't know why it is, but whenever I'm in close proximity to him, I feel kind of giddy. It's hard to describe, it's like someone you dislike on first sight, even though you have no idea what kind of person they are.

I've spent most of the last year avoiding being in the same room as him as much as possible. There's nothing physically wrong with the guy, and he's certainly one of the more quiet and obedient of the platoon. I correct myself as I think this – there is no platoon, it's just us now. I feel a bit better about that, in an odd sort of way. The Last Chancers, the *real* Last Chancers, are only ever a handful of soldiers. Maybe the Colonel started out with a four thousand-strong legion a couple of years ago, but the rest were just baggage really. They were being tested and only a few of us survived long enough to get to Coritanorum.

Oahebs is sitting comfortably, hands clasped in his lap, gnawing at his bottom lip. I can see that his fingernails are worn and ragged too, so it's easy to see how he deals with his nerves. Beside him, Kelth squirms uncomfortably, casting looks at Oahebs every couple of minutes, brow knitted. So it isn't just me that finds him awkward to be around.

And finally, there's the Colonel. Unflappable, unlovable and unkillable, I can feel him on my right like a rock. With parade ground stiffness, he just sits there, a hand on each knee, staring straight ahead. He doesn't even glance at the panel to check our progress. It's like he's deactivated on something, like a lasgun with the safety on, just waiting for someone, or something, to flick the switch and put him into action again. That said, I can see the subtle tic of his jaw muscles, the only sign I've ever noticed of stress or anger.

Sensing my gaze, he turns his head slowly towards me, his icy eyes boring into me. He doesn't say anything, he just stares at me.

'How long before entry, sir?' I ask, eager to break the crushing silence.

'Two and a half minutes,' he replies without even needing to check the display.

'Any idea where we'll crash-land?' I say, leaning forward to look at the meaningless scrolling runes and numbers of the telemetry panel.

He finally breaks his stare to look at the display, and then reaches inside his coat to pull out a battered-looking map. He unfolds it and then refolds it, glancing up at the co-ordinates glowing from the screen, until he's found the area he wants.

'The good news is that we are not likely to land in water,' he says, putting the map away.

'The bad news?' I say.

'There is a good chance that we will make planetfall somewhere in the jungles,' he says.

He doesn't have to add anything. From Greyt's briefing, we know that the jungle is teeming with ork activity, despite several fire missions to clear it out. Our only hope is that someone at Cerberus base notices us crash and sends out a search and rescue party.

There's little chance of that, I reckon. With all the problems they have, I figure that a saviour pod coming down is going to be the last thing they're worried about. They're virtually under siege from the orks and have got much better things to do with their time.

'That is assuming we do not get caught in an electrical storm and go off our current projected trajectory,' the Colonel adds.

There are a few groans around the pod, one of them my own. Not for the first time, and probably not the last, I ask myself whether this was worth the satisfaction of killing my sergeant. In the great balance of things, I should've just let him have the girl. Still, regret's for the weak. I cast my own die and the Emperor took the bet and left me here, so all that I can do now is deal with it. I've long since stopped blaming anyone else for my predicament; it makes it so much easier to deal with. Once you stop looking elsewhere for the reasons why crap happens to you, you realise it's all your own doing, one way or another. Unfortunately, I guess that's one of life's little wisdoms that are denied to us until after we've made an important mistake. We don't normally get the chance to learn from it.

THE INTERIOR OF the pod begins to heat up considerably, to the point where it starts getting difficult to breathe. We look at each other with consternation, wondering if this is a prelude to exploding into a ball of fire, the heat shielding tearing away, the metal casing melting and our bodies vaporising into nothing. The capsule begins to shake, jarring us from side to side and we can really start to feel the pull of the gravity well and our own velocity. Candlerick starts swearing, under his breath. Kin-Drugg laughs and we all stare at him.

'If the atmosphere's thickened enough to make things turbulent, then we've entered okay,' he says with a grin. 'Just the landing to worry about. Or maybe I should say impact.'

'Thanks for pointing that out,' mutters Dunmore, shaking his head. 'You really are a bonehead, aren't you?'

Kin-Drugg laughs and shrugs, and then seeing that we're not sharing the joke, points to Brownie's shining scalp.

'He's calling me a bonehead?' Kin-Drugg says.

'You want me to slap that smirk off your face?' says Dunmore, bringing his hand back across his chest to emphasise the point.

The vibrations become more and more violent as we dive down through the sky of Armageddon, and then stop suddenly. For a couple of minutes it feels like we're just floating, but then we hit the solid fume cover that fills the Armageddon air with thick clouds, and the turbulence starts again.

'Not long now,' says Kin-Drugg, checking the bindings on his harness.

'Let's just hope the retros didn't get fragged with the other systems,' I say, earning myself scowls from the others. 'I'm just saying what we're all thinking, so don't give me that.'

THERE'S A TANGIBLE release of tension when the pod shudders and a dull roar emanates from beneath us as the retrorocket fires. I can feel us slowing, the weightlessness of our descent disappearing. As the retro grows to full power the deceleration pushes us down into our seats and I feel blood rushing to my head, making me dizzy. There's another jolt as the chutes open and the retro burns off, leaving us, with any luck, drifting down to a not-too-speedy landing.

A few minutes later and the capsule tilts slightly to one side, accompanied by the metallic clang of branches slapping and snapping against the hull. We shudder to a stop, and I'm slightly hanging to my left in the seat strap. There are a few creaks and groans and I feel us settling little more. Candlerick slaps the release on his buckle and pushes himself up.

'Wait!' says the Colonel, just as I'm opening my mouth.

We're both too late.

As Candlerick steps forward, the weight in the capsule shifts. There's more snapping of branches and we drop. I'm spinning to my left and pitching forward, and Candlerick is thrown clear across the pod, ricocheting off the central control column and smashing head-first into the hull just to my right. His face explodes on impact and his head snaps back. I don't hear anything over the crashing through the branches, but his body lolls across me and then falls away, his dangling neck all the evidence I need. His neck snapped as easily as the branches outside.

With an impact that sends a shudder up my legs and along my spine, and jars my head back against the pod wall, we slam down to the ground. The pod rolls back and forth a little as it settles.

We sit there, waiting for further movement. I can hear Spooge whimpering, and out of the corner of my eye see Brownie clenching and unclenching his fists, muttering under his breath. Kin-Drugg is gripping tightly to his harness, head back against the wall. Gideon is staring at Candlerick's corpse lying bunched up against his feet. He nervously kicks it away, but at the angle we've landed it rolls straight back against his shins.

'I think we're done,' says Lorii, looking at me, and then the Colonel, who nods and undoes his straps. I notice him pulling out his pistol as he hauls himself up using the display column. Undoing my own restraint harness, I fish the shotgun out from where I stowed it beneath the seat, tucked behind one of the chair supports. I'm glad I did, because the last thing we needed was a loaded firearm tumbling about the pod as we fell.

As the rest of them free themselves, the Colonel pulls himself across to the door, which is slightly higher up than the ground, and at a shallow angle. He peers through the condensation-covered port-hole, looking outside.

'It appears clear to this side,' he says. 'No immediate threat, at least.'

'What's the plan?' asks Brownie, steadying himself with a hand on his seat and wringing a kink out of his neck. The Colonel turns and looks at each of us in turn as he speaks.

'We secure a perimeter around the pod, and then make a further appraisal,' he says.

'What are we going to secure a perimeter with, sir?' asks Kin-Drugg. 'Apart from Kage's shotgun and your pistol, all we've got are knives.'

The Colonel tosses his bolt pistol to Kin-Drugg, who catches the heavy sidearm awkwardly.

'I want you twenty metres out from doorward. Kage, you are to position yourself on the opposite side,' Schaeffer says, gripping the door lock. 'Understood?'

I give him the nod, and Kin-Drugg follows suit after a dubious look.

The Colonel spins the lock and thrusts the door outwards. As it clangs against the hull, I let Kin-Drugg out first, even though I'm closest to the opening. If there is something out there waiting for us, there is no reason to be in a rush to meet it, I figure.

The drop trooper clambers through, and I follow him a few seconds later. Pulling myself out of the opening, I see that we're definitely in the jungle, as if there was any doubt. The burned shell of the pod is resting on a litter of dried leaves and freshly broken branches. Leaping down to the jungle floor, shotgun in hand, I peel right and work my way around to the other side of the pod. The two white chutes lie in tatters a few metres above us, hanging like signal flags from the trees.

It's damn hot, and the air is thick with moisture. I'm already sweating buckets and it's difficult to breathe properly. There's an edge to the air that catches in the throat, making me feel as if I'm choking. It's pretty dark too: most of the light is coming through the hole in the canopy made by the crashing pod. Beyond that circle, the jungle looms dark, and other than the vague shapes of twisting trunks, I can't see anything beyond twenty metres or so. Gigantic fungi erupt out of warped roots and branches, and thin, thorny bushes somehow leech an existence from the dry ground. It's deadly quiet; any birds or beasts in the vicinity were obviously put to flight by our dramatic entrance. Seeing nothing, I bang on the pod with the butt of the shotgun.

'All clear,' I say, not too loudly because I don't want my voice to carry too far.

I drop to a crouch and work my way forwards away from the capsule, scanning left and right as I move. I'm moving slowly but surely, controlling the urge to just get in place and then burrow down. There're two things that are bound to attract notice. One of them is something absolutely still when everything else is moving. The other is quick movement, which will attract the eye faster than anything. Ever been jumpy? Ever been looking left and right constantly, thinking you saw something moving? That's pure survival instinct, and that's what I'm relying on right now.

There's scattered undergrowth, clawing for life in the little light that gets through the mass of foliage above us. Dark, prickly bushes and trailing vines criss-cross the jungle floor. As I settle down between two trees, shotgun laid in front of me, I do another quick scan ahead but see nothing. But once I'm in place an uneasy feeling starts to creep up my spine. Not a feeling, more of a memory. I recall a planet called False Hope that I visited with the Colonel. It was a jungle deathworld, and contact had been lost with the station there. What we found was one of the most fragged up, strangest things I've ever encountered, but you wouldn't believe it unless you'd been there yourself.

The memories of that jungle fight, the smell of burning vegetation from the flamers and the screaming of men being torn apart, rush back to me. I keep my finger over the trigger of the shotgun, ready to pull it into position.

I hear the sound of footsteps behind me, but resist the temptation to turn around. I've been told to keep watch and, whatever else you think of me, I'm a bloody good soldier these days and I do what I'm told. Whatever I'm told.

'The Colonel says we're setting off,' says Lorii. I push myself to my feet and look back at her.

'Which way?' I ask, and she nods to the right. 'What's that way?'

'Doesn't matter,' she says with a shrug. She turns and starts to walk off. 'We haven't got a clue where we are anyway, so the Colonel just picked a direction. Keep walking long enough, we'll find something to orientate ourselves.'

'Fair enough,' I say, slinging the strap of the shotgun over my shoulder and heading after her.

THE GOING IS tough, and I'm seriously short of breath after just a few hundred metres. The Colonel says that Armageddon's air is so full of pollutants that it can kill a man in three days. We're lucky we landed in the jungle, where the trees make it a little more bearable. Out in the desert, we'd have been coughing and choking the moment we were out of the pod. What with the thick air and the exhausting effort of wading through dead leaves, uniform-snagging bushes and sometimes having to saw our way through vines with our knives, it's an arduous march.

Things scuttle away through the brush at our approach. Beetles the size of my fist with glowing wings buzz to and fro in the gloom. The shrieking and cackling of birds and branch-dwellers hidden in the treetops announce our advance, and destroy any chance of our going undetected.

Brownie's up ahead on point, and I'm the man at the back. We're spaced out at ten metre intervals. Well, most of us are. Kelth and Erasmus are walking as a pair in the middle of the group. The scribe's been well behaved since we came down. The motor's gone in his servo-skull, but he insists on carrying it with him. So far they don't seem to be slowing us up, but we'll see how long that lasts.

We're not quite sure how long until last light, but we'll have to allow plenty of time to find a good lying up point to make camp. I reckon we've still got a good couple of hours marching ahead of us. Although the going isn't great, there's no reason why we can't cover at least ten kilometres before finding ourselves a bolt hole.

As we go further, the jungle seems to take on a little more character. There are a few shallow streams and pools across our line of advance, and we're steadily working uphill. Although we've scrambled in and out of gullies and depressions, I know it isn't my imagination that the climbs out have been higher than the routes in.

The Colonel advises us not to drink any of the water. Thousands of years of industry have contaminated pretty much everything on Armageddon. It's a wonder the jungle flourishes as it does. I guess sometimes plants know how to hang on to life just as much as a Last Chancer.

Every now and then, Brownie indicates a particular feature, like a large exposed boulder, a small cave under a tree's roots, a particularly splendid splay of red fungus, or a fallen trunk. As he passes between two gargantuan trees whose roots form an archway above him, Dunmore points to the ground again. Kelth drops back from Erasmus and falls in beside me.

'Why does he keep doing that?' the Navigator asks.

'Meeting points,' I tell him. 'If we run into some kind of trouble, and the Colonel tells us to bug out, that's where we meet up. Just remember where the last rendezvous is, and if there's any kind of a crisis, just head for it as best you can. Better tell Spooge too, in case he doesn't know.'

'I will,' he says, glancing over his shoulder behind me.

'Look,' I say, giving him a shove. 'Get out of my fraggin' way, you're right in my line of sight.'

'Sorry,' he says, stumbling ahead. I shake my head as he catches up with Erasmus.

'Bloody amateurs,' I mutter to myself, checking to the left and right as we continue on.

WE FIND AN area of high ground just as the twilight is making it difficult to see more than ten or twenty metres. The trees are sparser here, and so the undergrowth is a lot thicker, providing perfect cover to hide us from view. There's nothing to eat or drink, and despite the humidity my throat is parched. I feel my stomach growling empty as well. I hand the shotgun to Kin-Drugg, who's drawn first watch with Lorii.

The Colonel's already sitting with his back against a tree root, his eyes are closed, and he is breathing shallowly. I help Kin-Drugg scout out a good vantage point, nestled under the root of a tree a little further down the bank but with a view of the surrounding area.

'The Colonel will give me the tap when it's time to relieve you,' I say, and Kin-Drugg nods and crawls into the lookout position, shotgun across his knees. I walk over to the other side of the hill and find Lorii lying under the spreading thorns of a dark blue bush. The bolt pistol is under her right hand, just to her side, a few leaves scattered on top of it to hide it from view.

'You're being cautious,' I say, nodding to the pistol. 'There's going to be barely enough light to see your hand in front of your face, never mind enough to glint off metal.'

'And thinking you can relax is one of the best ways I know of getting yourself killed,' she replies, not turning around.

'You have to wind down some time,' I say, sitting down next to her.

'Piss off, Kage,' she says, not harshly, but with enough edge to her voice that I know she means it. She sounds more resigned than angry. 'Don't start pretending now that you cared.'

I open my mouth to answer, but think better of it. With a shrug, I push myself to my feet and walk back through the ferns and bushes to our camp. Spooge is near the Colonel, sitting cross-legged in the dead leaves, the hatch in the bottom of his servo-skull open. He's prodding around with his finger, a despondent look on his face.

Spooge's skull is cracked wide open, split asunder, his brains bulging out of the wound. I prod it with my fingers, exploring its depths, pulling it apart. I lick the fluids off my fingers, enjoying the sensation of the taste. The feel is rubbery in my hands, and I run my palm along the jagged edge of the broken skull to compare the harsher sensation. My sense of touch sends an ecstatic thrill through me; it is one of immense pleasure. I giggle as a shard nicks the flesh and my own blood bubbles out to mix with the scribe's life fluid.

I stumble, momentarily dizzy. Spooge looks up at me with his watery eyes and smiles. There's a flicker of memory for an instant, something to do with Erasmus. I can remember the taste of blood, but can't place it. There's a rippling at the back of my head, and it moves forward. But this isn't the crushing pain of a vision; it's just a pleasant little tremor that sets my skin tingling.

'Could you have a look at my skull, please?' says Erasmus and I stand there looking at him for a moment, feeling the urge to laugh, though I don't know why.

I suppress the notion, and sit down next to Erasmus. He proffers me the servo-skull and I take it from him. It weighs more than I thought, and I'm amazed he's carried it with him this far. I look at him out of the corner of my eye, so that he won't see me looking at him. I turn the skull over in my hands, pretending to examine it. He looks at me with eager expectation.

'I'm no tech,' I say, handing him back the lump of inert machinery.

'No, you're a soldier, aren't you?' says Erasmus, placing the quill-skull on the ground beside him.

'Yes, I'm a soldier,' I say, looking straight at him, trying to detect some kind of insult or criticism. 'What of it?'

'Do you know that I used to want to be a soldier?' he says. I shake my head. He could've wanted to be a glow-globe for all I care.

'I had to follow my father though, did you know that?' he says, with a quick glance towards the servo-skull. 'Did you know that the Departmento Munitorum gives an extra surrogacy allowance if you father a son to assume your position when you've passed on to the Emperor?'

'No, I never knew that,' I say.

'I was a scribe-apparent for thirty-five years. Don't you think that's a long time to wait for your calling in life?' he says.

'I have no idea,' I tell him. 'I'm not sure, but I don't think I'm even thirty-five years old. It's never been much of an issue. I was a kid, then I was a factory worker and then I was in the Guard.'

'You don't know how old you are?' he asks, incredulous. I shouldn't be surprised by his reaction; after all, he does surround himself with numbers and figures every day. I think statistics and records are his lifeblood. 'Give or take a couple of years for transit deviation, mistranslation and primary reference error, you're not even thirty Terran standard.'

I'm about to reply when I stop myself. I notice something about what he just said.

'That wasn't a question,' I say to him, turning full on to face him.

'What wasn't a question?' he says. 'Is that important?'

'Not important,' I guess,' I say to him, brow furrowed. 'It's just that… Well, you always…'

'Just what?' he says, concern on his face. 'I always what?'

'Have you always talked by asking questions?' I say, smirking to myself to see what his reaction is. I know he probably isn't even aware of it, but it's about bloody time he stopped.

'Have I always talked by asking questions?' he asks, staring up at me with his wide, honest eyes. 'Do you think it would be strange if I didn't?'

'Never mind,' I say, standing up. 'Get some shut-eye, we'll be heading off before first light.'

'How do you sleep in these conditions?' he says as I turn away. I stop and think for a moment, before replying. I don't look at him when I speak.

'Close your eyes,' I say. 'Then try not to remember all of the shit that's happened to you. That usually does the trick for me.'

DAWN IS JUST a glimmer above the treetops when we set out. I did my stint on watch around midnight, near as I could tell in this lightless, starless dump. Nothing happened. Brownie snored until the Colonel gave him a kick. There were a few bats, or possibly night birds, flapping about in the trees. I was sitting on a nest of ants for half the time, and I count myself lucky that the worst I got was that creepy sensation of having the little bastards in my clothes for a while. I've heard tales, one of them from False Hope, of insects that could poison or devour a man in a few minutes. I'll pay more attention in the future.

It's a monotonous, grinding leg for most of the morning. Dehydration is becoming a serious problem. All the moisture in the air counts for bugger all if none of it's inside. Combined with the acrid tang of the atmosphere, my throat's harsh and ragged by the time the Colonel calls a stop after four hours of marching. Kelth and Erasmus, who's still carrying that bloody skull, look completely done in. The rest of us aren't looking too great either.

Wheezing, coughing up gobbets of phlegm, drenched in sweat, we take a short break in the overhang of a long, shallow ridge. The Colonel uses a tree root to pull himself up the bank, and though I'm loth to miss any second of rest, I push myself to my feet and follow him.

'We can't keep pushing on like this, not without something to eat, or at least a drink,' I say. 'Sir,' I add as he glances at me with that icy look of his.

'There is no telling how long we must survive on our own resources before we reach new supplies,' he says. 'We must conserve what we have and not waste it at the outset.'

'We'll make better time with a little something in our bellies and a drink,' I say. 'There were enough rations in the pod for two days, I reckon. There's no harm in having some now before we set off.'

'Very well, but we eat and drink on the march,' he replies. He looks about to say something else, but is distracted by something off through the trees.

'What is it, sir?' I ask. He doesn't reply, so I follow his gaze. There's a darkness out there, but oddly better lit. It's about two hundred metres away. 'A clearing, do you think, sir?'

He grunts and looks back at me.

'Bring me my bolt pistol, and get Lorii to bring the shotgun,' he says. 'Tell the others to stay here while we have a look.'

I nod and jump back down the bank, passing on his orders to the squad. They ask what the fuss is about, but I don't tell them anything. I don't really know myself. It's just a clearing. Armed, we set off for the strange patch of sunlight, the Colonel waving us down to a crawl, as we get close. Through the trees, I can see that it is indeed an opening, with bright yellow light pouring in from above. The clearing is actually the edge of the jungle.

As we cautiously move forwards, we find the jungle filled with blackened, charred tree stumps and shattered trunks. Ash covers the ground, ankle deep. Wandering through this blasted maze, the destruction gets worse, and after about another kilometre we come out into the direct sunlight.

A massive open space is laid out in front of us, burned to the ground as far as I can see. In the distance, at the top of a rise, the light glints off metal, but it's too far too see what it is. Perhaps it's some kind of structure, but there's no way to be sure.

We do a quick circuit, checking for any sign of tracks, but draw a blank. The Colonel sends Lorii back to fetch the others while we head out into the open, keeping low all the same. Ash and charred wood crumbles underfoot as we make our way down the rim of the crater. Under the unfiltered sunlight, the heat is almost unbearably hot. I can feel it burning on my forehead and hands. The shotgun, which I took from Lorii before she left, gets very warm in my hands, and is rapidly becoming uncomfortable to hold. I see that the Colonel has holstered his pistol.

'Some kind of incendiary, sir?' I venture.

'It found it's mark, whatever it was,' the Colonel says, kicking over a lump of charred branch. Underneath, gleaming in the bright light is a piece of shattered bone.

'Looks old,' I say, crouching down and pulling it free. It's part of a skull, much thicker than a man's. 'It's ork.'

As I toss the fragment back into the ash and begin to pace around, I find other bits and pieces that survived the attack. A long knife with a crudely serrated edge lies next to the finger bones of the hand that was holding it. I see the muzzle of a gun protruding from underneath a shattered half-log and eagerly dig it up. I let it drop from my fingers, disappointed to see that the rest of the pistol has fused into an unusable lump. I look over at the Colonel, who's glaring up into the sky, one hand shielding his eyes from the sun.

'We will be too exposed if we make for that,' the Colonel says, looking towards the glint in the distance. 'It will be best if we keep to the cover of the jungle.'

'I don't think there's anything to help us here, sir,' I say, eager to get out of the sun that is beating on my head like a jackhammer on a plate-press. 'We should move on.'

He gives the crater another quick sweep with his gaze and then nods, heading off towards the edge of the jungle to our right. I glance back and see the others have caught up with us. They are looking around the massive crater with the same curiosity that we had.

'We're moving out,' I call to them, waving them onwards. As Brownie comes up to me, I toss him the shotgun. 'You can be on point, get going.'

His bald head prickling with sweat, he stares dumbly at the shotgun for a second, and then sees my impatient look. He hawks and spits before heading off at a jog to get ahead of the Colonel.

The inferno engulfs Dunmore, lighting him up like a candle. The stench, like burning swine, drifts on the smoke that fills my nostrils. His screams, choked and hoarse, are a symphony in my ears. They are accompanied by the crackling of the flames. His skin blisters and tears, creating circular patterns pleasing to the eye, before the blood boils away. The fireball strips him down to muscle, the fat hissing and spitting off him like a delicious roasted haunch. Shrivelling to ash, the muscles turn to powdery cinders that blow up in the thermal of the fire, dancing motes of greyness that look like dark snow. His organs rupture as his bones crack and wither, each popping noise is like a lover's kiss on my soul. His suffering emanates in a palpable wave that sends a shiver down my spine, arousing and satisfying. The last thing to go is his shining scalp: the last beads of moisture from his burning brain sizzle away into nothing.

With a start, I open my eyes and see Oahebs staring at me, his face full of concern. I don't remember closing my eyes. The light from the sun hurts and the heat makes me dizzy. Despite that, I feel a chill shiver run along my spine. I'd swear it was a cold sweat if it hadn't started at the bottom of my spine and worked its way up to the base of my skull.

'I think the heat's getting to me,' I admit, waving away Gideon's frowning face. He lingers for a moment longer, his eyes seeming to be looking at a point somewhere inside my skull. Then he slowly turns away. A few steps on, he glances over his shoulder at me, before pressing on after Brownie and the Colonel.

SIX
JUNGLE GHOSTS

DARKNESS FINDS us with no sign of Cerberus Base, so we set up another laying up point, this time in the hollow between the root systems of two immense trees. It is deep enough for a man to stand and not be seen from a couple of metres away. Following the routine of the night before, we set up the sentry points and allocate watches.

I feel ever so weak now, as do the rest of us. Even the Colonel is showing early signs of dehydration. We have only had a few sips of water every couple of hours to keep us going. I actually saw the Colonel stop once and lean against a tree to get his breath back briefly. It doesn't sound like much, but when you've been with him as long as I have, you know it must be getting bad for him just doing that. The Colonel's the most stubborn, unstoppable son-of-an-ork you'll ever meet. I saw him with his arm blown off once, and it barely even slowed him down. Emperor knows how the hell he got a new one. I suspect the tech-priests did something for him, but just what it was, I haven't got a clue.

I've only just closed my eyes after bedding down after first watch when there's an urgent whisper in my ear. Moving slowly, I sit up, to see the face of Oahebs right in front of me in the darkness. As I look at him, I feel a churning in my stomach. I tell myself it's just the dehydration, but I know it's him really.

'Movement,' he says, gesturing over his shoulder with a thumb. I crawl across the floor of the dell after him, and pull myself up the side to lie next to the Colonel. He has his pistol in hand and is

Gav Thorpe

peering through the ferns along the edge of the hollow. I glance at Oahebs and he hands me the shotgun without hesitation. The others are crouched under the overhanging roots, white eyes staring at me out of the darkness.

Not far away, perhaps twenty metres, I can see shadowy figure in the gloom. I can't make much out, just shifting shapes between the trees. Listening, I hear the soft crunching of the dead leaves under foot.

'Not orks,' I say and the Colonel grunts in agreement.

'Not moving that quietly,' he says.

He thumbs the safety catch of the bolter as the group, perhaps no more than a dozen strong, passes about fifteen metres in front of us. Behind me I hear the scrape of a boot searching for a footing. I resist the urge to glance back, knowing that a sudden movement might attract attention.

'Ours?' I say, my voice so low, it's little more than a breath. The Colonel nods slowly. I can't understand why he's so damned paranoid if he reckons they're on our side.

'I do not want to be shot in the dark,' he whispers, as if reading my thoughts. I understand immediately. I know that if I was one of the guys up there, and we suddenly sprang up, my trigger finger would work quicker than my eyes.

The Colonel slowly reaches up his hand and lifts up an old twig from the jungle floor just in front of us. With deliberate care, he snaps it between his fingers, the noise as loud as a gunshot in the still night.

The troops out there are good; I'll give them that. There's no sudden rushing for cover, no hectic movement. Over the next few seconds, they simply melt from view. The vague silhouettes just vanish into the bushes and trees. I know they're still out there, and they're probably just as worried about what's going to happen in the next few minutes as we are.

I wait, heart hammering on my chest, peering intently into the darkness. I can't see anything except the faint swishing of the wind through the ferns and long grasses. It's then that I feel something cold and round press against the side of my neck. I let go of the shotgun, easing my hands away, and slowly turn my head to the left.

There, just a metre away from me, autogun still at my throat, is a jungle-fighter. His eyes stare at me from out of the camouflage across his face. He's sprawled headfirst down the bole of one of the trees we were sheltering under. His free hand and toes are rammed into the thick cracks in the bark to hold himself in place.

With measured precision, the gun muzzle not wavering more than a centimetre, he spins himself around until his feet are on the floor. He winks at me and then makes a purposeful glance over my shoulder. I turn and look back into the hollow to see the others with their hands up. There're three more troopers on the far bank, guns levelled at the rest of the squad. They notice my stare and one of them points up. I follow the gesture with my gaze. As my eyes focus, I see the faintest of glimmers from a scope right above us, and then a movement that my brain only recognises after a moment.

It's a sniper waving at us.

'WELL, YOU'RE BLOODY well up a vagrin tree without a knife, aren't you?' says the lieutenant of the Armageddon Ork Hunter platoon after the Colonel has explained how we ended up on their patrol route. He says a few words to his platoon sergeant, and a few minutes later we're passing around their spare water canteens and scoffing down the rations offered.

We're sitting about a kilometre from where they met us, with the platoon's first squad spread out in a defensive cordon around us. The lieutenant, Golder Fenn, is the one who climbed down the tree to get the jump on me. He's a big guy, a little taller than me, and muscled like an ogryn. He's handsome, in a rugged, scarred sort of way, and seems always ready to use his smile.

'You did bloody well to get this far, I'll give you that,' he says with an appreciative nod. 'You were right, Colonel, to head this way. It's another hundred and twenty kilometres further than you thought it was though. And this sector is teeming with bloody orks. Hundreds of them, in fact. Nice lair you had there, as well.'

'It didn't stop you finding us easily,' says Brownie, tearing off a chunk of salted meat and chewing heavily. 'We might as well have stood in the open with signs on our heads, shouting at the top of our lungs.'

'That's just your bad luck, actually,' says the platoon sergeant, an older, heavy-set man named Thorn. 'That's one of our regular observation posts. Fenn's right, if we hadn't been heading for it anyway, we might have walked straight past. Our poor sniper Daffer, had to sit there all night watching you!'

'We're on our way back to Cerberus, as it happens,' says Fenn. 'We have to finish our sweep first, but we'll be back there by dawn the day after next. You're welcome of the company.'

The Colonel looks dubious.

'We need proper supplies as soon as we can get them,' he says. 'I think we might be more of a hindrance in our current state.'

'Well, we'll be stopping by one of our caches anyway,' says Thorn with a glance at his lieutenant. 'You can arm up there for the duration. It's only about three kilometres from here. We'll be there by first light.'

'You patrol by night?' asks Kin-Drugg. 'Isn't that dangerous?'

'It is for the orks,' laughs Fenn. 'They still haven't learned not to light fires. We can see them kilometres off. Anyway, I do strongly suggest you come with us tomorrow.'

'Strongly suggest?' says the Colonel, turning the full force of his stare on the Armageddon officer. Fenn shrugs it off without batting an eyelid.

'Well, actually, I insist,' he says. 'There's all kinds of traps and trip-wires as you get near Cerberus and I can't spare one of my men as a guide. Plus, I wouldn't have it on my conscience if you didn't make it. Think of it as welcome hospitality.'

We sit in silence for a while as the Colonel chews this over. It's Oahebs who speaks up, his voice the barest whisper.

'I notice your platoon doesn't have a commissar,' he says, looking around.

'They tend to have accidents in the jungle,' says Thorn, glancing round at the rest of the command squad, who give knowing nods.

'Their greatcoats aren't good for jungle work,' says one of them, a comm-set strapped to his back.

'Too ready to rush in when you should be falling back,' adds another, slowly sharpening his long hunting knife on a whetstone. 'Gotta be nice and careful out here, nice and quiet, like. No good running about bellowing orders when you've got an ambush set up, is it?'

'Most of them stay back at Cerberus,' explains Fenn. 'Those that venture out tend not to come back, I'm afraid.'

'Sometimes they're even got by the orks,' mutters one of the men, to the stifled laughs of the others. Fenn scowls.

The lieutenant glances at the Colonel.

'Don't listen to them,' he says with a dismissive wave of his hand.

'I'm well aware of the reputation of jungle fighters like yourselves,' says the Colonel heavily. 'When do we move out?'

Fenn checks a chronometer from his webbing.

'Oh, about another hour or so,' he says. 'I'll send out the first patrol in a few minutes and we'll see what they have to say.'

'Good,' I say, and Fenn looks at me with a puzzled expression. 'Time to grab a bit of sleep. It's good not having to be on watch. Wake me when you're ready.'

I shuffle off and find a boulder to use as a pillow, folding my fatigue jacket over it and curling up. There are thirty-five Guardsmen who grew up in these jungles out there, and they've been fighting the orks for over fifty years – ever since Ghazghkull's first invasion. Sleep comes easily when you feel safer than you've done in years.

First light gives us a better look out our new companions. Like Fenn and Thorn, they're all well built, raised from the hardy stock of many generations that have lived in these savage conditions. They're almost as barbaric as the aliens they're fighting. Dawn reveals necklaces and ear-piercings of ork fangs and heavy green tattoos beneath the camouflage. Fenn himself has the lower jawbone of an ork strapped beneath his helmet along the chinstrap. I didn't see it last night because he'd left it in his pack.

They certainly seem raring to go, which is more than can be said for the Last Chancers. I kick Kin-Drugg awake and send him to rouse the others. Moaning and stretching, they assemble around the Colonel as he waits for the signal from Fenn.

It's then that I notice someone is missing.

'Where's Spooge?' I say, looking around the encampment.

'I think he's talking with one of the squads,' says Kelth, picking at the tattered threads of his robe. 'Something about his skull.'

'For Emperor's sake,' I say, and I'm about to send Brownie to look for him when I notice him clawing his way up the bank towards us, servo-skull under one arm.

'No fixers?' says Lorii, seeing the little man cradling the quill-skull. He just shakes his head sadly and then looks at Fenn.

'Do you have tech-priests at Cerberus?' Erasmus asks, hope suddenly returning to his face.

'A few,' the lieutenant replies. Spooge nods happily to himself. 'Let's move out.'

After only a short while, we're at their supply cache, hidden in a cave between two tumbled boulders, a fallen log concealing the entrance. Inside are several packs full of water and rations, as well as ammo crates, spare autoguns, heavy stubber barrels and power packs.

The platoon begins to gear up properly and Fenn invites us to join in. I snatch myself an autogun and five mags of ammo, and while

I'm at it I snaffle a couple of frag grenades. Lorii passes out full water bottles, which we thirstily drink from, having had only a few mouthfuls since we crashed down. We spend the next few minutes checking magazines, finishing off part-full water bottles to avoid them making noise, all that kind of stuff. After a few minutes, Fenn gives us the nod, and we move out again.

With one squad out ahead, and one out to each flank, we march off, keeping a steady pace. The Colonel splits us into two groups, Kelth and Spooge under the watchful eye of Kin-Drugg and Oahebs, while the rest of us accompany Fenn's command squad.

A couple of hours in, Fenn signals a halt. From up ahead, one of the scouts emerges from the jungle, moving at a fast jog.

'We've got ork sign, about three kilometres ahead,' the ork hunter reports. 'A large group, perhaps forty or fifty of them.'

'Headed west like the last ones?' asks Thorn, kneeling down beside Fenn. The scout nods.

'Alright, assemble the platoon,' says Fenn. 'Squad one to stay on scout and follow the trail. Squad two move ahead, and set up an ambush a couple of kilometres ahead of them. Squad three is reserve. I'll provide regroup back-up and second reserve.'

I like the way Fenn includes himself with the platoon, not at all like a lot of lieutenants I've known. There's very little ceremony, something I've noticed with a lot of the wilderness-based regiments. I guess they realise that getting it right out on the battlefield is more important than shining buttons and sharp salutes. On top of that, these guys have been fighting together for years now. I can vaguely remember that kind of bond, when you know you can't trust the guy next to you not to spit in your coffee, but when the bullets and lasbolts start flying he'll be watching your back, because he knows you're the one watching his.

As the squad sergeants begin to filter back through the brush, Fenn briefs each of them in turn, giving them precise instructions and checking they understand. A few ask questions about positioning and timing. It's all very relaxed, but without being careless or casual. Thorn stands up and walks over to us, where we're sitting on the edge of a narrow stream having a quick break.

'You'll be staying with us, secondary line,' he says, looking at the Colonel to see if he has any objection. Schaeffer just nods in agreement. 'When Fenn gives the signal, we'll close up with the front squads and provide support.'

He nods over to the other members of the command squad. One of them has a 25mm heavy stubber across his shoulders, and the other two are stripping down and oiling their heavy bolters.

'How come you use autoguns instead of lasguns?' asks Lorii. 'Surely lasguns are more practical for extended patrols, what with being able to recharge the packs?'

Thorn smiles. The black and green camouflage twists across his face, his bright teeth showing.

'It's a platoon-by-platoon thing,' he says, pulling his autogun off his shoulder and patting it. 'Carrying ammo can be a bitch, you're right, but we don't mind trading that hardship for the added psychological effect.'

'What psychological effect?' asks Brownie. I notice with a smile that he managed to find a heavy stubber for himself. He has ammo belts looped over his shoulder, and spare shells thrust into pouches in his belt.

'You have to understand how an ork thinks to fight him properly,' says Thorn, getting serious. 'Autoguns make a lot of noise and bright muzzle flare, and that's something they can respect. There are not many things orks are scared of, but you can be sure we're one of them. When a platoon lets rip with these beauties from hiding, the air's filled with hot metal and it's an almighty din. Especially at night, when we usually operate. Orks just don't care about the pissy little zip-zip-zip of lasguns, it just doesn't register as proper weapons fire for them.'

'Weight of fire counts for a lot, too,' adds Fenn, and we glance up, not noticing that the sergeants have dispersed and he's joined us. He moves so damn quietly all the time, despite his bulk. 'When you're laying down fire into the bush, you're not looking for precision, aimed shots. Hell, that's why we got snipers in each platoon. And when one of them big green uglies is legging straight at you, you want to put as much fire into him as possible, 'cos it don't matter whether you shoot him in the leg, the head or the chest most of the time.'

Makes sense to me. Fenn makes it clear that it's time to head out, so we grab our gear and file off behind him. About thirty minutes later, and even I can see where the orks have been. The undergrowth is trampled flat, and there are hundreds of boot marks in the mud, overlapping each other. Fenn falls back to walk beside us.

'These are from seconders,' he says, and, seeing our perplexed expressions at the term, explains: 'Firsters are the orks that came down or are descended from the first invasion, fifty years ago. They've gone very feral, but they're heaps more jungle-wise than the ones we're following. Their weapons might be cruder, but they're cunning as a foxrat and it's almost impossible to find their camps.'

'So these orks are newly arrived?' says the Colonel, looking ahead through the trees as if he could see them.

'Yeah, it's a worry really,' says Fenn. 'We've come across more and more of them in the patrol, at least four groups. All heading west or north. This is the only one we've been close enough to follow.'

There's the distant crackle of fire from up ahead. Fenn doesn't seem the least bit concerned. He is marching along and chatting quietly with the Colonel. The rest of his squad are similarly relaxed. I can feel my heart beating faster in my chest. I tighten my grip in the autogun, checking once again to make sure that the safety's off.

'Erasmus?' I call out to the scribe, who's just ahead of me. He turns and stops, waiting for me to catch up. I nod towards Brownie. 'Go and act as loader for Dunmore.'

'You w-want me to help him?' he says, staring at me in disbelief. 'In combat?'

'You're an armourer, you know how that twenty-five mil works, don't you?' I tell him. He nods. 'Well, go and tell Brownie that I've assigned you as loader.'

Spooge jogs off, casting another worried glance back at me, then he joins Brownie. They exchange a few words and Brownie looks over in my direction and then heads towards me.

'What's your game, mate?' he says through clenched teeth. 'Why you dumping that useless fatball on me?'

'Because he's better off doing that than firing a gun,' I say, not looking at Dunmore. 'Better to have him loading for you than a soldier who should be putting down fire.'

I can almost hear gears in his brain trying to work out a flaw in my logic, but he doesn't come up with anything, so he simply scowls and stalks off. I check the safety is off on the autogun again, and out of the corner of my eye see the trooper with the comms-set holding the headpiece to his ear, listening. He gestures to Fenn, who jogs over and listens to the relayed message. The lieutenant looks in our direction and then walks over to us. He points to a fallen tree alongside the ork trails, about twenty metres away.

'Set up a position around there,' he says, looking at the Colonel. He gives Schaeffer the order as if he was one of the platoon. He turns around and points behind us, opposite the fallen tree. 'That's the area of engagement, no firing anywhere else. Orks have pulled back from the ambush, squad one will be following them up and we'll be on the diagonals to catch them. I don't want any stray shots catching our own guys.'

He turns to walk away and then changes his mind.

'I'm sure I don't have to tell you this, but I will anyway,' Fenn says, looking at each of us, his normally smiling face deadly serious. 'Nobody opens fire until we spring the trap. You mess this one up, and you're walking to Cerberus on your own.'

I expect the Colonel to reply, but he just stands there, unclipping the cover on his holster and then looks at me.

'You have your orders, Kage,' Schaeffer says, turning his back on Fenn as the Armageddon officer walks away. 'Detail fire teams to cover our position, and make sure you have someone covering our rear.'

I nod and start snapping out orders to the Last Chancers, pointing to various hiding places and vantage points in the area assigned to us. They break apart, heading to their individual places, leaving me with the Colonel and Kelth. I look at the Navigator.

'What am I going to do with you?' I say.

'I will find myself a safe refuge,' he says, looking around. 'Perhaps with Lieutenant Fenn.'

'Everyone fights,' says the Colonel, pointing to the laspistol hung at his belt, taken from the ork hunters' cache earlier that morning.

'Not me,' Kelth says, shaking his head slightly, eyes meeting the Colonel's stare. 'My abilities are far too rare to risk in some pointless skirmish.'

The click of the bolt pistol in Schaeffer's hands sounds ridiculously loud, and his brings his arm up, aiming straight at Kelth.

'Are your abilities too rare to waste getting shot *avoiding* a pointless skirmish?' the Colonel asks, his arm as steady as a rock, his icy glare burning into Kelth. The Navigator glances at me, looking for some sign that Schaeffer's bluffing, and then looks away, seeking Fenn or one of his men. They're all out of sight, there's nobody but him and the Colonel.

'This is ridiculous,' says Kelth. 'And it is also in contravention of my charter as Navigator. You are supposed to uphold the law, Colonel, not break it.'

The Colonel's finger curls inside the trigger guard.

'Under regulations, our escape qualifies as a military crisis,' the Colonel says. 'All present are therefore subject to military law. As I said in the saviour capsule, anyone guilty of cowardice will be executed.'

Kelth's look of disbelief turns to resignation and he pulls the laspistol from his belt. There's a barely audible whine as he presses the charge button. The Navigator looks at me.

'Where would I be most useful, lieutenant?' he asks, eyes narrowed.

'Stick with me, you'll be fine,' I say, leading him away from the Colonel to a narrow depression a few metres in front of the fallen log.

Brownie and Erasmus have set up the heavy stubber at one end of the log, facing the trail. They are hidden behind a clump of ferns and the log itself. There's a loud clank as Dunmore cocks the slide and moves the first round into place. He gives me a thumbs-up signal as I settle down.

It's not long before I can hear the orks approaching, the snapping of twigs and rustling of dead leaves underfoot. I can see them moving straight back down the trail, dumb green bastards that they are. I can't tell how many there are, not yet, but my guess would be two dozen or so. Glancing to my left, I can't see a trace of Fenn and his squad, so well hidden are they behind rocks, bushes and in depressions. Not even a single muzzle is in view. There are no sounds from them either, just the gentle wind in the trees above. In contrast, I can hear feet scraping behind me, the click of a safety being released, and a stifled snort.

The orks are coming forward in small groups of threes and fours, hurrying but not rushing headlong towards our position. They stumble along with their characteristic stooped gait, long arms swinging beside their short legs. Their green skin blends in with the colour of the jungle, but their dark clothes, rusting belts and chains, show up easily enough. A few of them stop to fire off shots behind them, at the pursuing squad I guess, or perhaps just at shadows. I don't know how closely they're being followed, and I suspect they don't either.

The front group is about fifty metres away now and I can make out their features more clearly. Their leader is at the front; it is larger and more heavier set than the others, with crude metal plates of armour riveted to its jerkin, a tight helmet on its bucket-jawed head. It's snarling something to the others, exposing a ragged row of long fangs, in a jaw powerful enough to crush a man's skull. I know, I've seen them do it, almost had my faced gouged off by one of them in the past.

At thirty metres, all hell breaks loose.

The bushes to our left erupt with muzzle flare and the chatter of autoguns. This is swiftly accompanied by the roar of the 25mm opening up. The front orks go down in the first concentrated hail of fire, bloody eruptions stitching across stomachs and chests, heads blown apart by heavy stubber fire. The heavy bolter opens up with a distinctive rapid booming, each shot hurling a rocket a little bit bigger than my thumb. The first shot explodes against a tree trunk, hurling bark and sap into the air. The gunner adjusts his aim quickly, the second bolt smacks cleanly into the chest of the leader and explodes, tearing the ork boss apart from inside, scattering ripped entrails.

It's all happened in just a few seconds and I realise that Brownie's been firing from behind me, the zip of heavy stubber bullets zinging past a few metres to my right. I pull the autogun round and squeeze the trigger, letting off a four shot burst to get the feel of the gun. It's got a bit of a kick to it and with my next burst I aim low at an orks that's raising its crude gun towards Fenn's position. Three shots rip out, the first missing, but the next two stick it in the abdomen. It swings back from the shots, its own gun roaring wildly into the trees. I down it with my third burst, putting a few rounds into its chest and neck.

The orks are running towards Fenn's position, not realising where we are, and I open fire again. A longer burst shatters the kneecaps of another ork, sending it tumbling into the leaves and dirt. It howls and then swings towards us on its belly, its bulky pistol erupting, sending bullets chewing into the dirt a little to my left. Before I can finish it off, Dunmore's heavy stubber chatters again, a line of impacts bursting in front of the ork until the fire intersects with it, gouging lumps out of its face and tearing into its shoulders. It slumps down, dead this time, and I pick another target.

The trail is littered with ork bodies, half of them dead already, and I realise with a shock it's only been about ten seconds since Fenn's group opened fire. Some of the orks are scattering into the jungle, while a five-strong group, much braver then the rest, charge towards us, brutal cleaver-like knives raised, pistols and guns hurling metal in all directions, chewing lumps out of the fallen tree just behind me.

They're about ten metres from us, and I'm about to stand up ready to flee when there's a burst of fire from behind them. The pursuing squad opens fire, adding to the din of autofire, and three of the orks go down in the surprise salvo, their backs ruptured and bloody. One of the orks falters and turns, only to get a heavy bolter shell in the ribs under its half-raised arm, its chest exploding outwards from the detonation.

The last hurls itself towards me, bringing its wicked cleaver down in a long arc. I roll to my right, finger on the trigger of the autogun as I throw myself clear. The point-blank fire tears into its left arm and stomach. It grunts and sways, and then steps forward again. Out of the corner of my eye, I see the Colonel rise up from the undergrowth to my right, bolt pistol in both hands.

He plants the shot straight into the side of the ork's low forehead; its head disintegrates a moment later. The steaming remnants of an eyeball plop onto my leg as the ork's headless corpse falls across me. Kicking it free, I leap to my feet, searching for another target, but the orks have scattered. I can hear bursts of autogun fire out in the jungle, and see occasional muzzle flashes in the gloom, as the other two ork hunter squads stalk through the murk, earning their title.

Fenn stands up from the tangled roots of a tree about twenty metres to my right, slapping another magazine into his autogun and waving for his squad to emerge. He sees the blood and shit all over me and grins. Striding over to me, he slings his firearm over one shoulder on its strap, and drags free a combat knife about as long as my forearm.

'Got yourself a couple there, eh, Kage?' he says, stooping down and rolling the ork over.

He digs into the remnants of its face with the knife and his bloodied hand emerges a few seconds later, proffering me four large tusks. He nods for me to take them and I hold out my hand. He tips the fangs into my palm and steps back. I look at them for moment and then he laughs, a deep noise, and steps forward to slap me on the shoulder, leaving a bloody handprint.

'Keep them safe,' he says with a smile. 'You've just killed your first ork on Armageddon. There's millions of the ugly green bastards out there for you to get, but always remember that first one!'

I look around to see the other Last Chancers being given similar prizes by the rest of Fenn's command squad. Erasmus staggers up to me, servo-skull under one arm, outstretched hand with a bloody ork tooth thrust towards me.

'Did I do alright?' he says, his stare slightly vacant. I take his fingers and close them over the fang, and give him a wink.

'Welcome to Armageddon, Erasmus,' I say. 'Welcome to the green hell.'

He smiles, nods slightly, and then faints.

SEVEN
ALONG THE CHAERON

I'M NOT SURE what I was expecting Cerberus Base to look like, but it's nothing like what I would have said if you'd asked me. I was thinking of some huge armoured bastion, with towers and ramparts and everything. What I find out, as Fenn leads us through the gap in the fourth concentric ring of razor wire surrounding the Imperial station, is that it's a huge camp. And it looks a complete mess.

The jungle is scorched and ripped up for about a kilometre in every direction, craters dotting the landscape. There are wooden watchtowers placed along the razor wire and minefield defences, and I can see mortar and artillery emplacements dug down into the earth behind wood-reinforced revetments. Here and there I spy a bunker roof, buried under sod and leaves, heavy stubber and lascannon muzzles protruding menacingly from their dark interiors. Trench works criss-cross the whole hill as it rises up from the jungle, overlooking the surrounding wilderness for kilometres on all sides.

As we pick our way through the traps, receiving waves from hidden snipers and gun post officers, I see a huge bonfire about half a kilometre to our left, a thick column of black smoke rising into the yellow sky. Out in the open, we're subjected to the full force of the sun, as it beats its way through the permanent low cloud, heating the air like an oven. I'm drowning in sweat after the first few metres, and I can already feel my face burning.

Fenn looks over at the bonfire, a concerned look on his face. He urges us to hurry on, without giving us a reason, but I collar Thorn and ask him what the blaze is all about.

'Ork bodies have to be burned,' the platoon sergeant says, glancing at the bonfire. 'Standard practice.'

'Yeah, so what's strange about that?' I ask. I've heard that advice given many times before, something to do with orks reproducing with spores or some other stupid theory the tech-priests have.

'A fire that size means there must have been a pretty serious attack,' Thorn says. 'We received a recall for defence when we were out on patrol, but Fenn figured it wasn't anything too major. I guess we know where all those seconders were going to or coming from now.'

Set just below the crest of the long low hill at the centre of the base is an armoured portal, its steel gates open. I can see rows of figures coming and going. Just above it, comms aerials sprout out of the ground like metal ferns, spreading high into the air, relaying and sending signals to all the patrols across the jungle, and to the high command out past the edges of the tree and in orbit.

Negotiating another kink in the trail through the razor wire, we start heading further uphill, towards the command bunker. As we move on, the other squads peel off to the right, heading for their own digs in a trench further around the hill. Only Fenn and his command squad are left with us.

IT'S A BLESSED relief to walk in through the open gates of the command complex, into the shade. Although it's still hot and humid as hell, it's good to be out of the direct heat, and with the change my sweat suddenly feels icy cold.

Suppressing a shiver, I stop for a moment, allowing my eyes to adjust to the gloom. The interior is carved out of the hill itself, and is reinforced in places with metal plates and spares. Corridors and rooms lead up, down, left and right. It's a total rats' nest, and my experienced eye notices some of the little details, such as loopholes in the walls covering the entrance so that any attacker can be fired on through the walls. Looking up, I see that as well as the main gates themselves, there are two more blast doors ready to be dropped down across the accessway. It'd be hard to imagine any enemy getting that far.

More ork hunter squads are heading out, giving nods and waves to Fenn and his men, and casting interested glances at us. A few tech-priests scurry about, and Erasmus tries to attract the attention of one but is ignored as the red-robed adept of the Machine God drifts past. There are a few officers floating around, chatting to each other, looking at maps as they walk, or carrying steaming mugs. It's all quite civilised really, considering there are thousands of orks out in the jungle, all of them intent on wiping this place from existence.

'There are a few secondary camps further north and south,' says Fen. It is the first thing he's said since we came in sight of Cerberus. 'They used to be training bases, but of course you can get all the training you need these days, just a day's march out into the jungle! We also used to have another major base to the northeast, Wolf Outpost. The orks almost overran it until the commander blew the self-destruct. You might have seen the remains, actually, made a hell of a mess for twenty kilometres in every direction.'

Well, that explains a lot. As we walk down the tunnels, turning left and right, seemingly doubling back on occasion, Fenn gives us a running commentary. The main comms room, buzzing with equipment, low chattering voices and radio static, opens up on our left. The hall down to the main armoury leads away a little further on. Steps that wind up to the artillery and observation posts are dotted at regular intervals along our route, along with officers' mess rooms, kitchens, cells, storerooms and all the other assorted junk you'd find in any Imperial military base. We've been walking about ten minutes when I realise how far down we've gone.

'Just how big is this place?' I ask Fenn, my voice loud in the confined space.

'It goes through the entire hill, with a few tertiary corridors out into the jungle itself,' he says. 'They've been sealed; the only way in or out now is through the main gates. It's too hard to defend that many entrances. We learned that in the first few days after the second invasion began.'

By the expression on Fenn's face, I know not to ask more. I can imagine what brutal fighting must have occurred when the orks got inside; fighting at close quarters where they're at their best.

'Here we are,' says Fenn, leading us through an open doorway to the right.

Inside is the command hub: an open room with a large table emblazoned with the Imperial eagle at the centre and a huge map hung on the wall. There are red and blue scrawls all over the chart, and there's a handful of officers moving back and forth in front of it, updating the annotations and making cryptic marks as they refer to scribbled notes on the pads they carry.

Through another doorway we walk into the real nerve centre, with comms panels all around the walls, linked to the various other stations in the hill I guess. Monitor servitors and lexmechanics churn out data from the incoming flow, scribbling the intelligence on long reams of parchment that spill onto the floor. Every now and then a map officer walks back in, tears free a strip and then goes back to update the map again.

At the far end, sitting in what can only be described as a metal throne hooked up with monitors, is a broad man, leaning over talking to a huddle of tech-priests and a man with the markings of a major on his cap. He looks up as we approach, smoothes his thick moustache with a gloved hand, and then slicks back his short greying hair.

'Ah, you've decided to come back after all, Lieutenant Fenn,' he says, his voice a cracked wheeze. I notice the scars of two puncture marks in the side of his throat. I guess that he's had his fair share of run-ins with orks before being cocooned in this command centre.

I then notice that he's not actually sitting in the throne, he is wired into it. He has no legs, the stumps sitting in metallic cups. Out of the corner of my eye, I see the Colonel do his best to straighten his dress coat and brush off the worst of the burrs and scratches inflicted by the jungle trek.

'Marshal Vine?' says the Colonel, stepping forward and saluting sharply. 'Colonel Schaeffer, commanding officer of the 13th Legion, sir.'

'Ah, you're the Last Chancers man, are you?' says Vine. 'I'm afraid you'll have to come to me so I can shake your hand, since my bloody chair isn't working!'

These last words are shouted at a thunderous bellow, directed towards the major and the tech-priests who visibly flinch. The Colonel takes a couple of steps forward and takes the proffered hand, giving it a short shake, and then steps back.

'Ah, I heard you ran into a spot of trouble,' says Vine, wheezing, folding his hands in his laps. 'Sorry about the welcome, but our intelligence is out of date all the bloody time!'

Again this damning criticism is delivered as a deafening roar, aimed this time at the map officers scurrying back and forth from the other chamber. I see Fenn suppressing a smirk, but not soon enough for the hawk-eyed marshal to miss it.

'Ah, you can stand there and smile all you bloody well like, Fenn, you piece of tree rat shit!' Vine shouts, pointing an accusing finger at the lieutenant. His hoarse voice turns shrill. 'Ignore my orders? Ignore my orders? I'll have you strung up as ork bait, you insubordinate little arse.'

'To return would have compromised our patrol security,' says Fenn, calmly taking in the commander's enraged glare.

'Ah, I don't care if you had to wade through a sea of bloody greenskins,' says Vine. 'When I tell you to get your smug arse back here, you do as you're told! How the hell am I supposed to run this bloody war, surrounded by incompetents and know-it-all arrogant ork fondlers like you?'

He breaks down into a hissing, wheezing fit, and the major steps forwards and proffers a handkerchief. Vine snatches it from him and uses to dab at the spittle dribbling down his chin.

'Ah, you're a good man, but I'm not having this, not having this at all,' he says after he composed himself again. He flings the sodden piece of cloth back at the major, who hurriedly tries to catch it before it hits him in the face. 'An order's an order, and if you disobey, that's insubordination. Am I right, Colonel?'

It takes Schaeffer a moment to realise that the marshal is now looking at him. He clears his throat purposefully. I guess he's buying time to work out what he's going to say.

'Failure to comply with a direct order is a charge of gross misconduct,' says the Colonel evenly, not looking at Fenn, but directing all his attention to Vine instead. 'It is punishable by flogging or other physical chastisement, incarceration not exceeding twenty years, or death.'

'Ah, hear that, Lieutenant Fenn?' says Vine, leaning forward as far as the bindings holding him to the chair allow. 'Do you deny that you did not comply with my orders? My bloody direct orders?'

'Is this a court-martial, sir?' says Fenn, stiffening to attention. 'If so, I think there are procedures to follow, and such.'

The Colonel looks at Fenn and then studies his glittering eyes. I can see something in them, something he's thinking quickly about.

'In a military crisis, jurisdiction and enforcement of Imperial law resides solely with the commanding officer in charge,' says Schaeffer.

'Ah, hear that too, Fenn?' wheezes Vine. 'Bloody well judge and executioner, that's what you're looking at here. So, did you receive my orders or not? I can check your signals record, so don't give me any ratshit about crossed wires or anything.'

'I received your signals, sir,' says Fenn, sighing heavily. He looks at the Colonel, eyes narrowing.

'Ah, and did you drag your sorry arse back here to protect Cerberus against attack, given that I'd issued the recall order to your platoon?' says Vine, his dark eyes glowering at the lieutenant.

'I did not, sir,' says Fenn.

'Ah, then what am I supposed to do, you daft bastard?' roars Vine, his anger reducing him to a coughing wreck again for a few seconds. His voice is a low hiss when he speaks again. 'Everybody knows you could make captain as quick as piss runs downhill, but I can't play favourites, can I?'

'No, sir, you cannot,' Fenn says, his voice quiet. I see him take a deep gulp. He really is taking this seriously, but it's just a bawling out, I'm pretty sure of that.

'Ah, discipline has to be maintained,' the marshal continues, scratching at one ear. 'So, do you want to be flogged, jailed or shot, you disobedient monkey-rat?'

'If I might offer an alternative, Marshal Vine,' says the Colonel before Fenn can reply. 'There is an alternative.'

I look at Fenn, who notices my glance. You poor bastard, I think. I've just realised what the Colonel's going to suggest. With just the look in my eyes and a slight shake of the head, I try to communicate to Fenn that he should go for the flogging, but he has to look back at Marshal Vine when the commander clears his throat.

'Ah, what have you got in mind, Colonel Schaeffer?' he says, sitting back heavily, causing his support chair to wobble slightly. I glance down at the floor and see that it's on narrow tracks, but one of the drive wheels is hanging off at an odd angle. No wonder he's annoyed with the tech-priests if they can't fix something that simple.

'It is within my power, under special considerations of the Imperial Commissariat as a penal legion commander, to commute any sentence, sir,' says the Colonel.

'Ah, so I don't have to flog this worthless idiot then?' says Vine.

'You have to sentence him first, sir, for the powers to be active,' prompts the Colonel.

'Ah, alright then,' says the marshal, leaning forward again. 'Golder Fenn, Lieutenant First Class, commanding officer of the third platoon, first company, fourth Armageddon Jungle Fighters Regiment. I hereby find you guilty of gross misconduct by order of insubordination, through deliberate failure to obey a direct order.'

Vine and Fenn look expectantly at Schaeffer. He blinks a couple of times, his ice blue eyes regarding them both. He then looks up at Vine.

'You have to pass sentence, sir,' he says.

'Ah, right, I sentence you to...' Vine's hand flaps for a moment, in mock indecision. 'Death by firing squad. Yes, I sentence you to the full penalty of Imperial Law.'

Oh frag. If only he'd stuck with the flogging. Now Fenn's up to his ears in the brown stuff and sinking quick. The Colonel turns smartly towards Fenn, eying him up and down.

'Golder Fenn,' he says, and I know the exact words that are coming next. 'You are sentenced to death for insubordination bringing about gross misconduct. Sentence commuted to penal servitude under the special supervision of Colonel Schaeffer, commanding officer of the 13th Penal Legion. Do you accept this new sentence?'

'What?' says Fenn, his brain catching up with the Colonel's words. I hear a spluttering cough from Vine as he also realises what's happened. 'Penal servitude?'

'What the hell are you doing, Schaeffer?' spits Vine.

'I need good soldiers,' the Colonel says, eyeing Fenn.

'Well, you can't have him, he's one of mine,' says the marshal. 'I can't have such a thing.'

'By the laws that you yourself invoked, Fenn can come with me or he can be put to death,' says the Colonel. 'It is the choice you gave him. My credentials with the Commissariat are of the highest authority, and I do have the power to remove you from command.'

'You wouldn't dare!' says Vine, shaking with anger. 'We're at bloody war, or didn't you notice?'

'It is for the successful conclusion of this war that I do this,' says Schaeffer. 'He will be mine with or without your approval. The association with countermanding an officer of the Commissariat will be enough to ruin you.'

'I'm sorry,' Vine says, looking at Fenn, and then looking away. 'I'm sorry.'

I take a couple of steps and lean forward to whisper in Fenn's ear. 'Gotcha!'

THE CHUGGING OF the barge's engine mixes with the slapping ripples of the water as we inch our way along the Chaeron River. Unsurprisingly, Marshal Vine was less than happy after the Colonel's little coup to snatch Golder Fenn, and Fenn himself hasn't spoken a word to any of us since. The marshal had us geared up and shipped out to the Chaeron docks within six hours, not even giving us time to get some sleep before we departed on a rescheduled supply hopper. Two bumpy, turbulent hours eastwards in the air and we were out of the jungle. Then we were dropped down at the docks where the Chaeron River comes down from the Diablo Mounts far to the east and enters the jungle. I managed to snatch a couple of hours at the wharfs while we waited for the barge to be readied, and then the Colonel took us aboard and we were off.

That was two days ago. Two days of dull, monotonous routine. There's barely room to swing a rat on board, and so we have to spend most of our time up on the deck or the roof, in the fume-filled air. The barge is low and wide, with a reinforced hull rusted and stained by the polluted waters. The roof is coated in layer after layer of peeling protective paint, eaten away by the air itself. Luckily, Schaeffer managed to commandeer us some rebreathers from Cerberus, but that still doesn't stop the stinging in your eyes, or the feeling of your skin being constantly etched away.

The Chaeron itself is a sluggish, bubbling tar-flow of chemical residues, thick with streaks of green and red. I would have thought it was impossible for anything to survive in that toxic soup, but telltale bubbles betray the creatures beneath the surface. Now and then I see vicious-looking, fin-backed lizards slipping into the murk from the banks, trailing after us for a few kilometres before deciding that none of us are going to fall overboard and provide them with a meal.

The barge is captained by Hauen Raqir. He is a wizened old man, his face shrivelled to a husk by the elements, his skin almost black with ingrained grit and dust. With his two sons, he keeps the engine coaxed into life, shovelling raw, solidified sewage into the burner to keep it ticking over just enough to propel us along. There's little other traffic on the river that we've seen, although I've seen abandoned Imperial gun emplacements along the banks in places, and the corroding shells of tanks, APCs, and a few ork vehicles too. Now and then, there are contrails in the sky high above us, left by Imperial interceptors or bombers, or maybe ork aircraft.

It's pretty lazy-going in comparison to the jungle, but we still have to keep a tight ration on food and water. Apparently both are valuable commodities everywhere. The orks have continually attacked the water pumping stations far to the south and according to Raqir, millions have died from dehydration in the hives and whole regiments have deserted their positions looking for water.

It's mid-afternoon and I'm sitting up on the roof of the barge as normal, near the front, playing cards with Brownie, Kin-Drugg and the captain's eldest, Yaidh. The rounded prow bobs up and down through the water ahead of us, the wind blowing smoke from the exposed engines back along the length, covering us in fumes, but the rebreathers keep the worst out of our lungs. There's frag all to actually bet with, but we make do with spent casings taken from the hold.

Raqir spends his time sifting through the desert looking for anything that can be taken back to the forges and smelted down again. Apparently metal is in pretty scarce supply too these days. It reminds me of the care taken to protect the transports in the convoy that brought us here.

'I'm sure you cheat, but can't see how,' says Yaidh, throwing up his hand with a grin. I scoop my winnings into a pile in front of me.

I pick up one of the spent cartridges while Brownie shuffles the deck.

'So how many of these have you got on board?' I ask.

'Nearly two thousand,' says Yaidh. 'Fifty of them worth a ration pack, hundred will get you a half-charged power pack.'

'Fifty for a rations tab?' says Kin-Drugg, looking at my stash. 'You've got my breakfast and lunch there, Kage.'

'Wish I'd kept all those we fired off in the jungle,' says Brownie, passing the deck to Yaidh to cut. With a deft flip of his fingers, Dunmore brings the two halves back together and starts to deal.

'So how many shells for the love of a good woman?' he asks with a grin. Yaidh smiles and taps the side of his nose.

'I know good place, but take more than empty casings to buy affection,' he says.

'Brownie's got nothing but empty casings anyway,' laughs Kin-Drugg, earning himself a punch on the arm. 'Why do you think he likes the biggest guns. He has to compensate somehow.'

I pick up my cards, keeping my face blank as I look at my abysmal hand. Brownie fidgets with his stake, toying with the casings with his left hand. He's got a good one, because every time he's bluffed so far, he's occupied himself with his right hand. Yaidh scratches his chin and takes a snort through his rebreather. He's gonna fold.

Kin-Drugg I haven't been able to read yet, but he's such a bad player he hasn't got any consistency to base my observations on. Hey, I spent two years on garrison duty on Stygies, I had to learn something while I was there, and cards was the main attraction. Thinking about it, it was the gambling that got me in trouble eventually. A bet with a woman as a stake, and a bad loser for a sergeant. Funny how things repeat themselves.

I fold.

As the others throw in their stakes and start the betting, I glance over to the bank, a couple of hundred metres to starboard. The ash wastes of Armageddon stretch out to the horizon, bleak and virtually featureless. Around here, the ground's not even proper ash dunes, just tiny rocks and pebbles, kilometre after kilometre of flatness. I'd hate to get lost out there, because except for an hour each way at dusk and dawn, you can't even tell where the sun is, and I haven't seen a star in the night sky since I got here. High-level smog covers the whole desolate planet. Doesn't stop it getting damn hot though, I think, pulling at my collar as if to let some of the heat out. A trickle of warm sweat runs down my chest.

'Do you think Fenn will ever come round?' says Kin-Drugg, tossing in his hand. He's obviously smarter than Yaidh, who doubles his bet.

'We'll have to see,' is all I say.

'How come he stays down below all the time?' asks Brownie, matching Yaidh and raising him again. The bargeman grins victoriously and then immediately matches the bet.

'Yeah, an outdoor man like him should enjoy all this fresh air,' says Kin-Drugg with a snort.

'He likes his open spaces to be not so open,' I tell them quietly. 'He's never been out of the jungle before, it's kind of creeping him out. He's not used to so much sky.'

'Oh great. Good one, Colonel,' says Kin-Drugg, pulling the stopper from his water bottle and taking a swig. Brownie lays down his cards and Yaidh starts muttering in some local dialect we can't understand. I'm pretty certain he's swearing his head off.

'I was sort of the same for a little while,' I say, pointing at Kin-Drugg to shuffle and deal. 'I grew up in a hive, so I never really knew you could get distances more than a hundred metres. Imagine how I felt when I was on the shuttle going up to orbit. I saw this massive hive that I only knew a tiny bit of, dwindle to a little blob. Damn near pissed my pants. And I really had never seen the sky before, although my grandpa used to tell us what lay outside the hive.'

'Well, Stralia's kind of average really,' says Brownie. 'Lot of islands, so I pretty much everyone grows up on the coast. I couldn't sleep for two weeks, not hearing waves nearby, or smelling salt.'

'Well, Kator's renowned for its grav-chute regiments because we pretty much live in the sky,' says Kin-Drugg. 'Gas harvesters mostly, a few sub-orbital cities. I'm the opposite from you, Kage. I never set foot on proper ground 'til I joined the guard.'

'And I was born on a boat that runs on shit,' says Yaidh. 'Less talk, more cards. Deal the cards. I win this time.'

SEVERAL MORE DAYS' travel brings us to the intersection with the Krynnan canal. A series of huge locks, fifteen in total over two kilometres, bring ships up seven hundred metres from the lowlands to the south. It's here that we part company with the Raqirs. We're due to meet with some kind of military transport heading up the canal, which will take us on to Infernus Quay. After that, I've got no idea, the Colonel didn't tell us any more. He obviously knows exactly where we're heading but for some reason is reluctant to tell us. That worries me, because last time he was so cagey about a mission, it was because nobody would have believed it.

I'm expecting something a bit like Raqir's barge, perhaps with a bit more accommodation, but when dawn reveals the transport pulling in to dock the next morning, I have to admit I'm a little bit more impressed.

Over two hundred metres long, the heavily-armoured barge cruises through the murky river waters at speed, a bow wave foaming ahead. It leaves smaller vessels bobbing madly in its wake. Smoke billows from three exhaust stacks, the clanking of powerful engines clearly audible over the noise of the dock. Two gun turrets jut out of her prow deck, each housing two large-bore cannon, and a third smaller gun is mounted on her rear. As she slows and pulls up at the wharf, a long metal gangplank hisses out on hydraulics, clanging down onto the ferrocrete. The Colonel walks up and talks to one of the officers by the boarding ramp, signing something and then waving us on. We grab our kit bags, scrounged from the ork hunters before we left Cerberus, and jog on board.

At the top, a corporal gives us a surly look and directs us to the lower deck. Heading down the stairwell, we find ourselves in a bunkroom, large enough for a hundred men, with kit lockers down the length of the ship. The hull vibrates even with the engines just ticking over, rattling bolts in their holes and causing tremors to run up my leg.

'This is a bit more like it,' says Kin-Drugg, dumping his bag on one of the upper bunks.

'Nice to have a bit of space,' says Brownie, wandering to the far end.

We stop as we hear the thumping of boots on the deck above. Lots of boots.

'Bugger,' says Brownie as a sergeant leads his squad down the steps, barking orders for them to sort themselves out. We drift down to the far end as two whole platoons file in. The last to arrive stand looking confused, looking for non-existent empty bunks. Then the Colonel strides in and the Guardsmen all leap up from their lounging, jump into line and snap off salutes. He marches over to us.

'I hope you are not occupying bunks needed by proper soldiers,' he says, nodding to the door through the next bulkhead.

With a sinking feeling, I lead the Last Chancers through. Sure enough, it's an empty storeroom, or more likely an ammo magazine. There's even shelving around the walls. Not a bed in sight, not even a scrap of mattress or blanket. A single yellow glowglobe illuminates the cramped chamber. It's dark, and below the waterline, and the throbbing of the engines is even more powerful. It makes my teeth rattle. There's a constant sloshing of backwash against the hull as the barge rides the river swells.

'Come on Last Chancers, make yourselves comfortable,' I snap, directing a venomous look at the Colonel's back as he steps out. The door swings shut behind him, and we hear the sound of a lockwheel squealing into place. I notice there's no wheel on the inside. Why would there be? It's a storeroom after all, it's not like cargo needs to let itself out. And that's all we are, human cargo.

EIGHT
DEATH IN THE RUINS

ANOTHER DAY AND a half, getting only brief exercise and five meal periods. Then the door opens again.

'Full kit, combat readiness,' says the corporal who welcomed us aboard. 'Muster aft.'

As he turns sharply on his heel and marches away, we look at each other.

Once we're up on deck, rebreathers in place, lasguns charged and ready to go, we find out what all the fuss is about. About half a kilometre down the river is Infernus Quay, a sprawling maze of ruined warehouses, docks and factories. Smoke fills the sky, and the steady pounding of artillery can be heard from the southern shore, about three hundred metres to our starboard.

With a roar of jets, a flight of three attack planes scream over, rockets rippling out from pods slung under their wings. Detonations erupt a few hundred metres inside the quay buildings. There are the constant sounds of small arms fire and grenades. Shells from the ork guns explode along the quay and send up massive plumes of water from the river. Another transport barge, slightly smaller than the one we're on, takes a direct hit. Its stern is flung into the air, and propellers splinter and fly off. The men on board are plunged into the murky water; they struggle briefly before the corrosive soup eats through their uniforms and sucks them below.

Half-ruined wharfs and piers jut into the Chaeron, swarming with Guardsmen pouring off barges, lighters and rickety old steamers.

They surge forward into the ruins. As we close, I can see the black coats of commissars, chainswords waving the troops on, and I can just hear their shouts blended in with the cacophony of battle, exhorting their men to their greatest efforts.

The Colonel appears, bolt pistol in hand, a newly acquired power sword hanging in a scabbard at his coat belt. He doesn't look at us, instead he fixes his attention on the mangled remnants of a pier about two hundred metres away, evidently our destination.

The other troops on board clump up the stairs onto deck, and it's then that I realise how young and old most of them are: some of them are barely old enough to shave, while others have thinning and greying hair. Their officer, a gangling lieutenant, moves along the line, checking weapons and packs. Behind the visor of his gasmask I can see wide, scared eyes.

The barge shudders as the engines are put in reverse, slowing us down for the approach to the pier. Looking out over Infernus Quay, I can see that there are very few buildings more than two storys high. A half ruined steeple of a shrine rears up near the centre of the complex, the wing of a massive golden eagle hanging forlornly from its twisted brackets. The whole place is littered with rubble, burnt out tanks and transports and piles of bodies.

'This doesn't look fun,' mutters Brownie, standing just behind me. I ignore him, focussing my attention on the landing place as the metal gangway soars down, clanging against the twisted platform. The Colonel turns and points at us, then heads off down the ramp.

'Come on Last Chancers, time to die!' I shout, breaking into a run.

With my boots thudding on the metal walkway, I hurl myself down the boarding ramp at full tilt, following the Colonel into a shattered office building just to our left. Glancing over my shoulder I see Brownie following, the heavy stubber slung over one shoulder, and Erasmus running behind him with loops of ammo belt.

Lorii leaps across a pile of bricks and slams into the wall next to me, breathing hard. She glances out of the jagged frame of a window just behind me, lasgun held ready. The others follow quickly, taking up covered positions in this room and the one next door.

I glance down at the rubble we're crouched on, and notice skeletal fingers protruding from underneath a twisted metal roofing beam. Putting it to the back of my mind, I scoot forward to kneel beside the Colonel, who's peering out of a doorway to the front.

'The orks hold the west quarter,' he says, pointing off to the left. 'This is a counter-attack to push them back. I want the heavy stubber up in that roof two hundred metres down the road, half the squad to its right, the other with you circling left.'

I nod and point to Brownie, Erasmus, Kelth, and Oahebs.

'You're with the Colonel, straight ahead, don't slow down,' I say. 'The rest of you, follow me.'

Without waiting for an acknowledgement, I put my head down and slide out of the door, keeping close to the wall. A squad of Armageddon guard, gas masks on, trench coats flapping, crosses the street about seventy metres further on and I head after them, running across the road into the building opposite. Finding myself in a large, corrugated-metal warehouse choked with smashed crates and splintered pallets; I head across, scrambling over the debris.

Scuttling from building to building, we cover about two hundred metres in the next few minutes. I'm breathing hard; my heart is hammering in my chest as I crouch at a corner, peering left and right, my whole body tense. Taking a deep breath, I force myself to relax and focus. There's sporadic firing from our right, and the crump of mortar shells falling not far ahead. To our left, past a fallen archway, a Leman Russ tank smokes fitfully, its tracks thrown, the turret dislodged from its ring. Ahead, a multi-storey building has collapsed across the road, filling it with rubble and chunks of masonry. I duck back when I see a flitting movement just beyond the mound.

Easing my head back around the corner, I look over the rubble, scanning to the left and right. I hear a barked order; it's obviously one of our squads.

'Come on, the Colonel will be waiting,' I say, heading forward at a jog, lasgun held in both hands.

Reaching the pile of rubble, I drop to my stomach and pull myself forward, ignoring the scrapes and scratches from the jagged debris cutting through my fatigues. Reaching the crest, I see three mortar teams huddled behind a sandbag wall, inside a large shell crater. Looking further ahead, I can see more movement, orks massing in a couple of half-demolished storehouses about three hundred metres away. The mortars are laying down constant fire on their position, but it'll only be a matter of time before the orks take their chances and head forwards.

Scrambling over the rubble, bricks and crumbling mortar cascading down over my boots, I make my way over to the mortar squad. Their sergeant glances around at the noise, laspistol ready, and then relaxes when he sees us. It's at that moment that I dearly wish we had a comms-set to communicate with the Colonel, or somehow find out what's going on. Looking down the side street to the right, I can see the position of the others, the nose of the heavy stubber poking out from a large crack in the wall on the third floor, the position covered from above by a slope of cracked roof.

'Wait here,' I tell the others, and they fan out into cover on either side of the road. I run down the street towards the Colonel, ducking instinctively as a shell screams overhead; it explodes on the far side of the block. Running into the ground floor, I see Oahebs by the door, lasgun resting against the frame.

'Where's the Colonel?' I ask, and he jabs a thumb over his shoulder towards the next room on.

I walk through and the Colonel's there, talking to Kelth. He looks over at me.

'We're down the street near the mortar battery,' I tell him. 'There's a good number of orks ahead, getting ready to attack. We'll be better off in front of the mortars to give them some protection.'

'Very well,' he says with a nod. 'This will be our fallback position if we need to retreat. Have your team secure the left side of the approach, we will be up shortly.'

I turn and start running back to Lorii and the others, hoping that the Colonel gets a move on. It'll be over very quickly if the orks advance on us before we have any support. Jumping down into the cracked plaster behind a wall, I glance around at the others. I point to a building across the junction and gesture for them to move up. As I do so, I see a couple of squads of Guardsmen coming up to our position from the rear. I recognise their lieutenant from the barge. Not wanting to exchange pleasantries, I head after the rest of the team before they get within talking distance, running at a crouch across the ruptured ferrocrete.

'What are they waiting for?' asks Kin-Drugg, looking at the orks. There's a fair few of them now, under bombardment from the mortars, splinters and shrapnel scything through the buildings and across the road. 'They're getting a pasting just sitting there.'

I shrug, not knowing the answer. I don't really care, as long as they hang back for a few more minutes. Ahead and to the left is a stairwell, leading up to the remnants of the floor above. I lead the others up, directing them to move along the level which seems to stretch for about fifty metres up the street. I poke my head out of a window, the glass crunching underfoot, to see what's going on. The sound of orkish chanting carries to me over the distant explosions and rattle of fire. They're definitely working themselves up for something.

'Any way up at the far end?' I ask Fenn. He turns to me, face as white as snow, blinking slowly. He opens his mouth and then shuts it again without saying a word. 'Come on, this is the urban jungle. It's just the same, only you've got rubble for undergrowth and walls for trees. Pull it together!'

He stares blankly at me for a second and then recognition lights up his eyes. He blinks a couple more times.

'No,' he says finally. 'There is no way up at the far end, unless they climb on each other's backs.'

'I want you down there, with grenades ready in case they try to get underneath us,' I tell him. 'Have you got that?'

He nods and turns away, to be replaced by Lorii.

'You'd better see this,' she says, and her expression makes my stomach knot.

I follow her along a ledge that leads out to the remnants of a bridge that once crossed from this building to the opposite side of the road, some ten metres away. The tangled wreckage of metal lies on the street below us. I can hear a loud rumbling, and creeping forward on my belly, stick my head out to look at the ork position. I can see them swarming through the buildings now, but it isn't that which is causing my heart to skip a beat.

Grinding along the road is a huge armoured vehicle, larger than a Leman Russ, three turrets pointed at the mortar section down the road. Its iron-rimmed wheels crush masonry and corpses under its weight as it rolls forward, oily smoke fuming from a cluster of exhaust stacks at its rear, filling the street with a reeking stench. Crude banners flap from flagpoles attached to its main turret.

'Battle fortress!' I turn and shout to the others. Glancing back, I see the orks pressing in behind it, using its bulk for cover. A mortar shell lands just in front of it, kicking up chunks of ferrocrete that bound harmlessly off its thick hull. The stutter of heavy stubber fire echoes down the street as Brownie opens up, bullets zinging of the metallic beast and cutting through the orks to either side.

'Hold your fire,' I say, making myself relax my grip on my lasgun, massaging some life back into my hand. 'Fenn, Kin-Drugg, I want covering fire against the infantry when we attack. Lorii, ready with grenades.'

She nods, pulling two from the pouches at her belt.

'Wait for my signal,' I say, my voice an urgent hiss, as I see Fenn crouching down, bringing his lasgun up to his shoulder.

With a great belch of flame and smoke, the battle fortress's main gun opens fire. A split second later the wall of a building across the street explodes outward in a shower of steel splinters and ferrocrete shards. The two secondary guns open up, raking the ground line with large calibre shells, tearing more pockmarks into the road and surrounding buildings. Sitting in hatches thrown back, two orks man heavy autoguns, their staccato firing interrupted frequently as the crude guns jam.

The battle fortress rumbles to a stop just beneath us. Orks move forward around it like a green wave breaking across a rock. The main gun fires again and I can feel the pressure wave slapping across my face, only a couple of metres above it. The sound makes my ears ring, as it echoes off the inside of the half-ruined room.

'Let's do it!' I shout over the din, bringing up my lasgun and firing off shots at the nearest cupola. It swings the gun around towards me and bullets rattle along the brickwork just below me, causing me to duck back. After the expected pause when the weapon jams again, I lean back out, this time putting two shots into the ork's head as it bends down, examining the breach of the gun. It slumps forward. All around me the others are opening fire, a torrent of lasbolts tearing into the orks that clamber around the immense vehicle.

Fire from the others and another mortar salvo join the attack, heavy stubber and lasfire cutting down half a dozen orks. Their bodies are flung into the air by the detonation of the mortar bombs; dirt and limbs scatter across the road and the hull of the battle fortress. Firing off another few shots in rapid succession, I lean back out of harm's way and check on the others.

Fenn is throwing a grenade underarm into the room below us; it bounces off the twisted remnants of a metal stairway. The growling cries of wounded orks follow the bang of the grenade's detonation. Kin-Drugg is snapping off shots left, right and centre, and I can already see a discarded power pack next to him. Each of those is good for forty shots, so he's been busy. Lorii's close by, crouched a couple of metres behind me, waiting for my signal.

A series of explosions ripples along the wall in front of me, and shards of ferrocrete fly inwards, grazing my face and tearing at my uniform. I look at Lorii and give her the nod. Leaning back out, I rake the second cupola with fire, only to discover that the ork's already dead, its finger tightened on the trigger, spraying bullets wildly into the air as the turret turns and it flops to one side. Lorii jumps past me, dropping down the metre and a half to the top of the battle fortress's roof. I sling my lasgun over my shoulder and follow.

Keeping low, we scuttle to the two hatches, readying our grenades. Lasbolts skip off the armour in bright flashes, and bullets scream past within centimetres of my face. With another glance at each other, we each toss two frag grenades in. With a running jump, I leap back, grabbing hold of a twisted bridge support jutting from the wall. Wrapping my legs around it I reach up a hand, which Lorii grabs, and I swing her up.

Below us, as we hurl ourselves behind the shattered wall, the grenades detonate. Shrapnel scythes through the interior of the battle fortress. The secondary guns fall silent and the huge tank begins to lurch forwards again. I guess the driver has either died at the controls or has decided it's better to keep moving. The main gun booms out again, the shot sailing high into the distance, the gunner's aim spoiled by the sudden movement. If it gets away, it'll roll over the position at the end of the road with no trouble.

'Again?' says Lorii and I nod, pulling another grenade from my belt.

'Kin-Drugg, get your arse over here, and give me your grenades!' The ex-grav chuter pulls back from the edge of the floor where he's been firing down into the orks, and legs it towards me, keeping his head down. I see that he's limping, blood streaming from his right leg.

'It's no bother,' he says between gritted teeth, noticing the line of my gaze. He hands me a grenade and shrugs. 'It's the only one I've got left.'

He makes his way back to his firing post and pulls his lasgun round. A second later, the ferrocrete explodes underneath him, and a whole section of the floor gives way with a crash and the screech of torn reinforcing rods. He's alright though, I can hear him shouting and shooting. Fenn glances down and then jumps over the edge after him.

'Looks like we're going downstairs then,' I say to Lorii, scuttling out onto the remnants of the bridge and then leaping down onto the top of the battle fortress as it crawls forwards. An ork sticks its head up through the nearest cupola and I ram my boot into its face as Lorii moves past, headed for the front of the tank. I slam the hatch shut, and then drop to my stomach as a bullet grazes my left shoulder. Crawling forwards, I hang over the edge of the track guards.

The clanking of wheels deafens me, but I see an air grille just to my left and smash it in with the butt of my lasgun. Throwing the grenade inside, I leap away, flattening myself against the hull as the orks around the tank fire up at us. Flames billow out of the exhausts and my ears are suddenly torn apart by the shrieking of metal grinding on metal as gears topple off, and the engine is torn to shreds.

The battle fortress slews to the left for a few seconds, crushing orks beneath it, before crashing into a building and coming to a stop. Debris showers down around me, but I can't stop myself grinning. It makes all those days spent on the ship with our mock tank worthwhile.

The sound of a shell, much heavier than a mortar bomb, whines overhead and a moment later the road just behind the battle fortress erupts, tossing orks into the air and causing the immobilised tank to shudder. As the smoke clears, it reveals a deep crater. I can just imagine the forward observation officer's next words. Concealed somewhere around here, he'll be saying, 'Fire for effect.'

It's time to get the hell out of here.

Lorii has the same idea, leaping clear and disappearing into the building where Kin-Drugg and Fenn are. I imagine I hear the distant boom of massive artillery pieces, though I doubt it's true, and I jump down, stumbling over the ork bodies littering the road.

'Run!' I scream at them, slapping Lorii on the back to get her moving.

Kin-Drugg has one arm around Fenn's shoulder. His trousers are soaked with blood from his injured leg. I grab his other arm, and between the two of us, we race towards the Colonel's position. Bullets skip off the walls and whistle around us as we put our heads down and sprint as best we can over the uneven surface.

Hurling ourselves through a shattered window into the street, we pick ourselves up and start across the roadway. A second later, there's an immense series of detonations. The building explodes into dust under the artillery bombardment, and the shockwave hurls us from our feet again. For several seconds the salvo continues, the floor shaking under the impacts, the air filled with choking smoke and dust. After the tumult dies down, it starts raining body parts. Green-skinned gobbets of flesh and dark blood spatter down onto the street around us, ash sticking to the gore as it settles slowly.

Kin-Drugg pulls himself up to a sitting position and looks back across to where the street had stood. The buildings are now nothing more than a crater-pocked wasteland about two hundred metres across.

'Why couldn't have they done that ten minutes ago?' he moans, grasping his leg tightly, spitting in pain. 'Bloody artillery crews.'

'What, and have the infantry complain they don't get any fun?' I say, mopping crap from my face with a dusty sleeve.

I hear a trumpet in the distance, signalling a general advance, and within a minute, squad after squad of troops are pounding down the street to reoccupy the position the orks were in. We sit there as the platoons march past us at the double, gazing around in astonishment. A shadow falls over me and I look up to see the Colonel silhouetted against the yellow sky.

'Where did all these late fraggers come from?' I say, pushing myself to my feet and picking up my lasgun.

'It was good that we stalled the ork advance,' he assures me, looking across now at the hundreds of men moving into place.

I wonder. There are at least two companies here, I suspect less than a dozen Last Chancers would not have made much of a difference. Still, better to be busy than bored, I suppose.

HEADING EAST ACROSS Infernus Quay, we pass hastily rebuilt barricades and emplacements, and thousands of Guardsmen digging in for the next ork assault. We take it in turns to help Kin-Drugg. We steadily make our way up through the centre of the complex and to the higher ground to the east. There's a medical station about halfway up the slope of one of the hills and we stop there to get treatment for Kin-Drugg. Sitting him down, we all turn and gaze east and north towards the ork lines.

You can easily see them out in the ash wastes, even a few kilometres away. The ground is swarming with them: huge mobs camped out in the harsh dunes, buggies and bikes roaring back and forth. The smoke from the fires and engines casts a pall for kilometres in every direction.

As we watch, something draws our attention to the horizon. They start out as specks, and at first I think I'm imagining it, but as the orderlies come and take Kin-Drugg, I stand there watching the distant shapes. As the minutes pass they grow larger, changing from specks to blobs. To be able to see them at this distance, they must be immense.

'Gargants,' says Fenn, shielding his eyes against the glare. 'Massive war engines, larger than a Warlord Titan. Three of them by the looks of it, plus a load of battle fortresses.'

The orks on the plains seem to be content to wait for their reinforcements to arrive. There's a cry of pain from Kin-Drugg inside the makeshift bloodstation. Nobody turns round.

I look over the defences arrayed against the orks, from the batteries of cannons and howitzers on the far bank of the Chaeron, to the legion of troopers in and around the buildings themselves.

All around on the hillside are the wounded, lying in lines along the sides of the road. The lucky ones have blankets to cover themselves from the burning sun, but most of them don't. A little way to our right, amongst the ruins of an old pumping station, dozens of men wearing the white armbands signifying punishment duty are digging a massive hole for the pile of bodies behind them. There must be at least two hundred corpses there, swarming with flies and rats. Luckily the breeze is blowing the other way, so the stench isn't too bad.

One of the orderlies comes out and stretches, his dark uniform crusted with dried blood. He notices us looking at the mass grave.

'That's just the ones that we've sent out this morning,' he says, rubbing a bloodied finger along his nose at an itch. 'There are fourteen more medic stations around here. Well, there were, a couple of them got bombed out by fighter-bombers this morning. On average, we're losing about fifteen hundred men a day. When the orks attack, that doubles, but on quiet days we just have to worry about lung poisoning, infected rat bites, the usual stuff.'

We look down at the dockside and see more troop transports unloading their cargoes of new soldiers. There are so many of them, marching up the piers and disappearing into the ruins.

'A real meatgrinder, eh?' says Brownie.

'It has been,' says the orderly. He proffers a hand to each of us, which we shake. All except that Colonel that is, because he's disappeared off somewhere in the last few minutes. 'The name's Syzbra, I'm with, well was with, the 14th Vastan Armoured Infantry.'

'We're Last Chancers,' I tell him. He gives me a puzzled look. 'Penal troopers. Anyway, it doesn't matter. What do you mean "was with"? Where's your unit now?'

'Well, with all the attacks and counter-attacks, we're pretty much scattered all along the north bank of the Chaeron as far as I can tell. I sort of ended up here, and it seemed there was plenty to do.'

'And what did you mean, it has been a real meatgrinder?' asks Lorii, picking up on his earlier choice of words. 'Are you expecting it to stop soon?'

Syzbra points to the ork horde stretching around Infernus Quay.

'Last time they came in with just one gargant, they almost overran us in a few hours,' he says. 'Luckily we had orbital support back then. I hear it's needed elsewhere at the moment, somewhere near Tartarus

I think. They've got three of them this time. I figure you guys turned up at a really bad time. Things are going to go from meatgrinder to slaughterhouse tomorrow.'

I hear Brownie swearing under his breath and Lorii's shaking her head. Kelth slumps to the ground, burying his head in his hands between his knees. I turn to face Syzbra.

'So what are you going to do?' I ask him.

'Keep patching up the bits they throw me, then start using this,' he says, pulling a bolt pistol out from the waistband of his fatigues. 'I figured the commissar who coughed up his lungs all over me the other day wouldn't need it.'

Kin-Drugg comes out, hobbling badly, his face ashen.

'Your friend lost a lot of blood. Lucky you got him here in time,' says Syzbra. 'Any other time, I'd recommend keeping the weight off it for a few days, but that just ain't going to happen is it?'

The Colonel reappears, a quartermaster sergeant trailing behind him. He glances at Kin-Drugg's leg and then looks at the rest of us.

'Grab your gear and move out,' he says. 'There is a supply train back into the Diablo Mounts, and we are going to be on board. Kin-Drugg, you will be staying here. Congratulations, you've survived the 13th Penal Legion.'

The drop trooper smiles for a moment, and then the expression turns to one of anger.

'Hold on, I'm not staying anywhere,' he says, limping forward. 'I heard what you guys were talking about. I'll be dead within the day I reckon. I'm sticking with you, Colonel.'

'Nonsense,' says Schaeffer with a snort. 'We cannot possibly accommodate walking wounded on this mission. You will slow us down.'

'I'll bloody well sprint if I have to,' says Kin-Drugg, lifting up his good leg and standing on the injured one to try and prove how strong he is.

'I said no, you are staying here,' the Colonel says, turning and walking away.

'I demand my redemption!' Kin-Drugg calls after him, and when the Colonel turns around he continues. 'Die or succeed, you said! They're the only two ways I got of redeeming myself in the eye of the Emperor, you said. Well, the mission's not over, and I'm pretty damn sure that if I was dead I wouldn't be looking at this bunch of ugly wasters. So I demand you take me with you.'

Colonel stares at him for a long while, and I expect him to reach for his pistol and blow his brains out. He'd be dead and redeemed then. It's just the sort of thing the Colonel would do. He gives a depressed shake of the head and then looks at me.

'Kage, if this man falls behind, no one goes back for him,' he says before stalking off.

'Too bloody right,' mutters Brownie, stomping after the Colonel. The others follow, leaving Kin-Drugg standing there, watching them go.

'What you waiting for?' I snap at him and he flinches. 'On the double, move out!'

He hobbles off as fast as he can, my laughter following him every painful step.

NINE

THROUGH THE MOUNTAINS

WHEN THE COLONEL had said we were travelling on a supply locomotive, I had been expecting some rickety old steam engine. The reality is very different. The glistening black armour is scuffed and dented in places and covered in ash, but the six carriages and engine look pretty impregnable at first glance. About three times higher than I am tall, the ten-metre long armoured compartments are each protected by anti-aircraft cupolas with twin multilasers, while the carriage behind the engine boasts a modified tank turret.

Climbing up the ladder into the central wagon, I note the thick armour plating spaced a little way off from the carriage sides. Inside it's sparse though, it is still a supply train after all. There are no windows, and as the crew slam the door shut we're plunged into darkness. We sit ourselves down on the reinforced steel floor, feeling something gritty underfoot. I don't know what it was delivering, but there's still some of its previous cargo scattered across the floor.

The train shudders as the engines growl into life and a fitful light emanates from the glow-globe set into the ceiling. At each end, hand and foot holds are set into the wall to allow access to the cupolas above. I pull myself up and open the hatch, allowing more light to spill in. Dragging myself up to look out of the roof, I see the track stretching ahead of us and up into the mountains.

'Check the other gun, Dunmore,' I call down, pulling the securing catch free on the multilasers in front of me.

Settling myself against the edge of the hatch, I swing the guns left and right along the rail. They've got a good traverse, moving around three-quarters of a circle to the front and sides. The elevation is good, almost going up to the vertical, although the size of the wagons themselves means that they're little use for clearing the ground unless the target's a few hundred metres away. Hearing the other hatch clang open, I glance over my shoulder to see Brownie pulling himself up. Turning my attention back to the guns, I press the power up switch and read the charge meter. Both power packs are almost full, which is good. Overall, everything seems to be in good order. Stowing the multilasers back into their locked position, I take the opportunity to have a look around.

We're already travelling at some speed, rocking gently side-to-side along the track accompanied by the rhythmic clattering of the wheels. To the right, the Chaeron is disappearing behind the ash dunes, and turning around I see the smoke-shrouded buildings of Infernus Quay are already a few kilometres behind us. To my left, the ash wastes of Armageddon stretch out: kilometre after kilometre of barren wasteland as far as I can see. All in all, it could be worse. I'm glad I'm not marching across those lifeless tracts.

As NIGHT CLOSES in, I give the word to break out our rations. I realise that we left most of the kit on the barge in the Colonel's eagerness to get into the fighting. It's just what we've got in the pouches on our belts, probably enough food and water for three days. I hope that it's either a short journey, or the Colonel has made other plans. I've already had enough of being hungry and thirsty.

Gnawing on a piece of bland dried meat substitute, I take a swig from my canteen to soften the rations.

'So what's the deal with you, then?' I say, looking at Gideon Oahebs. His face looks even more thin and pinched than normal in the dim yellow glow of the compartment, the shadows dark in his sunken cheeks.

'Nothing special,' he says, tearing a chunk out of his ration bar and stuffing it in his mouth.

'Come on,' says Brownie. 'It's been a year now, and we hardly know anything about you. So come on, Gideon, what got you into the Last Chancers?'

'I'd rather not talk about it,' he says, gazing down at the floor, and fiddling with the rations wrapper.

'Alright then, we'll ask Lorii,' I say.

'Don't drag me into this,' she says. 'I'm not going to talk as if he isn't here.'

'It can't be anything as bad as we're imagining,' I say, focussing on Oahebs again. I walk over and sit next to him.

'Just leave the guy alone,' says Fenn. 'If he doesn't want to talk, he doesn't have to.'

'You're just pissed because the Colonel got you good and proper,' says Kin-Drugg.

'Like any of you volunteered,' replies the ork hunter, tossing his crumpled-up wrapper at Kin-Drugg. 'I'm sure you were all queuing up for the penal legions.'

'Some of us had a choice,' says Brownie, looking at Lorii. 'So what's with that, eh? Did you miss your old mate Kage too much?'

She gives him a venomous stare.

'Who's got the cards?' I say, trying to break the uneasy silence.

'Don't change the subject,' says Kin-Drugg between slurping chews of his rations. 'Tell us, Lorii. Tell us what the hell you were thinking when you signed back on with Schaeffer?'

'It's none of your Emperor-damned business,' she says, giving them each a glare. 'I have my reasons, that's all you need to know.'

'I think we deserve more than that,' says Brownie. 'You too, Gideon. If I'm putting my arse on the line for you in a firefight, I want to know who I'm with. The rest of these meatheads I know, but you two are a mystery. How do we know you're not going to bug out in the middle of a scrap?'

Lorii pushes herself to her feet and walks towards Brownie, who hurriedly stands up, his arms raised to defend himself. She stands right in front of him, eyeballing him.

'I can look after myself, no need to make sacrifices on my account,' she says, and I can't help noticing the emphasis on the word "sacrifices". 'In fact, I'd feel safer knowing that I wasn't relying on you.'

'Is that so?' says Brownie, bristling with anger. 'And why would that be?'

'You're a show-off,' says Lorii, crossing her arms and leaning back on her heels. She glances over at the heavy stubber stowed in the corner. 'Without your big guns, you're nothing, are you?'

Kin-Drugg stands up next to Brownie, sneering.

'And what's so special about you?' says the drop trooper. 'Apart from being a white-skinned freak, obviously.'

Oh frag. He had to go and say something like that, didn't he? I launch myself to my feet in an instant, throwing myself in front of

Lorii. My right fist cracks straight into Kin-Drugg's jaw, the sudden blow knocking him to the floor.

'Back off, everyone!' I snap, shoving Brownie back a step. 'Anyone here want to pick a fight with me?'

Kin-Drugg scrambles to his feet, hands balled into fists, but I dart him a look that stops him in his tracks.

'Back down,' I say to him, my voice quiet. Behind me, I hear Lorii snort and walk to the far end of the compartment. Glancing over my shoulder, I see her slump down against the wall, eyes closed.

'What the hell did you do that for?' hisses Kin-Drugg, rubbing his jaw.

'You'll have a bruise, nothing more,' I tell him. 'Count yourself lucky I didn't let Lorii have a go at you.'

'She's not that tough,' he says, puffing up his chest.

'Yes she is,' I tell him. 'I don't need any more corpses at the moment, so don't start throwing around words like "freak", okay?'

He sees the sincerity in my eyes, and opens his mouth to say something but then shuts up. It's the first sensible thing he's done in the last five minutes. With an exaggerated shrug, he steps back and sits down, his gaze avoiding everyone else.

'And you,' I say, turning on Brownie. 'You just keep your mouth shut before someone here puts their fist into it.'

He nods and looks down at his feet. I take a few steps back so that I can look at them all. Kelth is sitting in the corner, eyes closed, apparently meditating or something. Oahebs is just sitting quietly toying with a rations wrapper, folding int and unfolding it. Next to him, Fenn has knife and whetstone out; slowly sharpening the blade with smooth, gentle motions. The others are looking at me, trying to guess what I'll do next.

'Listen up,' I say, raising my voice. 'I don't know what the Colonel has in store for us, but you can believe me that it won't be pretty and it certainly won't be easy. There will be enough fighting and dying to be done before we see this thing out; we haven't got the luxury of doing the orks' job for them. I don't give a rat's arse if you hate each other's guts. Hell, I despise most of you myself. That isn't the point. You're still fraggin' soldiers, and you're still damn well fighting for the Emperor. The next one of you to step out of line will have more than a sore jaw to worry about. You're damn lucky the Colonel isn't here to see you squabbling like kids. He'd probably shoot one of you, just to show he's not to be messed with, and I wouldn't blame him. We are going to be in the cack again pretty damn soon, so stay sharp, because the moment one of you misses a trick, we could all be dead.'

Lecture over, I pick a spot along one of the walls, pull off my jacket and ball it up into a pillow. I lie down, closing my eyes. Soldiers always need to let off steam now and then, and particular after they've been in action. It won't be the last time, I reckon. With any luck, they'll soon be too busy fighting for their lives to worry about their petty personal problems. Whatever happens next, I figure there's no sense in losing sleep over it.

THE SCREECHING OF brakes wakes me instantly, and I can feel us slowing rapidly. Pushing myself to my feet, I throw on my jacket, grab my lasgun off the floor and step over to the compartment doors. The others are stirring too. Fenn's on his feet already, Lorii's reaching out for her weapon. Feeling us shudder to a halt, and the jolt unbalancing me for a moment, I grab the door lock lever and pull, sliding the door open.

Bright light from lamps all along the side of the train floods in, painful after the gloom of the wagon. Shielding my eyes against the glare, I jump down to the ground, feeling rocky scree underfoot. Looking around, I see that we're heading up some kind of wide defile, ten to fifteen metre high cliffs punctuated by gullies and caves on either side. Silhouetted against the lights, I see other figures emerging from up near the engine.

Lorii's next out, instantly alert, scanning the top of the nearest cliff for signs of movement. Fenn and Brownie follow soon after, Brownie turning to take his heavy stubber from Kin-Drugg who lowers it out of the compartment. The drop trooper then helps Erasmus down, coils of belt feed in his arms.

Fenn ducks between the large wheels and heads under the train, and I motion for Lorii to go with him. As the others scramble out, Kelth brings up the rear with his laspistol drawn. I head off towards the front of the train.

The Colonel meets me a couple of carriages along, bolt pistol drawn, power sword glowing in his hand. His face betrays nothing of what's happening.

'There is a blockage on the rail ahead,' he says. 'Boulders across the track. It could be some type of ambush. Sergeant Manners and his squad will protect the crew clearing the rocks. I want you to lead the team up onto the cliffs to give them covering support. I will take

Dunmore, Kin-Drugg, Oahebs and Spooge up the left, the others go with you.'

'How long do you reckon it'll be, sir?' I ask, and he replies with a shake of his head.

'I am not sure,' he says, glancing over his shoulder as a work crew with picks and shovels jump of the wagon behind the engine and head along the track. 'An hour at least, I think.'

Calling out orders, I head back to the others. The Colonel's team hurries past me to join Schaeffer.

'Two man teams, one defile each,' I say. 'Kelth and Fenn, Lorii and me. You two, take that gully on the left, we'll go further up the track.'

Watching them head across the rocky ground to the defile, I head forwards, Lorii just behind me. Getting to the front of the train, I see that the track is well and truly blocked. Starkly lit by the searchlights on top of the engine, a pile of boulders as tall as me lies across the tracks and spills out several metres either side. Workmen are already crawling over the heap, pulling free the smaller rocks and tossing them clear. Just ahead and fanned out to the left and right are the men of Sergeant Manner's contingent, taking up positions along the foot of the cliffs and behind boulders.

'That's deliberate,' says Lorii, looking at the obstruction. 'If it was a natural rock fall, surely it would have spilled down from one side of the gorge.'

'All the more reason to get into position quick, then,' I say, searching for some way up the cliff.

About twenty metres ahead of the train, the canyon wall shallows, and I can see what looks like a natural trench running back up the slope. I head for it, my eyes adjusting slowly when we're out of the lights and into the pre-dawn gloom. Just before sunrise is a perfect time to attack.

I check the safety on my lasgun is on before slinging it across my shoulder. It's not too difficult to climb up to the crack in the rock face, there are plenty of handholds, and it's only a matter of minutes until I'm wedged into the crevice. Pulling my lasgun free, I crawl forwards, ducking under a natural arch of rock into a short tunnel and then out into a low gully. I guess this used to be the bed of a stream, carved through the rock thousands of years ago before the industrialisation of Armageddon and the exhaustion of all the water supplies except for the polar ice caps.

Remarkably, there's even a few scrubby, thorny bushes along the gully's edge, and it's then that I notice that the air's a little easier to breathe, although it gets thin at this altitude. I guess the crap that's in the air either rises up to form the permanent cloud layer or settles as smog near the ground. There's quite a strong wind, blowing straight into my face, dust gets in my eyes and down the front of my jacket.

The night is cool and crisp, and there's not a shred of moonlight. The glow from the train's lights doesn't extend very far past the cliff edge, and in front of us is a huge expanse of darkness. I crawl forward on my belly, eyes scanning for any sign of an enemy. Looking over my shoulder, I see Lorii emerging from the crevice and with a wave of my hand, send her a little way off to the right.

Trying to make as little noise as possible, I crawl to my left, lasgun held out in front of me, until I see a large boulder sticking up out of the ground.

A stubby little tree clings to existence in the lee of the rock. I rise to my feet and scuttle over, taking cover in the shadow of the boulder, looking out from the canyon wall. Now that my eyes have adjusted, I can see that we're in the valley between two peaks, a pass up into the heart of the Diablo Mounts. There's cover everywhere, the valley is cut into by meandering gullies and dotted with boulders. Too much cover for my liking, any enemy could be right on top of us before we noticed.

WE DON'T WAIT long before the orks make their move. A hundred metres to our right, there's a bright flash as Fenn opens fire with his lasgun, the bolt flaring off the rocks ahead of us. He fires again, and now Kelth joins in with his laspistol, and in that brief moment of illumination I can see shapes moving through the rocks, running from shadow to shadow. There's no return fire, which is puzzling, and I bring my lasgun up to my shoulder and scan along the ground ahead of me. There are fuzzy after-images flashing across my eyes, and I can't see a damned thing.

Thinking it's better to do something that nothing, I swivel round on my belly until I can see where Fenn and Kelth are firing. The orks are in amongst a rocky area of scrub, ducking down behind the boulders, running from one to the next. I pick a likely looking patch of shadow and fire. The flash of the lasbolts illuminates something just to my left, about ten metres away. It's an ork face emerging from a hole in the ground.

'Enemy to the left!' I roar, bringing my lasgun round, but the ork is up and running at me.

It lopes towards me and I pull the trigger, but my reflex shot goes wide. Everything slows down as it charges towards me, just a few strides away. It seems like an age has passed as I hear the recharging power cell whining in my ear. The beast is skinnier than other orks I've seen, dressed in a ragged loincloth, a long hatchet in one hand, and a jagged knife in the other. Human scalps hang from a rope belt around its waist. I can see other shadows emerging from the ground behind it. I can feel my blood rushing in my ears, and my heart pounding in my chest as the ork raises the axe over its head.

A bolt from Lorii takes it square in the chest, scorching flesh and knocking it sideways. Its faltering step is all the time I need as the firing light on my lasgun flicks on and I pull the trigger again. Everything is suddenly happening at once. I put three more shots into it as it crumples to the ground, and then turn my fire on the aliens storming forward from the cave entrance. I can't believe I missed it, but I can see it clearly now: a narrow hole about ten metres to my left, slightly obscured by a bush. Luckily it's only wide enough for them to come out one at a time, and between Lorii's fire and mine, we down four out of the next six to emerge.

'Fall back,' I yell, leaping to my feet and starting backwards, firing from the hip. The nearest ork, by some dint of lucky or divine intervention, seems to skip through the salvo without being touched and is barely metres from me. My next shot scorches across its left shoulder but it doesn't even notice; it continues charging towards me, fangs bared.

'Frag,' I mutter, snatching my lasgun by the barrel in both hands.

I step forwards and swing upwards; the attack catches the ork by surprise. The butt of the lasgun smashes into its jaw, shattering a tooth, and it stumbles, falling to one knee. Swinging the lasgun from overhead, I slam my weapon into the side of its head, flattening it. I'm about to swing again when I see that there are more of them just behind. I don't have time to finish the green bastard off.

I turn and run, realising that none of the orks have guns, and as I pass the position, Lorii stands up, still firing, and then turns and joins me.

'Back to the gully, we'll hold them off there,' I shout in her ear, though there's no need to yell because she's right next to me. My blood is rushing through my veins after the close encounter with the ork, and I can feel myself slipping out of control.

Leaping down into the gully, I turn and fire off a few shots without even aiming. I am gasping heavily. My random volley is rewarded with another ork tumbling to the ground. Lorii shoves me aside and down, a grenade in her other hand. She tosses it just in front of the charging orks, and we throw ourselves flat.

The grenade explodes, raining dirt down onto us, and I'm back up and firing again in a split second, spitting grit from my lips. Three orks lie writhing in the smoke of the grenade detonation, grasping onto shredded limbs and guts, their howls echoing off the mountainsides.

I risk a glance over towards Kelth and Fenn, and see that it's fallen quiet where they are. Are they dead? Have they staved off the orks? There's no obvious answer, so I have to assume the worst.

Leaning on the edge of the natural culvert next to me, Lorii keeps up a steady rate of fire, and I notice that orks aren't charging forwards any more. I can see them keeping to cover, spreading out to the left, trying to surround us. Perhaps they're scared of more grenades. I hope so.

I notice the shot counter on my gun is down to the last few, so I use the lull to rip out the power pack and stow it in my belt, drawing out a fresh one and slamming it home. I wait for the gun to recharge and then bring it up to my shoulder, sighting along the barrel.

'Save your ammo for clear targets,' I say to Lorii, without looking. I keep my eyes focussed on a small ridgeline about twenty metres ahead of me. I'm sure there are some orks behind there.

I pray the orks don't realise that one concerted charge and they'll be all over us. There are too many for two soldiers with lasguns to stop. I'm pretty sure it's only the threat of more grenades that's keeping them back, but then again maybe none of them wants to be the first one to make the charge. Even if they work out that they can storm us, they'll know that we'll take a few of them down.

'Keep your head down,' I tell Lorii, scrambling out of the trench and sprinting to a shallow depression to my left.

Throwing myself down, I pull a grenade from my belt. From here I can see along the ridgeline. Pulling the pin, I get up to a crouch and then throw, placing the grenade right where I wanted it. As it goes off, I run back to Lorii, and leap back down.

'What do you think?' I say, bringing my lasgun up to the firing position.

'I've got one grenade and one power cell left,' she says, looking at me out of the corner of her eye. 'We can hold them for a little while longer I reckon.'

I nod, squeezing off a shot as a shadow moves to my right. I see that both Kelth and Fenn are alive and well as more lasbolts flicker off to our right.

'Okay, we'll hold here for the moment,' I say. 'Save the grenade in case we need to cover a retreat.'

FOR THE NEXT half hour or so, we stay there, firing the occasional shot as an ork head appears out of the gloom. I can hear lasfire echoing along the canyon, so I know that we're not the only ones under attack. It's a tense time, because I haven't got a clue whether the orks have another way down into the canyon, or whether they're about to work their way up behind us and chop us into a bloody pulp. I don't know if Schaeffer's still alive, though I suspect he is, or if anyone else is dead or wounded. Most of all, I don't know how long I'm going to have to stand in this fragging gully, the chill biting through my fatigues.

The first glowing touch of dawn starts to spread across the clouds ahead, but too little to improve visibility. I figure the orks know that they've got to push ahead now, or they'll stand no chance in the light. I tighten my grip, blink a couple of times to clear the dust from my eyes, and get ready.

In the sudden quiet, I can hear the shouting of the train crew, the wind stirring up dust devils and rustling through the scattered thorn bushes. I can hear Lorii's shallow, steady breathing next to me, and feel the body heat in the pre-dawn chill.

Waves of heat emanate from the open wounds across Lorii's chest, as bright red blood spills across her white skin. The blood is as hot as lava flows as it settles under her breasts and leaks down the sides of her gashed stomach. Like the heart of a volcano, her heart continues to throb inside her, spilling the crimson heat from within shattered ribs. Her pale flesh is like ice, steaming and hissing as the blood flows across it, a heat haze shimmering into the air.

Lorii's looking at me funny, and it's only then that I realise that I'm holding my knife, and my lasgun is on the ground. I don't remember turning around.

'What are you doing?' she says, staring at me with suspicion. I look at her dumbly, and then sheath the knife without answering.

Picking up my lasgun, I hear an echoing cry from the canyon, calling us back to the train.

'You go first, I'll go rearguard,' I say. She hesitates, still looking at me in an odd way, before turning and worming her way back down the gully.

Hearing the echo of her passing through the archway, and seeing nothing of the orks ahead, I turn and follow her, squeezing back down into the defile and out onto the cliff face. As I climb down the rocks, I keep glancing up, expecting to see ork faces leering at me from out of the gully, ready to leap down on top of me. No such thing happens, and I reach the ground safely.

The track's cleared – the rocks are now in a couple of piles to the side of the track. I see the Colonel and his team working their way down the cliff on the opposite side and I walk back to our carriage, a few metres behind Lorii. I stop as something occurs to me. I turn to look at the piles of rocks again. I grin to myself as I come up with something special for the orks the next time they try blocking the rail.

'Hey Lorii,' I call out and she stops and turns. 'Give me your grenade.'

She walks back and hands it over, a questioning look on her face. I give her a nod to follow me as I walk over to the nearest rock pile. I hand her my lasgun so that both my hands are free. Pulling the pin on the grenade, but without letting the spring clip come free, I lift up one of the rocks and wedge the grenade into the gap underneath, using the weight of the rock to hold the clip in place. I repeat this with the other pile and the last grenade from my belt, and turn around smiling.

'Let's see how much they like grenades after today, shall we?' I say, dusting my hands off with satisfaction.

As THE TRAIN starts moving off again and the wagon begins to sway side-to-side under the motion, I notice that Fenn has a particularly smug look.

'What are you so happy about?' I ask him, sitting down with my back to the wall. The others have done likewise around me.

'Nothing special,' he says, still smiling. 'Just always happy to be killing orks.'

'How come these had no guns then?' asks Brownie. 'It was like being back on a firing range, them running about, taking them down without a shot in return.'

'Well, the orks up here are firsters,' explains Fenn, pulling out his knife and running his whetstone along the edge. 'They've gone really feral. There's nothing up here for them to scavenge except what we bring up ourselves, and there's few enough people up here anyway. Knives, cleavers and their fangs, that's what they rely on. Doesn't make them any less dangerous though. Like them back in the jungle, they've got natural cunning to make up for it. Doesn't surprise me, them springing a trap like that. You see, most folks think that orks are just plain stupid, but not in my experience. They can't think things out like you and me, that's for sure, but it doesn't make them dumb.'

'You seem to know a lot about orks,' says Kin-Drugg, nursing his injured leg.

'Been fighting them all my life,' says Fenn. 'You learn a thing or two about your enemy after thirty years, that's for sure. And my father fought in the first invasion before me, and passed on a thing or two he'd learnt.'

'You're still fighting the remnants and descendants of the attack fifty years ago,' says Lorii. She pulls a rag out of her pocket and starts cleaning the dust from her lasgun. 'What makes you think you'll ever drive them out, or get rid of them completely?'

'Never said we would, did I?' says Fenn with a grim smile. 'Once you've got that many orks planet side, I reckon you'll never get rid of them completely. You can hunt them down, burn the bodies from here to world's end but there'll always be a few left. And all it takes is a few to start breeding, and than you've got a problem again before your sons are grown up.'

'So what do they want here, anyway?' asks Kelth. He looks drawn and tired, his robes tattered, stained and dusty.

'Who cares?' says Kin-Drugg. 'What do they ever want? They're interplanetary vermin, that's all. It's like going to a cheap whore, once you've been you might never cure the consequences.'

'I reckon I know why Ghazghkull's back,' says Oahebs, and we all turn and look at him. He hardly ever speaks. I think this is the first time he's ever volunteered information. We gaze at him expectantly, and suddenly self-conscious, he looks down, occupying himself with his bootlaces.

'Well then?' I say, when it becomes obvious that he's not going to say anything else. He looks up at me, and then at the others, uncertainty in his eyes.

'It's just a theory,' he says, his voice subdued. He pauses, obviously gearing himself up for the explanation. 'Orks never know when to give up, do they? You shoot them, they retreat, regroup and come back again. The last time Ghazghkull came, Commissar Yarrick kicked his arse good and proper, with the help of Commander Dante of course. What was one of the first things that happened, Fenn?'

The ork hunter thinks about it for a moment before replying.

'Well, obviously there was the space battles, but in terms of the ground assault, I guess that was when the rocks forts came down,' he says. 'Big asteroids hollowed out and protected with force fields, like mobile bases with engines fitted.'

'Yeah, we know what they are,' says Kin-Drugg, shaking his head with bitterness. 'Why the hell do you think we decided to drop in to the jungle and say hello?'

'And when the fortresses were coming down, the orks dropped a huge great big asteroid on Hades Hive, yes?' says Oahebs. He doesn't wait for confirmation, having got up a head of steam now. 'Hades is where Yarrick held out last time, giving the Spaces Marines enough time for their counter-attack. So what does Ghazghkull do this time? Flattens it completely, wiping it out in one go to make sure that doesn't happen again.'

We all sit digesting this idea for a while.

'So you mean that we got dragged across the galaxy for Emperor-knows-what because some ork warlord's pissed off and wants to get his own back?' says Brownie.

'Could be,' says Oahebs.

'Just why the hell are we here anyway?' says Kin-Drugg. 'There are millions, tens of millions, of Guard and Space Marines on Armageddon, what the hell is Schaeffer expecting us to achieve?'

'Something none of the rest can do,' I say, scratching at my belly. Sand and dust got in under my clothes while I was crawling about outside and now I've got itches in dozens of places.

'Something Space Marines can't do?' asks Fenn, his disbelief obvious from his tone. 'I can't imagine that.'

'Perhaps it's something the Space Marines won't do,' says Lorii. She looks at me with a pointed expression. 'Remember Coritanorum, Kage?'

'Course I do,' I say. What a stupid question.

'A handful of Last Chancers, and a city to destroy,' she says. 'Four people got out alive, two of them are in this wagon. Nobody else could have done it.'

'So, we're heading east, right,' says Brownie. 'What's so important to the east?'

'For all I know it could be something in the mountains, or on the other side of the planet,' I say. 'Look, the Colonel will tell us in good time, when he's ready. It's not going to be anything we can think of, I'm sure of that. Better off not wasting time dwelling on it.'

'So, where's this Coritanorum place?' asks Kin-Drugg.

'Nowhere,' Lorii says quietly. 'It isn't anywhere any more. Not even a pile of ash to remember, to mark the spot.'

She has a far away look in her eye and I know exactly what she's thinking about. She's thinking about her twin brother's blood splashing across her face; his head blown apart.

I wonder again just why it is she decided to come back. Surely she'd be better off burying the memories as far away from the Colonel as possible. Or perhaps not. It's been over two years since that mission, and in that time I've seen more blood, more killing, and suddenly Coritanorum doesn't seem that bad after all. Perhaps if she dives into a sea of blood, she'll no longer be able to tell if it's Loron's or not.

Whatever it is she's after, I'm glad she's here all the same. It's good to know that at least one other person, other than the Colonel, has some idea what might be in store. I don't think about it any more. I just take each day as it comes, each battle, each firefight's just the latest in a long line that stretches out until the end of my life. Nothing's going to change that now, so there's no point fretting about it.

In a week, in a day, in an hour, I could be dead. It doesn't matter, even high lords die eventually I guess. If I get another hour, another day or another week, then that's fine with me. When you're in my position, it doesn't matter what you can or can't do with your life. It's just enough to still be alive.

TEN
AMBUSH

We spend another two days rattling around in that wagon before we finally come to a stop. Stiff and tired, we jump down out of the train to find ourselves in a marshalling yard on the slopes of a mountain. Rickety, temporary-looking sheds and storehouses line the track, watched over by a high tower with skyward pointing. Beyond is a mass of shattered buildings, their skeletal ruins rising up against the dark, tar and dust covered slopes beyond.

Not far on, the rail track comes to an abrupt end as it disappears into a crater several hundred metres across. The rock has fused in strange organic shapes from some immensely hot detonation. The mountains are obscured just a few hundred metres higher up the slopes by a thick layer of cloud. It has a dirty, reddish tint to it, clinging to the mountainsides. I make a silent plea to the Emperor that we don't have to go up into the deadly-looking smog.

The place is half-deserted; a few men are hurrying around swathed in robes and scarves to ward away the chill mountain air. Without a word, the Colonel leads us between the buildings, heading uphill.

'Where the hell are we now?' asks Brownie, gazing around at the empty buildings.

'I think it's Diabolus forge,' says Erasmus, staggering along with heavy stubber ammo under one arm and his servo-skull under the other.

'And what's Diabolus?' says Kin-Drugg. 'Looks like the arse-end of nowhere to me.'

'It's where I was due to be stationed on my arrival,' Erasmus says quietly. 'It's a Departmento Munitorum outpost, set up during the second Armageddon War. As you can see, it's very low priority now. The mine has been abandoned since the latest invasion, so there's not much to protect any more.'

'You knew we were coming here and you didn't say anything,' I ask, rounding on Spooge. 'Why didn't you tell us?'

'Was I supposed to have told you?' he says, cringing back from me. 'When did anyone ask me? And how was I supposed to know you were all coming here too?'

'Just ignore him,' says Brownie, wrapping an arm around Erasmus's shoulders, his skin seeming even darker against the pallid neck of the scribe.

'Since when have you two been friends?' I say, taken aback by this show of support. It's not like Spooge is really one of us, he's just been tagging along because there's been nowhere else for him to go.

'Razzy here's the best damn loader I've ever had,' says Brownie, patting the scribe on the head. 'Not had a belt jam yet, have we, mate?'

'Razzy?' I say, trying not to laugh.

'Well, Erasmus such a mouthful, isn't it?' says Brownie. 'And so's Spooge. I like Razzy.'

'Well, you better start saying your fond farewells,' I say with a snarl. 'It's the end of the line for Razzy, and I bet that we're not going to be hanging around any longer than necessary.'

I quicken my stride and walk ahead. Brownie's gone soft in the head, worrying about a damn scribe. He'll be glad to be rid of him once the serious fighting starts. I've had some pretty desperate company in the past, but this group are really starting to wind me up. Kelth's a stuck up Navigator who's just as keen to crawl into a hole as fire a gun. Emperor knows what's going on in Lorii's head and I've got a gut feeling that something's going to crack before the mission's over. I can't stand to be within five metres of Oahebs, he makes me feel physically nauseous. Fenn's scared of the bloody sky, and Kin-Drugg is a loudmouth with a quick temper. I'd happily trade them in for the team we had on Typhos Prime, even for Kronin who was utterly insane and could only speak in litanies and Ecclesiarchy teachings.

THE COLONEL TAKES us a to a large, low building just outside the railhead itself, and we follow him inside into a small, bare chamber. There are no windows, and other than the door leading in, the only feature is another scuffed steel door at the other end.

'Make yourselves comfortable,' he says, and we slump down against the wall.

'We have recently suffered some setbacks,' says the Colonel, slowly pacing back and forth in front of us. 'However, we have overcome these, and now the mission is ready to proceed as originally planned. It was expected that there would be losses, but now the success or failure of our mission depends solely upon your abilities and determination. You have fought well so far, but it is not your fighting skills that have ever been in doubt. The road ahead will test your resolve and your discipline, and many of you will fail. The reward is the same as it always has been, the chance for absolution through success or death. There are no other alternatives.'

He stops and looks at us, eyeing each of us in turn, and weighing us up. It might be my imagination, but it seems his gaze lingers on me for longer than the others.

'You are all wondering just what it is that we few can do in a war that has killed millions,' he says, resuming his pacing, hands clasped behind his back. 'The status of Armageddon is finely poised. A shift in power either way may yet decide the fate of the planet. Victory on Armageddon is more than just a strategic necessity; it is also a spiritual and moral test. If the forces of the Emperor cannot prevail here, where we are in such strength, then what hope is there for those worlds far from Terra, out on the Eastern Fringe, in the far-flung stars? The Imperium needs hope now more than ever, because enemies surround us on all sides. This is a test of our fortitude that we have not seen the likes of for hundreds of years. If Armageddon can endure, then the realm of the Immortal Emperor can also endure.'

His eyes shine as he speaks. He gazes over our heads, through the wall and into the galaxy beyond. His voice rings with faith, assurance, and authority. Once again I'm struck by how strongly he believes. His faith in the Emperor, in the Imperium and in himself provides him with his invulnerability, like a physical shield. Despite what he's done to us, and to me in particular, I have to admire his conviction. He's never failed. Never. The reason for that is simple – he's never even considered it a possibility. Whatever he sets out to do, he does, with never a moment of doubt.

'Our mission here is simple, and yet the consequences of what we do will reach out beyond this world, out beyond this system into the farthest reaches of the glorious Imperium,' he pauses for a moment, head bowed, before continuing. 'Armageddon, and our victory here, will shine like a beacon, reminding those who doubt that the

Imperium still fights on that mankind has not yet laid rest to its
claim to the galaxy. Such a victory could well depend upon one man.
One man could hold the key to winning the Third Armageddon War.'

He walks close, passing along the line just out of arm's reach, gauging us again.

'That man is Imperial Commander Herman von Strab,' he says.
'And we are here to either rescue him or kill him.'

WE TAKE THIS news in silence for the moment, until Brownie raises
his hand.

'Yes, Dunmore?' says the Colonel striding over to stand in front of
him.

'Rescue or kill?' says Brownie. 'Kind of opposite ends of a piece of
string, aren't they? Which is it?'

The Colonel coughs, clearing his throat, and then walks back to the
other side of the room. He pulls his map from his pocket and opens
it up, spreading it across the bare floor. He motions for us to gather
round.

'We are here, in the Diablo Mounts,' he says, drawing a circle on the
map with his finger. His finger moves quite a distance. 'Von Strab is
here, in Acheron Hive.'

'But I thought Acheron was declared purgatus?' says Lorii, kneeling
down beside the Colonel. 'Hasn't it fallen to the orks?'

'That is the first part of our mission,' says Schaeffer. 'We must determine if Acheron is irretrievably lost to the enemy. Part of that task
will be to determine the loyalties of von Strab.'

'He's turned traitor,' says Fenn with a growl. 'He disappeared after
the last war and led Ghazghkull back three years ago. Acheron's his
now, from what I hear. He even has orks fighting for him.'

'The reality may not be so simple,' says the Colonel, sitting back. 'It
is suspected that those orks are just as likely to be enforcing
Ghazghkull's will on von Strab as the other way round. Acheron Hive
is being held hostage, in effect, forcing von Strab to comply. There is
evidence that the former overlord has indeed provided intelligence
information to Ghazghkull and his warlords. However, the latest
news from our agents inside Acheron say that von Strab has begun to
recruit what he has called the "Army for the Liberation of Armageddon". It is unsure what he intends to do with this army. It may be that
he intends to use it to overthrow ork domination of Acheron, in
which case we will assist him in whatever way we can before extract-
ing him to safety.'

'And if it's not for that?' I ask.

'If the Army for the Liberation of Armageddon is a counter-Imperial militia, then we must kill von Strab,' says the Colonel. 'The military importance of such a traitor army, and the moral damage it would do to our resistance against the orks, could swing the balance of power on Armageddon. Von Strab still commands great respect and loyalty amongst the local nobility, some of the hive rulers and even senior military officers. If we discover that he is not acting under duress, then we have orders to remove him by any means necessary. He cannot be allowed to stand as a figurehead for anti-Imperial sentiment.'

'So what was the original plan?' I ask. 'You obviously didn't mean for us to crash in the jungle. How do we get to Acheron?'

'We walk,' says the Colonel. 'There's a disused pipeline from this mine that leads across the ash wastes and down into the Acheron underhive. The wastes are devoid of any major activity, and any kind of transportation would soon be noticed and reported. In particular, the wastes nomads are thought to be working for von Strab. As it is, a small group of us can masquerade as deserters to gain entry to the hive if we are discovered.'

'That's hundreds of kilometres across barren wasteland,' says Fenn. 'We're never going to survive that on foot. We've got no food or water, no environmental protection gear or camping equipment. We wouldn't survive to the first dusk.'

'That has already been considered,' says the Colonel. He turns to Erasmus. 'You were given something when sent your orders to report here, I believe.'

Standing, Erasmus reaches inside his jacket and pulls free a thick neck chain, with three large brass keys hanging from it. He steps forward to hand them to the Colonel, but Schaeffer backs away and waves a hand to the door leading out of the room.

'It is time to assume your new office,' says the Colonel.

Erasmus walks over to the door. Glancing at the lock, he picks a key and inserts it. It turns with a heavy click, and with a short push, Erasmus opens the door. A dark void lies beyond. As he steps through, lights begin to flicker into life from a high ceiling and we stand and crowd through the door after him.

As glowstrips illuminate the chamber, they reveal row after row of high shelf units, stretching across the large warehouse. The storeroom is full of supplies. Just from the door I can see ammo boxes, stacks of blankets, power pack chargers, and thousands of rations cartons.

'What is this?' I ask the Colonel, walking right into the warehouse, and gazing in wonder at the stacked shelves receding fifty metres to the left and right.

'When the Departmento Munitorum withdrew from the Diablo Mounts, there was a certain oversight in its stock records,' says the Colonel, prompting a gasp from Erasmus.

'An oversight?' the scribe says. 'But… but that's impossible, isn't it?'

'No, not impossible,' says Schaeffer. 'And especially possible if certain documents are requisitioned and classified by the Inquisition.'

'The Inquisition?' I say, instantly suspicious. I knew it had to be too good to be true. Nothing's ever straightforward when the Inquisition is involved.

'The Inquisition has had a strong presence on Armageddon,' says the Colonel, as we walk between the shelves of stores. 'Given the nature of most of its activities, it is only prudent for them to maintain facilities and resources overlooked by normal channels.'

'Lucky for us,' I mutter, picking up an empty autogun magazine and pretending to examine it.

Erasmus is pacing back and forth with small steps, looking around with wide eyes.

'The Inquisition?' he says, his voice quiet with awed reverence. 'This all belongs to the Inquisition?'

I notice that most of the others are also walking around with the same sort of expression. I'd forgotten that for all but a few, the Inquisition is little more than a myth. Sometimes it's a shadowy threat used to elicit obedience from children and adults alike, other times it is composed of secretive heroes who hold the power of the Imperium in the palms of their hands.

My experience has been slightly different. My dealings with them on the last two missions has led me to believe that they are overly paranoid, political, and quite possibly power-hungry. Their open mandate, to protect the Emperor and Imperium from any threat by whatever means deemed necessary, is so vulnerable to abuse, I have to wonder who it is who watches the protectors of humanity.

I then realise that Lorii is watching the Colonel carefully, and Oahebs too is paying him a lot of attention. I remember that they were working closely with Inquisitor Oriel before they joined the Colonel, and they both look slightly nervous with this talk about the Inquisition. I suspect they have seen things and done things that most people would never want to know about.

'It does not belong to anyone,' says the Colonel. 'Officially, this place does not exist. That is the point.'

'But, doesn't that mean that if we take anything, we will be looting?' says Spooge, taking the magazine from my hands and carefully placing it on the shelf. 'I can't be party to looting, can I? I mean, if everybody thought they could just help themselves to stores, where would we end up?'

I stroll along to the next set of shelves, which are stacked far above my head with ammunition cases. Bolter ammunition by the look of it.

'I can just about understand the Inquisition's motives here,' I say. 'A potentially renegade Imperial commander has thrown in his lot with alien invaders. Yes, that's very much their bag. What I can't understand is you, I mean us, being here.'

The Colonel gives me a quizzical look and I continue.

'Why the Last Chancers?' I say. 'It took a lot of resource and clout to get us all the way over here from the Eastern Fringe. Now, I know you've got a good record of success, but I can't believe that we're the only ones who could do this.'

The Colonel looks thoughtful for a moment, probably trying to work out if he should answer, and how much he can tell us, or whether he even wants to tell us.

'Several attempts have already been made to ascertain the loyalty of von Strab,' he says slowly. 'They have proved unsuccessful. Other agents and organisations have also made attempts on the Imperial commander's life, and except for news of their failure, they have been unable to provide any accurate intelligence.'

'But why us?' I say insistently. 'With the Inquisition involved, I'd like to know what you've gotten us into.'

'It is just a mission,' the Colonel says, his expression sharp with anger. 'News of our success with the Brightsword operation was recognised by individuals in the hierarchy of the Inquisition and the decision was made to give me the opportunity to effect an attempt.'

'Kage has got a point,' says Kin-Drugg, walking just ahead of the group. He stops and turns, arms crossed. 'A full assault on Acheron wouldn't work, I can see that, but there are all kinds of specialist forces on Armageddon. What about the Space Marines, for instance? Or Stormtroopers? I would think that they could probably do a pretty successful raid to take out this von Strab.'

'Any kind of regular forces are out of the question,' the Colonel says, staring flatly at Kin-Drugg. 'The Inquisition is doing all that it can to suppress knowledge of von Strab's personal army. If this information were to become more widely known, it would lead to uncertainty at best, and at worst, we would be facing the possibility of mass desertions, even fighting within our own ranks. Our efforts here cannot tolerate such a situation. Even the intervention by non-line forces would cause questions to be raised. Their absence from the fighting for any period of time would be noticed and have to be accounted for, as would any failure of them to return.'

'I get it now,' says Brownie. 'Nobody knows we're here, so nobody's going to miss us when we're dead, is that it?'

'That is one way of looking at it, yes,' says the Colonel, resuming his walking. 'The other is that there has been no chance of us developing any kind of pro-liberation sympathies. We have been free of exposure to the propaganda put out by von Strab.'

'And what if we fail?' says Lorii, casting a sideways glance at me. I'm not sure whether the look is one of accusation, or seeking support. I keep my expression blank.

'I have already spoken of the potential disaster to the war effort if von Strab is indeed a traitor and allowed to continue,' the Colonel says, looking away.

He seems uncomfortable with the questioning, but he's not got much choice. This is the part of the mission when everything hangs in the balance for him. Up until now, we've had no choice but to follow his orders. They have been backed up by the full force of the Imperium, from the Commissariat provosts on the ship to the Imperial Guard we've been amongst since reaching Cerberus Station. Now there's nothing except discipline and his own force of will to stop us simply walking away. We're covert, so nobody knows we're here, there's nobody to back him up. He can't threaten us any more, so now he has to get us to understand what it is we're doing, and why we have no choice but to comply.

'You know what I mean,' says Lorii. 'There is always a last resort, a fall back plan. What will happen if we can't take out von Strab?'

The Colonel doesn't answer straight away; instead he looks at each of us. He has our full attention.

'Considering what is at stake, the Inquisition will use extreme measures to ensure that von Strab cannot turn the course of the war against us,' he says, expression impassive. 'If we fail, they will have no choice but to ensure the complete destruction of Acheron Hive.'

'But surely that would be a blow just as deadly?' says Fenn. 'If only for morale, which is everything in this war at the moment.'

'Then we must not fail,' says the Colonel briskly, regaining his usual business-like self. He turns to me. 'You will work with Armourer-scribe Spooge to draw supplies suitable for the remainder of the mission. I want every eventuality covered.'

'Right, sir,' I say. I look at the others and then sweep open my arms in a gesture that encapsulates the whole warehouse. 'Let's find out what we've got to play with.'

ELEVEN
ACROSS THE WASTES

WE SPEND TWO days getting ready. The secret storehouse has pretty much anything we want: there are weapons and ammunition obviously, but also rations, canteens, blankets, packs, picks, shovels, knives, mugs, bowls, magnoculars, cold weather suits, mountaineering equipment, gas masks, rebreathers, eyeshades, portable cookers, lanterns, tents, poles, rope and a hundred other things besides.

The time not spent hunting down rogue boxes of ammunition or searching through piles of foil-wrapped bagging for ration bars we spend asleep or resting. We find blankets and bedrolls and make ourselves a cosy little camp in one corner of the warehouse amongst the shelves of crates. The Colonel seems pretty lax about keeping watch, but I continue to keep the practice going so that we stay sharp. I get the impression that he's giving us the time to regain our strength and build up our energy reserves for the next push.

At first it looked as if there wouldn't be any problems, but then we worked out just how much this stuff weighed. There was no way we would be able to carry it on foot. The problem is, the heavier your pack, the slower your progress. And the slower your progress, the more water and rations you need, which in turn weigh more and take up more space. We can't rely on getting any kind of re-supply until we reach the hive, and given the uncertain terrain we'll be crossing, as well as the possibility of bad weather, we could be hiking for anything up to three weeks to cover the hundreds of kilometres to Acheron.

We lay out each pack and its contents in the small antechamber, and it becomes obvious that some things are just too big to carry. In the end, with the help of Spooge and advice from Fenn – who knows a thing or two about extended missions – we narrow our needs down to essentials, and then we all have a little space to bring some of our own preferences.

Brownie, for example, insists that as well as the heavy stubber he's dragged all the way from the jungles, and five hundred rounds for it, a light mortar would be extremely useful. Fenn, on the other hand, is all for carrying extra water to be on the safe side. Hidden in a dusty corner, amongst piles of tent poles and coils of rope, I found a few innocent-looking boxes not even listed on Erasmus's inventory. Prying one open, I discovered that it was full of gold coins. I guess the Inquisition isn't above greasing a few palms.

A few years ago, such a find would have seemed a golden opportunity to make something for myself, but not now. Where the hell am I going to be able to exchange coin? What am I going to spend it on? For a start, I'd have to desert from the Colonel, and that's a lot harder than you might think. I got away from him once, legitimately, but he was waiting for me as soon as I screwed it up. However, you never know what fate might deal you, so I make a secret compartment inside the lining of my pack and stash twenty of the coins.

The others take a selection of spare side-arms, ammo, or extra rations, according to their own needs and desires. While the others are packing the Colonel goes over our planned route to Acheron with Fenn, Oahebs and me. I have to say it doesn't look appealing.

To get down from the Diablo Mounts, we have to get past the lovely-titled Ork Mountain. It's a huge volcano not far north of where we are, and it is teeming with feral orks. Down on the plains, we'll be south of the ruins of Hades Hive. It's too risky to join the Hades-Acheron highway, because it's bound to be used by both Imperial forces and orks as the battle lines shift back and forth between the two hives. And the nature of our mission means we have to stay away from both sides.

We'll be cutting across the wastes south of the highway, until we reach Avernas, a forge complex that sits across the road outside Acheron. From there, the Colonel tells us, there's a disused pipeway that leads across the wastes to the Acheron underhive, allowing us to infiltrate von Strab's domain from within. It'll neatly bypass the Imperial forces around the hive, as well as the long-ranging patrols from the heavily fortified Hemlock cordon. The whole area is also littered with ork drop sites, so the greenskins are constantly sallying forth from landed rok fortresses across the ash wastes and along the rivers.

Generally I'm confident, though far from happy. It's not the orks that are going to be the problem. Nobody's going to find a small group like us in those vast stretches of wilderness unless they happen to roll straight into us, and we're more than capable of dealing with the odd scouting force or roaming ork band.

No, the problem is the wilderness itself. The terrain is going to be hard going all the way, and there'll be no respite until we reach Averneas. If we can get that far in good time, we'll have broken the back of the trek and we can start preparing for Acheron itself. But I won't dwell on what we can do once we reach the hive itself. It's far better just to concentrate on getting us there.

Oahebs proves to be a brilliant navigator: he studies the sketchy maps constantly and questions the Colonel or Fenn about landmarks, route and the conditions we're likely to encounter. Throughout the discussion I feel that same uneasy feeling I get when I'm around him. I can't shake the notion that he seems to be keeping an eye on me for some reason. I still don't know anything about him, or why Oriel saw fit to send him to Schaeffer. I'll be watching him just as closely from now on. Anyone who's had dealings with the Inquisition deserves scrutiny, because you can be sure they've got some hidden plan or agenda. You just have to wait it out, and hope they aren't out to frag you too much.

Although we'll be almost impossible to spot, particularly since nobody should be looking for us, the Colonel decides to travel by night and hole up during the day. Fenn warns us that it can get freezing cold in the wastes and that we should not skimp on cold weather clothing. Later we sit down with the rest of the squad, and I pass the message on.

'It'll be tricky,' says Fenn, who is leaning against the wall, with an unopened ration pack in his hand. 'It'll be hot during the day and cold at night. We need to look for shaded campsites wherever possible. Storm season is just around the corner too.'

'This just gets better and better,' says Kin-Drugg, shaking his head. He nurses his wounded leg. 'Perhaps I should have stayed at Infernus Quay, I'm not going to be making good progress on this.'

'If you fall behind, you stay behind,' the Colonel says, standing in the doorway of the bare room. 'You carry your share, too.'

Crumpling his ration wrapper and angrily tossing it to the floor, Kin-Drugg hauls himself up and limps outside, muttering under his breath. We watch him go, exchanging glances. We know the Colonel's right: we can't afford to move at the speed of the slowest.

'I have intercepted a communication from high command on one of the comms sets,' says the Colonel, stepping forward. We look at him attentively. 'The orks have launched a serious offensive against Helsreach, so a lot of our forces will be drawn south. There will be a lot of activity, but it means that everyone's attention will be diverted from Hades and Acheron.'

'Have you heard anything about the weather?' asks Fenn, peeling open his rations and looking at it with a glimmer of distaste. 'What's the storm forecast like?'

'I haven't received any specific storm warnings,' says the Colonel. 'However, there is little comfort to be drawn from that. If we get caught in a storm, our priority must be to weather it. We have to make the best possible progress we can, because things will only get worse if we lag. We must reach Averneas before the season of storms begins in earnest.'

'And what news from Acheron?' I ask.

'No further intelligence,' replies the Colonel. 'However, there are rumours that Thraka himself visited the hive not long ago, with fresh instructions for von Strab. But these are unconfirmed.'

'Have we any idea what those instructions might be?' says Lorii.

'It is likely that the warlord is merely reinforcing his authority,' replies the Colonel. He pulls a chronometer from his pocket and snaps the case open. 'There has been no change in activity to indicate a new strategy. Sundown is in little over an hour. Kage, have everyone ready to move out in thirty minutes.'

'Yes sir,' I say, standing up, and dusting crumbs from my trousers. 'Okay Last Chancers, eat up and gear up. Last one ready carries the heavy stubber.'

THE SQUAD ASSEMBLES outside in a ragged line in the descending darkness with their bulging packs at their feet. The jagged silhouettes of ruined buildings jutting up above the warehouse merge into the night sky. I head back into the storehouse and find the Colonel in conversation with Spooge and Kelth.

'But my orders were to take office here in Diabolus Forge,' Erasmus is saying. His skin is reddened from exposure, but the flabbiness has disappeared with his recent exertions. 'I cannot disobey the directives of my masters.'

'Do you have a copy of your orders?' says the Colonel, holding out a hand. Spooge delves into the recesses of his clothing, pulls out a tattered scroll and hands it to Schaeffer. The Colonel reads it briefly, and then hands it back to Spooge.

'It says you are to report to your post here for duties,' says Schaeffer. 'And I am giving you your new duties.'

'As much as I agree with you, Colonel, I'm afraid it's impossible,' says Spooge. 'An Imperial Guard officer does not hold authority over an adept of the Departmento Munitorum.'

I pull my laspistol from my belt and stride forward, pointing it at Spooge.

'I think you can safely say that you've done everything you can to fulfil your orders,' I say, stopping with the pistol an arm's length from his face.

'You're not offering me any choice, are you?' he asks with gratitude on his face.

I shake my head and then pivot on the spot to aim at Kelth. The tall Navigator looks down his nose at me, and sneers.

'This is ridiculous,' he snorts. 'There is no reason to subject me to this imposition. What possible use can I be? I'm not a soldier, I have made that quite obvious.'

'Everyone is useful,' says the Colonel, walking over and placing his hand on my arm, to make me lower my weapon. 'Until now you have had no choice but to accompany me. I could force you to continue, but you are right, that would serve little purpose.'

'So let me go,' says Kelth, crossing his arms. 'Let me walk away.'

'For security reasons, I cannot do that either,' says Schaeffer, walking over to Kelth, his hands clasped behind his back. He pauses for a moment, then looks deep into the Navigator's grey eyes.

'What we're doing here is not a game,' the Colonel says finally. 'I do not dress up the importance of my missions, and this operation ranks amongst the highest I have ever led. Armageddon hangs in the balance, and the slightest nudge in either direction could turn the war.'

He walks away, head bowed, before turning again, an arm outstretched towards Kelth. The Navigator watches him with a wary expression, occasionally glancing at me with distaste.

'Von Strab is hiding out in the Acheron underhive,' the Colonel says. 'The forces drawn into Acheron by his presence are far beyond any military threat posed by this so-called army of liberation. However, the moral threat he poses is greater than any other on the planet. We cannot allow Ghazghkull to have such a man under his sway, whether it be as a pawn or an ally.'

'I am not trained for your war,' says Kelth with a heavy shrug. 'I am of the Navis Nobilite, and I have a higher calling than crawling around in the dirt dodging bullets. I was born to steer mighty ships through the ether, and to bring warships to battle. I am no use to you.'

'I'll say it again,' says Schaeffer. 'Everyone is useful. None of us can see how this will end. It may be that the Emperor has some part for you to play. You are here, now. All the starships in the fleet, and all the soldiers of the Imperial Guard, have battered themselves against this ork horde, grinding this war into a stalemate. Now we have a chance, a lone, slim chance, to be victorious. Can you honestly walk away from this? Would you ever forgive yourself for passing up an opportunity to do something real, something genuine in your life? Will the Emperor forgive you?'

Kelth is amazed by the passion in the Colonel's voice. But his expression changes back to its usual one of superiority and suspicion. I don't know why the Colonel's so keen to have him with us, perhaps he really believes we have been brought together by the Emperor. It doesn't matter. If the Colonel wants him, I'll deliver him.

'We're called the Last Chancers,' I say, and Kelth turns on me, eyes narrowed. 'We're all given a last chance because we have wronged the Emperor with our crimes. Perhaps you deserve a last chance to do something truly exceptional with your life. Even if you don't do it for the Imperium and the Emperor, think of yourself and your family. Few people will know what we do here, but those in power, those whose words shape our futures, they will find out. Think what good it will do for the standing of your family to be associated with a great victory. Those Imperial commanders, those nobles, will owe you a debt of honour, so your future can be prosperous.'

I'm surprised by my own conviction, and a turn of phrase I didn't think I was capable of. As a devious, calculating look enters Kelth's eyes, I wonder what's brought this sudden surge of loyalty in me. The Navigator interrupts my thoughts.

'I would need some form of assurance,' he says, stroking his chin. 'A letter. Write me a letter detailing the events that have occurred here. Have it sealed and sent to High Command. I want it to be forwarded to our estates on Terra.'

The Colonel thinks for a moment and then nods.

'Spooge, come with me and we will draft this letter,' he says. The scribe heads off into the recesses of the storehouse. The Colonel gives Kelth a hard look before turning and following him.

The Navigator looks at me, a smug smile on his face.

'The Colonel will be true to his word,' he says.

'Yes he will,' I say, walking right up to him to stare him right in the eye. 'And that means you're one of us now. One of his. One of mine. You can start by grabbing your pack.'

I ignore his disconcerted look and I walk off chuckling to myself.

WITH NEW UNIFORMS, boots and weapons, and carrying full belts and packs, we're ready to set off at last light. In single file, we keep to the shadows. In the dark sky above us, the odd flicker of a jet soars overhead, while the evening air echoes with the distant thump of heavy artillery. The sky to the south is illuminated by the detonations.

Lorii leads the way, a little ahead of the rest of us, as we make our way over cratered ferrocrete roads, and march between broken piles of brocks and half-ruined walls. Banks of earth are piled up as crude, abandoned defences across some streets. A deep dip in the ground turns out to be the footprint of a passing Titan. Its weight pulverised the brick into dust and compacted the mud into a rock-hard surface.

Erasmus starts panting under the weight of his pack after just a few minutes. Kelth falls to the rear alongside Kin-Drugg. At least the drop trooper has the excuse of a busted leg, the other two are just out of shape. After a few days' hard slog we'll soon see if they can make it all the way or not. If they're still with us in five days' time, I reckon they'll be good for the whole trek. If not, the scavenging rats of the ash wastes will strip every morsel of flesh from their bones.

While we march between the shattered shells of Infernus Forge, I marvel at how much destruction has been heaped upon Armageddon. I've been to war zones before – from the tyranid-scourged fields of Ichar IV to the trench lines of Coritanorum – but I've never seen a world so wholly torn up.

Fenn sees me looking around and drops back to fall in beside me.

'This all happened in the first few days of the invasion,' he says, waving a hand to encompass the ruined complex. 'It was once teeming with Adeptus Mechanicus, but then the gargants came. Only the adepts' Titans could match the firepower of the ork war machines. The whole place was virtually destroyed in the crossfire.'

We pass a toppled monument, a larger-than-life-size statue of a Space Marine, his ornate armour emblazoned with a winged blood drop.

'That's the Dante Memorial,' says Fenn, stopping to gaze sadly at the fallen sculpture. He shakes his head. 'The Blood Angels were our saviours in the second war, when Ghazghkull first came here. There are monuments right across the planet. There's even a shrine of thanks at Cerberus.'

'You seem bitter,' I say, noticing the deep frown creasing the ork hunter's forehead.

'Monuments, memorials, arches and statues!' he spits, rounding on me with a snarl. 'Instead of rebuilding our defences or repairing the factories, von Strab has squandered our resources on these effigies. And more than half of them are dedicated to him. We won't see it, but there's a huge arch on the approaches to Acheron, that commemorates his part in the second war; it was erected by his cronies after he disappeared.'

We stop as the Colonel signals from ahead. He is standing at a junction between the remnants of two huge smelting plants, and conferring with Lorii and Oahebs.

'You'll have to fill me in,' I say. 'History was never my strong point, especially not when it concerns events on the other side of the galaxy.' I squat down on a piece of fallen masonry. Fenn sits next to me, and pulls free his knife and whetstone, as he always does when we take a break. The others sense an opportunity for a quick rest, even though we've barely been going an hour, and they set themselves down on the side of the rubble-strewn roadway.

'Even in the last war, it was rumoured that von Strab had sided with the orks,' says Fenn. His words are punctuated by the scrape of the whetstone. 'Armageddon is so important, strategically, that his family have been given free rein for tens of generations. Even before the wars, life here was never easy – except for the overlord's family and his so-called advisors. But the tanks rolled off the production lines, minerals were shipped out according to the tithes, so no one cared. Not until the orks arrived, anyway. Then von Strab suddenly became the centre of attention.'

He stops sharpening the knife and tests the blade with his thumb. A small bead of blood drops from its tip. He nods up ahead and I look to see the Colonel waving us on. Sheathing his knife, Fenn stands up and stretches. The rest of us pull ourselves to our feet, and help each other with the weight of our packs.

'If it hadn't been for Commissar Yarrick holding out at Hades, Ghazghkull would have overrun us last time,' Fenn says as we start walking again. 'Von Strab said he had some master plan to win the war; it turned out his family had a stash of virus missiles they'd been keeping secret for centuries. I don't know what they thought they might be used for, but I'm pretty bloody sure it wasn't in the event that the orks invaded. Anyway, that's beside the point. The missiles were so ancient that half of them malfunctioned and fell on our own troops. After that, Yarrick made moves to have von Strab removed from power but he disappeared with Ghazghkull after the Blood Angels' attack on the main ork headquarters. Nobody heard anything from him until Ghazghkull came back, transmitting his messages from Acheron.'

'What messages?' asks Brownie, who is just a little way behind us.

Fenn waves a hand for Kin-Drugg to join us, and he fishes around in the drop trooper's pack. He pulls out the compact comm-link receiver and switches it on. Static and chopped messages squawk out from the speaker message as Fenn twists the frequency dial. He stops and we listen to a reedy voice just discernible between the crackling and hissing.

'Brave citizens of Armageddon, I beseech you to unite with me and cast off the shackles of Imperial oppression! Join us in our holy cause. Your prince has returned to lead you to freedom!' There's more hissing and an audible clicking before the voice starts again. 'The glorious...'

Fenn snaps the comm-link off as the Colonel comes striding back down the road towards us. He snatches the comm-link and rams it back into Kin-Drugg's pack, a growl in his throat.

'Nobody uses the link!' Schaeffer barks, angrily tightening the cords on the pack. The force jerks Kin-Drugg backwards, and almost pulls him off his feet.

'Are you afraid we might get swayed by such persuasive rhetoric?' asks Kelth, coming up from behind.

'You should know better,' the Colonel says in a low hiss. 'Sound carries far at night. No talking until we are clear of the forges.'

He waves us on, but puts his hand on my shoulder to stop me. He turns me round to face him.

'You in particular should know what is at stake,' he whispers. Even in the darkness I can see the angry glint of his icy eyes. 'We must succeed.'

'Why?' I say, stepping out of his grasp. 'Why the frag are we so Emperor-damned important? I don't believe your crap about us being the only ones who can do this.'

The Colonel checks ahead and, once satisfied that the others are out of earshot, motions me to start walking. He strides alongside me on those long pegs of his, looking straight ahead, and not even glancing at me as he talks.

'There are currently those in the Inquisition who are working on a more drastic solution to the von Strab problem,' he says, the words quiet and clipped. 'We are to be the last attempt at a covert conclusion.'

'Covert conclusion?' I ask, glancing down as my foot catches a piece of rubble and sends it skittering over the rockcrete. The noise bounces back off the dark, hollow shells of buildings around us. Suddenly I feel very exposed and understand the Colonel's anger at the use of the comm-link.

'The troops inside Acheron have achieved nothing in their search for von Strab,' the Colonel says. 'There are inquisitors who believe that the threat he poses to the stability of the sector is such that any sacrifice pales in comparison.'

'Like Coritanorum?' I can tell where the Colonel is going with this. 'They want to destroy Acheron?'

'Yes,' the Colonel says, finally glancing at me for the briefest moment.

'We destroyed Coritanorum,' I say. 'If what you say is true, then perhaps these inquisitors are right.'

'Coritanorum was irrevocably infected,' Schaeffer replies. 'Even those who had not been directly corrupted by the genestealer infestation were exposed to its spiritual heresy. There is a strong resistance movement inside Acheron, not to mention the thousands of our own troops who are conducting operations in there.'

'Yes, but they'll be pulled out before any strike, won't they?' The Colonel shakes his head. 'Why the hell not?'

'To do so would let von Strab guess our intentions,' he says. 'Giving him the opportunity to escape justice.'

'That comms signal is obviously a recording, so how does anyone know that von Strab is still in Acheron?' I ask. Somehow a stone has worked its way into my boot and is pressing into my big toe. I wriggle my toes to shift it, trying to concentrate on the Colonel at the same time.

'Nobody knows if he is still there,' the Colonel says heavily. 'These hard-line inquisitors are prepared to sacrifice Acheron just to be sure.

You were telling Kelth about the last chance. Well, we are the last chance for Acheron. One of the inquisitors opposed to this course of action is an old colleague of Inquisitor Oriel. When he heard about the operation against Brightsword he specifically requested that Oriel intervene and ask me to deal with the situation.'

'But who would be willing to carry out such orders?' I say. 'Surely there will be resistance to the annihilation of a hive full of people?'

'The resistance has been our ally, until now,' he says. He looks up into the cloud-covered night sky, as if to look into space. 'However, a battle barge of the Marines Malevolent is currently disengaging itself from its current duties and will be preparing for the bombardment.'

'So that's the great hurry,' I say, realisation hitting me. 'Someone's been buying time for us?'

'Buying it with the lives of Imperial soldiers and Space Marines,' the Colonel murmurs, his face grim. 'Despite our best efforts, time is running short. Desperately short, in fact. We have twenty days, twenty-five at the most, before the destruction of Acheron begins. In twenty days, if we have not removed von Strab, millions of soldiers and citizens in Acheron will die under Imperial guns.'

TWELVE
THE LONG MARCH

We march all night, taking short breaks every couple of hours to catch our breath, and take air from our breather tanks. It would have been impossible for us to carry enough air for the whole journey, and so all we can do is periodically clear our lungs of the gas and filth that clings to the Diablo Mounts like the tar on the rocks.

Our faces are covered in grime and our fatigues hang heavy with accumulated dust and filth. And this is after only the first night. My clothes are greasy on my skin and dirt stirred up by the wind has worked its way into every opening in my uniform. Grit inside the neckline chafes my throat, my hands are raw from scraping against the grip of my lasgun, and my heavy pack bites deep into my shoulders. My back aches, my calf muscles are tighter than coiled steel and my eyes are gummed up with sweat and dust. The wind is bitterly cold, and the layers of clothes I'm wearing do little to blunt its bite.

I'd rather be someplace else.

Dawn finds us huddled in a depression in a large boulder. I'm on first watch, and as light slowly seeps across the sky, dull through the thick clouds, I finally get to see the pass in the ash wastes below. Munching on a ration bar, I look down at the valley that stretches down between two low, rounded peaks. The rocks glisten like an oil slick in the yellow light. A few pale, twisted trees rise out of cracks and crevices in large rocks.

Behind me I can hear the squad slumbering fitfully; their snorts, coughs and snores blend with the shrill noise of the wind that comes down the mountainsides. I can barely see them – they are hidden under their bedrolls in nooks and crannies.

Tendrils that drip with blood erupt from the ground, spraying the still bodies with gore and dirt. Blissfully unaware of the danger, they continue to sleep. The grey tentacles wrap around them squeezing them tight. They awake with chokes and screams. Their necks snap, and their organs burst out under the pressure. Their faces are crushed by the tendrils. Lifted into the air, the ragged shapes erupt with blood that sprays from ruptured arteries. Their limbs are pulled from their sockets and waved around as trophies. A victorious scream fills the silent air as the tentacles swirl the blood and dust into obscene patterns. The air starts to shimmer, and half-seen forms appear out of the bloody mist that wells up from the dismembered corpses. I realise the scream is mine, that I am revelling in the slaughter before me, and am infused with the power of the sacrifice. I feel hot, in the throes of ecstatic revelation, and energy courses through my body.

'Your watch is over.'

I almost yelp with surprise. Oahebs is standing in front of me, leaning down over the lip of the hollow I'm secreted in.

'Where the frag did you come from?' I snap. 'Emperor's tits, man, I could have sodding shot you!'

He eyes me darkly, his gaze lingering on my face.

'You look tired, Kage,' he says eventually. 'Your eyes are very bloodshot.'

'Of course I'm tired, you meathead,' I say, rising to my feet. 'I've been awake for the last twenty hours straight. Are there any other meaningful observations you'd like to make, any other pearls of wisdom you want to drop in my direction?'

'It looked like you were in a trance,' he says, obviously picking his words with care. 'You were staring at the camp. I thought you were asleep with your eyes open.'

I look sharply at him, trying to read his thoughts, but his face is as passive as ever. I feel a cramp in my stomach and dizziness momentarily grips me.

'Just keep yourself awake, alright?' I snap, pushing past him.

He doesn't reply. I stomp down into the sheltered depression where the others are still sleeping. Kin-Drugg gives me a wordless nod as he comes in from the other side, where he's been watching the route we came in by. I give him a hurried wave and then throw myself down next to my pack. Pulling at my blanket, I roll over, with my back to the others.

My thoughts are racing. One moment I was looking down the valley, and the next Oahebs was right in front of me. There's no way he could have come up on me without making some kind of sound, and I'm pretty keen-eyed and keen-eared.

The nausea has subsided, but I'm left with a little edge of panic. Breathing deeply, I close my eyes. I am bone tired. I wish sleep would sweep over me, but the more I long for it, the more awake I become. I can hear the blood rushing in my ears, and I can feel every stone and lump underneath me. My heart is hammering in my chest. I sense a distant whispering, a voice just on the edge of my hearing, and I roll over and open one eye to see who it is. Everyone else is still asleep.

As my fatigue finally pulls me into sleep, the voices start to get louder.

LORII WAKES ME just before dusk. After a quick bite to eat and some water from my canteen, I'm ready to go. The Colonel leads off, heading down the pass to the left of the main track. He weaves a path through the scattered boulders and stubby bushes. After about an hour, the pass makes a bit of a hump – a last rise before plunging down towards the wastes below. Schaeffer heads further to the left, up the side of a steep ridge.

'Aren't we silhouetting ourselves?' asks Brownie nervously. 'It's not even dark yet.'

'There is something I want you to see,' replies the Colonel, pointing out to the north-east. In the evening gloom, we can see right across the wastes. Just before the horizon is a dark blot, from which hundreds of columns of smoke and vapour rise into the air. A small mountain-like shape rising out of the wastes, surrounded by smaller blobs. The place is lit from within by innumerable fires; some are just flickers, but others rise high into the air.

'Hades Hive,' says Fenn, bowing his head and making the sign of the eagle across his chest.

'There's nothing left,' says Brownie.

'On the contrary, millions of refugees, soldiers, Space Marines and orks are out there,' says the Colonel. 'It is still a constant battle for control of the ruins. Commissar Yarrick declared that Hades would never fall. Blood is spilt to ensure that he does not have to break his word.'

'Is that what could become of Acheron?' I ask. The Colonel glares at me. I'd forgotten he hadn't told the others about the Inquisition's plan to flatten the place.

'It is a possible fate for all the hives on Armageddon,' the Colonel says, smoothing over the subject. 'The orks will ravage this world, and without Armageddon's factories, without the forges and the hives, worlds a hundred light years from here will weaken and wane, in a long chain that stretches back to Holy Terra itself. Acheron could be the turning point in preventing that. Alternatively our failure could see the beginning of the end for the Imperium.'

'That sounds overly dramatic,' says Kelth. He's taken his pack off and has leaned it against a rock. To do so is a mistake, because he'll only have to struggle to put it on again.

'I wish this were a simple melodrama,' says the Colonel. 'And I wish I was merely making speeches to rouse you. But I am not. We are beset on all sides by a galaxy full of enemies. Our foes are held back only by the Emperor's vast fleets, his armies, and the might of the Space Marines. If those foes sense weakness, they will descend on us like a pack of scavengers and pick apart the Imperium piece by piece. A squad is only as good as its weakest member, and the Imperium is only as strong as the weakest world.'

We contemplate this in silence as the Colonel leads us back down the ridge. The sight of a smouldering, ruined hive that once teemed with hundreds of millions of lives is certainly one that I'll never forget. I've seen horror: in the eyes of a strangled woman and on a battlefield literally heaving with the wounded crawling over the dead. Even the crater that was left from Coritanorum, the death place of over three million souls, was nothing compared to the ruination of Hades.

I can understand why Yarrick won't abandon the desolate hive. He made his stand there against Ghazghkull's first invasion. Like the Colonel says, if you falter for just a moment, you're dead. If you show the smallest hint of weakness, or mercy, then you will be taken out and fragged, good and proper. In a small way, it's a shame that we're going to Acheron. I'd like to fight in defence of Hades. It somehow seems appropriate for the Last Chancers to fight for something broken.

'Hey, move your arse,' says Kin-Drugg from behind me, breaking into my melancholy thoughts. I realise I've slowed down.

'Piss off,' I say to him, without turning around. I pick up the pace, eager to put the ruins of Hades behind me.

IF I THOUGHT that the jungle was hard-going, and the Diablo Mounts an ordeal, then the ash wastes have to be the worst terrain I have ever had to cross – and that includes the our forced march across the ice fields of Kragmeer.

Discoloured sand and ash stretch as far as the eye can see. Heat shimmers off the undulating dunes. The wind blows constantly, whipping a constant mist of ash into your face; its touch burns the skin with alchemical pollution. With our hoods pulled tight over our heads, rebreathers in our mouths and our noses clamped shut, each of us is enclosed in our own personal world. We are unable to communicate even with the person just a few metres in front.

The ground is constantly shifting underfoot. Each step sees you sinking to your ankles into the orange and red ash. Our pace slows to a crawl. The Colonel pushes us on for longer than before so that we make camp only when the pre-dawn glow touches the horizon.

During the night, the temperature drops rapidly. Our sweat freezes on our skin, and our breath billows from our filters like tank exhaust fumes. It's the only moisture there is – the ash underfoot stays just the same, because there's no water in it to freeze. Occasionally we see explosions far off that we steer away from, or hear the roar of a jet passing low overhead. On the second night, a huge wave of Imperial bombers passed over us, attacking a position no more than ten kilometres away. We stopped to watch the display: cluster bombs and incendiaries lit up the sky for nearly an hour.

Each step is painful. I drag my foot from the sucking ash and plant it in front of me, hauling myself forward. The pack on my back seems to hold the weight of the galaxy. Breathing shallowly to conserve the air tanks, we claw our way up dunes on our hands and knees and the wind drags dust to obscure our tracks behind us.

Sometimes the ground is rockier, as we breast some ridge of escarpment, so we pick up the pace. Kin-Drugg is in almost constant agony, he is literally dragging his bad leg behind him towards the end of each night's hike.

At other times the wastes are like an ocean. The ash has no substance; it is just thin dust that the winds slice through, creating constantly moving waves. Just like water, we wade through it, or swim across the top of it on our stomachs, craning our necks back so that the toxic dust doesn't get into our rebreathers.

We almost lost Erasmus at one point. Crossing an ash lake, he forged forwards, with loops of heavy stubber ammo around his chest and waist and his malfunctioning servo-skull crammed under one arm. He lost his footing and slipped forwards. The weight of the bullets began to drag him under. Brownie managed to get his hands under Erasmus's chin and hold his head free while the rest of us clawed at the dust, trying to scoop him out. As the ground shifted and settled, we ended up waist-deep in the ash, and floundered around for a few minutes until Oahebs found some sturdier ground a little way off. Now we use our lasguns to probe the ground ahead of us, checking to see how solid it is.

He was lucky we found him. Visibility is no more than a couple of metres in the darkness. It was thanks to his shouts and the clanking of his bullet belts that we could zero in on his position. Emperor alone knows how the Colonel and Oahebs lead us in the right direction. Except for first and last light, the sun's glow is pretty much constant in all directions. We can only judge by the prevailing winds that come from ahead and to our left that we're not travelling in circles. Well, I hope we're not.

Each day as the light of the sun begins to glow through the clouds, we pitch our crude shelters to protect against the wind, each little more than a two-sided sheet held up on a pole. There's nothing for the pegs to bite into, so we hold down the guy ropes with ammo cans and packs. After setting camp each day, we break out the rations and use one of the low-detection stoves that the ork hunters take into the jungle. A ration bar crumbled into a little boiled water makes a passable broth. We cluster around the heat from the plate with our gloves off, taking it in turns to bask in the relative warmth.

With the coming of the sun, the heat of the day steadily grows, until it's like a furnace. We daren't remove our protective gear, any pieces of exposed flesh are touched by the elements are raw and blistered. We wear tinted goggles for the most part, which shade our eyes from the glare reflecting off the rising mounds and ridges on every side. My cheeks are cracked and started bleeding yesterday. Only four days into the march, and my eyebrows have started falling out.

We slumber fitfully in our shelters, each of us exhausted from the day's toil, but too uncomfortable to find solace in sleep. We don't even pretend to be keeping watch. We can barely see twenty metres in the dust and heat haze. Nobody's looking for us, and in any case they'd have to walk straight over us to spot us. Better that time is spent resting, digging into those reserves of energy for the next night's march, our bodies slowly thawing as the morning turns to afternoon.

The constant temperature changes are playing havoc with the equipment. I'm pretty sure the barrel of my lasgun has warped and points slightly to the right now. I don't think it'd be much use in a fire fight anyway, now that grit has got into the lenses and trigger mechanism. I make a point of remembering to tell everyone to clean and check their weapons before bedding down each day, so that if trouble does come along we might at least fire back.

When it's time to break camp, we almost have to dig ourselves out. Ash and dust gathers on the shelters, and leaves a layer over our packs. Each of us spends several minutes excavating in the dying light to find hidden magazines or spare boots.

SEVEN DAYS IN and we're all fit to drop. I'm so dog-tired I'm staggering from one step to the next, every fibre in my body, every moment of my concentration is focussed on taking the next step. I hear voices on the wind, but I know they can't be real voices: I would only to be able to hear the others over the wind and through my thick hood if they stood right next to me and shouted. The wastes turn into an undulating morass of greens and oranges, deep reds and blackened ash. The laces in my boots have been eaten away by the corrosive dust, and my coat is frayed and torn in places.

My face burns, my eyes water constantly and my throat feels as if red-hot needles have been shoved into it. Even taking off my rebreather to take a gulp of water is an arduous task. We have to try not to breathe in the toxic fumes that swirl around us.

We pass a lake of oil that burns with a green flame. There are remnants of twisted machinery at its heart. The heat is welcome in the freezing night so we stay there for a short while, not caring that we can be seen silhouetted against the blaze. There's nothing out here to see us. There's nothing out here at all.

Or so I think.

We're just getting ready to camp on the eighth dawn when shimmering figures appear in the gloom, about fifty metres away. I think I'm seeing things again, but they soon solidify into the shape of a small group of men riding on the backs of strange mounts. Despite our fatigued state and numbed brains, we react quickly.

I sling off my pack and drop to the ground, lasgun ready. Ahead and to my right, Erasmus hurries forward with the ammo for Brownie's heavy stubber. The Colonel has his pistol in his hand and waves Kin-Drugg and Kelth to circle to the left. Lorii and Fenn have already broken to the right. Oahebs takes cover behind his pack a few metres behind me and to my left. He rests his lasgun across the pack, and squints through his goggles along its length.

The riders see us and halt. One of them comes forward, pulling a rifle from a sling that hangs behind his leg. The six-legged creature he's riding is covered in long, shaggy fur, and has a pointed snout and heavy shoulders. Its broad, webbed feet step across the surface of the ash without sinking, and it tosses its head from side to side, snorting constantly. I can't see any obvious eyes or ears.

The rider is swathed from head to foot in ragged cloth. Over this he wears heavy black robes, two bandolers cross over his chest. His legs are protected by a long quilted skirt split to the groin, under which are heavy trousers. Dark goggles glint from under the scarf across his face, but I can see nothing of his expression. He rides forward with his rifle pointing up, his other hand on the reins of his beast.

He stops about fifteen metres away, glancing left and right. I train my lasgun on his chest, my finger easing on to the trigger. I spare a second to use my sleeve to wipe grime from my eyeshades, before taking aim again.

To the right, there's a stutter of autogun fire and muzzle flare in the swirling dust. The Colonel brings up his pistol immediately, but I've squeezed the trigger first. So too does Oahebs. The two las-bolts strike the rider almost simultaneously: my shot detonates some of the ammunition on a bandoler, and the other punches through his right shoulder.

The beast rears as Brownie opens up. The roar of the heavy stubber sounds over the wind and two of the riders further out pitch from their saddles. There's more autogun fire from the right, replied to with the zip of lasguns. Suddenly every one of my senses works just fine. I fire off shots at the cluster of riders, as they're turning their mounts to run. I catch one of their steeds in the flank and it jinks wildly, almost toppling its rider, before they both disappear into the gloom.

We continue to fire after them, not knowing whether we're hitting anything or not. The lead rider is slumped across the neck of his mount, which just stands there dumbly until the Colonel puts a bolt into its skull. It falls sideways in a cloud of ash and dust. Brownie lets off another couple of bursts before everything falls silent again except for the hissing of the wind.

There are another few shots from the right and I think I hear a shout, but I can't be sure. We wait to see if they've regrouped for another attack. A minute passes, then another, and another, and still we don't move. After days of monotonous slog, the sudden action infuses my body, making me almost twitch with energy. I strain every nerve to stay calm.

We all turn as two figures emerge from our right, dragging something between them. We relax when we see Fenn and Lorii, bringing back a trophy of their own fight. With Oahebs, Fenn, Brownie and Spooge still standing watch, we gather around the dead rider. He looks like the others we downed: hidden beneath layer after layer of clothes. Kelth pulls the scarf from the rider's head, to reveal a face pitted and worn with exposure; the skin thick and leathery. Scabs and boils are clustered around his lips, and his teeth are little more than blackened stumps. Lorii briefly pulls out her rebreather to speak, trying not to breathe in too much.

'There were four more of them, trying to get behind us,' she says, pausing to inhale through her rebreather. 'One of them saw Fenn and opened fire.'

The Colonel nods before pulling out his own mouth-piece.

'Nomad raiders,' he says. 'There could be more. We will move in case they return. Set watch during the day.'

I nod as he turns at me for acknowledgement. Placing his pistol in its holster, he waves for us to move out. His head turns from left to right as he scans for any sign of the raiders. Already the ash is covering up the bodies, and by the time we sort ourselves out and moved away in single file, the only evidence of them is a few dark mounds. As we slip away into the swirling dust, a distant, haunting cry carries along on the wind. It's a signal, there's no doubt. Clutching our weapons tighter, we cast nervous glances around us, and hurry off.

WE PRESS ON as fast as we can for the next two nights. Finally, as dawn approaches on the tenth day, a darkness can be seen on the horizon to the north. The coming of daylight sees us taking shelter in the shade of an overhanging cliff, the red face soaring out of the dunes to a hundred metres above us. There's been no further contact with the nomads, although occasionally one of us thinks we have glimpsed shapes in the distance, either ahead or behind us.

We find a small cave, half filled with sand and dust, at the foot of the cliff, and dig our way in. We find ourselves in a spacious cavern, high enough to stand in, and twenty metres across at its broadest. While the others make camp, the Colonel asks Oahebs and me to join him. Leaving the cave, we make our way along the cliff until it descends to a ridge that we climb up. With thick boots and gloved hands, the climb isn't easy, but we eventually make it to the top. From here, we can see kilometres around, over the layer of dust-fog that sweeps across the wastes below.

And there, about twenty kilometres away, we can see the Hades-Acheron highway as it cuts across the wastes on high pillars; it is like a ribbon of grey against the orange and red. And slightly to the east, Averneas Forge sprawls out into the dunes and hills, a black oily cloud of soot hanging above it. It looks like Infernus Forge, only much more intact. Chimneystacks hundreds of metres high pierce the dark cloud and a tangle of dome-roofed Mechanicus factory-temples radiate out from a large, slab-sided structure at the centre. It's impossible to make out any more detail from this distance.

The smoking remnants of a gargant – seventy metres of ruptured metal plates and jutting many-barrelled cannons – stand a few kilometres from the complex. There are swarms of movement around its base. Although it's impossible to make out any details through the dust cloud kicked up, it's obvious the orks are there in force. Flickers of light from the forges are accompanied a few seconds later by the tinny, distant thumps of heavy gunfire.

Oahebs points to the west of the forge, and there we can see the shadowy shapes of two Battle Titans; Warlord-class I'd guess by their size. They are standing watch over the industrial complex. Like huge sentinels, sixty metres tall; they stand immobile, their giant plasma reactors dormant and their huge weapons silent. A column of vehicles, tanks and personnel carriers is making its way along the highway in front of the nearest titan. They look like toys compared to the armoured titans; each is smaller than its head. I can imagine the crew in the carrier manning their stations, waiting for the order to unleash the destructive potential of their war machine.

Pulling out his map, the Colonel fumbles in his pocket. He produces a short pencil and makes a few notes on the map before passing it to Oahebs. I look over his shoulder as he traces a route under the highway west of Averneas, around the end of the ork lines and then into the complex itself. The Colonel nods, takes the map back and folds it away. We head back down the ridge to rejoin the others.

I DON'T SLEEP at all well that day, thinking about ash wastes nomads finding us and knowing that a battle rages so close. We can hear the occasional explosion. We're going to have to sneak in to Averneas, and the battle may actually turn out to work in our favour. Nobody's going to give a squad a second thought as it hurries through the half-ruined complex – there are troops all over the place. The only concern is that we don't get too caught up in the fighting itself.

As day turns to night, the dark sky is once again lit by detonations and muzzle flashes. We cut across the wastes towards Averneas. Our progress is slower than normal as we make sure we don't run into anything unexpectedly. Myself, Lorii and Fenn each make regular forays ahead to scout out any enemy positions, but there's nothing for the first hour.

The noise of the ork attack is loud now; it's only a few kilometres away. We start to skirt west, away from the brightness of the battlefield. As we get closer, we can see lights from vehicles that move along the highway. They are the tanks and supply convoys that reinforce Averneas from other fronts. We pass under the highway itself between the huge supporting struts, and climb over mounds of debris and wrecks of vehicles. The rockcrete pillars are pocked with shell craters and bullet holes, and the tangled ruins of the combatants stretch out of sight to the left and right, testimony to the battles fought for control of the road.

We hear odd noises over the rumbling of vehicles above: the sound of scratching on metal, the skitter of a dislodged stone down a rubble pile. There are odd glimpses of movement in the gloom. They are probably just desert rats or solitary scavengers picking an existence from the ruin of war. Whatever it is, it knows better than to face us. As we clear the tangled wreckage, we make a quick sweep behind us, which reveals nobody following. Two kilometres ahead and to the east lie the outlying buildings of the forge complex. Its smokestacks jut from roofs, billowing fumes, and the glow of forges and furnaces spills out from shattered windows and shuttered doors.

With jets roaring above us and tracer fire crossing the sky, we sneak into Averneas, cutting our way through a battered mesh fence that surrounds a windowless building on the outskirts. We climb a wall on the far side into a dumping compound of some kind. Piles of warm slag smoke fitfully on the frost-hardened ground, illuminated by the flare of fire from an anti-aircraft gun on the roof of the nearby forge house.

A guardhouse stands at the gate into the accessway beyond the forge, and we slip around it, keeping to the shadows, before making our way along the surrounding fence. We duck into pools of darkness as a squad of Steel Legion troop past, following their Chimera APC along the road.

To our right, a spotlight springs into life; it points up into the air, and reflects off the clouds. It's joined by others, and soon a dozen patches of light criss-cross the night sky, occasionally showing up the silhouettes of large ork bombers. Flak and tracer fire screams up into the sky as we cut through the fence and push through. But the bombers don't attack; they disappear from view as they head eastwards towards Acheron Hive.

The Colonel points left and we hurry on, leaping over abandoned sandbag barricades into empty gun pits, into the heart of Averneas, skirting along gantries over dormant firepits. A misplaced shell explodes ahead of us, bringing down the wall of a brick outbuilding. We turn away as a fire crew appears on a steam-driven tender, and pick our way along another route to our objective. The Colonel leads us steadily north and east, taking a circuitous route to avoid contact with the defending forces.

About half a kilometre inside Averneas, a ruined refinery soars above the landscape, its chimneys and towers toppled, the maze of pipes and tanks now a dark warren of twisted metals and ruptured ferrocrete.

'This is it,' the Colonel says, voice muffled by his rebreather. He waves me to lead the way in.

Something crunches under my foot, and I look down to see a half-rotted ork skull. Other remnants lie close by, alien and human, and it's obvious that the refinery has changed hands several times before. A twisted, spire-like pumping tower leans precariously onto a bent network of high-level gangways. The Colonel leads us towards it, signalling that we are to enter the shattered building at its foot.

Passing through, we see faces reflected in blank, cracked display screens. We step past overturned chairs and have to avoid cracked plates and mugs that have been dropped on the floor. We find ourselves at the top of a spiralling staircase that plunges deep into Averneas. The Colonel pulls a small lantern from his pack and lights it with a match. Then he leads us down, pistol in hand.

Five storeys down, we come to another landing. The Colonel turns off the stairs, ducking through the collapsed arch of a doorway. Beyond, we come into a room full of pipes and gauges, the pumping machinery long silent. The length of the chamber is dominated by a single massive pipe, twice the height of a man. Near to where it comes in the wall is a maintenance hatch. It creaks alarmingly as Oahebs winds it open.

Shining his lantern inside, the Colonel reveals the interior of the dark pipe. The sides are smeared with scum and residue, and the bottom of the pipe is slicked with a thin stream of shiny, thick fluid. The smell is acrid; it stings my eyes and lips even through my protective gear. The Colonel ducks and steps through the hatch into the pipe, his boots ringing dully on the thick, corroded metal. Shining the lantern to the left, east towards Acheron, he waves us on.

THIRTEEN
NO LIGHT AT THE END OF THE TUNNEL

THE AIR IN THE pipe is old and stale; it hangs with the cloying tastes of oil, but is purer than anything we've breathed since we arrived on Armageddon. We take off the rebreathers and talk as we walk. It helps to break up the monotony of trudging kilometre after kilometre, day after day. We follow the bobbing glow of the Colonel's lantern. After a kilometre or so underground when it has cleared Averneas, the pipeline rises sharply and breaks out overground into the ash wastes.

Occasionally the pipe takes a turn to the left or the right, or rises and dips over some obstruction. Here and there, battle has taken its toll and the pipeline is ruptured. We have to don the rebreathers as we pass such sections, through which the light from outside blinks. Our feet scrape on the dust and ash blown in from the wastes.

At one point, the pipeline is so mangled and torn by some huge explosion that we have to climb over the twisted remnants. We step out into the wastes from the shattered pipe to see Acheron rearing up in the distance, about thirty kilometres away. Thousands of metres tall, it spears the sky like a dark spear, the upper spires obscured by the low toxic cloud. Flames burn from its ravaged shell, and there are still signs of heavy fighting as artillery batteries bombard its lower reaches.

Like a giant stalagmite, it rises up from the wastes, pocked with shuttle docks and entryways. Even at this distance, we can see the smoke issuing from a million flues, the haze rising and clinging to the hive's upper reaches, adding to the smog that obscures its lofty pinnacle. Buttresses that housed tens of thousands splay outwards, scarred and ravaged with shell holes and craters. The ferrocrete skin is worn by millennia of erosion into strangely flowing, organic shapes. It looks like a massive fire-ant mount, excreted up from the core of the planet.

It reminds me of Olympas, my home, and not since fighting around the hives of Ichar IV have I felt so far from there.

The pipeline starts again less than a hundred metres away, but I take every second to drink in the dark majesty of Acheron. I can imagine the thousands of factories within, the millions of souls labouring in forges and mills, workshops and garages. The thump of engines, the clanging of hammers will be resounding through the hive city; the sounds of my childhood. Generations live and die without ever breathing air that has not been reclaimed for millennia, and without drinking water that has not been the piss of five hundred generations before. Most have never seen light except from a glow-globe. Many of them don't even know such things exist.

This could be last sight of a hive I see in all of its glory, a great mound of humanity's industry with a life and personality of its own. In just two weeks, it might not be there. It might become like Hades, a ruined wasteland of craters, testament to the orbital fury of the Marines Malevolent. Those millions – no billions – of souls exist in ignorance of the doom that hangs over them. They are condemned simply because it would be pointless trying to save them. So it has always been, and so it must be, for the Imperium does not count in millions or billions of lives. Such numbers are insignificant. What does the Emperor care, all-seeing from the Golden Throne of Terra, if a billion souls die so that a world is held against the darkness? It is a mere drop in a sea, amongst a million oceans.

Armageddon must hold.

I linger for a few seconds as the others clamber back into the pipe way and continue on. I can't let Acheron die. If Acheron dies, then so could Geidi Hive on Olympas. No matter what has happened to me, or happens to me, I've always felt sure that Geidi would live on, as old as the Imperium itself, enduring war, poverty, insurrection and upheaval. The people change, regimes come and go, but Geidi will always be Geidi. Now that might not be true. Perhaps even now it is a flaming pyre for three billion people, destroyed by orks, or eldar, the tau or the traitors of Abyssal Chaos. Perhaps the soldiers of the Emperor have obliterated it. If Acheron can survive, then so can Geidi and part of what I am will last for eternity.

* * *

A FEW KILOMETRES on, after five days of walking, the pipeway dips sharply, and heads down into the rock beneath the ash wastes towards the Acheron underhive. We decide to rest for a few hours before making a concerted effort towards our goal on the next march. Everything is still down here, not even the wind brushing against the pipe to break the silence. I close my eyes but sleep refuses to come.

Hearing a scraping noise, I open one eye to see Brownie dragging his knife across his bald scalp, shaving off non-existent stubble. I sit up and he turns and looks at me. His eyes are white in his dark face, and they peer at me out of the gloom. Standing up, he shuffles past the sleeping form of Fenn and sits next to me.

'Nearly there,' he says, his voice kept low to avoid disturbing the others. I nod, not sure whether I'm in the mood to talk or not. 'How long do you think it'll take to find him?'

'Hard to say,' I shrug. 'There've been Guard regiments looking for him for almost a year now, without so much as a glimpse, or so Fenn reckons.'

'And so how are we supposed to find him?' he says with a frown. 'We could be here weeks, months, even years.'

'It won't come to that,' I say, and he looks at me sharply.

'How do you know? What have you heard?'

'The Colonel always has a plan,' I tell him. 'I bet he probably already knows where von Strab is, and if he doesn't, then he'll have a way of tracking him down in no time.'

'You seem very confident,' he says.

'Experience,' I reply after a moment. 'The Colonel's never failed.'

'I'd never heard of him before he turned up at the prison tower,' says Brownie, glancing over to Schaeffer's sleeping form. The Colonel is lying on his back with his head on his pack. His greatcoat is pulled up to his chin like a blanket. He looks as still as a corpse except for the shallow rising and falling of his chest. 'If he was such a hero, surely someone would know who he is, or where he's from?'

'Ever heard of a place called Typhos Prime?' I ask, leaning closer. He shakes his head. 'How about False Hope? Kragmeer? Deliverance?'

'Nope, never heard of any of them,' says Brownie. 'Why?'

'That's my point,' I say. 'You don't hear about the Colonel because he doesn't want you to. Does anybody know exactly where he's been? What he's done? Perhaps Inquisitor Oriel and few of his shadowy friends do. Maybe the odd Warmaster or sector marshal. I don't know him from the next man. He could be the son of a Terran High Lord, or the bastard spawn of a pit slave for all I know. We once thought that perhaps he was a daemon in the body of a man.'

Brownie laughs, before casting a nervous glance at the others.

'That's a bit much, isn't it?' he says.

'I saw him get his arm blown off by a plasma bolt,' I tell him. Brownie looks over, seeing the Colonel's arms crossed over his chest like a body waiting to be interred in its coffin.

'They look normal enough to me,' he says. 'Are you saying he's not human?'

'Don't listen to him,' says Lorii, rolling over to her side on my left. 'The Colonel's as human as you or me.'

Brownie can't stop himself from giving her a second glance. He is obviously looking at her alabaster skin and pure white hair.

'Why?' he says. 'Kage might have a point.'

Lorii gives me a long, hard look, and I glance away, wondering what she knows. What did Oriel tell her about me? What about Oahebs, for that matter? Oriel knows, or suspects, that I'm a witch. Did he voice those suspicions to anyone else? Lorii taps a finger into her temple and my heart skips a beat.

'Kage isn't quite all there, are you, Kage?' she says. I scowl at her. 'He's got a bit missing, cut out of him on his last mission.'

'What's that got to do with the Colonel?' I ask, raising my voice. 'You thought there was something not right with him too.'

A shadow looms over us in the yellow glow of the lantern. We look up to see the Colonel standing over us, his face in shadow. His head turns to look at each of us, the whites of his eyes barely a slit. With the fingers of his left hand, he pulls off his right glove and holds his arm out. I expect to see the metal of an augmetic, but the skin is tough and wrinkled; small hairs stand out from his wrist. He leans forward and waves it in front of my face.

'They grew a new one for me,' he says, bending close.

'Who?' asks Brownie, before flinching as the Colonel turns his gaze to him.

'The tech-priests, of course,' he says, pulling his glove back on. 'It took three weeks of constant pain, feeling bone growing, new flesh knitting to old flesh, and skin hardening under the glare of special lamps.'

'You never mentioned it before,' I say, and the Colonel straightens up.

'Why would I?' he asks. 'You may fear and loathe the Inquisition, but they are powerful allies and have their uses. A new arm took a while, but not as long as it took them to rebuild my spine after I was crushed by a tank.'

He leans forward again, centimetres from me.

'Do you think I was born with these eyes, Kage?' he asks, his whisper sending a shiver down my spine. 'Even they cannot grow eyes, did you know that? These were donated.'

'Who was the donor?' Lorii asks in a hushed voice, peering at the Colonel closely. Her hand unconsciously moves to touch him.

'A heretic who sinned against the Machine God,' Schaeffer says. 'A mindless servitor now, with no need of eyes to monitor the power fluctuations in a plasma reactor aboard a battleship.'

'That's so fragged,' I say, shaking my head. 'What else have they done to you?'

He gives me a confused look.

'You make it sound like a punishment,' the Colonel says. Behind him, I see that the others have woken up and are listening intently. Erasmus looks as if his eyes are going to burst, they're bulging so much. 'It is not a sentence, it is a gift. I have been kept alive for six times the natural span of a human, that's nearly three hundred years. Three centuries of service to the Emperor – three centuries of dedication.'

'Three centuries cheating death, and knowing nothing but war?' suggests Lorii, earning herself a bitter laugh from Schaeffer.

'Life is war, Lorii, you of all people know that,' he says. 'I was not created for battle like you, but in his wisdom the Emperor has granted me a gift that is seldom seen. I have never failed, and as long as I live, I never will.'

'What does he mean, you were created for battle?' asks Brownie, looking at Lorii. 'What does that mean?'

Lorii says nothing, she just grimaces at the Colonel.

'What is the matter, Lorii?' Schaeffer says. 'It is not a guilty secret to be ashamed of and kept hidden. Not like some low-born lover to a governess. Tell them who you are, and be proud of it.'

Her expression turns to one of sadness. She looks pleadingly at the Colonel, who steps back and looks away, arms crossed. She looks at the others, and then at me.

'I was one of five hundred brothers and sisters,' she says, looking down, head bowed. 'We were bred from the seed of Macharius himself in an incubator. We were fed on artificial stimulants, and combat doctrine was pumped straight into our minds.'

She falls silent, hands tightly balled into fists in her lap, her shoulders shaking with anger.

'They thought they could make a perfect soldier,' the Colonel says, without turning around. 'They took the seed of the great Macharius without his knowledge just before he died. For centuries they laboured in secret, their goal shunned by other tech-priests. They did well, considering. Five hundred healthy babies were created out of fifty thousand attempts. Five companies of soldiers were raised from their unnatural births to fight.'

'I'm the last one,' says Lorii, still gazing at the oil-slicked floor. Then she looks up, her eyes brimming with tears. She looks at me, and her anger returns. 'When Loron died, I was the only one left. You think you suffered, believing you were the only one of us to survive Coritanorum? What if you were the only living proof of an obscene experiment performed by outcasts and heretics?'

'The tech-priests understand the working of the body, even the mind, and the ways it can be manipulated,' says the Colonel. 'But they know nothing of the soul. In all their teachings they forgot about one thing. Faith. Faith in the Emperor.'

'So what happened to the others?' I ask. 'I know your company was all but wiped out in an air attack, but what happened to the other four?'

'Killed in battle, all of them,' says Lorii. 'On Ichar IV, Methusala, Lazarus Saecunda. They were on their own, shunned by the other regiments – easy targets.'

We absorb this in silence. Then Dunmore stands up.

'Well, since we seem to be getting everything in the open, I have something to tell you,' he says. 'Why do you think I'm called Brownie?'

'I thought it was because of your dark skin,' says Kin-Drugg, but Brownie shakes his head.

'First time I was in battle,' he says, looking at his feet. 'First time the firing started, I shit myself. Literally, shit myself. That's why they called me Brownie.'

We greet this in stunned silence, and it's Lorii who starts laughing first. Her cackle degenerates into snorts as we all join in, except the Colonel who stands there in stony silence.

'Seriously?' Lorii manages to say between gulps of air. 'You're called Brownie because you shed your cargo in your first fight?'

Brownie's laughing too; his teeth gleaming white in the gloom.

'Damn straight I cacked myself,' he says with a grin. 'A shell went off about twenty metres in front of me; it covered me in blood and guts. I dumped my load as I lay there screaming. That's when I decided that I was going to learn how to use the biggest guns we've got. I even tried to join an artillery regiment, but they found out I was already enlisted and kicked me back.'

'Meathead,' I mutter, slumping back against the side of the pipe, and closing my eyes. I've no desire to confess anything at the moment.

Everyone drifts apart again, some still chuckling. I drift away too, and sleep finally claims me.

IT DOESN'T FEEL like any time has passed before the shuffling of feet and scraping wakens me. I didn't realise just how dog-tired I was. My brain still numb, I gather my gear together and fall into line behind Kin-Drugg. It doesn't take much to start walking, swinging one leg in front of the other. I focus on the buckle of Kin-Drugg's pack a couple of metres in front of me.

Why do I feel so lethargic? Looking past Kin-Drugg's shoulder, I see that the others are stumbling and shuffling along too. We're all so tired; mindless zombies from the fatigue. My legs are cramping and I can feel a pain in my chest every time I breathe in. The sores on my face throb and open. Blood dribbles down my cheeks and chin. I see the Colonel sway slightly, and reach out a hand to steady himself. The lantern drops from his fingers and clatters into the skin of oil gathered in the bottom of the pipe.

That's when I realise there's more to this than just exhaustion.

'Rebreathers!' I croak, but nobody seems to hear me. I'm sweating hard, my face is burning hot, and my hands greasy with perspiration.

I stumble past Kin-Drugg and grab the Colonel.

'Gas,' I manage to wheeze, pointing to the rebreather at Schaeffer's belt. 'Bad air!'

He nods dumbly but does nothing. I fumble for my own rebreather, my fingers feeling thick and clumsy, like fat sausages. I manage to pull on the rebreather. The filtered air fills my lungs. A few short breaths clear my head enough to pull the Colonel's rebreather free and slip it over his face. He waves me away and I help Kin-Drugg with his. Slowly, like they're underwater or in zero-grav, the rest of the team begin to pull on their masks, flailing with the straps and buckles.

I haul off my pack and retrieve my goggles from a pocket. The filtered lenses blot out almost all the light from the lantern, but the stinging stops almost immediately. Fenn stumbles up to me, pointing desperately at his rebreather. Bending forward, I peer at his face and see a short crack in the mask, just under the nose filter. Ignoring my pack, I grab hold of him and drag him forwards, past the Colonel. I'm hoping that the gas pocket will come to an end shortly.

Fenn begins to convulse in my grasp. His fingers claw at my sleeve, his feet kick spasmodically as he tries to walk. I heft a shoulder under his arm and half-drag, half-carry him along. The light of the lantern fades behind us and we plunge into darkness. Something cracks and crunches underfoot and the floor becomes slippery. A couple of times the weight of Fenn overbalances me and we fall down into a heap. As I struggle up with him, I put my hand into a soft, furry mass. Things writhe under my fingertips and I snatch my hand back, gagging from the sensation. I pull us to our feet and hurry on as quickly as possible, part of me glad I can't see anything in the darkness.

I'm not sure how much further we have to go, or how long he's got. Occasionally the pipeline bends without me noticing, and it's only as I slip on the sloping sides that I know we've changed direction. At one point, I feel a gust of air on the side of my face, and I turn and look but can't see anything. Perhaps there's a secondary pipe or some kind of vent. I consider stopping, hoping that it'll be bringing in fresher air. I stop myself though, equally conscious that the toxins could be coming from there instead.

I can't tell how far we've gone, perhaps two desperate kilometres, before Fenn starts to calm down. I can't see him, so I risk pulling out my rebreather. I swallow a lungful of stale air, but it's the usual stale air of the pipe. I take off the ork hunter's mask and he's gulping it in. He bends double, hacking and coughing. Then he slumps sideways, falling from my grasp, and I fumble around in the pitch black until my hands find him again.

I dump myself down next to him. Both of us are panting heavily, not able to spare a breath for words. We sit in silence, in the total darkness, hoping that the others will catch up with us soon. Hoping that they're not all dead.

It can't actually be more than half an hour until we see a glow from further up the pipe, though it feels like half a day to us. There are definitely things in the darkness, creatures skittering past, brushing under my legs, scratching at my boots.

As the light draws closer I make out the Colonel, and the others close behind him. He doesn't even give us a second glance as he walks past. Brownie dumps my pack at my feet and offers a hand to haul me up. Lorii pulls up Fenn. Nodding his thanks, Fenn falls into line. I pull on my pack and take up the rear, following behind Kin-Drugg as he limps along.

FOURTEEN
THE UNDERHIVE

THE PIPELINE IS teeming with rats that scurry underfoot and dart through the glow of the lantern into the darkness. Here, lower down the pipe, they swarm in front of us, hissing, screeching. Some of them are as long as a man is tall, their tails fat ropes of pink flesh.

Many of the rats are misshapen, with hunched backs, bony protuberances, overlong fangs and are covered in scabs and boils. They nip at our ankles, bare their fangs and whip their tails in agitation as we kick them aside. Here and there, the pipeline is cracked, and the rats hide in the shadows; their glittering eyes regarding us menacingly. They seem to plague Kin-Drugg more than the rest of us. Perhaps they sense that he is wounded and is the easiest prey. I have no doubt that had he strayed from the circle of light they would have been on him as quick as possible.

I reckon any one of us would probably be easy meat, for that matter, the hunger of the rats only kept in check by their fear of our numbers. I figure it was the skeletons of those that had unwisely ventured into the gas pocket that we had been crunching through in the pitch black.

After several hours, the rat population slowly begins to dwindle and we start to hear noises. The pipe shudders almost imperceptibly with a distant thumping. The rats here are leaner and more active than their cousins further up the pipe. As we march, the thumping becomes more pronounced and blends in with sounds of other machinery whirring and grinding.

The Colonel stops and shuts off the lantern for a while. As my eyes adjust, I detect a tinge of light from far ahead. It gets brighter as we walk, and I become steadily more aware of the clumping of our boots on the hollow metal of the pipe. I realise that it's no longer burrowing through the ground.

Smaller pipes spring off from the main one, heading left and right, up and down, to different parts of the Acheron underhive. The route branches into two pipes roughly half the size of the one we stand in and the Colonel leads us to the left, stooping and shuffling through the much narrower space. It's not far, less than half a kilometre and the pipe suddenly ends, opening out into a wide, low tank. Dropping to its bottom, we find ourselves knee-deep in thick, oily sludge that sucks at our boots. Dull light streams in from an open hatch in the roof ahead of us, and iron rungs, corroded and broken, stick out of the tank's wall. The Colonel switches off the lantern, stowing it in Lorii's pack and signals for me to lead the way up the ladder.

Poking my head out of the hatch, I find that we're in a high chamber, filled with similar rectangular tanks arranged in a regular pattern over a ferrocrete store. Dust, centimetres thick, lies over everything, stirred gently by large fans rotating solely behind grilles in the ceiling.

There's no sign of life so I pull myself out, readying my lasgun. I crouch on top of the tank and gesture to the others to come up.

We fan out across the room, securing the two wide doorways at either end, both barred from the inside with steel slide-locks. I look to the Colonel for further instructions but he just shakes his head and then points to the door next to me.

'We are inside the underhive,' Schaeffer says, keeping his voice low. 'From here we will have to establish our exact location and commence our search for von Strab. Remember that there are the native underhivers, Imperial forces, von Strab's Army of Liberation and the orks. And none of them will necessarily be sympathetic to our cause. We must acquire suitable disguises at the earliest opportunity and preferably a guide of some kind. We must not be discovered.'

He nods for me to slide back the bar on the door. It squeals as rust flakes off and drops into the dust. Kin-Drugg puts a hand on the door and thrusts it open. It swings out noisily on corroded hinges, revealing another chamber, much like the one we're in, but filled with spherical tanks ruptured from within. The floor is sticky with ancient chemicals. Flickering glow-globes cast moving shadows over the gauges and control panels, and reflect off another doorway opposite.

I scoot forward, my boots sticking to the tacky floor, holding my lasgun in a tight grip. The others follow, spreading out to the left and right, picking their routes between the abandoned machinery. The glass in the gauges is cracked; the pipes between them are split and frayed and a moss-like growth is spread over most of the tanks.

'Water reclamation,' I say quietly, remembering the parasitical algae that I was tasked with cleaning off the tanks when I was four years old.

The next door swings open with little noise; its hinges have more recently been oiled. Instantly, we're all alert, realising that whoever oiled them could be close by, perhaps living in the area. Oahebs points at the ground and I glance down, seeing obvious boot tracks in the grime of the floor. Behind me, Brownie whispers to Erasmus to prepare the heavy stubber ammo, and he pulls out the bipod from its barrel, ready to drop down and give covering fire at a moment's notice.

The roof is low, buckled inwards in places, sprouting coils of pipes and cables, covered with grilles and hatches. We're on some kind of landing, a stairwell spirals up through the roof and drops down beneath us. Other doorways open up from the walls around us, some into darkness, others into brightly lit areas. From below comes the flickering orange glow of flames.

As we move to the stairwell, we see that the handrail is dotted with small spikes, made from short nails crudely welded to it. Fenn motions for us to stop where we are and stalks forward, crouching, examining the steps. He bends down to look through the railing and then sits back.

'Trip-wire,' he says, running his finger along a fine wire strung across the front of the first step.

'Attached to what?' the Colonel asks, stepping forwards.

'Bolts, metal plates, spoons,' says Fenn. 'It's an alarm, not a booby trap. Everyone watch where they tread.'

He leads the way, the Colonel following, as we step carefully down the stairway. I glance over the rail into the darkness below, and there's an unmistakable glow of flames from near to the base of the stairs some thirty metres below. I'm sure I see movement, and Lorii's glance over her shoulder at me confirms that I haven't imagined it. Without a word, and trying to make as little noise as possible, we spread out, allowing a gap of a few steps to open up between each of us. Looking up, it's easy to see the crude tripwire and rattling, clanging alarm system suspended from the steps above.

Suddenly, Fenn freezes and we all stop immediately, weapons brought up to the firing position, ready for anything. He hands his lasgun back to the Colonel and draws his knife, keeping it behind his back to prevent any reflection from the firelight below. The Colonel lets him to disappear further down the steps. Shortly afterwards there's a muffled groan, and the sound of boots scraping on metal. Then a heavy sigh.

Receiving some signal from Fenn that we can't see, the Colonel carries on downwards, and we follow, catching up with Fenn a dozen steps on, stooped over a body, his lasgun reclaimed from the Colonel. The man is thin to the point of being wasted. He is dressed in ragged breeches and jerkin and his arms are tattooed with a pattern of interlocking black squares. On his head he wears a black and red scarf, tied in an intricate knot at the base of his skull. The tattered ends drip with blood from the ragged wound across his throat.

I glance at Fenn and he gives me a 'him-or-us' sort of look. I nod in understanding. We're close enough to the fire now to hear the crackling of flames and the murmur of voices. It's only about ten more steps down, and by crouching we can see into the low room below through the spiralling banister. The substantial fire is a little off to our right, and there are seven or eight figures sitting around it on blankets.

The room itself, ruddy from the firelight, is some kind of old slaughterhouse. Hooks on belts hang from the ceiling, rusted gears seized together from the ancient mechanism that used to move them. Blood channels are cut into the floor, angling down towards one wall into a gutter and down into a sinkhole, even redder than the rest of the room.

Along one wall is a long, rusted metal bench, covered with junk of all kinds: broken knives, hammer heads, corroded spanners, planks of wood, nests of wire and stretched springs, leaking power packs and pieces of broken glass.

At that moment, one of the figures by the fire half turns to look over its shoulder straight at me. It's a woman, she has long straggles of hair sticking out of her headscarf. Her mouth is open as if she's about to speak and her right hand is raised holding a bottle. Her eyes lock on mine for an eternity, and I can do nothing but stare back at her.

Her invitation for a drink turns to a shout of warning.

The others around the fire boil up from their places, grabbing weapons and shouting. Fenn leaps down the steps, followed by the

Colonel and the rest of us. The crack of gunfire echoes around the room and bullets whiz past me as I jump down the last few steps, almost losing my footing.

Lasbolts and muzzle flares blot out the firelight as we return fire. A bullet plucks at the material of my trousers just below the knee. Hurling myself to the left, I fire from the hip, aiming at the woman who is crouched down with a pistol held in both hands.

The first shot is high, but the second takes her in the shoulder and the third low in the stomach. She sprawls backwards, pistols flying from her grip, and clutches her stomach.

Brownie curses to my right, sheltering behind the iron of the staircase, fumbling with the heavy stubber as Spooge slaps an ammo belt into the breech. The Colonel's bolt pistol roars in my ear. One of the enemy is flung backwards by a hit in the chest, onto the fire. His ragged clothes erupt into flames and his piercing shrieks can be heard over the noise of the fire fight.

In a few seconds, all but one of them is down, dead or wounded and the last one bolts for an archway to the left of the fire.

'We need him alive,' snaps the Colonel, knocking aside Fenn's lasgun with his pistol as he takes aim.

'Got him!' I shout, and I sprint forwards after the getaway.

I don't spare a glance at the groaning wounded as I duck through the arch, which opens out into a high chamber, vaulted with buttresses and pillars. Ancient, defunct machinery fills the room, soaring above my head with banks of dials and gauges, creating a maze of pathways. Water drips down from rusted pipes that criss-cross the ceiling. A splash to my right sends me heading in that direction. I jog along, half-crouched and alert, wary of an ambush. To my left I see a deep puddle rippling against the base of the machines and turn to follow my prey.

I catch a glimpse of him in the gloom, about twenty metres ahead. He ducks to the right and out of sight. Speeding up, I leap over the puddle, lasgun grasped in both hands as I pound up the rockcrete aisle.

Skidding around the corner, I have to spin and twist to avoid the knife thrust at my face as the man jumps out of the shadows at me. Instinctively, I drop and roll to the left using the momentum of my run to come back up to my feet, grabbing my lasgun by the barrel and swinging it. The butt connects with the man's arm above the elbow; it knocks him off balance and jars the knife from his fingers.

I step in to drive the toe of my left boot into his family jewels. I almost lift him off the ground. With an agonised squeal he drops like a sack of synthi-spuds, grasping his crotch, coughing and choking. I loom over him, and he looks up at me, pleading in his eyes.

He's older than me, I would guess thirty-five years at least, his face thin, his premature wrinkles lined with grease and grime. His eyes are watery and weak. They are filled with tears from the pain in his nuts, his lips cracked and raw as he wordlessly mouths his agony. Like the others, he's dressed in breeches and jerkin, which is open to reveal a tight, wiry body tattooed with the same overlapping boxes design on the sentry. His scarf is pinned in place with gaudy brooches shaped as cogs and skulls.

I hear the others making their way through the room and I call out to them. Slinging my rifle over my shoulder, I offer him a hand and pull him to his feet. He stamps several times on the ground, trying to get his balls to settle properly. He is still bent over.

'What's your name?' I ask him, and he looks at me with hate-filled eyes.

'Derflan Kierck,' he wheezes. 'By the Great Cog, who are you?'

'We're your new best friends,' I tell him as the others gather behind me. 'Say hello to the Last Chancers.'

FIFTEEN
TRAITOR CITY

THE UNDERHIVE IS lit with thousands of burning braziers. They stand on poles and are slung from chains from the high plasteel rafters that soar above the small conglomeration of huts and hovels. They are wedged into spaces between the banks of gigantic pistons that seized up thousands of years ago.

We're standing at the top of a wide sweep of stairs that leads down into the vast hall. We are now dressed in rags and headscarves taken from the dead underhivers. Our packs have been swapped for ragged, rope-strapped sacks, our lasguns swathed in strips of dirty cloth to conceal their well-maintained appearance. It turns out that the group we killed were tool merchants, who scavenge and repair whatever they can find to sell. It was a workshop we'd found them in. They used to spend half their time travelling from settlement to settlement.

KIERCK STANDS AT the front of our group, the Colonel right behind him, ready to grab him if he tries to do a runner.

'Is Firehole,' the underhiver says, grinning and revealing his stubby, brown-stained teeth. 'Good tradin' at Firehole. Allas plenty of tradin' at Firehole.'

He looks at me and flinches. His expression changing into an oily, sycophantic smile before he looks away.

'We will circle around,' says the Colonel. 'We should avoid contact as much as possible.'

'No!' says Kierck, his voice a nasal whine wholly in keeping with his scrawny, withered appearance. 'They seen us already. Wonder why we not come in if we leave now. Is good, no worries. We trade, we go on, they not know where we go next.'

The Colonel considers this for moment and nods.

'We will do this your way,' he says. 'But if we run foul, you will be the first to die, understand?'

'No worries, Derflan not run you foul, you see, yes,' Kierck says, almost bowing because he's so hunched over, the same ingratiating smile on his face. 'Derflan talk, we sell, they buy. Is allas good, yes?'

The Colonel nods again and Kierck leads us down the steps. He pulls a small hammer from his belt and then produces a triangular sheet of metal hung on a chain. Holding the chain, he begins to rap the hammer against the sheet, ringing out a sharp clang every few steps. He begins to holler, his accent so broad I can't understand what he's saying.

'No talk,' he says, looking over his shoulder at us. He eyes us critically, obviously not pleased with our disguise. A leering look enters his eye as he examines Lorii. 'Mouths give you away as outsiders. I say you cousins, brother-keepers of the Great Cog. You learnin' tool tradin' from ole Derflan. You promise keep ears open and mouths shut, that why you not talk, yes?'

As we approach, people emerge from the hovels of Firehole. Most are semi-naked, dressed in leather aprons, heavy kilts and thick breeches, their chests bare. This goes for the women too, and like the men who emerge, they're also painted with orange and red flame designs from navel to shoulder. Some show branding scars on their faces, breasts and arms, and the men have a strange F-shaped runes burnt into their foreheads. A few have small children with them, unmarked as yet. In all, about thirty or forty gather around us as we walk into the middle of the settlement.

I can feel heat rising up from the ground and I guess that there are some kind of forges or furnaces below us, that once worked the huge pistons, but are now turned to some other use. The fact that they're fire-worshippers is as plain as the nose on my face, and their whole lives are based on this valuable resource so they've built their settlement on top of it.

One of them comes forwards from the group, his bald head glistening in the light of the braziers. His skin is swarthy. He looks at us with dark eyes. He's broad and muscled; the flame designs dancing as his chest and biceps twitch. He looks about thirty years old, no more.

'Praise the Imperial flame,' he says, holding his hands above his head. There's a murmured echo from the other gathered folk. 'Long has it been since the people of the Great Cog visited us. I am Firefather Supurnis, and you are welcome in my town.'

He extends a hand, his arm rippling with taut muscles and Kierck shakes it, bowing ever so slightly in his cringing fashion.

'The Great Cog has sent us,' says Kierck, nodding ferociously. 'Yes, with bounty he has sent us. Bounty for the tradin'. Our halls grow dim and cold, and we bring the gifts of the Great Cog to trade for the warmth of the Imperial fire. My cousins here, they come from the distant halls, strangers who allas wanted to see the magnificent Imperial flame.'

The leader of Firehole looks at us, head cocked to one side.

'You are welcome to Firehole, distant travellers,' he says. 'Perhaps I might show you the Imperial flame once we have completed out business?'

'Allas good to see,' says Kierck. 'Sorries for my cousins, for they have vowed not to speak except in the hall of the Great Cog, for none worthy of words except the Great Cog. Their thanks you have, I sure of. Tradin! Down to tradin', we here for that.'

As we pull forth our sacks of salvaged hammers and spanners, gears, shovels and other assorted junk, Kierck squats down and spreads out a large oil-stained sheet pulled from his pack. Taking our wares, he lays them out, carefully grouping them by function and, from left to right, in ascending order of repair. We lay out everything from broken bits of wood to fully functioning hand drills.

The people of Firehole crowd close, pointing at various items, and muttering to each other. Some items they pick up and pass around to examine, until all are happy with what's on display.

'Wares seen,' says Firefather Supurnis, looking over the crowd and receiving nods of agreement. 'Let the trading begin.'

Chaos breaks loose as a disorganised auction begins, with everyone bidding for different items, waving their fists in the air, bellowing their offers, pushing and shoving to point at the objects of their bids. The Firefather is in there with the rest of them, shouting his own bid.

Kierck squats, looking up at the press of bodies, mentally taking note, nodding, shaking his head, and bargaining with twenty people at once. Now and then, an agreement is reached and he picks up something from his sheet and hands it over. He receives a handful of tatty pieces of paper in return. Slowly, piece by piece, the sheet is emptied until only a few items remains and the crowd has drifted away, content with their purchases.

Firefather Supurnis and a few of his devotees linger as Kierck packs his sheet away, handing back the items to those who gave them to him. He presses a greasy length of chain into my hand.

'Tradin' over,' Kierck says happily, waving a fistful of notes above his head. He grins at us. 'Allas good tradin' in Firehole, dint I say, yes? Allas good tradin'.'

'Come,' says Supurnis, waving an arm in a broad sweep to usher us forward. 'You shall see a sight that has become one of the marvels of Acheron.'

He leads us through the twisting maze of pistons and hovels, his henchmen behind us, until we come to a great block in the centre of the settlement. Archways have been carved into it, the ferrocrete structure daubed with bad paintings of flames, scrawled script written across it like graffiti.

Entering into the hollowed-out block, we find a conveyor cage, its open ironwork box is suspended on chains that are looped around gears hanging from the ceiling above us. From the shaft billows smoke and heat, causing sweat to spring up on my face. Distant sounds of industry, the clanking of metal and the crackle of flames, echoe up from below. Swinging open the conveyor door, he waves us inside. We cram into the small space, and Supurnis pulls a brake lever. The gears begin to slowly shift into motion, lowering us down into the shaft.

The elevator is obviously not part of the original piston room above. The walls are chipped and hand-carved from the ferrocrete. Small alcoves here and there contain burning lamps that scarcely illuminate the dark passage. We pass down about twenty or thirty metres until the shaft opens out, replaced with metal girders that guide the elevator.

Beneath us stretches a massive furnace room that eventually disappears into the smoky gloom. The heat is intense from the high open furnace doors; everything is bathed in a red glow. Hundreds, perhaps thousands, toil at great coal heaps, with pails and shovels, to feed the furnaces. From young children to old women, their painted flames are smeared with sweat and toil. Their labour keeps the fires burning. Braziers gutter everywhere, lending their smoke to the fumes of the furnaces.

As the elevator touches down with a loud crunching clang, Supurnis opens the door and we step out. He swings the door shut and slaps loudly on the framework of the cage, which lifts off a moment later, clanking back up into the gloom.

It's then that the noise hits me properly. There's the crackle of flames, the creaking of great steam wheels and the hiss of boiling water. But there are also groans, moans and the crack of whips. Through the gloom I see large, stooped shapes shuffling amongst the lines of workers, barbed whips in their hands, cudgels and clubs occasionally raised to beat a flagging worker about the back and shoulders.

They're unmistakeably orks.

I look to the Colonel, who's also spotted them. Before he can do anything, shapes loom out of the shadows behind us. More orks, five of them, are carrying heavy cleavers and maces. Their thick green skin catches the red hue of the furnace fires and the flames glint off their dagger-like tusks and pug-like noses. Their red eyes regard us malignly.

We freeze, none of us willing to make a move for our weapons. They have the advantage of surprise. A look from the Colonel warns us to play it cool. Kierck begins to whimper, and there's a wet, dripping noise as he soils himself. He cowers on the ground, covering his head with his arms. I catch Brownie's eye as he shifts nervously. A heavy poncho over his shoulders conceals the loaded heavy stubber and loop of ammo trails from his pack.

'Behold the Fires of Supurnis!' the Firefather declares, spreading his arms wide, his face a picture of exultation. 'The Imperial flame was great, but the flames of Supurnis are mightier still. See the fires that never dim, hotter and brighter than ever before under a hundred Firefathers.'

We say nothing, and he reads the fear and anger in our eyes. The zealous look is replaced by a business-like expression.

'I know you, assassins,' he says with a cruel smile. '*Emperor* von Strab warned me that you would come for me.'

'Emperor von Strab?' blurts Kin-Drugg before he can stop himself. A triumphant gleam enters the Firefather's eyes, or perhaps it's just a trick of the light.

'I knew you were no cousins of this wretch!' he says. He bends down and snatches the notes still gripped in Kierck's hand and waves them at us. 'Jealous out-hivers, that's who you are, isn't it? You heard that Firehole was strong again, bringing warmth and life to everyone. The great Emperor von Strab is generous in his gifts and you wish to claim them for yourselves.'

He looks at the orks and smiles.

'His needs are great, and he must protect his interests,' he says. 'Without them, the fires would dim, the furnaces would grow cold and the palaces of the Emperor would be lifeless. Bountiful was the great day when the messengers of the Emperor came to me. See what I have here? These labourers, they labour for me and me alone.'

'Slaves,' the Colonel snaps. 'You have made slaves of your own people.'

'Oh no,' says Supurnis with a horrified look. 'They are new converts, brought together under the fires of Supurnis. My people share in the generosity of Emperor von Strab, for I am not a tyrant.'

The Colonel snorts.

'And what of us?' he says. 'What do you think you will do with us?'

'You shall pass through the cleansing flames and join the great works of Supurnis,' the Firefather says. 'Is it not fitting that those sent to slay me should end their lives in the great furnaces they tried to quench?'

The Colonel says nothing, and I look around, desperately seeking some way out. The conveyor has gone, the orks are behind us and there is nothing in front of us except an endless stretch of furnaces and slaves, with more orks among them.

I can't see any obvious route of escape.

'Bind them,' Supurnis says, receiving a questioning grunt from one of the orks. He shakes his head in disbelief. He grabs Kierck's arms, drags them behind his back and imitates wrapping something around his wrists. 'Tie their hands up, you idiots.'

The orks step forwards, and one reaches out and grabs my left arm. I act without thinking, wrenching my knife from my belt, driving it up into the soft underjaw of the alien. It becomes buried to the handle. Lorii's clubbed down by a brutal backhand slap, she spins to the floor with blood flying from her split lips.

The Colonel whips out his power sword, turning the motion into a sweep that cleanly severs the arm of the closest ork. It bellows and punches him in the face, knocking him backwards. Brownie grabs Spooge and they dive clear of the scrum, trying to drag the heavy stubber free. Kin-Drugg is knocked from his feet by a club to the back of his head, smashing his nose on the bare ferrocrete.

I just have time to pull my knife free and duck as another ork swipes at me with its cleaver. The blade whooshes past my right cheek and tears through the fleshy part of my shoulder. The Colonel spins and chops the ork's head off in a single stroke, the blood fizzing and spitting along the length of the power sword's glowing blade.

I see Kelth huddled on the ground, trying to crawl away, but he catches a boot in the ribs that rolls him over with a shocked shout. Another ork lunges for me and I spin away, coming face to face with Supurnis. The Firefather batters a huge fist into my jaw. My legs threaten to buckle under me.

With a roar I drive my left fist into his nose, splintering the bridge and driving the cartilage into his skull. He flies backwards, blood spraying from his broken nose and I dive on top of him, my knife at his throat. I wrestle him between myself and the ork.

'Stop or your master dies,' I shout, and the ork pauses for just a second before bringing its blade down onto the Firefather's head, splitting it to the cheek. It gives a guttural chuckle as it wrenches the blade free, blood and brain fluid dripping from its hand.

'Not master,' it says, its large jaw twisting obscenely to form the words. 'Slave.'

I throw the Firefather's body into the ork and scramble away. I manage to get to my feet as the ork flings the corpse of the Firefather aside. Lorii rears up behind it, swinging her lasgun like a club with all her strength. The stock connects with the back of the ork's head. The creature merely grunts before turning around and swinging wildly with its broad cleaver. The blade chews a notch in the lasgun and sticks. The ork pulls towards it, tearing the lasgun from Lorii's grasp. I dive towards its exposed back, my knife held fast in two hands, and plunge it downwards into its skull. The force of my charge bowls it forwards into the ground.

By now, other orks are running towards us from the slave lines, yelling and growling. They wade through the press of bodies with their clubs and whips, clearing a path. That's until a woman, younger than me, her long black hair matted with blood and filth, drives the edge of her shovel into the face of one of her enslavers. Another ork batters her across the side of her head with its cudgel, smashing her face in and toppling her. But her act has ignited the whole mob. Like a ripple in a pool, her resistance spreads through the slave mob.

Flailing with buckets and shovels, clawing and biting, the slaves rise up against the orks. Emperor knows how much degradation and impoverishment has turned to hatred and anger in an instant. The two dozen or so orks react viciously, breaking bones, crushing skulls and tearing off limbs. But the mass of humanity is too much for them as the seething crowd overwhelms them; their raw loathing demands the destruction of its creators. The orks disappear under a pile of bodies, some dead, some alive, but all crushed by the sheer weight of their foes.

We watch in stunned silence as the crowd begins to part. Some of the slaves wield gory trophies such as a severed head or hand, and wave them in the air. It is all over in less than a minute. The cheering begins, and the bodies of the orks are hoisted into the air and over the heads of the freed slaves before being tossed into the furnaces. Some start singing and dancing, but most of them flood towards us, and we retreat quickly until our backs hit a metal wall behind us.

The celebrating mass presses in towards us, shouting thanks, clamouring for a touch. I fear for my life more than ever. It looks like they'll mash us to death with their praise. I step on something soft, and glance down to see Kierck cowering behind me, my foot on his hand. I drag him to his feet, and push him away from me.

'Get back!' the Colonel bellows, brandishing his power sword.

The crowd falters for a moment and then sweeps on. The people at the front are pushed into us by the weight of those behind. We thrust them away as best we can, shouting for them to stay back. After a few minutes of breathless wrestling with the mob, we manage to push them back far enough to get some breathing space There's still shouting and cheering, and a sea of grinning yelling faces and waving hands in front of us. The Colonel grabs one of the freed slaves, an elderly man with whip marks across his shoulders; his face caked in coal dust and soot.

'How do we get out of here?' Schaeffer demands, sheathing his sword and grabbing hold of the man's arms.

'Out?' the man says, his eyes crazed, half-vacant. 'No way out. No, stay here, no way out.'

'The coal ramp,' says a bearded man from behind the old-timer. 'We can climb out of there.'

He turns and speaks to the people behind him, pointing over their heads. The message is passed through the crowd. Eventually the consensus is reached and the mob begins to move away, flowing down the wide aisle between coal piles and furnaces like a filthy tide. They begin to scramble up over the fuel, some forging ahead, others stopping to help the children and the elderly.

We look at each other, dumbfounded by the rapid turn of events.

'Ever started a revolution?' Kin-Drugg asks of no one in particular.

'Twice,' says the Colonel, walking forward to peer up the conveyor shaft. 'The Firefather must have had some way to call down the elevator.'

'Perhaps he just shouted,' suggests Brownie, craning his neck to look up into the darkness.

'Unlikely,' says the Colonel.

'Why don't we just follow them?' I ask, pointing to the men and women clambering up the ramps where the coal is dumped.

'We are here to hunt von Strab, not liberate the hive,' says Schaeffer. 'We must avoid complications.'

'Won't they wonder who we are?' says Kin-drugg. 'Word's bound to spread.'

'All the more reason to get as much distance as possible between ourselves and this place, then,' says the Colonel. 'Now, look for something to call the elevator.'

We examine the area, looking for some kind of comms or lever, but there's nothing but battered old pails, broken shovels and dirt.

'He must have been worried that the slaves might try to storm the lifter,' says Lorii. 'Perhaps it's hidden.'

We recommence our search, examining the walls and floor. Oahebs gives a cry of triumph as he peels back a piece of sacking hanging from a large nail. Suddenly it seems so very out of place. Behind it is a small rope hanging from a hole in the wall. Oahebs tugs the rope, and far above rings a tinny bell that echoes down the conveyor shaft. A few seconds later machinery grumbles into life and we see the elevator rumbling down towards us.

We step back and ready our guns in case it's carrying more orks or some other hired thugs in the dead Firefather's employ. As it rattles into view, we see a single man in the elevator; his wide-eyed astonishment makes me chuckle. He desperately looks around, as if to magically find some way of stopping the conveyor.

'Don't think about shouting,' I warn him, my lasgun pointed at his head as the conveyor shakily drops down the last few metres. He holds up his hands as Kelth steps forward and pulls open the door, waving him out with the barrel of his laspistol.

'We heard fighting, I thought the Firemaster was in trouble,' he says, looking around. His gaze rests on the corpse of Supurnis and his shattered skull. He looks at us with horror. 'You killed the Firefather!'

'Actually, that did,' says Brownie, pointing to the dead ork I knifed in the neck.

'You profited from this slavery,' the Colonel says, his voice deathly quiet. The angrier he gets, the quieter he gets, and his voice is barely a whisper. He raises his pistol.

'I... I...' the man stammers, stepping backwards. The Colonel's bolt pistol booms and the fire worshipper's head disintegrates in a cloud of blood and splintered bone, his headless corpse collapsing to the floor in front of the conveyor.

'Bring him,' the Colonel says, pointing to Kierck, who's curled up by the wall, one hand over his eyes, the other clutching and wringing his tunic nervously.

Lorii grabs the underhiver by the collar and drags him up, guiding him into the lifter. We follow and the Colonel shifts the lever. The cogs above hoist us into the air. We ready our guns, crouched and standing around the outside of the conveyor. We're sitting targets in here if anyone has a mind to attack.

It's a tense half-minute as we clatter up the shaft, waiting for some shout that we've been spotted, anticipating the gears to clank to a halt and the conveyor cage to be sent plummeting to the ground below. Nothing happens though, and as we top the shaft, we can see that the block room is deserted, save for the two twisted corpses in the corner. Blood is pooled over the floor and leads out the door in the prints of several pairs of bare feet. The slaves got here first then. The fire worshipper was the lucky one, judging by the battered and bloodied bodies. At least he died quickly.

We cautiously exit the conveyor room and find Firehole living up to its name. The hovels are ablaze, some with burning corpses visible inside, others empty. The screaming and shouting of the slaves as they tip over braziers and put the settlement to the torch can be heard a short distance away. It's a form of justice, that Firehole should die by the flames that were kept burning by the labour of its slaves.

'This way, this way,' says Kierck, suddenly animated and pointing out of the settlement. 'We go quick, tetraptors wake up soon, must cross valley first.'

'The what?' asks Oahebs. 'Tetraptors? What are they?'

'Not matter, we not see them, we go quickly, now!' says the underhiver, heading off at a trot, waving us to follow. 'Come, we cross valley then sleep.'

SIXTEEN
EVIL AWAKENING

'THE VALLEY', IT turns out, is a great gash across the underhive. At some distant time in the past, the crust of Armageddon gave way under the weight of the hive city, and opened up a fissure that plunges down several kilometres. Heat and steam issue forth and the glow from deep lava illuminates the whole chasm. For level after level below us, and soaring half a kilometre above us, the rip extends. Like a ragged cross-section of the whole underhive, you can see the twisted, crushed depths and the more spacious, populated upper levels, before the fissure heals itself far above us meeting the hive city proper.

The levels just stop, chambers broken in half, walls crumbling from centuries of subsidence. The gap, some two hundred metres wide, is criss-crossed with bridges of all types, from ferrocrete spans to chain-link, rope bridges to metal structures, all bowing under their own weight.

The lip of the fissure is teeming with crowds and other life. Spiders the size of dogs scuttle out of holes and drop from above to feast on discarded rubbish, and bats swirl overhead; darting from shadow to shadow and feasting on the clouds of insects hovering in the thermal updrafts. Small birds, no larger than my thumb, flit to and fro, their chirps resounding along with the chirruping of fire crickets.

Gantries extend across the gap, from rickety wharfs made of charred wood to elegant half-arches jutting out from several levels above us. There's a great throng of people gathered over the fiery chasm, some with nets trying to catch the flitting birds, others on their knees praying.

As we walk onto the rubble-strewn lip, a priest dressed in a red robe is performing a wedding a few metres to our right, mumbling the rites in High Gothic. The couple, dressed in their best rags by the look of it, offer him two dead rats, which he casts into the molten rock below, blessing their unions. Others are casting their possessions into the flames, chanting, slapping themselves, baring their loins and indulging in all manner of other bizarre behaviour.

Kierck stops and we admire the view for a moment, shaking our heads. Sweat prickles on my face from under the headscarf; it runs down my cheeks and the back of my neck. There are lots of people here, I guess thousands, if not tens of thousands stretching up, down, left and right as far as I can see; those more than about half a kilometre away disappearing in the heat haze.

In front of us is a swaying rope bridge with metal bars for a floor. On it people squeeze past each other as they meet coming in opposite directions. It attaches to a metal A-frame dug into the ferrocrete of the opposite floor, and leads into a low, dark tunnel. We have to wait for a short while as a large group of men swathed in robes and hung with chains made from finger bones, hurry across the bridge, casting nervous glances downwards.

Walking out over the inferno, I feel a tremor of fear, but it's more than just the natural disquiet of walking across a ramshackle bridge over a raging inferno two kilometres down. No, I'm reminded of the warp-dream, in which I fall into a purifying inferno.

I glance over the edge of the bridge, one hand grasping the rope guideline tightly. My eyes sting from the heat. I can't see anything except the red glow and the roiling steam.

Then I notice the silence. Suddenly the chasm is deserted. Even the birds and insects have disappeared. Lorii has her head craned up to see above us, and the Colonel turns, shoulders his way past me and grabs Kierck by the arm.

'What happened?' he demands. 'Where have they gone?'

'Too late!' wails Kierck, flapping his hands against the top of his head with terror. 'Run! Run now!'

He tears himself free from Schaeffer's grasp and, head down, ploughs past me, his spindly little legs moving at speed. Below us is an ominous rumble and the walls of the chasm begin to shiver. Stones topple off the edge into depths. The rumbling grows louder, and steam belches up around us. I glance over the edge and see a dark cloud racing up towards us. After a moment I realise that it's thousands of winged creatures, rushing straight up out of the chasm. These must be the tetraptors.

'Run!' I bellow, sprinting after Kierck.

The others need no encouragement, and as fast as we can, we haul ourselves across the bridge, which sways violently from side to side, causing us to lose our footing, slipping forward on the metal rungs polished smooth by generations of feet.

We're not fast enough.

With a deafening flap of wings, the tetraptor swarm engulfs us. Each is only the size of my hand, with four broad bat-like wings. On thin necks, their beaked heads swivel and peck, tearing at our clothes and skin, their small claws shredding and gripping. Several are biting at my headscarf, their wings battering my face; others hang from my arms as I flail around. My face is bleeding from a dozen tiny cuts in an instant, bitten, or caught with the tip of their talons as the things fly past.

I can't see any of the others in the black morass of flying beasts. I bow my head and charge, stomping tetraptors underfoot, stumbling forwards with no idea how far it is to the other side. I can feel their greasy, furred bodies pushing at me through tears in my flesh. I have to pause to rip one free; it is trying to claw its way through the groin of my trousers. I fling it aside in disgust. I'm snorting heavily as I run, breathing through my nose. I am scared of opening my mouth in case one of them gets in there.

My foot lands on solid ground and, not expecting it, I trip, falling forwards, crushing more tetraptors underneath me. Scrabbling forwards on all fours, I feel someone grab me under the arms and haul me to my feet. I half-run, half-dive, suddenly finding myself clear of the living cloud in a small passageway, lying on top of Kierck. A couple of the creatures are still attached to me and I stand up to pull them free, throwing them down to the ground. I grind them to pulp with the heel of my boot.

The Colonel bursts out next, swiping with his hands at lingering tetraptors. He is swiftly followed by Lorii and then Spooge, who's whimpering from the dozens of lacerations torn into his flesh. Brownie comes out next, panting heavily, dragging the weight of the heavy stubber behind him. He collapses to the ground next to me, dabbing a ragged sleeve at the cuts on his forehead. His headscarf has gone completely.

The others appear in a large clump, falling over each other in their desperation to get clear. Kelth yells as the rest land on top of him in

a heap at my feet. We watch in horrid fascination as the swarm continues: thousands upon thousands of the creatures all heading up the
chasm, until it begins to slow after another minute or so. Two minutes later they're gone, having disappeared up beyond our view.

'What in all holy crap was that?' moans Kin-Drugg, cradling his leg,
blood streaming down from his reopened wound.

'Tetraptors,' says Kierck. 'I warn you, we be quick, but not quick
enough, yes?'

'What are they?' says Lorii, still looking up the chasm, as if expecting them to return. 'Where did they come from?'

'Live down in the depths of the valley,' says Kierck. 'In holes and
gutters, nooks and crannies. Each night the valley rocks, the river of
fire surges, and they come free, flying higher for food. Each morning
they return. Not good to be in the valley when that happens, yes?'

He gives a guttural chuckle, and slaps his thigh.

'You think Derflan look ragged, eh?' he says, pointing at us. 'You
proper underhivers now, yes? Ha!'

As the others pick themselves up, tugging at torn clothes and nursing their wounds, the colonel grabs Kierck by the shoulder. He pulls
him close, his voice harsh.

'If I were a suspicious man I would say you were trying to betray us,'
he says.

Kierck recoils from the Colonel's anger. 'First there is the debacle at
Firehole, and now this. I said that if we run foul, you would be the
first to die.'

The Colonel pulls his pistol out and thrusts Kierck against the wall.
The tool trader flings himself prostrate at the Colonel's feet, sobbing
and muttering, stroking the Colonel's bloodstained boots.

'No, no!' he gibbers. 'Not betray the Colonel. Derflan like Last
Chancers, he does. Free those people, go to kill the overlord, yes?
Derflan not lie, he almost slave in the firepits, yes? Not know evil in
Firefather's heart, not know anythin', not been to Firehole for many
years. Overlord to blame, not poor Derflan. Must cross the valley to
get to the overlord, oh yes we must!'

The Colonel looks down at him with a disgusted expression and
then kicks him away, holstering his pistol.

'How far to von Strab?' he asks, crossing his arms.

'One more day, Colonel, one more day,' Kierck says, his forehead
still pressed against the metal mesh of the floor. 'Rest tonight, Derflan know good place for sleepin'. Tomorrow we go through the
tunnels, then we by the overlord palace, tomorrow night at latest.'

'And where are these tunnels?' says Schaeffer. 'What will we find in them?'

'Nothing in tunnels, nothing 'cept rats,' says Kierck, trying to cringe even lower. 'Only way to overlord, less you wantin' more orks. Orks everywhere, Overlord army everywhere this side of the valley.'

'How dangerous is it?' the Colonel says.

'Derflan not lie, is dangerous, yes, dangerous,' he says. 'But Derflan travel the valley side many times, I know secret ways, rat ways. Orks not find us, overlord army not find us.'

'Lorii, Kage, scout out tonight's camp,' says Schaeffer. 'Come back here if it is clear.'

'Is close,' says Kierck. 'Down this tunnel, take first tunnel on right. Crawl tunnel, big enough for us and rats. Too small for orks. Derflan hide there before. Is sixth gratin' on floor, drops down into fan well. Yes, sixth gratin'. Fan well has other tunnels, check them too. Find rats, no orks I reckon.'

'Did you get that?' I ask Lorii and she nods.

'Come on, let's not hang around,' she says with a strangely expectant expression.

KIERCK WASN'T LYING, the tunnels he sends us to are a complete rat's nest of interlocking passages, ducts, sewers and alcoves, teeming with giant rodents. They flee when we approach, their chittering echoing off the metal and stone walls. Using hand-held glowstrips, we find the fan cover he talked about, and, prising it open, drop down into the room below. The fan is motionless, its hub a solid mass of rust; the blades broken and lying on the ground. The chamber itself is low, forcing us to crouch, but broad enough to accommodate all of us. Vents, some large enough to crawl through, radiate out from the chamber, some head up, others down. A large access hatch lies off its hinges on one wall, revealing a dark room beyond.

'Looks quiet enough,' I say, and Lorii grunts in agreement. She shines her torch at the hatchway.

'We should look through there, to make sure nothing's in there,' she says. 'You first.'

Ducking through the door, lasgun in one hand, torch in the other, I find myself in a room high enough to stand up in. Walkways lead up to doors on each side, and old factory machinery lies dormant; it is a labyrinth of conveyor belts, gears and metal boxes.

Something cannons into my back, sending me flying forward. Spinning to my back, I drop my torch and reach for my lasgun.

Lorii steps forward, lashing out with her foot to send my weapon tumbling out of my grasp. She pulls up her lasgun, the barrel pointed straight at my face.

'Go for your knife,' she says. 'Please.'

I slowly pull the dagger free, and as her finger closes around the trigger of her lasgun, I toss it away, clattering under a machine that looks like a splayed ribcage.

'What are you doing?' I ask, keeping my voice steady.

'I've been waiting for this for over a year, you bastard,' she says, spittle flying from her lips. 'In fact, ever since you left Typhos Prime.'

'This is about Coritanorum, isn't it?' I say. I start to sit up, but she signals me to lie back down with a thrust of her rifle.

'You guessed that all on your own, did you?' she says, sneering. 'Whatever gave you that idea?'

'Loron's death wasn't my fault.'

'No, it was the bullet through his head that killed him,' she says, her voice dripping with bitterness.

'He got slack, didn't pay attention,' I utter, slowly edging away. 'I'm not responsible.'

'It was a war, idiot,' she snaps. 'You heard how we were brought up. We were bred for fighting. We expected to die in battle.'

'And that's what happened to Loron,' I retort.

'Yes,' she says. 'But this isn't about Loron, it's about me.'

'Look, I'm sorry that you're the last one left, but it's better than being dead, isn't it?' I cast around for some kind of weapon. There's nothing.

'Are you really sorry?' she asks.

'Actually, no,' I admit with a shrug. 'It's not my fault, is it? It's your problem, you deal with it.'

'I'm about to,' she says. 'But the only reason I'm here is because of Inquisitor Oriel. He was the one who got me out of there. You left me behind.'

'We thought you were dead!' I snap, my anger rising. 'You charged off and we thought you were shot!'

'You didn't check, did you?' she snarls, her pale skin yellow in the light of the glow-strip. 'I might have been wounded, but you didn't care. Just one more dead freak, I bet.'

'I never thought that,' I say, shaking my head. 'You were a Last Chancer. We're all freaks one way or another.'

'You didn't think anything, did you?' she says, taking her hand away from her lasgun for a moment to swipe away a frond of hair. A moment later, she's focussed on me again, her eyes daring me to make a move. 'There wouldn't have been one of us left, would there? None of us, none of us to remember what we were, where we came from. Just a bunch of dead soldiers.'

'Don't blame me,' I say with a curl of my lip. 'I didn't make you. Frag you!'

I stand up slowly, my stare fixed on her.

'So what?' I snap. 'You're going to kill me because I was more concerned with my own survival than some stupid woman who ran off? Because you're a freak of nature that should never have existed?'

'Because you're so proud you're still alive,' she says. 'You're a survivor, aren't you? Inviolable, painless, survivor Kage. That's you isn't it? You'll outlast the Colonel, you think. But you don't deserve it, do you? You've done nothing, you even threw away your Last Chance.'

'I've never pretended otherwise,' I say, exasperated. 'Just fraggin' shoot me and have done with it, for Emperor's sake.'

'Oriel told me about you,' she says with an arch expression. 'You're tainted, evil. I'll be doing you a favour.'

'Oriel can fraggin' talk!' I sneer. 'He reads minds, you know.'

'Actually, he just lets people read his,' she says. 'Otherwise he would have never let me rejoin the Last Chancers, he'd know I wanted to kill you.'

'Perhaps he did know, I wouldn't be surprised,' I say, crossing my arms. 'He's not the type to do his own dirty work, is he?'

'No, he didn't know,' she says confidently. 'It's why he sent Oahebs. He's to keep an eye on you, and make sure your evil doesn't take you over.'

'You're either going to shoot me or not, so get it over with,' I say, staring straight at her.

'I'm not going to shoot you,' she says, grabbing her lasgun by the barrel and letting it drop beside her.

'So what the soddin' hell was that all about?' I gasp.

'I'm going to use my hands,' she says.

LORII CRACKS HER knuckles and smiles at me.

'You're good, but you'd best shoot me instead,' I say with a laugh.

Her first punch is lightning fast, and as I pick myself up rubbing my jaw, I remember just what she was like in Coritanorum. Deadly with her hands and feet.

I duck the next punch, only to find out it's a feint as the toe of her right boot cracks into my chin, snapping my head backwards and sending me back on to my arse again. This isn't funny any more.

She lets me stand up, and I launch myself at her, throwing a quick left-right-left combo that she bats aside with her forearms, twisting quickly and sending a back heel kick to my knee. I topple to the ground. She says nothing, just stands there bouncing on her toes as she waits for me to get back to my feet.

The bitch is just taunting me. She thinks she can kill me; she wants me to feel pain. No holding back any more. I'll teach her pain. I claw my fingers and rake at her face, grabbing the wrist of the arm she shoots out to stop the blow. Bending sideways, I twist, wrenching her arm out of the socket. Her shrill cry sounds like sweet music in my ears.

She tries to punch me and I block the blow, slapping her arm away, driving the fingers of my free hand into her stomach, just below the ribs. She falls, gasping for breath. I kick her in the face, splitting her nose open. Her head slams against the floor, the red blood vivid against her pale skin. The sight of it sends a thrill down my spine. Leaning forward I grasp her hair, longer after a month without being cut, and drag her head forwards. My fingers find her eyes, and I dig deep into the sockets.

I wonder whether to stop, but the sight of the crimson patterns across her white flesh brings out an urge from deep within me. This is what I exist for.

Leaving her mewling on the ground, I get up and stalk across the room, stooping to fish out my discarded knife from where it lies. The blade feels cold as I hold it against my cheek. I walk back over to her, as she tries to crawl away. I grab a leg and haul her back, and she twists, trying to kick me; her good arm flailing in thin air. I can hear the breath whistling out of her lungs. I want to see them.

I LICK THE *knife clean when I'm finished. Blood tastes saltier than I remember.*

I CAN TASTE blood as I wake up, and in a moment of recollection, I remember the fight with Lorii. I snap my eyes open, disorientated. There's blood on my hands, and my knife lies next to me. I'm sitting with my back propped up against a machine, and I can see the toe of a boot poking out around the corner. Not sure what I'll find, I pull myself up, feeling dizzy. Leaning on the machine, I stagger to the corner, trying to ignore the pounding in my head.

What I find is a ragged, bloody mess, almost unidentifiable. All except the shock of white hair on the scalp.

I throw up.

SEVENTEEN
THE REALM
OF THE OVERLORD

I RUN. IT's the only thing I can do. I don't care where I'm going. I twist, turn and crawl through air vents, and splash along sewer pipes, just trying to get as far away as possible. I tell myself it's for the safety of the others, that there's something I can't control happening. I know that it's really just to save my skin. When the others find out what's happened they'll kill me for sure. Perhaps I deserve it, but I'm not going to wait around for it to happen.

I enjoyed every minute of it. Every touch, every scream, every whimper, every drop of blood and bile. It was like a symphony of the senses.

I shudder, images appearing in my mind as I duck under coils of cables and squeeze between filtration tanks. I want to bury myself in the industrial morass of the underhive. For hours I keep moving, in the same general direction, ignoring the squealing of the rats, and the flutter of things against my face in the darkness. Here and there I pass through a lighted section, flickering glow-globes casting a sickly yellow light over a tunnel junction or sewer entrance. I abandoned my pack a while ago, unable to squeeze it through an observation hatch. I took only the rations I could fit in my belt, and the gold coins taken from the Inquisition stockpile in Infernus Forge. My flight takes me up and down, through wells and sinkholes lined with algae, across swaying bridges of rope and wood, skirting the glow of fires, and the indistinct babble of voices.

I stop as I'm crawling through a ventilation duct. It ends in a grille, and through the mesh of wire I can see an open area beyond, brightly lit from above. It looks like some kind of forecourt. As I look to the right, I can see two large gates made from plates of steel, heavily riveted. There's a handful of orks outside, carrying large calibre guns, and a few men with red forage caps on, autoguns and lasguns in their hands.

Without trying, I've found von Strab. This is obviously a major entrance to his domain. It's hard to see how the Imperial forces could have failed to find it after months of looking. Perhaps it's better hidden than it seems. This is the last place I want to be, on the edge of the fortress of the man I was sent to kill.

This is perfect. Von Strab will give me sanctuary. He will protect me from the Colonel and the others. All I have to do is go and warn him, show him my good intentions. I don't want to kill him, not now. Now he is my saviour.

I kick out the grille, which clatters noisily to the ground. The guards come running over, the orks lumber up behind, grunting and growling. I throw down my lasgun and hold up my hands in surrender.

'Who are you?' demands one of the sentries, a young man with a pointed black beard and a tattoo of a dagger on his cheek. 'What are you doing here?'

'I need to see the overlord,' I say, lowering my hands. 'I have important news for him.'

'You can tell me,' the guard says.

'No, it's too important,' I reply. 'I have to speak with von Strab himself. I'm from outside the hive.'

'I can see you're an outhiver,' the man says, glancing over his shoulder towards the gate. 'Curfew's on, I can't let anybody inside, especially not some outhiver stranger.'

I step closer, fixing the man with an intent stare.

'This is important,' I say to him, speaking slowly, earnestly. 'The overlord could die if you don't let me see him right now. You can't ignore this, not with witnesses to say that you met me.'

The man shuffles nervously. He looks at his companions, who offer him only shrugs and shakes of the head for support. The orks look on, bemused, perhaps not understanding the conversation. They look to the man I'm talking to, waiting for the order to smash me to a pulp.

I toss my knife to the ground in front of him. I spend a moment wistfully remembering the feeling of the sharp blade slicing through Lorii's white skin. I recall carving an elegant tracery of red on the canvas of her naked body.

'I'm unarmed,' I say, focussing on the matter in hand. 'You can search me.'

'I will,' the guard says.

'So you'll let me in then?' I say.

'If the overlord is displeased, you'll die before me,' he says with a scowl. 'Follow me.'

He turns and the whole group of us troop to the gate. One of them has picked up my knife and lasgun. I can see now that there's a watchtower behind the gates, mounted on the side of a white marble pillar that stretches up to the roof. The snouts of three heavy weapons poke through vision slits cut into the sheets of metal. The sentry leader signals to the tower and I hear a muffled voice calling out. A short while later, metal grinds on metal and the gate is pushed open. The man grabs me by the arm and leads me inside. With a clang the gates shut behind me again, and I see two men lowering a thick iron bar into place.

The four of us are in a wide plaza, lined with marble pillars, littered with broken and toppled columns and statues. Cracked flagstones line the floor, thick red moss growing between them. At the far end, a wide set of steps leads up, also made of marble. At the top is a set of high double doors, carved from wood. They are decorated with Imperial eagles that have been burnt and hacked at; the symbols of the Emperor defaced by the ancient cathedral's new occupants. Headless busts of saints line the stone wall; obscene graffiti scrawled over the frescos of great triumphs of the distant past. Guttering torches are mounted on the pillars, and in the shadows I see movement. I can hear grunts and crude, barking words. More orks.

The guard leads me up the steps and opens a small porter door in the cathedral entrance, pushing me through before stepping in behind me. The inside of the cathedral is crumbling and ruined. Tapestries have been torn down from the walls and scorched, the stained glass windows have been shattered. More torches in sconces bathe the interior with fluttering red light. Four more men emerge from the left to join us. They wear red forage caps too, and makeshift uniforms scavenged from various Imperial regiments. 'Strip,' says the bearded man.

I pull off my headscarf and drop it to the ground, and follow with the ragged clothes taken from the tool merchants. I stand naked while they search through the garments. They find the rations in my belt, and then one of them empties out the pouch containing the gold coins.

'What do we have here?' says the man in the white tunic.

'Gifts for the loyal soldiers of the Army of Liberation,' I say.

They look at me with suspicion for a moment, and then their greed takes over. They count the coins and divide them between them, hiding them away in pockets and pouches.

'Okay, get dressed,' says the bearded man.

This done, he leads me down through the pews, on which more men sleep, grey blankets over their still forms. A few wake with coughs and snorts, and watch us as we walk down the aisle towards the overturned altar at the far end.

'This way,' he says, pointing to a winding staircase that leads up to the right.

Halfway up, the staircase is replaced by a metal ladder, which enters a hole in the roof. The ceiling is shored up with metal beams and timbers. There are cracks in the plaster and stone – evidence of the great weight that crushes down upon the ancient cathedral. That's how it is in the underhive. One generation's homes become the sewers and basements of the next. And then another layer is built right on top of that, and another and another. For thousands of years the hive grows, its foundations the rubble of the buildings below, until it becomes the mighty tower that today stretches up into the clouds.

The ladder leads us into a small, bare room with a single door leading from it. Following the guard, I walk through the door into a narrow corridor lined with portraits that have been scrawled over and ripped. At the far end of the gallery we pass through another door and down a short flight of steps.

For several minutes we walk, sometimes passing the silent machines of a factory workshop, other times we return to the spires of the cathedral. Up ladders and down stairs, through the maze. I wonder if he's deliberately taking the long route, trying to disorientate me. If he is it's working admirably, because I haven't got a clue where I am now.

He brings us to halt in a small chamber with thick red carpet on the floor, muddied and trampled by many booted feet. A low couch lies along one wall, with a small table next to it. On the table sits a crystal decanter and a glass.

'Sit down,' he says, directing me towards the couch. I do as he says. He pours a clear liquid from the decanter into a glass and hands it to me.

'That's very civil of you,' I say, sniffing the liquid. It's odourless.

'It's water,' he explains. 'The overlord insists that his visitors be refreshed when he greets them.'

'Very sensible,' I say, not sipping the water. It could be poisoned or drugged. The guard sees my distrusting look and, with an annoyed sigh, grabs the goblet from my hand and takes a swig.

'It's perfectly safe, what do you take us for? Barbarians?' he says.

Still unsure, I take a small sip. It's clear, tasteless, unlike the scummy liquid I've been surviving on since boarding the starship over a year ago.

'Yes, it really is fresh,' the man says with a smile, reading my expression. 'The overlord had a few tankers full before… before his unplanned

migration. We managed to bring one with us. It's almost used up now, so make the most of it.'

I nod in thanks and take another sip while the guard knocks gently on the door and then lets himself in. The door closes with a click behind him and I can hear a muffled conversation. Suddenly there's the sharp retort of a pistol, and something bangs against the door. A moment later, the door opens and another man steps out, an old style revolver smoking in his hand. This one looks mean, with a hard edge about his grey eyes. He has a scar across his chin and his greying black hair is slicked back over his head. He's dressed in a long gown of patchy purple velvet, the leather belt with a holster looking out of place around his waist. I stand up to meet him.

'I am Sorious von Spenk,' he says with a cursory bow of the head. 'I am Emperor von Strab's chancellor.'

'Ex-Lieutenant Kage, formerly of the Imperial 13th Penal Legion,' I say, bowing stiffly with my hands by my side, in the manner I've seen a certain type of officer use in the past.

'A penal legionary?' says von Spenk, cocking his head to one side and examining me. 'How interesting.'

'Can I see von Strab now?' I say. 'It is urgent.'

'The Emperor will see you in a moment,' he says, emphasising von Strab's new self-proclaimed title. 'Please, finish your water.'

We stand in silence, with me pretending to examine the interior of the antechamber and von Spenk blatantly looking me up and down, his brow furrowed. After what seems like a long while, he holsters the revolver. After a tortuous wait, which must have only been a few minutes but felt like an eternity, there's a bellow from inside the door. Von Spenk opens it and I step through, almost stumbling over the body of the bearded guard who is lying next to it, blood dribbling out of a hole in his forehead.

'I apologise for the mess,' murmurs von Spenk, steering me forward with a hand on my shoulder, closing the door with the other. 'The Emperor does so dislike being disturbed at this hour.'

The walls of the short, wide chamber are hung with deep red drapes, looped over rails. It's only at a second glance that I notice that the rails are made from wired-together bones. The carpet underfoot was once white, but now is stained with mud, blood and who knows what else. Two sets of double doors lead off from either side, and I note with fascination that the handles have been replaced with small jaw bones. I look up and see a chandelier made from fused ribs, and I can guess what fat was used to make the candles by the distinctive smell. At the far end, sitting on a throne-like chair carved from dark wood, sits von Strab. Other than him and us, the room is empty.

He is heavily built, his jowls wobbling as he sits forward to peer at me out of one piggy eye. The other has been replaced with an artificial lens, the glass and metal protruding from his pallid, veiny skin. He sits with his hands on his knees in what I supposed is meant to be a regal pose. The whole effect is somewhat spoiled by the fact that the so-called Emperor is dressed in a grubby off-white bed robe and a pointed nightcap, complete with tassel.

'Humble greetings, your excellency,' says von Spenk, with a low bow. 'My profuse apologies for this disturbance. May I present Lieutenant Kage, a messenger from the outside.'

Von Strab lifts a hand and waves me forward. He speaks quietly, his voice strong and proud.

'Let me see you,' he says, leaning forwards.

I stand in front of him, hands clasped behind my back, waiting patiently. He looks at me from toe to scalp, lips moving wordlessly. He gives a grunt and sits back.

'Ugly sort, aren't you, lieutenant?' he says.

'Kage,' I say automatically.

'Hmm? What's that?' says von Strab.

'Just call me Kage, your excellency,' I say. 'And yes, my features are as harsh as my life has been.'

'Well, Kage, don't keep me waiting,' the overlord says. 'What do you want?'

'I have been sent here to kill you,' I say.

Von Strab recoils in horror, and instantly von Spenk is by my side, his revolver pointing at my right temple.

'Do not move, assassin,' says von Spenk. I sigh.

'Obviously I'm not going to do it,' I say, keeping my eyes on von Strab. 'I'm here to warn you.'

Von Strab recovers slightly, and peers at me suspiciously. He waves a hand at von Spenk, who lowers his pistol, though I note he doesn't holster it.

'Warn me that you are sent to kill me?' says the overlord.

'The rest of my team are still in the underhive, and they intend to either kill you or abduct you,' I say. And then, as if that would explain everything, 'We were sent by the Inquisition.'

'The Inquisition, you say?' says von Strab. He laughs, a soft, gurgling sound. 'Well, that's no surprise at all, is it von Spenk?'

'No your excellency,' says the chancellor-bodyguard. 'I imagine it is they who are responsible for the previous attempts on your life.'

'Of course they are,' I say. 'They think that the fate of Armageddon could rest in your hands. You are quite a threat to them.'

'This team of yours, tell me about them.' says von Strab.

I tell him everything. Everything about the Last Chancers, the Colonel, our journey here and our arrival. I explain about Derflan Kierck and his tunnel system. I save the best until last.

'And if we fail, then you're still doomed,' I say. 'A Space Marine battle barge is readying to flatten the whole of Acheron from orbit.'

Von Strab accepts this with a nod. He rests his elbows on the arms of the chair and steeples his fingers under his chin.

'You're not surprised?' I say.

'Of course not,' says the overlord. 'Everything they say is true. My grand Army of Liberation is fast becoming a force to be reckoned with. Do you know why they haven't found me yet? Deserters, like you. I'm always a step ahead of them. The rewards for loyalty to me are worthwhile, as I'm sure you'll find out. I have ten thousand trained soldiers, natives and others, and ten times that number as auxiliaries. The hive will be ours again.'

'You can stop the Colonel, with my help,' I say, stepping forward. Von Spenk tenses but I ignore him. 'But there's nothing you can do about that battle barge. In less than two weeks there'll be no hive to retake.'

'Let me worry about that, Kage,' says von Strab. He smiles and nods. 'I think I like you, Kage. I think I'll let you live, for now.'

'For now?' I say, raising an eyebrow.

'For now,' he says. 'Be thankful for that. Now, I must retire, I am bone-weary. Von Spenk will find you suitable quarters for tonight, and I'll see you bright and early in the morning. Oh, and make sure you get him cleaned up, von Spenk, he smells as bad as he looks.'

'Yes, your excellency,' von Spenk says with another bow. 'I'm sure we can accommodate your guest.'

He leads me through the door to the left and we pass through a series of rooms, each decorated in the same macabre opulence as the audience chamber. One is a trophy room, and amongst the strange and mutated rat skulls, stuffed lizard heads and other creatures are a number of human skulls and half-decayed heads.

'Hunting has always been the sport of the Emperor's forefathers,' explains von Spenk, noticing my gaze lingering on the contorted face of a woman. I can see maggots crawling in her empty eye sockets, making her cheeks twitch with a semblance of life. 'He refuses to let circumstances stand in the way of family traditions and makes do with what he can.'

After passing through several rooms, von Spenk brings me into a bare stone corridor, the walls slimed with mould. Rickety wooden steps lead down into a small basement with barred doors leading off. Von Spenk opens

734   Gav Thorpe

one and shoves me through. I bang my head on the low ceiling, and see a bare room, no larger than two metres square.

'Surely von Strab…' I begin, turning to von Spenk. He smashes me round the head with the butt of his pistol.

EIGHTEEN
THE MAD COURT

I WAKE UP, my head thumping with pain. I raise a hand to my forehead to feel a lump the size of an egg and scabbed blood. It's dark, a thin trickle of light seeps out of a door in front of me. I stand up and crack the top of my skull against a ceiling. Crouching down, I crawl across the cold, hard floor, feeling with my hand in front of me. I feel the grain of wood on the door, and by moving to the left and right find that I'm in a cell just a little wider than my outstretched arms.

Where am I?

More to the point, how did I get here? I try to concentrate through the pain of my throbbing head, trying desperately to remember. I mentally recoil from the image of Lorii, and try to recall what happened after that. My memory ends in an air vent, looking at the gates to von Strab's realm. After that, I haven't got a clue. I consider banging on the door, but disregard the idea. In my experience, if someone puts you in a cell, they intend you to stay there until they're ready for you to come out. If you make a fuss, you're just as likely to increase the length of your stay. With this in mind, I sit with my back to a wall, hugging my knees to my chest as I try to think.

It's pointless. I can't remember a damned thing. I don't know where I am, whether I actually want to get out of here, or what's waiting for me beyond that door. As has happened so many times in my life, I'm left with just one option. I have to sit and wait to see what happens.

I don't have to wait long. Soon there's the rattle of a key in the lock and it swings inwards, dim light streaming in. A man stands there in a faded purple robe, a gun belt at his waist.

'Come and get washed up for the emperor,' he says, stepping back. 'We'll see if he's still approving of you this morning.'

I think it best to say nothing yet. Anything I do say is bound to get me in more trouble. If I just play it steady, go along with whatever happens unless it gets life threatening, I could come out of this without too much pain. I just hope there isn't a test later.

I'M LED OUT of the cell and up a set of steps, and we turn into a shower block. The water is freezing cold but I don't mind. It's the first opportunity I've had to wash the grime of the ash wastes and the pipeline and the underhive out of my hair and from under my fingernails. I realise just how filthy I am as the blackened water spills down the plughole. I'm not one to worry about getting dirty, but it is nice not to be caked in crap like this every once in a while.

My rags have been replaced with robes of black silk, patched in a few places, with a white belt. It feels airy and light, and quite strange after a lifetime of combat fatigues and constricting uniforms. Lastly, there's a red forage cap, which I ram onto my head.

'The emperor will approve, I'm sure,' says the scarred man, looking me up and down, then leaning forward to straighten my collar. 'Follow me.'

He leads me through a succession of rooms decorated with ghastly human remains. Bones, foetid organs and rotting skulls are used to adorn portrait rails, chandeliers, doors and furniture.

The stench is unbelievable, and it sticks in my throat. I try to hold my breath, but soon that doesn't work and I resort to merely breathing through my mouth. Now I can taste the sickness in the air.

We finally enter a crowded room, filled with men and women of all ages; some dressed in simple robes like I am, others with gaudy officers' uniforms. Young boys wind through the crowd with tarnished silver trays, offering up a selection of local delicacies. My escort has disappeared into the throng, and one of the serving boys comes over and proffers the tray beneath my nose. It is dominated by a pyramid of small brown balls, edged with slices of meat.

'What's that?' I ask, pointing at a small, grey sliver of flesh.

'Sandrat bladder,' he chirps. 'Broiled over sump-oak branches. Very bitter, they say.'

'And these?' I say, using my fingertips to pick up one of the balls, which looks like excrement rolled in wood shavings.

'Oven-roasted kernuckle, with a savoury coating of fresh mudstool,' the young waiter replies.

'Kernuckle?' I say.

The boy sighs and despite being less than half my age, gives me a superior look.

'It's taken from the loins of a phundra,' he says with a condescending tone.

'The loins?' I say, plopping it back onto the plate and wiping the grease from my fingers on the boy's white smock. 'It's a bollock, you mean? Must be rare.'

'They have six each. It is an acquired taste,' answers the boy. With a mock sorrowful shake of his head he turns away and melts into the crowd, in search of someone who's obviously acquired more taste than I have.

The crowd is gossiping and mingling, but soon a hush spreads out from the far corner of the room. I shoulder my way through the people, earning myself the odd elbow in the ribs in the process, until I can see to the front.

I see a balding fat man dressed in a grey greatcoat lined with red thread. He wears a long parade sword at his belt, and a pistol grip inlaid with glittering gems protrudes from a leather holster. If he ever tried to fire that it'd rip his palm to shreds. His right eye has been replaced with a mechanical implant, the lens glowing with inner energy. He has a napkin tucked into the front of his coat, stained dark red. The man who took me from the cell appears at his shoulder and plucks the napkin free, using a corner to dab at a couple of specks at the corner of his master's mouth.

'Thank you, von Spenk,' the man says, the crowd parting in front of him as he waddles forward. He sees me and I flinch trying not to catch his attention. But he marches straight towards me, and suddenly I'm right in front of him.

'Glad you could make it, Kage,' he says, and my heart begins to pound in my chest. How the frag does he know my name? What the hell has been happening to me? 'I trust that your new vestments are to your liking.'

I look down at the flimsy robe, suddenly uncomfortable as I realise that it barely hides my nakedness.

'I'm more used to a uniform,' I say, looking at the fat man and shrugging. There's an almost inaudible murmur of disapproval from the crowd.

'This robe belonged to the youngest half-son of his excellency, Gabro von Strab,' says the man in the velvet robes. 'It is an honour to wear it.'

Von Strab? This is overlord von Strab? I'm about to open my mouth to apologise but the overlord speaks first.

'Nonsense, von Spenk!' says von Strab, pushing him away and stepping closer to me. He lays a beringed hand across my shoulders and turns me to face the crowd. 'Gabro was a noisome little prick who didn't even have the decency to scream when I throttled him. Kage is a military man, through and through, aren't you?'

'I... I've never been anything more than a soldier,' I say, hoping it doesn't look like I'm squirming too much.

'Such humility!' booms von Strab. 'See, Kage is a fighting man, a veteran of the hack and slash of war. He doesn't want the throw-offs of some poxy boy-lover. Take it off, I'll find you something better.'

'Now?' I whisper. 'Take it off now?'

I'm not usually self-conscious. I've spent untold hours in the shower blocks in a garrison or aboard a ship in front of my fellow soldiers, men and women. But there's something about the expectation, the leer in the eyes of these lackeys that makes me want to keep myself covered up. Von Strab unbuckles the belt and whips up the robe.

'You've certainly got nothing to hide, Kage,' he says, casting the silk robe aside. I stand there covering my troopers with my hands as a gasp ripples through the audience. 'Why, look at all these scars. I thought it might have just been your face.'

A short, thin woman steps forward. She is wearing a wig that makes her twice as tall as she should be.

'Are you... intact?' she asks, glancing suggestively at my crotch. I pull my hands away and she titters and grins. 'Oh no, most intact!'

'You there, von Guerstal,' says von Strab, pointing to a man in a bright blue uniform with a thick moustache, his thinning grey hair plastered over a scalp shining with perfumed lotion. 'You've let a bunch of assassins into the underhive. I'm stripping you of your title and giving it to Kage.'

The man stands mouthing wordlessly, his hands flapping ineffectually at his sides. Von Strab clicks his fingers and his henchman, von Spenk, steps forwards with a revolver in his hand. A single shot through the left eye blows the man's brain out and he flops to the floor.

'As well as your title, I'm stripping you of your clothes,' von Strab continues, as if the man could still hear him. He turns to me. 'Congratulations, Marshal Kage.'

Standing there naked, with everyone's gaze upon me, I'm not sure what to do. I bow formally and murmur my thanks. Von Strab rounds on the crowd,

'Well, don't leave the man standing there with his pride hanging out,' he bellows.

The crowd surge around the dead man like scavengers, fighting each other to pull off his clothes. They pounce on me next, lifting me up and turning me as they dress me. Having been pinched, pulled and spun around a few times, I'm deposited back on my feet a little unsteadily. I stand swaying in front of von Strab. The uniform, with its bright blue jacket and red sash, is a little too big for me: the cuffs hang past my wrists, the hose wrinkles around my ankles.

'Splendid, now you look like a Marshal of Acheron,' von Strab says, grabbing me by a shoulder and slowly turning me around. 'Once we're done here, you can assume your duties.'

'Duties?' I say.

'Well, von Spenk will fill you in on the details, I'm sure,' says von Strab. 'But a damned good start would be hunting down these assassins of yours.'

THE 'EMPEROR' IS listening to petitions from his court, and judging a few cases brought to his attention by underhivers brave enough to dare enter his lair. While von Strab settles a dispute between a small man dressed in a red smock with a golden laurel nailed into the flesh of his head and a tall, pinched-faced man with a ridiculous blue wig, von Spenk takes me to one side.

'You do nothing,' he says, the fingers of his hand digging painfully into my arm. 'If the emperor asks anything, just say that it is all in order and being looked after. I arrange the security around here, you just have to take the credit.'

'Or the blame?' I say.

'Look at him,' von Spenk says, nodding towards von Strab, who now has the two plaintiffs balancing on one leg, to see who falls over first. 'Centuries of intra-family breeding never gave him the best start in life, but this whole business with the beast has made him worse than he ever was.'

'The beast?' I stammer.

'Ghazghkull, you halfwit,' snaps von Spenk, his voice a whisper. 'Didn't Oriel tell you anything?'

I stay silent, stunned by the question. How does he know Inquisitor Oriel? What have I got myself into?

'Look,' he says, calming down. 'I'll make it simple for you. Oriel recommended the Last Chancers to me for this job. I'm the one trying to make sure this place doesn't get blown to hell and back, so for Emperor's sake, listen carefully.'

'You could've killed him last night,' I say, stepping back. 'One shot, and this'll be over.'

'That's my back-up plan, yes,' says von Spenk. 'Ideally, I want to take him alive. We need him on board, and to find out what he knows.'

'And risk millions of lives?' I snap, glancing over my shoulder as I realise how loud I spoke.

'Yes,' says von Spenk, his face set. 'Like you say, I can finish this any time I like. I'm his bodyguard, I have been for twenty years, you idiot. Do you think I just happened to be in the right place at the right time? If we can't get him out alive, his corpse will do fine, and we still have sixteen days.'

'I didn't realise,' I say.

'You're not meant to – you're a trooper, Kage, just stick to following orders,' says von Spenk. 'I'll make sure Schaeffer and the others can get to von Strab, you just keep your head down and cover for me. It's your neck on the line, not mine, so you best play the…'

He stops suddenly and looks up. I follow his gaze. Von Strab is looking at both of us, arms crossed, tapping his foot.

'What are you two colluding about, eh?' he barks.

'Marshal von Kage was just outlining his plans for tracking down and detaining the interlopers, your excellency,' von Spenk says, giving me a gentle push in the back.

'Von Kage?' I whisper, holding my ground.

'It's the name of a noble, get used to it,' von Spenk whispers back. 'Everyone's bloody von something or other around here, so pay attention or you'll get confused.'

I totter forward after a more hearty push from von Spenk. Glancing past the overlord, I can see two men wrestling on the ground, clawing and biting at each other, tearing out lumps of hairs and scratching at each other's faces. Von Strab notices my gaze.

'A stroke of genius, though I say it myself,' the overlord says with a smug grin. 'If they can't decide which of them gets the woman, they should fight like women for the right.'

The woman in question is watching the fight with distaste, her loose white gown open at the front to leave little to the imagination.

'Of course,' says von Strab, leaning close to whisper in my ear. 'I might just take the girl myself. What do you think?'

'She's certainly a fine woman,' I say.

The two men are panting heavily, bleeding from dozens of cuts and scratches, their tussling grows slower and weaker. Von Strab watches them, a finger held to his pursed lips in a studied pose of thought. He glances at me and winks. He claps his hands together and the two wrestlers stop and look up at him.

'Abysmal, absolutely abysmal,' the overlord says in a matter-of-fact tone. 'Von Spenk, since neither of these two is man enough to claim her, I claim her for myself. And since they're not man enough for that, I claim their manhood too. Have them castrated.'

The two men haul themselves to their feet. They grasp at their ragged robes, protesting and pleading. Red-capped guards appear as if from nowhere and haul them off, their screams resounding from the white-plastered walls and ceiling.

Von Strab beckons the woman forward with his finger. She has long dark hair that hangs around her shoulder in curls, and her stomach is tattooed with an interweaving snake and rose.

'You can have her, Kage, as a reward for dealing with this whole matter so well,' says von Strab. The woman looks at me, and her expression is none too pleased as she takes in my scarred face and blunted nose.

'You are very generous,' I manage to say. It's been many years since I've been with a woman, I'm not sure I remember what to do.

'Well, don't mess about, Kage, get on with it,' says von Strab, and my mouth gapes in disbelief. He wants me to do the deed right here? Then to my relief he says, 'That door behind us, you'll find your new bedchamber through the hall and the second door on the left. Take your time, I'm sure you've earned it.'

Seeing a hint of annoyance in the overlord's eye, the woman steps forward, eyes cast demurely to the ground, and takes my hand. The gathered mock officers and gentry begin to clap and cheer as she leads me out through the door. My heart begins to race, the feeling of her hand in mine causing a sweat to prickle on my skin. Desires I've not felt for a long time begin to rise.

The female's hand is hot and clammy, and I can feel her blood rushing through her veins. Her heart pounds as fast as mine, and I can hear her breath begin to shorten from fear or excitement. I don't care which. She opens the door to my chamber, revealing a wide, high-ceilinged room with a ragged-looking pair of armchairs, an ornate night stand and a bed the size of a small spaceport. It's covered in stained white covers decorated with fraying embroidered flowers.

The woman lets go of my hand and crosses to the bed, slipping the robe from her shoulders. She turns and reveals herself to me, before lying back onto the sheets. She looks at me past her generous breasts. I can sense her fear, her unwillingness.

'You can do what you like with me, marshal,' she lies. Her voice betrays her coldness. I notice cloudy glass goblets and tarnished silver cutlery on a tray on the night stand. I smile at her.

'I will,' I say.

I LEAVE THE bloodied cutlery and shards of glass in a crimson pool on the tray. Someone will clean it up for me, I'm sure. I feel spent, exhausted, but I know there's something I've got to do before I can rest.

I leave the bedchamber with its blood-soaked sheets and the ragged corpse of the harlot, and walk back to the room where I met von Strab. Opening the door, I find it empty, except for the serving boy who is now crawling across the floor on his hands and knees, picking up crumbs, bones and pieces of discarded food.

'Where is von Strab?' I ask him and he shrugs.

'Dunno,' he says, his pompous tone now gone.

I walk over to him and grab his curling golden hair in a fist, dragging him to his feet. He squirms in my grasp and I give him a little shake to quieten him down. When he goes limp, I twist my wrist so that he's looking at me.

'Don't make me ask again,' I say. Something wet dribbles down his leg onto my foot. He begins to cry.

'He'll be in the throne room,' he stammers between sobs, pointing to an archway on my right. I let him go. As he turns to crawl away, I kick him in the stomach, turning him over. Pinning him to the ground with my soiled boot, I give him a look. Pulling a cloth from the belt of his tunic, he wipes the piss from my shoe. With another kick, I send him on his way.

Walking through the arch, I find myself in a columned gallery overlooking a deep pit on one side. Naked bodies writhe and moan on the ground. At first I think it's sounds of pleasure, but then I notice the fattened, blood-slicked forms of rats weaving their way through the morass of exposed humanity. They're being eaten alive. None of them seem to be putting up any kind of fight as the rats, some with multiple tails, two heads, elongated fangs and other mutations, gnaw at their skin, nibble on fingers and toes, or burrow their way into their warm guts. I stand watching the tableau, caught up in the decaying artistry and beauty of the scene. I have to tear *my gaze away, remembering that I have an important errand before I can take all this pleasure for granted.*

I find the throne room at the far end of the gallery. It looks to have been a warehouse some time in the past. A mezzanine runs around for a higher level, partly blocked off by the collapsed roof. Metal girders criss-cross the wide span of the ceiling, held up by more steel beams. Light green paint peels off the walls, revealing crumbling dark red brick. The floor is tiled with white squares, greening at the edges. The wide space is littered with detritus. A few decaying bodies are slumped here and there, and there are clothes scattered all over, some of them neatly folded and stacked, others ripped and torn, thrown haphazardly everywhere or in half-burned piles.

At the far end of the hall von Strab is sitting in a large plain chair, vacantly looking around the room. He hears my boots clicking on the tiles as I cross to him, and looks up quickly, a haunted expression on his face. He seems to recognise me only after a moment, and then relaxes. His left cheek is bruised and his eye red-rimmed as if he'd been crying.

'Where's von Spenk?' I ask, looking around.

'Oh, he had something to attend to, over in the oil sump district,' says von Strab.

'How much do you trust him?' I say, bending forward and whispering in a conspiratorial fashion.

'With my life, every day,' he replies, looking at me with a quizzical expression. 'Why?'

'I think he's a traitor,' I say, looking to the left and right as if someone might overhear us. 'I think he wants to kill you.'

'I don't believe you,' von Strab says, shaking his head.

'But he confided in me earlier, about a plot of his,' I say, taking the gamble. 'He's in league with Colonel Schaeffer.'

'I know he is,' hisses von Strab. 'Keep your voice down! He's trying to get me out of here, isn't he.'

I can't think of anything to say for the moment, taken aback by this admission.

'You mean you want to go back?' I say, amazed. 'They'll kill you for sure.'

'I have nothing to fear,' von Strab says, pulling himself up haughtily. 'Yarrick may be their golden boy at the moment, but he has no breeding. No breeding at all, and that will shine through. Besides, what makes you think Schaeffer will keep me? Once I'm out of Acheron, that's another business entirely.'

'But why risk it?' I say, trying to keep the pleading out of my voice.

'If I stay here, they'll kill me for sure, you know that,' says von Strab.

'It doesn't have to be that way,' I say, crouching in front of the overlord, leaning forward with a hand on the arm of his chair. 'I can get you out of here. I'll deal with von Spenk and Schaeffer, no problem. You'll be a lord again, and I'll be your right hand man. Think of the pleasures we could indulge in!'

'And the orks, what will you do about them?' he says, spittle flying from his lips.

'What about them?' I say, rocking back on my heels. 'Ditch them or bring them with us, it's up to you.'

'You don't understand,' says von Strab, nervously looking past me. 'Who do you think von Spenk is trying to rescue me from?'

I SQUAT THERE in silence, absorbing this information, trying to work out what it means. I give up.

'What does that mean?' I ask von Strab, who has a manic look in his eye now, and is gripping the arms of the chair so tightly his pudgy knuckles have gone white.

'I didn't have any choice, did I?' he says. His eyes rove around the large hall. 'Yarrick was going to have me tried as a traitor. I tried my best, I really did. This is my planet, not his, damn it! But he wanted me dead, so I had to get away. It seemed the only choice was with Thraka. When he said he was going to return, I was overjoyed. But he was going to kill me. I had to tell him about the orbital defences, about the battle fleet. What was I supposed to do?'

'You did the right thing,' I say to him, soothing him with my soft tone. 'Like you said, you would have died. You have to look after yourself.'

'Precisely, Kage, precisely,' he says, finally meeting my gaze. 'He gave me Acheron back, and the nobles flocked here, but he didn't leave me alone. You think those green-skinned thugs are my guards? They're my jailers. They have a leader, Urkug they call him. He's as brutal as Thraka himself. He's not stupid, not like you would think an ork to be. He thinks, he listens and he tells Thraka what I'm up to. I had to concoct the whole Army of Liberation scheme so I could at least get some of my own men. But Urkug keeps me away from them; his brute squads are barracked with them and they intimidate them.'

'We'll take care of it, you and me,' I assure him, radiating confidence. 'I've been in deeper shit than this in the past. I'll have your army licked into shape in no time, and I'll personally take care of von Spenk and this Urkug if you want me to.'

There's a clatter of heavy boots from behind me and von Strab falls silent, sitting back in his chair and assuming an air of indifference. I swivel round on my haunches and see a group of six orks entering through the archway. The one in front is a head taller than the rest, an immense green bastard with arms as thick as my legs. Scalps hang from his heavy belt and his hands are covered with thick spiked knuckledusters.

'Ah, Urkug, there you are!' beams von Strab, stepping off the chair and bringing me to my feet with a hand on my arm. 'I was just telling Kage here who you are. He's my new marshal, by the way.'

'Shut up!' grunts the ork leader, shoving me aside and barging into von Strab. He forces him back into his chair. 'My boys 'ave been tellin' me fings. Who are dese killers dat have come fer you? Who's 'im?'

He jabs a clawed thumb over his shoulder at me. I'm suddenly acutely aware of the green hunks of muscle looming up behind me. I feel nothing from them, except their stench. You'd think I could sense their rage, their bestial hungers, but they're as blank as the chair von Strab sits on. It's not like they love violence, or loathe their enemies. It's just what they do, without thought and without feeling.

'That's Kage, I just told you, Urkug,' says von Strab, squirming as a rope of saliva drips from the ork's jutting jaw onto his face. 'He's the one who told me about the assassins. That's why I made him a marshal.'

'He killed some of my boys,' says Urkug, turning on me. Behind him, von Strab gets to his feet and tries to walk away, but he stops as Urkug reaches back with a clawed hand and plants it on his chest, thrusting him back into the chair.

'I killed them,' I say. Stepping forward, and staring the ork straight in his red eyes. 'With my knife, not a gun.'

'Yer look too small,' the ork says. 'My boyz could eat you alive.'

There's only one thing orks really understand. I drive my forehead into Urkug's jaw, snapping a tooth. The ork squints down at me, his jaw working as he thinks, his fangs carving grooves in the thick flesh of his lips. He starts to laugh, a rolling, gurgling noise, and slaps me hard on the shoulder.

'You got a good wun dis time,' Urkug says, his congratulatory slap sending me staggering away. 'I like 'im.'

With the ork won over, my next job becomes a little easier.

'Would you like to join us?' I say, looking at Urkug. 'We were just about to conduct an inspection of the oil sump district, check on security, that sort of thing.'

Von Strab's eyes widen as he remembers that's where von Spenk is waiting for the Colonel.

'I'm sure Urkug and his boys have something else they should be doing, isn't that right, Urkug?' he says quickly, frowning in concentration. He's *probably trying to work out whether I've intentionally betrayed him or not, or whether this is some elaborate plan to help him escape.*

'Inspekshun sounds gud,' says Urkug. 'Me an' the boys will come wiv you.'

'Lead the way, your Excellency,' I say to von Strab, and I see the horror in his eyes as it dawns on him that we're not playing for the same team any more. There's only one player on my team, and that's me. Just like old times, looking out for number one. Frag the Colonel and his mission, it's time I put myself first again.

NINETEEN
BETRAYAL

VON STRAB TRIES *to come up with something else for Urkug to busy himself with, but the ork leader is single-minded and determined to make a sweep of the sumps located a few levels below us. Ultimately, von Strab is just selfish and power-hungry. Once von Spenk and the Colonel are dead, he'll probably forget all about this stupid idea of giving himself up. With my help and encouragement, we'll get out of Acheron before the bombardment hits, and start anew someplace else. Perhaps we'll be able to make something in Hades, perhaps we could return to Acheron after the devastation has been unleashed and lead the scattered survivors to a great new life in gratitude and servitude. People in that position need strong leadership, and will accept it from just about anyone who shows them the way. Yes, with the fires still burning in the hive, Acheron will be ripe for the plucking.*

I try to urge the orks on, without making it look as if that's what I'm trying to do. I've got no doubt that von Spenk is down here waiting to meet up with the Colonel. With any luck we'll catch him before the rendezvous and we'll be able to set a trap for the Last Chancers. I'm also interested to see whether von Spenk blows his cover. I reckon he won't.

The orks seem to know their way around pretty well, which isn't all that surprising since they've been in Acheron since the invasion began and von Strab returned. We haven't passed any substantial doors or gates and I haven't seen any boundary walls so I guess we're still inside the overlord's 'palace'.

We pass by areas plunged into blackness and I can feel chill draughts flowing from darkened doorways, the air damp and clinging. I guess the episode at the Firefather's little slave empire has begun to have its effects. The power from his furnaces is gone now, leaving areas of the underhive devoid of light and warmth.

The air gets even more stale as we descend, mildew and the tang of oil hanging in my nostrils. We pass between huge riveted steel tanks, the steady thump-thump-thump of unseen engines vibrating the floor and walls. This must be the oil sump district.

There are a few of von Strab's red-capped Army of Liberation soldiers stationed at intersections and doorways. They give us surprised, nervous looks as we approach. They look especially worried when Urkug and his boys give them menacing stares and growls. I wonder if they're in on the whole plan, or if they've simply been duped by von Spenk. I bet their loyalties would be different if they learned that Acheron was soon going to be turned into a smouldering lump of molten metal and rock, reduced to rubble by plasma and cyclotronic bombardment.

In fact, as soon as I sort out this current situation, I think I'll make it a priority to spread the news as far as possible. Not only will there be a stampede and chaos of godly proportions, resulting in thousands of wonderful deaths, but the uproar should give us the opportunity to take our leave of this god-forsaken place.

As we take a right down a flight of steps to another sub-level, the walls oozing with sticky green fluid, the corpses of rats and other vermin stuck in the adhesive flow, I wonder whether we should take Urkug and his boys with us. It might be worth getting them to help in the escape. They might not be that bright, but they are good hired brawn, which could come in handy. Once they've outlived their usefulness they can be disposed of easily enough. I don't want to feel Ghazghkul leering over my shoulder watching my every move through the eyes of his green-skinned enforcer.

The sump area is a maze of intersecting corridors, and we ask after von Spenk. The men of the Army of Liberation wander around guarding doorways and access shafts. Following their grunted directions, some of them contradictory, we eventually make our way down a winding set of steps. I note that it's been several minutes since we've seen any of the red-capped soldiers.

Through an archway ahead I can see von Spenk. He's pacing back forth in an open chamber that has a sump overflow pipe jutting down towards the centre from one of the walls. He seems agitated, stepping from foot to foot, glancing around. I know he's waiting for Schaeffer to make contact somehow, and it looks like the Last Chancers are running a little late. When he sees us, he freezes.

'Just seeing how your sweep is getting along, von Spenk,' says the overlord with a weak attempt at a cheery wave. 'It looks like everything is in hand, so we'll be getting along now.'

I have to stall them. I know Urkug won't want to hang around too long, so I need to keep him busy. I turn to the ork, keeping one eye on von Spenk at the same time.

'So, you're one of Ghazghkul's top boys then?' I say. He squints down at me with his blood red eyes.

'Da boss knows I can take care of meself,' he grunts. He stomps forward and slaps a meaty paw onto von Strab's shoulder, making him wince. 'Emperor and me 'ave got everyfing stitched up, ain't we?'

Von Strab has begun to regain some of his senses, and a cunning look enters his eye. The broken, slumped man I found in the throne room is disappearing as he straightens his shoulders, then glances at von Spenk before addressing the ork leader.

'Certainly, Urkug, certainly,' the overlord says. 'We need each other, don't we? And to make sure that nothing happens to me, we need to search this area thoroughly.'

'You 'eard summink?' Urkug says, cocking his head to one side, his lips rippling as he thinks.

'Assassins might be coming here to kill me,' says von Strab. 'I'm sure von Spenk has everything under control, and his soldiers are doing a fine job, but I would feel safer if you were to have your boys join the search.'

Von Spenk and the overlord are trying to get rid of the orks, but I definitely want to be around for the meeting with the Last Chancers. I haven't got a weapon, and if Urkug leaves I'll be alone with von Spenk. The Colonel will be here soon and the overlord will be whisked away. Then I'll be stuck here. Or worse.

'On the other hand,' I say quickly, stepping forward, 'It might also be good to make sure the emperor has his bodyguards close, in case the killers slip through the net.'

Urkug pauses, trying to decide what to do.

'I'll have von Spenk to watch out for me,' says von Strab, walking over to pat the gunman on the shoulder. 'I'm sure he won't let anything untoward happen to me.'

Urkug is still undecided. A glance at von Spenk confirms that he's getting increasingly nervous. His lack of calm is betrayed by his furtive glances towards the outflow pipe, and his fingers hovering over his holster. Von Strab, on the other hand, is a picture of calm composure, the statesman in him coming to the fore.

'The emperor must be our primary concern,' I say, crossing the chamber to stand on the other side of von Spenk. 'I've been with this team. They have a native guide, and will slip into our midst without warning. They're like shadows, like ghosts.'

Just as I finish, Urkug's nostrils flare and his pointed ears twitch as he frowns. He looks at the other orks, who are also sniffing the air. There's a resounding thump from beyond the wall that echoes along the pipe to us; it is accompanied by a small cloud of dust and shower of gravel spilling from the end. A moment later, Erasmus comes tumbling into view, his servo-skull flying from his hands and clattering across the floor.

I pounce first, clamping a hand over his mouth and dragging him to one side. There's a pregnant pause as Urkug and his greenskins pull pistols and cleavers from their belts.

'We should take them alive,' hisses von Spenk, and surprisingly the ork nods in agreement.

Spluttering on the cloud of dust, Brownie follows next, his look of astonishment when he sees us is priceless. Urkug steps forward and smashes his pistol across Dunmore's jaw, hurling him to the ground, out cold. There's scuffling and rattling inside the pipe, and I guess the others are trying to decide whether to come down or not. Urkug waves his orks to close in around the opening, waving them to step back out of sight.

'It's Kage,' I say in a loud whisper that echoes up the pipe. 'I've got something waiting for you down here.'

I hear a muffled exchange of words that I can't quite make out, followed by a series of bumps. My ruse has worked, as first Fenn, then the Colonel drop out of the inflow. The Colonel takes everything in with a single glance, his gaze resting on me. There's no accusation in his eyes, no resignation. He simply looks at me with his blank expression and raises his hands away from his bolt pistol and power sword.

Kin-Drugg is next, still nursing his wounded leg, along with the under-hiver, Derflan Kierck. The tool trader gives a panicked squeak and turns to haul himself back into the pipe, but one of Urkug's boys grabs his ragged robe and hauls him back, dumping to the ground and placing a heavy boot on him to stop him crawling away.

Next is Kelth, who delicately slithers out of the pipe with his back to us. As he turns around, his jaw drops. Without hesitation, he sweeps his hand up, pulling back his headscarf to reveal his warp eye.

To my left, von Strab and von Spenk both start screaming, flinging themselves to the ground with their hands clawing at their faces. Urkug stands mesmerised for a moment, his eyes glazing over, and a rope of drool dripping from his jaw. Then he topples to the ground, stiff as a board. The other *orks react with a mixture of terrified wails and angry roars, firing their pistols at unreal phantoms. One of them stares for a long moment before its eyeballs explode and it crumples into a heap on the ground. The other Last Chancers are in similar comatose or panicked sates. Brownie is squatting on the ground gibbering softly. Kin-Drugg starts tearing wildly at the bandages on his leg, driven by some personal mania.*

I just look at the Navigator, the swirling, ever-changing deep vortex in his skull nothing new for me. I can feel the warmth of his immaterial stare wash over me as he turns in my direction. This time it is Kelth whose eyes widen in horror as he looks at me with his warp eye for the first time, seeing my true form.

'Daemon!' he hisses, recoiling, his natural eyes scanning left and right for some avenue of escape. 'Get away from me, foulest of the foul!'

'That's enough of this bollocks,' I say, stepping forward and delivering a sharp punch to the navigator's face, breaking his nose and sending him to the ground.

I kick him in the side of the head and he rolls over. Snatching the scarf from his limp hand, I quickly bind his third eye again, pulling the rope belt from his rags to tie his hands behind his back. Looking up, I see that everyone else in the room is starting to recover.

His boots thumping on the ferrocrete, Oahebs leaps out of the pipe, wrapping his arms around my shoulders and bundling me to the ground.

THE NEEDLES BEING driven through my head are total agony and I scream at the top of my lungs, wrestling against the weight bearing down on me. My eyes are dark, full of stinging pain, and my own yelling voice feels muted and distant in my ears. I thrash around, feeling something constricting me as my sight slowly returns. Suddenly the weight lifts and I see the face of Oahebs close to mine. He is crouched over me. A trail of blood dribbles from his nostrils and one of his eyes is cloudy, the pupil almost obscured.

'What?' I manage to say, my voice suddenly unnaturally loud, ringing in my ears. More pain stabs through my head but I ignore, it, concentrating on Oahebs. He covers my mouth with his hand to stop me speaking.

'Shut up, listen hard,' he says, the words coming so quickly and quietly I almost can't understand them. 'You're a psyker, you've been possessed by a daemon. I'm a soulguard, an earthing rod for psychic energy. When you're away from me, the daemon will try to come back. You must fight it. Believe me, try with all your will and soul!'

I'm in a bare chamber, looking at a wide pipe jutting in from one wall. Just ahead of me, the other Last Chancers are lying on the ground, moaning and clutching their heads and faces. There is a handful of orks nearby, recovering from something. I see von Strab beyond them, kneeling on the ground and vomiting. His bodyguard, von Spenk, is crouched behind him with his revolver pointing at me.

One of the orks has regained enough presence of mind to drag Oahebs from me. Retching, the Last Chancer doubles up, and I see blood clotting in his ears and strange burn-like marks on the back of his neck. He glances back at me, his left eye now completely white, pain etched across his face. I feel weak, sickened and dizzy and push myself to my feet to stagger away from him. The orks have their pistols in their hands again, surrounding the Last Chancers. I fall to all fours, resting my head against the cold, slightly damp floor, feeling trembling exhaustion course through my body.

Then I notice my hands.

They're almost claw-like, the nails extended and pointed, the skin thin and brittle; the bones threatening to break through the wasted flesh. Shaking uncontrollably, I push myself to my feet and stagger to the wall, leaning against it, breathing hard. I look over my shoulder, vaguely remembering Oahebs's words. Something about a daemon.

The largest ork is disarming the Last Chancers, casually tossing their weapons aside. Three red-capped soldiers run into the chamber, lasguns ready. They stop short at the sight that meets them. They look at the orks, and then von Spenk and the overlord, trying to work out what's going on. It's von Strab who takes the lead.

'These are the assassins,' he says. 'Lock them up! We shall deal with them later. Von Spenk, Kage, Urkug, we have plans to make. Acheron is proving far too troublesome. It is time the Army of Liberation made its mark!'

TWENTY
FREEDOM

THE LAST CHANCERS have been bundled away, presumably to the cells where I woke up. Von Strab leads myself, von Spenk and Urkug back up through the sumps and then through the halls and galleries of his palaces, with their grisly, bloody decorations. A throne carved from dark reddish wood sits at one end. The walls are covered with heavy drapes. There are only the four of us here.

Von Spenk carefully closes the door behind us after we enter. I have only flashes of recollection from after the last time we were together. I remember there was a girl, and I have an image of von Strab on a throne weeping, but nothing else. Outwardly, I try to keep my expression as calm as possible, but on the inside my thoughts are in turmoil. Oahebs's warning comes back in full. A daemon is inside me! I don't know when or how, but it doesn't really matter. I thought the blackouts, the nausea, were tied to my witching abilities. Now it makes more sense. Something inside me is wrestling for control of my body. Even now its corruption is lurking inside me. He said to fight it, but how? How can I fight something I don't even begin to understand?

Already I'm changing. Its presence inside me is warping my flesh. I can feel it now that I know it is there. My hands are becoming obscene claws, and I can feel bones breaking and knitting inside them and elsewhere. The thump of my heart sounds different, faster, more erratic. There's a pain in my chest I've never had before; it feels like my ribs are fusing together. Never before have I been so aware of

753

myself and my body. Like a cancerous growth, the essence of the dae-mon is sitting inside me, gripping my body and soul.

'The assassination attempt has failed,' declares von Strab, sitting down in his chair with a flourish, his good eye staring at me mani-cally. 'Thanks to the prompt, nay miraculous, action of Marshal Kage, we are still alive. This is a state of affairs we wish to continue long into the future. Acheron itself is under threat, and we must therefore concede to quit our palaces and locate to fresher ground.'

Von Spenk is agitated in the extreme. Not once does he tear his gaze from me except to glance cautiously at Urkug. His fingers are hovering above his holster pistol in anticipation of drawing the weapon. He looked dangerous enough when I saw him before, but in this mood he looks downright murderous, and totally unpre-dictable.

As they discuss their withdrawal from the hive, I let my mind dwell on other plans. The overlord, the inquisitor-cum-bodyguard and the ork leader are all ignoring me, so I try to straighten things out in my head, although my thoughts keep returning to the creature festering inside me.

I've never been one for politics, but I think I can figure what is going on by piecing together snippets of remembered observations and conversations. Through von Spenk, or whatever his real name is, von Strab has heard about the planned bombardment of Acheron. He wants to get out, understandably, and having gained von Spenk's confidence will double-cross him before he is handed over to the Imperial authorities. That much makes sense so far, and explains his remarkable recovery when things turned awry.

Though he's as mad as a bag of spanners, the overlord is certainly not inexperienced when it comes to scheming. He probably has at least one back-up plan at any given time. His allegiance however tem-porary, with von Spenk and the Colonel allow him to shake off the orks and the grip of Ghazghkull.

For his part, as far as I know, von Spenk is trying to get von Strab out of Acheron as well, to prevent its destruction and win a little coup of his own over his rivals who want to flatten the hive. He said that he'd kill the overlord if necessary, but I'm doubtful. He seems more likely to throw caution to the wind and just cut and run. I'm pretty sure there's more than a little self-interest here and he obvi-ously wants to save his own skin. With Urkug hanging around like a fart in an APC, I don't think he's willing to pull the trigger and risk his own neck.

And as far as I can tell, Urkug is the only straightforward one here, which isn't surprising. His orders from Ghazghkull are to keep von Strab alive and well, and to keep an eye on him so he can't betray the warlord. Von Strab thinks he's playing a subtle game, with his Army of Liberation and his plotting, but he's admitted that Urkug is smarter than he appears. Even he hasn't figured out what's going on, it's clear that Ghazghkul is intelligent enough to be aware of von Strab's potential double-crosses.

And stuck in the middle of all this are the Last Chancers, locked up somewhere below us, probably condemned to death. I don't know how it all went wrong, or why Urkug turned up at the meeting point, but it's obvious that the plan's gone to hell and isn't coming back. All of which leaves me thoroughly fragged as far as I can tell.

I have no weapon, and little chance of getting one at the moment. I haven't a doubt that if I make the wrong move, von Spenk will take me down in an instant.

Trouble is, I haven't got a fragging clue what the wrong move might be. Urkug's the same, so that's double the fun, and I can't even begin to work out how I'm going to figure in von Strab's schemes. At best the three of them consider me a disposable asset, at worst a potential threat.

The obvious course of action is to get the frag out of here and leave them to it. That's easier said than done though, with von Spenk and Urkug both keeping an eye on me. The only friends, for want of a better term, that I have are the Last Chancers, and I'm not even sure where they are. As far as I can tell, the only way out of this for me is to get the plan rolling again. If I can kill or seize von Strab, the Colonel and the others will be the best way of getting out of here. So I'd best start listening to what's happening, otherwise things could get even further out of my control.

'…narrow thinking,' von Strab is saying. 'What should we care if they all die? They are my army, and their duty is to protect me. If that is to be a diversion, then so be it. You never know, it might actually come good and do some damage to the lap dogs of Yarrick.'

'If dere's a fight, my boys will show you what dey're made of,' says Urkug, thumping a clawed fist into the palm of his other hand. 'We's not had a proper fight for ages, and the lads is getting bored.'

'But throwing away your forces just to cover your escape could prove unwise, your excellency,' says von Spenk, his smooth tone having returned as he tries to manipulate the overlord. 'We cannot guarantee what sort of reception you will receive wherever we end up relocating to.'

'I think I know how to do this,' I say, trying not to flinch as they all suddenly turn their attention on me. Von Spenk has his eyebrows raised in doubt, von Strab is looking at me with one narrowed eye and Urkug is frowning, although he seems to do that most of the time.

I feel something squirm inside me, not physically but in my mind, in my soul. I ignore it, fighting it back into the dark recesses.

'Colonel Schaeffer must have had some plan for getting out again, he always does,' I say, the idea only forming properly as I talk. 'I might be able to get it out of him. At the moment, his mission has failed. If I can offer him a chance to succeed, he might just take it.'

'What makes you think he'll trust you, a traitor?' says von Strab, leaning back in his chair. 'After all, you have betrayed him twice now.'

I have? I don't remember anything like that. That makes things more complicated, but as I'm trying to concoct an argument, it's von Spenk who steps in. He is pointedly not looking at me now, but something tells me he's guessed what I have in mind.

'He may have something, your excellency,' says von Spenk. 'There is nothing to lose by trying, as I see it. I will personally escort him to the prisoners, to assist if necessary.'

'I dun like it,' grunts Urkug. 'We should kill 'em before dey make more trouble.'

'We'll get rid of them, one way or the other, when they are no longer useful,' says von Strab.

Urkug stands his ground, his muscles flexing as he tenses, glaring at the overlord.

'I dun trust anywun any more,' he says. 'Dere's been too much secret talking, and I dun want no more of it.'

'You can come with me as well,' I say, and the ork's bucket-jawed head swings in my direction, fixing me with an evil stare. Behind him, von Spenk gives an almost imperceptible nod, confirming that he thinks we can take the ork out between us if necessary. In fact, as I think about it, it could be to our advantage to remove the ork leader as early as possible. 'If you don't trust us, that is.'

'I dun,' Urkug says. 'Let's do it now, no more talking!'

I WAS RIGHT: they are being kept down in the same cells where I had been for Emperor-knows how long. Von Spenk leads the way, down through the ornate audience chambers and portrait galleries, and then into the slime-covered stone depths in the levels below. The three of us stop at the bottom of the steps leading into a cell-lined hallway. Urkug pulls his pistol from his belt as von Spenk hands me the keys.

'I fink you doin' summink wrong, I plug you, right?' the ork says and I nod.

I walk down the line of cells, to the third on the left, which von Spenk tells me is the one where I'll find the Colonel. I pause outside the door, the heavy brass key between my fingers, figuring out how to make this work. I can't guarantee that von Spenk can take out Urkug with his revolver. Even a point blank shot to the head isn't always fatal to an ork.

On the other hand, if Urkug nails one of us with his heavy pistol, it's going to be all over pretty damn quickly.

I think perhaps the best way will be to lure Urkug towards the cell so that von Spenk can perhaps shoot him in the neck while the Colonel and I tackle him from the rear. A quick shout should bring the huge ork running in our direction, and then it'll be up to von Spenk. After that, we'll release the others and set about getting von Strab out of here.

If we can get von Strab out on his own, I doubt we'll have a problem keeping him safe and sound. He may be planning to double-cross von Spenk and avoid being taken in, but with the Last Chancers around that'll be near impossible. Of course, we'll still have to get him back to friendly lines intact, but since we managed to actually get here against the odds, a few kilometres to the Imperial cordon outside Acheron shouldn't be too difficult.

I slip the key into the lock, trying to keep my hand steady. The lock clunks loudly as I turn the key, and I tense as I pull the door outwards. As the sickly light from the glow-globes seeps into the room, I see the Colonel. He's sitting with his back to the wall facing the door. His eyes bore straight into me from the dim light. I stand there for a moment as we just look at each other, the Colonel's blank face betraying no clue as to his mood.

He stands up slowly to straighten his rags as if he were still in uniform, and takes a step forward. I hold up a hand to stop him, swinging the door almost closed behind me, cutting off all but a sliver of light.

As I turn round, the Colonel leaps forward, his right fist slamming into my jaw, knocking me backwards. I throw up my right hand to block the next punch, a fraction too late. Blood wells from a cut on my lip as his knuckles smash into my face, knocking back another step.

I open my mouth to tell him to stop, but he wades in with a boot, forcing me to sway to one side. I catch his ankle in my left hand. Instinctively, I bring my leg round to sweep away his standing leg, but he leans forward and catches my knee with a blocking forearm, spinning on his heel and wrenching himself free from my grasp.

Without pause, he attacks again, raining punch after punch towards my throat and face, forcing me to duck and weave, blocking with my hands and shoulders, slowly forcing me away from the door. A feint and a right uppercut catch me off guard, slamming my head back against the wall and stunning me. As I blink sweat out of my eyes, I see him stepping towards me, his face filled with murderous intent, his lips twisted into a snarl. It's the first time I've ever feared for my life at the hands of another man.

With a smile, I lunge forwards, the fingers of my hand driving towards Schaeffer's eyes. I can get this body to work faster than he ever imagined. I go on the offensive, striking with left and right blows, taking him on the chin and above the eyes. Turning my attention lower, I drive a fist into his gut, lifting him to his toes, and then slam a punch into the side of his head, making him stagger sideways.

'Idiot,' I hiss at him, driving a booted foot into his chest, leaving him leaning up against the wall gasping for breath. 'I was going to get you out of here. Now that's never going to happen. I'm going to enjoy watching you die.'

He looks up at me, chest heaving; his face a picture of hatred.

'He is one of mine,' he spits. 'I want him back!'

He takes me by surprise, hurling himself off the wall, driving a shoulder into my midriff and bundling me into the far wall. My spine cracks against the stonework. The pain is easy to ignore, as he batters my face with combinations left and right punches. My right eye swells and closes up, my nose spills blood down onto my lips. He's panting badly now and I slap him with the back of my hand, my bony knuckles tearing the skin from his cheeks.

Clawing my fingers, I rake my hand across his face. My new talons tear off the lobe of his left ear and he sways to avoid the blow. He throws out a hasty punch, which is easily stopped. Grabbing his wrist, I trap it under my arm and wrench upwards. His elbow bends the wrong way with an audible snap. He hasn't once groaned or cried out in pain yet. That's a shame.

'You can't blame me,' I say, grabbing the front of his ragged clothes and slamming him into the wall. 'I'm not the Kage I used to be.'

He breaks my grip and forces his arms between us, throwing me backwards.

'I know,' he says. 'You are a creature of the abyss, a weak, despicable cacodaemon. I want him back, fiend of Horus, leech of the void!'

'But I'm right here,' I say with a laugh. 'I am Kage, you know it. This is what I'm really like. This is what I want to be like. This is what is inside me, in my soul. It was easy to release myself, my psychic gifts saw to that. Now I can be free, from you, from the accursed Emperor, from duty and guilt.'

'You are never free from me,' snarls Schaeffer, smashing a fist into my chest, and cracking a rib. I laugh. It won't take long to heal, not now that I've unleashed my true potential. A few more modifications and this body will be perfect for me.

I stop his next punch in the palm of my hand and my long fingers close around his fist, crushing knuckles and pulverising the flesh. I force him down on to one knee and then let go, bringing my hand across his face with the same movement, splitting his bottom lip.

'Ever since I first met you, I wanted to do this,' I say, cracking my bloodied knuckles. 'Sure, you remember? I stuck a knife in you. This time I won't bother with the knife.'

I take a step forward, but at that moment light spills into the room, and I freeze. Urkug and von Spenk crowd into the door, their pistols drawn. I step back and lower my hands to my sides.

'He wouldn't co-operate, so I'm trying to force it out of him,' I say quickly, possibly too quickly as von Spenk's eyes narrow in suspicion. 'I just need a couple more minutes.'

'I think you've done enough,' von Spenk says, pushing past Urkug into the room. The ork grunts in annoyance and shoves him to one side to cram his bulk through the narrow space.

'I dun like dis, you stop it now,' Urkug says, waving me towards the door with his blunt-barrelled pistol. 'I say we just shoot dem now and forget about dem.'

'No!' says von Spenk, stepping in front of the ork's raised pistol. 'The emperor wants to dispose of them himself, you heard him say so. We'll get rid of them his way, and then we will get out of here and start again.'

Something gurgles in the ork's throat as he considers this and then he backs off, lowering his pistol.

'We go soon,' he says. 'Tonight. I might just get bored of your emperor if I have to hang around ere any longer. I get rid of fings when I'm bored wiv dem.'

Schaeffer is lying on the ground, clasping his broken arm. He is looking up at us with simmering abhorrence. Von Spenk motions with his pistol for *me to leave the cell, but before I do, I crouch down next to Schaeffer and whisper in his bleeding ear.*

'You always knew it would be one of your own that did for you,' I say. 'You made me, and now I've destroyed you. I hope you think about that when you're dying.'

Von Strab doesn't *seem too put out by the news of what happened when we return to the audience chamber. The manic look has returned to his eyes, and he looks at me closely as von Spenk informs him of what they found in the cell.*

'Couldn't pass up the opportunity to settle the score, eh, Kage?' *he says with a chuckle.* 'It's quite naughty lying to me like that, but I can understand your reasons. I bet he made your life a living hell.'

'Yes he did,' *I say.* 'And he's overseen the deaths of hundreds, thousands of good soldiers and innocent civilians. If ever there was a man who embodied the evil that the Imperium represents, Schaeffer was that man. The sooner we're rid of him, the better.'

'Well, yes, but let's not be too hasty,' *he says and I try not to show my disappointment.* 'I have something special planned for these Last Chancers and their commander. Tonight, they'll be seeing the valley again, although I doubt they'll enjoy the view much.'

True to his *word, a few hours later, a great entourage is making its way through the underhive to the massive fire chasm called the valley. Soldiers and courtiers numbering over a hundred file through the twisting corridors, across silent machine rooms, down spiralling stairs and along crumbling boulevards.*

Von Strab walks at the head of the procession, and some of the Army of Liberation are obviously clearing the route ahead. With him are four bearers, carrying a patched canvas shelter over his head. The purpose of this becomes clear when we pass through a high chamber, its vaulted ceiling about two hundred metres above us. It writhes with bats, millions of them, and their shit rains down on us in steady drips, spattering our uniforms and robes. I try not to look up.

Flanked by orks and redcaps, we wind our way up a twisting causeway that arches out over a desolate, cratered hall. I can see a few ragged figures slipping between the shadows, digging in the pocked earth with small shovels.

'Who are they?' *I ask, looking over the balustrade into the dim depths. The man behind me stops and leans over. He's dressed in a bright orange uniform coat, with jewelled roses set into the lapels. A cluster of medallions, many of them tarnished, hang on his chest, and he holds a cockaded hat under his arm. I can't help but notice that he has no trousers or boots on, and his left big toe is pointing out of a hole in his damp, stained hose.*

'Bone prospectors,' he says, and then seeing my ignorance, continues. 'The fighting in the underhive has moved around a lot in the last three years. This was one of the earlier battles. About a hundred and fifty dead orks, maybe a thousand human remains. They were all buried in the mud when the level above collapsed, dropping the contents of the sewer tanks onto them. They dig around in the stuff looking for valuables. Apparently there are some people who cook the bones down, to eat, for glue, that kind of thing.'

'Just my sort of place, shame it has to go,' I say.

'Hmm? Go?' my new companion asks. 'What's going?'

'Nothing, nothing really,' I say with a smile, turning away and rejoining the column.

At the front of the line, chained hand and foot, come the Last Chancers. Kelth is easily picked out, a head taller than the rest with a crude iron mask, a lot like a pail, chained over his head. I guess von Strab doesn't want another attack of the warp-jeebies. The Colonel walks proudly at their head, the others either skulking along avoiding any attention, or looking around at their surroundings with startled gapes. Brownie looks like he hasn't got a clue what's going on. He keeps stopping and looking over his shoulder to talk to Erasmus behind him until the orks turn up and club him into moving again.

Somehow, Spooge is still carrying that bloody broken servo-skull, tucked under his arm. Before the little fragger dies, I want to smash it into pieces in front of him. I want to tear out all the mechanics and gears and cognitive analysers and scatter them to the winds. Maybe then he'll understand that it's not fun and games to be a soldier.

The others are obscured by the press of people; mock military officers and the local dignitaries, some of them prodding the prisoners with walking canes, or spitting on them. We eventually reach a large semi-circular area with an ornate iron fence around the outside. Beyond that, I can see the jagged, bridged chasm of the valley, bathed in a red glow from below. A walkway juts out about fifty metres over the artificial canyon, lined with ropes on each side.

The overlord's lackeys and retainers spread out across the large balcony, pushing and elbowing each other to get the best view of the coming proceedings. Von Strab beckons for me, von Spenk and Urkug to follow him out onto the gangway. Ahead of us, the Last Chancers are herded along the pathway to its end. It's immediately clear what von Strab is intending to do.

It's a wonderful feeling, standing above that massive precipice, looking down over the edge into its ruddy depths. The heat drifts up and around me, the air dry on my skin. It's the closest I've come to remembering the soaring, gliding freedom of the warp. It's an odd memory, tinged with senses that my body no longer possesses.

I look up, seeing the roof has collapsed just a few levels above our heads, jutting stalactites of metal and ferrocrete point down at me. There's a wonderful stillness, a momentary hush of the underhive.

I turn to von Strab, who stands in front of the Last Chancers, von Spenk on one side, Urkug on the other. He opens out his arms; palms held up to the low artificial sky, his head arched back.

'Behold the great valley of Acheron!' the overlord declares. 'For a hundred generations, it has brought life and light and warmth to the underhive. Gods have been born in its depths, and blessings bestowed by robed priests basking in its holy heat. It has spawned its own creatures, its own tribes, its own prophecies. It is an extension of the will of Armageddon itself. These fiery depths have witnessed births and deaths, marriages and dissolutions, miracles and martyrdoms! And now it is time to commit the bodies of Armageddon's enemies to its burning embrace.'

A great cheer resounds from the gathered dignitaries, echoing off the roof, resounding back from the far wall of the valley. But I can sense the hollowness in their voices. The cheer is as much for the orks behind them as for their ruler and his rites of execution. Acheron is under the heel of von Strab, and if only it wasn't going to get annihilated in fourteen days, I would have had it made here. Still, there are other things to look forward to.

Brownie is the first in the line of Last Chancers, and he's starting to realise his predicament. He tries to wipe a hand over his bald scalp, but the chains between his wrists and ankle stop him. Sweat drips down his face as he looks over the edge. He shuffles backwards, and tries to run as Urkug steps forward and grabs him.

He shouts; his voice cracking into a scream as the burly ork hauls him towards the lip of the half-bridge, holding him out over the valley. Von Strab makes a theatrical flourish with his hand and Urkug shoves Brownie over the edge, flinging him into the empty space. In my mind's eye he hangs there for a second, mouth stretched open. He tries to flail his arms and legs, and drops from view, his shriek growing quieter and more hoarse as he falls to his doom.

There's baying and clapping from the crowd, and cries of 'Shame!' and 'Kill the traitors!'

Their fear-fuelled anger washes over me. It is mixed with genuine hatred. I shudder and my eyelids flutter. I glance around to make sure no one noticed.

Urkug turns and gives a gurgling laugh, and von Strab claps his hands quickly like an excited child about to receive a present. Beside the overlord, von Spenk looks decidedly irritated, his arms folded across his chest. The Colonel looks typically stoical, jutting his chin forward and regarding von Strab coolly.

Erasmus, behind the Colonel in line, gives an agonised shout and tries to rush forward, but one of von Strab's guards steps in and batters him around the side of the head with the butt of his shotgun.

Next up is Kelth, standing there with his head covered, unaware of what's going on. I wonder whether it's a cruelty or a kindness that he can't see what's happening. It's probably better for him, which is a shame because the arrogant bastard deserves more suffering in his life.

There's polite clapping from the crowd this time, following the overlord's lead. The ripple of applause seems civilised and tame compare to the emotions I can feel emanating from the frightened, heated mob.

Urkug hoists the lanky Navigator above his head with a roar and strides to the precipice. Kelth struggles vainly in the grip of the green monster, his chains rattling against the ork's skull. With a triumphant shout, Urkug flexes his powerful arms and flings the Navigator into the void. I laugh, feeling the waves of fear washing from the remaining Last Chancers. It's like a drug, swilling around inside me, buoying up my released soul.

Casually, the ork strolls back towards the line and grabs the rags of the underhiver, Derflan Kierck. The scrawny little man writhes in Urkug's clawed grasp, but to no effect. With almost contemptuous ease, the ork hurls Kierck over the edge into the chasm, holding up his other fist over his head in celebration. There's another great cheer and brash hooting from the audience, and hats are tossed into the air in celebration.

I stop when I see that it's to be the Colonel next. Urkug is stomping back from the end of the walkway, clenching his fists in anticipation.

'Wait!' I shout out, and the ork pauses. Everyone looks at me as I stride forwards. 'I think the honour of this should be mine!'

Von Spenk gives me a curious look, perhaps thinking this is some last minute gamble to save the Last Chancers. I'm happy to disappoint him.

'Of course, Marshall Kage,' says von Strab with an extravagant wave of his hand towards Schaeffer. 'You not only deserve it, but you have earned it.'

I walk forwards, my eyes focussed on the Colonel, and he returns my stare. Cold hatred burns there, willing me to explode from his sheer force of will. I smile at him, and then the smile turns into a grin, exposing my newly reshaped fangs. I hear a hiss from von Spenk behind me and a shout from one of the other Last Chancers. I ignore them.

I'm a few metres from the Colonel, when I remember Oahebs is still alive. Frag.

LIKE A DROWNING man bursting to the surface of a tossing sea, I awake with a gasp for breath. With a force of will I cling on to the memories of the departing daemon, and through the pain surging through my heart and head, remember everything. In a single moment of clarity, I feel myself, more aware of who and what I am than I have ever been in my life.

In a single glance, I see the Colonel looking at me, a snarl on his lips. Next to him, Erasmus cowers, tears streaming down his now-sunken cheeks. To my right is von Strab, with von Spenk just behind him. And ahead of me is the massive ork, Urkug. I can feel the heat of the distant fire chasm washing up over the edges of the walkway. Sweat prickles on my skin. I can taste the blood from my bleeding gums where my sharpened fangs bite into them. My body feels tense and strong, twisted and warped by the daemon.

In that single moment, my entire soul becomes focussed in on itself, like a collapsing warp hole. I suddenly understand everything. I look at Oahebs, and see the blank white orb of his eye and the scars left across his face from the psychic energy that is coursing through him from me.

I see Fenn, standing tall beside the anti-psyker, a haunted look in his eye as he gazes out into the wideness of the valley, his nightmare of open spaces about to become a reality. Then there's Spooge, the last weeks of hardship etched onto his face. Gone are the rounded edges the blubbery cheeks. Still mortally afraid, and caught up in something far beyond what he could have comprehended a year ago, he nevertheless manages to spit at me. He cradles the servo-skull of his father like a totem, protecting it to the last.

And then there's the Colonel. Cold, hard as rock, unflinching and remorseless. A man who has endured pain, hardship and injury for over three centuries. A man who has dedicated his life to the Emperor and never once asked why; his faith is more solid than the foundations of a hive city. His body has been broken innumerable times and yet he's stayed alive; they have healed him and thrown him back into the eternal war.

He has never failed.

It all becomes as clear as crystal in that moment of awakening. Sacrifice, the Imperium is built on it. The sayings are all true. The Blood of Martyrs is the Seed of the Imperium. The Loyal Slave Learns to Love the Lash. Only in Death does Duty End.

For ten thousand years we have endured, sometimes we have thrived, other times merely survived. For a hundred centuries we have fought and died, spilt the blood of our enemies and our own over an uncountable number of battlefields. Mankind has sacrificed itself, for itself, so that it might last for another generation, and another, and another. Those sacrifices are for no greater cause than for the acts themselves. It is done in the unspoken hope that some day, perhaps in another ten thousand years, a generation will live without sacrifice and mankind's destiny is fulfilled for eternity.

The Emperor will not remember you by your medals and diplomas, but by your scars.

It is not only in death that we offer up our lives to Him, but also in life. We are not judged merely by the manner of our deaths, we do not earn His eternal grace merely by dying in His name. It is by the way we live out our lives before we die that defines who we were. It is easy to sacrifice a body, for it's nothing more than a mortal shell for our soul. To sacrifice your life, not your death, is the ultimate test of faith.

It is a test I have always failed. I have lied and cheated and killed my fellow men for my own reasons. I have squandered the opportunities for glory that I was given. Time and again I have stood upon the precipice of true sacrifice and turned away.

Von Strab's look of triumph turns to horror as I fling my arms around him, lifting him off the ground. I see von Spenk's astonished face flash past as I drive forwards with the overlord in my arms, the panicked bellows of Urkug sounding in my ears.

His legs hit the rope barrier and buckle, and my momentum carries us forward, toppling us head over heels into the precipice.

Now I truly understand what it means to have a Last Chance. I'm glad I finally took it.

ABOUT THE AUTHOR

Gav Thorpe works for Games Workshop in his capacity as Lead Background Designer, overseeing and contributing to the Warhammer and Warhammer 40,000 worlds. He has a dozen or so short stories to his name (maybe less, he can't remember), and over half a dozen novels.